SELECTED
STORIES OF
ANTON CHEKHOV

SELECTED
STORIES OF
ANTON CHEKHOV

*Translated by Richard Pevear
and Larissa Volokhonsky*

MODERN LIBRARY
NEW YORK

Published in the United States by Modern Library,
an imprint of The Random House Publishing Group,
a division of Random House, Inc., New York.

MODERN LIBRARY and the TORCHBEARER Design
are registered trademarks of Random House, Inc.

Originally published in trade paperback in the United States by
Bantam Books, an imprint of The Random House Publishing Group,
a division of Random House, Inc., in 2000.

Grateful acknowledgment is made to HarperCollins Publishers, Inc. for permission
to reprint excerpts from *Letters of Anton Chekhov* by Michael Henry Heim and
Simon Karlinsky, copyright © 1973 by Harper & Row, Publishers, Inc.
Reprinted by permission of HarperCollins Publishers, Inc.

ISBN 978-0-553-38100-9
eBook ISBN 978-0-307-56828-1

Printed in the United States of America

www.modernlibrary.com

29

Contents

INTRODUCTION

In the autumn of 1844 a young writer named Dmitri Grigorovich was sharing rooms with a friend of his from military engineering school, the twenty-three-year-old Fyodor Dostoevsky, who was at work on his first novel, *Poor Folk*. Through Grigorovich the finished manuscript reached the hands of Vissarion Belinsky, the most influential critic of the time, whose enthusiasm launched Dostoevsky's career. More than four decades later, in 1886, this same Grigorovich, now an elder statesman of literature, came across the humorous sketches of someone who signed himself "Antosha Chekhonte," brought them to the attention of the publisher Alexei Suvorin, and thus "recognized" the last great Russian writer of the nineteenth century—Anton Chekhov.

Grigorovich also wrote to the young man himself, scolding him for not taking his work seriously and for hiding behind a pseudonym. Chekhov was astonished and deeply moved. In his reply, dated March 28, 1886, after apologizing for scanting his talent, though he suspected he had it, and thanking Grigorovich for confirming that suspicion, he explained:

> . . . In the five years I spent hanging around newspaper offices, I became resigned to the general view of my literary insignificance, soon took to looking down on my work, and kept plowing right on. That's the first factor. The second is that I am a doctor and up to my ears in medicine. The saying about chasing two hares at once has never robbed anybody of more sleep than it has me.
>
> The only reason I am writing all this is to justify my grievous sin in your eyes to some small degree. Until now I treated my literary work extremely frivolously,

casually, nonchalantly; I can't remember working on *a
single* story for more than a day, and "The Huntsman,"
which you so enjoyed, I wrote in a bathing house . . . All
my hope lies in the future. I'm still only twenty-six. I
may manage to accomplish something yet, though time
is flying . . .*

Just a month earlier, Chekhov had written to a friend saying that
his real commitment was to medicine, while literature was a mistress he would one day abandon. Now he likened the effect of
Grigorovich's letter on him to "a governor's order to leave town
within twenty-four hours." And he obeyed the order. He began to
write less and work more. The first story signed with his real name,
"Panikhida," appeared in Suvorin's magazine *New Time* that same
year—the start of a close and sometimes difficult collaboration between writer and editor that would continue for the rest of
Chekhov's life. Though a delight in the absurd and a sharp eye for
human folly remained central to his work, he was no longer merely
a humorist. The repentant sketch-writer had made his entry into
serious literature.

Chekhov's contemporaries were struck by his originality. He invented a new kind of story, which opened up areas of life that had
not yet been explored by Russian literature. Tolstoy saw it at once.
"Chekhov is an incomparable artist," he is quoted as saying, "an
artist of life . . . Chekhov has created new forms of writing, completely new, in my opinion, to the whole world, the like of which I
have not encountered anywhere . . . Chekhov has his own special
form, like the impressionists." Tolstoy was not alone in using the
term "impressionism" to describe Chekhov's art. We may see what
he meant if we look at "The Huntsman," the story that first caught
Grigorovich's eye. Written entirely in the present tense, it opens
with some fragmentary observations about the weather, a brief but
vivid and (typically for Chekhov) slightly anthropomorphized description of the fields and forest, a few spots of color—the red shirt
and white cap of the huntsman. A woman appears out of nowhere.
She and the huntsman talk, she tenderly and reproachfully, he

---

* Quotations of Chekhov's letters, unless otherwise noted, are from *Letters of Anton
Chekhov,* selection, introduction, and commentary by Simon Karlinsky, trans. by
Michael Henry Heim in collaboration with Simon Karlinsky, New York, 1973.

boastfully and casually. "Ashamed of her joy," she "covers her mouth with her hand." He scratches his arm, stretches, follows some wild ducks with his eyes. It is clear from what he says that they cannot live together. He gets up and leaves; she watches him go: "Her gaze moves over the tall, skinny figure of her husband and caresses and fondles it . . ." He turns, hands her a worn rouble, and goes on. She whispers, "Good-bye, Yegor Vlasych!" and "stands on tiptoe so as at least to see the white cap one more time." That is all. The story does not build to any moment of truth; it does not reach any significant conclusion. It simply stops.

In a letter of May 10, 1886, to his older brother Alexander, who had taken up writing before him with only modest success, Chekhov, from his new position as a recognized author, set forth six principles that make for a good story: "1. Absence of lengthy verbiage of a political-social-economic nature; 2. total objectivity; 3. truthful descriptions of persons and objects; 4. extreme brevity; 5. audacity and originality: flee the stereotype; 6. compassion." It is a remarkably complete description of Chekhov's artistic practice. Authorial commentary, if not entirely absent, is kept to an absolute minimum. The most ordinary events, a few trivial details, a few words spoken, no plot, a focus on single gestures, minor features, the creation of a mood that is both precise and somehow elusive— such is Chekhov's impressionism. "This seemingly slight adjustment of tradition," wrote the critic Boris Eikhenbaum, "had, in fact, the significance of a revolution and exerted a powerful influence not only on Russian literature, but also on the literature of the world."*

Chekhov's way of composition *wordlessly* extends the limited scope of the story by means of juxtaposition, alternation, simultaneity, that is, by means of a new kind of poetic logic. His art is constructive not in a narrative but in a musical sense, to borrow D. S. Mirsky's terms.** Not that he wrote "musical" prose; on the contrary, his language is perhaps the plainest in Russian literature; but he built his stories by musical means—curves, repetitions, modulations, intersecting tones, unexpected resolutions. Their essence, as Mirsky says, is not development but envelopment in a

---

*"Chekhov at Large" (1944), in *Chekhov: A Collection of Critical Essays*, ed. R. L. Jackson, Englewood Cliffs, N.J., 1967.
**See the chapter on Chekhov in his *History of Russian Literature*.

state of soul. They are "lyric constructions." That may partly explain the importance Chekhov gives to sounds, to precisely transcribed noises—night watchmen rapping on their wooden bars, the distinctive calls of corncrakes, cuckoos, bitterns, and "angry, straining frogs," the banging of shutters in a storm, the howling or singing of wood stoves, the humming of samovars, the ringing of bells—symbolic sounds, of which the most famous is the very last note in his work, the breaking string at the end of *The Cherry Orchard*.

Another aspect of Chekhov's originality is the inclusiveness of his world. He describes life in the capitals and the provinces, city life, village life, life in the new industrialized zones around the cities, life in European Russia, Siberia, the Crimea, the Far East, the life of noblemen, officials, clergy high and low, landowners, doctors, intellectuals, artists, actors, merchants, tradesmen, peasants, prisoners, exiles, pampered ladies, farm women, children, young men, old men, the sane, and the mad. "One of the basic principles of Chekhov's artistic work," Boris Eikhenbaum notes, "is the endeavor to embrace all of Russian life in its various manifestations, and not to describe selected spheres, as was customary before him. The Chekhovian grasp of Russian life is staggering; in this respect, as in many others, he cannot be compared with anyone . . ." His characters are not monumental personalities dramatically portrayed, like the heroes of Dostoevsky or Tolstoy, they are sharply observed types—the darling, the explainer, the fidget, the student, the malefactor, the man in a case, the heiress, the bishop, the fiancée. They are made of "the common stuff of humanity," as Mirsky has said, "and in this sense, Chekhov is the most 'democratic' of writers." There is something in them reminiscent of Chaucer's Canterbury pilgrims—the knight, the miller, the prioress, the parson, the manciple, the pardoner, the wife of Bath—but Chekhov's world is more scattered, and his people are transients of a more accidental sort: summer guests, doctors on call, hunters in the field, riders on ferries, passersby, city people displaced to the country, country people out of place in the city. Their pilgrimage has no definite goal.

Chekhov's early work was a popular success, and remains popular to this day among ordinary Russian readers, who do not share the common Western image of Chekhov as the pessimistic "poet of crepuscular moods," the "last singer of disintegrating trifles." His first collection, *Tales of Melpomene,* was published in 1884, the year he finished his medical studies; the second, *Motley Stories,* was published in 1886, and did so well that he gave up the idea of practicing medicine full-time and, with Grigorovich's blessing, devoted himself to writing. A year later came the collection *In the Twilight,* which was awarded the prestigious Pushkin Prize in 1888. Among the sketches and anecdotes of these early collections are some masterpieces of artistic concentration and force: not only "The Huntsman" but "The Malefactor," "Anyuta," "Easter Night," "Vanka," "Sleepy." Chekhov began writing plays at the same time, and with equal success. His first play, *Ivanov,* opened in Moscow on November 19, 1887. In January 1889 it was staged in Petersburg, where it was greeted with enthusiasm and much discussed in the newspapers and literary journals. The production later toured the provinces.

But, precisely because of its originality, Chekhov's work met with opposition from the established critics of the time. For decades literary criticism had been dominated by political ideologists, who judged literary works according to their social "message," their usefulness to the common cause. The writer was seen first of all as a pointer of the way, a leader in the struggle for social justice; his works were expected to be "true to life" and to carry a clear moral value. Faced with stories like "Anyuta" or "Easter Night," what were these critics to say? What were they to think of a writer whose first precept was the "absence of lengthy verbiage of a political-social-economic nature"? Chekhov's "impressionism" was seen as a form of art for art's sake, a denial of the writer's social role, and a threat to the doctrine of realism, and he was attacked for deviating from the canons of useful art.

In fact, just as Chekhov created a new kind of story, he also created a new image of the writer: the writer as detached observer, sober, restrained, modest, a craftsman shaping the material of prose under the demands of authenticity and precision, avoiding ideological excesses, the temptations of moral judgment, and the vainglory of great ideas. That is how Chekhov himself has most often been seen, and certainly it was in part what he wanted to be. He often joked about his ideological shortcomings. "I still lack a political, religious and philosophical world view," he wrote to Grigorovich on October 9, 1888. "I change it every month—and so I'll have to limit myself to descriptions of how my heroes love, marry, give birth, die, and how they speak." He considered that the writer's job, and thought it was enough. On October 27, 1888, he wrote to Alexei Suvorin:

> The artist must pass judgment only on what he under-stands; his range is as limited as that of any other special-ist—that's what I keep repeating and insisting upon. Anyone who says the artist's field is all answers and no questions has never done any writing or had any dealings with imagery. The artist observes, selects, guesses and syn-thesizes . . . You are right to demand that an author take conscious stock of what he is doing, but you are confus-ing two concepts: *answering the questions* and *formulating them correctly*. Only the latter is required of an author.

The leading critic of the time, the populist Nikolai Mikhailovsky, said that those who admired Chekhov admired him precisely for the "indifference and impassibility" with which he applied his excellent artistic apparatus to a swallow or a suicide, a fly or an elephant, tears or water—"a revelation they call 'the rehabilitation of reality' or 'pantheism.' All in nature . . . is equally worthy of artistic treatment, all can give equal artistic pleasure, and one must avoid selection ac-cording to a general idea or principle." Mikhailovsky considered this a waste of Chekhov's genuine talent. And Tolstoy, for all his admira-tion, was of a somewhat similar opinion. In August 1895, after Chekhov's first visit to his estate, he noted in his diary: "He is very gifted, must have a good heart, but up to now he has no definite point of view on things." The place Chekhov gave to contingency in his choice of themes and arrangement of details, the lack of any gen-eral idea to unify the whole, was considered his great originality or his great defect as an artist.

Chekhov privately defended himself against the attacks of his critics in a letter written on October 4, 1888, to Alexei Pleshcheev, literary editor of the *Northern Herald:*

> The people I am afraid of are the ones who look for tendentiousness between the lines and are determined to see me as either liberal or conservative. I am neither lib-eral nor conservative, nor gradualist, nor monk, nor in-differentist. I would like to be a free artist and nothing else, and I regret God has not given me strength to be

one. I hate lies and violence in all their forms, and consistory secretaries are just as odious to me as Notovich and Gradovsky [two unscrupulous left-wing journalists]. Pharisaism, dullwittedness and tyranny reign not only in merchants' homes and police stations. I see them in science, in literature, among the younger generation. That is why I cultivate no particular predilection for policemen, butchers, scientists, writers or the younger generation. I look upon tags and labels as prejudices. My holy of holies is the human body, health, intelligence, talent, inspiration, love and the most absolute freedom imaginable, freedom from violence and lies, no matter what form the latter two take. Such is the program I would adhere to if I were a major artist.

In his memoir *Chekhov with Us,* written not long after Chekhov's death in 1904, Kornei Chukovsky called this now-famous letter "a gauntlet flung in the face of an entire age, a rebellion against everything it held sacred." The anger in it is far from the sobriety of a detached observer of life. It is the anger of a man looking back over decades of empty rhetoric, of the posturings of literary professionals, of newspaper battles between various factions and tendencies, of general ideas that led nowhere, of new political and artistic movements that drew young people in, distorted their lives, and left them with nothing, of falsity and cruelty coming both from the authorities and from their opponents. Chekhov portrayed these things time and again in his stories and plays, obstinately opposing them in the name of his "holy of holies." The restraint of the cool scientist, which was his artistic ideal, was nourished by strong feeling and, as Chukovsky rightly says, by rebellion.

Chekhov's "impressionism" was not simply a literary manner: it corresponded to something much deeper in his perception of the world. The fragmentation of the picture into "separate brushstrokes" and the vagueness of the general outline reflect an inner state, perhaps best described by the old professor in "A Boring Story" (1889). This famous doctor, teacher, and man of science discovers something of a disturbingly non-scientific sort at the end of his life:

. . . in all the thoughts, feelings, and conceptions I form about everything, something general is lacking that would unite it all into a single whole. Each feeling and thought lives separately in me, and in all my opinions about science, the theater, literature, students, and in all the pictures drawn by my imagination, even the most skillful analyst would be unable to find what is known as a general idea or the god of the living man.

The professor's dilemma amounts to a commentary on Chekhov's artistic method. Like his hero, Chekhov refused to substitute a false god for the absent "god of the living man." In his revolt against general ideas, according to the philosopher Lev Shestov, he "finally frees himself from ideas of every kind, and loses even the notion of connection between the happenings of life. Herein lies the most important and original characteristic of his creation." Shestov's essay "Creation from the Void," written in 1908 and still one of the most penetrating discussions of Chekhov's art, contains the following description of the spiritual condition of that time:

To calculate beforehand is impossible. Impossible even to hope. Man has entered that stage of his existence wherein the cheerful and foreseeing mind refuses its service. It is impossible for him to present to himself a clear and distinct notion of what is going on. Everything takes on a tinge of fantastical absurdity. One believes and disbelieves—everything.

This was the condition within which, and against which, Chekhov worked. He was more acutely aware of it than most of his contemporaries, which is why we still read him with a sense of immediacy.

Chekhov came to literature by an unlikely path. He was born in 1860, in the town of Taganrog on the Sea of Azov. His grandfather was a serf, but bought freedom for himself and his family even before the emancipation of 1861. His father was a grocer. The family—there were three more brothers and a sister—was a very close one, and Chekhov always had the greatest respect for his parents, who were simple people, pious and not very educated. When he was seventeen, he wrote to his younger brother Mikhail: "Our parents are the only persons in the world for whom I will never stint in anything. If something becomes of me, it will be the work of their hands. The unlimited love they bear for their children is enough to put them beyond all praise and to cover up the faults provoked in them by a thankless life." He never separated from them, supported them as soon as he could, and in 1892, when he bought the small estate of Melikhovo, south of Moscow, brought them there to live with him, together with his sister and younger brother. Such family closeness was rare ("extremely rare," according to D. S. Mirsky) among the intelligentsia, but not among the peasants from whom Chekhov came.

From 1867 to 1879, he attended the Greek school in Taganrog, where he received an Orthodox religious education. His upbringing was also religious; he and his brothers sang in the church choir, conducted by their father; they read the Epistles and Psalms in church, served as altar boys and bell ringers. He looked back on the experience as rather gloomy, and later lost his faith, but his familiarity with church life shows in many of his stories, and his knowledge of the services and prayers was probably more precise than that of any other Russian writer. His work is also imbued with a Christian understanding of suffering. The critic Leonid Grossman has described him as "a probing Darwinist with the love of St. Francis of Assisi for every living creature."*

In 1876 Chekhov's father lost his business and to escape debtor's prison had to flee to Moscow, where his eldest son, Alexander, was studying. The rest of the family went with him, leaving the sixteen-year-old Anton to finish high school alone in Taganrog. He gave lessons to support himself, lived very poorly, but completed his studies in 1879, after which he joined his family in Moscow and entered medical school. Ten years later he gave an oblique description of the change he went through during this period of his life in a letter to Suvorin (January 7, 1889):

> What aristocratic writers take from nature gratis, the less privileged must pay for with their youth. Try and write a story about a young man—the son of a serf, a former grocer, choirboy, schoolboy and university student, raised on respect for rank, kissing priests' hands,

---

* "Chekhov as Naturalist" (1914), in *Chekhov*, ed. R. L. Jackson.

worshipping the ideas of others, and giving thanks for every piece of bread, receiving frequent whippings, making the rounds as a tutor without galoshes, brawling, torturing animals, enjoying dinners at the houses of rich relatives, needlessly hypocritical before God and man merely to acknowledge his own insignificance—write about how this young man squeezes the slave out of himself drop by drop and how, on waking up one fine morning, he finds that the blood coursing through his veins is no longer the blood of a slave, but that of a real human being.

To support his medical studies, and his family, Chekhov followed his brother Alexander's example and began to contribute brief sketches and stories to popular magazines, signing his work in various camouflaged ways, most often with the nickname "Antosha Chekhonte," bestowed on him by one of his teachers in Taganrog. He finished medical school in 1884, and though he never finally set up as a doctor, he always remained faithful to medicine and acknowledged that he owed a great deal to his study of the natural sciences and his acquaintance with the scientific method. "Both anatomy and belles-lettres are of equally noble descent," he once wrote to Suvorin, "they have identical goals and an identical enemy—the devil—and there is absolutely no reason for them to fight . . . Goethe the poet coexisted splendidly with Goethe the naturalist." During his years in Melikhovo, he organized clinics and gave free treatment to hundreds of peasants from the district. He helped to fight the cholera epidemics of 1891 and 1892, and worked for famine relief during the same period. He also built a school in Melikhovo in 1892, which came out so well that he was asked to build two more in neighboring villages during the next three years. He also built a bell tower for the village church. He donated thousands of books to the library in Taganrog and helped to set up a marine biology station in Yalta, where he lived after 1898. In practical matters, Chekhov was an enormously active man, and one can sense from his letters the relief he felt in taking up such work. Literature, his mistress, was a more ambiguous affair.

As early as 1888, he wrote to Suvorin expressing his admiration for men of action, in particular the explorer N. M. Przhevalsky:

I do infinitely love people like Przhevalsky. Their personality is a living document which shows society that beside the people who argue about optimism and pessimism, who, out of boredom, write trivial stories, unnecessary projects, and cheap dissertations, who lead a depraved existence in the name of denial of life, and who lie for the sake of a hunk of bread—beside the skeptics, mystics, psychopaths, Jesuits, philosophers, liberals, and conservatives—there are still people of another order, people of heroic action, of faith and a clear, conscious goal.*

It was in this same spirit that Chekhov decided, in 1890, to travel to Sakhalin Island, off the far eastern coast of Russia, to study conditions in this place that had been founded as a penal colony and to take a census of the population. "I owed a debt to medicine," he explained. The trip took him across the whole of Russia. He spent several months on the island, interviewed hundreds of people, took voluminous notes, and returned by ship via Hong Kong, Singapore, and Ceylon—an experience reflected in the story "Gusev."** The result of the trip was the documentary book *Sakhalin Island* (1893), which in turn resulted in certain reforms in the treatment of prisoners and the administration of the colony. Later Chekhov also sent shipments of books to the island's library.

Faithful to his family, to medicine, to the places that marked his life—Taganrog, Sakhalin, Melikhovo, Yalta—Chekhov was also faithful to his friends. A case in point is his resignation from the Russian Academy in quiet protest when the young Maxim Gorky was refused membership. His relations with Alexei Suvorin are another case in point, and a more telling one. The publisher of *New Time* became more and more conservative and pro-government as

---

* Trans. by Elizabeth Henderson, in *Chekhov,* ed. R. L. Jackson.

** According to the memoirs of his brother Mikhail, Chekhov sometimes swam off the ship with a towline and in that way once happened to observe the movements of a shark and a school of pilot fish. He also witnessed the burial of two men at sea: "When you see a dead man wrapped in sailcloth flying head over heels into the water . . . you grow frightened and somehow start thinking that you are going to die too and that you too will be thrown into the sea" (letter of Suvorin, December 9, 1890).

he grew older. Chekhov was far from sharing Suvorin's views and often wrote him caustic letters about them, but they remained friends. The only real break between them came over the Dreyfus affair. Chekhov had suffered a severe hemorrhage of the lungs in March of 1897 and was living in Nice when the Dreyfus case was reopened. He became a staunch Dreyfusard, and even went to Paris in April of the next year to meet with Dreyfus's brother and the journalist Bernard Lazare, whose articles had forced the reopening of the case, and offer them his support. Suvorin meanwhile took a strongly anti-Dreyfus and anti-Semitic position in his magazine, which so disgusted Chekhov that he stopped meeting and corresponding with him. But they made peace again before too long. Chekhov even managed to remain on good terms with his chief ideological opponent, Nikolai Mikhailovsky, whom he referred to privately as "an important sociologist and failed literary critic."

Chekhov was less faithful to the women who fell in love with him—and many did. There was Lika Mizinova, with whom he was "nearly" in love, but then failed to keep a rendezvous while traveling abroad in 1894. There was the novelist Lydia Avilova, whom he called to his bedside when he was hospitalized with consumption in 1897, and who left slightly deluded memoirs about their romance. There was also the mysterious "fiancée" he mentions in a letter, whose family nickname, "Missyus," he gave to the younger sister in "The House with the Mezzanine." It was only in 1899 that he met the woman he would finally marry: Olga Knipper, a young actress in the Moscow Art Theater. It was there, in the theater of Stanislavsky and Nemirovich-Danchenko, that his last plays were staged: *The Seagull,* which became the company's "totem," in 1898, followed by *Uncle Vanya* in 1899. In 1901, the year of their marriage, came the triumphant production of *Three Sisters,* and in 1904, just months before his death, the still greater triumph of *The Cherry Orchard.*

Chekhov's admiration for men of "heroic action" like Przhevalsky, and his own energetic activity as a doctor, a builder of schools and clinics, are oddly contradicted by the weakness, anguish, ineffectuality, and resignation of the protagonists in his stories and plays. In fact, contradiction runs deep in Chekhov's nature. It is not hard to find examples. He was the most humane of writers, yet his stories are as merciless as any ever written. He constantly portrayed himself in his work, and constantly denied it. His art has an air of impassivity, but is fueled by indignation and protest. He believed in progress, yet he shows only the natural and human waste it has caused. He scorned the new Symbolist movement in literature, but the surface objectivity of his work gives way time and again to a visionary symbolism of his own (of which "The Black Monk" is the most obvious, and least successful, example). This well-known Chekhovian ambiguity is not a halfhearted mixture of contraries. Resignation and revolt are equally extreme in his work and are mysteriously held together, though they ought to tear his world apart.

We may find the source of these contradictions in Chekhov's attitude toward science. "Goethe the poet coexisted splendidly with Goethe the naturalist," he wrote to Suvorin, expressing his own ideal. He had no doubt that his scientific training had been of benefit to his artistic work. "It significantly broadened the scope of my observations and enriched me with knowledge whose value for me as a writer only a doctor can appreciate . . . My familiarity with the natural sciences and the scientific method has always kept me on my guard; I have tried wherever possible to take scientific data into account, and where it has not been possible I have preferred not writing at all" (letter of October 11, 1899). But what sort of knowledge did he draw from science and the scientific worldview?

The chief thing it taught him was that the order of the world is implacable and indifferent to human suffering. He could observe its operation in the progress of his own illness, the first definite symptoms of which appeared in 1889, the year he wrote "A Boring Story," which marked the beginning of his maturity. He could also observe it in his medical practice, which, as Leonid Grossman has written, "brought home to Chekhov with remarkable fullness the horror of life, the cruelty of nature, and the impotence of man." Doctor-protagonists confront the same cruelty and impotence in scenes repeated throughout his work—with the brutality and indifference of human beings added to it, or simply making one with it.

Nikolai Stepanovich, the old professor in "A Boring Story," likes reading the current French authors, because "not seldom one finds in them the main element of creative work—a sense of personal freedom, which Russian authors don't have." Chekhov also preferred Flaubert, Zola, Maupassant, who, along with Tolstoy, were his acknowledged masters. Zola's notion of the writer-scientist and his concept of the "experimental novel" interested him, but formally speaking it was Maupassant who influenced him most. He learned much from Maupassant's handling of the short story, in which artistic refinement is hidden behind an apparent casualness and superficiality. As Leonid Grossman notes, Maupassant also "reinforced Chekhov's convictions about the colorlessness of life, the horror of death, the animal nature of man. Life in its basic nature is much simpler, shallower, and more insignificant than we are accustomed to think it—here is the hard core of Maupassant's work." But the contradictions in Chekhov were more profound and more fruitful than in the French naturalists. He absorbed their "dark tenets," but at the same time he rebelled against them with all his strength.

Andrei Yefimych, the doctor-protagonist of "Ward No. 6," meditating one night on the "life cycle," the naturalists' final solution to the question of human immortality, thinks to himself: "Only a coward whose fear of death is greater than his dignity can comfort himself with the thought that in time his body will live in grass, a stone, a toad . . . To see one's own immortality in the life cycle is as strange as to prophesy a brilliant future to the case after the costly violin has been broken and made useless." In a letter of April 16, 1897, Chekhov rejected Tolstoy's idealist notion of immortality in almost the same terms: "He recognizes immortality in its Kantian form, assuming that all of us (men and animals) will live on in some principle (such as reason or love), the essence of which is a mystery. But I can only imagine such a principle or force as a shapeless, gelatinous mass; my I, my individuality, my consciousness would merge with this mass—and I feel no need for this kind of immortality . . ."

Here we touch on the paradox that Lev Shestov finds at the heart of Chekhov's work:

> Idealism of every kind, whether open or concealed, roused feelings of intolerable bitterness in Chekhov. He found it more pleasant to listen to the merciless menaces of a downright materialist than to accept the dry-as-dust consolations of humanising idealism. An invincible power is in the world, crushing and crippling man—this is clear and even palpable. The least indiscretion, and the mightiest and the most insignificant alike fall victims to it. One can only deceive oneself about it as long

as one knows of it only by hearsay. But the man who has once been in the iron claws of necessity loses forever his taste for idealistic self-delusion.

And thus, says Shestov, "the only philosophy which Chekhov took seriously, and therefore seriously fought, was positivist materialism," which says that "man, brought face to face with the laws of nature, must always adapt himself and give way, give way, give way." The human spirit can only submit. And yet in Chekhov "the submission is but an outward show; under it lies concealed a hard, malignant hatred of the unknown enemy."

It is worth pursuing Shestov's argument, because it is easy to mistake his meaning. He calls Chekhov "the poet of hopelessness." This sounds like the same old accusation of pessimism and resignation that is so often leveled at Chekhov. But Shestov means something very different.

> Thus the real, the only hero of Chekhov, is the hopeless man. He has absolutely no *action* left for him in life, save to beat his head against the stones . . . He has nothing, he must create everything for himself. And this "creation out of the void," or more truly the possibility of this creation, is the only problem which can occupy and inspire Chekhov. When he has stripped his hero of the last shred, when nothing is left for him but to beat his head against the wall, Chekhov begins to feel something like satisfaction, a strange fire lights in his burnt-out eyes, a fire which Mikhailovsky did not call "evil" in vain.

Shestov is right to state the paradox in the most extreme terms. Chekhov, who admired men of action, has no *action* left except to beat his head against the wall. It is hardly a scientific way to proceed. But then, readily as he acknowledged his debt to science, it is precisely science that has "robbed him of everything." His only hope lies in utter hopelessness. Anything else would be a lie or a form of violence, a general idea or a utopia at gunpoint. And it is here, in this "void," that Chekhov begins "seeking new paths."

> Like Hamlet, he would dig beneath his opponent a mine one yard deeper, so that he may at one moment

blow engineer and engine into the air. His patience and fortitude in this hard, underground toil are amazing and to many intolerable. Everywhere is darkness, not a ray, not a spark, but Chekhov goes forward, slowly, hardly, hardly moving . . . An inexperienced or impatient eye will perhaps observe no movement at all. It may be Chekhov himself does not know for certain whether he is moving forward or marking time.

That is how Chekhov *formulates the question*. In a conversation with Ivan Bunin, he mentioned that his own favorite among his stories was "The Student," and wondered how people could call him a pessimist after that. The story is one of his shortest. It interweaves the student's grim thoughts about poverty and hunger and the surrounding emptiness and darkness—"all these horrors had been, and were, and would be, and when another thousand years had passed, life would be no better"—with his sudden recollection of Peter's denial of Christ. He tells the story to an old widow and her daughter, and they both begin to "weep bitterly," as Peter wept after his betrayal. The student goes on his way. "A cruel wind was blowing, and winter was indeed coming back, and it did not seem that in two days it would be Easter." He begins thinking about the widow: "If she wept, it meant that everything that had happened with Peter on that dreadful night had some relation to her . . ." And joy suddenly stirs in his soul: "The past, he thought, is connected with the present in an unbroken chain of events flowing one out of the other. And it seemed to him that he had just seen both ends of the chain: he touched one end, and the other moved." The student's thoughts are given only the slightest shade of irony, just enough to call his youthful "anticipation of happiness, an unknown, mysterious happiness" into question without demolishing it. That happiness remains, along with the tears of Peter and of the two women, along with the cold wind, the surrounding darkness, and the promise of Easter. "In his revelation of those evangelical elements," writes Leonid Grossman, "the atheist Chekhov is unquestionably one of the most Christian poets of world literature."

The old professor of "A Boring Story," who knows that he has only six months to live, finds something strange happening to him, despite his faith in science and indifference to "questions about the darkness beyond the grave."

In the midst of a lecture, tears suddenly choke me, my eyes begin to itch, and I feel a passionate, hysterical desire to stretch my arms out and complain loudly. I want to cry in a loud voice that fate has sentenced me, a famous man, to capital punishment, and that in six months or so another man will be master of this auditorium. I want to cry out that I've been poisoned; new thoughts such as I have never known before have poisoned the last days of my life and go on stinging my brain like mosquitoes. And at such times my situation seems so terrible that I want all my listeners to be horrified, to jump up from their seats and, in panic fear, rush for the exit with a desperate cry.

His stifled protest and hysteria have little in common with the dignity with which the bishop dies in almost the last story Chekhov wrote. But are the two men not essentially alike? The one belongs to the hierarchy of science, the other to the hierarchy of the Church, but life, which is given to us only once (how often Chekhov repeats that trite phrase!), is being taken from both of them, senselessly and ineluctably. Each of them is isolated from his family and friends in this incommunicable and incomprehensible experience. The bishop "goes to the Lord's Passion," to read the Gospel accounts of the crucifixion on Good Friday, and dies on Holy Saturday, before the bells joyfully announce the resurrection. What happens to him is the same as what happens to the old professor. By very different means, with opposite tonalities, both stories reveal the infinite value of what is perishing. Through the forms Chekhov finds to express this living contradiction, the world begins to show itself in a new way.

RICHARD PEVEAR

TRANSLATORS' NOTE

No one who makes a one-volume selection of Anton Chekhov's stories can help being painfully aware of what has been left out. Our selection represents all periods of Chekhov's creative life, from his first sketches to his very last story. We have included short pieces from different periods (it is interesting to see Chekhov return to the extreme brevity of his earliest work in "At Christmastime," written in 1900), and the most important of the longer stories, those of thirty-five to fifty pages. We have not included any of the "novelized stories" of eighty to a hundred pages—"The Steppe," "My Life," "The Duel," "Three Years"—thinking they would go better in a separate volume. As for the rest of the collection, it is meant to show the best of Chekhov's work in all its diversity.

Chekhov's prose does not confront the translator with the difficulties found in Gogol, Dostoevsky, or Leskov. "His temperament," as Nabokov remarked, "is quite foreign to verbal inventiveness." Words cannot be translated, but meanings can be, and rhythms can be. Every good writer has an innate rhythm, which "tells" the world in a certain way. Chekhov has a preference, especially in his later stories, for stringing clauses and sentences together with the conjunction "and": "Far ahead the windmills of the village of Mironositskoe were barely visible, to the right a line of hills stretched away and then disappeared far beyond the village, and they both knew that this was the bank of the river, with meadows, green willows, country houses, and if you stood on one of the hills, from there you could see equally vast fields, telegraph poles, and the train, which in the distance looked like a caterpillar crawling, and in clear weather you could even see the town." Often he begins sentences and even paragraphs with an "and," as if events keep accumulating without quite integrating. A related feature, and one more difficult to maintain in English, is his use of the continuous tense, with sudden shifts to the simple present or past and back again. We have tried as far as possible to keep these stylistic qualities in our translation.

We would like to express our gratitude to two Chekhovians, Cathy Popkin of Columbia University and Michael Finke of Washington University, for their suggestions of stories to be included. Limitations of space have kept us from following all of them, but without them the collection would not be what it is.

R. P., L. V.

The Death of a Clerk

One fine evening the no less fine office manager Ivan Dmitrich Cherviakov[1] was sitting in the second row of the stalls, watching *The Bells of Corneville*[2] through opera glasses. He watched and felt himself at the height of bliss. But suddenly . . . This "but suddenly" occurs often in stories. The authors are right: life is so full of the unexpected! But suddenly his face wrinkled, his eyes rolled, his breath stopped . . . he put down the opera glasses, bent forward, and . . . ah-choo!!! As you see, he sneezed. Sneezing is not prohibited to anyone anywhere. Peasants sneeze, police chiefs sneeze, sometimes even privy councillors sneeze. Everybody sneezes. Cherviakov, not embarrassed in the least, wiped his nose with his handkerchief and, being a polite man, looked around to see whether his sneezing had disturbed anyone. And now he did become embarrassed. He saw that the little old man sitting in front of him in the first row of the stalls was carefully wiping his bald head and neck with his glove and muttering something. Cherviakov recognized the little old man as General Brizzhalov,[3] who served in the Department of Transportation.

"I sprayed him!" thought Cherviakov. "He's not my superior, he serves elsewhere, but still it's awkward. I must apologize."

Cherviakov coughed, leaned forward, and whispered in the general's ear:

"Excuse me, Yr'xcellency, I sprayed you . . . I accidentally . . ."

"Never mind, never mind . . ."

"For God's sake, excuse me. I . . . I didn't mean it!"

"Ah, do sit down, please! Let me listen!"

Cherviakov became embarrassed, smiled stupidly, and began looking at the stage. He looked, but felt no more bliss. Anxiety began to torment him. In the intermission he went up to Brizzhalov, walked around him, and, overcoming his timidity, murmured:

"I sprayed you, Yr'xcellency . . . Forgive me . . . I . . . it's not that I . . ."

"Ah, come now . . . I've already forgotten, and you keep at it!" said the general, impatiently twitching his lower lip.

"Forgotten, but there's malice in his eyes," thought Cherviakov, glancing suspiciously at the general. "He doesn't even want to talk. I must explain to him that I really didn't mean it . . . that it's a law of nature, otherwise he'll think I wanted to spit. If he doesn't think so now, he will later! . . ."

On returning home, Cherviakov told his wife about his rudeness. His wife, it seemed to him, treated the incident much too lightly. She merely got frightened, but then, on learning that Brizzhalov served "elsewhere," she calmed down.

"But all the same you should go and apologize," she said. "He might think you don't know how to behave in public!"

"That's just it! I apologized, but he was somehow strange . . . Didn't say a single sensible word. And then there was no time to talk."

The next day Cherviakov put on a new uniform, had his hair cut, and went to Brizzhalov to explain . . . Going into the general's reception room, he saw many petitioners there, and among them was the general himself, who had already begun to receive petitions. Having questioned several petitioners, the general raised his eyes to Cherviakov.

"Yesterday, in the Arcadia, if you recall, Yr'xcellency," the office manager began, "I sneezed, sir, and . . . accidentally sprayed you . . . Forg . . ."

"Such trifles . . . God knows! Can I be of help to you?" the general addressed the next petitioner.

"He doesn't want to talk!" thought Cherviakov, turning pale. "That means he's angry . . . No, it can't be left like this . . . I'll explain to him . . ."

When the general finished his discussion with the last petitioner and headed for the inner rooms, Cherviakov followed him and murmured:

"Yr'xcellency! If I venture to trouble Yr'xcellency, it's precisely, I might say, from a feeling of repentance! . . . It wasn't on purpose, you know that yourself, sir!"

The general made a tearful face and waved his hand.

"You must be joking, my dear sir!" he said, disappearing behind the door.

"What kind of joke is it?" thought Cherviakov. "This is no kind of joke at all! A general, yet he can't understand! If that's the way it is, I won't apologize to the swaggerer any more! Devil take him! I'll write him a letter, but I won't come myself! By God, I won't!"

So Cherviakov thought, walking home. He wrote no letter to the general. He thought and thought, and simply could not think up that letter. So the next day he had to go himself and explain.

"I came yesterday to trouble Yr'xcellency," he began to murmur, when the general raised his questioning eyes to him, "not for a joke, as you were pleased to say. I was apologizing for having sneezed and sprayed you, sir . . . and I never even thought of joking. Would I dare joke with you? If we start joking, soon there won't be any respect for persons . . . left . . ."

"Get out!!" barked the general, suddenly turning blue and shaking.

"What, sir?" Cherviakov asked in a whisper, sinking with terror.

"Get out!!" the general repeated, stamping his feet.

Something in Cherviakov's stomach snapped. Seeing nothing, hearing nothing, he backed his way to the door, went out, and plodded off . . . Reaching home mechanically, without taking off his uniform, he lay down on the sofa and . . . died.

JULY 1883

SMALL FRY

D ear sir, father and benefactor!" the clerk Nevyrazimov[1] wrote in the draft of a letter of congratulations. "May you spend this bright day,[2] and many more to come, in good health and prosperity. And may your fam . . ."

The lamp, which was running out of kerosene, smoked and stank of burning. On the table, near Nevyrazimov's writing hand, a stray cockroach was anxiously running about. Two rooms away from the duty-room, the hall porter Paramon was polishing his Sunday boots for the third time, and with such energy that his spitting and the noise of the shoe brush could be heard in all the rooms.

"What else shall I write to the scoundrel?" Nevyrazimov reflected, raising his eyes to the sooty ceiling.

On the ceiling he saw a dark circle—the shadow of the lampshade. Further down were dusty cornices; still further down—walls that had once been painted a bluish-brown color. And the duty-room looked like such a wasteland to him that he felt pity not only for himself but even for the cockroach . . .

"I'll finish my duty and leave, but he'll spend his whole cockroach life on duty here," he thought, stretching. "Agony! Shall I polish my boots, or what?"

And, stretching once more, Nevyrazimov trudged lazily to the porter's lodge. Paramon was no longer polishing his boots . . . Holding the brush in one hand and crossing himself with the other, he was standing by the open vent window,[3] listening . . .

"They're ringing!" he whispered to Nevyrazimov, looking at him with fixed, wide-open eyes. "Already, sir!"

Nevyrazimov put his ear to the vent and listened. Through the vent, together with the fresh spring air, the ringing of the Easter bells came bursting into the room. The booming of the bells mingled with the noise of carriages, and all that stood out from the chaos of sounds was a pert tenor ringing in the nearest church and someone's loud, shrill laughter.

"So many people!" sighed Nevyrazimov, looking down the street, where human shadows flitted one after another past the lighted lamps. "Everybody's running to church . . . Our fellows must've had a drink by now and be hanging around the city. All that laughter and talking! I'm the only one so wretched as to have to sit here on such a day. And every year I have to do it!"

"Who tells you to get yourself hired? You weren't on duty today, it was Zastupov hired you to replace him. Whenever there's a holiday, you get yourself hired . . . It's greed!"

"The devil it's greed! What's there to be greedy about: two roubles in cash, plus a necktie . . . It's need, not greed! And, you know, it would be nice to go with them all to church now, and then break the fast[4] . . . Have a drink, a bite to eat, then hit the sack . . . You sit at the table, the kulich[5] has been blessed, and there's a hissing samovar, and some little object beside you . . . You drink a glass, chuck her under the chin, and it feels good . . . you feel you're a human being . . . Ehh . . . life's gone to hell! There's some rogue driving by in a carriage, and you just sit here thinking your thoughts . . ."

"To each his own, Ivan Danilych. God willing, you'll get promoted, too, and drive around in carriages."

"Me? No, brother, that I won't. I'll never get beyond titular councillor,[6] even if I burst . . . I'm uneducated."

"Our general hasn't got any education either, and yet . . ."

"Well, the general, before he amounted to all that, stole a hundred thousand. And his bearing is nothing like mine, brother . . . With my bearing you don't get far! And my name is so scoundrelly: Nevyrazimov! In short, brother, the situation's hopeless. Live like that if you want, and if you don't—go hang yourself . . ."

Nevyrazimov left the vent window and began pacing the rooms in anguish. The booming of the bells grew louder and louder . . . It was no longer necessary to stand by the window in order to hear it.

And the clearer the sound of the ringing, the noisier the clatter of the carriages, the darker seemed the brownish walls and sooty cornices, and the worse the smoking of the lamp.

"Maybe I'll skip work?" thought Nevyrazimov.

But escape did not promise anything worthwhile . . . After leaving the office and loitering around town, Nevyrazimov would go to his place, and his place was still grayer and worse than the duty-room . . . Suppose he spent that day nicely, in comfort, what then? The same gray walls, the same work for hire and letters of congratulations . . .

Nevyrazimov stopped in the middle of the duty-room and pondered.

The need for a new, better life wrung his heart with unbearable anguish. He passionately longed to find himself suddenly in the street, to merge with the living crowd, to take part in the festivity, in honor of which the bells were all booming and the carriages clattering. He wanted something he used to experience in childhood: the family circle, the festive faces of his relatives, the white table cloth, light, warmth . . . He remembered the carriage in which a lady had just passed by, the overcoat in which the office manager strutted about, the gold chain adorning the secretary's chest . . . He remembered a warm bed, a Stanislas,[7] new boots, a uniform with no holes in the elbows . . . remembered, because he did not have any of it . . .

"Maybe try stealing?" he thought. "Stealing's not hard, I suppose, but the problem is hiding it . . . They say people run away to America with what they steal, but, devil knows, where is this America? In order to steal, you also have to have education."

The ringing stopped. Only the distant noise of a carriage was heard, and Paramon's coughing, and Nevyrazimov's sadness and spite grew stronger and more unbearable. The office clock struck half-past midnight.

"Maybe write a denunciation? Proshkin denounced somebody and started rising in the world . . ."

Nevyrazimov sat down at his desk and pondered. The lamp, which had completely run out of kerosene, was smoking badly now and threatening to go out. The stray cockroach still scurried about the table and found no shelter . . .

"I could denounce somebody, but how write it out! It has to be with all those equivocations and dodges, like Proshkin . . . Not me!

I'll write something and get in trouble for it myself. A complete nitwit, devil take me!"

And Nevyrazimov, racking his brain for some way out of his hopeless situation, stared at the draft of the letter he had written. The letter was to a man he hated and feared with all his soul, and from whom he had been trying for ten years to obtain a transfer from a sixteen-rouble post to an eighteen-rouble . . .

"Ah . . . running about here, you devil!" With the palm of his hand he spitefully swatted the cockroach, which had had the misfortune of catching his eye. "What vileness!"

The cockroach fell on its back and desperately waved its legs . . . Nevyrazimov took it by one leg and threw it into the lamp. The lamp flared and crackled . . .

And Nevyrazimov felt better.

MARCH 1885

THE HUNTSMAN

A sultry and stifling day. Not a cloud in the sky ... The sun-scorched grass looks bleak, hopeless: there may be rain, but it will never be green again ... The forest stands silent, motionless, as if its treetops were looking off somewhere or waiting for something.

A tall, narrow-shouldered man of about forty, in a red shirt, patched gentleman's trousers, and big boots, lazily saunters along the edge of the clearing. He saunters down the road. To his right are green trees, to his left, all the way to the horizon, stretches a golden sea of ripe rye ... His face is red and sweaty. A white cap with a straight jockey's visor, apparently the gift of some generous squire, sits dashingly on his handsome blond head. Over his shoulder hangs a game bag with a crumpled black grouse in it. The man is carrying a cocked double-barreled shotgun and squinting his eyes at his old, skinny dog, who runs ahead, sniffing about in the bushes. It is quiet, not a sound anywhere ... Everything alive is hiding from the heat.

"Yegor Vlasych!" the hunter suddenly hears a soft voice.

He gives a start and turns around, scowling. Beside him, as if sprung from the ground, stands a pale-faced woman of about thirty with a sickle in her hand. She tries to peer into his face and smiles shyly.

"Ah, it's you, Pelageya!" says the hunter, stopping and slowly uncocking his gun. "Hm! ... How did you turn up here?"

"The women from our village are working here, so I'm here with them . . . Hired help, Yegor Vlasych."

"So-o . . ." Yegor Vlasych grunts and slowly goes on.

Pelageya follows him. They go about twenty steps in silence.

"I haven't seen you for a long time, Yegor Vlasych . . ." says Pelageya, gazing tenderly at the hunter's moving shoulders and shoulder blades. "You stopped by our cottage for a drink of water on Easter day, and we haven't seen you since . . . You stopped for a minute on Easter day, and that God knows how . . . in a drunken state . . . You swore at me, beat me, and left . . . I've been waiting and waiting . . . I've looked my eyes out waiting for you . . . Eh, Yegor Vlasych, Yegor Vlasych! If only you'd come one little time!"

"What's there for me to do at your place?"

"There's nothing to do there, of course, just . . . anyway there's the household . . . Things to be seen to . . . You're the master . . . Look at you, shot a grouse, Yegor Vlasych! Why don't you sit down and rest . . ."

As she says all this, Pelageya laughs like a fool and looks up at Yegor's face . . . Her own face breathes happiness . . .

"Sit down? Why not . . ." Yegor says in an indifferent tone and picks a spot between two pine saplings. "Why are you standing? Sit down, too!"

Pelageya sits down a bit further away in a patch of sun and, ashamed of her joy, covers her smiling mouth with her hand. Two minutes pass in silence.

"If only you'd come one little time," Pelageya says softly.

"What for?" sighs Yegor, taking off his cap and wiping his red forehead with his sleeve. "There's no need. To stop by for an hour or two—dally around, get you stirred up—and my soul can't stand living all the time in the village . . . You know I'm a spoiled man . . . I want there to be a bed, and good tea, and delicate conversation . . . I want to have all the degrees, and in the village there you've got poverty, soot . . . I couldn't even live there a day. Suppose they issued a decree that I absolutely had to live with you, I'd either burn down the cottage or lay hands on myself. From early on I've been spoiled like this, there's no help for it."

"Where do you live now?"

"At the squire Dmitri Ivanych's, as a hunter. I furnish game for his table, but it's more like . . . he keeps me because he's pleased to."

"It's not a dignified thing to do, Yegor Vlasych . . . For people it's just toying, but for you it's like a trade . . . a real occupation . . ."

"You don't understand, stupid," says Yegor, dreamily looking at the sky. "In all your born days you've never understood and never will understand what kind of a man I am . . . To you, I'm a crazy, lost man, but for somebody who understands, I'm the best shot in the whole district. The gentlemen feel it and even printed something about me in a magazine. Nobody can match me in the line of hunting . . . And if I scorn your village occupations, it's not because I'm spoiled or proud. Right from infancy, you know, I've never known any occupation but guns and dogs. Take away my gun, I'll get a fishing pole, take away the fishing pole, I'll hunt bare-handed. Well, and I also did some horse-trading, roamed around the fairs whenever I had some money, and you know yourself, if any peasant gets in with hunters or horse traders, it's good-bye to the plough. Once a free spirit settles in a man, there's no getting it out of him. It's like when a squire goes to the actors or into some other kind of artistry, then for him there's no being an official or a landowner. You're a woman, you don't understand, and it takes understanding."

"I understand, Yegor Vlasych."

"Meaning you don't understand, since you're about to cry . . ."

"I . . . I'm not crying . . ." says Pelageya, turning away. "It's a sin, Yegor Vlasych! You could spend at least one little day with me, poor woman. It's twelve years since I married you, and . . . and never once was there any love between us! . . . I . . . I'm not crying . . ."

"Love . . ." Yegor mutters, scratching his arm. "There can't be any love. It's just in name that we're man and wife, but is it really so? For you I'm a wild man, and for me you're a simple woman, with no understanding. Do we make a couple? I'm free, spoiled, loose, and you're a barefoot farm worker, you live in dirt, you never straighten your back. I think like this about myself, that I'm first in the line of hunting, but you look at me with pity . . . What kind of couple are we?"

"But we were married in church, Yegor Vlasych!" Pelageya sobs.

"Not freely . . . Did you forget? You can thank Count Sergei Pavlych . . . and yourself. The count was envious that I was a better shot than he was, kept me drunk for a whole month, and a drunk man can not only be married off but can even be seduced into a different faith. In revenge he up and married me to you . . . A huntsman to a cow girl. You could see I was drunk, why did you marry me? You're not a serf, you could have told him no! Of course, a cow girl's lucky to marry a huntsman, but we need to be reasonable. Well, so now you can suffer and cry. It's a joke for the count, but you cry . . . beat your head on the wall . . ."

Silence ensues. Three wild ducks fly over the clearing. Yegor looks at them and follows them with his eyes until they turn into three barely visible specks and go down far beyond the forest.

"How do you live?" he asks, shifting his eyes from the ducks to Pelageya.

"I go out to work now, and in winter I take a baby from the orphanage and nurse him with a bottle. They give me a rouble and a half a month."

"So-o . . ."

Again silence. From the harvested rows comes a soft song, which breaks off at the very beginning. It is too hot for singing . . .

"They say you put up a new cottage for Akulina," says Pelageya.

Yegor is silent.

"It means she's after your own heart . . ."

"That's just your luck, your fate!" says the hunter, stretching. "Bear with it, orphan. But, anyhow, good-bye, we've talked too much . . . I've got to make it to Boltovo by evening . . ."

Yegor gets up, stretches, shoulders his gun. Pelageya stands up.

"And when will you come to the village?" she asks softly.

"No point. I'll never come sober, and when I'm drunk there's not much profit for you. I get angry when I'm drunk . . . Good-bye!"

"Good-bye, Yegor Vlasych . . ."

Yegor puts his cap on the back of his head and, clucking for his dog, continues on his way. Pelageya stays where she is and looks at his back . . . She sees his moving shoulder blades, his dashing head, his lazy, nonchalant stride, and her eyes fill with sadness and a tender caress . . . Her gaze moves over the tall, skinny figure of her husband and caresses and fondles it . . . He seems to feel this gaze, stops, and looks back . . . He is silent, but Pelageya can see from his face, from his raised shoulders, that he wants to say something to her. She timidly goes up to him and looks at him with imploring eyes.

"For you!" he says, turning away.

He hands her a worn rouble and quickly walks off.

"Good-bye, Yegor Vlasych!" she says, mechanically accepting the rouble.

He walks down the long road straight as a stretched-out belt . . . She stands pale, motionless as a statue, and catches his every step with her eyes. But now the red color of his shirt merges with the dark color of his trousers, his steps can no longer be seen, the dog is indistinguishable from his boots. Only his visored cap can still be seen, but . . . suddenly Yegor turns sharply to the right in the clearing and the cap disappears into the greenery.

"Good-bye, Yegor Vlasych!" Pelageya whispers and stands on tiptoe so as at least to see the white cap one more time.

JULY 1885

THE MALEFACTOR

Before the examining magistrate stands a puny, exceedingly scrawny little peasant in a calico shirt and patched trousers. His face is overgrown with hair and eaten with pockmarks, and his eyes, barely visible through his thick, beetling brows, have an expression of sullen sternness. On his head a whole mop of long-uncombed, matted hair, which endows him with a still greater spiderlike sternness. He is barefoot.

"Denis Grigoriev!" the magistrate begins. "Come closer and answer my questions. On the seventh day of July instant the railroad watchman Ivan Semyonovich Akinfov, proceeding along the line in the morning, at the ninety-first mile post found you unscrewing one of the nuts by means of which the rails are fastened to the ties. Here is that nut! . . . With which nut he also detained you. Is that how it went?"

"Wha?"

"Did it all go as Akinfov explains?"

"Sure it did."

"Good. Now, why were you unscrewing the nut?"

"Wha?"

"Drop this 'wha?' of yours and answer the question: why were you unscrewing the nut?"

"If I didn't need it, I wouldn't have been unscrewing it," croaks Denis, looking askance at the ceiling.

"And why did you need this nut?"

"That nut there? We make sinkers out of 'em . . ."

"We who?"

"Us folk . . . the Klimovo peasants, that is."

"Listen, brother, don't play the idiot here. Talk sense. There's no point in lying about sinkers!"

"Never lied in all my born days, so now I'm lying . . ." mumbles Denis, blinking his eyes. "Could we do without a sinker, Your Honor? If you put a live worm or a minnow on a hook, how'll it ever go down without a sinker? Lying . . ." Denis smirks. "Who the devil needs live bait if it floats up top! Your perch, your pike, your burbot always bites on the bottom, and if the bait floats up top, it's only good for catching gobies, and even that's rare . . . Gobies don't live in our river . . . It's a fish that likes space."

"What are you telling me about gobies for?"

"Wha? But you asked yourself! The gentry here fish the same way, too. Not even the merest lad would go fishing without a sinker. Of course, if somebody's got no sense at all, he'll try and fish without a sinker. A fool is as a fool does . . ."

"So you tell me that you were unscrewing this nut in order to make a sinker out of it?"

"What else? Can't play knucklebones with it!"

"But you could use a bit of lead for a sinker, a bullet . . . a nail of some sort . . ."

"You won't find lead lying about, you've got to buy it, and a nail's no good. There nothing better than a nut . . . It's heavy, and it's got a hole in it."

"He pretends to be such a fool! As if he was born yesterday or fell from the moon! Don't you understand, dunderhead, what this unscrewing leads to? If the watchman hadn't spotted it, a train might have gone off the rails, people might have been killed! You'd have killed people!"

"God forbid, Your Honor! Why kill? Are we heathens or villains of some kind? Thank the Lord, my good sir, we've lived our life without any killing, such thoughts never even enter our head . . . Queen of Heaven, save us and have mercy . . . How could you, sir!"

"And what do you think causes train accidents? Unscrew two or three nuts, and you've got yourself an accident!"

Denis smirks and squints his eyes mistrustfully at the magistrate.

"Well! All these years the whole village has been unscrewing nuts and the Lord's preserved us, so now it's an accident . . . killing people . . . If I took away the rail or, let's say, put a log across the tracks, well, then the train might go off, but this . . . pah! a nut!"

"But you must understand, the nuts fasten the rail to the tie!"

"We understand that . . . We don't unscrew all of them . . . we leave some . . . We don't do it mindlessly . . . we understand . . ."

Denis yawns and makes a cross over his mouth.

"Last year a train went off the rails here," says the magistrate, "now I see why . . ."

"Beg pardon, sir?"

"Now, I said, I see why a train went off the rails last year . . . I understand!"

"That's what you get educated for, so you'll understand, most merciful judges . . . The Lord knew who to give understanding to . . . And here you've considered how and what, but a watchman's the same as a peasant, he's got no understanding, he just grabs you by the scruff of the neck and drags you off . . . Reason first, and then drag! Like they say—peasant head, peasant thoughts . . . Write this down, too, Your Honor, that he hit me twice in the teeth and the chest."

"When they searched your place, they found a second nut . . . When and where did you unscrew it?"

"You mean the one that was under the little red trunk?"

"I don't know where it was, I only know they found it. When did you unscrew it?"

"I didn't unscrew it, it was Ignashka, the son of one-eyed Semyon, gave it to me. I mean the one that was under the little trunk, and the one that was in the sledge in the yard I unscrewed along with Mitrofan."

"Which Mitrofan?"

"Mitrofan Petrov . . . You've never heard of him? He makes nets and sells them to the gentry. He needs a lot of these same nuts. Reckon maybe a dozen for each net . . ."

"Listen . . . Article one thousand and eighty-one of the Criminal Code says that any deliberate damage to the railways, in case it endangers the transport availing itself of those railways, and with the perpetrator's knowledge that the consequences thereof will be an accident—understand? knowledge! And you couldn't help knowing what this unscrewing would lead to—will be punishable by a term at hard labor."

"Of course, you know best . . . We're ignorant folk . . . what do we understand?"

"You understand everything! You're lying and dissembling!"

"Why lie? Ask in the village, if you don't believe me . . . Without a sinker you only get bleak. You won't even get gudgeon, the worst of the lot, without a sinker."

"Next you'll be talking about gobies again!" the magistrate smiles.

"We've got no gobies here . . . If we fish on top without a sinker, using butterflies for bait, we get chub, and even that's rare."

"Well, be quiet . . ."

Silence ensues. Denis shifts from one foot to the other, stares at the table covered with green baize, and blinks his eyes strenuously, as if what he sees before him is not baize but the sun. The magistrate is writing rapidly.

"Can I go?" asks Denis, after some silence.

"No. I must put you under arrest and send you to prison."

Denis stops blinking and, raising his thick eyebrows, looks questioningly at the official.

"That is, how do you mean—to prison? Your Honor! I haven't got time, I have to go to the fair, and also get three roubles from Yegor for the lard . . ."

"Quiet, don't disturb me . . ."

"To prison . . . If it was for something, I'd go, but like this . . . for a fleabite . . . Why? Seems I didn't steal, I didn't fight . . . And if you've got doubts about the arrears, Your Honor, don't believe the headman . . . Better ask mister permanent member . . . An ungodly fellow, that headman . . ."

"Quiet!"

"I'm quiet as it is . . ." mutters Denis. "I'll swear an oath the headman's accounts are a pack of lies . . . We're three brothers: Kuzma Grigoriev, that is, and Yegor Grigoriev, and me, Denis Grigoriev . . ."

"You're disturbing me . . . Hey, Semyon!" shouts the magistrate. "Take him away!"

"We're three brothers," mutters Denis, as two stalwart soldiers take him and lead him from the chamber. "Brother's not answer-

able for brother. Kuzma doesn't pay and you, Denis, have to answer . . . Judges! Our late master, the general, died, may he rest in
peace, otherwise he'd show you judges something . . . You've got to
judge knowingly, not just anyhow . . . Give a whipping, even, but
so as it's for a reason, in all fairness . . ."

JULY 1885

PANIKHIDA

In the church of the Mother of God Hodigitria,[1] the one in the village of Verkhnie Zaprudy, the morning liturgy has just ended. People have begun moving and pouring out of the church. The only one who does not stir is the shopkeeper Andrei Andreich, the Verkhnie Zaprudy intellectual and old-timer. He leans his elbow on the railing of the choir to the right and waits. His clean-shaven, fat face, bumpy from former pimples, on this occasion expresses two opposite feelings: humility before inscrutable destiny, and a dumb, boundless haughtiness before all those passing kaftans and motley kerchiefs. He is smartly dressed for Sunday. He is wearing a flannel coat with yellow ivory buttons, dark blue, straight-legged trousers, and stout galoshes, the same huge, clumsy galoshes that are met with only on the feet of people who are positive, sensible, and have firm religious convictions.

His swollen, lazy eyes are turned to the iconostasis.[2] He sees the long-familiar faces of the saints, the caretaker Matvei puffing his cheeks to blow out the candles, the darkened icon stands, the worn rug, the beadle Lopukhov, who rushes from the sanctuary and brings the warden a prosphora[3] . . . All this he has seen over and over again, like his own five fingers . . . One thing, however, is somewhat strange and unusual: Father Grigory is standing by the north door, still in his vestments, blinking angrily with his thick eyebrows.

"Who is he blinking at, God be with him?" thinks the

shopkeeper. "Ah, now he's beckoning with his finger! And, mercy me, stamping his foot . . . Holy Mother, what a thing! Who is it at?"

Andrei Andreich turns around and sees that the church is already quite empty. There are about a dozen people crowding at the door, and with their backs turned to the sanctuary.

"Come when you're called! Why are you standing there like a statue?" he hears the angry voice of Father Grigory. "It's you I'm calling!"

The shopkeeper looks at the red, wrathful face of Father Grigory and only now realizes that the blinking of the eyebrows and beckoning of the finger may be addressed to him. He gives a start, separates himself from the choir, and, stamping his stout galoshes, goes hesitantly towards the sanctuary.

"Andrei Andreich, was it you who sent in a note about the departed Maria?" the priest asks, angrily looking up at his fat, sweaty face.

"It was."

"So, then, it was you who wrote this? You?"

And Father Grigory angrily thrusts a little note into his eyes. And in this note, which Andrei Andreich sent in with a prosphora for the proskomedia,[4] there is written in big, unsteady-looking letters:

"For the departed servant of God, the harlot Maria."

"It was . . . I wrote it, sir . . ." the shopkeeper replies.

"But how did you dare to write that?" the priest draws out in a whisper, and in his hoarse whisper both wrath and fear can be heard.

The shopkeeper gazes at him in dumb astonishment, becomes perplexed and frightened himself: never before has Father Grigory spoken in that tone with the Verkhnie Zaprudy intellectual! For a moment the two are silent, peering into each other's eyes. The shopkeeper's perplexity is so great that his fat face spreads in all directions like spilled batter.

"How did you dare?" the priest repeats.

"Wh . . . what, sir?" Andrei Andreich's perplexity continues.

"You don't understand?!" Father Grigory whispers, stepping back in amazement and clasping his hands. "What's that on your shoulders—a head, or some other object? You send a note in to the sanctuary and write a word on it that is even indecent to say in the street! Why are you goggling your eyes? Don't you know the meaning of this word?"

"That is, concerning the harlot, sir?" murmurs the shopkeeper, blushing and blinking his eyes. "But the Lord, in his goodness, I mean . . . that is, he forgave the harlot . . . and prepared a place for her, and from the life of the blessed Mary of Egypt[5] we can see, in that same sense of the word, begging your pardon . . ."

The shopkeeper wants to give some further argument as an excuse, but gets confused and wipes his mouth with his sleeve.

"So that's how you understand it!" Father Grigory clasps his hands. "But the Lord forgave—you understand?—forgave, and you judge, denounce, call someone an indecent name—and who? Your own departed daughter! Not only in sacred, but even in secular writings you cannot find such a sin! I repeat to you, Andrei: don't get too clever! Yes, brother, don't get too clever! God may have given you a searching mind, but if you can't control it, you'd better give up thinking . . . Give up thinking and keep quiet!"

"But she was a sort of . . . begging your pardon . . . a play-actress!" pronounces the stunned Andrei Andreich.

"A play-actress! But whoever she was, you must forget it all after her death, and not go writing it in your notes!"

"That's so . . ." agrees the shopkeeper.

"You ought to have a penance laid on you." From inside the sanctuary comes the bass voice of the deacon, who looks contemptuously at Andrei Andreich's abashed face. "Then you'd stop acting smart! Your daughter was a famous artiste. Her death was even reported in the newspapers . . . Philosophizer!"

"That, of course . . . in fact . . ." mutters the shopkeeper, "is not a suitable word, but it wasn't by way of judging, Father Grigory, but to make it godly-like . . . so you could see better who to pray for. People do write different titles for commemoration, like, say, the child Ioann, the drowned Pelageya, the warrior Yegor, the murdered Pavel, and such like . . . That's what I wanted."

"None too bright, Andrei! God will forgive you, but next time watch out. Above all, don't get clever, just think as others do. Make ten bows and go."

"Yes, sir," says the shopkeeper, happy that the admonishment is over, and again giving his face an expression of gravity and importance. "Ten bows? Very good, sir, I understand. And now, Father, allow me to make a request . . . Because, since I'm her father, after all . . . you know, and she, whatever she was, she's my daughter, after all, I sort of . . . begging your pardon, I'd like to ask you to serve a panikhida[6] today. And I'd like to ask you, too, Father Deacon!"

"Now, that's good!" says Father Grigory, taking off his vestments. "I praise you for it. Meets my approval . . . Well, go! We'll come out at once."

Andrei Andreich gravely walks away from the sanctuary and stops in the middle of the church, flushed, with a solemnly panikhidal expression on his face. The caretaker Matvei places a little table with kolivo[7] before him, and in a short time the panikhida begins.

The church is quiet. There is only the metallic sound of the censer and the drawn-out singing . . . Beside Andrei Andreich stands the caretaker Matvei, the midwife Makaryevna, and her boy Mitka with the paralyzed arm. There is no one else. The beadle sings poorly, in an unpleasant, hollow bass, but the melody and the words are so sad that the shopkeeper gradually loses his grave expression and is plunged in sorrow. He remembers his little Mashutka. He recalls that she was born while he was still working as a servant for the master of Verkhnie Zaprudy. Owing to the bustle of his servant's life, he did not notice his girl growing up. For him the long period during which she formed into a graceful being with a blond little head and pensive eyes as big as kopecks went unnoticed. She was brought up, like all children of favorite servants, pampered, together with the young ladies. The gentlefolk, having nothing to do, taught her to read, write, and dance, and he did not interfere with her upbringing. Only rarely, accidentally, meeting her somewhere by the gate or on the landing of the stairs, did he remember that she was his daughter, and he began, as far as his time allowed, to teach her prayers and sacred history. Oh, even then he had a reputation for knowing the services and the holy scriptures! The girl, however grim and solemn her father's face, listened to him willingly. She yawned repeating prayers after him, but on the other hand, when he began telling her stories, stammering and adding flowery embellishments, she turned all ears. At Esau's mess of pottage, the punishment of Sodom, and the ordeals of the little boy Joseph,[8] she grew pale and opened her blue eyes wide.

Later, when he quit being a servant and opened a village shop with the money he had saved, Mashutka left for Moscow with the master's family.

Three years before her death, she came to see her father. He barely recognized her. She was a slender young woman with the manners of a lady and dressed like gentlefolk. She spoke cleverly, as if from a book, smoked tobacco, slept till noon. When Andrei Andreich asked her what she was, she boldly looked him straight in the eye and said: "I am an actress!" Such frankness seemed to the former servant the height of cynicism. Mashutka began boasting of her successes and of her artistic life, but seeing that her father only turned purple and spread his arms, she fell silent. And thus silently, without looking at each other, they spent some two weeks, until she left. Before leaving, she persuaded her father to go for a stroll with her along the embankment. Terrified though he was of going for a stroll with his actress daughter in broad daylight, in front of all honest people, he yielded to her entreaties . . .

"What wonderful places you have here!" she admired as they strolled. "Such dells and marshes! God, how beautiful my birthplace is!"

And she wept.

"These places only take up room . . ." thought Andrei Andreich, gazing stupidly at the dells and failing to understand his daughter's admiration. "They're about as useful as teats on a bull."

But she wept, wept and breathed greedily with her whole breast, as if sensing that she did not have long to breathe . . .

Andrei Andreich tosses his head like a stung horse and, to stifle the painful memories, starts crossing himself rapidly . . .

"Remember, O Lord," he murmurs, "the departed servant of God, the harlot Maria, and forgive her transgressions both voluntary and involuntary . . ."

The indecent word again escapes his mouth, but he does not notice it: what is stuck fast in his consciousness will not be dug out of it even by a nail, still less by Father Grigory's admonitions! Makaryevna sighs and whispers something, sucking in air. Mitka with the paralyzed arm ponders something . . .

". . . where there is no sickness, sorrow or sighing . . ." drones the beadle, putting his hand to his right cheek.

Bluish smoke streams from the censer and bathes in a wide,

slanting ray of sunlight that crosses the gloomy, lifeless emptiness of the church. And it seems that, together with the smoke, the soul of the departed woman herself hovers in the ray of sunlight. The streams of smoke, looking like a child's curls, twist, rush upwards to the window and seem to shun the dejection and grief that fill this poor soul.

FEBRUARY 1886

Anyuta

In the cheapest furnished rooms of the Hotel Lisbon, the third-year medical student, Stepan Klochkov, paced up and down and diligently ground away at his medicine. The relentless, strenuous grinding made his mouth dry, and sweat stood out on his forehead.

By the window, coated at the edges with icy designs, his roommate Anyuta sat on a stool. She was a small, thin brunette of about twenty-five, very pale, with meek gray eyes. Her back bent, she was embroidering the collar of a man's shirt with red thread. It was an urgent job . . . The clock in the corridor hoarsely struck two, but the room had not yet been tidied. A crumpled blanket, scattered pillows, books, clothes, a large, dirty basin filled with soapy swill, in which cigarette butts floated, litter on the floor—it all looked as if it had been piled in a heap, purposely confused, crumpled . . .

"The right lung consists of three sections . . ." repeated Klochkov. "The boundaries! The upper section reaches the fourth or fifth rib on the front wall of the chest, the fourth rib at the side . . . the *spina scapulae* in the back . . ."

Klochkov, straining to visualize what he had just read, raised his eyes to the ceiling. Getting no clear impression, he began feeling his own upper ribs through his waistcoat.

"These ribs are like piano keys," he said. "To avoid confusion in counting them, one absolutely must get used to them. I'll have to study it with a skeleton and a living person . . . Come here, Anyuta, let me try to get oriented!"

Anyuta stopped embroidering, took off her blouse, and straightened up. Klochkov sat down facing her, frowned, and began counting her ribs.

"Hm . . . The first rib can't be felt . . . It's behind the collarbone . . . Here's the second rib . . . Right . . . Here's the third . . . Here's the fourth . . . Hm . . . Right . . . Why are you flinching?"

"Your fingers are cold!"

"Well, well . . . you won't die, don't fidget. So then, this is the third rib, and this is the fourth . . . You're so skinny to look at, yet I can barely feel your ribs. The second . . . the third . . . No, I'll get confused this way and won't have a clear picture . . . I'll have to draw it . . . Where's my charcoal?"

Klochkov took a piece of charcoal and drew several parallel lines with it on Anyuta's chest, corresponding to the ribs.

"Excellent. All just like the palm of your hand . . . Well, and now we can do some tapping. Stand up!"

Anyuta stood up and lifted her chin. Klochkov started tapping and got so immersed in this occupation that he did not notice that Anyuta's lips, nose, and fingers had turned blue with cold. Anyuta was shivering and feared that the medical student, noticing her shivering, would stop drawing with charcoal and tapping, and would perhaps do poorly at the examination.

"Now it's all clear," said Klochkov, and he stopped tapping. "You sit like that, without wiping off the charcoal, while I go over it a little more."

And the medical student again began pacing and repeating. Anyuta, as if tattooed, black stripes on her chest, shrunken with cold, sat and thought. She generally spoke very little, was always silent and kept thinking, thinking . . .

In all her six or seven years of wandering through various furnished rooms, she had known some five men like Klochkov. Now they had all finished their studies, had made their way in life, and, of course, being decent people, had long forgotten her. One of them lived in Paris, two had become doctors, the fourth an artist, and the fifth was even said to be a professor already. Klochkov was the sixth . . . Soon he, too, would finish his studies and make his way. The future would no doubt be beautiful, and Klochkov would probably become a great man, but the present was thoroughly bad: Klochkov had no tobacco, no tea, and there were only four pieces of sugar left. She had to finish her embroidery as quickly as possible, take it to the customer, and, with the twenty-five kopecks she would get, buy tea and tobacco.

"Can I come in?" came from outside the door.

Anyuta quickly threw a woolen shawl over her shoulders. The painter Fetisov came in.

"I've come to you with a request," he began, addressing Klochkov and looking ferociously from under the hair hanging on his forehead. "Be so good as to lend me your beautiful maiden for an hour or two! I'm working on a painting, and I can't do without a model!"

"Ah, with pleasure!" Klochkov agreed. "Go on, Anyuta."

"What business do I have there?" Anyuta said softly.

"Well, really! The man's asking for the sake of art, not for some trifle. Why not help if you can?"

Anyuta began to dress.

"And what are you painting?" asked Klochkov.

"Psyche. A nice subject, but it somehow won't come out right. I have to use different models all the time. Yesterday there was one with blue feet. Why are your feet blue? I ask. My stockings ran, she says. And you keep grinding away! Lucky man, you've got patience."

"Medicine's that sort of thing, you have to grind away at it."

"Hm . . . I beg your pardon, Klochkov, but you live like an awful swine. Devil knows how you can live this way!"

"How do you mean? I can't live any other way . . . I get only twelve roubles a month from the old man, and it's a real trick to live decently on that."

"So it is . . ." said the artist, wincing squeamishly, "but all the same you could live better . . . A developed man absolutely must be an aesthete. Isn't that true? And here you've got devil knows what! The bed isn't made, there's swill, litter . . . yesterday's kasha on a plate . . . pah!"

"That's true," said the medical student, and he became embarrassed, "but Anyuta didn't manage to tidy up today. She's busy all the time."

When the artist and Anyuta left, Klochkov lay down on the sofa and began to study lying down, then accidentally fell asleep, woke up an hour later, propped his head on his fists and pondered gloomily. He remembered the artist's words, that a developed man absolutely must be an aesthete, and his room indeed seemed disgusting, repulsive to him now. It was as if he foresaw the future with his mental eye, when he would receive patients in his office, have tea in a spacious dining room in company with his wife, a respectable woman—and now this basin of swill with cigarette butts floating in it looked unbelievably vile. Anyuta, too, seemed homely, slovenly, pitiful . . . And he decided to separate from her, at once, whatever the cost.

When she came back from the artist's and began taking off her coat, he stood up and said to her seriously:

"The thing is this, my dear . . . Sit down and listen to me. We have to separate! In short, I don't wish to live with you anymore."

Anyuta had come back from the artist's so tired, so worn out. She had posed for so long that her face had become pinched, thin, and her chin had grown sharper. She said nothing in reply to the medical student's words, only her lips began to tremble.

"You must agree that we'll have to separate sooner or later anyway," said the medical student. "You're good, kind, and not stupid—you'll understand . . ."

Anyuta put her coat back on, silently wrapped her embroidery in paper, gathered up her needles and thread; she found the little packet with four pieces of sugar in it on the windowsill and put it on the table near the books.

"It's yours . . . some sugar . . ." she said softly and turned away to hide her tears.

"Well, what are you crying for?" asked Klochkov.

He walked across the room in embarrassment and said:

"You're strange, really . . . You know yourself that we have to separate. We can't be together forever."

She had already picked up all her bundles and turned to him to say good-bye, but he felt sorry for her.

"Why not let her stay another week?" he thought. "Yes, indeed, let her stay, and in a week I'll tell her to leave."

And, annoyed at his own lack of character, he shouted at her sternly:

"Well, why are you standing there! If you're going, go, and if you don't want to, take your coat off and stay! Stay!"

Silently, quietly, Anyuta took off her coat, then blew her nose, also quietly, gave a sigh, and noiselessly went to her permanent post—the stool by the window.

The student drew the textbook towards him and again began pacing up and down.

"The right lung consists of three sections . . ." he ground away. "The upper section reaches the fourth or fifth rib on the front wall of the chest . . ."

And someone in the corridor shouted at the top of his voice:

"Gr-r-rigory, the samovar!"

FEBRUARY 1886

Easter Night

I was standing on the bank of the Goltva and waiting for the ferry from the other side. Ordinarily the Goltva is a middling sort of stream, silent and pensive, sparkling meekly through the thick bulrushes, but now a whole lake was spread before me. The spring waters had broken loose, overflowed both banks and flooded far out on both sides, covering kitchen gardens, hayfields and marshes, so that you often came upon poplars and bushes sticking up solitarily above the surface of the water, looking like grim rocks in the darkness.

The weather seemed magnificent to me. It was dark, but I could still see trees, water, people . . . The world was lit by the stars, which were strewn massively across the sky. I do not recall ever having seen so many stars. You literally could not put a finger between them. There were some as big as goose eggs, some as tiny as hempseed . . . For the sake of the festive parade, all of them, from small to large, had come out in the sky, washed, renewed, joyful, and all of them to the last one quietly moved their rays. The sky was reflected in the water; the stars bathed in the dark depths and trembled with their light rippling. The air was warm and still . . . Far away on the other side, in the impenetrable darkness, a few scattered fires burned bright red . . .

Two steps away from me darkened the silhouette of a peasant in a tall hat and with a stout, knotty stick.

"There's been no ferry for a long while now," I said.

"It's time it came," the silhouette replied.

"Are you also waiting for the ferry?"

"No, I'm just . . ." the peasant yawned, "waiting for the lumination. I'd have gone, but, to tell the truth, I haven't got the five kopecks for the ferry."

"I'll give you five kopecks."

"No, thank you kindly . . . You use those five kopecks to light a candle for me in the monastery . . . That'll be curiouser, and I'll just stay here. Mercy me, no ferry! As if it sank!"

The peasant went right down to the water, took hold of the cable, and called out:

"Ieronym! Ierony-y-ym!"

As if in answer to his shout, the drawn-out tolling of a big bell came from the other side. The tolling was dense, low, as from the thickest string of a double bass: it seemed that the darkness itself had groaned. All at once a cannon shot rang out. It rolled through the darkness and ended somewhere far behind my back. The peasant took off his hat and crossed himself.

"Christ is risen!"[1] he said.

Before the waves from the first stroke of the bell congealed in the air, a second was heard, and immediately after it a third, and the darkness was filled with an incessant, trembling sound. New lights flared up by the red fires, and they all started moving, flickering restlessly.

"Ierony-y-ym!" a muted, drawn-out call was heard.

"They're calling from the other side," said the peasant. "That means the ferry's not there either. Our Ieronym's asleep."

The lights and the velvety ringing of the bell were enticing . . . I was beginning to lose patience and become agitated, but then, finally, as I peered into the dark distance, I saw the silhouette of something that looked very much like a gallows. It was the long-awaited ferry. It was moving so slowly that if it had not been for the gradual sharpening of its outline, one might have thought it was standing in place or moving towards the other shore.

"Quick! Ieronym!" my peasant shouted. "A gentleman's waiting!"

The ferry crept up to the bank, lurched, and creaked to a stop. On it, holding the cable, stood a tall man in a monk's habit and a conical hat.

"Why so long?" I asked, jumping aboard the ferry.

"Forgive me, for the sake of Christ," Ieronym said softly. "Is there anybody else?"

"Nobody . . ."

Ieronym took hold of the cable with both hands, curved himself into a question mark, and grunted. The ferry creaked and lurched. The silhouette of the peasant in the tall hat slowly began to recede from me—which meant that the ferry was moving. Soon Ieronym straightened up and began working with one hand. We were silent and looked at the bank towards which we were now moving. There the "lumination" which the peasant had been waiting for was already beginning. At the water's edge, barrels of pitch blazed like huge bonfires. Their reflection, crimson as the rising moon, crept to meet us in long, wide stripes. The burning barrels threw light on their own smoke and on the long human shadows that flitted about the fire; but further to the sides and behind them, where the velvet ringing rushed from, was the same impenetrable darkness. Suddenly slashing it open, the golden ribbon of a rocket soared skywards; it described an arc and, as if shattering against the sky, burst and came sifting down in sparks. On the bank a noise was heard resembling a distant "hoorah."

"How beautiful!" I said.

"It's even impossible to say how beautiful!" sighed Ieronym. "It's that kind of night, sir! At other times you don't pay any attention to rockets, but now any vain thing makes you glad. Where are you from?"

I told him where I was from.

"So, sir . . . a joyful day this is . . ." Ieronym went on in a weak, gasping tenor, the way convalescents speak. "Heaven and earth and under the earth rejoice. The whole of creation celebrates. Only tell me, good sir, why is it that even amidst great joy a man can't forget his griefs?"

It seemed to me that this unexpected question was an invitation to one of those "longanimous," soul-saving conversations that idle and bored monks love so much. I was not in the mood for much talking and therefore merely asked:

"And what are your griefs, my good man?"

"Ordinary ones, like all people have, Your Honor, but this day a particular grief happened in the monastery: at the liturgy itself, during the Old Testament readings, the hierodeacon Nikolai died . . ."

"Then it's God's will!" I said, shamming a monkish tone. "We all must die. In my opinion you should even be glad . . . They say whoever dies on the eve of Easter or on Easter day will surely get into the Kingdom of Heaven."

"That's so."

We fell silent. The silhouette of the peasant in the tall hat merged with the outline of the bank. The pitch barrels flared up more and more.

"And scripture clearly points out the vanity of grief and the need for reflection," Ieronym broke the silence, "but what makes the soul grieve and refuse to listen to reason? What makes you want to weep bitterly?"

Ieronym shrugged his shoulders, turned to me, and began talking quickly:

"If it was I who died or somebody else, maybe it wouldn't be so noticeable, but it was Nikolai who died! Nobody else but Nikolai! It's even hard to believe he's no longer in the world! I stand here on the ferry and keep thinking his voice will come from the bank any minute. He always came down to the bank and called out to me so that I wouldn't feel scared on the ferry. He got out of bed in the middle of the night especially for that. A kind soul! God, what a kind and merciful soul! Some people's mothers are not to them like this Nikolai was to me! Lord, save his soul!"

Ieronym took hold of the cable, but at once turned to me again.

"And such a bright mind, Your Honor!" he said in a sing-song voice. "Such sweet, good-sounding speech! Exactly like what they're about to sing in the matins: 'O how loving-kind! O how most sweet is thy word!'[2] Besides all the other human qualities, he also had an extraordinary gift!"

"What gift?" I asked.

The monk looked me up and down and, as if having assured himself that I could be entrusted with secrets, laughed gaily.

"He had the gift of writing akathists[3] . . ." he said. "A wonder, sir, and nothing but! You'll be amazed if I explain it to you! Our father archimandrite[4] is from Moscow, our father vicar graduated from the Kazan theological academy, there are intelligent hieromonks and elders among us, and yet, just imagine, not a single one of them could write akathists, but Nikolai, a simple monk, a hierodeacon, never studied anywhere and even had no external appeal, and yet he wrote! A wonder. A real wonder!"

Ieronym clasped his hands and, forgetting all about the cable, went on enthusiastically:

"Our father vicar has difficulty composing sermons; when he was writing the history of the monastery, he got all the brothers into a sweat and went to town ten times, but Nikolai wrote akathists! Akathists! A sermon or a history is nothing next to that!"

"So it's really difficult to write akathists?" I asked.

"There's enormous difficulty . . ." Ieronym wagged his head. "Wisdom and holiness won't do anything here, if God doesn't give you the gift. Monks who don't understand about it reckon you only need to know the life of the saint you're writing to, and then follow the other akathists. But that's not right, sir. Of course, a man who writes an akathist has to know the life extremely well, to the last little point. Well, and also to follow the other akathists, how to begin and what to write about. To give you an example, the first kontakion begins every time with 'the victorious' or 'the chosen' . . . The first ikos always has to begin with angels. In the akathist to the Most Sweet Jesus, if you're interested, it begins like this: 'Creator of angels and lord of hosts,' in the akathist to the Most Holy Mother of God: 'An angel was sent from heaven to stand before,' to Saint Nicholas the Wonderworker:[5] 'An angel in appearance, but of earthly nature,' and so on. There's always an angel at the beginning. Of course, you can't do without following, but the main thing is not in the life, not in the correspondence with the others, but in the beauty and sweetness. It all has to be shapely, brief, and thorough. There should be softness, gentleness, and tenderness in every little line, so that there's not a single coarse, harsh, or unsuitable word. It has to be written so that the one who is praying will rejoice and weep in his heart, but shake and be in awe in his mind. In the akathist to the Mother of God there are the words: 'Rejoice, height unattainable to human reason; rejoice, depth invisible to the eyes of angels!' In another place in the same akathist it says: 'Rejoice, tree of the bright fruit on which the faithful feed, rejoice, tree of good-shading leaves in which many find shelter!' "

Ieronym, as if frightened or embarrassed at something, covered his face with his hands and shook his head.

"Tree of the bright fruit . . . tree of good-shading leaves . . ." he murmured. "He really finds such words! The Lord gave him that ability! He puts many words and thoughts into one brief phrase, and it all comes out so smooth and thorough! 'Light-proffering lamp to those . . .' he says in the akathist to the Most Sweet Jesus. 'Light-proffering!' There's no such word in our speech, or in our books, and yet he thought it up, he found it in his mind! Besides smoothness and eloquence, sir, it's necessary that every little line be adorned in all ways, to have flowers in it, and lightning, and wind, and sun, and all things of the visible world. And every exclamation should be composed so that it's smooth and easy on the ear. 'Rejoice, lily of paradisal blossoming!' it says in the akathist to Nicholas the Wonderworker. It doesn't say simply 'lily of paradise,' but 'lily of paradisal blossoming'! It's sweeter and smoother on the ear. And that's precisely how Nikolai wrote! Precisely like that! I can't even express to you how he wrote!"

"In that case, it's a pity he died," I said. "However, my good man, let's get moving, otherwise we'll be late . . ."

Ieronym recovered himself and rushed to the cable. On the bank all the bells were ringing away. Probably the procession was already going around the monastery, because the whole dark space behind the pitch barrels was now strewn with moving lights.[6]

"Did Nikolai publish his akathists?" I asked Ieronym.

"Where could he publish them?" he sighed. "And it would be strange to publish them. What for? In our monastery nobody's interested in them. They don't like it. They knew Nikolai wrote them, but they paid no attention. Nowadays, sir, nobody respects new writings!"

"Are they prejudiced against them?"

"Exactly so. If Nikolai had been an elder, the brothers might have been curious, but he wasn't even forty years old. There were some who laughed and even considered his writings a sin."

"Then why did he write?"

"More for his own delight. Of all the brothers, I was the only one who read his akathists. I used to come to him on the quiet, so that the others wouldn't see, and he was glad I was interested. He embraced me, stroked my head, called me tender words as if I were a little child. He would close the door, sit me down next to him, and start reading . . ."

Ieronym left the cable and came over to me.

"We were like friends, he and I," he whispered, looking at me with shining eyes. "Wherever he went, I went, too. He missed me when I wasn't there. And he loved me more than the others, and all because I wept from his akathists. It moves me to remember it! Now I'm like an orphan or a widow. You know, in our monastery the people are all good, kind, pious, but . . . there's no softness and delicacy in any of them, they're all like low-class people. They talk loudly, stamp their feet when they walk, make noise, cough, but Nikolai always spoke quietly, gently, and if he noticed that anyone was asleep or praying, he would pass by like a gnat or a mosquito. His face was tender, pitiful . . ."

Ieronym sighed deeply and took hold of the cable. We were nearing the bank. Out of the darkness and silence of the river we gradually floated into an enchanted kingdom, filled with suffocating smoke, sputtering lamps, and tumult. People could be seen clearly moving about the pitch barrels. The flashing of the fire lent their red faces and figures a strange, almost fantastic expression. Occasionally, among the heads and faces, horses' muzzles appeared, motionless, as if cast in red copper.

"They're about to start the Easter canon . . ." said Ieronym, "and Nikolai isn't here, there's no one to grasp it . . . For him there was no writing sweeter than this canon. He used to grasp every word of it! You'll be there, sir, try to grasp what they sing: it will take your breath away!"

"And you won't be in church?"

"I can't be, sir . . . I have to take people across."

"But won't they relieve you?"

"I don't know . . . I should have been relieved between eight and nine, but as you see, I haven't been! . . . And, to tell the truth, I'd like to be in church . . ."

"Are you a monk?"

"Yes, sir . . . that is, I'm a novice."

The ferry ran into the bank and stopped. I gave Ieronym a five-kopeck piece for the ride and jumped onto dry land. At once a cart with a boy and a sleeping woman drove creaking onto the ferry. Ieronym, faintly colored by the lights, leaned on the cable, curved his body, and pushed the ferry off . . .

I took a few steps through the mud, but further on I had to follow a soft, freshly trampled path. This path led to the dark, cave-like gates of the monastery, through clouds of smoke, through a disorderly crowd of people, unharnessed horses, carts, britzkas. It was all creaking, snorting, laughing, and over it all flashed crimson light and wavy shadows of smoke . . . A veritable chaos! And in this turmoil they still found room to load the little cannon and sell gingerbreads!

There was no less bustle on the other side of the wall, in the churchyard, but there was more ceremoniousness and order to be observed. Here there was a smell of juniper and incense. There was loud talk, but no laughter or snorting. People with kulichi[7] and bundles huddled together among the tombstones and crosses. Obviously many of them had come a long way to have their kulichi blessed and were now tired. Over the cast-iron slabs that lay in a strip from the gates to the church door, busy young novices ran, loudly stamping their boots. In the bell tower there was also scurrying and shouting.

"What a restless night!" I thought. "How good!"

One would have liked to see this restlessness and sleeplessness in all of nature, beginning with the night's darkness and ending with the slabs, the graveyard crosses, and the trees, under which people bustled about. But nowhere did the excitement and restlessness tell so strongly as in the church. At the entrance an irrepressible struggle went on between ebb and flow. Some went in, others came out and soon went back again, to stand for a little while and then move again. People shuttle from place to place, loiter, and seem to be looking for something. The wave starts at the entrance and passes through the whole church, even disturbing the front rows where the solid and weighty people stand. To concentrate on prayer is out of the question. There are no prayers, but there is a sort of massive, childishly instinctive joy that is only seeking an excuse to burst and pour itself out in some sort of movement, be it only an unabashed swaying and jostling.

The same extraordinary mobility strikes one's eye in the paschal service itself. The royal doors[8] in all the chapels are wide open, dense clouds of incense smoke float in the air around the big candle stand; everywhere one looks there are lights, brilliance, the sputtering of candles . . . There are no readings in this service; the busy and joyful singing goes on till the very end; after every ode of the canon the clergy change vestments and come out to cense the church, and this is repeated every ten minutes.

I had just managed to take my place when a wave surged from the front and threw me back. Before me passed a tall, sturdy deacon with a long red candle; behind him the gray-haired archimandrite in a golden mitre hurried with a censer. When they disappeared from view, the crowd pushed me back to my former place. But ten minutes had not gone by before a new wave surged and the deacon appeared again. This time he was followed by the father vicar, the one who, according to Ieronym, was writing a history of the monastery.

As I merged with the crowd and became infected with the general joyful excitement, I felt unbearably pained for Ieronym. Why did they not relieve him? Why did someone less sensitive and impressionable not go to the ferry?

"Cast thine eyes about thee, O Zion, and behold . . ." sang the choir, "for lo! from the West and from the North, and from the sea, and from the East, as to a light by God illumined, have thy children assembled unto thee . . ."[9]

I looked at the faces. They all bore lively, festive expressions; but not one person listened to or tried to grasp what was being sung, and no one had their "breath taken away." Why did they not relieve Ieronym? I could picture this Ieronym to myself, humbly standing somewhere near the wall, bending forward and eagerly seizing upon the beauty of the holy phrase. All that was now slipping past the hearing of the people standing about me, he would be eagerly drinking in with his sensitive soul, he would get drunk to the point of ecstasy, of breathlessness, and there would be no happier man in the whole church. But now he was going back and forth across the dark river and pining for his dead brother and friend.

A wave surged from behind. A stout, smiling monk, playing with his beads and glancing over his shoulder, squeezed past me sideways, making way for some lady in a hat and velvet coat. In the lady's wake came a monastery server, holding a chair up over our heads.

I left the church. I wanted to look at the dead Nikolai, the unknown writer of akathists. I strolled near the churchyard fence where a row of monks' cells stretched along the wall, peered through several windows and, seeing nothing, went back. Now I do not regret not having seen Nikolai; God knows, perhaps if I had seen him I would have lost the image my imagination now paints for me. This sympathetic, poetic man, who came at night to call out to Ieronym and who strewed his akathists with flowers, stars, and rays of sunlight, lonely and not understood, I picture to myself as timid, pale, with gentle, meek, and sad features. In his eyes, alongside intelligence, tenderness should shine, and that barely re-strained, childlike exaltation I could hear in Ieronym's voice when he quoted the akathists to me.

When we left the church after the liturgy, it was no longer night. Morning was coming. The stars had faded and the sky was gray-blue, sullen. The cast-iron slabs, the tombstones, and the buds on the trees were covered with dew. There was a sharp feeling of fresh-ness in the air. Outside the churchyard there was no more of that animation I had seen at night. Horses and people seemed tired, sleepy, they barely moved, and all that was left of the pitch barrels was heaps of black ashes. When a man is tired and wants to sleep, it seems to him that nature is in the same state. It seemed to me that the trees and young grass were asleep. It seemed that even the bells did not ring as loudly and gaily as at night. The restlessness was over, and all that was left of the excitement was a pleasant languor, a desire for sleep and warmth.

Now I could see the river with both its banks. Hills of light mist hovered over it here and there. The water breathed out cold and severity. When I jumped aboard the ferry, someone's britzka already stood there, and some twenty men and women. The damp and, as it seemed to me, sleepy cable stretched far across the wide river and in places disappeared in the white mist.

"Christ is risen! Is there anybody else?" a quiet voice asked.

I recognized the voice of Ieronym. Now the darkness of night did not prevent me from seeing the monk. He was a tall, narrow-shouldered man of about thirty-five, with large, rounded features, half-closed, lazy-looking eyes, and a disheveled, wedge-shaped beard. He looked extraordinarily sad and weary.

"They still haven't relieved you?" I was surprised.

"Me, sir?" he asked, turning his chilled, dew-covered face to me and smiling. "Now there won't be anyone to relieve me till morn-ing. They'll all go to the father archimandrite's to break the fast, sir."[10]

He and some little peasant in a red fur hat that looked like the bast pots they sell honey in, leaned on the cable, gave a concerted grunt, and the ferry moved off.

We floated along, disturbing the lazily rising mist as we went. Everyone was silent. Ieronym mechanically worked with one hand. For a long time he looked us over with his meek, dull eyes, then rested his gaze on the rosy, black-browed face of a young merchant's wife, who stood next to me on the ferry and silently shrank away from the mist that embraced her. He did not take his eyes off her face all the while we crossed.

This prolonged gaze had little of the masculine in it. It seems to me that in the woman's face Ieronym was seeking the soft and tender features of his deceased friend.

APRIL 1886

VANKA

Vanka Zhukov, a nine-year-old boy, sent three months earlier to be apprenticed to the shoemaker Aliakhin, did not go to bed on Christmas eve. He waited till master and apprentices went to church, then took a bottle of ink and a pen with a rusty nib from the master's cupboard, spread out a rumpled sheet of paper in front of him, and began to write. Before tracing the first letter, he looked fearfully several times at the doors and windows, cast a sidelong glance at the dark icon, surrounded on both sides by long shelves of shoe lasts, and heaved a choking sigh. The paper lay on a bench, and he himself knelt down by the bench.

"Dear grandpa, Konstantin Makarych!" he wrote. "So I'm writing you a letter. I wish you a Merry Christmas and all good things from the Lord God. I have no father or mother, you are the only one I have left."

Vanka's eyes moved to the dark window, in which the reflection of his candle flickered, and vividly imagined his grandfather, Konstantin Makarych, who worked as a night watchman at the Zhivarevs'. He was a small, skinny, but remarkably nimble and lively old fellow of about sixty-five, with an eternally laughing face and drunken eyes. He spent his days sleeping in the servants' quarters or bantering with the kitchen maids, and during the night, wrapped in a roomy winter coat, he walked around the estate beating on his clapper.[1] Behind him, their heads hanging, trotted the old bitch Chestnut and little Eel, so called because of his black color and long, weasel-like body. This Eel was remarkably respectful and gentle, looked with equal tenderness on his own people and on strangers, but enjoyed no credit. His respectfulness and humility concealed a most Jesuitical insidiousness. No one knew better than he how to sneak up and nip you on the leg, how to get into the cellar or steal a peasant's chicken. He had been beaten to pulp more than once, twice he had been hung, every week he was thrashed till he was half dead, but he always recovered.

His grandfather is probably standing by the gate now, squinting his eyes at the bright red windows of the village church, stamping his felt boots, and bantering with the servants. His clapper hangs from his belt. He clasps his hands, hunches up from the cold, and, with an old man's titter, pinches a maid or a kitchen girl.

"How about a little snuff?" he says, offering his snuffbox to the women.

The women take snuff and sneeze. His grandfather goes into indescribable raptures, dissolves in merry laughter, and shouts:

"Tear it off, it's frozen!"

They also give snuff to the dogs. Chestnut sneezes, turns her nose away, and goes off feeling offended. But Eel, being respectful, does not sneeze and wags his tail. And the weather is magnificent. The air is still, transparent, and fresh. The night is dark, but the whole village can be seen, the white roofs with little curls of smoke coming from the chimneys, the trees silvered with hoarfrost, the snowdrifts. The whole sky is strewn with merrily twinkling stars, and the Milky Way is as clearly outlined as if it had been washed and scoured with snow for the feast . . .

Vanka sighed, dipped his pen, and went on writing:

"And yesterday they gave me what-for. The master dragged me out to the yard by the hair and thrashed me with a belt, because I was rocking their baby in the cradle and accidentally fell asleep. And last week the mistress told me to clean a herring, and I started with the tail, so she took the herring and began shoving its head into my mug. The apprentices poke fun at me, send me to the pothouse for vodka, and tell me to steal pickles from the master, and the master beats me with whatever he can find. And there's nothing to eat. They give me bread in the morning, kasha for dinner, and bread again in the evening, and as for tea or cabbage soup, that the masters grub up themselves. And they make me sleep in the front hall, and when their baby cries I don't sleep at all, I rock the cradle.

Dear grandpa, do me this mercy, take me home to the village, I just can't stand it . . . I go down on my knees to you, and I'll pray to God eternally for you, take me away from here or I'll die . . ."

Vanka twisted his lips, rubbed his eyes with his black fist, and gave a sob.

"I'll rub your tobacco for you," he went on, "pray to God for you, and if there's ever any reason, you can whip me like a farmer's goat. And if you think there'll be no work for me, I'll ask the steward for Christ's sake to let me polish the boots or go instead of Fedka to help the shepherd. Dear grandpa, I can't stand it, it's simply killing me. I thought of running away on foot to the village, but I have no boots, I'm afraid of freezing. And when I grow up, I'll feed you for it, and I won't let anybody harm you, and when you die, I'll pray for the repose of your soul, as I do for my mama Pelageya.

"And Moscow is a big city. All the houses are manors, there are lots of horses, but no sheep, and the dogs aren't fierce. There's no children's procession with the star[2] here, and they don't let anybody sing in the choir,[3] and once in the window of a shop I saw hooks for sale with lines for all kinds of fish, really worth it, there was even one hook that would hold a thirty-pound sheatfish. And I saw shops selling all kind of guns like our squire's, worth maybe a hundred roubles each . . . And in the butcher shops there are blackcock, and hazel grouse, and hares, but where they go to hunt them the shop clerks won't tell.

"Dear grandpa, when the masters have a Christmas tree party with treats, take a gilded nut for me and hide it in the green chest. Ask the young miss, Olga Ignatievna, and tell her it's for Vanka."

Vanka sighed spasmodically and again stared at the window. He remembered how his grandfather always went to the forest to fetch a Christmas tree for the masters and took his grandson with him. They had a merry time! His grandfather grunted, and the frost grunted, and, looking at them, Vanka also grunted. Usually, before cutting down the tree, his grandfather smoked his pipe or took a long pinch of snuff, while he chuckled at the freezing Vaniushka . . . The young fir trees, shrouded in hoarfrost, stand motionless, waiting to see which of them is to die. Out of nowhere, a hare shoots like an arrow across the snowdrifts . . . His grandfather cannot help shouting:

"Catch him, catch him . . . catch him! Ah, the short-tailed devil!"

The cut-down tree would be lugged to the master's house, and there they would start decorating it ... The young miss, Olga Ignatievna, Vanka's favorite, was the busiest of all. When Vanka's mother Pelageya was still alive and worked in the master's house as a maid, Olga Ignatievna used to give Vanka fruit drops and, having nothing to do, taught him to read, to write, to count to a hundred, and even to dance the quadrille. But when Pelageya died, the orphaned Vanka was packed off to his grandfather in the servants' kitchen, and from the kitchen to Moscow, to the shoemaker Aliakhin ...

"Come, dear grandpa," Vanka went on, "by Christ God I beg you, take me away from here. Have pity on me, a wretched orphan, because everybody beats me, and I'm so hungry, and it's so dreary I can't tell you, I just cry all the time. And the other day the master hit me on the head with a last, so that I fell down and barely recovered. My life is going bad, worse than any dog's ... And I also send greetings to Alyona, to one-eyed Yegorka, and to the coachman, and don't give my harmonica away to anybody. I remain your grandson, Ivan Zhukov, dear grandpa, come."

Vanka folded the written sheet in four and put it into an envelope he had bought the day before for a kopeck ... After thinking a little, he dipped his pen and wrote the address:

To Grandpa in the Village.

Then he scratched his head, reflected, and added: "Konstantin Makarych." Pleased that he had not been disturbed at his writing, he put on his hat and, without getting into his coat, ran outside in just his shirt ...

The clerks at the butcher shop, whom he had asked the day before, had told him that letters are put in mailboxes, and from the mailboxes are carried all over the world on troikas of post-horses with drunken drivers and jingling bells. Vanka ran over to the nearest mailbox and put the precious letter into the slot ...

Lulled by sweet hopes, an hour later he was fast asleep ... He dreamed of a stove. On the stove sits his grandfather, his bare feet hanging down. He is reading Vanka's letter to the kitchen maids ... Eel walks around the stove, wagging his tail ...

DECEMBER 1886

SLEEPY

Night. The nanny Varka, a girl of about thirteen, is rocking a cradle in which a baby lies, and murmuring barely audibly:

> Hush-a-bye, baby,
> I'll sing you a song . . .

A green oil lamp is burning before an icon; a rope is stretched across the whole room from corner to corner, with swaddling clothes and large black trousers hanging on it. A big green spot from the icon lamp falls on the ceiling, and the swaddling clothes and trousers cast long shadows on the stove, the cradle, and Varka . . . When the icon lamp begins to flicker, the spot and the shadows come alive and start moving as if in the wind. It is stuffy. There is a smell of cabbage soup and shoemaker's supplies.

The baby is crying. He became hoarse and exhausted from crying long ago, but he goes on howling, and no one knows when he will quiet down. And Varka is sleepy. Her eyes close, her head droops down, her neck aches. She cannot move her eyelids or her lips, and it seems to her that her face has become dry and stiff and her head is as small as the head of a pin.

"Hush-a-bye, baby," she murmurs, "I'll feed you by and by . . ."

A cricket chirps from the stove. In the next room, behind the door, the master and his apprentice Afanasy are snoring . . . The cradle creaks pitifully, Varka herself is murmuring—and all this merges into the lulling night music that is so sweet to hear when you are going to bed. But now this music is only vexing and oppressive, because it makes her drowsy, yet she cannot sleep. God forbid that Varka should fall asleep, or the masters will give her a beating.

The icon lamp flickers. The green spot and the shadows begin to move, getting into Varka's fixed, half-open eyes and forming dim reveries in her half-sleeping brain. She sees dark clouds chasing each other across the sky and crying like babies. But now the wind has blown, the clouds have vanished, and Varka sees a broad highway covered with liquid mud. Down the highway stretches a string of carts, people trudge along with bundles on their backs, and some sort of shadows flit back and forth. Forest can be seen on both sides through the cold, harsh fog. Suddenly the shadows and the people with bundles drop down in the liquid mud. "Why is that?" asks Varka. "To sleep, to sleep," comes the answer. And they fall fast asleep, sleep sweetly, and crows and magpies sit on the telegraph wires, crying like babies, trying to wake them up.

"Hush-a-bye, baby, I'll sing you a song . . ." murmurs Varka, and now she sees herself in a dark, stuffy cottage.

Her late father, Yefim Stepanov, is thrashing on the floor. She does not see him, but she hears him moaning and rolling on the floor in pain. His rupture, as he puts it, "is acting up." The pain is so intense that he cannot utter a single word and only sucks in air, his teeth chattering like a drum roll:

"Rat-a-tat-tat-tat . . ."

Her mother Pelageya has run to the manor to tell the masters that Yefim is dying. She has been gone for a long time and ought to be back. Varka lies on the stove, awake, and listens to her father's "rat-a-tat-tat." But now she hears someone drive up to the cottage. The masters have sent the young doctor, who came from town for a visit. The doctor enters the cottage. He cannot be seen in the darkness, but she hears him cough and clack the door.

"Light a lamp," he says.

"Rat-a-tat-tat . . ." answers Yefim.

Pelageya rushes to the stove and starts looking for the crock of matches. A minute passes in silence. The doctor feels in his pockets and lights his own match.

"One moment, good man, one moment," says Pelageya, rushing out of the cottage and coming back shortly with a candle end.

Yefim's cheeks are pink, his eyes shine, and his gaze is somehow sharp, as if Yefim can see through both the cottage and the doctor.

"Well, so? What's this you're up to?" the doctor says, bending over him. "Aha! Have you had it long?"

"What, sir? It's time to die, Your Honor . . . I'm done living . . ."

"Enough of that nonsense . . . We'll cure you!"

"As you like, Your Honor, my humble thanks, only we do understand . . . Since death has come, there's no use."

The doctor fusses over Yefim for a quarter of an hour. Then he gets up and says:

"I can do nothing . . . You must go to the hospital, they'll do surgery on you. Go right now . . . Go without fail! It's a bit late, everybody's asleep there, but never mind, I'll give you a note. Do you hear me?"

"How is he going to get there, good man?" says Pelageya. "We have no horse."

"Never mind, I'll ask the masters, they'll give you a horse."

The doctor leaves, the candle goes out, and again she hears "rat-a-tat-tat" . . . Half an hour later somebody drives up to the cottage. The masters have sent a gig to go to the hospital. Yefim gets ready and goes . . .

Now comes a fine, clear morning. Pelageya is not home: she has gone to the hospital to find out what is happening with Yefim. Somewhere a baby is crying, and Varka hears someone singing with her own voice:

"Hush-a-bye, baby, I'll sing you a song . . ."

Pelageya comes back. She crosses herself and whispers:

"They set it during the night, but by morning he gave up his soul to God . . . The kingdom of heaven, eternal rest . . . They say they caught it too late . . . He should have come earlier . . ."

Varka goes to the woods and weeps there, but suddenly somebody hits her on the back of the head so hard that she bumps her forehead against a birch. She lifts her eyes and sees before her the shoemaker, her master.

"What's this, you mangy girl?" he says. "The little one's crying, and you sleep?"

He twists her ear painfully, and she shakes her head, rocks the cradle, and murmurs her song. The green spot and the shadows of the trousers and swaddling clothes ripple, wink at her, and soon invade her brain again. Again she sees the highway covered with liquid mud. Shadows and people with bundles on their backs sprawl about, fast asleep. Looking at them, Varka passionately longs to sleep; it would be such a pleasure to lie down, but her mother Pelageya walks beside her and hurries her. They are hastening to town to find work.

"Give alms, for Christ's sake!" her mother asks passersby. "Show God's mercy, merciful people."

"Give me the baby!" somebody's familiar voice answers her. "Give me the baby!" the same voice repeats, angrily and sharply now. "Sleeping, you slut?"

Varka jumps up and, looking around her, understands what is the matter: there is no road, no Pelageya, no passersby, but only her mistress standing in the middle of the room, come to nurse her baby. While the fat, broad-shouldered mistress nurses and quiets the baby, Varka stands and looks at her, waiting till she is finished. Outside the windows the air is turning blue, the shadows and the green spot on the ceiling are becoming noticeably paler. It will soon be morning.

"Take him!" says the mistress, buttoning her nightshirt over her breasts. "He's crying. Must be the evil eye."

Varka takes the baby, lays him in the cradle, and again begins to rock. The green spot and the shadows gradually disappear, and there is nothing left to get into her head and cloud her brain. And she is as sleepy as before, so terribly sleepy! Varka lays her head on the edge of the cradle and rocks with her whole body, so as to overcome sleep, but her eyes keep closing all the same and her head is heavy.

"Varka, light the stove!" the master's voice comes from behind the door.

That means it is time to get up and start working. Varka leaves the cradle and runs to the shed to fetch firewood. She is glad. When you run and walk, you do not feel so sleepy as when you are in a sitting position. She brings the firewood, lights the stove, and feels how her stiffened face relaxes and her thoughts become clear.

"Varka, set up the samovar!" cries the mistress.

Varka splits some splinters, and has barely had time to light them and put them under the samovar when she hears a new order.

"Varka, clean the master's galoshes!"

She sits on the floor, cleans the galoshes, and thinks how good it would be to put her head into a big, deep galosh and have a nap there . . . Suddenly the galosh grows, swells, fills the whole room. Varka drops the brush, but immediately shakes her head, rolls her eyes, and tries to look at things in such a way that they do not grow and move as she looks.

"Varka, wash the front steps, it's shameful for the customers!"

Varka washes the steps, tidies the rooms, then lights the other stove and runs to the grocer's. There is much work, and not a free moment.

But nothing is harder than to stand in one spot at the kitchen table and peel potatoes. Her head droops on the table, potatoes flash in her eyes, the knife keeps falling from her hand, and around her paces the fat, angry mistress, with her sleeves rolled up, talking so loudly that it makes her ears ring. It is also a torment to serve at the table, do the laundry, sew. There are moments when she longs to forget everything, collapse on the floor, and sleep.

The day passes. Looking at the darkening windows, Varka clutches her stiffening temples and smiles, not knowing why herself. The evening darkness caresses her closing eyes, promising a sound sleep soon. In the evening her masters have guests.

"Varka, set up the samovar!" cries the mistress.

Their samovar is small, and before the guests have had enough tea, she has to heat it some five times. After tea, Varka stands in one spot for a whole hour, looking at the guests and awaiting orders.

"Varka, run and fetch three bottles of beer!"

She tears herself from the spot and tries to run faster so as to drive sleep away.

"Varka, run and fetch vodka! Varka, where's the corkscrew? Varka, clean the herring!"

But now, finally, the guests have gone, the lights are put out, the masters go to sleep.

"Varka, rock the baby!" comes the last order.

A cricket chirps from the stove. The green spot on the ceiling and the shadows of the trousers and swaddling clothes again get into Varka's half-closed eyes, flicker, and cloud her head.

"Hush-a-bye, baby," she murmurs, "I'll sing you a song . . ."

And the baby cries and gets exhausted from crying. Again Varka sees the muddy highway, the people with bundles, Pelageya, her father Yefim. She understands everything, recognizes everyone, but through her half sleep she simply cannot understand what power binds her hand and foot, oppresses her, and keeps her from living.

She looks around, seeking this power in order to rid herself of it, but she cannot find it. Finally, worn out, she strains all her powers and her vision, looks up at the flickering green spot, and, hearing the crying, locates the enemy that keeps her from living.

That enemy is the baby.

She laughs. It amazes her: how is it that she was unable to understand such a simple thing before? The green spot, the shadows, and the cricket, too, seem to laugh and be amazed.

A false notion takes hold of Varka. She gets up from the stool and, smiling broadly, without blinking her eyes, walks about the room. She is pleased and tickled by the thought that she is about to rid herself of the baby that binds her hand and foot . . . To kill the baby, and then sleep, sleep, sleep . . .

Laughing, winking, and shaking her finger at the green spot, Varka steals up to the cradle and bends over the baby. After strangling him, she quickly lies down on the floor, laughing with joy that she can sleep, and a moment later is already fast asleep, like the dead . . .

JANUARY 1888

A Boring Story

FROM AN OLD MAN'S NOTES

I

There is in Russia an honored professor named Nikolai Stepanovich So-and-so, a privy councillor and chevalier. He has so many Russian and foreign decorations that when he has to wear them all, the students call him "the iconostasis."[1] His acquaintances are of the most aristocratic sort; at least for the last twenty-five or thirty years in Russia there is not and has not been a single famous scholar with whom he has not been closely acquainted. Now he has no one to be friends with, but if we speak of the past, the long list of his glorious friends ends with such names as Pirogov, Kavelin and the poet Nekrasov,[2] who offered him the warmest and most sincere friendship. He is a member of all the Russian and three foreign universities. And so on and so forth. All this and many other things that might be said constitute what is known as my name.

This name of mine is popular. In Russia it is known to every literate person, and abroad it is mentioned from podiums with the addition of well-known and esteemed. It is one of those few fortunate names which it is considered bad tone to abuse or take in vain, in public or in print. And so it should be. For my name is closely connected with the notion of a man who is famous, richly endowed, and unquestionably useful. I'm as staunch and hardworking as a camel, which is important, and I'm talented, which is still more important. Besides that, be it said in passing, I'm a well-bred, modest, and honorable fellow. Never have I poked my nose into literature and politics, or sought popularity in polemics with ignoramuses, or given speeches either at dinners or over the graves of my colleagues . . . Generally, there is not a single blot on my learned name, and it has nothing to complain of. It is happy.

The bearer of this name, that is, myself, has the look of a sixty-two-year-old man with a bald head, false teeth, and an incurable tic. As my name is brilliant and beautiful, so I myself am dull and ugly. My head and hands shake from weakness; my neck, as with one of Turgenev's heroines,[3] resembles the fingerboard of a double bass, my chest is sunken, my shoulders narrow. When I speak or read, my mouth twists to one side; when I smile, my whole face is covered with an old man's deathly wrinkles. There is nothing imposing in my pathetic figure; except perhaps that when I have my tic, I acquire some peculiar expression, which evokes in anyone looking at me the stern and imposing thought: "This man will evidently die soon."

I still lecture fairly well; I can hold the attention of my listeners for two hours at a stretch, as I used to. My passion, the literary quality of my exposition, and my humor make almost unnoticeable the defects of my voice, which is dry, shrill, and sing-song, like a hypocrite's. But I write badly. The part of my brain in charge of writing ability refuses to work. My memory has weakened, my thoughts lack consistency, and each time I set them down on paper it seems to me that I've lost the intuition of their organic connection, the constructions are monotonous, the phrasing impoverished and timid. I often write something other than what I mean; when I get to the end, I no longer remember the beginning. I often forget ordinary words, and always have to waste much energy avoiding superfluous phrases and unnecessary parenthetical clauses in my writing—both clearly witnessing to a decline of mental activity. And, remarkably, the simpler the writing, the more excruciating is the strain. With a learned article I feel myself far more free and intelligent than with a letter of congratulations or a report. Another thing: it's easier for me to write in German or English than in Russian.

As for my present way of life, first of all I must make note of the insomnia from which I've been suffering lately. If I were to be asked: What now constitutes the main and fundamental feature of your existence? I would answer: Insomnia. As before, out of habit, I get undressed and go to bed exactly at midnight. I fall asleep quickly, but I wake up again before two o'clock, and with a feeling as if I haven't slept at all. I have to get up and light the lamp. For an hour or two I pace the room from corner to corner and gaze at the long-familiar paintings and photographs. When I get tired of pacing, I sit down at my desk. I sit motionless, not thinking about anything and not feeling any desires; if there's a book lying in front of me, I mechanically draw it towards me and read without any interest. Thus, recently, in a single night I mechanically read an entire novel with the strange title *What the Swallow Sang*.[4] Or else, to occupy my attention, I make myself count to a thousand or picture the face of one of my colleagues and begin recalling: in what year and under what circumstances did he take up his post? I like listening to sounds. Two doors away my daughter Liza says something rapidly in her sleep, or my wife crosses the living room with a candle and unfailingly drops the box of matches, or a cupboard creaks from dryness, or the lamp flame suddenly starts to hum—and for some reason all these sounds trouble me.

Not to sleep during the night means to be aware every moment of your abnormality, and therefore I wait impatiently for morning and daylight, when I have the right not to sleep. A long, wearisome time goes by before the cock crows in the yard. He is my first bearer of good tidings. Once he crows, I know that in an hour the hall porter will wake up below and, coughing gruffly, come upstairs for something. And then little by little the air outside the windows will turn pale, voices will be heard in the street . . .

My day begins with the coming of my wife. She enters my room in a petticoat, her hair not yet done, but already washed, smelling of flower cologne, and with the air of having come in by chance, and each time she says one and the same thing:

"Excuse me, I'll only stay a moment . . . You didn't sleep again?"

Then she puts out the lamp, sits down by the desk and begins to talk. I'm no prophet, but I know beforehand what the talk will be about. It is the same every morning. Usually, after anxious inquiries about my health, she suddenly remembers our son, an officer serving in Warsaw. After the twentieth of each month we send him fifty roubles—that mainly serves as the theme of our conversation.

"Of course, it's difficult for us," my wife sighs, "but until he finally gets on his feet, it's our duty to help him. The boy is in a foreign land, his pay is small . . . However, if you like, next month we'll send him not fifty but forty. What do you think?"

Everyday experience might have convinced my wife that expenses are not diminished by our frequent talking about them, but my wife does not recognize experience and tells me regularly each morning about our officer, and that the price of bread has gone down, thank God, but sugar has gone up two kopecks—and all this in such a tone as if she were telling me some news.

I listen, mechanically saying yes, and strange, useless thoughts come over me, probably because I haven't slept all night. I look at my wife and am astonished, like a child. In perplexity, I ask myself: Can it be that this old, very stout, ungainly woman with a dull expression of petty care and fear over a crust of bread, with eyes clouded by constant thoughts of debt and poverty, only capable of talking about expenses and only smiling at bargains—can it be that this woman was once that same slender Varya whom I passionately loved for her good, clear mind, her pure soul, her beauty, and, as Othello loved Desdemona, "that she did pity" my science? Can this be that same wife Varya who once bore me a son?

I peer intently into the flabby, ungainly old woman's face, searching for my Varya in her, but nothing has survived from the past except her fear for my health and her way of calling my salary *our* salary and my hat *our* hat. It pains me to look at her, and to comfort her at least a little I let her say whatever she likes, and even say nothing when she judges people unfairly or chides me for not having a practice or publishing textbooks.

Our conversation always ends in the same way. My wife suddenly remembers that I have not had my tea yet and becomes alarmed.

"What am I doing sitting here?" she says, getting up. "The samovar has long been on the table, and I sit here chattering. Lord, I've become so forgetful!"

She goes out quickly but stops in the doorway to say:

"We owe Yegor for five months. Do you know that? It won't do to fall behind with the servants' pay, I've said so many times! Paying ten roubles a month is much easier than going five months and paying fifty!"

She gets through the door, stops again, and says:

"There's no one I pity so much as our poor Liza. The girl studies at the conservatory, she's always in good society, and she's dressed

God knows how. It's shameful to go out in such a coat. If she were someone else's daughter, it would be nothing, but everybody knows her father is a famous professor, a privy councillor!"

And, having reproached me with my name and rank, she finally leaves. So my day begins. The sequel is no better.

While I'm having tea, my Liza comes in with her coat and hat on, holding some scores, all ready to go to the conservatory. She's twenty-two years old. She looks younger, is pretty, and slightly resembles my wife when she was young. She kisses me tenderly on the temple and on the hand, and says:

"Good morning, papa. Are you well?"

As a child she was very fond of ice cream, and I often took her to the pastry shop. For her, ice cream was the measure of all that was beautiful. If she wanted to praise me, she would say: "You're ice cream, papa." One little finger was named pistachio, another vanilla, another raspberry, and so on. Usually, when she came and said good morning to me, I would take her on my knee and, kissing her fingers, repeat:

"Vanilla . . . pistachio . . . lemon . . ."

And now, for old times' sake, I kiss Liza's fingers, murmuring: "Pistachio . . . vanilla . . . lemon . . ." but it turns out all wrong. I'm cold as ice cream and feel ashamed. When my daughter comes to me and brushes my temple with her lips, I give a start as if I'd been stung by a bee, smile tensely, and turn my face away. Ever since I began to suffer from insomnia, a question has been lodged in my brain like a nail: my daughter often sees me, an old man, a celebrity, blush painfully because I owe money to a servant; she sees how often the worry over petty debts makes me abandon my work and spend whole hours pacing back and forth, pondering, but why has she never once come to me, in secret from her mother, and whispered: "Father, here is my watch, my bracelets, my earrings, my dresses . . . Pawn it all, you need money . . ."? Why, seeing how her mother and I, surrendering to a false feeling, try to hide our poverty from people, does she not give up the expensive pleasure of studying music? Not that I'd accept any watch, or bracelets, or sacrifices, God forbid—I don't need that.

And then I also remember my son, the officer in Warsaw. He's an intelligent, honest, and sober man. But I don't find that enough. I think if I had an old father and if I knew that he had moments when he was ashamed of his poverty, I would give my officer's post to someone else and go to do day labor. Such thoughts about my children poison me. What's the point? To harbor spiteful feelings against ordinary people for not being heroes is possible only for a narrow-minded or embittered man. But enough of that.

At a quarter to ten I must go to my dear boys and give a lecture. I get dressed and follow a road that has been familiar to me for thirty years now and has its own history for me. Here is a big gray house with a pharmacy; a small house once stood there, and in it there was a beer parlor; in that beer parlor I thought over my dissertation and wrote my first love letter to Varya. I wrote it in pencil, on a page with the heading "Historia morbi."[5] Here is the grocery shop; it was formerly run by a little Jew who sold me cigarettes on credit, then by a fat woman who loved students because "each of them has a mother"; now there's a red-haired shopkeeper sitting there, a very indifferent man, who drinks tea from a copper teapot. And here are the gloomy university gates, which have long needed repair; the bored caretaker in a sheepskin coat, his besom, the heaps of snow ... Such gates cannot make a healthy impression on a fresh boy, come from the provinces, who imagines that the temple of learning really is a temple. In the history of Russian pessimism, the general decrepitude of the university buildings, the gloomy corridors, the grimy walls, the inadequate light, the dismal look of the stairs, cloakrooms and benches, occupy one of the foremost places in the series of causes predisposing ... And here is our garden. It seems to have become neither better nor worse since I was a student. I don't like it. It would be much smarter if, instead of consumptive lindens, yellow acacias, and sparse trimmed lilacs, there were tall pines and handsome oaks growing here. The student, whose mood is largely created by the surroundings of his place of learning, should see at every step only the lofty, the strong, the graceful ... God save him from scrawny trees, broken windows, gray walls, and doors upholstered with torn oilcloth.

When I come to my entrance, the door opens wide, and I am met by my old colleague, coeval, and namesake, the porter Nikolai. Letting me in, he grunts and says:

"Freezing, Your Excellency!"

Or else, if my coat is wet:

"Raining, Your Excellency!"

Then he runs ahead of me and opens all the doors on my way. In the office, he carefully helps me off with my coat, and meanwhile manages to tell me some university news. Owing to the close acquaintance that exists among all university porters and caretakers, he knows everything that goes on in the four faculties, in the chancellery, in the rector's office, in the library. What doesn't he know! For instance, when the latest news is the retirement of the rector or a dean, I hear him name the candidates as he talks with the young caretakers, and explain straight off that so-and-so will not be approved by the minister, that so-and-so will decline, and then go into fantastic detail about some mysterious papers received in the chancellery, about a secret talk that supposedly took place between the minister and a member of the board, and so on. Generally, apart from these details, he almost always turns out to be right. The character references he gives for each candidate are original, but also correct. If you need to know in which year someone defended his thesis, or took up his post, or retired, or died, avail yourself of the vast memory of this old soldier, and he will tell you not only the year, the month, and the day, but also the details that accompanied this or that circumstance. Only one who loves can remember so well.

He is the guardian of university tradition. From his porter predecessors he has inherited many legends of university life, has added to this wealth a considerable quantity of his own goods, acquired during his service, and, if you wish, will tell you many tales both long and short. He can tell of extraordinary wise men who knew *all*, of remarkably hard workers who didn't sleep for weeks at a time, of numerous martyrs and victims of science; with him good triumphs over evil, the weak always overcome the strong, the wise the stupid, the humble the proud, the young the old . . . There is no need to take all these legends and tall tales at face value, but sift them and what you need will be left in the filter: our good traditions and the names of true heroes recognized by all.

In our society all information about the world of scholars is summed up in anecdotes about the extraordinary absentmindedness of old professors and two or three quips ascribed to Gruber, or to me, or to Babukhin.[6] For educated society that is not enough. If it loved learning, scholars and students as much as Nikolai does, its literature would long have had whole epics, sagas, and saints' lives, such as it unfortunately does not have now.

Having told me the news, Nikolai puts a solemn expression on his face, and we begin to talk business. If at that moment some outsider should hear how freely Nikolai handles terminology, he might think that he was a scholar disguised as a soldier. Incidentally, the rumors about the learnedness of university caretakers are greatly exaggerated. True, Nikolai knows more than a hundred Latin names, can assemble a skeleton, prepare a slide on occasion, make the students laugh with some long, learned citation, but so unsophisticated a thing as the theory of the circulation of the blood is as obscure for him now as twenty years ago.

At the table in my office, bending low over a book or a slide, sits my prosector Pyotr Ignatievich, a hardworking, humble, but untalented man of about thirty-five, already bald and with a big stomach. He works from morning to night, reads voluminously, remembers everything he reads excellently—and in that respect he's not a man, he's pure gold; in all the rest he's a cart horse, or, to put it differently, an educated dolt. The characteristic features that distinguish the cart horse from a talented man are these: his horizon is narrow and sharply limited by his profession; outside his profession he is as naïve as a child. I remember coming into the office one morning and saying:

"Imagine, what a misfortune! They say Skobelev[7] is dead."

Nikolai crossed himself, but Pyotr Ignatievich turned to me and asked:

"Which Skobelev is that?"

Another time—this was a little earlier—I announced that Professor Perov[8] had died. Dear old Pyotr Ignatievich asked:

"What did he teach?"

I believe if Patti[9] started singing right in his ear, if hordes of Chinese invaded Russia, even if there was an earthquake, he wouldn't stir a single limb and would quite calmly go on peering with his screwed-up eye into his microscope. In short, Hecuba is nothing to him.[10] I'd pay dearly to see how that dry crust sleeps with his wife.

Another feature: a fanatical faith in the infallibility of science and above all of everything the Germans write. He's sure of himself, of his slides, he knows the goal of life, and is totally unacquainted with the doubts and disappointments that turn talented heads gray. A slavish worship of authority and a lack of any need for independent thinking. To talk him out of anything is difficult, to argue with him is impossible. Try arguing with a person who is profoundly convinced that the best science is medicine, the best people are doctors, the best traditions are medical traditions. The nefarious past of medicine has survived only in one tradition—the white tie now worn by doctors; for the scientist and for the educated man in general, only university-wide traditions can exist, with no divisions into medical, legal, and so on, but Pyotr Ignatievich finds it hard to agree with that, and he is prepared to argue with you till doomsday.

His future I can picture clearly. In his lifetime he will prepare several hundred slides of an extraordinary neatness, write a lot of dry but quite decent papers, make a dozen or so conscientious translations, but he won't set the world on fire. To set the world on fire, you need fantasy, inventiveness, intuition, and Pyotr Ignatievich has nothing of the sort. To put it briefly, in science he is not a master, but a servant.

Pyotr Ignatievich, Nikolai and I are talking in low voices. We're slightly ill at ease. You feel something peculiar when the auditorium murmurs like the sea behind the door. In thirty years I've never gotten used to that feeling, and I experience it every morning. I nervously button my frock coat, ask Nikolai unnecessary questions, get angry . . . It looks as if I turn coward, yet this is not cowardice, but something else I can neither name nor describe.

I needlessly look at my watch and say:

"Well, we must go."

And we proceed in the following order: in front walks Nikolai with the slides or atlases, I come after him, and after me, his head humbly lowered, strides the cart horse; or else, if necessary, a cadaver is carried in first, after the cadaver walks Nikolai, and so on. At my appearance, the students rise, then sit down, and the murmur of the sea suddenly grows still. Calm ensues.

I know what I will lecture about, but I don't know how I will lecture, what I will begin with and where I will end. There is not a single ready-made phrase in my head. But I have only to look over the auditorium (it is built as an amphitheater) and pronounce the stereotypical "In the last lecture we stopped at . . ." for a long string of phrases to come flying out of my soul and—there the province goes scrawling![11] I speak irrepressibly quickly, passionately, and it seems no power can stem the flow of my speech. To lecture well, that is, not boringly and with some profit for your listeners, you must have not only talent but a certain knack and experience, you must possess a very clear notion of your own powers, of those to whom you are lecturing, and of what makes up the subject of your talk. Besides that, you must be self-possessed, keenly observant, and not lose your field of vision even for a second.

A good conductor, as he conveys a composer's thought, does twenty things at once: reads the score, waves his baton, watches the singer, gestures now towards the drum, now towards the French horn, and so on. It is the same with me when I lecture. Before me are a hundred and fifty faces, no two alike, and three hundred eyes looking me straight in the face. My goal is to conquer this many-headed hydra. If, as I lecture, I have at every moment a clear notion of the degree of its attention and the power of its comprehension, then it is in my control. My other adversary sits inside myself. It is the infinite diversity of forms, phenomena, and laws, and the host of thoughts, my own and other people's, that they call forth. At every moment I must be adroit enough to snatch what is most im-portant and necessary from this vast material and, in pace with my speech, to clothe my thinking in such form as will be accessible to the hydra's understanding and arouse its attention, and at the same time I must observe keenly that the thoughts are conveyed, not as they accumulate, but in a certain order necessary for the correct composition of the picture I wish to paint. Furthermore, I try to make my speech literary, my definitions brief and precise, my phrasing as simple and elegant as possible. At every moment I must rein myself in and remember that I have only an hour and forty minutes at my disposal. In short, it's no little work. I have to figure at one and the same time as a scientist, a pedagogue, and an orator, and it's a bad business if the orator in you overwhelms the peda-gogue and scientist, or the other way round.

You lecture for a quarter, a half hour, and then you notice that the students have started looking up at the ceiling, at Pyotr Ignatievich, one feels for his handkerchief, another tries to settle more comfortably, a third smiles at his own thoughts . . . This means their attention is flagging. Measures must be taken. Availing myself of the first opportunity, I make some quip. All hundred and fifty faces smile broadly, eyes shine merrily, there is a momentary murmur of the sea . . . I, too, laugh. Attention has been refreshed, and I can go on.

No argument, no amusement or game ever gave me such plea-sure as lecturing. Only while lecturing could I give myself entirely to passion and understand that inspiration is not an invention of poets but exists in reality. And I imagine that Hercules, after the most piquant of his great deeds, did not feel such sweet exhaustion as I experienced each time after a lecture.

That was before. Now lectures are nothing but torture for me. Before half an hour has gone by, I begin to feel an insuperable weakness in my legs and shoulders; I sit down in a chair, but I'm not accustomed to lecturing while seated; after a minute I get up, go on standing, then sit down again. My mouth is dry, my voice is hoarse, my head spins . . . To conceal my condition from my listeners, I keep drinking water, cough, blow my nose frequently, as if I were bothered by a cold, produce inappropriate quips, and in the end announce the break sooner than I should. But the main thing is that I'm ashamed.

My conscience and intelligence tell me that the best thing I could do now is give the boys a farewell lecture, speak my last words to them, bless them, and yield my place to a man who is younger and stronger than I. But, God be my judge, I lack the courage to follow my conscience.

Unfortunately, I'm not a philosopher and not a theologian. I know very well that I have no more than another six months to live; it would seem I should now be most occupied with questions about the darkness beyond the grave and the visions that will haunt my sepulchral sleep. But for some reason my soul rejects those questions, though my mind is aware of all their importance. As twenty or thirty years ago, so now in the face of death I am interested only in science. Breathing my last, I will still believe that science is the most important, the most beautiful and necessary thing in man's life, that it has always been and always will be the highest manifestation of love, and that only by science will man conquer nature and himself. This faith may be naïve and incorrect in its foundations, but it is not my fault that I believe thus and not otherwise; in myself I cannot overcome this faith.

But that is not the point. I only ask indulgence for my weakness and the understanding that to tear away from his lectern and his students a man who has greater interest in the fate of bone marrow than in the final goal of the universe, is tantamount to having him nailed up in his coffin without waiting till he's dead.

From insomnia and as a result of the intense struggle against mounting weakness, something strange is happening to me. In the midst of a lecture, tears suddenly choke me, my eyes begin to itch, and I feel a passionate, hysterical desire to stretch my arms out and complain loudly. I want to cry in a loud voice that fate has sentenced me, a famous man, to capital punishment, and that in six months or so another man will be master of this auditorium. I want to cry out that I've been poisoned; new thoughts such as I have never known before have poisoned the last days of my life and go on stinging my brain like mosquitoes. And at such times my situation seems so terrible that I want all my listeners to be horrified, to jump up from their seats and, in panic fear, rush for the exit with a desperate cry.

It is not easy to live through such moments.

II

After the lecture I sit at home and work. I read journals or dissertations, or prepare the next lecture, or sometimes I write something. I work with many breaks, because I'm obliged to receive visitors.

The bell rings. It's a colleague stopping by to talk shop. He comes into my room with his hat and stick, hands me the one and the other, and says:

"For a moment, a moment! Sit down, *collega*! Just a couple of words!"

At first we try to show each other that we are both extraordinarily polite and very glad to see each other. I offer him an armchair, and he offers me an armchair; as we do so we cautiously stroke each other's waists, touch each other's buttons, and it looks as if we're palpating each other and are afraid of getting burnt. We both laugh, though we haven't said anything funny. Sitting down, we lean our heads towards each other and begin talking in low voices. Cordially disposed as we are to each other, we can't help gilding our talk with all sorts of Orientalia, like: "As you were pleased to observe so justly," or "As I have already had the honor of telling you," nor can we help laughing if one of us produces some witticism, even an unfortunate one. Having finished his shop talk, my colleague abruptly stands up and, waving his hat in the direction of my work, starts taking his leave. Again we palpate each other and laugh. I see him to the front hall; there I help my colleague into his coat, but he does everything to avoid this high honor. Then as Yegor opens the door, my colleague assures me that I am going to catch cold, as I make a show of even being ready to follow him outside. And when I finally return to my study, my face goes on smiling, probably from inertia.

A short while later the bell rings again. Someone comes into the front hall, spends a long time removing his things, coughs. Yegor announces that a student has appeared. Show him in, I order. A moment later a pleasant-looking young man comes in. It's already a year since our relations became strained: he gives me execrable answers at examinations, and I give him F's. Every year I wind up with about seven of these fine fellows, whom, to use student language, I grill or flunk. Those who can't pass the examination owing to inability or illness usually bear their cross patiently and don't bargain with me; those who do bargain and come to see me at home are the broad, sanguine natures, whose failure at an examination spoils their appetite and interferes with their regular attendance at the opera. The former I treat benignly; the latter I grill for the whole year.

"Sit down," I say to the visitor. "What do you have to say?"

"Excuse me for bothering you, Professor . . ." he begins, stammering and not looking in my face. "I wouldn't have ventured to bother you if it hadn't been . . . I've taken your examination five times and . . . and failed. I beg you, be so kind as to pass me, because . . ."

The argument that all lazy students give in their own favor is ever the same: they have passed all their courses splendidly and failed only mine, which is the more surprising since they have always studied my subject most diligently and have an excellent knowledge of it; if they have failed, it is owing to some inexplicable misunderstanding.

"Excuse me, my friend," I say to the visitor, "but I cannot pass you. Go read over the lectures and come back. Then we'll see."

A pause. The urge comes over me to torment the student a bit for liking beer and the opera more than science, and I say with a sigh:

"In my opinion, the best thing you can do now is abandon the study of medicine entirely. If, with your abilities, you cannot manage to pass the examination, then you obviously have neither the desire nor the vocation for being a doctor."

The sanguine fellow pulls a long face.

"Excuse me, Professor," he grins, "but that would be strange on my part, to say the least. To study for five years and suddenly . . . quit!"

"Why, yes! It's better to waste five years than to spend your whole life afterwards doing something you don't like."

But I feel sorry for him at once and hasten to say:

"However, you know best. So, do a little more reading and come back."

"When?" the lazy fellow asks in a hollow voice.

"Whenever you like. Even tomorrow."

And in his kindly eyes I read: "Yes, I can come, but you'll throw me out again, you brute!"

"Of course," I say, "you won't acquire any more knowledge by taking the examination with me another fifteen times, but it will season your character. And thanks be for that."

Silence ensues. I get up and wait for the visitor to leave, but he stands there, looks out the window, pulls at his little beard, and thinks. It becomes boring.

The sanguine fellow's voice is pleasant, juicy, his eyes are intelligent, mocking, his face is good-natured, somewhat flabby from frequent consumption of beer and prolonged lying on the sofa; clearly he could tell me a lot of interesting things about the opera, about his amorous adventures, about friends he likes, but, unfortunately, to speak of such things isn't done. And I'd have listened eagerly.

"Professor! I give you my word of honor that if you pass me, I'll . . ."

As soon as it comes to the "word of honor," I wave my hands and sit down at my desk. The student thinks a moment longer and says dejectedly:

"In that case, good-bye . . . Excuse me."

"Good-bye, my friend. Be well."

He walks irresolutely to the front hall, slowly puts his coat on, and, as he goes out, again probably thinks for a long time. Having come up with nothing to apply to me except "the old devil," he goes to a bad restaurant, drinks beer and has dinner, and then goes home to sleep. May you rest in peace, honest laborer!

A third ring. A young doctor comes in, wearing a new black two-piece suit, gold-rimmed spectacles, and, sure enough, a white tie. He introduces himself. I invite him to sit down and ask what I can do for him. Not without excitement, the young priest of science begins telling me that he passed his doctoral examination this year and that the only thing he has left to do is write a dissertation. He would like to work for a while with me, under my guidance, and I would greatly oblige him if I gave him a topic for a dissertation.

"I would be very glad to be of use, *collega*," I say, "but let's first agree on what a dissertation is. In the accepted understanding, the word refers to a piece of writing that represents a product of independent work. Isn't that so? A piece of writing on someone else's topic, produced under someone else's guidance, goes by a different name . . ."

The doctoral candidate is silent. I flare up and jump to my feet.

"Why do you all come to me? I don't understand it," I shout angrily. "Am I running a shop or something? I don't deal in topics! For the thousand and first time I beg you all to leave me in peace! Forgive my indelicacy, but I'm finally sick of it!"

The doctoral candidate is silent, only a slight color appears around his cheekbones. His face expresses profound respect for my famous name and learning, but by his eyes I can see that he despises my voice, and my pathetic figure, and my nervous gestures. I seem odd to him in my wrath.

"I'm not running a shop!" I say angrily. "And it's an astonishing thing! Why don't you want to be independent? Why are you so against freedom?"

I talk a lot, but he remains silent. In the end I gradually calm down and, of course, give in. The doctoral candidate will get a topic from me that isn't worth a brass farthing, will write under my guidance a dissertation that nobody needs, will stand with dignity through a boring defense, and receive a learned degree that he has no use for.

The rings could follow one another endlessly, but here I'll limit myself to only four. The bell rings a fourth time, and I hear familiar footsteps, the rustle of a dress, a dear voice . . .

Eighteen years ago my oculist colleague died, leaving a seven-year-old daughter, Katya, and sixty thousand roubles. In his will he appointed me her guardian. Katya lived in my family till she was ten, then was sent to boarding school and spent only the summer months in my house, during vacations. I had no time to occupy myself with her upbringing, I observed her only in snatches and therefore can say very little about her childhood.

The first thing I remember and love in my memories is this—the extraordinary trustfulness with which she came into my home, and let herself be treated by doctors, and which always shone on her little face. She might be sitting somewhere out of the way, with a bandaged cheek, but she was sure to be looking attentively at something; if just then she should see me writing or looking through a book, or my wife bustling about, or the cook in the kitchen peeling potatoes, or the dog playing, her eyes would invariably express the same thing—namely: "All that goes on in this world is beautiful and wise." She was inquisitive and liked very much to talk with me. She would sit at the desk facing me, following my movements, and ask questions. She was interested in knowing what I read, what I did at the university, whether I was afraid of cadavers, what I did with my salary.

"Do the students fight at the university?" she would ask.

"Yes, they do, dear."

"Do you make them stand on their knees?"

"I do."

And she thought it was funny that the students fought and that I made them stand on their knees, and she laughed. She was a meek, patient, and kind child. Not seldom I happened to see how things were taken from her, or she was punished for no reason, or her curiosity went unsatisfied; at those moments the constant expression of trustfulness on her face would be mixed with sadness—and that was all. I wasn't able to intercede for her, but only felt a longing, when I saw her sadness, to draw her to me and pity her in the tone of an old nanny: "My dear little orphan!"

I also remember that she liked to dress well and sprinkle herself with scent. In that respect she was like me. I, too, like fine clothes and good scent.

I regret that I had no time or wish to follow the beginning and development of the passion that already filled Katya by the time she was fourteen or fifteen years old. I'm referring to her passionate love for the theater. When she came home from boarding school for vacation and lived with us, she spoke of nothing else with such pleasure and such ardor as of plays and actors. She wore us out with her constant talk about the theater. My wife and children didn't listen to her. I was the only one who lacked the courage to deny her my attention. When she had a wish to share her raptures, she would come to my study and say in a pleading voice:

"Nikolai Stepanych, let me talk with you about the theater!"

I would point to the clock and say:

"I'll give you half an hour. Go on."

Later she started bringing home dozens of portraits of the actors and actresses she adored; then she tried a few times to take part in amateur productions, and finally, when she finished school, she announced to me that she was born to be an actress.

I never shared Katya's theatrical infatuation. I think, if a play is good, there's no need to bother with actors for it to make the proper impression; it's enough simply to read it. And if a play is bad, no performance will make it good.

In my youth I often went to the theater, and now my family reserves a box twice a year and takes me for an "airing." Of course, that is not enough to give one the right to judge about the theater, but I will say a little about it. In my opinion, the theater has become no better than it was thirty or forty years ago. As before, I can never find a glass of clean water either in the corridors or in the theater lobby. As before, the ushers fine me twenty kopecks for my coat, though there's nothing reprehensible about wearing warm clothes in winter. As before, they needlessly play music during the intermissions, adding to the impression of the play a new and unwanted one. As before, men go to the buffet during intermissions to drink alcoholic beverages. If no progress is to be seen in small things, it would be futile to start looking for it in major things. When an actor, bound from head to foot in theatrical traditions and preconceptions, tries to read the simple, ordinary monologue "To be or not to be" not simply, but for some reason with an inevitable hissing and convulsing of his whole body, or when he tries to convince me by one means or another that Chatsky, who talks so much with fools and loves a foolish woman, is a very intelligent man, and that *Woe from Wit*[12] is not a boring play, I feel the same routine wafting from the stage that I already found boring forty years ago, when I was treated to a classical howling and beating of the breast. And I leave the theater each time more conservative than when I entered it.

The sentimental and gullible crowd may be convinced that the theater in its present form is a school. But no one acquainted with school in the true sense can be caught on that hook. I don't know what will happen in fifty or a hundred years, but in the present circumstances the theater can serve only as entertainment. But this entertainment is too expensive for us to go on resorting to it. It robs the country of thousands of young, healthy, and talented men and women, who, if they had not devoted themselves to the theater, might have been good doctors, tillers of the soil, teachers, army officers; it robs the public of the evening hours—the best hours for mental labor and friendly conversation. To say nothing of the money spent and of the moral losses suffered by the spectator, who sees murder, adultery, and slander incorrectly interpreted on stage.

But Katya was of quite a different opinion. She assured me that the theater, even in its present state, was higher than the auditorium, higher than books, higher than anything in the world. The theater was a force that united all the arts in itself, and actors were missionaries. No art or science by itself was capable of having so strong and so sure an effect on the human soul as the stage, and it was not without reason that an actor of the average sort enjoyed far greater popularity in the country than the best scholar or artist. And no public activity could afford such pleasure and satisfaction as that of the stage.

And one fine day Katya joined a troupe and left—for Ufa, I think—taking with her a lot of money, a host of bright expectations, and aristocratic views of the matter.

Her first letters from the road were extraordinary. I read them and was simply amazed that those small pages could contain so much youth, inner purity, holy innocence, together with subtle, sensible opinions that would have done credit to a sound male mind. The Volga, nature, the towns she visited, her comrades, her successes and failures—she did not so much describe as sing them; every line breathed the trustfulness I was accustomed to seeing in her face—and with all that, a mass of grammatical errors and an almost total lack of punctuation.

Before half a year went by, I received a highly poetical and rapturous letter, beginning with the words: "I am in love." Enclosed in this letter was a photograph showing a young, clean-shaven man in a broad-brimmed hat, with a plaid thrown over his shoulder. The letters that followed this one were as splendid as before, but punctuation marks appeared in them, the grammatical errors disappeared, and they gave off a strong male smell. Katya began writing to me about how good it would be to build a big theater somewhere on the Volga, as a stock company, to be sure, and to attract rich merchants and shipowners to the enterprise; there would be lots of money, enormous receipts, the actors would perform on cooperative principles ... Maybe it was all indeed good, but it seemed to me that such ideas could only proceed from a man's head.

Be that as it may, for a year or two everything appeared to prosper. Katya was in love, believed in her work, and was happy; but then I began to notice clear signs of a decline in her letters. It began with Katya complaining to me about her comrades—that was the first and most ominous symptom. If a young scholar or writer begins his activity by complaining bitterly about scholars or writers, it means he's already worn out and not fit for work. Katya wrote to me that her comrades did not attend rehearsals and never learned their parts; that the preposterous plays they produced and the way they behaved on stage betrayed in each of them a total lack of respect for the public; in the interest of the box office, which was all they talked about, dramatic actresses lowered themselves to singing chansonettes, and tragic actors sang ditties making fun of cuckolded husbands and the pregnancies of unfaithful wives, and so on. Generally, it was a wonder that provincial theater had not died out yet, and that it could hold on by such a thin and rotten little thread.

In reply I sent Katya a long and, I confess, very boring letter. Among other things, I wrote to her: "I have not infrequently had occasion to exchange words with old actors, the noblest of people, who accorded me their sympathy; from talking with them I was able to see that their activity is directed not so much by their own reason and freedom as by fashion and the mood of society; the best of them had been obliged, during their lives, to play in tragedies, and in operettas, and in Parisian farces, and in fairy pageants, yet they always had the same feeling of following a straight path and being useful. And so, as you see, the cause of the evil must be sought not in actors, but deeper, in the art itself and how the whole society relates to it." This letter only annoyed Katya. She replied to me: "You and I are singing in different operas. I wrote to you not about the noblest of people, who accorded you their sympathy, but about a band of swindlers who have nothing in common with nobility. They're a herd of wild people, who wound up on the stage only because they wouldn't have been accepted anywhere else, and who call themselves artists only out of insolence. Not a single talent, but a lot of giftless people, drunkards, intriguers, and gossips. I can't tell you how bitter it is for me that the art I love so much has fallen into the hands of people I find hateful; how bitter that the best people see evil only from a distance, do not want to come closer, and, instead of intervening, write heavy-handed common-places and totally needless moral pronouncements . . ." and so on, all in the same vein.

A little more time went by, and I received this letter: "I have been brutally deceived. I cannot live any longer. You may dispose of my money as you see fit. I loved you as a father and my only friend. Forgive me."

It turned out that her *he* also belonged to the "herd of wild peo-ple." Later I was able to guess from certain hints that there had been an attempt at suicide. It seems Katya tried to poison herself. It must be supposed that she was seriously ill afterwards, because the next letter I received was from Yalta, where, in all likelihood, the doctors had sent her. Her last letter to me contained a request to send her a thousand roubles in Yalta as soon as possible, and it ended like this: "Excuse me for such a gloomy letter. Yesterday I buried my baby." After spending about a year in the Crimea, she returned home.

She had been away for about four years, and for all those four years, I must confess, I played a rather strange and unenviable role in regard to her. When she had announced to me earlier that she was going to become an actress, and then wrote to me about her love, when she was periodically possessed by a spirit of prodigality and I had time and again to send her, on her demand, now a thou-sand, now two thousand roubles, when she wrote to me about her intention to die and then about the death of the baby, I was at a loss each time and all my concern for her fate expressed itself only in my thinking a lot and writing long, boring letters, which I might as well not have written. And yet I had taken the place of her real fa-ther and loved her like a daughter!

Now Katya lives half a mile from me. She has rented a five-room apartment, and has furnished it quite comfortably and in her own taste. If anyone should undertake to depict her furnishings, the predominant mood of the picture would be indolence. Soft couches, soft seats for an indolent body, carpets for indolent feet, pale, dull, or matte colors for indolent eyes; for an indolent soul, an abundance of cheap fans on the walls and little pictures in which an originality of execution dominates content, a superfluity of little tables and shelves filled with totally useless and worthless objects, shapeless rags for curtains . . . All that, along with the fear of bright colors, symmetry, and open space, testifies not only to inner indolence but also to a perversion of natural taste. For whole days Katya lies on a couch and reads books, mostly novels and stories. She leaves the house only once a day, in the afternoon, to come and see me.

I'm working, and Katya is sitting not far away on the sofa, silent and wrapped in a shawl, as if she felt cold. Either because I find her sympathetic, or because I became accustomed to her frequent visits when she was still a little girl, her presence does not keep me from concentrating. From time to time I mechanically ask her some question, and she gives me a very brief answer; or, to rest for a moment, I turn to her and watch her pensively looking through some medical journal or newspaper. And then I notice that her face no longer has its former trustful expression. Her expression is cold now, indifferent, distracted, as with passengers who have to wait a long time for a train. She still dresses beautifully and simply, but carelessly; you can see that her clothes and hair have to put up with a lot from the couches and rocking chairs she lies in all day long. And she's not as curious as she used to be. She asks me no questions now, as if she has already experienced everything in life and doesn't expect to hear anything new.

Towards four o'clock there begins to be movement in the hall and the drawing room. Liza has come home from the conservatory and brought some girlfriends with her. They can be heard playing the piano, trying out their voices, and laughing. Yegor is setting the table in the dining room and clattering the dishes.

"Good-bye," says Katya. "I won't see your family today. They must excuse me. I have no time. Come by."

As I see her off to the front door, she looks me up and down sternly and says in vexation:

"And you keep losing weight! Why don't you see a doctor? I'll go and invite Sergei Fyodorovich. Let him examine you."

"There's no need, Katya."

"I don't understand where your family is looking! Good ones they are!"

She puts her coat on impetuously, and as she does so, two or three hairpins are bound to fall from her carelessly done hair. She's too lazy to put it right, and she has no time; she awkwardly tucks the loose strands under her hat and leaves.

When I go into the dining room, my wife asks me:

"Was Katya with you just now? Why didn't she stop and see us? It's even strange . . ."

"Mama!" Liza says to her reproachfully. "If she doesn't want to, God be with her. We're not going to kneel to her."

"As you like, but it's disdainful. To sit in your study for three hours and not give us a thought! However, as she likes."

Varya and Liza both hate Katya. This hatred is incomprehensible to me, and one probably has to be a woman to understand it. I'll bet my life that of the hundred and fifty-odd young men I see almost every day in my auditorium, and the hundred older ones I have to meet each week, it would be hard to find even one who is able to understand their hatred and loathing for Katya's past—that is, for her pregnancy out of wedlock and her illegitimate child; and at the same time I simply cannot recall even one woman or girl among those I know who would not consciously or instinctively share those feelings. And that is not because women are purer or more virtuous than men: purity and virtue scarcely differ from vice, if they're not free of malice. I explain it simply by the backwardness of women. The dejected feeling of compassion and pained conscience experienced by a contemporary man at the sight of misfortune speak much more to me of culture and moral development than do hatred and loathing. Contemporary women are as tearful and coarse of heart as in the Middle Ages. And, in my opinion, those who advise that they be educated like men are quite reasonable.

My wife also dislikes Katya for having been an actress, for her ingratitude, for her pride, for her eccentricity, and for a whole host of vices that one woman is always able to find in another.

Besides my family and myself, we also have dining with us two or three of my daughter's girlfriends, and Alexander Adolfovich Gnekker, Liza's admirer and the pretender to her hand. He is a blond young man, no more than thirty, of average height, very stout, broad-shouldered, with red side-whiskers at his ears and a waxed little mustache that gives his plump, smooth face a sort of toylike expression. He is wearing a very short jacket, a bright-colored waistcoat, trousers of a large checked pattern, very wide above and very narrow below, and yellow shoes without heels. He has prominent crayfish eyes, his tie resembles a crayfish tail, and it seems to me that the whole of the young man exudes a smell of crayfish soup. He calls on us every day, but no one in my family knows what his origins are, where he studied, or what he lives on. He neither plays nor sings, but is somehow connected with music and singing, sells somebody's grand pianos somewhere, is often at the conservatory, is acquainted with all the celebrities, and takes a hand in concerts. He pronounces on music with great authority, and I've noticed that everybody willingly agrees with him.

Rich people are always surrounded by spongers; so are people of science and art. It seems no science or art in the world is free of the presence of "foreign bodies" like this Mr. Gnekker. I'm not a musician, and may be mistaken concerning this Gnekker, whom, moreover, I know only slightly. But his authority, and the dignity with which he stands by the piano and listens while someone sings or plays, strike me as all too suspicious.

You can be a gentleman and a privy councillor a hundred times over, but if you have a daughter, nothing can protect you from the bourgeois vulgarity that is often introduced into your house and into your state of mind by courtships, proposals, and weddings. I, for instance, am quite unable to reconcile myself to the solemn expression my wife acquires each time Gnekker sits down with us, nor can I be reconciled to the bottles of Lafite, port, and sherry that are served only for his sake, to give him ocular evidence of the luxury and largesse of our life. I also can't stand Liza's jerky laughter, which she learned at the conservatory, or her way of narrowing her eyes when we have gentleman visitors. And above all I simply cannot understand why it is that I am visited every day by and have dinner every day with a being who is totally alien to my habits, my learning, the whole mode of my life, and who is totally different from the people I like. My wife and the servants whisper mysteriously that he is "the fiancé," but even so I don't understand his presence; it arouses the same perplexity in me as if a Zulu were seated at my table. And it also seems strange to me that my daughter, whom I am accustomed to consider a child, should love that necktie, those eyes, those soft cheeks . . .

Formerly I either liked dinner or was indifferent to it, but now it arouses nothing but boredom and vexation in me. Ever since I became an Excellency[13] and was made dean of the faculty, my family has for some reason found it necessary to change our menu and dining habits. Instead of the simple dishes I became accustomed to as a student and a doctor, I'm now fed puréed soup with some sort of white icicles floating in it, and kidneys in Madeira. Renown and the rank of general have deprived me forever of cabbage soup, and tasty pies, and goose with apples, and bream with kasha.[14] They have also deprived me of the maid Agasha, a talkative old woman, quick to laugh, instead of whom the dinner is now served by Yegor, a dumb and arrogant fellow with a white glove on his right hand. The intermissions are short, but they seem far too long, because there is nothing to fill them. Gone are the former gaiety, unconstrained conversation, jokes, laughter, gone is the mutual tenderness and joy that animated my children, my wife and myself when we used to come together in the dining room; for a busy man like me, dinner was a time to rest and see my wife and children, and for them it was a festive time—short, it's true, but bright and joyful—when they knew that for half an hour I belonged not to science, not to my students, but to them alone and no one else. No more the ability to get drunk on a single glass, no more Agasha, no more bream with kasha, no more the noise produced by small dinner scandals, like a fight between the cat and dog under the table or the bandage falling from Katya's cheek into her plate of soup.

Describing our present-day dinners is as unappetizing as eating them. My wife's face has an expression of solemnity, an assumed gravity, and her usual worry. She glances uneasily over our plates and says: "I see you don't like the roast . . . Tell me: don't you really?" And I have to answer: "You needn't worry, my dear, the roast is quite delicious." And she: "You always stand up for me, Nikolai Stepanych, and never tell the truth. Why, then, has Alexander Adolfovich eaten so little?" and it goes on in the same vein throughout the meal. Liza laughs jerkily and narrows her eyes. I look at the two of them, and only now, at dinner, does it become perfectly clear to me that their inner life escaped my observation long ago. I have the feeling that once upon a time I lived at home with a real family, but now I'm the dinner guest of someone who is not my real wife and am looking at someone who is not the real Liza. An abrupt change has taken place in them both, I missed the long process by which this change came about, and it's no wonder I don't understand anything. Why did the change take place? I don't know. Maybe the whole trouble is that God gave my wife and daughter less strength than He gave me. Since childhood I've been accustomed to standing up to external circumstances, and I've become rather seasoned; such catastrophes in life as renown, the rank of general, the change from well-being to living beyond one's means, acquaintance with the nobility, and so on, have barely touched me, and I've remained safe and sound; but on my weak, unseasoned wife and Liza it all fell like a big block of snow, and crushed them.

The young ladies and Gnekker are talking about fugues, counterpoint, about singers and pianists, about Bach and Brahms, and my wife, afraid to be suspected of musical ignorance, smiles at them sympathetically and murmurs: "That's lovely . . . Really? You don't say . . ." Gnekker eats gravely, cracks jokes gravely, and listens condescendingly to the young ladies' observations. Every once in a while he feels a desire to speak bad French, and then for some reason he finds it necessary to address me as *votre excellence*.

And I am morose. Obviously I inhibit them all, and they inhibit me. Never before have I been closely acquainted with class antagonism, but now I'm tormented precisely by something of that sort. I try to find only bad features in Gnekker, quickly find them, and am tormented that in the suitor's place there sits a man not of my circle. His presence affects me badly in yet another respect. Usually, when I'm by myself or in the company of people I like, I never think of my own merits, and if I do begin to think of them, they seem as insignificant to me as if I had become a scientist only yesterday; but in the presence of people like Gnekker, my merits seem like a lofty mountain, its peak disappearing into the clouds, while at its foot, barely visible to the eye, the Gnekkers shift about.

After dinner I go to my study and there light my pipe, the only one of the whole day, a leftover from a long-past bad habit of puffing smoke from morning till night. While I'm smoking, my wife comes in and sits down to talk with me. Just as in the morning, I know beforehand what the talk will be about.

"I must have a serious talk with you, Nikolai Stepanych," she begins. "It's about Liza . . . Why aren't you paying attention?"

"Meaning what?"

"You make it seem as if you don't notice anything, but that's not good. It's impossible to be unconcerned . . . Gnekker has intentions towards Liza . . . What do you say?"

"That he's a bad man I cannot say, since I don't know him, but that I dislike him, I've already told you a thousand times."

"But this is impossible . . . impossible . . ."

She gets up and paces in agitation.

"It's impossible to deal this way with such a serious step . . ." she says. "When it's a question of your daughter's happiness, you must set aside everything personal. I know you dislike him . . . Very well . . . If we reject him now, break it all off, what assurance do you have that Liza won't complain about us for the rest of her life? There aren't so many suitors nowadays, and it may so happen that no other party comes along . . . He loves Liza very much, and she apparently likes him . . . Of course, he has no definite position, but what can we do? God willing, he'll get himself established somewhere in time. He's from a good family and he's rich."

"How do you know that?"

"He said so. His father has a big house in Kharkov and an estate near Kharkov. In short, Nikolai Stepanych, you absolutely must go to Kharkov."

"What for?"

"You can make inquiries . . . You have acquaintances among the professors there, they'll help you. I'd go myself, but I'm a woman. I can't . . ."

"I won't go to Kharkov," I say morosely.

My wife gets alarmed, and an expression of tormenting pain appears on her face.

"For God's sake, Nikolai Stepanych!" she implores me, sobbing. "For God's sake, relieve me of this burden! I'm suffering!"

It's becoming painful to look at her.

"Very well, Varya," I say tenderly. "If you wish, so be it, I'll go to Kharkov and do whatever you like."

She presses her handkerchief to her eyes and goes to her room to cry. I remain alone.

A little later a lamp is brought in. Familiar shadows I've long since grown weary of are cast on the walls and floor by the chairs and the lamp shade, and when I look at them, it seems to me that it's already night and that my cursed insomnia is beginning. I lie down, then get up and pace the room, then lie down again . . . Usually after dinner, before evening, my nervous agitation reaches its highest pitch. I start weeping for no reason and hide my head under the pillow. In those moments I'm afraid somebody may come in, afraid I may die suddenly; I'm ashamed of my tears, and generally there is something unbearable in my soul. I feel that I can no longer stand the sight of my lamp, the books, the shadows on the floor, or the sound of voices coming from the drawing room.

Some invisible and incomprehensible force is roughly pushing me out of the house. I jump up, hastily put on my coat and hat, and cautiously, so that the family won't notice, go outside. Where to?

The answer to that question has long been sitting in my brain: to Katya.

III

As usual, she's lying on a Turkish divan or couch and reading something. On seeing me, she raises her head indolently, sits up, and gives me her hand.

"And you're always lying down," I say, after pausing briefly to rest. "That's unhealthy. You ought to find something to do!"

"Eh?"

"I said, you ought to find something to do."

"What? A woman can only be a menial worker or an actress."

"Well, then? If you can't be a worker, be an actress."

Silence.

"Why don't you get married?" I say half jokingly.

"There's nobody to marry. And no reason to."

"You can't live like this."

"Without a husband? A lot it matters! There are men all over, if anybody's interested."

"That's not nice, Katya."

"What's not nice?"

"What you just said."

Noticing that I'm upset, and wishing to smooth over the bad impression, Katya says:

"Come. Over here. Look."

She leads me to a small, very cozy room and says, pointing to the writing table:

"Look . . . I've made it ready for you. You can work here. Come every day and bring your work. At home they only bother you. Will you work here? Do you want to?"

To avoid upsetting her by saying no, I reply that I will work in her place and that I like the room very much. Then the two of us sit down in this cozy room and begin to talk.

The warmth, the cozy atmosphere, and the presence of a sympathetic person now arouse in me not a feeling of contentment, as before, but a strong urge to complain and grumble. For some reason it seems to me that if I murmur and complain a bit I'll feel better.

"Things are bad, my dear!" I begin with a sigh. "Very bad . . ."

"What's wrong?"

"The thing is this, my friend. The best and most sacred right of kings is the right to show mercy. And I always felt myself a king, because I made boundless use of that right. I never judged, I was tolerant, I willingly forgave everybody right and left. Where others protested and were indignant, I merely advised and persuaded. All my life I tried only to make my company bearable for my family, students, colleagues, and servants. And this attitude of mine towards people, I know, was an education to all those around me. But now I'm no longer a king. Something is going on inside me that is fit only for slaves: spiteful thoughts wander through my head day and night, and feelings such as I've never known before are nesting in my soul. I hate and despise, I feel indignant, outraged, afraid. I've become excessively severe, demanding, irritable, ungracious, suspicious. Even something that before would have given me an occasion for one more quip and a good-natured laugh, now produces a heavy feeling in me. My logic has also changed in me: before I only despised money, now I harbor a spiteful feeling not for money but for the rich, as if they were to blame; before I hated violence and tyranny, but now I hate the people who use violence, as if they alone were to blame and not all of us, because we're unable to educate each other. What does it mean? If my new thoughts and feelings proceed from a change of convictions, where could that change have come from? Has the world become worse and I better, or was I blind and indifferent before? And if this change has proceeded from a general decline of physical and mental powers—I'm sick and losing weight every day—then my situation is pathetic: it means that my new thoughts are abnormal, unhealthy, that I should be ashamed of them and consider them worthless . . ."

"Sickness has nothing to do with it," Katya interrupts me. "It's simply that your eyes have been opened, that's all. You've seen something that for some reason you didn't want to notice before. In my opinion, you must first of all break with your family and leave."

"What you're saying is absurd."

"You don't love them, so why this duplicity? And is that a family? Nonentities! They could die today, and tomorrow nobody would notice they were gone."

Katya despises my wife and daughter as much as they hate her. In our day one can hardly talk of people's right to despise each other. But if one takes Katya's point of view and acknowledges that such a right exists, one can see that after all she has the same right to despise my wife and Liza as they have to hate her.

"Nonentities!" she repeats. "Did you have dinner today? How is it they didn't forget to call you to the dining room? How is it they still remember your existence?"

"Katya," I say sternly, "I ask you to be quiet."

"And do you think I enjoy talking about them? I'd be glad not to know them at all. Listen to me, my dear: drop everything and leave. Go abroad. The sooner the better."

"What nonsense! And the university?"

"The university, too. What is it to you? There's no sense in it anyway. You've been lecturing for thirty years now, and where are your disciples? Have you produced many famous scientists? Count them up! And to multiply the number of doctors who exploit ignorance and make hundreds of thousands, there's no need to be a good and talented man. You're superfluous."

"My God, how sharp you are!" I say, horrified. "How sharp you are! Be quiet, or I'll leave! I don't know how to reply to your sharpness!"

The maid comes in and invites us to have tea. At the samovar our conversation changes, thank God. Since I've already complained, I want to give free rein to my other old man's weakness—reminiscence. I tell Katya about my past and, to my great astonishment, inform her of such details as I didn't even suspect were still preserved in my memory. And she listens to me with tenderness, with pride, with bated breath. I especially like telling her how I once studied at the seminary[15] and dreamed of going to university.

"I used to walk in our seminary garden . . ." I tell her. "The squeak of an accordion and a song from a far-off tavern would come on the wind, or a troika with bells would race past the seminary fence, and that was already quite enough for a sense of happiness suddenly to fill not only my breast, but even my stomach, legs, arms . . . I'd listen to the accordion or to the fading sound of the bells, and imagine myself a doctor and paint pictures—one better than the other. And so, as you see, my dreams have come true. I've received more than I dared dream of. For thirty years I've been a beloved professor, have had excellent colleagues, have enjoyed honorable renown. I've loved, married for passionate love, had children. In short, looking back, my whole life seems to me like a beautiful composition, executed with talent. Now it only remains for me not to ruin the finale. For that I must die like a human being. If death is indeed a danger, I must meet it as befits a teacher, a scientist, and the citizen of a Christian country: cheerfully and with a peaceful soul. But I'm ruining the finale. I'm drowning, I run to you asking for help, and you say to me: drown, that's how it should be."

But here the bell rings in the front hall. Katya and I recognize it and say:

"That must be Mikhail Fyodorovich."

And, indeed, a moment later in comes my colleague, the philologist Mikhail Fyodorovich, a tall, well-built man of around fifty, clean-shaven, with thick gray hair and black eyebrows. He is a kind man and an excellent comrade. He comes from an old aristocratic family, very fortunate and talented, which has played a notable role in the history of our literature and education. He himself is intelligent, talented, very cultivated, but not without his oddities. To a certain degree we're all odd, we're all eccentrics, but his oddities seem to his acquaintances to be something exceptional and not entirely harmless. Among those acquaintances I know not a few who are totally unable to see his many virtues through his oddities.

He comes into the room, slowly removes his gloves, and says in a velvety bass:

"Good evening. Having tea? That's quite appropriate. It's hellishly cold."

Then he sits at the table, takes a glass, and immediately starts talking. The most characteristic thing in his manner of talking is his permanently jocular tone, a sort of blend of philosophy and banter, as with Shakespeare's gravediggers. He always talks about serious things, but never talks seriously. His opinions are always sharp, abusive, but owing to his soft, smooth, jocular tone, it somehow turns out that his sharpness and abuse do not grate on the ear, and you quickly get used to them. Every evening he brings along five or six anecdotes from university life, and when he sits at the table, he usually begins with them.

"Oh, Lord!" he sighs, with a mocking movement of his black eyebrows. "Such comedians there are in the world!"

"And so?" asks Katya.

"I'm leaving after my lecture, and on the stairs I meet that old idiot of ours, X . . . He's walking along with his horse's jaw thrust out as usual, looking for somebody to complain to about his migraine, his wife, and the students, who don't want to attend his lectures. Well, I think, he's seen me—that's it, I'm lost . . ."

And so on in the same vein. Or else he begins like this:

"Yesterday I was at our Y's public lecture. It surprises me that our alma mater—not to speak of the devil—ventures to show the public such patent oafs and dimwits as this Y. He's a fool on a European scale! Good heavens, you wouldn't find another like him in all of Europe, not even with a candle in broad daylight! He lectures, if you can imagine, just as if he's sucking a candy: ssk-ssk-ssk . . . He gets cold feet, can't make out his own notes, his wretched little thoughts barely move, like a monk on a bicycle, and above all there's no way to tell what he's trying to say. Flies die of boredom. The boredom can only be compared with what we have in our big auditorium at commencement, when the traditional speech is being read, devil take it."

And at once a sharp transition:

"Some three years ago, as our Nikolai Stepanych remembers, I had to deliver that speech. Hot, stuffy, uniform tight under the arms—you could die! I read for half an hour, an hour, an hour and a half, two hours . . . Well, I think, thank God, only ten pages left. And at the conclusion there were four pages I could omit altogether, so I counted on not reading them. That leaves only six, I thought. Then, imagine, I glance up and see some beribboned general and a bishop sitting next to each other in the front row. The poor souls are stiff with boredom, they roll their eyes so as not to fall asleep, and yet they still try to keep an attentive look on their faces and pretend that they like and understand my lecture. Well, I think, since you like it, you're going to get it! For spite! And I up and read all four pages."

When he talks, only his eyes and eyebrows smile, as generally with people given to mockery. There is no hatred or spite in his eyes at these moments, but a good deal of sharpness and that peculiar foxy cunning that is seen only in very observant people. To go on about his eyes, I've noticed another peculiarity in them. When he takes a glass from Katya, or listens to some remark of hers, or follows her with his eyes when she momentarily leaves the room for some reason, I notice in his glance something meek, prayerful, pure . . .

The maid removes the samovar and puts a big piece of cheese and some fruit on the table, along with a bottle of Crimean champagne, a rather bad wine that Katya came to like when she lived in the Crimea. Mikhail Fyodorovich takes two decks of cards from the shelf and lays out a game of patience. According to him, some varieties of patience call for considerable cleverness and concentration, but he still never stops entertaining himself with talk, even while he plays. Katya follows the cards attentively and helps him more with looks than with words. She drinks no more than two glasses of wine all evening, I drink a quarter of a glass; the rest of the bottle falls to Mikhail Fyodorovich, who can drink a lot and never gets drunk.

Over patience we resolve various questions, mostly of a higher order, and what gets the most punishment from us is what we love most—that is, science.

"Science has outlived itself, thank God," Mikhail Fyodorovich says measuredly. "Its song has been sung. Yes, sir. Mankind is already beginning to feel the need to replace it with something else. It sprang from the soil of superstition, was nourished by superstition, and is now as much the quintessence of superstition as the grandmothers it has outlived: alchemy, metaphysics, and philosophy. And what, indeed, has it given people? The difference between learned Europeans and the Chinese, who have no science themselves, is quite negligible and purely external. The Chinese don't know science, but what have they lost because of it?"

"Flies don't know science either," I say, "but what of that?"

"You needn't get angry, Nikolai Stepanych. I'm saying it here, among us . . . I'm more cautious than you think, and am not about to say it publicly, God forbid! The superstition persists among the masses that science and the arts are higher than agriculture and trade, higher than the handicrafts. Our sect feeds on that superstition, and it's not for you or me to destroy it. God forbid!"

Over patience the younger generation also comes in for rough treatment.

"Our public has become paltry these days," sighs Mikhail Fyodorovich. "I'm not even talking about ideals and all that, but they don't even know how to work or think properly! It's precisely: 'In sorrow I gaze upon our generation.' "[16]

"Yes, terribly paltry," Katya agrees. "Tell me, have you had at least one outstanding student in the last five or ten years?"

"I don't know about other professors, but I don't remember any among mine."

"I've seen lots of students in my time, and your young scientists, and lots of actors . . . And what? Never once was I deemed worthy of meeting not only a hero or a talent, but even simply an interesting human being. They're all gray, giftless, puffed up with pretensions . . ."

All these conversations about paltriness give me the feeling each time of having accidentally overheard some nasty conversation about my own daughter. It offends me that the accusations are so sweeping and built on such worn-out commonplaces, such bogeys, as paltriness, lack of ideals, or references to the beautiful past. Any accusation, even if it's spoken in the company of ladies, must be formulated as definitely as possible, otherwise it's not an accusation but empty maligning, unworthy of decent people.

I'm an old man, I've been teaching for thirty years, but I don't see any paltriness or lack of ideals, nor do I find it worse now than before. My porter Nikolai, whose experience in this case is valid, says that today's students are no better or worse than before.

If I were asked what I do not like in my present students, I would not answer at once or at length, but I would be sufficiently definite. I know their shortcomings and therefore have no need to resort to a fog of commonplaces. I do not like it that they smoke, use alcoholic beverages, and marry late; that they are careless and often indifferent to such a degree that they suffer people to go hungry in their midst and do not pay into the student aid society. They don't know modern languages and speak Russian incorrectly; just yesterday a colleague of mine, a hygienist, complained to me that he had to lecture twice as long, because they have a poor knowledge of physics and are totally unacquainted with meteorology. They willingly submit to the influence of modern writers, and not even the best of them, but are completely indifferent to such classics as Shakespeare, Marcus Aurelius, Epictetus, or Pascal, and this inability to distinguish great from small betrays most of all their everyday impracticality. All difficult questions of a more or less social character (resettlement, for instance) they solve by subscriptions, and not by means of scientific research and experiment, though the latter are entirely at their disposal and best correspond to their purposes. They willingly become orderlies, assistants, laboratory technicians, adjuncts, and are ready to occupy those positions till the age of forty, though independence, a sense of freedom, and personal initiative are no less necessary in science than, for instance, in art or in trade. I have students and auditors, but no helpers or heirs, and therefore, though I feel love and tenderness for them, I am not proud of them. And so on and so forth.

Such shortcomings, numerous though they are, can produce a pessimistic or abusive spirit only in a fainthearted and timid man. They all have an accidental, transient character and are totally dependent on life's circumstances; some ten years are enough for them to disappear or yield their place to new and different shortcomings, which it is impossible to do without and which, in their turn, will frighten the fainthearted. I'm often vexed by my students' sins, but this vexation is nothing compared with the joy I've experienced for thirty years, when I talk with my students, lecture to them, study their relations, and compare them with people in other circles.

Mikhail Fyodorovich maligns, Katya listens, and neither notices what a deep abyss this apparently innocent amusement of judging their neighbors draws them into. They don't feel how their simple conversation gradually turns into jeering and scoffing, and how they both even start using slanderous methods.

"Some specimens are killingly funny," says Mikhail Fyodorovich. "Yesterday I come to our Yegor Petrovich and find a *studiosus,* one of your medics, in his third year, I think. A face in the . . . the Dobrolyubov[17] style, the stamp of profundity on his brow. We get to talking. 'Thus and so, young man,' I say. 'I read that some German—I forget his name—has obtained a new alkaloid, idiotine, from the human brain.' And what do you think? He believed me and his face even showed respect: That's our boys for you! Then the other day I come to the theater. I sit down. In the row just in front of me these two are sitting: one of 'our boyth,' apparently doing law, the other all disheveled—a medic. The medic is drunk as a cobbler. Pays zero attention to the stage. Keeps dozing and nodding his head. But as soon as some actor starts loudly reciting a monologue or simply raises his voice, my medic gives a start, nudges his neighbor in the side, and asks: 'What's he saying? Something no-o-oble?' 'Something noble,' answers the one from our boyth.

'Brrravo!' bawls the medic. 'Something no-o-oble! Bravo!' You see, the drunken blockhead has come to the theater not for art but for nobility. He's after nobility."

And Katya listens and laughs. Her laughter is somehow strange: her inhalations alternate quickly and in regular rhythm with her exhalations, as if she were playing the harmonica, and yet all that laughs on her face are her nostrils. I'm dispirited and don't know what to say. Beside myself, I explode, jump up from my place and shout:

"Be quiet, finally! What are you doing sitting here like two toads poisoning the air with your breath? Enough!"

And without waiting for them to finish their maligning, I prepare to go home. And it's high time: past ten o'clock.

"I'll stay a little longer," says Mikhail Fyodorovich. "May I, Ekaterina Vladimirovna?"

"You may," Katya answers.

"*Bene*. In that case tell them to serve another little bottle."

The two of them see me off to the front door with candles, and while I'm putting my coat on, Mikhail Fyodorovich says:

"You've grown terribly thin and old recently, Nikolai Stepanych. What's the matter? Are you ill?"

"Yes, I'm a bit ill."

"And he won't be treated . . ." Katya puts in glumly.

"Why won't you be treated? My dear man, the Lord helps those who help themselves. Regards to your family and my apologies for not visiting them. One of these days, before I go abroad, I'll stop and say good-bye. Without fail! I leave next week."

I go out of Katya's annoyed, frightened by the talk of my illness, and displeased with myself. I ask myself: should I not, indeed, consult one of my colleagues? And I immediately imagine how my colleague, having auscultated me, goes silently to the window, ponders, then turns to me, and, trying to keep me from reading the truth on his face, says in an indifferent tone: "So far I see nothing special, but all the same, *collega*, I'd advise you to stop working . . ." And that will deprive me of my last hope.

Who doesn't have hopes? Now, diagnosing myself and treating myself, there are moments when I hope that my own ignorance is deceiving me, that I'm also mistaken about the protein and sugar I find in myself, and about my heart, and about the swelling I've noticed twice now in the morning; re-reading the manuals on therapy with the zeal of a hypochondriac and changing my medications daily, I keep thinking I'll hit on something comforting. It's all paltry.

Whether the sky is covered with clouds, or the moon and stars are shining in it, each time I return home, I look up at it and think that death will soon take me. One would think that at such moments my thoughts should be deep as the sky, bright, striking . . . But no! I think about myself, my wife, Liza, Gnekker, my students, people in general; my thoughts are bad, paltry, I'm tricking myself, and in those moments my worldview can be expressed in the words which the famous Arakcheev[18] said in one of his private letters: "Nothing good in the world can be without bad, and there is always more bad than good." That is, everything is muck, there is nothing to live for, and the sixty-two years I've lived should be considered a waste. I catch myself in these thoughts and try to convince myself that they are accidental, temporary, and not lodged deeply in me, but at once I think:

"If so, then what is it that draws you to those two toads every evening?"

And I swear to myself that I will not go to Katya's anymore, though I know I'll go to her again tomorrow.

Ringing my doorbell and then going up the stairs, I feel that I no longer have a family and have no wish to return to it. Clearly, the new Arakcheevian thoughts are not lodged in me accidentally or temporarily, but govern my whole being. With a sick conscience, dejected, indolent, barely moving my limbs, as if a thousand pounds had been added to my weight, I lie down in bed and soon fall asleep.

And then—insomnia . . .

IV

Summer comes, and life changes.

One fine morning Liza enters my room and says in a joking tone:

"Let's go, Your Excellency. Everything's ready."

My Excellency is taken outside, put into a carriage, and driven somewhere. I ride along and, having nothing better to do, read the signboards from right to left. The word "pothouse" comes out "esuohtop." That would suit an ancient Egyptian: the pharaoh Esuohtop. I go on over a field past the cemetery, which makes precisely no impression on me at all, though I'll soon be lying in it; then I go through a woods and another field. Nothing interesting. After a two-hour drive, My Excellency is led into the bottom floor of a summer house and installed in a very cheerful little room with light blue wallpaper.

At night there's the usual insomnia, but in the morning I'm not awake and listening to my wife, but lying in bed. I don't sleep, but experience that drowsy, half-oblivious state when you know you're not asleep, and yet have dreams. At noon I get up and, out of habit, sit at my desk, but I don't work now, I entertain myself with the French books in yellow covers that Katya sends me. Of course, it would be more patriotic to read Russian authors, but I confess I'm not especially in favor of them. Except for two or three older writers, all modern literature seems to me not literature but some sort of handicraft, which exists only so as to be encouraged, though one is reluctant to use its products. Even the best products of handicraft cannot be called remarkable and cannot be praised without a "but." The same can be said of all the literary novelties I've read over the last ten or fifteen years: not one is remarkable, and there's no avoiding a "but." Intelligent, noble, but not talented; talented, noble, but not intelligent; or, finally, talented, intelligent, but not noble.

I'm not saying that French books are talented, and intelligent, and noble. They don't satisfy me either. But they're less boring than the Russian ones, and not seldom one finds in them the main element of creative work—a sense of personal freedom, which Russian authors don't have. I can't remember a single new book in which the author doesn't do his best, from the very first page, to entangle himself in all possible conventions and private deals with his conscience. One is afraid to speak of the naked body, another is bound hand and foot by psychological analysis, a third must have "a warm attitude towards humanity," a fourth purposely wallows for whole pages in descriptions of nature, lest he be suspected of tendentiousness . . . One insists on being a bourgeois in his work, another an aristocrat, etc. Contrivance, caution, keeping one's own counsel, but no freedom nor courage to write as one wishes, and therefore no creativity.

All this refers to so-called belles-lettres.

As for serious Russian articles, for instance on sociology, art, and so on, I avoid reading them out of sheer timidity. In my childhood and youth I was for some reason afraid of doormen and theater ushers, and that fear has stayed with me. I'm afraid of them even now. They say we fear only what we don't understand. And, indeed, it's very hard to understand why doormen and ushers are so important, so arrogant, and so majestically impolite. When I read serious articles I feel exactly the same vague fear. The extraordinary importance, the facetiously pontifical tone, the familiar treatment of foreign authors, the knack of augustly pouring from empty into void—I find it all incomprehensible, frightening, and nothing like the modesty and gentlemanly calm tone I'm accustomed to in reading what doctors and natural scientists write. Not only articles, it's even painful for me to read the translations done or edited by serious Russian people. The conceited, benevolent tone of the prefaces, the abundance of translator's notes, which disturb my concentration, the parenthetical question marks and *sic*'s that the translator generously scatters through the article or book, are for me like an encroachment both upon the person of the author and upon my independence as a reader.

I was once invited to the circuit court as an expert; during a break, one of my fellow experts drew my attention to the prosecutor's rude treatment of the defendants, among whom were two women of the intelligentsia. I don't think I was exaggerating in the least when I answered my colleague that this treatment was no more rude than that displayed towards each other by the authors of serious articles. Indeed, it is such rude treatment that one cannot speak of it without pain. Either they treat each other and the authors they criticize with excessive deference, forgetting all dignity, or the reverse, they handle them with greater boldness than I use in these notes, and in my thoughts, towards my future son-in-law Gnekker. Accusations of irresponsibility, of impure intentions, and of all sorts of criminality are the usual adornments of serious articles. And that, as young doctors like to put it in their articles, is the *ultima ratio*![19] Such relations cannot fail to be reflected in the morals of the younger generation of writers, and therefore I'm not surprised in the least that in the new books our literature has acquired over the last ten or fifteen years, the heroes drink gallons of vodka and the heroines are insufficiently chaste.

I read my French books and keep glancing out the window, which is open; I see the teeth of my fence, two or three scrawny trees, and beyond the fence a road, a field, then a wide strip of ever-green forest. I often admire how a certain little boy and girl, both towheaded and ragged, climb up the fence and laugh at my bald head. In their bright little eyes I read: "Go up, thou bald head!"[20] They're probably the only people who care nothing about my rank and renown.

Now I don't have visitors every day. I will mention only the visits of Nikolai and Pyotr Ignatievich. Nikolai usually comes on feast days,[21] seemingly on business, but more just to see me. He arrives rather tipsy, which never happens with him in the winter.

"What's up?" I ask, coming to meet him in the front hall.

"Your Excellency!" he says, pressing his hand to his heart and looking at me with the rapture of a lover. "Your Excellency! May God punish me! May I be struck by lightning on this very spot! *Gaudeamus igitur juvenestus!*"[22]

And he greedily kisses me on the shoulders, sleeves, buttons.

"Is everything all right with you there?" I ask him.

"Your Excellency! As God lives . . ."

He won't stop swearing needlessly by God, I soon get sick of him and send him to the kitchen, where they serve him dinner. Pyotr Ignatievich also comes on feast days, especially to see how I am and to share his thoughts with me. He usually sits by my desk, modest, neat, sensible, not daring to cross his legs or lean on his elbow; and all the while, in his soft, even little voice, smoothly and bookishly, he tells me what he thinks are various extremely interesting and spicy bits of news that he has come across in journals and books. These items are all alike and boil down to this: a certain Frenchman made a discovery; another man—a German—caught him out, by proving that this discovery had already been made in 1870 by some American; and a third—also a German—outwitted them both, proving that they were a pair of dupes who mistook air bubbles for dark pigment under the microscope. Even when he wants to make me laugh, Pyotr Ignatievich tells everything at length, thoroughly, as if defending a thesis, with a detailed list of his printed sources, trying not to make any mistakes in the dates, or in the numbers of the journals, or in names, and he never simply says Petit, but always Jean-Jacques Petit. Occasionally he stays for dinner with us, and then he tells the same spicy stories all through dinner, which plunges everyone at the table into gloom. If Gnekker and Liza start talking about fugues and counterpoint, about Brahms and Bach, he modestly looks down and gets embarrassed; he's ashamed that such banalities should be talked about in the presence of such serious people as he and I.

In my present mood five minutes are enough to make me as sick of him as if I'd seen and heard him for all eternity. I hate the wretched fellow. I wither from his soft, even voice and bookish language, I grow dumb from his stories . . . He has the best feelings for me and talks with me only to give me pleasure, and I pay him back by looking at him point-blank, as if I wanted to hypnotize him, and thinking: "Go away, go away, go away . . ." But he doesn't succumb to my mental suggestion and stays, stays, stays . . .

All the while he stays with me, I'm unable to rid myself of the thought: "It's quite possible that when I die, he'll be appointed to replace me," and in my imagination my poor auditorium looks like an oasis in which the spring has dried up, and I'm unpleasant, silent, and sullen with Pyotr Ignatievich, as if he were to blame for these thoughts and not I myself. When he begins his habitual praise of German scientists, I no longer joke good-naturedly, as before, but mutter sullenly:

"Your Germans are asses . . ."

This is like the episode when the late professor Nikita Krylov, swimming at Revel[23] once with Pirogov, got angry with the water for being very cold and swore: "Scoundrelly Germans!" I behave badly with Pyotr Ignatievich, and only when he leaves, and I see his gray hat flash outside the window, beyond the fence, do I want to call out to him and say: "Forgive me, my dear fellow!"

Our dinners are more boring than in winter. The same Gnekker, whom I now hate and despise, dines with us almost every day. Formerly I suffered his presence silently, but now I send little barbs at him, which make my wife and Liza blush. Carried away by spiteful feeling, I often say simply stupid things and don't know why I say them. It happened once that I gave Gnekker a long, scornful look and then, out of nowhere, fired off at him:

> Eagles may fly lower than the hen,
> But no hen ever soared into the clouds . . . [24]

And the most vexing thing is that the hen Gnekker proves to be much smarter than the eagle professor. Knowing that my wife and daughter are on his side, he sticks to the following tactics: he responds to my barbs with an indulgent silence (the old man's cracked, what's the point of talking to him?), or good-naturedly makes fun of me. It's astonishing how paltry a man can become! I'm capable of dreaming all through dinner of how Gnekker will turn out to be an adventurer, and how Liza and my wife will realize their mistake, and how I will taunt them—to have such absurd dreams when I've got one foot in the grave!

Misunderstandings also happen now which I knew before only from hearsay. Ashamed as I am, I'll describe one that occurred the other day after dinner.

I'm sitting in my room smoking my pipe. My wife comes in as usual, sits down, and begins saying how nice it would be now, while it's still warm and I have free time, to go to Kharkov and there find out what sort of man our Gnekker is.

"All right, I'll go . . ." I agree.

My wife, pleased with me, gets up and goes to the door, but comes back at once and says:

"Incidentally, one more request. I know you'll be angry, but it is my duty to warn you . . . Forgive me, Nikolai Stepanych, but there has begun to be talk among all our neighbors and acquaintances that you visit Katya rather often. She's intelligent, educated, I don't dispute it, one may enjoy spending time with her, but at your age and with your social position, you know, it's somehow strange to find pleasure in her company . . . Besides, her reputation is such that . . ."

All the blood suddenly drains from my brain, sparks shoot from my eyes, I jump up and, clutching my head, stamping my feet, shout in a voice not my own:

"Leave me! Leave me! Get out!"

My face is probably terrible, my voice strange, because my wife suddenly turns pale and cries out loudly in a desperate voice, also somehow not her own. At our cries, Liza, Gnekker, then Yegor come running in . . .

"Leave me!" I shout. "Get out! Out!"

My legs go numb, as if they're not there, I feel myself fall into someone's arms, briefly hear someone weeping, and sink into a swoon that lasts for two or three hours.

Now about Katya. She calls on me every day towards evening, and, of course, neighbors and acquaintances cannot fail to notice it. She comes for just a minute and takes me for a ride with her. She has her own horse and a new charabanc, bought this summer. Generally, she lives in grand style: she has rented an expensive separate summer house with a big garden and moved all her town furniture into it; keeps two maids, a coachman . . . I often ask her:

"Katya, how are you going to live when you've squandered all your father's money?"

"We'll see then," she replies.

"That money deserves a more serious attitude, my friend. A good man earned it by honest labor."

"You already told me about that. I know."

First we drive through the field, then through the evergreen forest that can be seen from my window. I still find nature beautiful, though a demon whispers to me that none of these pines and firs, birds and white clouds in the sky will notice my absence when I die three or four months from now. Katya enjoys driving the horse and is pleased that the weather is nice and that I'm sitting beside her. She's in fine spirits and doesn't say anything sharp.

"You're a very good man, Nikolai Stepanych," she says. "You're a rare specimen, and there's no actor who could play you. Even a bad actor could play me, or Mikhail Fyodorych, for instance, but no one could play you. And I envy you, envy you terribly! Because what am I the picture of? What?"

She thinks for a moment and asks:

"I'm a negative phenomenon—right, Nikolai Stepanych?"

"Right," I answer.

"Hm . . . What am I to do?"

What answer can I give her? It's easy to say "work," or "give what you have to the poor," or "know yourself," and because it's easy to say, I don't know how to answer.

My general-practitioner colleagues, when they teach medical treatment, advise one "to individualize each particular case." One need only follow that advice to be convinced that the remedies recommended by textbooks as the best and wholly suitable for the standard case, prove completely unsuitable in particular cases. The same is true for moral illnesses.

But answer I must, and so I say:

"You have too much free time, my friend. You must occupy yourself with something. Why indeed don't you become an actress again, since you have the calling?"

"I can't."

"Your tone and manner make it seem that you're a victim. I don't like that, my friend. It's your own fault. Remember, you started by getting angry at people and their ways, but you did nothing to make them better. You didn't fight the evil, you got tired, and you are the victim not of the struggle, but of your own weakness. Well, of course, you were young then, inexperienced, but now everything might go differently. Really, try it again! You'll work and serve holy art . . ."

"Don't dissemble, Nikolai Stepanych," Katya interrupts me. "Let's agree once and for all: we can talk about actors, about actresses, or writers, but we'll leave art alone. You're a wonderful, rare person, but you don't understand art well enough to regard it in good conscience as holy. You have neither the feel nor the ear for art. You've been busy all your life, and you've had no time to acquire the feel for it. Generally . . . I don't like these conversations about art!" she goes on nervously. "I really don't! It has been trivialized enough, thank you!"

"Trivialized by whom?"

"Some have trivialized it by drunkenness, the newspapers by familiarity, clever people by philosophy."

"Philosophy has nothing to do with it."

"Yes, it has. If anybody starts philosophizing, it means he doesn't understand."

To keep things from turning sharp, I hasten to change the subject and then remain silent for a long time. Only when we come out of the forest and turn towards Katya's place do I come back to the former conversation and ask:

"You still haven't answered me: why don't you want to be an actress?"

"Nikolai Stepanych, this is cruel, finally!" she cries out and suddenly blushes all over. "You want me to speak the truth aloud? All right, if that . . . if that's your pleasure! I have no talent! No talent and . . . and enormous vanity! There!"

Having made this confession, she turns her face away from me and grips the reins hard to hide the trembling of her hands.

As we approach her place, we can already see Mikhail Fyodorovich in the distance, strolling about the gate, impatiently waiting for us.

"Again this Mikhail Fyodorych!" Katya says with vexation. "Rid me of him, please! I'm sick of him, he's played out . . . Enough of him!"

Mikhail Fyodorovich should have gone abroad long ago, but he keeps postponing his departure each week. Certain changes have taken place in him lately: he has become somehow pinched, wine now makes him tipsy, which never happened before, and his black eyebrows have begun to turn gray. When our charabanc stops at the gate, he doesn't conceal his joy and impatience. He bustles about, helps me and Katya out of the carriage, hurriedly asks questions, laughs, rubs his hands, and that meek, prayerful, pure something that I noticed only in his eyes before is now spread all over his face. He's glad, and at the same time ashamed of his gladness, ashamed of this habit of visiting Katya every evening, and he finds it necessary to motivate his coming by some obvious absurdity, such as: "I was passing by on business, thought why don't I stop for a moment."

The three of us go in; first we have tea, then on the table appear the two long-familiar decks of cards, the big piece of cheese, the fruit, and the bottle of Crimean champagne. Our topics of conversation are not new, they're all the same as in the winter. The university, students, literature, theater all come in for it; the air gets thicker and stuffier with malignant gossip, it is poisoned by the breath not of two toads now, as in the winter, but of all three. Besides the velvety baritone laugh and the laugh that resembles a harmonica, the maid who serves us also hears an unpleasant, cracked laughter, like that of a vaudeville general: haw, haw, haw . . .

V

There are terrible nights of thunder, lightning, rain, and wind, which among the people are known as sparrow nights. There was one such sparrow night in my personal life . . .

I wake up past midnight and suddenly jump out of bed. It seems to me for some reason that I'm suddenly just about to die. Why does it seem so? There's not a feeling in my body that would point to an imminent end, but my soul is oppressed by such terror as if I had suddenly seen some enormous, sinister glow.

I quickly light the lamp, drink water straight from the carafe, then rush to the open window. The weather outside is magnificent. There's a smell of hay and of something else very good. I can see the teeth of the fence, the sleepy, scrawny trees by the window, the road, the dark strip of the forest; a calm, very bright moon in the

sky, and not a single cloud. Silence, not a leaf stirs. I feel as if everything is looking at me and listening in on how I'm going to die . . .

Eerie. I close the window and run to my bed. I feel my pulse
and, not finding it in my wrist, search for it in my temples, then
under my chin, then again in my wrist, and it's all cold, clammy
with sweat. My breath comes quicker and quicker, my body trembles, all my insides are stirred up, my face and bald head feel as if
they're covered with cobwebs.

What to do? Call the family? No, no need. I don't know what
my wife and Liza will do if they come to me.

I hide my head under the pillow, close my eyes, and wait,
wait . . . My back is cold, it's as if it were being drawn into me, and
I have the feeling that death will surely come at me from behind,
on the sly . . .

"Kee-wee, kee-wee!" a piping suddenly sounds in the silence of
the night, and I don't know where it is—in my breast, or outside?

"Kee-wee, kee-wee!"

My God, how frightening! I'd drink more water, but I'm scared
to open my eyes and afraid to raise my head. The terror I feel is unconscious, animal, and I'm unable to understand why I'm frightened: is it because I want to live, or because a new, still unknown
pain awaits me?

Upstairs, through my ceiling, someone either moans or
laughs . . . I listen. Shortly afterwards I hear footsteps on the stairs.
Someone hurriedly comes down, then goes back up. A moment
later there are footsteps downstairs again; someone stops by my
door, listening.

"Who's there?" I cry.

The door opens, I boldly open my eyes and see my wife. Her
face is pale and her eyes tearful.

"You're not asleep, Nikolai Stepanych?" she asks.

"What is it?"

"For God's sake, go and look at Liza. Something's the matter
with her . . ."

"All right . . . with pleasure . . ." I mutter, very pleased that I'm
not alone. "All right . . . this minute."

I follow my wife, listen to what she tells me, and understand
nothing in my agitation. Bright spots from her candle leap over the
steps of the stairway, our long shadows quiver, my legs get tangled
in the skirts of my dressing gown, I'm out of breath, and it seems to

me as if something is pursuing me and wants to seize me by the back. "I'm going to die right now, here on the stairs," I think. "Right now . . ." But the stairs and the dark corridor with the Italian window are behind us, and we go into Liza's room. She's sitting on her bed in nothing but her nightgown, her bare feet hanging down, and moaning.

"Oh, my God . . . oh, my God!" she murmurs, squinting at our candle. "I can't, I can't . . ."

"Liza, my child," I say. "What's wrong?"

Seeing me, she cries out and throws herself on my neck.

"My kind papa . . ." she sobs, "my good papa . . . My dearest little papa . . . I don't know what's wrong with me . . . I'm so sick at heart!"

She embraces me, kisses me, and babbles tender words such as I heard from her when she was a little girl.

"Calm yourself, my child, God be with you," I say. "You mustn't cry. I'm sick at heart, too."

I try to cover her with a blanket, my wife gives her a drink, the two of us fuss confusedly around the bed; my shoulder brushes her shoulder, and in that moment the recollection comes to me of how we used to bathe our children together.

"Help her, help her!" my wife implores. "Do something!"

But what can I do? I can't do anything. The girl has some burden on her heart, but I don't know or understand anything, and can only murmur:

"Never mind, never mind . . . It will go away . . . Sleep, sleep . . ."

As if on purpose, a dog's howling suddenly comes from our yard, first soft and uncertain, then loud, in two voices. I've never ascribed any particular significance to such omens as the howling of dogs or the hooting of owls, but now my heart is painfully wrung and I hasten to explain this howling to myself.

"Nonsense . . ." I think. "The influence of one organism on another. My intense nervous strain transmitted itself to my wife, to Liza, to the dog, that's all . . . This sort of transmission explains presentiments, premonitions . . ."

When I go back to my room a little later to write a prescription for Liza, I no longer think I'll die soon, I simply feel a heaviness, a tedium, in my soul, so that I'm even sorry I didn't die suddenly. I stand motionless for a long time in the middle of the room, trying to think up something to prescribe for Liza, but the moaning through the ceiling quiets down, and I decide not to prescribe anything, and still I stand there . . .

There's a dead silence, such a silence that, as some writer has said, it even rings in your ears. Time moves slowly, the strips of moonlight on the windowsill don't change their position, as if frozen . . . Dawn is still far off.

But now the gate in the fence creaks, someone steals up and, breaking a branch from one of the scrawny trees, cautiously taps on the window with it.

"Nikolai Stepanych!" I hear a whisper. "Nikolai Stepanych!"

I open the window, and think I'm dreaming: by the window, pressing herself to the wall, stands a woman in a black dress, brightly lit by the moon, gazing at me with big eyes. The moon makes her face look pale, stern, and fantastic, as if made of marble. Her chin trembles.

"It's me . . ." she says. "Me . . . Katya!"

In the moonlight all women's eyes look big and black, people look taller and paler, which is probably why I didn't recognize her at first.

"What's the matter?"

"Forgive me," she says. "For some reason I felt unbearably sick at heart . . . I couldn't stand it and came here . . . There was light in your window and . . . and I decided to knock . . . Excuse me . . . Oh, if only you knew how sick at heart I am! What are you doing now?"

"Nothing . . . Insomnia."

"I had a sort of presentiment. Anyhow, it's nonsense."

Her eyebrows rise, her eyes glisten with tears, and her whole face lights up with that familiar, long-absent expression of trustfulness.

"Nikolai Stepanych!" she says imploringly, reaching out to me with both arms. "My dear, I beg you . . . I implore you . . . If you don't disdain my friendship and my respect for you, agree to do what I ask you!"

"What is it?"

"Take my money from me!"

"Well, what will you think up next! Why should I need your money?"

"You'll go somewhere for a cure . . . You need a cure. Will you take it? Yes? Yes, my dearest?"

She peers greedily into my face and repeats:

"You'll take it? Yes?"

"No, my friend, I won't . . ." I say. "Thank you."

She turns her back to me and hangs her head. I probably refused her in such a tone as to prohibit any further discussion of money.

"Go home to bed," I say. "We'll see each other tomorrow."

"So you don't consider me your friend?" she asks glumly.

"I didn't say that. But your money is of no use to me now."

"Forgive me . . ." she says, lowering her voice a whole octave. "I understand you . . . To be indebted to a person like me . . . a retired actress . . . Anyhow, good-bye . . ."

And she leaves so quickly that I don't even have time to say good-bye to her.

VI

I'm in Kharkov.

Since it would be useless, and beyond my strength, to struggle with my present mood, I've decided that the last days of my life will be irreproachable at least in the formal sense; if I'm not right in my attitude towards my family, which I'm perfectly aware of, I will try to do what they want me to do. If it's go to Kharkov, I go to Kharkov. Besides, I've become so indifferent to everything lately that it makes absolutely no difference to me where I go, to Kharkov, to Paris, or to Berdichev.[25]

I arrived here around noon and put up at a hotel not far from the cathedral. On the train I got seasick and suffered from the drafts, so now I'm sitting on the bed, holding my head and waiting for my tic. I ought to go and see the professors I know here, but I haven't the urge or the strength.

The old servant on my floor comes to ask whether I have bed linen. I keep him for about five minutes and ask him several questions about Gnekker, on whose account I've come here. The servant turns out to be a native of Kharkov, knows it like the palm of his hand, but doesn't remember a single house that bears the name of Gnekker. I ask about country estates—same answer.

The clock in the corridor strikes one, then two, then three . . . These last months of my life, as I wait for death, seem to me far longer than my whole life. And never before was I able to be so reconciled to the slowness of time as now. Before, when I waited at the station for a train or sat at an examination, a quarter of an hour seemed like an eternity, but now I can spend the whole night sitting motionless on my bed and think with perfect indifference that tomorrow the night will be just as long and colorless, and the night after . . .

In the corridor it strikes five o'clock, six, seven . . . It's getting dark.

There's a dull pain in my cheek—the tic is beginning. To occupy myself with thoughts, I put myself in my former point of view, when I was not indifferent, and ask: why am I, a famous man, a privy councillor, sitting in this small hotel room, on this bed with its strange gray blanket? Why am I looking at this cheap tin washbasin and listening to the trashy clock clanking in the corridor? Can all this be worthy of my fame and my high station among people? And my response to these questions is a smile. The naïveté with which, in my youth, I exaggerated the importance of renown and the exclusive position celebrities supposedly enjoy, strikes me as ridiculous. I'm well known, my name is spoken with awe, my portrait has been published in *Niva* and *World Illustrated*,[26] I've even read my own biography in a certain German magazine—and what of it? I'm sitting all alone in a strange town, on a strange bed, rubbing my aching cheek with my palm . . . Family squabbles, merciless creditors, rude railway workers, the inconvenience of the passport system,[27] expensive and unwholesome food in the buffets, universal ignorance and rudeness of behavior—all that and many other things it would take too long to enumerate, concern me no less than any tradesman known only in the lane where he lives. How, then, does the exclusiveness of my position manifest itself? Suppose I'm famous a thousand times over, that I'm a hero and the pride of my motherland; all the newspapers publish bulletins about my illness, expressions of sympathy come to me by mail from colleagues, students, the public; but all that will not prevent me from dying in a strange bed, in anguish, in utter solitude . . . No one's to blame for that, of course, but, sinner that I am, I dislike my popular name. It seems to me that it has betrayed me.

Around ten o'clock I fall asleep and, despite my tic, sleep soundly and would go on sleeping for a long time if no one woke me up. Shortly after one o'clock there is a sudden knock at the door.

"Who's there?"

"Telegram!"

"You might have brought it tomorrow," I grumble as I take the telegram from the servant. "Now I won't fall back to sleep."

"Sorry, sir. You had a light burning, I thought you weren't asleep."

I open the telegram and look at the signature first: from my wife. What does she want?

"Yesterday Gnekker and Liza secretly married. Come back."

I read this telegram and am frightened for a moment. What frightens me is not what Gnekker and Liza have done, but the indifference with which I receive the news of their marriage. They say philosophers and wise men are indifferent. Wrong. Indifference is a paralysis of the soul, a premature death.

I lie down in bed again and begin inventing thoughts to occupy myself with. What to think about? It seems everything has already been thought through, and there's nothing now that is capable of stirring my mind.

When dawn comes I'm sitting in bed with my arms around my knees and, since I have nothing to do, am trying to know myself. "Know yourself"[28]—what splendid and useful advice; too bad the ancients never thought of showing how to use this advice.

Formerly, when I would feel a desire to understand someone, or myself, I would take into consideration not actions, in which everything is relative, but wishes. Tell me what you want and I'll tell you who you are.

And now I examine myself: what do I want?

I want our wives, children, friends, and students to love in us not the name, not the brand or label, but the ordinary person. What else? I'd like to have helpers and heirs. What else? I'd like to wake up in a hundred years and have at least a glimpse of what's happened with science. I'd like to live another ten years or so . . . And what more?

Nothing more. I think, I think for a long time, and can't think up anything else. And however much I think, however widely my thought ranges, it's clear to me that my wishes lack some chief thing, some very important thing. In my predilection for science, in my wish to live, in this sitting on a strange bed and trying to know myself, in all the thoughts, feelings, and conceptions I form about everything, something general is lacking that would unite it all into a single whole. Each feeling and thought lives separately in me, and in all my opinions about science, the theater, literature, students, and in all the pictures drawn by my imagination, even the most skillful analyst would be unable to find what is known as a general idea or the god of the living man.

And if there isn't that, there's nothing.

Given such poverty, a serious illness, the fear of death, the influence of circumstances or of people, would be enough to overturn and smash to pieces all that I used to consider my worldview, and in which I saw the meaning and joy of my life. And therefore it's not at all surprising that I should darken the last months of my life with thoughts and feelings worthy of a slave and a barbarian, and that I'm now indifferent and do not notice the dawn. When a man lacks that which is higher and stronger than any external influence, a good cold really is enough to make him lose his balance and begin to see an owl in every bird and hear a dog's howl in every sound. And at that moment all his pessimism or optimism, together with his thoughts great and small, have the significance of mere symptoms and nothing more.

I am defeated. If so, there's no point in continuing to think, no point in talking. I'll sit and silently wait for what comes.

In the morning the servant brings me tea and a copy of the local newspaper. I mechanically read through the announcements on the first page, the editorial, the excerpts from other newspapers and magazines, the news reports . . . In the news I find, among other things, the following item: "Yesterday our famous scientist, the acclaimed professor Nikolai Stepanovich So-and-so, arrived in Kharkov on the express train and is staying at such-and-such hotel."

Evidently, great names are created so as to live by themselves, apart from their bearers. Now my name is peacefully going about Kharkov; in some three months, inscribed in gold letters on a tombstone, it will shine like the sun itself—while I'm already covered with moss . . .

A light tap at the door. Someone wants me.

"Who's there? Come in!"

The door opens and I step back in surprise, hastily closing the skirts of my dressing gown. Katya stands before me.

"Good morning," she says, breathing heavily after climbing the stairs. "You didn't expect me? I . . . I've come here, too."

She sits down and continues, stammering and not looking at me.

"Why don't you wish me good morning? I've come, too . . . today . . . I found out you were in this hotel and looked you up."

"I'm very glad to see you," I say, shrugging my shoulders, "but I'm surprised . . . It's as if you dropped from the sky. Why are you here?"

"Me? I . . . simply up and came."

Silence. Suddenly she gets up impetuously and steps towards me.

"Nikolai Stepanych!" she says, turning pale and clasping her hands to her breast. "Nikolai Stepanych! I can't live like this any longer! I can't! For the love of God, tell me quickly, this very moment: what am I to do? Tell me, what am I to do?"

"But what can I say?" I'm perplexed. "There's nothing."

"Tell me, I implore you!" she goes on, choking and trembling all over. "I swear to you, I can't live like this any longer! It's beyond my strength!"

She drops into a chair and begins to sob. She throws her head back, wrings her hands, stamps her feet; her hat has fallen off her head and dangles from an elastic, her hair is disheveled.

"Help me! Help me!" she implores. "I can't go on!"

She takes a handkerchief from her traveling bag, and along with it pulls out several letters that fall from her knees onto the floor. I pick them up from the floor and on one of them recognize Mikhail Fyodorovich's handwriting, and unintentionally read a bit of one word—"passionat . . ."

"There's nothing I can tell you, Katya," I say.

"Help me!" she sobs, seizing my hand and kissing it. "You're my father, my only friend! You're intelligent, educated, you've lived a long time! You've been a teacher! Tell me: what am I to do?"

"In all conscience, Katya, I don't know . . ."

I'm at a loss, embarrassed, touched by her sobbing, and barely able to keep my feet.

"Let's have breakfast, Katya," I say with a forced smile. "Enough crying!"

And I add at once in a sinking voice:

"I'll soon be no more, Katya . . ."

"Just one word, one word!" she weeps, holding her arms out to me. "What am I to do?"

"You're a strange one, really . . ." I murmur. "I don't understand!

Such a clever girl and suddenly—there you go, bursting into tears! . . ."

Silence ensues. Katya straightens her hair, puts her hat on, then crumples the letters and stuffs them into her bag—and all this silently and unhurriedly. Her face, breast, and gloves are wet with tears, but the expression of her face is already dry, severe . . . I look at her and feel ashamed that I'm happier than she is. I've noticed the absence in me of what my philosopher colleagues call a general idea only shortly before death, in the twilight of my days, but the soul of this poor thing has known and will know no refuge all her life, all her life!

"Let's have breakfast, Katya," I say.

"No, thank you," she replies coldly.

Another minute passes in silence.

"I don't like Kharkov," I say. "Much too gray. A gray sort of city."

"Yes, perhaps so . . . Not pretty . . . I won't stay long . . . Passing through. I'm leaving today."

"Where for?"

"The Crimea . . . I mean, the Caucasus."

"Ah. For long?"

"I don't know."

Katya gets up and, smiling coldly, gives me her hand without looking at me.

I want to ask: "So you won't be at my funeral?" But she doesn't look at me, her hand is cold, like a stranger's. I silently walk with her to the door . . . Now she has left my room and walks down the long corridor without looking back. She knows I'm following her with my eyes and will probably look back from the turn.

No, she didn't look back. The black dress flashed a last time, the footsteps faded away . . . Farewell, my treasure!

NOVEMBER 1889

GUSEV

I

It has grown dark, it will soon be night.

Gusev, a discharged private, sits up on his cot and says in a low voice:

"Can you hear, Pavel Ivanych? A soldier in Suchan told me their ship ran over a big fish as it went and broke a hole in its bottom."

The man of unknown status whom he is addressing and whom everyone in the ship's sick bay calls Pavel Ivanych, says nothing, as if he has not heard.

And again there is silence . . . The wind plays in the rigging, the propeller thuds, the waves splash, the cots creak, but the ear is long accustomed to it all, and it seems as if everything around is asleep and still. It is boring. The other three patients—two soldiers and a sailor—who played cards all day long, are now asleep and muttering to themselves.

It seems the ship is beginning to toss. The cot under Gusev slowly goes up and down, as if sighing—it does it once, twice, a third time . . . Something hits the floor with a clank: a mug must have fallen.

"The wind has snapped its chain . . ." says Gusev, listening.

This time Pavel Ivanych coughs and replies irritably:

"First you've got a ship running over a fish, then the wind snaps its chain . . . Is the wind a beast that it can snap its chain?"

"That's how Christian folk talk."

"And Christian folk are as ignorant as you are . . . What else do they say? You have to keep your head on your shoulders and think. Senseless man."

Pavel Ivanych is subject to seasickness. When the ship tosses, he usually gets angry and the least trifle irritates him. But there is, in Gusev's opinion, absolutely nothing to get angry about. What is so strange or tricky, for instance, even in the fish, or in the wind snapping its chain? Suppose the fish is as big as a mountain, and its back is as hard as a sturgeon's; suppose, too, that at the world's end there are thick stone walls, and the angry winds are chained to the walls . . . If they have not snapped their chains, why are they rushing about like crazy all over the sea and straining like dogs? If they do not get chained up, where do they go when it is still?

Gusev spends a long time thinking about fish as big as mountains and thick, rusty chains, then he gets bored and begins thinking about his homeland, to which he is now returning after serving for five years in the Far East. He pictures an enormous pond covered with snow . . . On one side of the pond, a porcelain factory the color of brick, with a tall smokestack and clouds of black smoke; on the other side, a village . . . Out of a yard, the fifth from the end, drives a sleigh with his brother Alexei in it; behind him sits his boy Vanka in big felt boots and the girl Akulka, also in felt boots. Alexei is tipsy, Vanka is laughing, and Akulka's face cannot be seen—she is all wrapped up.

"Worse luck, he'll get the kids chilled . . ." thinks Gusev. "Lord, send them good sense," he whispers, "to honor their parents and not be cleverer than their mother and father . . ."

"You need new soles there," the sick sailor mutters in a bass voice while he sleeps. "Aye-aye!"

Gusev's thoughts break off, and instead of a pond, a big, eyeless bull's head appears out of nowhere, and the horse and sleigh are no longer driving but are whirling in the black smoke. But all the same he is glad to have seen his family. Joy takes his breath away, gives him gooseflesh all over, quivers in his fingers.

"God has granted me to see them!" he says in his sleep, but at once opens his eyes and feels for water in the darkness.

He drinks and lies down, and again the sleigh is driving, then again the eyeless bull's head, the smoke, the clouds . . . And so it goes till dawn.

II

First a blue circle outlines itself in the darkness—it is a round window; then Gusev gradually begins to distinguish the man on the cot next to his, Pavel Ivanych. This man sleeps in a sitting position, because when he lies down he suffocates. His face is gray, his nose long, sharp, his eyes, owing to his great emaciation, are enormous; his temples are sunken, his little beard is thin, the hair on his head is long . . . Looking into his face, it is hard to tell what he is socially: a gentleman, a merchant, or a peasant? Judging by his expression and his long hair, he seems to be an ascetic, a monastery novice, but when you listen to what he says—it turns out that he may not be a monk. Coughing, stuffiness, and his illness have exhausted him, he breathes heavily and moves his dry lips. Noticing Gusev looking at him, he turns his face to him and says:

"I'm beginning to guess . . . Yes . . . Now I understand it all perfectly."

"What do you understand, Pavel Ivanych?"

"Here's what . . . I kept thinking it was strange that you gravely ill people, instead of staying in a quiet place, wound up on a ship, where the stuffiness, and the heat, and the tossing—everything, in short, threatens you with death, but now it's all clear to me . . . Yes . . . Your doctors put you on a ship to get rid of you. They're tired of bothering with you, with brutes . . . You don't pay them anything, you're a bother to them, and you ruin their statistics for them by dying—which means you're brutes! And it's not hard to get rid of you . . . For that it's necessary, first, to have no conscience or brotherly love, and, second, to deceive the ship's authorities. The first condition doesn't count, in that respect we're all artists, and the second always works if you have the knack. In a crowd of four hundred healthy soldiers and sailors, five sick men don't stand out; so they herded you onto the ship, mixing you in with the healthy ones, counted you up quickly, and in the turmoil didn't notice anything wrong, but when the ship got under way what did they see: paralytics and terminal consumptives lying around on deck . . ."

Gusev does not understand Pavel Ivanych; thinking that he is being reprimanded, he says, to justify himself:

"I lay on the deck because I had no strength. When they unloaded us from the barge onto the ship, I caught a bad chill."

"Outrageous!" Pavel Ivanych goes on. "Above all, they know perfectly well you won't survive this long passage, and yet they put you here! Well, suppose you get as far as the Indian Ocean, but what then? It's terrible to think . . . And this is their gratitude for loyal, blameless service!"

Pavel Ivanych makes angry eyes, winces squeamishly, and gasps out:

"There are some who ought to be thrashed in the newspapers till the feathers fly."

The two sick soldiers and the sailor are awake and already playing cards. The sailor is half lying on a cot, the soldiers are sitting on the floor in the most uncomfortable positions. One soldier has his right arm in a sling and a whole bundle wrapped around his wrist, so he holds his cards under his right armpit or in the crook of his arm and plays with his left hand. The ship is tossing badly. It is impossible to stand up, or have tea, or take medicine.

"You served as an orderly?" Pavel Ivanych asks Gusev.

"Yes, sir, as an orderly."

"My God, my God!" says Pavel Ivanych, shaking his head ruefully. "To tear a man out of his native nest, drag him ten thousand miles away, then drive him to consumption, and . . . and all that for what, you may ask? To make him the orderly of some Captain Kopeikin or Midshipman Dyrka.[1] Mighty logical!"

"The work's not hard, Pavel Ivanych! You get up in the morning, polish his boots, prepare the samovar, tidy his rooms, and then there's nothing to do. The lieutenant draws his plans all day, and you can pray to God if you want, read books if you want, go out if you want. God grant everybody such a life."

"Yes, very good! The lieutenant draws his plans, and you sit in the kitchen all day, longing for your homeland . . . Plans . . . It's a man's life that counts, not plans! Life can't be repeated, it must be cherished."

"That's sure, Pavel Ivanych, a bad man's cherished nowhere, not at home, not in the service, but if you live right, obey orders, then who has any need to offend you? The masters are educated people, they understand . . . In five years I was never once locked up, and I was beaten, if I remember right, no more than once . . ."

"What for?"

"For fighting. I've got a heavy fist, Pavel Ivanych. Four Chinks came into our yard, bringing firewood or something—I don't remember. Well, I was feeling bored, so I roughed them up, gave one a bloody nose, curse him ... The lieutenant saw it through the window, got angry, and cuffed me on the ear."

"You're a foolish, pathetic man ..." whispers Pavel Ivanych. "You don't understand anything."

He is totally exhausted by the tossing and closes his eyes; his head gets thrown back, then falls on his chest. He tries several times to lie down, but nothing comes of it: suffocation prevents him.

"And why did you beat the four Chinks?" he asks after a while.

"Just like that. They came into the yard, and I beat them."

And silence ensues ... The cardplayers play for a couple of hours, with passion and cursing, but the tossing wearies them, too; they abandon the cards and lie down. Again Gusev pictures the big pond, the factory, the village ... Again the sleigh is driving, again Vanka laughs, and foolish Akulka has opened her coat and shows her legs: "Look, good people, my boots aren't like Vanka's, they're new."

"She's going on six and still has no sense!" Gusev says in his sleep. "Instead of sticking your legs up, you'd better bring your soldier uncle some water. I'll give you a treat."

Here Andron, a flintlock on his shoulder, comes carrying a hare he has shot, and after him comes the decrepit Jew Isaichik and offers him a piece of soap in exchange for the hare; here is a black heifer in the front hall, here is Domna, sewing a shirt and weeping about something, and here again is the eyeless bull's head, the black smoke ...

Someone overhead gives a loud shout, several sailors go running; it seems as if something bulky is being dragged across the deck or something has cracked. Again there is running. Has there been an accident? Gusev raises his head, listens, and sees: the two soldiers and the sailor are playing cards again; Pavel Ivanych is sitting and moving his lips. It is stifling, he does not have strength enough to breathe, he wants to drink, but the water is warm, disgusting ... The tossing will not let up.

Suddenly something strange happens to one of the cardplaying soldiers ... He calls hearts diamonds, mixes up his score and drops his cards, then gives a frightened, stupid smile and gazes around at them all.

"Just a minute, brothers ..." he says and lies down on the floor.

They are all perplexed. They call out to him, he does not answer.

"Maybe you're not well, Stepan? Eh?" asks the other soldier with his arm in a sling. "Maybe we should call the priest? Eh?"

"Drink some water, Stepan . . ." says the sailor. "Here, brother, drink."

"Well, why shove the mug in his teeth?" Gusev says crossly. "Can't you see, dunderhead?"

"What?"

"What!" Gusev repeats mockingly. "There's no breath in him! He's dead! That's 'what' for you! Such senseless folk, Lord God! . . ."

III

There is no tossing, and Pavel Ivanych has cheered up. He is no longer angry. The look on his face is boastful, perky, and mocking. As if he wants to say: "Yes, now I'm going to tell you such a joke that you'll split your sides with laughing." The round window is open, and a soft breeze is blowing on Pavel Ivanych. Voices are heard, the splashing of oars in the water . . . Just under the window somebody is whining in a thin, disgusting little voice: it must be a Chinaman singing.

"So we're in harbor," says Pavel Ivanych with a mocking smile. "Another month or so and we'll be in Russia. Yes, my esteemed gentlemen soldiers. I'll get to Odessa, and from there go straight to Kharkov. In Kharkov I have a friend who is a writer. I'll go to him and say: 'Well, brother, abandon for a bit your vile stories about female amours and the beauties of nature, and start exposing these two-legged scum . . . Here are some stories for you . . .' "

He thinks about something for a moment, then says:

"Do you know how I tricked them, Gusev?"

"Who, Pavel Ivanych?"

"Them . . . You see, there's only first and third class on this ship, and the only ones allowed to travel third class are peasants—that is, boors. If you're wearing a suit or look like a gentleman or a bourgeois, from a distance at least, then kindly travel first class. You dish up five hundred roubles, even if it kills you. 'Why have you set up such rules?' I ask. 'Do you hope to raise the prestige of the Russian intelligentsia?' 'Not in the least. We won't let you in there, because a decent man cannot travel third class: it's much too nasty and vile.'

'Really, sir? Thank you for being so concerned for decent people. But in any case, whether it's nasty or not there, I don't have five hundred roubles. I haven't robbed the treasury, haven't exploited the racial minorities, haven't engaged in smuggling or flogged anyone to death, so you decide: do I have the right to be installed in first class and, what's more, to count myself among the Russian intelligentsia?' But you can't get them with logic . . . I had to resort to trickery. I dressed up in a peasant kaftan and big boots, put on a drunken, boorish mug, and went to the ticket agent: 'Gimme a little ticket, Your Honor . . . ' "

"And what estate are you from?" asks the sailor.

"Clerical. My father was an honest priest. He always told the truth in the faces of the great ones of the world, and for that he suffered a lot."

Pavel Ivanych is out of breath and tired of talking, but he goes on all the same:

"Yes, I always tell the truth in people's teeth . . . I'm not afraid of anybody or anything. In that sense there's an enormous difference between me and you. You are ignorant, blind, downtrodden people, you don't see anything, and what you do see you don't understand . . . You're told that the wind can snap its chain, that you are brutes, Pechenegs,[2] and you believe it; you get it in the neck, and kiss the man's hand; some animal in a raccoon coat robs you, then tosses you a fifteen-kopeck tip, and you say: 'Allow me, sir, to kiss your hand.' You're pathetic people, pariahs . . . With me it's different. I live consciously, I see everything, like an eagle or a hawk when it flies over the earth, and I understand everything. I am protest incarnate. When I see tyranny, I protest. When I see a bigot and hypocrite, I protest. When I see a triumphant pig, I protest. And I'm invincible, no Spanish inquisition can silence me. No . . . Cut out my tongue and I'll protest with gestures. Wall me up in a cellar and I'll shout so loud it will be heard a mile away, or I'll starve myself to death, so there'll be another fifty pounds on their black consciences. Kill me and I'll come back as a ghost. My acquaintances all tell me: 'You're a most insufferable man, Pavel Ivanych!' I'm proud of that reputation. I served for three years in the Far East and left a memory behind that will last a hundred years: I quarreled with everybody. My friends write me from Russia: 'Don't come back!' But I will, I'll come back just to spite them . . . Yes . . . That's life, as I understand it. That's what can be called life."

Gusev is not listening, he is looking out the window. A boat, all flooded with blinding, hot sunlight, is rocking on the transparent, soft turquoise water. Naked Chinamen are standing in it, holding up cages of canaries and shouting:

"He sing! He sing!"

Another boat knocks against this boat, a steam-launch passes by. And here is a third boat: in it sits a fat Chinaman, eating rice with chopsticks. The water ripples lazily, white seagulls fly lazily over it.

"Be nice to give that fat one a punch . . ." thinks Gusev, gazing at the fat Chinaman and yawning.

He dozes off, and it seems to him that the whole of nature is dozing. Time runs fast. The day passes imperceptibly, darkness comes imperceptibly . . . The ship is no longer standing still, but going on somewhere.

IV

Two days pass. Pavel Ivanych is not sitting now, but lying down; his eyes are closed, his nose seems to have grown sharper.

"Pavel Ivanych!" Gusev calls to him. "Hey, Pavel Ivanych!"

Pavel Ivanych opens his eyes and moves his lips.

"Are you unwell?"

"Not at all . . ." Pavel Ivanych gasps. "Not at all, on the contrary . . . I'm better . . . You see, I can lie down now . . . It's eased off . . ."

"Well, thank God, Pavel Ivanych."

"When I compare myself with you, I feel sorry for you . . . wretches. My lungs are good, and this is a stomach cough . . . I can endure hell, not just the Red Sea! Besides, I take a critical attitude both towards my sickness and towards medications. But you . . . you're in the dark . . . It's hard for you—very, very hard!"

There is no tossing, it is calm, but on the other hand it is stifling and hot as a steambath; not only talking, but even listening is difficult. Gusev has put his arms around his knees, laid his head on them, and is thinking of his homeland. My God, in such stifling heat what a delight it is to think of snow and cold! You are riding in a sleigh; suddenly the horses get frightened by something and bolt . . . Heedless of roads, ditches, ravines, they race madly through the whole village, across the pond, past the factory, then over the fields . . . "Stop them!" factory workers and passersby shout at the top of their lungs. "Stop them!" But why stop them? Let the sharp, cold wind lash your face and nip at your hands, let the lumps of snow flung up by the horses' hooves fall on your hat, on your neck behind the collar, on your chest, let the runners squeal and the harness and swingletree snap, devil take it all! And what a delight when the sleigh turns over and you go flying headlong into a snowdrift, your face right in the snow, and then you get up all white, icicles on your mustache; no hat, no mittens, your belt undone . . . People laugh, dogs bark . . .

Pavel Ivanych half opens one eye, looks at Gusev with it, and asks softly:

"Gusev, did your commander steal?"

"Who knows, Pavel Ivanych! We don't know, it doesn't get to us."

And then a long time passes in silence. Gusev thinks, mutters, sips water every so often; it is hard for him to speak, hard for him to listen, and he is afraid someone may start talking to him. An hour passes, another, a third; evening comes, then night, but he does not notice it and goes on sitting and thinking about frost.

He seems to hear somebody come into the sick bay, there are voices, but another five minutes pass and everything quiets down.

"The Kingdom of Heaven and eternal rest to him," says the soldier with his arm in a sling. "He was a restless man!"

"What?" asks Gusev. "Who's that?"

"He died. They just took him topside."

"Well, so there," Gusev mutters, yawning. "God rest his soul."

"What do you think, Gusev?" the soldier with the sling asks after some silence. "Will God rest his soul or not?"

"Who do you mean?"

"Pavel Ivanych."

"He will . . . he suffered long. And another thing, he was from the clerical estate, and priests have big families. They'll pray for him."

The soldier with the sling sits down on Gusev's cot and says in a low voice:

"And you, Gusev, you're not long for this world. You won't make it to Russia."

"Was it the doctor or his assistant that told you?" asks Gusev.

"It's not that anyone says it, but you can see . . . You can see at once when a man's going to die soon. You don't eat, you don't drink, you've grown so thin it's frightening to look at you. Consumption, in short. I say it not to alarm you, but in case you may want to take communion and be anointed.³ And if you have any money, you should place it with a senior officer."

"I haven't written home . . ." sighs Gusev. "I'll die and they won't know."

"They'll know," the sick sailor says in a bass voice. "When you die, they'll record it in the ship's log, in Odessa they'll give an extract to the military commander, and he'll send it to the local office or wherever . . ."

Gusev feels eerie after such a conversation and begins to suffer from some sort of yearning. He drinks water—it's not that; he leans to the round window and breathes the hot, humid air—it's not that; he tries thinking about his homeland, about the frost—it's not that . . . In the end it seems to him that if he spends another minute in the sick bay, he will surely suffocate.

"It's bad, brothers . . ." he says. "I'm going topside. Take me topside, for Christ's sake!"

"All right," the soldier with the sling consents. "You won't make it, I'll carry you. Hold on to my neck."

Gusev puts his arm around the soldier's neck, the soldier grasps him with his good arm and carries him topside. Discharged soldiers and sailors are lying asleep on deck; there are so many of them that it is hard to pick your way.

"Stand on your feet," the soldier with the sling says softly. "Follow me slowly, hold on to my shirt . . ."

It is dark. There are no lights on deck, nor on the masts, nor on the surrounding sea. Right at the bow the man on watch stands motionless, like a statue, and it looks as if he, too, is asleep. As if the ship has been left to its own will and is going wherever it likes.

"They'll throw Pavel Ivanych into the water now . . ." says the soldier with the sling. "In a sack and into the water."

"Yes. That's how it's done."

"It's better to lie in the ground at home. At least your mother can come to the grave and cry a little."

"That's a fact."

There is a smell of dung and hay. Oxen are standing along the rail, their heads hanging. One, two, three . . . eight head! And here is a little horse. Gusev reaches out to stroke it, but it tosses its head, bares its teeth, and tries to bite his sleeve.

"Cur-r-rse you . . ." Gusev says angrily.

The two of them, he and the soldier, quietly make their way to the bow, then stand side by side and silently look up, then down. Above them is the deep sky, bright stars, peace and quiet—exactly as at home in the village—but below is darkness and disorder. The high waves roar for no known reason. Each wave, whichever you look at, tries to rise higher than all, and pushes and drives out the last; and noisily sweeping towards it, its white mane gleaming, comes a third just as fierce and hideous.

The sea has no sense or pity. If the ship were smaller and not made of thick iron, the waves would break it up without mercy and devour all the people, saints and sinners alike. The ship, too, has a senseless and cruel expression. This beaked monster pushes on and cuts through millions of waves as it goes; it fears neither darkness, nor wind, nor space, nor solitude, it cares about nothing, and if the ocean had its own people, this monster would also crush them, saints and sinners alike.

"Where are we now?" asks Gusev.

"I don't know. Must be the ocean."

"There's no land to be seen . . ."

"Land, hah! They say it'll be seven days before we see land."

The two soldiers look at the white foam gleaming with phosphorus, and think silently. Gusev is the first to break the silence.

"There's nothing frightening," he says. "It's just eerie, like sitting in a dark forest, but if, say, they lowered a boat now, and the officer told me to go fifty miles out to sea and start fishing—I'd go. Or say a Christian fell into the water now—I'd fall in after him. I wouldn't go saving a German[4] or a Chink, but I'd go in after a Christian."

"But isn't it frightening to die?"

"It is. I'm sorry about our farm. My brother at home, you know, he's not a steady man: he gets drunk, beats his wife for nothing, doesn't honor his parents. Without me it'll all be lost, and my father and the old woman, for all I know, may have to go begging. Anyhow, brother, my legs won't hold me up, and it's stifling here . . . Let's go to bed."

V

Gusev goes back to the sick bay and lies down on his cot. As before he suffers from some vague yearning, and he cannot figure out what he wants. There is a weight on his chest, a throbbing in his head, his mouth is so dry that he can hardly move his tongue. He dozes and mutters and, tormented by nightmares, coughing, and stuffiness, falls fast asleep towards morning. He dreams that they have just taken the bread out of the oven in the barracks, and he gets into the oven and has a steambath, lashing himself with birch branches. He sleeps for two days, and on the third day two sailors come from topside and carry him out of the sick bay.

He is sewn up in canvas and, to weight him down, two iron bars are put in with him. Sewn up in canvas, he comes to resemble a carrot or a black radish, wide at the head, narrow towards the foot . . . Before sunset he is taken out on deck and laid on a plank; one end of the plank rests on the rail, the other on a box placed on a stool. Discharged soldiers and the ship's crew stand around him with their hats off.

"Blessed is our God," the priest begins, "always, now, and ever, and unto ages of ages!"

"Amen!" sing three sailors.

The discharged soldiers and the crew cross themselves and keep looking askance at the waves. It is strange that a man has been sewn up in canvas and will presently be thrown into the waves. Can it really happen to anyone?

The priest sprinkles Gusev with some soil and bows. They sing "Memory Eternal."[5]

The man on watch lifts the end of the plank. Gusev slides off, falls head down, then turns over in the air and—splash! Foam covers him, and for a moment he seems to be wrapped in lace, but the moment passes—and he disappears into the waves.

He goes quickly towards the bottom. Will he get there? The bottom, they say, is three miles down. After some ten or twelve fathoms he begins to go slower and slower, sways rhythmically, as if pondering, and, borne by the current, drifts more quickly sideways than down.

But now he meets on his way a school of little fish, which are known as pilot fish. Seeing a dark body, the fish stop stock-still, and suddenly they all turn around at once and disappear. In less than a minute, swift as arrows, they rush back at Gusev, piercing the water in zigzags around him . . .

After that another dark body appears. It is a shark. Grandly and casually, as if not noticing Gusev, it swims under him, and he comes down on its back, then it turns belly up, basking in the warm, transparent water, and lazily opens its jaws with their twin rows of teeth. The pilot fish are delighted; they have stopped and wait to see what will happen. After playing with the body, the shark casually puts its jaws under it, touches it warily with its teeth, and the canvas rips open the whole length of the body, from head to foot; one of the bars falls out and, frightening the pilot fish, striking the shark on the side, quickly goes to the bottom.

And up above just then, on the side where the sun goes down, clouds are massing; one cloud resembles a triumphal arch, another a lion, a third a pair of scissors . . . A broad green shaft comes from behind the clouds and stretches to the very middle of the sky; shortly afterwards a violet shaft lies next to it, then a golden one, then a pink one . . . The sky turns a soft lilac. Seeing this magnificent, enchanting sky, the ocean frowns at first, but soon itself takes on such tender, joyful, passionate colors as human tongue can hardly name.

DECEMBER 1890

Peasant Women

In the village of Raibuzh, just across the street from the church, stands a two-storied house with a stone foundation and an iron roof. The owner, Filipp Ivanovich Kashin, nicknamed Dyudya, lives on the lower floor with his family, and on the upper floor, which is usually very hot in summer and very cold in winter, he lodges passing officials, merchants, and landowners. Dyudya rents out plots of land, runs a pothouse on the high road, trades in tar, honey, cattle, and sable, and has already saved up some eight thousand, which he has sitting in the bank in town.

His elder son Fyodor works as a senior mechanic in a factory and, as the peasants say of him, has risen so high in the world that nobody can touch him. Fyodor's wife Sofya, a homely and sickly woman, lives in her father-in-law's house, weeps all the time, and goes to the clinic for treatment every Sunday. Dyudya's second son, hunchbacked Alyoshka, lives in his father's house. He was recently married to Varvara, who was taken from a poor family: she is a young woman, beautiful, healthy, and smartly dressed. When officials and merchants stop there, they always ask that the samovar be served and the beds be made by no one but Varvara.

On one June evening, when the sun was setting and the air smelled of hay, warm manure, and fresh milk, a simple cart drove into Dyudya's yard carrying three people: a man of about thirty in a cotton suit, beside him a seven- or eight-year-old boy in a long black frock coat with big bone buttons, and a young fellow in a red shirt as driver.

The fellow unharnessed the horses and went to walk them up and down in the street, and the traveler washed, prayed facing the church, then spread out a rug by the cart and sat down with the boy to have supper; he ate unhurriedly, gravely, and Dyudya, who had seen many travelers in his day, recognized him by his manners as a practical and serious man who knew his own worth.

Dyudya sat on the porch in his waistcoat, without a hat, and waited for the traveler to speak. He was used to travelers telling all sorts of stories in the evening before bed, and he liked it. His old wife Afanasyevna and his daughter-in-law Sofya were milking the cows in the shed; the other daughter-in-law, Varvara, was sitting at an open window upstairs eating sunflower seeds.

"The boy would be your son, then?" Dyudya asked the traveler.

"No, he's adopted, an orphan. I took him in for the saving of my soul."

They fell to talking. The traveler turned out to be a garrulous and eloquent man, and Dyudya learned from the conversation that he was a tradesman from town, a house-owner, that his name was Matvei Savvich, that he was now on his way to look at the orchards he rented from German colonists, and that the boy's name was Kuzka. It was a hot and stuffy evening, and nobody felt like sleeping. When darkness came and pale stars twinkled here and there in the sky, Matvei Savvich began to tell where he got his Kuzka from. Afanasyevna and Sofya stood a little way off and listened. And Kuzka went to the gate.

"This, grandpa, is a detailed story in the extreme," Matvei Savvich began, "and if I was to tell you everything as it was, the night wouldn't be long enough. About ten years ago in our street, just next to my place, in a little house that's now a candle factory and a creamery, there lived an old widow named Marfa Simonovna Kapluntsev, and she had two sons: one worked as a conductor for the railway, and the other, Vasya, the same age as me, lived with his mother. The late old man Kapluntsev kept horses, five pair, and sent carters around town; his widow kept up the business and ordered the carters about no worse than the deceased, so that some days she cleared up to five roubles in profit. And the boy, too, made a bit of money. He bred pedigree pigeons and sold them to fanciers; he used to spend all his time on the roof, throwing a broom up and whistling, and his tumbler pigeons would fly up into the sky, but it wasn't high enough, he wanted them to fly still higher. He caught finches and starlings, made cages . . . A trifling thing, but the trifles would add up to ten roubles a month. Well, sir, after a while the old woman lost the use of her legs and took to her bed. Owing to that fact, the house was left without a mistress, and that's the same as a man without an eye. The old woman stirred herself and decided to get her Vasya married. The matchmaker was sent for, this and that, women's talk, and our Vasya went to look himself up a bride. He picked out the widow Samokhvalikha's Mashenka. Without more ado the couple got blessed and the whole thing was put together in a week. The girl was young, about seventeen, short, scanty, but with a fair and pleasant face, and with all the qualities, like a young lady; and the dowry wasn't bad either—five hundred roubles in cash, a cow, linen . . . And three days after the wedding, as if her heart could sense it, the old woman departed for the heavenly Jerusalem, where there's no sickness or sighing.[1] The young couple paid her their respects and began life together. They lived in splendid fashion for about half a year, then suddenly a new woe. Misfortunes never come singly: Vasya was summoned to the office to draw lots. They took him, the dear heart, as a soldier and didn't even shorten his term. They shaved his head and drove him to the Kingdom of Poland. It was God's will, nothing to be done. He was all right as he took leave of his wife in the yard, but when he gave a last look at the hayloft with his pigeons, he dissolved in floods of tears. It was a pity to see. At first, so as not to be bored, Mashenka took in her mother; the mother stayed till this Kuzka was born, then went to Oboyan to her other daughter, also married, and Mashenka was left alone with the baby. Five carters, all drunken folk, mischievous; horses, wagons, then a fence would collapse, or the soot would catch fire in the chimney—not a woman's business, so she started turning to me, in neighborly fashion, for every trifle. Well, I'd come and take care of it, give her advice . . . You know, there was nothing for it but to go in, have some tea, talk a bit. I was a young man, of a mental sort, liked to talk about various subjects, and she was educated and polite, too. She dressed neatly, went about with a parasol in summer. I'd start on divinity or politics with her, and she'd be flattered and treat me to tea and preserves . . . In short, not to embroider on it, I'll tell you, grandpa, that before a year was out the unclean spirit, the enemy of the human race, got me worked up. I began to notice that if I didn't go to her one day, I'd feel out of sorts, bored. And I kept inventing some reason to go to her. 'It's time you put your winter sashes in,' I'd say, and I'd spend the whole day loitering around her place, putting the sashes in and doing it so as there were two sashes left for the next day. 'I must count up Vasya's pigeons, to make sure none gets lost,' and the like. I kept talking with her over the fence, and in the end, to save going the long way round, I made a little gate in it. There's a lot of evil and all sorts of vileness in this world from the female sex. Not only us sinners but even holy men have been led astray. Mashenka didn't do anything to turn me away from her. Instead of remembering her husband and minding herself, she fell in love with me. I began to notice that she was bored, too, and kept walking near the fence and looking into my yard through the cracks. The brains in my head whirled with fantasy. On Thursday in Holy Week,[2] early, at daybreak, I went to the market, and as I passed her gate, the unclean one was right there. I looked—her gate had a little lattice at the top—and she was already up and standing in the middle of the yard feeding the ducks. I couldn't help myself and called to her. She came up and looked at me through the lattice. Fair little face, tender eyes, still sleepy . . . I liked her very much and began paying her compliments, as if we weren't by the gate but at a birthday party, and she blushed, laughed, and kept looking right into my eyes without blinking. I lost my mind and started explaining my amorous feelings to her . . . She opened the gate and let me in, and from that morning on we began to live as husband and wife."

Hunchbacked Alyoshka came into the yard from outside and, breathless, not looking at anyone, ran into the house; a moment later he came running out with an accordion, the copper money jingling in his pocket, and disappeared through the gate, cracking sunflower seeds as he ran.

"And who's that one?" asked Matvei Savvich.

"Our son, Alexei," Dyudya answered. "Gone carousing, the scoundrel. God wronged him with a hump, so we don't ask too much."

"And he keeps on carousing, carousing with the boys," Afanasyevna sighed. "We married him off before Lent, thinking he'd get better, but he got even worse."

"Useless. Just gave a stranger girl a stroke of good luck for nothing," said Dyudya.

Somewhere behind the church they started singing a magnificent, melancholy song. It was impossible to make out the words, only the voices could be heard: two tenors and a bass. Everyone began to listen, and it became very quiet in the yard . . . Two voices suddenly broke off the song with a peal of laughter, while the third, a tenor, went on singing and struck such a high note that everyone inadvertently looked up, as if the voice in its high pitch had reached to the very sky. Varvara came out of the house and, shielding her eyes with her hand as if from the sun, looked at the church.

"It's the priest's sons and the schoolmaster," she said.

Again the three voices sang together. Matvei Savvich sighed and went on.

"That's how it was, grandpa. About two years later a letter came from Vasya in Warsaw. He wrote that his superiors were sending him home to recuperate. He was sick. By then I'd gotten that silliness out of my head, and a good match had been found for me, and I only didn't know how to loose myself from this little love of mine. Every day I meant to talk with Mashenka, only I didn't know how to approach her so as to avoid any female screaming. The letter untied my hands. Mashenka and I read it, she turned white as snow, and I said: 'Thank God, now you'll be your husband's wife again.' And she to me: 'I won't live with him.' 'But he's your husband, isn't he?' I say. 'It's easy for you . . . I never loved him and married him against my will. My mother told me to.' 'Don't go dodging, foolish woman,' I say, 'tell me: were you married in church or not?' 'I was,' she says, 'but I love you and will live with you till I die. Let people laugh . . . I don't care . . . ' 'You're pious,' I say, 'you read the Scriptures, and what does it say there?' "

"You married a husband, you must live with your husband," said Dyudya.

"Husband and wife are one flesh. 'You and I have sinned,' I say, 'and enough, we should be ashamed and fear God. Let's confess to Vasya,' I say, 'he's a peaceable man, timid—he won't kill us. And it's better,' I say, 'to suffer torment in this world from your lawful husband than gnash your teeth at the Last Judgment.' The woman won't hear any of it, she stands her ground, and that's that. 'I love you,' is all she says! Vasya came on Saturday, on the eve of the

Trinity,[3] early in the morning. I could see everything through the fence: he ran into the house, came out a moment later with Kuzka in his arms, laughing and crying and kissing Kuzka, and looking at the hayloft—he's sorry to leave Kuzka, but wants to see his pigeons. A tender man he was, a sensitive one. The day passed well, quietly and modestly. The bells rang for the evening vigil, and I think: to-morrow's the Trinity, why don't they decorate the gates and fence with greenery?[4] Something's wrong, I think. I went over to them. I see him sitting on the floor in the middle of the room, his eyes wandering like a drunk man's, tears running down his cheeks, his hands shaking; he's taking pretzels, beads, gingerbread, and other treats from his bundle and scattering them around the floor. Kuzka—he was three years old then—is crawling around, chewing gingerbread, and Mashenka is standing by the stove, pale, trembling all over, and murmuring: 'I'm not your wife, I don't want to live with you'—and all sorts of foolishness. I bow down at Vasya's feet and say: 'We're guilty before you, Vassily Maximych, forgive us for Christ's sake!' Then I got up and said this to Mashenka: 'You, Marya Semyonovna,' I say, 'should wash Vassily Maximych's feet now and drink the dirty water. And be his obedient wife, and pray to God for me, that He in His mercy,' I say, 'may forgive me my trespass.' I was as if inspired by an angel in heaven, so I admonished her, and I spoke with such feeling that I was even moved to tears. A couple of days later, Vasya comes to me. 'I forgive you, Matyusha, you and my wife, God be with you,' he says. 'She's a soldier's wife, it's women's business, she's young, it's hard for her to mind herself. She's not the first, and she won't be the last. Only,' he says, 'I ask you to live as if there was nothing between you and never show anything, and I'll try to please her in everything,' he says, 'so she'll come to love me again.' He gave me his hand, had some tea, and left feeling cheerful. Well, I thought, thank God, and I was glad that everything had come out so well. But as soon as Vasya left, Mashenka came. A real punishment! She hangs on my neck, cries and begs: 'For God's sake, don't abandon me, I can't live without you.' "

"What a slut!" sighed Dyudya.

"I shouted at her, stamped my feet, dragged her to the front hall, and hooked the door. 'Go to your husband!' I shouted. 'Don't shame me in front of people, fear God!' And every day it's the same story. One morning I was standing in my yard near the stable, mending a bridle. Suddenly I see her running through the gate into my yard, barefoot, in nothing but her petticoat, and coming straight towards me. She took hold of the bridle, got all smeared with tar, was shaking and weeping . . . 'I can't live with the hateful man, it's beyond me! If you don't love me, you'd better kill me!' I got angry and hit her twice with the bridle, and at the same time Vasya comes running through the gate and shouts in a desperate voice: 'Don't beat her! Don't beat her!' And he ran up himself like a demented man, and swung and started beating her with his fists as hard as he could, then he threw her on the ground and started trampling her with his feet. I tried to protect her, but he took some reins and went at her with the reins. He's beating her and giving little shrieks all the while like a colt: hee, hee, hee!"

"They should take the reins and give it to you the same way . . ." Varvara grumbled, walking off. "You prey on women, curse you all . . ."

"Shut up!" Dyudya shouted at her. "You mare!"

"Hee, hee, hee!" Matvei Savvich went on. "A carter came running from his yard, I called my hired man, and the three of us took Mashenka away from him and led her home under the arms. The shame of it! That same evening I went to visit her. She was lying in bed, all wrapped up in compresses, only her eyes and nose visible, and staring at the ceiling. I say: 'Good evening, Marya Semyonovna!' Silence. And Vasya is sitting in the other room, holding his head and weeping: 'I'm a villain! I've ruined my life! Send me death, O Lord!' I sat by Mashenka for a little half hour and admonished her. Put a fright into her. 'The righteous,' I say, 'will go to Paradise in the other world, and you to the fiery Hyena[5] along with all the harlots . . . Don't oppose your husband, go and bow at his feet.' Not a word from her, not even a blink, as if I'm talking to a post. Next day Vasya took sick with something like cholera, and by evening I heard he was dead. They buried him. Mashenka didn't go to the cemetery, didn't want to show people her shameless face and bruises. And talk soon spread among the townsfolk that Vasya hadn't died a natural death, that Mashenka had done him in. It came to the authorities. They dug Vasya up, cut him open, and found arsenic in his belly. The thing was clear as day; the police came and took Mashenka away, and penniless Kuzka along with her. She was put in prison. The woman had it coming, God punished her . . . Eight months later there was a trial. She sits on the bench, I remember, in a white kerchief and gray smock, so thin, so pale, sharp-eyed, a pity to see. Behind her a soldier with a gun. She wouldn't confess. At the trial some said she poisoned her husband, and some tried to prove that the husband poisoned himself from grief. I was one of the witnesses. When they asked me, I explained it all in good conscience. 'The sin is on her,' I said. 'There's no hiding it, she didn't love her husband, and she was temperamental . . . ' The trial started in the morning, and that night they reached a verdict: to send her to hard labor in Siberia for thirteen years. After the verdict, Mashenka sat in our jail for three months. I used to visit her, and brought her tea and sugar out of human kindness. But when she saw me, she'd start shaking all over, waving her arms and muttering: 'Go away! Go away!' And she'd press Kuzka to her as if she was afraid I'd take him. 'This is what you've come to,' I say. 'Ah, Masha, Masha, you're a lost soul! You didn't listen to me when I taught you reason, so you can weep now. It's your own fault and nobody else's.' I'm admonishing her, and she says: 'Go away! Go away!'—and presses herself and Kuzka to the wall and trembles. When she was sent from here to the provincial capital, I went to see her off at the station and put a rouble into her bundle to save my soul. But she didn't get as far as Siberia . . . In the provincial capital she came down with a fever and died in jail."

"A dog's death for a dog," said Dyudya.

"Kuzka was brought back home . . . I thought a little and took him in. Why not? Though he's a jailbird's spawn, he's still a living soul, a Christian . . . It's a pity. I'll make him my manager, and if I don't have children of my own, I'll make a merchant out of him. Now, whenever I go somewhere, I take him with me—let him get used to it."

All the while Matvei Savvich was telling his story, Kuzka sat on a stone by the gate, his head propped in his hands, looking at the sky. From a distance, in the twilight, he looked like a little stump.

"Kuzka, go to bed!" Matvei Savvich shouted to him.

"Yes, it's time," said Dyudya, getting up. He yawned loudly and added: "They've just got to live by their own minds, not listening to anybody, and so they get what's coming to them."

The moon was already sailing in the sky above the yard; it raced quickly in one direction, while the clouds below it raced in the other; the clouds went on their way, but the moon could still be seen above the yard. Matvei Savvich prayed facing the church and, wishing everyone good night, lay down on the ground by the cart. Kuzka also said a prayer, lay down in the cart, and covered himself with his frock coat. To be more comfortable, he made a depression in the straw and curled up so that his elbows touched his knees. From the yard Dyudya could be seen lighting a candle in his downstairs room, putting his spectacles on, and standing in the corner with a book. He spent a long time reading and bowing.

The travelers fell asleep. Afanasyevna and Sofya went over to the cart and began looking at Kuzka.

"The little orphan's asleep," the old woman said. "So thin, so skinny, nothing but bones. He's got no mother, there's nobody to feed him properly."

"My Grishutka must be a couple of years older," said Sofya. "He lives at the factory, like a prisoner, without a mother. The master probably beats him. As I looked at this little lad today and remembered my Grishutka, my heart just bled."

A minute passed in silence.

"He surely doesn't remember his mother," said the old woman.

"How could he!"

Big tears poured from Sofya's eyes.

"All curled up . . ." she said, sobbing and laughing with tenderness and pity. "My poor orphan."

Kuzka gave a start and opened his eyes. He saw before him an ugly, wrinkled, tear-stained face, beside it another face, an old woman's, toothless, with a sharp chin and hooked nose, and above them the fathomless sky with racing clouds and the moon, and he cried out in terror. Sofya also cried out; an echo answered both of them, and anxiety passed through the stuffy air; the watchman rapped at the neighbor's, a dog barked. Matvei Savvich murmured something in his sleep and rolled over on his other side.

Late in the evening, when Dyudya and the old woman and the neighbor's watchman were already asleep, Sofya went out the gate and sat on a bench. She needed air, and her head ached from weeping. The street was wide and long; about two miles to the right, the same to the left, and no end to be seen. The moon had left the yard and stood behind the church. One side of the street was flooded with moonlight, and the other was black with shadow; the long shadows of poplars and birdhouses stretched across the whole street, and the shadow of the church, black and frightening, lay broadly, having swallowed up Dyudya's gate and half the house.

The place was deserted and quiet. From time to time, barely audible music came from the end of the street; it must have been Alyoshka playing his accordion.

Someone was walking in the shadow by the church fence, and it was impossible to make out whether it was a man, or a cow, or perhaps no one at all, but only a big bird rustling in the trees. But then a figure emerged from the shadow, stopped and said something in a man's voice, then vanished into the lane by the church. A while later another figure appeared about five yards from the gate; it walked from the church straight towards the gate and, seeing Sofya on the bench, stopped.

"Varvara, is that you?" asked Sofya.

"And what if it is?"

It was Varvara. She stood for a moment, then came up to the bench and sat down.

"Where have you been?" asked Sofya.

Varvara did not answer.

"Watch out that you don't come to grief, girl, with your wanderings," said Sofya. "Did you hear how Mashenka got it with feet and reins? You may get yourself the same thing."

"Who cares."

Varvara laughed into her kerchief and said in a whisper:

"I've just been with the priest's son."

"You're babbling."

"By God."

"It's a sin!" Sofya whispered.

"Who cares . . . What's there to be sorry about? If it's a sin, it's a sin, but I'd rather be struck down by lightning than live such a life. I'm young, healthy, and my husband's hunchbacked, hateful, harsh, worse than that cursed Dyudya. Before I got married, I never had enough to eat, I went barefoot, so I left that wicked lot, got tempted by Alyoshka's riches, and got snared like a fish in a net, and it would be easier for me to sleep with a viper than with that mangy Alyoshka. And your life? I don't even want to look at it. Your Fyodor drove you away from the factory back to his father and found himself another woman; they took your boy from you and put him into bondage. You work like a horse and never hear a kind word. It's better to pine away unmarried all your life, better to take fifty kopecks from the priest's son, to beg for alms, better to go head first down a well . . ."

"It's a sin," Sofya whispered again.

"Who cares."

Somewhere behind the church the same three voices—two tenors and a bass—started up a melancholy song again. And again it was impossible to make out the words.

"Night owls . . ." laughed Varvara.

And she began to tell in a whisper how she spends nights out with the priest's son, and what he says to her, and what sorts of friends he has, and how she had spent time with traveling officials and merchants. The melancholy song called up a free life, Sofya began to laugh, she felt it was sinful, and scary, and sweet to listen, and she was envious and sorry that she had not sinned herself when she was young and beautiful . . .

In the old cemetery church it struck midnight.

"Time for bed," said Sofya, getting up, "or else Dyudya will catch us out."

The two women slowly went into the yard.

"I left and didn't hear what he told afterwards about Mashenka," said Varvara, making up a bed under the window.

"She died in jail, he says. Poisoned her husband."

Varvara lay down beside Sofya, thought a little, and said softly:

"I could do in my Alyoshka and not regret it."

"You're babbling, God help you."

As Sofya was falling asleep, Varvara pressed herself to her and whispered in her ear:

"Let's do in Dyudya and Alyoshka!"

Sofya gave a start but said nothing, then opened her eyes and gazed at the sky for a long time without blinking.

"People would find out," she said.

"No, they wouldn't. Dyudya's old already, it's time he died, and they'll say Alyoshka died of drink."

"It's scary . . . God would kill us."

"Who cares . . ."

The two women lay awake and thought silently.

"It's cold," said Sofya, beginning to tremble all over. "Must be nearly morning . . . Are you asleep?"

"No . . . Don't listen to me, dear heart," Varvara whispered. "I'm bitter against the cursed lot of them, and don't know what I'm saying myself. Sleep, dawn's already coming . . . Sleep . . ."

They both fell silent, calmed down, and soon went to sleep.

The old woman was the first to wake up. She roused Sofya, and they went to the shed to milk the cows. Hunchbacked Alyoshka came, thoroughly drunk, without his accordion; his chest and knees were covered with dust and straw—he must have fallen down on his way. Staggering, he went to the shed and, without undressing, dropped into a sledge and at once began to snore. When the rising sun flamed brightly on the crosses of the church and then on the windows, and the shadows of the trees and the well-sweep stretched across the yard over the dewy grass, Matvei Savvich jumped up and started bustling about.

"Kuzka, get up!" he cried. "It's time to harness the cart! Look lively!"

The morning turmoil began. A young Jewess in a brown dress with ruffles led a horse into the yard for watering. The well-sweep creaked pitifully, the bucket banged . . . Kuzka, sleepy, sluggish, covered with dew, sat in the cart, lazily putting on his frock coat and listening to the splashing of water from the bucket in the well, and he shuddered from the cold.

"Auntie," Matvei Savvich shouted to Sofya, "nudge my lad, so he'll go and harness up!"

And just then Dyudya shouted out the window:

"Sofya, take a kopeck from the Jewess for the watering! No keeping them away, mangy Yids."

In the street sheep were running up and down, bleating; women shouted at the shepherd, and he played his pipe, cracked his whip, or answered them in a heavy, hoarse bass. Three sheep ran into the yard and, unable to find the gate, poked about at the fence. The noise awakened Varvara, she gathered up her bedding and went to the house.

"You might at least drive the sheep out!" the old woman shouted at her. "A fine lady!"

"What else! I should start working for you Herods!" Varvara growled, going into the house.

They greased the cart and harnessed the horses. Dyudya came out of the house, an abacus in his hands, sat down on the porch, and began counting up how much the traveler owed for the night, the oats, and the watering.

"You're putting in a lot for oats, grandpa," said Matvei Savvich.

"If it's too much, don't take any, merchant. Nobody's forcing you."

When the travelers went to get into the cart and go, they were detained for a minute by one circumstance. Kuzka's hat had disappeared.

"Where'd you put it, little swine?" Matvei Savvich shouted angrily. "Where is it?"

Kuzka's face twisted in terror, he rushed around the cart and, not finding it there, ran to the gate, then to the shed. The old woman and Sofya helped him to look.

"I'll tear your ears off!" shouted Matvei Savvich. "You rascal, you!"

The hat was found at the bottom of the cart. Kuzka brushed it off with his sleeve, put it on, and timidly, still with a look of terror on his face, as if afraid of being hit from behind, climbed into the cart. Matvei Savvich crossed himself, the young fellow jerked the reins, the cart started moving and rolled out of the yard.

JUNE 1891

The Fidget

I

All of Olga Ivanovna's friends and good acquaintances were at her wedding.

"Look at him: there's something in him, isn't there?" she said to her friends, nodding towards her husband, as if she wished to explain why she had married this simple, very ordinary and in no way remarkable man.

Her husband, Osip Stepanych Dymov, was a doctor and held the rank of titular councillor.[1] He worked in two hospitals: as an intern in one, and as a prosector in the other. Every day from nine o'clock till noon he received patients and was busy with his ward, and in the afternoon he took a horse-tram to the other hospital, where he dissected dead patients. His private practice was negligible, some five hundred roubles a year. That was all. What more could be said of him? And yet Olga Ivanovna and her friends and good acquaintances were not exactly ordinary people. Each of them was remarkable for something and of some renown, already had a name and was considered a celebrity or, if not yet a celebrity, held out the brightest hopes. An actor in the theater, a big, long-recognized talent, a graceful, intelligent, and humble man and an excellent reader, who taught Olga Ivanovna recitation; an opera singer, a fat, good-natured man, who sighed as he assured Olga Ivanovna that she was ruining herself: that if she stopped being lazy and took herself in hand, she would become an excellent singer; then several artists, chief among them the genre, animal, and landscape painter Ryabovsky, a very handsome young man of about twenty-five, who was successful at exhibitions and whose last picture had sold for five hundred roubles; he corrected Olga Ivanovna's studies and said that something might come of her; then a cellist, whose instrument wept and who confessed sincerely that, of all the women he knew, Olga Ivanovna alone was able to accompany him; then a writer, young but already known, who wrote novellas, plays, and stories. Who else? Well, there was also Vassily Vassilyich, squire, landowner, dilettante illustrator and vignette painter, who had a strong feeling for the old Russian style, heroic song and epic; he literally performed miracles on paper, porcelain, and smoked glass. Amidst this artistic, free, and fate-pampered company, delicate and modest, true, but who remembered the existence of all these doctors only when they were sick, and for whom the name Dymov sounded as nondescript as Sidorov or Tarasov—amidst this company Dymov seemed foreign, superfluous, and small, though he was a tall and broad-shouldered man. It seemed as if he were wearing someone else's tailcoat and had a salesman's beard. However, if he had been a writer or an artist, they would have said his little beard made him look like Émile Zola.

The actor told Olga Ivanovna that in her wedding dress, and with her flaxen hair, she very much resembled a slender cherry tree in spring, when it is covered all over with tender white blossoms.

"No, listen!" Olga Ivanovna said to him, seizing his hand. "How could this suddenly happen? Listen, listen . . . I must tell you that my father worked in the same hospital as Dymov. When my poor father fell ill, Dymov spent whole days and nights watching at his bedside. Such self-sacrifice! Listen, Ryabovsky . . . And you, writer, you listen, too, it's very interesting. Come closer. So much self-sacrifice and genuine sympathy! I also stayed up nights, sitting by my father, and suddenly—hello! the fine fellow's conquered! My Dymov is smitten and head over heels in love. Really, fate is sometimes so whimsical. Well, after my father's death he called on me occasionally, or I'd meet him in the street, and one fine evening suddenly—bang!—he proposed . . . like a ton of snow on my head . . . I cried all night and fell infernally in love myself. And so, as you see, I've become a wife. There's something strong, brawny, bear-like in him, isn't there? His face is turned three-quarters to us now, and poorly lit, but when he turns this way, look at his forehead. Ryabovsky, what do you say of that forehead? Dymov, we're talking about you!" she called out to her husband. "Come here. Give your honest hand to Ryabovsky . . . That's it. Be friends."

Dymov, with a naïve and good-natured smile, gave Ryabovsky his hand and said:

"Delighted. I finished my studies with a man named Ryabovsky. Is he a relation of yours?"

II

Olga Ivanovna was twenty-two years old, Dymov thirty-one. They started life excellently after the wedding. Olga Ivanovna hung all the walls of the drawing room with her own and other people's studies, framed and unframed, and around the grand piano and furniture she arranged a beautiful clutter of Chinese parasols, easels, colorful rags, daggers, little busts, photographs . . . In the dining room she covered the walls with folk prints, hung up bast shoes and sickles, put a scythe and rake in the corner, and thus achieved a dining room in Russian style. In the bedroom, she draped the ceiling and walls with dark cloth to make it look like a cave, hung a Venetian lantern over the beds, and placed a figure with a halberd by the door. And everybody found that the young spouses had themselves a very sweet little corner.

Every day, getting out of bed at around eleven, Olga Ivanovna would play the piano or, if it was sunny, would paint something in oils. After that, between noon and one, she would go to her dressmaker. Since she and Dymov had very little money, barely enough, she and her dressmaker had to be very clever if she was to appear frequently in new dresses and amaze people with her outfits. Often an old, re-dyed dress, some worthless scraps of tulle, lace, plush, and silk, would be turned into a wonder, something enchanting, not a dress but a dream. From the dressmaker's, Olga Ivanovna usually went to see some actress she knew, to find out the theater news and incidentally try to get a ticket for the opening night of a new play or for a benefit performance. From the actress, she would have to go to an artist's studio or a picture exhibition, then to see some celebrity—to make an invitation or return a visit, or for a simple chat. And everywhere she was met gaily and amiably, and was assured that she was nice, sweet, rare . . . Those whom she called famous and great received her like one of themselves, like an equal, and in one voice prophesied that with her talents, taste, and intelligence, she would have great success if she did not disperse herself. She sang, played the piano, painted, sculpted, took part in amateur theatricals, and all of it not just anyhow, but with talent; whether it was making lanterns for a fête, or putting on a disguise, or tying someone's tie—everything she did came out extraordinarily artistic, graceful, and pretty. But nothing showed her talent so strikingly as her ability to become quickly acquainted and on close terms with celebrities. The moment anyone became the least bit famous and was talked about, she made his acquaintance, became his friend that same day, and invited him to her house. Every new acquaintance was a veritable feast for her. She idolized celebrities, took pride in them, and saw them every night in her dreams. She thirsted for them and was never able to quench her thirst. Old ones would go and be forgotten, new ones would come to replace them, but she would get used to them, too, or become disappointed in them, and begin searching greedily for more and more new great people, find them, and search again. Why?

Between four and five she had dinner at home with her husband. His simplicity, common sense, and good nature moved her to tenderness and delight. She kept jumping up, impulsively embracing his head, and showering it with kisses.

"You're an intelligent and noble person, Dymov," she said, "but you have one very important shortcoming. You're not interested in art. You reject music and painting."

"I don't understand them," he said meekly. "I've studied natural science and medicine all my life, and haven't had time to get interested in the arts."

"But this is terrible, Dymov!"

"Why? Your acquaintances don't know natural science and medicine, and yet you don't reproach them for it. To each his own. I don't understand landscapes and operas, but I think like this: if some intelligent people devote their entire lives to them, and other intelligent people pay enormous amounts of money for them, then it means they're needed. I don't understand them, but not to understand doesn't mean to reject."

"Allow me to shake your honest hand!"

After dinner Olga Ivanovna would visit some acquaintances,

then go to the theater or a concert, and return home past midnight. And so it went every day.

On Wednesdays she had soirées. At these soirées the hostess and her guests did not play cards or dance, but entertained themselves with various arts. The actor recited, the singer sang, the artists did drawings in albums, of which Olga Ivanovna had many, the cellist played, and the hostess herself also drew, sculpted, sang, and accompanied. Between the recitations, music, and singing, they talked and argued about literature, the theater, and painting. There were no ladies, because Olga Ivanovna considered all ladies, except for actresses and her dressmaker, to be boring and banal. Not a single soirée went by without the hostess, giving a start at each ring of the bell, saying with a triumphant expression: "It's him!"—meaning by the word "him" some new celebrity she had invited. Dymov would not be in the drawing room, and no one remembered his existence. But at exactly half-past eleven, the door to the dining room would open, and Dymov would appear with his meek, good-natured smile and say, rubbing his hands:

"A bite to eat, gentlemen."

They would all go to the dining room, and each time would see the same things on the table: a plate of oysters, a ham or veal roast, sardines, cheese, caviar, mushrooms, vodka, and two carafes of wine.

"My sweet maître d'hôtel!" Olga Ivanovna would say, clasping her hands in delight. "You're simply charming! Gentlemen, look at his forehead! Dymov, turn in profile. Look, gentlemen: the face of a Bengal tiger, and an expression as kind and sweet as a deer's. Oh, my sweet!"

The guests ate and, looking at Dymov, thought: "A nice fellow, actually," but they soon forgot him and went on talking about the theater, music, and painting.

The young spouses were happy and their life went swimmingly. However, the third week of their honeymoon passed not altogether happily, even sadly. Dymov caught erysipelas in the hospital, spent six days in bed, and had to shave his beautiful black hair. Olga Ivanovna sat with him and wept bitterly, but when he felt better, she put a white scarf around his cropped head and began painting him as a Bedouin. And they both felt merry. About three days after he recovered and began going to the hospital again, he suffered another mishap.

"I have no luck, mama!" he said over dinner. "Today I had to do four dissections, and I cut myself on two fingers at once. And I only noticed it when I got home."

Olga Ivanovna became alarmed. He smiled and said it was nothing and that he often cut himself while doing dissections.

"I get carried away, mama, and don't pay attention."

Olga Ivanovna worriedly anticipated blood poisoning and prayed to God at night, but nothing bad happened. And again their peaceful, happy life flowed on without sorrows or alarms. The present was beautiful, and it would be replaced by the approaching spring, already smiling from afar and promising a thousand joys. There would be no end of happiness! In April, May, and June a dacha[2] far from town, walks, sketching, fishing, nightingales, and then, from July right till fall, an artists' trip to the Volga, and Olga Ivanovna would take part in that trip, too, as a permanent member of the *société*. She had already had two simple linen traveling outfits made, and had bought some paints, brushes, canvases, and a new palette to take along. Ryabovsky came to her almost every day, to see what progress she had made in painting. When she showed him her paintings, he thrust his hands deep into his pockets, pressed his lips tightly, sniffed, and said:

"Well, now . . . This cloud you've made too loud—it's not evening light. The foreground is somehow chewed up, and there's something off here, you see . . . And your little cottage is choking on something and squealing pitifully . . . this corner could be a bit darker. But in general it's not bad at all . . . My compliments."

And the more incomprehensibly he spoke, the more easily Olga Ivanovna understood him.

III

On the day after Pentecost, Dymov bought some snacks and sweets after dinner and went to his wife at the dacha. He had not seen her for two weeks and missed her sorely. Sitting on the train and then looking for his dacha in the big woods, he felt hungry and tired all the while, and dreamed of having a leisurely supper with his wife and then dropping off to sleep. And it cheered him to look at his bundle, with its wrapped-up caviar, cheese, and white salmon.

By the time he found his dacha and recognized it, the sun was already setting. The old maid said that the lady was not at home but would probably be back soon. The dacha was very unattractive to look at, with low ceilings pasted over with writing paper and cracks between the uneven floorboards, and it consisted of only three rooms. In one room stood a bed, in the second there were canvases, brushes, greasy paper, and men's jackets and hats lying about on the chairs and windowsills, and in the third Dymov found three men he did not know. Two were dark-haired with little beards, and the third was clean-shaven and fat, apparently an actor. A samovar was boiling on the table.

"What can I do for you?" the actor asked in a bass voice, giving Dymov an unsociable look. "Is it Olga Ivanovna you want? Wait, she'll come soon."

Dymov sat down and began to wait. One of the dark-haired men, glancing at him sleepily and sluggishly, poured himself some tea and asked:

"Want some tea?"

Dymov wanted to drink and to eat, but he declined the tea so as not to spoil his appetite. Soon footsteps and familiar laughter were heard; the door banged, and Olga Ivanovna, in a broad-brimmed hat and carrying a paint box, ran into the room, followed by the gay, red-cheeked Ryabovsky with a big parasol and a folding chair.

"Dymov!" Olga Ivanovna cried out and blushed with joy. "Dymov!" she repeated, putting her head and both hands on his chest. "It's you! Why haven't you come for so long? Why? Why?"

"How could I, mama? I'm always busy, and whenever I'm free, it always turns out that the train schedule doesn't suit."

"But I'm so glad to see you! I dreamed of you all night, all night, and I was afraid you were sick. Ah, if only you knew how sweet you are, how timely you've come! You'll be my savior. You alone can save me! Tomorrow they're having the most original wedding here," she went on, laughing and knotting her husband's tie. "A young telegraphist from the train station, a certain Chikeldeev, is getting married. A handsome young man, well, and not at all stupid, and with something, you know, strong and bear-like in his face . . . He'd be a good model for a young Viking. All of us summer people sympathize with him and have given our word of honor to come to his wedding . . . He's a poor man, lonely, timid, and of course it would be a sin to deny him our sympathy. Imagine, after the liturgy there'll be the wedding, then we all go on foot from the church to the bride's place . . . you understand, the woods, the birds singing, patches of sun on the grass, and all of us like colored spots against the bright green background—most original, in the style of the French Impressionists. But, Dymov, what am I to wear to church?" Olga Ivanovna said, and made a tearful face. "I've got nothing here, literally nothing! No dress, no flowers, no gloves . . . You must save me. Since you've come, it means fate itself is telling you to save me. Take the keys, my dear, go home and get my pink dress from the wardrobe. You remember, it's hanging in front . . . Then, in the closet, on the floor to the right, you'll see two boxes. Open the top one and you'll see tulle, tulle, tulle, and all sorts of scraps, and flowers under them. Take all the flowers out carefully, darling, try not to crush them, I'll choose what I want later . . . And buy some gloves."

"All right," said Dymov. "I'll go tomorrow and send it all."

"Why tomorrow?" Olga Ivanovna asked and looked at him in surprise. "You won't have time tomorrow. The first train leaves at nine tomorrow, and the wedding's at eleven. No, dearest, it has to be today, absolutely today! If you can't come back tomorrow, send it with a courier. Well, go . . . The train must be coming right now. Don't be late, darling."

"All right."

"Ah, how sorry I am to let you go," said Olga Ivanovna, tears brimming her eyes. "And why was I such a fool as to give the telegraphist my word?"

Dymov quickly drank a cup of tea, took a pretzel, and, smiling meekly, went to the station. And the caviar, cheese, and white salmon were eaten by the two dark-haired gentlemen and the fat actor.

IV

On a quiet, moonlit July night Olga Ivanovna stood on the deck of a Volga steamer and gazed now at the water, now at the beautiful banks. Beside her stood Ryabovsky, who was saying to her that the black shadows on the water were not shadows but a dream, that at the sight of this magical water with its fantastic gleam, at the sight of the fathomless sky and melancholy, pensive banks that speak of the vanity of our life and the existence of something lofty, eternal, blissful, it would be good to fall into oblivion, to die, to become a

memory. The past is banal and uninteresting, the future insignificant, and this wondrous night, unique in their life, will soon end,
will merge with eternity—why then live?

And Olga Ivanovna listened now to Ryabovsky's voice, now to
the silence of the night, and thought she was immortal and would
never die. The turquoise color of the water, such as she had never
seen before, the sky, the banks, the black shadows, and the unac-
countable joy that filled her heart, told her that she would become
a great artist, and somewhere beyond the distance, beyond the
moonlit night, in infinite space, success awaited her, fame, people's
love . . . When she looked into the distance for a long time without
blinking, she imagined crowds of people, lights, the festive sounds
of music, shouts of delight, she herself in a white dress, and flowers
pouring on her from all sides. She also thought that beside her,
leaning his elbows on the bulwark, stood a truly great man, a genius, one of God's chosen . . . Everything he had created so far was
beautiful, new, and extraordinary, and what he would create in
time, when his rare talent was strengthened by maturity, would be
astounding, immeasurably lofty, and this could be seen by his face,
by his manner of expressing himself, and by his attitude towards
nature. Of the shadows, the evening hues, the shining of the moon,
he spoke somehow specially, in his own language, so that one inadvertently felt the charm of his power over nature. He himself was
very handsome, original, and his life, independent, free, foreign to
everything mundane, was like the life of a bird.

"It's getting cool," said Olga Ivanovna, shivering.

Ryabovsky wrapped his cloak around her and said sorrowfully:

"I feel I am in your power. I am a slave. What makes you so be-
witching today?"

He gazed at her all the while, not tearing himself away, and his
eyes were terrible, and she was afraid to look at him.

"I love you madly . . ." he whispered, breathing on her cheek.
"Say one word to me, and I'll cease living, I'll abandon art . . ." he
murmured in great agitation. "Love me, love . . ."

"Don't speak like that," said Olga Ivanovna, closing her eyes.
"It's terrible. And Dymov?"

"What of Dymov? Why Dymov? What do I care about Dymov?
The Volga, the moon, beauty, my love, my ecstasy, and there isn't
any Dymov . . . Ah, I know nothing . . . I need no past, give me
one instant . . . one moment."

Olga Ivanovna's heart was pounding. She wanted to think of her husband, but the whole of her past, with the wedding, with Dymov, with her soirées, seemed small to her, worthless, faded, unnecessary, and far, far away . . . What Dymov, indeed? Why Dymov? What did she care about Dymov? Did he really exist in nature, or was he merely a dream?

"For him, a simple and ordinary man, the happiness he has already received is enough," she thought, covering her face with her hands. "Let them condemn me *there,* let them curse me, and I'll just up and ruin myself, ruin myself to spite them all . . . One must experience everything in life. Oh, God, how scary and how good!"

"Well, what? What?" the artist murmured, embracing her and greedily kissing her hands, with which she tried weakly to push him away. "You love me? Yes? Yes? Oh, what a night! A wondrous night!"

"Yes, what a night!" she whispered, looking into his eyes, glistening with tears. Then she glanced around quickly, embraced him, and kissed him hard on the lips.

"Approaching Kineshma!" someone said on the other side of the deck.

Heavy footsteps were heard. It was a man from the buffet walking by.

"Listen," Olga Ivanovna said to him, laughing and crying from happiness, "bring us some wine."

The artist, pale with excitement, sat down on a bench, looked at Olga Ivanovna with adoring, grateful eyes, then closed his eyes and said, smiling languidly:

"I'm tired."

And he leaned his head against the bulwark.

V

The second day of September was warm and still, but gray. Early in the morning a light mist wandered over the Volga, and after nine a drizzling rain set in. And there was no hope that the sky would clear. Over tea Ryabovsky was saying to Olga Ivanovna that painting was the most ungrateful and boring of arts, that he was not an artist, and that only fools thought he had talent, and suddenly, out of the blue, he seized a knife and scratched the best of his studies. After tea he sat gloomily by the window and looked at the Volga. And the Volga was without a gleam, dull, lusterless, and cold-looking. Everything, everything recalled the approach of melancholy, dismal autumn. And it seemed as if nature now stripped the Volga of the luxurious green carpets on its banks, the diamond glints of the sun, the transparent blue distance, and all that was smart and showy, and packed it away in trunks till next spring, and the crows flew about the Volga, teasing her: "Bare! Bare!" Ryabovsky listened to their cawing and thought that he was already played out and had lost his talent, and that everything in this world was conventional, relative, and stupid, and that he should not have tied himself to this woman . . . In short, he was in a foul and splenetic mood.

Olga Ivanovna sat on the bed behind the partition and, fingering her beautiful flaxen hair, imagined herself now in the drawing room, now in the bedroom, now in her husband's study; her imagination carried her to the theater, to the dressmaker's, and to her famous friends. What were they doing now? Did they remember her? The season had already begun, and it was time to be thinking of soirées. And Dymov? Dear Dymov! How meekly and with what childlike plaintiveness he asked her in his letters to come home soon! Every month he sent her seventy-five roubles, and when she wrote to him that she owed the artists a hundred roubles, he sent her the hundred as well. What a kind, generous man! Olga Ivanovna was tired of traveling, she was bored and wanted to get away quickly from these peasants, from the smell of river dampness, and to shake off the feeling of physical uncleanness she had experienced all the while she had been living in peasant cottages and migrating from village to village. If Ryabovsky had not given the artists his word of honor that he would stay with them till the twentieth of September, they might have left that same day. And how good it would be!

"My God," moaned Ryabovsky, "but when will there finally be some sun? I can't go on working on a sunny landscape without the sun! . . ."

"But you have a study with a cloudy sky," said Olga Ivanovna, appearing from behind the partition. "Remember, a woods to the right and a herd of cows or some geese to the left. You could finish it now."

"Eh!" the artist winced. "Finish it! Maybe you think I myself am so stupid that I don't know what I should do!"

"How you've changed towards me!" Olga Ivanovna sighed.

"Well, splendid."

Olga Ivanovna's face trembled, she went over to the stove and began to cry.

"Yes, we only lacked tears. Stop it! I have a thousand reasons to cry, but I don't cry."

"A thousand reasons!" Olga Ivanovna sobbed. "The main reason is that I'm already a burden to you. Yes!" she said, and burst into tears. "If the truth were told, you're ashamed of our love. You try to keep the artists from noticing it, though it's impossible to hide it and they've all known for a long time."

"Olga, I ask one thing of you," the artist said pleadingly, placing his hand on his heart, "just one thing: don't torture me! I don't need anything else from you!"

"But swear that you still love me!"

"This is torture!" the artist said through his teeth and jumped up. "It will end with me throwing myself into the Volga or losing my mind! Let me be!"

"Then kill me, kill me!" cried Olga Ivanovna. "Kill me!"

She burst into tears again and went behind the partition. Rain began to patter on the thatched roof of the cottage. Ryabovsky clutched his head and paced from corner to corner, then, with a resolute face, as if wishing to prove something to someone, he put on his cap, shouldered his gun, and walked out of the cottage.

After he left, Olga Ivanovna lay on the bed for a long time and cried. First she thought it would be good to poison herself, so that Ryabovsky would find her dead when he came back, then she was carried in her thoughts to the drawing room, to her husband's study, and she imagined herself sitting motionless beside Dymov, enjoying the physical peace and cleanness, and sitting in the theater in the evening listening to Mazzini.[3] And the longing for civilization, for city noise and famous people, wrung her heart. A peasant woman came into the cottage and began unhurriedly to fire the stove in order to cook supper. There was a smell of burning, and the air turned blue with smoke. Artists in dirty high boots and with rain-wet faces came in, looked at their studies and said, to comfort themselves, that the Volga had its charm even in bad weather. And the cheap clock on the wall said: tick, tick, tick . . . Chilled flies crowded into the front corner by the icons and buzzed there, and cockroaches could be heard stirring in the fat portfolios under the benches . . .

Ryabovsky returned home as the sun was going down. He threw his cap on the table and, pale, worn out, in dirty boots, sank onto a bench and closed his eyes.

"I'm tired . . ." he said and moved his eyebrows in an effort to raise his eyelids.

To show her tenderness and let him know that she was not angry, Olga Ivanovna went over to him, kissed him silently, and passed her comb over his blond hair. She wanted to comb it for him.

"What's that?" he asked with a start, as if something cold had touched him, and he opened his eyes. "What's that? Leave me alone, I beg you."

He moved her aside with his hands and walked away, and it seemed to her that his face expressed disgust and vexation. Just then the woman was carefully carrying a plate of cabbage soup to him with both hands, and Olga Ivanovna saw her thumbs dip into the soup. The dirty woman with her cross-tied belly, and the soup that Ryabovsky began eating greedily, and the cottage, and that whole life, which she had liked so much at the beginning for its simplicity and artistic disorder, now seemed horrible to her. She suddenly felt offended and said coldly:

"We must part for a time, otherwise we may quarrel seriously out of boredom. I'm sick of it. I'll leave today."

"How? Riding on a stick?"

"Today is Thursday, which means the steamer will be coming at nine-thirty."

"Ah, yes, yes . . . Well, go then . . ." Ryabovsky said gently, wiping his mouth with a towel instead of a napkin. "You're bored here and have nothing to do, and one would have to be a great egoist to keep you here. Go, and we'll see each other after the twentieth."

Olga Ivanovna packed cheerfully, and her cheeks even burned with pleasure. Could it be true, she asked herself, that she would soon sit painting in a living room, and sleep in a bedroom, and dine on a tablecloth? Her heart felt relieved, and she was no longer angry with the artist.

"I'll leave the paints and brushes for you, Ryabusha," she said. "Bring back whatever's left . . . See that you don't get lazy here without me, or splenetic, but work. I think you're a fine fellow, Ryabusha."

At nine o'clock Ryabovsky kissed her good-bye, to avoid, as she thought, having to kiss her on the steamer, in front of the artists, and brought her to the wharf. The steamer soon came and took her away.

She arrived home two and a half days later. Not taking off her hat and waterproof, breathless with excitement, she went to the drawing room and from there to the dining room. Dymov, in his shirtsleeves, his waistcoat unbuttoned, was sitting at the table and sharpening his knife on his fork; on a plate in front of him lay a grouse. As Olga Ivanovna was entering the apartment, she felt convinced that it was necessary to hide everything from her husband, and that she would have skill and strength enough to do it, but now, when she saw his broad, meek, happy smile and his shining, joyful eyes, she felt that to hide anything from this man was as base, as loathsome, and as impossible and beyond her strength, as to slander, steal, or kill, and she instantly resolved to tell him all that had happened. After letting him kiss and embrace her, she sank to her knees before him and covered her face.

"What? What is it, mama?" he asked tenderly. "You missed me?"

She raised her face, red with shame, and looked at him guiltily and imploringly, but fear and shame prevented her from telling the truth.

"Never mind . . ." she said. "I'm just so . . ."

"Let's sit down," he said, raising her up and sitting her at the table. "There . . . Have some grouse. You must be hungry, poor little thing."

She greedily breathed in the air of her home and ate the grouse, and he gazed at her lovingly and laughed with joy.

VI

Apparently, by the middle of winter Dymov began to suspect that he was being deceived. As if his own conscience were not clean, he could no longer look his wife straight in the eye, did not smile joyfully when he met her, and, to avoid being alone with her, often brought to dinner his friend Korostelev, a crop-headed little man with a crumpled face, who, as he spoke with Olga Ivanovna, in his embarrassment would undo all the buttons of his jacket and button them up again, and then would start twisting his left mustache with his right hand. Over dinner the two doctors spoke of the irregular heartbeat that sometimes occurs if the diaphragm is positioned high, or of how multiple neuritis had become more prevalent lately, or how the day before, having dissected a corpse diagnosed as having "malignant anemia," Dymov had found cancer of the pancreas. And it looked as if the two men conducted a medical conversation only so that Olga Ivanovna could keep silent—that is, not lie. After dinner Korostelev sat down at the piano, and Dymov sighed and said to him:

"Eh, brother! Well, now! Play us something sad."

Hunching his shoulders and spreading his fingers wide, Korostelev played a few chords and began singing "Show me such a haven where the Russian muzhik does not groan"[4] in a tenor voice, and Dymov sighed again, propped his head on his fist, and fell to thinking.

Lately Olga Ivanovna had been behaving very imprudently. She woke up every morning in a bad mood and with the thought that she no longer loved Ryabovsky, and thank God it was all over. But after coffee she would realize that Ryabovsky had taken her husband from her, and that she now had neither husband nor Ryabovsky; then she would recall what her acquaintances had said about Ryabovsky preparing something astounding for the exhibition, a mixture of landscape and genre painting in the style of Polenov,[5] over which everyone who visited his studio was in ecstasies; but this, she thought, he had created under her influence, and generally, thanks to her influence, he had changed greatly for the better. Her influence was so beneficial and essential that, if she were to leave him, he might even perish. And she also recalled that he had come to her last time in some gray little frock coat with flecks and a new tie, and had asked languidly: "Am I handsome?" And, graceful, with his long hair and blue eyes, he was indeed very handsome (or perhaps only seemed so), and he was tender with her.

Having recalled and realized many things, Olga Ivanovna would get dressed and, in great agitation, go to see Ryabovsky in his studio. She would find him cheerful and delighted with his indeed magnificent painting; he would clown, hop about, and answer serious questions with jokes. Olga Ivanovna was jealous of the painting and hated it, but out of politeness she would stand silently before it for some five minutes and, sighing as one sighs before some sacred thing, say softly:

"Yes, you've never yet painted anything like that. You know, it's even frightening."

Then she would begin imploring him to love her, not to abandon her, to have pity on her, poor and unhappy as she was. She would weep, kiss his hands, demand that he swear his love for her, insist that without her good influence he would go astray and perish. And, having ruined his good spirits and feeling humiliated herself, she would go to her dressmaker or to some actress acquaintance to obtain a ticket.

If she did not find him in his studio, she would leave a note for him, in which she swore that if he did not come to her that day, she would certainly poison herself. He would get alarmed, come to her, and stay for dinner. Unembarrassed by her husband's presence, he would say impertinent things to her, and she would respond in kind. They both felt that they were hampering each other, that they were despots and enemies, and they were angry. And in their anger, they did not notice that they were being indecent, and that even crop-headed Korostelev understood everything. After dinner, Ryabovsky would hurriedly say good-bye and leave.

"Where are you going?" Olga Ivanovna would ask him in the front hall, looking at him with hatred.

Wincing and narrowing his eyes, he would name some lady of their acquaintance, and it was clear that he was making fun of her jealousy and wanted to vex her. She would go to her bedroom and lie down on the bed; from jealousy, vexation, a feeling of humiliation and shame, she would bite her pillow and begin crying loudly. Dymov would leave Korostelev in the drawing room, come to the bedroom, and, embarrassed and perplexed, say softly:

"Don't cry so loudly, mama . . . Why? You must keep it quiet . . . You mustn't show . . . You know you can't mend what's happened."

Not knowing how to suppress her painful jealousy, which even made her temples ache, and thinking that things could still be put right, she would wash, powder her tear-stained face, and fly to the lady acquaintance. Not finding Ryabovsky there, she would go to another, then a third . . . In the beginning she was ashamed of going around like that, but then she got used to it, and it would happen that in one evening she would visit all the ladies of her acquaintance, searching for Ryabovsky, and they all understood it.

She had once said of her husband to Ryabovsky:

"The man crushes me with his magnanimity!"

She liked the phrase so much that, whenever she met artists who knew about her affair with Ryabovsky, she would say of her husband, with an energetic gesture of the hand:

"The man crushes me with his magnanimity!"

The order of life was the same as the year before. There were soirées on Wednesdays. The actor recited, the artists painted, the cellist played, the singer sang, and at half-past eleven, unfailingly, the door to the dining room would open, and Dymov, smiling, would say:

"A bite to eat, gentlemen."

As before, Olga Ivanovna sought great people, found them and was unsatisfied, and sought again. As before, she returned home late every night, but Dymov would not be asleep, as last year, but sitting in his study and working on something. He would go to bed at around three and get up at eight.

One evening, as she was standing in front of the pier glass getting ready for the theater, Dymov came into the bedroom in a tailcoat and white tie. He was smiling meekly and, as before, looked joyfully straight into his wife's eyes. His face was beaming.

"I've just defended my thesis," he said, sitting down and patting his knees.

"Successfully?" asked Olga Ivanovna.

"Uh-huh!" he laughed and craned his neck so as to see his wife's face in the mirror, as she went on standing with her back to him, straightening her hair. "Uh-huh!" he repeated. "You know, it's very likely I'll be offered a post as assistant professor of general pathology. It's in the air."

It was clear from his blissfully beaming face that, if Olga Ivanovna could share his joy and triumph with him, he would forgive her anything, both present and future, and forget everything, but she did not understand what an assistant professor of general pathology was, and besides she was afraid to be late to the theater, and so she said nothing.

He sat for a couple of minutes, smiled guiltily, and left.

VII

This was a most troublesome day.

Dymov had a bad headache. He did not have tea in the morning, did not go to the hospital, and spent the whole time lying on the Turkish divan in his study. After twelve, as usual, Olga Ivanovna went to Ryabovsky to show him her study for a *nature morte* and ask him why he had not come the day before. The study was nothing to her, and she had painted it only so as to have a further pretext for calling on the artist.

She went in without ringing the bell, and as she was removing her galoshes in the front hall, she seemed to hear something run softly across the studio, a rustling as of a woman's dress, and when she hastened to peek into the studio, she saw just a bit of brown skirt flash for a moment and disappear behind a big painting which, together with its easel, was covered to the floor with black cloth. There was no possible doubt, it was a woman hiding. How often Olga Ivanovna herself had taken refuge behind that painting! Ryabovsky, obviously quite embarrassed, seemed surprised by her visit, gave her both hands, and said with a forced smile:

"A-a-ah! Very glad to see you. What's the good news?"

Olga Ivanovna's eyes filled with tears. She felt ashamed, bitter, and not for any amount would she have consented to speak in the presence of a strange woman, a rival, a liar, who was now standing behind the painting, probably tittering gleefully.

"I've brought you a study . . ." she said timidly, in a thin little voice, and her lips trembled, "a *nature morte*."

"A-a-ah . . . a study?"

The artist took the study and, as he examined it, went as if mechanically into the other room.

Olga Ivanovna obediently followed him.

"*Nature morte* . . . best sort," he muttered, choosing a rhyme, "resort . . . port . . . wart . . ."

Hurried footsteps were heard in the studio and the rustle of a dress. It meant *she* had gone. Olga Ivanovna wanted to shout loudly, hit the artist on the head with something heavy, and leave, but she could see nothing through her tears, was crushed by her shame, and felt herself no longer an Olga Ivanovna, nor an artist, but a little bug.

"I'm tired . . ." the artist said languidly, looking at the study and shaking his head to overcome his drowsiness. "It's sweet, of course, but it's a study today, and a study last year, and in a month another study . . . Aren't you bored? If I were you, I'd drop painting and take up something seriously, music or whatever. You're not an artist, you're a musician. Anyhow, I'm so tired! I'll have tea served . . . Eh?"

He left the room, and Olga Ivanovna heard him give some order to his servant. So as not to say good-bye, not to explain, and, above all, not to burst into tears, she quickly ran to the front hall before Ryabovsky came back, put on her galoshes, and went outside. There she breathed easily and felt herself free forever from Ryabovsky, and from painting, and from the heavy shame that had so oppressed her in the studio. It was all finished!

She went to her dressmaker, then to the actor Barnay,[6] who had arrived the day before, from Barnay to a music shop, thinking all the while of how she was going to write Ryabovsky a cold, stern letter, filled with dignity, and how in the spring or summer she and Dymov would go to the Crimea, there definitively free themselves of the past, and start a new life.

She returned home late in the evening and, without changing her clothes, sat down in the drawing room to write the letter. Ryabovsky had told her that she was not an artist, and she, in revenge, would write to him that he painted the same thing every year and said the same thing every day, that he was stuck, and nothing would come from him except what had already come. She also wanted to write that he owed a lot to her good influence, and if he acted badly, it was only because her influence was paralyzed by various ambiguous persons, like the one who had been hiding behind the painting that day.

"Mama!" Dymov called from the study, without opening the door. "Mama!"

"What's the matter?"

"Mama, don't come in, just come to the door. The thing is . . . Two days ago I caught diphtheria in the hospital, and now . . . I'm not well. Send for Korostelev quickly."

Olga Ivanovna had always called her husband, as she did all the men she knew, not by his first but by his last name. She did not like his first name, Osip, because it reminded her of Gogol's Osip[7] and of the tongue twister: "Osip's hoarse, his horse has pip." But now she cried out:

"Osip, it can't be!"

"Send quickly! I'm not well . . ." Dymov said behind the door, and she heard him go to the divan and lie down. "Send quickly!" came his muted voice.

"What does it mean?" thought Olga Ivanovna, turning cold with terror. "But this is dangerous!"

Quite unnecessarily she took a candle and went to her bedroom, and there, trying to think what she must do, she accidentally looked at herself in the pier glass. With a pale, frightened face, in a puff-sleeved jacket, yellow flounces on her breast, and an unusual pattern of stripes on her skirt, she appeared dreadful and vile to herself. She suddenly felt painfully sorry for Dymov, for his boundless love for her, for his young life, and even for this orphaned bed of his, in which he had not slept for a long time, and she remembered his usual meek, obedient smile. She wept bitterly and wrote an imploring letter to Korostelev. It was two o'clock in the morning.

VIII

As Olga Ivanovna, her head heavy after a sleepless night, her hair undone, looking guilty and unattractive, emerged from the bedroom at around eight in the morning, some black-bearded gentleman, apparently a doctor, passed her on his way to the front hall. There was a smell of medications. Korostelev stood by the door of the study, twisting his left mustache with his right hand.

"Sorry, I can't let you see him," he said glumly to Olga Ivanovna. "You might catch it. And in fact there's no need. He's delirious anyway."

"He has real diphtheria?" Olga Ivanovna asked in a whisper.

"Those who ask for trouble really should be taken to court," Korostelev muttered without answering Olga Ivanovna's question. "Do you know how he caught it? On Tuesday he sucked diphtherial membranes from a sick boy's throat with a tube. And what for? Stupid . . . Just like that, foolishly . . ."

"Is it dangerous? Very?" asked Olga Ivanovna.

"Yes, they say it's an acute form. In fact, we ought to send for Schreck."

A little red-headed man with a long nose and a Jewish accent came, then a tall one, stoop-shouldered, disheveled, looking like a protodeacon; then a young one, very fat, with a red face and in spectacles. They were doctors, come to attend their colleague's sickbed. Korostelev, having finished his turn, did not go home, but stayed and wandered like a shadow through all the rooms. The maid served tea to the attending doctors and kept running to the pharmacy, and there was no one to put the rooms in order. It was quiet and dismal.

Olga Ivanovna sat in her bedroom and thought that this was God punishing her for deceiving her husband. A silent, unprotesting, incomprehensible being, depersonalized by his own meekness, characterless, weak from excessive kindness, suffered mutely somewhere on his divan, and did not complain. And if he should complain, even in his delirium, the attending doctors would learn that it was not diphtheria alone that was to blame. They should ask Korostelev: he knew everything, and it was not without reason that he looked at his friend's wife with such eyes, as if she were the chief, the real villain, and diphtheria were only her accomplice. She no longer remembered the moonlit evening on the Volga, or the declarations of love, or the poetic life in the cottage, but remembered only that for an empty whim, an indulgence, she had become smeared all over, hands and feet, with something dirty, sticky, that could never be washed off . . .

"Ah, how terribly I lied!" she thought, remembering the turbulent love between her and Ryabovsky. "A curse on it all! . . ."

At four o'clock she had dinner with Korostelev. He ate nothing, only drank red wine and scowled. She also ate nothing. First she prayed mentally and vowed to God that if Dymov recovered, she would love him again and be a faithful wife. Then, oblivious for a moment, she gazed at Korostelev and thought: "Isn't it boring to be a simple, completely unremarkable and unknown man, with such a crumpled face and bad manners besides?" Then it seemed to her that God would kill her that very instant, because, for fear of catching the illness, she had not once gone near her husband's study. And generally there was a dull, dismal feeling and a certainty that life was already ruined and nothing could put it right . . .

After dinner it grew dark. When Olga Ivanovna went out to the drawing room, Korostelev was sleeping on a couch, with a gold-embroidered silk pillow under his head. "Khi-puah," he snored, "khi-puah."

And the doctors who came to attend the sick man and then left, did not notice this disorder. That there was a strange man sleeping in the drawing room and snoring, and the studies on the walls, and the whimsical furnishings, and that the hostess had her hair undone and was carelessly dressed—all that did not arouse the slightest interest now. One of the doctors accidentally laughed at something, and this laughter sounded somehow strange and timid, and even felt eerie.

The next time Olga Ivanovna came out to the drawing room, Korostelev was not asleep but sitting and smoking.

"He has diphtheria of the nasal cavity," he said in a low voice. "His heart is already not working very well. In fact, things are bad."

"Send for Schreck," said Olga Ivanovna.

"He's already been here. It was he who noticed that the diphtheria had passed into the nose. Eh, and what of Schreck! In fact, Schreck's nothing. He's Schreck, I'm Korostelev—nothing more."

The time dragged on terribly long. Olga Ivanovna lay on the bed, unmade since morning, and dozed. She imagined that the whole apartment, from floor to ceiling, was taken up by a huge piece of iron, and if only the iron could be taken away, everybody would be cheerful and light. Coming to herself, she remembered that this was not iron, but Dymov's illness.

"*Nature morte,* port . . ." she thought, sinking into oblivion again, "sport . . . resort . . . And how about Schreck? Schreck, wreck, vreck . . . creck. And where are my friends now? Do they know about our misfortune? Lord, save us . . . deliver us. Schreck, wreck . . ."

And again the iron . . . The time dragged on long, and the clock on the ground floor struck frequently. And the doorbell kept ringing all the time; doctors came . . . The maid came in with an empty cup on a tray and asked:

"Shall I make the bed, ma'am?"

And, receiving no answer, she left. The clock struck downstairs, she had been dreaming of rain on the Volga, and again someone came into the bedroom, a stranger, she thought. Olga Ivanovna jumped up and recognized Korostelev.

"What time is it?" she asked.

"Around three."

"Well, so?"

"So, I've come to tell you: he's going . . ."

He sobbed, sat down on the bed beside her, and wiped the tears with his sleeve. She did not understand at once, but turned all cold and slowly began to cross herself.

"He's going . . ." he repeated in a thin little voice and sobbed again. "He's dying, because he sacrificed himself . . . What a loss for science!" he said bitterly. "Compared to us all, he was a great, extraordinary man! So gifted! What hopes we all had in him!" Korostelev went on, wringing his hands. "Lord God, he'd have been a scientist such as you won't find anywhere now. Oska Dymov, Oska Dymov, what have you done! Ai, ai, my God!"

Korostelev covered his face with both hands in despair and shook his head.

"And what moral strength!" he went on, growing more and more angry with someone. "A kind, pure, loving soul—not a man, but crystal! He served science and died from science. And he worked like an ox, day and night, nobody spared him, and the young scientist, the future professor, had to look for patients, to do translations by night, in order to pay for these . . . mean rags!"

Korostelev looked hatefully at Olga Ivanovna, seized the sheet with both hands, and tore at it angrily, as if it were to blame.

"He didn't spare himself, and no one else spared him. Ah, there's nothing to say!"

"Yes, a rare person!" some bass voice said in the drawing room.

Olga Ivanovna recalled her whole life with him, from beginning to end, in all its details, and suddenly understood that he was indeed an extraordinary, rare man and, compared with those she knew, a great man. And, recalling the way her late father and all his fellow doctors had treated him, she understood that they had all seen a future celebrity in him. The walls, the ceiling, the lamp, and the rug on the floor winked at her mockingly, as if wishing to say: "You missed it! You missed it!" In tears, she rushed from the bedroom, slipped past some unknown man in the drawing room, and ran into her husband's study. He lay motionless on the Turkish divan, covered to the waist with a blanket. His face was terribly pinched, thin, and of a gray-yellow color such as living people never have; and only by his forehead, his black eyebrows, and the familiar smile could one tell that this was Dymov. Olga Ivanovna quickly touched his chest, forehead, and hands. His chest was still warm, but his forehead and hands were unpleasantly cold. And his half-open eyes looked not at Olga Ivanovna but down at the blanket.

"Dymov!" she called loudly. "Dymov!"

She wanted to explain to him that this was a mistake, that all was not lost yet, that life could still be beautiful and happy, that he was a rare, extraordinary, and great man, and that she would stand in awe of him all her life, worship him and feel a holy dread . . .

"Dymov!" she called to him, patting him on the shoulder and refusing to believe that he would never wake up. "Dymov, but, Dymov!"

And in the drawing room Korostelev was saying to the maid:

"What is there to ask? Go to the church caretaker and find out where the almshouse women live. They'll wash the body and prepare it—they'll do everything necessary."

JANUARY 1892

In Exile

Old Semyon, nicknamed the Explainer, and a young Tartar whose name no one knew, sat on the bank near a bonfire; the other three boatmen were inside the hut. Semyon, an old man of about sixty, lean and toothless, but broad-shouldered and still healthy-looking, was drunk; he would have gone to bed long ago, but he had a bottle in his pocket, and he was afraid the fellows in the hut might ask him for vodka. The Tartar was sick, pining away, and, wrapping himself in his rags, was telling how good it was in Simbirsk province and what a beautiful and intelligent wife he had left at home. He was about twenty-five years old, not more, and now, in the light of the bonfire, pale, with a sorrowful, sickly face, he looked like a boy.

"It's sure no paradise here," the Explainer was saying. "See for yourself: water, bare banks, clay everywhere, and nothing else . . . Easter's long past, but there's ice drifting on the river, and it snowed this morning."

"Bad! Bad!" said the Tartar, and he looked around fearfully.

Some ten paces away from them the dark, cold river flowed; it growled, splashed against the eroded clay bank, and quickly raced off somewhere to the distant sea. Close to the bank a big barge loomed darkly. The boatmen called it a "barridge." On the far bank, lights crawled snakelike, flaring up and dying out: this was last year's grass being burnt. And beyond the snakes it was dark again. Small blocks of ice could be heard knocking against the barge. Damp, cold . . .

The Tartar looked at the sky. The stars were as many as at home, there was the same blackness around, but something was missing. At home, in Simbirsk province, the stars were not like that at all, nor was the sky.

"Bad! Bad!" he repeated.

"You'll get used to it!" the Explainer said and laughed. "You're still a young man, foolish, not dry behind the ears, and like a fool you think there's no man more wretched than you, but the time will come when you say to yourself: 'God grant everybody such a life.' Look at me. In a week's time the water will subside, we'll set up the ferry here, you'll all go wandering around Siberia, and I'll stay and start going from shore to shore. It's twenty-two years now I've been going like that. And thank God. I need nothing. God grant everybody such a life."

The Tartar added more brushwood to the fire, lay down closer to it, and said:

"My father is a sick man. When he dies, my mother and wife will come here. They promised."

"And what do you need a mother and wife for?" asked the Explainer. "That's all foolishness, brother. It's the devil confusing you, damn his soul. Don't listen to the cursed one. Don't let him have his way. He'll get at you with a woman, but you spite him: don't want any! He'll get at you with freedom, but you stay tough—don't want any! You need nothing! No father, no mother, no wife, no freedom, no bag, no baggage! You need nothing, damn it all!"

The Explainer took a swig from his bottle and went on:

"I'm no simple peasant, brother dear, I'm not of boorish rank, I'm a beadle's son, and when I was free and lived in Kursk, I went around in a frock coat, and now I've brought myself to the point where I can sleep naked on the ground and have grass for my grub. God grant everybody such a life. I need nothing, and I fear nobody, and to my way of thinking there's no man richer or freer than I am. When they sent me here from Russia, I got tough the very first day: I want nothing! The devil got at me with my wife, my family, my freedom, but I told him: I need nothing! I got tough and, you see, I live well, no complaints. And if anybody indulges the devil and listens even once, he's lost, there's no saving him: he'll sink into the mire up to his ears and never get out. Not only your kind, foolish peasants, but even noble and educated ones get lost. About fifteen years ago a gentleman was sent here from Russia. He quarreled with his brothers over something, and somehow faked a will. They said he was a prince or a baron, but maybe he was just an official—who knows! Well, this gentleman came here and, first thing, bought himself a house and land in Mukhortinskoe. 'I want to live by my own labor,' he says, 'by the sweat of my brow, because,' he says, 'I'm no longer a gentleman, I'm an exile.' Why not, I say, God help you, it's a good thing. He was a young man then, a bustler, always busy; he went mowing, and fishing, and rode forty miles on horseback. Only here's the trouble: from the very first year he started going to Gyrino, to the post office. He used to stand on my ferry and sigh: 'Eh, Semyon, it's long since they sent me money from home!' No need for money, Vassily Sergeich, I say. Money for what? Give up the old things, forget them as if they'd never been, as if it was only a dream, and start a new life. Don't listen to the devil—he won't get you anything good, he'll only draw you into a noose. You want money now, I say, and in a little while, lo and behold, you'll want something else, and then more and more. If you wish to be happy, I say, then first of all wish for nothing. Yes . . . Since fate has bitterly offended you and me, I say to him, there's no point asking her for mercy or bowing at her feet, we should scorn her and laugh at her. Otherwise it's she who will laugh at us. That's what I said to him . . . About two years later, I take him to this side, and he rubs his hands and laughs. 'I'm going to Gyrino,' he says, 'to meet my wife. She's taken pity on me,' he says, 'and she's coming. She's a nice woman, a kind one.' And he's even breathless with joy. So two days later he arrives with his wife. A young lady, beautiful, in a hat; with a baby girl in her arms. And a lot of luggage of all sorts. My Vassily Sergeich fusses around her, can't have enough of looking at her and praising her. 'Yes, brother Semyon, people can live in Siberia, too!' Well, I think, all right, you won't be overjoyed. And after that he began to visit Gyrino nearly every week, to see if money had come from Russia. He needed no end of money. 'For my sake,' he says, 'to share my bitter lot, she's ruining her youth and beauty here in Siberia, and on account of that,' he says, 'I must offer her all sorts of pleasures . . .' To make it more cheerful for the lady, he began keeping company with officials and all sorts of trash. And it's a sure thing that all such people have to be wined and dined, and there should be a piano, and a shaggy lapdog on the sofa—it can croak for all of me . . . Luxury, in short, indulgence. The lady didn't live with him long. How could she? Clay, water, cold, no vegetables, no fruit, drunken, uneducated people everywhere, no civility at all, and she's a spoiled lady, from the capital . . . And, sure enough, she got bored . . . And her husband, say what you like, is no longer a gentleman, he's an exile—it's not the same honor. In about three years, I remember, on the eve of the Dormition,[1] a shout comes from the other bank. I went over in the ferry, I see—the lady, all wrapped up, and a young gentleman with her, one of the officials. A troika . . . I brought them over to this side, they got in and— that's the last I ever saw of them! They passed out of the picture. And towards morning Vassily Sergeich drove up with a pair. 'Did my wife pass by here, Semyon, with a gentleman in spectacles?' She did, I say, go chase the wind in the field! He galloped after them, pursued them for five days. Afterwards, when I took him back to the other side, he fell down and began howling and beating his head on the floorboards. There you have it, I say. I laugh and re- mind him: 'People can live in Siberia, too!' And he beats his head even harder . . . After that he wanted to get his freedom. His wife went to Russia, and so he was drawn there, too, to see her and get her away from her lover. And so, brother dear, he began riding nearly every day either to the post office or to see the authorities in town. He kept sending and submitting appeals to be pardoned and allowed to return home, and he told me he'd spent two hundred roubles on telegrams alone. He sold the land, pawned the house to the Jews. He turned gray, bent, his face got as yellow as a consump- tive's. He talks to you and goes hem, hem, hem . . . and there are tears in his eyes. He suffered some eight years like that with these appeals, but then he revived and got happy again: he came up with a new indulgence. His daughter's grown up, you see. He looks at her and can't have enough. And, to tell the truth, she's not bad at all: pretty, with dark eyebrows, and a lively character. Every Sunday he took her to church in Gyrino. The two of them stand side by side on the ferry, she laughs and he can't take his eyes off her. 'Yes, Semyon,' he says, 'people can live in Siberia, too. There's happiness in Siberia, too. Look,' he says, 'what a daughter I have! I bet you won't find one like her for a thousand miles around!' The daughter's nice, I say, it's really true . . . And to myself I think: 'Just wait . . . She's a young girl, her blood is high, she wants to live, and what

kind of life is there here?' And she began to languish, brother . . .
She pined and pined, got all wasted, fell ill, and took to her bed.
Consumption. There's Siberian happiness for you, damn its soul,
there's 'people can live in Siberia' for you . . . He started going for
doctors and bringing them to her. As soon as he hears there's some
doctor or quack within a hundred or two hundred miles, he goes to
get him. He's put an awful lot of money into these doctors, and in
my view it would have been better to drink the money up . . . She'll
die anyway. She's absolutely sure to die, and then he'll be totally
lost. He'll hang himself from grief or run away to Russia—it's a
fact. He'll run away, get caught, there'll be a trial, hard labor, a taste
of the whip . . ."

"Good, good," the Tartar muttered, shrinking from the chill.

"What's good?" the Explainer asked.

"The wife, the daughter . . . Hard labor, yes, grief, yes, but still
he saw his wife and daughter . . . Need nothing, you say. But nothing—bad. His wife lived with him three years—that was a gift from
God. Nothing bad, three years good. How you don't understand?"

Trembling, straining to find Russian words, of which he did not
know many, and stammering, the Tartar began to say that God forbid he get sick in a foreign land, die and be put into the cold, rusty
earth, that if his wife came to him, be it for a single day and even
for a single hour, he would agree to suffer any torment for such
happiness and would thank God. Better a single day of happiness
than nothing.

After that he told again about what a beautiful and intelligent
wife he had left at home, then, clutching his head with both hands,
he wept and began assuring Semyon that he was not guilty of anything and had been falsely accused. His two brothers and his uncle
stole horses from a peasant and beat the old man half to death, but
the community gave them an unfair trial and sentenced all three
brothers to Siberia, while his uncle, a rich man, stayed home.

"You'll get u-u-used to it!" said Semyon.

The Tartar fell silent and fixed his tear-filled eyes on the fire; his
face showed bewilderment and fright, as if he were still unable to
understand why he was there in the dark and the damp, among
strangers, and not in Simbirsk province. The Explainer lay down
near the fire, grinned at something, and struck up a song in a low
voice.

"What fun is it for her with her father?" he said after a while.

"He loves her, takes comfort in her, it's true; but don't go putting your finger in his mouth, brother: he's a strict old man, a tough one. And young girls don't want strictness . . . They need tenderness, ha-ha-ha and hee-ho-ho, perfumes and creams. Yes . . . Eh, so it goes!" Semyon sighed and got up heavily. "The vodka's all gone, that means it's time to sleep. Eh, I'm off, brother . . ."

Left alone, the Tartar added more brushwood, lay down, and, gazing at the fire, began thinking of his native village and his wife; let his wife come for just a month, just a day, and then, if she wants, she can go back! Better a month or even a day than nothing. But if his wife keeps her promise and comes, what will he give her to eat? Where will she live here?

"If no food, how live?" the Tartar asked out loud.

Because now, working day and night with an oar, he earned only ten kopecks a day; true, travelers gave them tips for tea and vodka, but the boys divided all the income among themselves and gave nothing to the Tartar, but only laughed at him. And need makes one hungry, cold, and afraid . . . Now, when his whole body aches and trembles, it would be nice to go into the hut and sleep, but there he has nothing to cover himself with, and it is colder than on the bank; here he also has nothing to cover himself with, but at least he can make a fire . . .

In a week, when the water fully subsided and the ferry was set up, none of the boatmen would be needed except for Semyon, and the Tartar would start going from village to village, begging and asking for work. His wife was only seventeen; she was beautiful, pampered, and shy—could she, too, go around the villages with her face uncovered and beg for alms? No, it was horrible even to think of it . . .

Dawn was breaking; the outlines of the barge, the osier bushes in the rippling water, could be seen clearly, and, looking back, there was the clay cliffside, the hut roofed with brown straw below, and a cluster of village cottages above. In the village the cocks were already crowing.

The red clay cliffside, the barge, the river, the unkind strangers, hunger, cold, sickness—maybe none of it exists in reality. Probably I am only dreaming it all, thought the Tartar. He felt that he was asleep and heard his own snoring . . . Of course he is at home, in Simbirsk province, and as soon as he calls his wife's name, she will call back to him; and his mother is in the next room . . . Sometimes one has such frightful dreams! What for? The Tartar smiled and opened his eyes. What river is this? The Volga?

It was snowing.

"Hallo-o-o!" someone was shouting from the other bank. "Ba-a-arridge!"

The Tartar came to his senses and went to wake up his comrades, so that they could cross to the other side. Putting on their ragged sheepskin coats as they went, cursing in hoarse, just-awakened voices, and hunching up against the cold, the boatmen appeared on the bank. The river, which exhaled a piercing cold, probably seemed disgusting and eerie to them after sleep. They clambered unhurriedly into the barridge . . . The Tartar and the three boat-men took hold of the long, broad-bladed oars, which in the dark resembled crayfish claws; Semyon heaved the weight of his belly against the long tiller. The shouting from the other side went on, and two pistol shots rang out, probably with the thought that the boatmen were asleep or had gone to the pothouse in the village.

"All right, you'll get there!" the Explainer said in the tone of a man convinced that in this world there is no need to hurry, "nothing good will come of it anyway."

The heavy, clumsy barge detached itself from the bank and floated among the osier bushes, and only by the fact that the osiers were slowly dropping behind could one tell that it was not standing in place but moving. The boatmen swung the oars regularly, in unison; the Explainer lay his belly against the tiller and, describing a curve in the air, flew from one gunwale to the other. In the darkness it looked as if people were sitting on some antediluvian animal with long paws and floating on it towards some cold, gloomy land such as one sometimes sees in nightmares.

They passed the osiers and emerged into the open. On the other bank the knocking and regular splashing of the oars could already be heard, and there came a shout of "Hurry! Hurry!" Another ten minutes passed and the barge bumped heavily against the wharf.

"It just keeps pouring down, pouring down!" Semyon muttered, wiping the snow from his face. "Where it comes from God only knows!"

On the other side an old man was waiting, lean, not tall, in a jacket lined with fox fur and a white lambskin hat. He stood apart from the horses and did not move; he had a grim, concentrated expression, as if he were at pains to remember something and angry with his disobedient memory. When Semyon came up to him, smiling, and removed his hat, he said:

"I'm rushing to Anastasyevka. My daughter's gotten worse again, and I've heard a new doctor has been appointed to Anastasyevka."

They pulled the tarantass onto the barge and went back. The man whom Semyon called Vassily Sergeich stood motionless all the while they crossed, his thick lips tightly compressed and his eyes fixed on one point; when the coachman asked permission to smoke in his presence, he made no answer, as if he had not heard. And Semyon, laying his belly against the tiller, looked at him mockingly and said:

"People can live in Siberia, too. Li-i-ive!"

The Explainer's face wore a triumphant expression, as if he had proved something and was glad it had come out exactly as he had predicted. The wretched, helpless look of the man in the jacket lined with fox fur seemed to afford him great pleasure.

"It's messy traveling now, Vassily Sergeich," he said, as the horses were being harnessed on the bank. "You should hold off going for a couple of weeks, until it gets more dry. Or else not go at all . . . As if there's any use in your going, when you know yourself how people are eternally going, day and night, and there's still no use in it. Really!"

Vassily Sergeich silently gave him a tip, got into the tarantass, and drove off.

"There, galloping for a doctor!" said Semyon, hunching up from the cold. "Yes, go look for a real doctor, chase the wind in the field, catch the devil by his tail, damn your soul! Such odd birds, Lord, forgive me, a sinner!"

The Tartar came up to the Explainer and, looking at him with hatred and revulsion, trembling and mixing Tartar words into his broken language, said:

"He good . . . good, and you—bad! You bad! Gentleman a good soul, excellent, and you a beast, you bad! Gentleman alive, and you dead . . . God created man for be alive, for be joy, and be sorrow, and be grief, and you want nothing, it means you not alive, you stone, clay! Stone want nothing, and you want nothing . . . You stone—and God not love you, but love gentleman."

Everybody laughed. The Tartar winced squeamishly, waved his arm and, wrapping himself in his rags, went towards the fire. The boatmen and Semyon trudged to the hut.

"It's cold!" croaked one of the boatmen, stretching out on the straw that covered the damp clay floor.

"Yes, it's not warm!" another agreed. "A convict's life! . . ."

They all lay down. The wind forced the door open, and snow blew into the hut. Nobody wanted to get up and shut the door: it was cold, and they were lazy.

"And I'm fine!" Semyon said as he was falling asleep. "God grant everybody such a life."

"We know you, a convict seven times over. Even the devils can't get at you."

Sounds resembling a dog's howling came from outside.

"What's that? Who's there?"

"It's the Tartar crying."

"Look at that . . . Odd bird!"

"He'll get u-u-used to it!" said Semyon, and he fell asleep at once.

Soon the others also fell asleep. And so the door stayed open.

MAY 1892

WARD No. 6

I

In the hospital yard stands a small annex surrounded by a whole forest of burdock, nettles, and wild hemp. The roof is rusty, the chimney is half fallen down, the porch steps are rotten and overgrown with grass, and only a few traces of stucco remain. The front façade faces the hospital, the back looks onto a field, from which it is separated by the gray hospital fence topped with nails. These nails, turned point up, and the fence, and the annex itself have that special despondent and accursed look that only our hospitals and prisons have.

If you are not afraid of being stung by nettles, let us go down the narrow path that leads to the annex and see what is going on inside. Opening the first door, we go into the front hall. Here whole mountains of hospital rubbish are piled against the walls and around the stove. Mattresses, old torn dressing gowns, trousers, blue-striped shirts, worthless, worn-out shoes—all these rags are piled in heaps, crumpled, tangled, rotting and giving off a suffocating smell.

On top of this rubbish, always with a pipe in his mouth, lies the caretaker Nikita, an old retired soldier with faded tabs. He has a stern, haggard face, beetling brows, which give his face the look of a steppe sheepdog, and a red nose; he is small of stature, looks lean and sinewy, but his bearing is imposing and his fists are enormous.

He is one of those simple-hearted, positive, efficient, and obtuse people who love order more than anything in the world and are therefore convinced that *they* must be beaten. He beats them on the face, the chest, the back, wherever, and is certain that without that there would be no order here.

Further on you enter a big, spacious room that takes up the entire annex, except for the front hall. The walls here are daubed with dirty blue paint, the ceiling is as sooty as in a chimneyless hut—clearly the stoves smoke in winter and the place is full of fumes. The windows are disfigured inside by iron grilles. The floor is gray and splintery. There is a stench of pickled cabbage, charred wicks, bedbugs, and ammonia, and for the first moment this stench gives you the impression that you have entered a menagerie.

In the room stand beds bolted to the floor. On them sit or lie people in blue hospital gowns and old-fashioned nightcaps. These are madmen.

There are five of them in all. Only one of them is of noble rank, the rest are tradesmen. First from the door, a tall, lean tradesman with a red, gleaming mustache and tearful eyes sits with his head propped on his hand and gazes at a single point. Day and night he grieves, shaking his head, sighing and smiling bitterly; he rarely takes part in conversation and usually does not reply to questions. He eats and drinks mechanically, when offered. Judging by his painful, racking cough, his thinness and the flush of his cheeks, he is in the first stages of consumption.

Next to him is a small, lively, extremely agile old man, with a pointed little beard and dark hair curly as a Negro's. During the day he strolls about the ward from window to window, or sits on his bed, his legs tucked under Turkish-fashion, and whistles irrepressibly like a bullfinch, sings softly, and giggles. He displays a childlike gaiety and lively character at night as well, when he gets up to pray to God, that is, to beat his breast with his fists and poke at the door with his finger. This is the Jew Moiseika, a half-wit, who went crazy about twenty years ago when his hatter's shop burned down.

Of all the inhabitants of Ward No. 6, he alone is allowed to go outside the annex and even outside the hospital yard. He has enjoyed this privilege for years, probably as a hospital old-timer and a quiet, harmless half-wit, a town fool, whom people have long been used to seeing in the streets surrounded by boys and dogs. In a flimsy robe, a ridiculous nightcap and slippers, sometimes barefoot and even without trousers, he walks about the streets, stopping at gates and shops and begging for a little kopeck. In one place they give him kvass, in another bread, in a third a little kopeck, so that he usually returns to the annex feeling rich and well-fed. Everything he brings with him Nikita takes for himself. The soldier does this rudely, vexedly, turning his pockets inside out and calling God to be his witness that he will never let the Jew out again and that for him disorder is the worst thing in the world.

Moiseika likes to oblige. He brings his comrades water, covers them up when they sleep, promises to bring each of them a little kopeck from outside and to make them new hats. He also feeds his neighbor on the left, a paralytic, with a spoon. He acts this way not out of compassion, nor from any humane considerations, but imitating and involuntarily submitting to Gromov, his neighbor on the right.

Ivan Dmitrich Gromov, a man of about thirty-three, of noble birth, a former bailiff and provincial secretary, suffers from persecution mania. He either lies curled up on the bed or paces from corner to corner, as if for exercise, but he very rarely sits. He is always agitated, excited, and tense with some vague, unfocused expectation. The slightest rustle in the front hall or shout in the yard is enough to make him raise his head and start listening: is it him they are coming for? Is it him they are looking for? And his face at those moments expresses extreme anxiety and revulsion.

I like his broad, high-cheekboned face, always pale and unhappy, reflecting as in a mirror his soul tormented by struggle and prolonged fear. His grimaces are strange and morbid, but the fine lines that deep and sincere suffering has drawn on his face are sensible and intelligent, and there is a warm, healthy brightness in his eyes. I like the man himself, polite, obliging, and of extraordinary delicacy in dealing with everyone except Nikita. When anyone drops a button or a spoon, he quickly jumps from his bed and picks it up. Every morning he wishes his comrades a good morning, and on going to bed he wishes them a good night.

Besides his permanently tense state and grimacing, his madness also expresses itself as follows. Sometimes in the evening he wraps himself in his robe and, trembling all over, teeth chattering, begins pacing rapidly from corner to corner and between the beds. It looks as if he has a very high fever. From the way he suddenly stops and gazes at his comrades, it is clear that he wants to say something very important, but, evidently realizing that he would not be listened to or understood, he shakes his head impatiently and goes on pacing. But soon the wish to speak overcomes all other considerations, and he gives himself free rein and speaks ardently and passionately. His speech is disorderly, feverish, like raving, impulsive, and not always comprehensible, yet in it, in his words and in his voice, one can hear something extremely good. When he speaks, you recognize both the madman and the human being in him. It is hard to convey his insane speech on paper. He speaks of human meanness, of the violence that tramples on truth, of the beautiful life there will be on earth in time, of the grilles on the windows, which remind him every moment of the obtuseness and cruelty of the oppressors. The result is a disorderly, incoherent potpourri of old but still unfinished songs.

II

Some twelve or fifteen years ago there lived in town, right on the main street, in his own private house, the official Gromov, a solid and well-to-do man. He had two sons: Sergei and Ivan. When he was a fourth-year student, Sergei fell ill with galloping consumption and died, and this death seemed to mark the beginning of a whole series of misfortunes that suddenly rained down on the Gromov family. A week after Sergei's funeral, the old father was taken to court for forgery and embezzlement, and soon afterwards died of typhus in the prison hospital. The house and all the moveable property was auctioned off, and Ivan Dmitrich and his mother were left without any means.

Formerly, when his father was alive, Ivan Dmitrich, who lived in Petersburg and studied at the university, received sixty or seventy roubles a month and had no notion of poverty, but now he was abruptly forced to change his life. He had to work from morning till night, giving penny lessons, doing copying work, and still go hungry, because all his earnings went to support his mother. Ivan Dmitrich proved unable to endure such a life, he lost heart, wasted away, and, quitting the university, went home. Here in town, through connections, he obtained a post as teacher in the local high school, but he did not get along with his colleagues, the students did not like him, and soon afterwards he quit the post. His mother died. For half a year he went without work, living on nothing but bread and water, then he was hired as a bailiff. That position he occupied until he was dismissed on account of illness.

Never, even in his young student years, did he give the impression of being a healthy person. He was always pale, thin, subject to colds, ate little, slept badly. One glass of wine made him dizzy and hysterical. He was always drawn to people, but, owing to his irritable character and mistrustfulness, he never became close to anyone and had no friends. He always spoke scornfully of the townspeople, saying that he found their coarse ignorance and sluggish animal existence loathsome and repulsive. He spoke in a tenor voice, loudly, ardently, and not otherwise than with indignation and exasperation, or with rapture and astonishment, and always sincerely. Whatever you touched upon with him, he brought it all down to one thing: life in town is stifling and boring, society has no higher interests, it leads a dull, meaningless life, finding diversion in violence, coarse depravity, and hypocrisy; the scoundrels are sleek and well-dressed, while honest men feed on crumbs; there is a need for schools, for a local newspaper with an honest trend, a theater, public readings, a uniting of intellectual forces; society needs to become aware of itself and be horrified. In his judgments of people he laid the paint on thick, only white and black, not recognizing any shades; mankind was divided for him into honest people and scoundrels; there was no middle ground. Of women and love he always spoke passionately, with rapture, but he was never once in love.

Despite his nervousness and the sharpness of his judgments, he was liked in town and, behind his back, was affectionately called Vanya. His innate delicacy, obligingness, decency, moral purity, and his worn little frock coat, sickly appearance, and family misfortunes, inspired a kindly, warm, and sad feeling; besides, he was educated and well-read, knew everything, in the townspeople's opinion, and around town was something of a walking reference book.

He read a great deal. He used to sit in the club all the time, nervously pulling at his beard and leafing through magazines and books; one could see by his face that he was not reading but devouring, with barely any time to chew. It must be assumed that reading was one of his morbid habits, since he used to fall with equal appetite upon whatever was at hand, even the past year's newspapers and calendars.[1] At home he always read lying down.

III

One autumn morning, the collar of his coat turned up, splashing through the mud, Ivan Dmitrich was making his way by lanes and backyards to some tradesman to collect on a court claim. He was in a dark mood, as always in the morning. In one lane he met two prisoners in chains, being escorted by four armed soldiers. Ivan Dmitrich had often met prisoners before, and each time they called up feelings of compassion and awkwardness in him, but this time the encounter made a special, strange impression on him. For some reason it suddenly seemed to him that he, too, could be put in chains and led in the same way through the mud to prison. Returning home after calling on the tradesman, he met near the post office a police inspector he knew, who greeted him and walked a few steps down the street with him, and for some reason he found that suspicious. At home he could not get the prisoners and armed soldiers out of his head all day, and an incomprehensible inner anxiety kept him from reading and concentrating. He did not light the lamp in the evening, and during the night he did not sleep, but kept thinking about the possibility of his being arrested, put in chains, and taken to prison. He was not guilty of anything that he knew of and could pledge that he would never kill, or burn, or steal; yet it was not difficult to commit a crime accidentally, inadvertently, and was slander or, finally, a judicial error impossible? Not for nothing has age-old popular experience taught us that against poverty and prison there is no guarantee. And a judicial error, given present-day court procedures, was very possible, and it would be no wonder if it happened. Those who take an official, business-like attitude towards other people's suffering, like judges, policemen, doctors, from force of habit, as time goes by, become callous to such a degree that they would be unable to treat their clients otherwise than formally even if they wanted to; in this respect they are no different from the peasant who slaughters sheep and calves in his backyard without noticing the blood. With this formal, heartless attitude towards the person, a judge needs only one thing to deprive an innocent man of all his property rights and sentence him to hard labor: time. Only the time to observe certain formalities, for which the judge is paid a salary, and after that—it is all over. Then go looking for justice and protection in this dirty little town two hundred miles from the railroad! And is it not ridiculous to think of justice when society greets all violence as a reasonable and expedient necessity, and any act of mercy—an acquittal, for instance—provokes a great outburst of dissatisfied, vengeful feeling?

In the morning Ivan Dmitrich got out of bed in horror, with cold sweat on his brow, already quite convinced that he could be arrested at any moment. If yesterday's oppressive thoughts had not left him for so long, he thought, it meant there was a portion of truth in them. They could not, indeed, have come into his head without any reason.

A policeman unhurriedly passed by the windows: not for nothing. Here two men stopped near the house and stood silently. Why were they silent?

And painful days and nights began for Ivan Dmitrich. All who passed by his windows or entered the yard seemed like spies or sleuths to him. At noon the police chief usually drove down the street with his carriage and pair; he was coming to the police station from his outlying estate, but to Ivan Dmitrich it seemed each time that he was driving too fast and with some special expression: obviously he was hastening to announce that a very important criminal had appeared in town. Ivan Dmitrich jumped at each ring or knock at the gate; he suffered each time he met a new person at his landlady's; when he met policemen or gendarmes he smiled and began to whistle in order to appear indifferent. He did not sleep for whole nights, expecting to be arrested, but he snored loudly and sighed like a sleeping man, so that his landlady would think he was asleep; because if he did not sleep, it meant he was suffering from remorse—what evidence! Facts and logical sense insisted that all these fears were absurd and psychopathic, that, once one took a broader view, there was nothing especially terrible in arrest and prison—as long as his conscience was at ease; but the more sensible and logical his reasoning was, the more intense and painful his inner anxiety became. It resembled the story of the recluse who wanted to clear a little spot for himself in a virgin forest; the more zealously he worked with the axe, the deeper and thicker the forest grew. Seeing in the end that it was useless, Ivan Dmitrich abandoned reasoning altogether and gave himself up entirely to fear and despair.

He began to seek solitude and avoid people. His work had disgusted him even before, but now it became unbearable to him. He was afraid that someone might do him a bad turn, put a bribe in his pocket surreptitiously and then expose him, or that he himself might make a mistake tantamount to forgery in some official papers, or lose someone else's money. Strangely, his thought had never before been so supple and inventive as now, when he invented thousands of different pretexts every day for seriously fearing for his freedom and honor. But, on the other hand, his interest in the external world, particularly in books, weakened considerably, and his memory began to fail him badly.

In the spring, when the snow melted, two half-decayed corpses—of an old woman and a boy, with signs of violent death— were found in the ravine near the cemetery. These corpses and the unknown murderers became the only talk of the town. To make sure that people would not think he killed them, Ivan Dmitrich went about the streets smiling, and, on meeting his acquaintances, turned pale, then blushed and began assuring them that there was no meaner crime than the murder of the weak and defenseless. But he soon wearied of this lie and, after some reflection, decided that in his situation the best thing would be—to hide in his landlady's cellar. In that cellar he sat for a day, then a night, then another day, became very chilled, and, waiting till dark, made his way on the sly, like a thief, to his room. He stood till dawn in the middle of the room, motionless, listening. Early in the morning, before daybreak, some stovemakers came to his landlady's. Ivan Dmitrich knew very well that they had come to reset the stove in the kitchen, but fear whispered to him that they were policemen disguised as stovemakers. He quietly left the apartment and, gripped by terror, ran down the street without his hat and frock coat. Dogs chased after him, barking, a peasant shouted somewhere behind him, the wind whistled in his ears, and it seemed to Ivan Dmitrich that the violence of the whole world had gathered at his back and was pursuing him.

He was stopped, brought home, and the landlady went for the doctor. Dr. Andrei Yefimych, of whom we shall speak further on, prescribed cold compresses and laurel water, shook his head sadly, and left, telling the landlady that he would not come anymore, because people should not be prevented from losing their minds. Since there was no money for expenses and medications at home, Ivan Dmitrich was soon sent to the hospital, where he was put in the ward for venereal patients. He did not sleep at night, fussed and disturbed the patients, and soon, on orders from Andrei Yefimych, was transferred to Ward No. 6.

Within a year Ivan Dmitrich was completely forgotten in town, and his books, which the landlady dumped into a sleigh in the shed, were pilfered by street boys.

IV

Ivan Dmitrich's neighbor on the left, as I have already said, is the Jew Moiseika, and his neighbor on the right is a fat-swollen, nearly spherical peasant with a dumb, completely senseless face. He is an inert, gluttonous, and slovenly animal, who long ago lost the ability to think and feel. He constantly gives off a pungent, suffocating stench.

Nikita, who cleans up after him, beats him terribly, with all his might, not sparing his fists; and the terrible thing here is not that he is beaten—that one can get used to—but that this dumb animal does not respond to the beating either by sound or by movement, or by the expression of his eyes, but only rocks slightly like a heavy barrel.

The fifth and last inhabitant of Ward No. 6 is a tradesman who once worked as a sorter in the post office, a small, lean, blond fellow with a kind but somewhat sly face. Judging by his calm, intelligent eyes, which have a bright and cheerful look, he keeps his own counsel and has some very important and pleasant secret. He keeps something under his pillow or mattress that he does not show to anyone, not from fear that it might be taken away or stolen, but from bashfulness. Sometimes he goes to the window and, turning his back to his comrades, puts something on his chest and looks, craning his neck; if anyone approaches him at that moment, he gets embarrassed and tears the something off his chest. But his secret is not hard to guess.

"Congratulate me," he often says to Ivan Dmitrich, "I've been recommended for the Stanislas, second degree, with star.[2] The second degree with star is only given to foreigners, but for some reason they want to make an exception in my case," he smiles, shrugging his shoulders in perplexity. "I must confess, I really didn't expect it!"

"I understand nothing about that," Ivan Dmitrich says glumly.

"But do you know what I'll get sooner or later?" the former sorter continues, narrowing his eyes slyly. "I'm sure to get the Swedish 'Polar Star.'³ It's a decoration worth soliciting for. A white cross and a black ribbon. Very beautiful."

Probably nowhere else is life so monotonous as in this annex. In the morning the patients, except for the paralytic and the fat peasant, wash themselves from a big tub in the front hall, wiping themselves with the skirts of their robes; after that they have tea in tin mugs, which Nikita brings from the main building. Each of them gets one mug. At noon they eat pickled cabbage soup and kasha, and in the evening they have the kasha left over from dinner. In between they lie down, sleep, look out the windows, or pace up and down. And so it goes every day. Even the former sorter talks about the same decorations.

New people are seldom seen in Ward No. 6. The doctor long ago stopped accepting new madmen, and there are not many in this world who enjoy visiting madhouses. Once every two months the barber, Semyon Lazarich, visits the annex. Of how he gives the madmen haircuts, and how Nikita helps him to do it, and what commotion among the patients each appearance of the drunken, grinning barber causes, we will not speak.

Apart from the barber, no one comes to the annex. The patients are condemned to see only Nikita day after day.

Recently, however, a rather strange rumor spread through the hospital.

The rumor went around that the doctor had started visiting Ward No. 6.

V

Strange rumor!

Dr. Andrei Yefimych Ragin is a remarkable man in his way. They say that he was very pious in his youth, was preparing for a clerical career, and that, on graduating from high school in 1863, he intended to enter a theological academy, but that his father, a doctor of medicine and a surgeon, supposedly mocked him venomously and said categorically that he would not consider him his son if he became a priest. How much truth there is to it I do not know, but Andrei Yefimych himself admitted more than once that he never felt any vocation for medicine or generally for any particular science.

However that may be, having completed his studies in the medical faculty, he did not become a priest. He showed no devoutness, and resembled a clergyman as little at the start of his medical career as he does now.

His appearance is heavy, coarse, peasant-like; with his face, his beard, his lank hair and sturdy, clumsy build, he resembles a highway innkeeper, overfed, intemperate, and tough. His face is stern, covered with little blue veins, his eyes are small, his nose red. Tall and broad-shouldered, he has enormous hands and feet; it looks like one whack of his fist would be lights out. But he walks softly, and his gait is cautious and furtive; meeting you in a narrow corridor, he always stops first to make way, and says, not in a bass but in a high, soft tenor: "Excuse me!" He has a small growth on his neck that prevents him from wearing stiff, starched collars, and therefore he always goes about in soft linen or cotton shirts. Generally, he does not dress in doctorly fashion. He goes about in the same suit for some ten years, and new clothes, which he usually buys in a Jewish shop, seem as worn and wrinkled on him as the old; he receives patients, eats dinner, and goes visiting in the same frock coat; but that is not from stinginess, but from a total disregard for his appearance.

When Andrei Yefimych came to take up his post in town, the "charitable institution" was in a terrible state. In the wards, the corridors, and the hospital yard, it was hard to breathe for the stench. The peasant caretakers, nurses, and their children slept in the wards along with the patients. People complained that there was no bearing with the cockroaches, bedbugs and mice. Erysipelas had installed itself permanently in the surgery section. There were only two scalpels and not a single thermometer in the entire hospital; the baths served for storing potatoes. The superintendent, the matron, and the doctor's assistant robbed the patients, and of the old doctor, Andrei Yefimych's predecessor, it was said that he had secretly traded in hospital alcohol and had started a real harem for himself among the nurses and female patients. The townspeople were well aware of these disorders and even exaggerated them, but they viewed them calmly; some justified them by saying that only tradesmen and peasants stayed in the hospital, who could not be displeased, since they lived much worse at home than in the hospital—no one was going to feed them on grouse! Others said in justification that the town alone, without the help of the zemstvo,[4] was unable to maintain a good hospital; thank God they at least had a bad one. And the young zemstvo would not open a clinic either in town or near it, explaining that the town already had its own hospital.

Having inspected the hospital, Andrei Yefimych came to the conclusion that it was an immoral institution and highly detrimental to the health of the citizens. In his opinion, the most intelligent thing that could be done would be to discharge the patients and close the place down. But for that he reckoned that his will alone was not enough and in any case it would be useless; when physical and moral uncleanness was driven out of one place, it went to another; one had to wait until it dispersed of itself. Besides, if people had opened the hospital and put up with it in their town, it meant they needed it; prejudice and all this everyday filth and muck are necessary, because in time they turn into something useful, as dung turns into black earth. There is nothing good in the world that does not have some filth in its origin.

On taking over the post, Andrei Yefimych treated these disorders with apparent indifference. He merely asked the peasant caretakers and nurses not to sleep in the wards, and installed two cabinets with instruments. The superintendent, the matron, the assistant doctor, and the surgical erysipelas stayed where they were.

Andrei Yefimych is extremely fond of intelligence and honesty, but he lacks character and faith in his right to organize an intelligent and honest life around him. He is positively incapable of ordering, prohibiting, or insisting. It looks as if he has taken a vow never to raise his voice or speak in the imperative. To say "give" or "bring" is hard for him; when he wants to eat, he coughs irresolutely and says to his cook: "How about some tea?" or "How about some dinner?" But to tell the superintendent to stop stealing, or to dismiss him, or to abolish the useless, parasitic post altogether—is completely beyond his strength. When Andrei Yefimych is deceived or flattered, or handed a false receipt to sign knowingly, he turns as red as a lobster and feels guilty, but all the same he signs the receipt; when the patients complain to him that they are hungry or that the nurses are rude, he gets embarrassed and mutters guiltily:

"All right, all right, I'll look into it later . . . There's probably some misunderstanding . . ."

At first Andrei Yefimych worked very assiduously. He received every day from morning till dinnertime, did surgery and even took up the practice of obstetrics. Ladies said of him that he was attentive and excellent at diagnosing illnesses, especially in children and women. But as time went on he became noticeably bored with the monotony and obvious uselessness of the work. Today you receive thirty patients, and tomorrow, lo and behold, thirty-five come pouring in, and the next day forty, and so it goes, day after day, year after year, and the town mortality rate does not go down, and the patients do not stop coming. To give serious aid to forty outpatients between morning and dinnertime was physically impossible, which meant, willy-nilly, that it was all a deceit. During the fiscal year twelve thousand outpatients were received, which meant, simply speaking, that twelve thousand people were deceived. To put the seriously ill in the hospital and care for them according to the rules of science was also impossible, because while there were rules, there was no science; and to abandon philosophy and follow the rules pedantically, as other doctors did, you first of all needed cleanliness and ventilation, not filth, and wholesome food, not soup made from stinking pickled cabbage, and good assistants, not thieves.

Then, too, why prevent people from dying, if death is the normal and natural end of every man? So what if some dealer or clerk lives for an extra five or ten years? If the purpose of medical science is seen as the alleviation of suffering by medication, then, willy-nilly, the question arises: why alleviate it? First, they say that suffering leads man to perfection, and, second, if mankind really learns to alleviate its suffering with pills and drops, it will completely abandon religion and philosophy, in which it has hitherto found not only a defense against all calamities, but even happiness. Pushkin suffered terribly before death, poor Heine lay paralyzed for many years: why should there be no illness for some Andrei Yefimych or Matryona Savishna, whose life is insipid and would be completely empty and similar to the life of an amoeba were it not for suffering?

Oppressed by such reasoning, Andrei Yefimych threw up his hands and stopped going to the hospital every day.

VI

His life goes like this. Ordinarily he gets up in the morning at around eight, dresses and has tea. Then he sits in his study and reads or goes to the hospital. There, in the hospital, in a dark, narrow corridor, the outpatients sit waiting to be received. Peasants and nurses rush past them, their boots stomping on the brick floor, skinny patients in robes pass by, dead bodies and pots of excrement are carried out, children cry, a drafty wind blows. Andrei Yefimych knows that for the feverish, the consumptive, and the impressionable sick in general, such an atmosphere is torture, but what can he do? In the receiving room he is met by his assistant, Sergei Sergeich, a small, fat man with a clean-shaven, well-scrubbed, plump face, with soft, smooth manners, wearing a roomy new suit and looking more like a senator than an assistant doctor. He has an enormous practice in town, wears a white tie, and considers himself more knowledgeable than the doctor, who has no practice at all. In the corner of the receiving room stands a big icon in a case, with a heavy icon lamp, beside it a candle stand under a white cover; on the walls hang portraits of bishops, a view of the Svyatogorsk monastery, and wreaths of dried cornflowers. Sergei Sergeich is religious and a lover of the beauteous. The icon was installed at his expense; on Sundays one of the patients, on his orders, reads an akathist[5] aloud in the receiving room, and after the reading Sergei Sergeich himself makes the rounds of all the wards carrying a censer and censing everybody.

The patients are many, but time is short, and so the business is confined to a brief questioning and the dispensing of some sort of medicine like camphor ointment or castor oil. Andrei Yefimych sits with his cheek propped on his fist, deep in thought, and asks questions mechanically. Sergei Sergeich also sits rubbing his little hands and occasionally mixes in.

"We get sick and suffer want," he says, "because we don't pray properly to the merciful Lord. Yes!"

Andrei Yefimych does not do any surgery during receiving hours; he got out of the habit long ago, and the sight of blood upsets him unpleasantly. When he has to open a child's mouth to look down his throat, and the child shouts and resists with his little hands, the noise in his ears makes him giddy and tears come to his eyes. He hastens to prescribe some medicine and waves his arms, so that the peasant mother will quickly take the child away.

While receiving, he quickly becomes bored with the patients' timidity, their witlessness, the proximity of the beauteous Sergei Sergeich, the portraits on the walls, and his own questions, which he has been asking unvaryingly for twenty years now. And he leaves after receiving five or six patients. The assistant doctor receives the rest without him.

With the agreeable thought that, thank God, he has had no private practice for a long time, and that no one will bother him, Andrei Yefimych goes home, sits down immediately at the desk in his study, and begins to read. He reads a lot, and always with great pleasure. Half of his salary goes on books, and of the six rooms of his apartment, three are heaped with books and old magazines. He likes writings on history and philosophy most of all; in the field of medicine, he subscribes to *The Doctor,* which he always starts reading from the back. Each time the reading goes on uninterruptedly for several hours without tiring him. He does not read quickly and impulsively, as Ivan Dmitrich used to, but slowly, sensitively, often lingering over places that please or puzzle him. Beside the book there always stands a little carafe of vodka, and a pickled cucumber or apple lies directly on the baize, without a plate. Every half hour, without taking his eyes off the book, he pours himself a glass of vodka and drinks it, then, without looking, feels for the pickle and takes a bite.

At three o'clock he warily approaches the kitchen door, coughs, and says:

"Daryushka, how about some dinner . . ."

After dinner, rather poor and slovenly, Andrei Yefimych paces about his rooms, his arms folded on his chest, and thinks. It strikes four, then five, and still he paces and thinks. Occasionally the kitchen door creaks, and Daryushka's red, sleepy face peeks out.

"Andrei Yefimych, isn't it time you had your beer?" she asks worriedly.

"No, not yet . . ." he replies. "I'll wait a bit . . . wait a bit . . ."

Towards evening the postmaster, Mikhail Averyanych, usually comes, the only man in town whose company Andrei Yefimych does not find burdensome. Mikhail Averyanych was once a very rich landowner and served in the cavalry, but he was ruined and, out of need, joined the postal service in his old age. He has a hale and hearty look, magnificent gray side-whiskers, well-bred manners, and a loud, pleasant voice. He is kind and sensitive, but hottempered. When a client at the post office protests, disagrees, or simply begins to argue, Mikhail Averyanych turns purple, shakes all over, and in a thundering voice shouts: "Silence!" so that the post office has long since acquired the reputation of an institution one fears to visit. Mikhail Averyanych respects and loves Andrei Yefimych for his education and nobility of soul, but to the rest of the townspeople he behaves haughtily, as to his own subordinates.

"And here I am!" he says, coming in to Andrei Yefimych's. "Good evening, my dear! You must be tired of me by now, eh?"

"On the contrary, I'm very glad," the doctor replies. "I'm always glad to see you."

The friends sit down on the sofa in the study and smoke silently for a time.

"Daryushka, how about some beer!" says Andrei Yefimych.

The first bottle is also drunk silently—the doctor deep in thought, and Mikhail Averyanych with a merry, animated air, like a man who has something very interesting to tell. It is always the doctor who begins the conversation.

"What a pity," he says slowly and softly, shaking his head and not looking his interlocutor in the eye (he never looks anyone in the eye), "what a great pity, my esteemed Mikhail Averyanych, that our town is totally lacking in people who enjoy and are capable of carrying on an intelligent and interesting conversation. That is an enormous privation for us. Even the intelligentsia is not above banality; the level of its development, I assure you, is no whit higher than in the lower estates."

"Quite right. I agree."

"You yourself are aware," the doctor continues softly and measuredly, "that everything in this world is insignificant and uninteresting except the higher spiritual manifestations of human reason. Reason draws a sharp distinction between animal and man, hints at the divinity of the latter, and for him, to a certain degree, even takes the place of immortality, which does not exist. Hence, reason is the only possible source of pleasure. We, however, neither see nor hear any reason around us—which means we are deprived of pleasure. True, we have books, but that is not at all the same as live conversation and intercourse. If you will permit me a not entirely successful comparison, books are the scores, while conversation is the singing."

"Quite right."

Silence ensues. Daryushka comes from the kitchen and, with an expression of dumb grief, her face propped on her fist, stops in the doorway to listen.

"Ah!" sighs Mikhail Averyanych. "To ask reason of people nowadays!"

And he talks about how life used to be wholesome, gay, and interesting, what a smart intelligentsia there was in Russia and how highly it placed the notions of honor and friendship. Money was lent without receipt, and it was considered a disgrace not to offer a helping hand to a needy comrade. "And what campaigns, adventures, skirmishes there were, what comrades, what women! And the Caucasus—what an astonishing country! And the wife of one of the battalion commanders, a strange woman, used to dress up as an officer and ride off into the mountains in the evening alone, without an escort. They said she was having a romance with some princeling in a village there."

"Saints alive . . ." Daryushka sighs.

"And how they drank! How they ate! What desperate liberals they were!"

Andrei Yefimych listens and hears nothing; he ponders something and sips his beer.

"I often dream about intelligent people and conversations with them," he says unexpectedly, interrupting Mikhail Averyanych. "My father gave me an excellent education, but, influenced by the ideas of the sixties,[6] he forced me to become a doctor. I think that if I hadn't obeyed him, I would now be at the very center of the intellectual movement. I would probably be a member of some faculty. Of course, reason is not eternal and also passes, but you already know why I am well disposed towards it. Life is a vexing trap. When a thinking man reaches maturity and attains to adult consciousness, he involuntarily feels as if he is in a trap from which there is no escape. Indeed, against his will he is called by certain accidents from non-being into life . . . Why? He wants to learn the meaning and aim of his existence, and he is not told or else is told absurdities; he knocks—it is not opened; death comes to him—also against his will. And so, as people in prison, bound by a common misfortune, feel better when they come together, so also in life the trap can be disregarded when people inclined to analysis and generalization come together and spend time exchanging proud, free ideas. In this sense reason is an irreplaceable pleasure."

"Quite right."

Without looking his interlocutor in the eye, softly and with pauses, Andrei Yefimych goes on talking about intelligent people and his conversations with them, and Mikhail Averyanych listens to him attentively and agrees: "Quite right."

"And you don't believe in the immortality of the soul?" the postmaster suddenly asks.

"No, my esteemed Mikhail Averyanych, I do not believe in it and have no grounds for doing so."

"I confess that I, too, have doubts. Though, incidentally, I have the feeling that I'll never die. Hey, I think to myself, you old duffer, it's time for you to die! And a little voice in my soul says: don't believe it, you won't die! . . ."

After nine, Mikhail Averyanych leaves. Putting his fur coat on in the front hall, he says with a sigh:

"But what a hole the fates have brought us to! The most vexing thing is that we'll have to die here as well. Ah! . . ."

VII

After seeing his friend off, Andrei Yefimych sits down at the desk and again begins to read. The stillness of the evening and then the night is not broken by any sound, and time seems to stop, transfixed, with the doctor over the book, and it seems that nothing exists except for this book and the lamp with its green shade. The doctor's coarse, peasant face gradually lights up with a smile of tenderness and delight at the movements of the human spirit. Oh, why is man not immortal? he thinks. Why brain centers and convolutions, why sight, speech, self-awareness, genius, if it is all doomed to sink into the ground and in the final end to cool down along with the earth's crust and then whirl without sense or purpose, for millions of years, with the earth around the sun? For that cooling down and whirling around there was no need at all to bring man out of non-being, along with his lofty, almost divine reason, and then, as if in mockery, turn him into clay.

The life cycle! But what cowardice to comfort oneself with this surrogate of immortality! The unconscious processes that occur in nature are even lower than human stupidity, for in stupidity there is still consciousness and will, while in these processes there is nothing. Only a coward whose fear of death is greater than his dignity can comfort himself with the thought that in time his body will live in grass, a stone, a toad . . . To see one's own immortality in the life cycle is as strange as to prophesy a brilliant future to the case after the costly violin has been broken and made useless.

When the clock strikes, Andrei Yefimych throws himself back in his armchair and closes his eyes in order to think a little. And inadvertently, under the influence of the good thoughts he has found in his book, he casts a glance over his past and present. The past is repulsive, better not to recall it. And the present is the same as the past. He knows that all the while his thoughts are whirling together with the cooled-down earth around the sun, in the big building next door to the doctor's apartment people are languishing in disease and physical uncleanness; perhaps someone is lying awake and battling with insects, or someone is coming down with erysipelas or moaning because his bandage is too tight; perhaps the patients are playing cards with the nurses and drinking vodka. Twelve thousand people have been deceived during the fiscal year; the whole hospital business, just as twenty years ago, is built on theft, squabbles, gossip, chumminess, crude charlatanism, and, just as before, the hospital is an immoral institution, highly detrimental to the townspeople's health. He knows that in Ward No. 6, behind the grilles, Nikita is beating the patients, and that Moiseika goes around town every day begging for alms.

On the other hand, he knows perfectly well that a fabulous change has come over medicine in the last twenty-five years. When he was studying at the university, it seemed to him that the same lot that had befallen alchemy and metaphysics would soon befall medicine, but now, when he reads at night, medicine touches him and arouses astonishment and even rapture in him. Indeed, what unexpected splendor, what a revolution! Owing to antiseptics, such operations are performed as the great Pirogov[7] considered impossible even *in spe*.[8] Ordinary zemstvo doctors dare to perform resections of the knee, only one out of a hundred Caesarean sections ends in death, and gallstones are considered such a trifle that no one even writes about them. Syphilis can be radically cured. And the theory of heredity, hypnotism, the discoveries of Pasteur and Koch,[9] hygiene, and statistics, and our Russian zemstvo doctors? Psychiatry, with its present-day classification of illnesses, its methods of diagnosis and treatment, is a whole Mt. Elbrus[10] compared to what it used to be. No one pours cold water over madmen's heads now, or puts them in straitjackets: they are kept like human beings and, as the newspapers report, even have performances and balls organized for them. Andrei Yefimych knows that, given present-day views and tastes, such an abomination as Ward No. 6 is perhaps only possible two hundred miles from the railroad, in a town where the mayor and all the councilmen are semi-literate bourgeois, who see a doctor as a sort of priest who is to be believed without any criticism, even if he starts pouring molten tin down people's throats; anywhere else the public and the newspapers would long ago have smashed this little Bastille to bits.

"Well, so?" Andrei Yefimych asks himself, opening his eyes. "What of it? Antiseptics, and Koch, and Pasteur, but the essence of the matter hasn't changed at all. The rates of sickness and mortality remain the same. Balls and performances are organized for the mad, but even so they're not released. That means it's all nonsense and vanity, and in essence there's no difference between the best clinic in Vienna and my hospital."

But sorrow and a feeling akin to envy interfere with his indifference. It must be from fatigue. His heavy head sinks onto the book, he puts his hands under his face to make it softer, and thinks:

"I serve a harmful cause, and I receive a salary from the people I deceive. I am dishonest. But by myself I'm nothing, I'm merely a particle of an inevitable social evil: all provincial officials are harmful and receive their salaries for nothing . . . So it is not I who am to blame for my dishonesty, but the times . . . If I had been born two hundred years later, I would be different."

When it strikes three, he puts out the lamp and goes to the bedroom. He does not feel like sleeping.

VIII

About two years ago the zemstvo waxed generous and decided to allot three hundred roubles annually to subsidize the reinforcement of medical personnel in the town hospital, until such time as the zemstvo hospital opened, and the town invited a district doctor, Evgeny Fyodorych Khobotov, to assist Andrei Yefimych. He is still a very young man—not yet thirty—tall, dark-haired, with broad cheekbones and small eyes; his ancestors probably belonged to a racial minority. He arrived in town without a cent, with a small suitcase and a homely young woman whom he calls his cook. This woman had a baby at the breast. Evgeny Fyodorych goes about in a peaked cap and high boots, and in winter wears a short jacket. He has become close with the assistant doctor, Sergei Sergeich, and with the treasurer, and for some reason calls the rest of the officials aristocrats and shuns them. There is only one book in his whole apartment: *Latest Prescriptions of the Vienna Clinic for 1881*. When he visits a patient, he always takes this book with him. In the evening, he plays billiards at the club, but he does not like cards. He has a great fondness for introducing into his conversation such words as "flim-flam," "mantifolia with vinegar," "you're just blowing smoke," and so on.

He comes to the hospital twice a week, makes the rounds of the wards, and receives patients. The total absence of antiseptics and the use of cupping glasses[11] make him indignant, but he does not introduce any new rules for fear of insulting Andrei Yefimych. He considers his colleague Andrei Yefimych an old swindler, suspects him of having great means, and secretly envies him. He would gladly take over his post.

IX

One spring evening at the end of March, when there was no more snow on the ground and the starlings were singing in the hospital garden, the doctor went outside to see his friend the postmaster to the gate. Just then the Jew Moiseika, returning from his hunt, came into the yard. He was hatless, had low galoshes on his bare feet, and was carrying a small bag of alms.

"Give me a little kopeck!" he addressed the doctor, shivering with cold and smiling.

Andrei Yefimych, who could never say no, gave him ten kopecks.

"This is so wrong," he thought, looking at his bare legs and red, skinny ankles. "It's wet out."

And, moved by a feeling akin to both pity and squeamishness, he followed the Jew to the annex, looking alternately at his bald spot and his ankles. As the doctor came in, Nikita jumped off the pile of rubbish and stood up straight.

"Hello, Nikita," Andrei Yefimych said softly. "How about giving this Jew some boots, otherwise he'll catch cold."

"Yes, Your Honor! I'll report it to the superintendent."

"Please do. Ask him on my behalf. Tell him I asked for it."

The door from the hall to the ward was open. Ivan Dmitrich, who lay in bed propped on one elbow, listened anxiously to the strange voice and suddenly recognized the doctor. He shook all over with wrath, jumped up, and, his face red and angry, his eyes popping, rushed to the middle of the room.

"The doctor has come!" he cried and burst into loud laughter. "At last! Gentlemen, I congratulate you, the doctor has bestowed a visit upon us! Cursed vermin!" he shrieked and stamped his foot in a frenzy such as had not been seen in the ward before. "Kill the vermin! No, killing's not enough! Drown him in the outhouse!"

Andrei Yefimych, hearing that, peeked into the room and asked softly:

"What for?"

"What for?" cried Ivan Dmitrich, approaching him with a menacing look and convulsively wrapping his robe around him. "What for? Thief!" he said with disgust, pursing his lips as if he were about to spit. "Charlatan! Hangman!"

"Calm yourself," said Andrei Yefimych, smiling guiltily. "I assure you, I've never stolen anything, and as for the rest, you are probably exaggerating greatly. I can see that you are angry with me. Calm yourself, if you can, I beg you, and tell me coolheadedly: why are you angry?"

"And why do you keep me here?"

"Because you are ill."

"Ill, yes. But dozens, hundreds, of madmen are walking around free, because in your ignorance you are unable to tell them from the sane. Why, then, must I and these unfortunates sit here for all of them, like scapegoats? In the moral respect, you, your assistant, the superintendent, and all your hospital scum are immeasurably lower than any of us, so why do we sit here and not you? Where's the logic?"

"Logic and the moral respect have nothing to do with it. It all depends on chance. Those who have been put here, sit here, and those who have not are walking around, that's all. That I am a doctor and you are a mental patient has no morality or logic in it—it's a matter of pure chance."

"I don't understand that gibberish . . ." Ivan Dmitrich said dully, and he sat down on his bed.

Moiseika, whom Nikita was embarrassed to search in the doctor's presence, laid out his pieces of bread, scraps of paper, and little bones on the bed and, still shivering with cold, began saying something rapidly and melodiously in Hebrew. He probably imagined he had opened a shop.

"Release me!" said Ivan Dmitrich, and his voice trembled.

"I can't."

"But why not? Why not?"

"Because it's not in my power. Consider, what good will it do you if I release you? Go now. The townspeople or the police will stop you and bring you back."

"Yes, yes, it's true . . ." said Ivan Dmitrich, and he rubbed his forehead. "It's terrible! But what am I to do? What?"

Andrei Yefimych liked Ivan Dmitrich's voice and his young, intelligent face with its grimaces. He wished to be kind to the young man and calm him down. He sat beside him on the bed, thought a little, and said:

"You ask, what is to be done? The best thing in your situation would be to run away from here. But, unfortunately, that is useless. You'll be stopped. When society protects itself from criminals, the mentally ill, and generally inconvenient people, it is invincible. One thing is left for you: to rest with the thought that your being here is necessary."

"Nobody needs it."

"Since prisons and madhouses exist, someone must sit in them. If not you, then me; if not me, some third person. Wait till the distant future, when there will be no more prisons and madhouses; then there will be no bars on the windows, no hospital robes. Such a time is sure to come sooner or later."

Ivan Dmitrich smiled mockingly.

"You're joking," he said, narrowing his eyes. "Gentlemen like you and your helper Nikita don't care about the future at all, but rest assured, my dear sir, that better times will come! My expressions may be banal, you may laugh, but the dawn of the new life will shine forth, truth will triumph, and—it will be our turn to celebrate! I won't live to see it, I'll croak, but somebody's great-grandchildren will see it. I greet them with all my heart, and I rejoice, I rejoice for them! Forward! May God help you, my friends!"

Ivan Dmitrich, his eyes shining, got up and, stretching his arms towards the window, went on in an excited voice:

"From behind these bars I bless you! Long live the truth! I rejoice!"

"I see no special reason for rejoicing," said Andrei Yefimych, who found Ivan Dmitrich's gesture theatrical, but at the same time liked it very much. "There won't be any prisons and madhouses, and truth, as you were pleased to put it, will triumph, but the essence of things will not change, the laws of nature will remain the same. People will get sick, grow old, and die, just as they do now. However magnificent the dawn that lights up your life, in the end you'll still be nailed up in a coffin and thrown into a hole."

"And immortality?"

"Oh, come now!"

"You don't believe in it. Well, but I do. In Dostoevsky or Voltaire somebody says if there were no God, people would have invented him.[12] And I deeply believe that if there is no immortality, sooner or later the great human mind will invent it."

"Well said," pronounced Andrei Yefimych, smiling with pleasure. "It's good that you believe. With such faith one can live beautifully even bricked up in a wall. You must have received some education?"

"Yes, I studied at the university, but I didn't finish."

"You're a thinking and perceptive man. You can find peace within yourself under any circumstances. Free and profound thought, which strives towards the comprehension of life, and a complete scorn for the foolish vanity of the world—man has never known anything higher than these two blessings. And you can possess them even if you live behind triple bars. Diogenes[13] lived in a barrel, yet he was happier than all the kings of the earth."

"Your Diogenes was a blockhead," Ivan Dmitrich said sullenly. "What are you telling me about Diogenes and some sort of comprehension?" He suddenly became angry and jumped up. "I love life, I love it passionately! I have a persecution mania, a constant, tormenting fear, but there are moments when I'm seized by a thirst for life, and then I'm afraid of losing my mind. I want terribly to live, terribly!"

He paced about the ward in agitation and said in a lowered voice:

"When I dream, I'm visited by phantoms. People come to me, I hear voices, music, and it seems to me that I'm strolling in some forest, on the seashore, and I want so passionately to have cares, concerns . . . Tell me, what's new there?" asked Ivan Dmitrich. "How are things?"

"Do you wish to know about the town or generally?"

"Well, first tell me about the town and then generally."

"How is it? In town, excruciatingly boring . . . There's nobody to talk to, nobody to listen to. There are no new people. Though the young doctor Khobotov came recently."

"He came while I was still there. A boor, or what?"

"Yes, an uncultivated man. It's strange, you know . . . To all appearances, there is no intellectual stagnation in our capitals, there is movement—meaning that there must be real people there—but for some reason they always send us such people that you can't stand the sight of them! A wretched town!"

"Yes, a wretched town!" Ivan Dmitrich said and laughed. "And how is it generally? What are they writing in the newspapers and magazines?"

It was already dark in the ward. The doctor got up and, standing, began to tell about what people were writing abroad and in Russia and what trends of thought could be observed at present. Ivan Dmitrich listened attentively and asked questions, but suddenly, as if recalling something terrible, clutched his head and lay down on the bed, his back to the doctor.

"What's wrong?" asked Andrei Yefimych.

"You won't hear another word from me!" Ivan Dmitrich said rudely. "Leave me alone!"

"But why?"

"Leave me alone, I tell you! What the devil do you want?"

Andrei Yefimych shrugged, sighed, and went out. Passing through the front hall, he said:

"How about cleaning up here, Nikita . . . It smells awful!"

"Yes, Your Honor!"

"What a nice young man!" thought Andrei Yefimych as he walked to his own quarters. "In all the time I've lived here, it seems he's the first with whom one can talk. He knows how to reason and is interested in precisely the right things."

Reading and then lying in bed, he kept thinking about Ivan Dmitrich, and waking up the next morning, he remembered that he had made the acquaintance of an intelligent and interesting man yesterday and resolved to visit him again at the first opportunity.

X

Ivan Dmitrich lay in the same posture as yesterday, his head clutched in his hands and his legs drawn up. His face could not be seen.

"Good day, my friend," said Andrei Yefimych. "Are you asleep?"

"First of all, I'm not your friend," Ivan Dmitrich said into the pillow, "and second, you're troubling yourself in vain: you won't get a single word out of me."

"Strange . . ." Andrei Yefimych murmured in embarrassment. "Yesterday we talked so peaceably, but for some reason you suddenly became offended and broke off all at once . . . I probably expressed myself somehow awkwardly, or perhaps voiced a thought that doesn't agree with your convictions . . ."

"Yes, I'll believe you just like that!" said Ivan Dmitrich, rising a little and looking at the doctor mockingly and with alarm; his eyes were red. "You can do your spying and testing somewhere else, you've got no business here. I already understood yesterday why you came."

"Strange fantasy!" smiled the doctor. "So you think I'm a spy?"

"Yes, I do . . . A spy or a doctor assigned to test me—it's all the same."

"Ah, really, what a . . . forgive me . . . what an odd man you are!"

The doctor sat down on a stool by the bed and shook his head reproachfully.

"But suppose you're right," he said. "Suppose I treacherously try to snatch at some word in order to betray you to the police. You'll be arrested and then tried. But will it be worse for you in court or prison than it is here? And if you're sent into exile or even to hard labor, is that worse than sitting in this annex? I suppose not . . . So what are you afraid of?"

These words obviously affected Ivan Dmitrich. He quietly sat up.

It was between four and five in the afternoon, the time when

Andrei Yefimych usually paced his rooms and Daryushka asked him whether it was time for his beer. The weather outside was calm and clear.

"I went for a stroll after dinner and stopped by, as you see," said the doctor. "Spring has come."

"What month is it now? March?" asked Ivan Dmitrich.

"Yes, the end of March."

"Is it muddy outside?"

"No, not very. There are footpaths in the garden already."

"It would be nice to go for a ride in a carriage somewhere out of town now," said Ivan Dmitrich, rubbing his red eyes as if he had just woken up, "then come back home to a warm, cozy study and . . . have a decent doctor treat your headache . . . I haven't lived like a human being for so long. It's vile here! Insufferably vile!"

After yesterday's agitation he was tired and sluggish and spoke reluctantly. His fingers trembled, and one could see by his face that he had a bad headache.

"There's no difference between a warm, cozy study and this ward," said Andrei Yefimych. "A man's peace and content are not outside but within him."

"How so?"

"An ordinary man expects the good or the bad from outside, that is, from a carriage and a study, but a thinking man expects them from himself."

"Go and preach that philosophy in Greece, where it's warm and smells of wild orange, it doesn't go with the climate here. Who was I talking about Diogenes with? Was it you, eh?"

"Yes, with me, yesterday."

"Diogenes didn't need a study and a warm room; it's hot there as it is. You can lie in a barrel and eat oranges and olives. But if he lived in Russia, he'd ask for a room not only in December but even in May. He'd be doubled up with cold."

"No. Like all pain in general, it's possible not to feel cold. Marcus Aurelius[14] said: 'Pain is the living notion of pain: make an effort of will to change this notion, remove it, stop complaining, and the pain will disappear.' That is correct. The wise man, or simply the thinking, perceptive man, is distinguished precisely by his scorn of suffering; he is always content and is surprised at nothing."

"Then I'm an idiot, since I suffer, am discontent, and am surprised at human meanness."

"You needn't be. If you reflect on it more often, you will understand how insignificant is everything external that troubles us. We must strive for the comprehension of life, therein lies the true blessing."

"Comprehension . . ." Ivan Dmitrich winced. "External, internal . . . Excuse me, but I don't understand that. I only know," he said, getting up and looking angrily at the doctor, "I know that God created me out of warm blood and nerves, yes, sir! And organic tissue, if it's viable, must react to any irritation. And I do react! I respond to pain with cries and tears, to meanness with indignation, to vileness with disgust. In my opinion, this is in fact called life. The lower the organism, the less sensitive it is and the more weakly it responds to irritation, and the higher, the more susceptible it is and the more energetically it reacts to reality. How can you not know that? You're a doctor and you don't know such trifles! To scorn suffering, to be always content and surprised at nothing, you must reach that condition"—and Ivan Dmitrich pointed to the obese, fat-swollen peasant—"or else harden yourself with suffering to such a degree that you lose all sensitivity to it, that is, in other words, stop living. Forgive me, I'm not a wise man or a philosopher," Ivan Dmitrich went on irritably, "and I understand nothing about it. I'm unable to reason."

"On the contrary, your reasoning is excellent."

"The Stoics, whom you are parodying, were remarkable people, but their teaching froze two thousand years ago and hasn't moved a drop further, and it won't, because it's neither practical nor vital. It was successful only with the minority who spend their life examining and relishing various teachings, but the majority didn't understand it. A teaching that preaches indifference to wealth, to the good things in life, scorn of suffering and death, is utterly incomprehensible for the vast majority, since that majority has never known either wealth or the good things in life; and for them scorn of suffering would mean scorn of life itself, because the whole essence of man consists in the sensations of hunger, cold, offense, loss, and a Hamletian fear of death. These sensations are the whole of life: you may be oppressed by it, you may hate it, but you cannot scorn it. Yes, so I repeat, the teaching of the Stoics can have no future, and progress, from the beginning of time down to this day, as

you see, belongs to struggle, the sensitivity to pain, the ability to respond to irritation . . ."

Ivan Dmitrich suddenly lost his train of thought, stopped, and
rubbed his forehead vexedly.

"I wanted to say something important, but I got confused," he
said. "What was it about? Yes! So, I was saying: one of the Stoics
sold himself into slavery in order to buy off his neighbor. You see,
so the Stoic, too, reacted to an irritation, because for such a magnanimous act as destroying yourself for the sake of your neighbor,
you must have an indignant, compassionate soul. Here in prison
I've forgotten everything I studied, otherwise I'd remember more.
But take Christ? Christ responded to reality by weeping, smiling,
grieving, being wrathful, even anguished; he didn't go to meet suffering with a smile, nor did he scorn death, but he prayed in the
garden of Gethsemane for this cup to pass from him."[15]

Ivan Dmitrich laughed and sat down.

"Suppose that man's peace and content are not outside but
within him," he said. "Suppose that we ought to scorn suffering
and be surprised at nothing. But what is your basis for preaching it?
Are you a wise man? A philosopher?"

"No, I'm not a philosopher, but everyone ought to preach it, because it's reasonable."

"No, I want to know why you consider yourself competent in
matters of comprehension, scorn of suffering, and the rest. Have
you ever suffered? Do you have any notion of suffering? Excuse me:
were you ever birched as a child?"

"No, my parents detested corporal punishment."

"Well, my father whipped me cruelly. My father was a tough,
hemorrhoidal official with a long nose and a yellow neck. But
let's talk about you. In all your life nobody ever laid a finger on you,
nobody frightened you, nobody beat you; you're sturdy as an ox.
You grew up under your father's wing and studied at his expense,
and then at once grabbed a sinecure. For more than twenty years
you've had free quarters, with heat, light, servants, besides having
the right to work as you want and as much as you want, or even not
to work at all. By nature you're a lazy man, a soft man, and therefore you tried to shape your life so that nothing would trouble you
or make you stir from your place. You shifted all the work onto
your assistant and other scum, and you yourself sat around, warm
and peaceful, saving up money, reading books, delighting yourself

with thoughts about all sorts of nonsense, and" (Ivan Dmitrich looked at the doctor's red nose) "tippling away. In short, you've never seen life, you don't know anything about it, and you're only theoretically acquainted with reality. And you scorn suffering and are surprised at nothing for a very simple reason: vanity of vanities, external and internal scorn of life, of suffering, and of death, comprehension, the true blessing—all that is a most suitable philosophy for a Russian lie-about. You see a peasant beating his wife, for instance. Why interfere? Let him beat her, they'll both die sooner or later anyway; and besides, the man who beats someone only insults himself, not the one he beats. To be a drunkard is stupid, indecent, but one drinks and dies, or does not drink and dies. A peasant woman comes with a toothache . . . So what? Pain is the notion of pain, and besides, one cannot live in this world without sickness, and we'll all die, so go away, woman, don't interfere with my thinking and my vodka drinking. A young man asks for advice, what to do, how to live; another man would stop and think before answering, but here the answer is ready: strive for comprehension, that is, for the true blessing. And what is this fantastic 'true blessing'? There is no answer, of course. We're kept behind bars here, to rot and be tortured, but that's beautiful and reasonable, because there's no difference between this ward and a warm, cozy study. A convenient philosophy: no need to do anything, and your conscience is clear, and you feel yourself a wise man . . . No, sir, that's not philosophy, not thinking, not breadth of vision, it's laziness, fakirism, a dreamy stupor . . . Yes!" Ivan Dmitrich became angry again. "You scorn suffering, but I suppose if you pinched your finger in the door, you'd howl your head off!"

"Maybe I wouldn't," said Andrei Yefimych, smiling meekly.

"Oh, surely! And if you were suddenly slapped with paralysis or, say, some brazen fool, taking advantage of his position and rank, insulted you publicly, and you knew he'd go unpunished—well, then you'd understand how it is to fob others off with comprehension and the true blessing."

"That's original," Andrei Yefimych said, laughing with pleasure and rubbing his hands. "I'm pleasantly surprised by your inclination to generalize, and the characterization of me that you've just produced is simply brilliant. I confess, conversation with you gives me great pleasure. Well, sir, I've heard you out, now you kindly hear me out . . ."

XI

This conversation went on for another hour or so and evidently made a deep impression on Andrei Yefimych. He began visiting the annex every day. He went in the morning and after dinner, and often the evening darkness found him conversing with Ivan Dmitrich. At first Ivan Dmitrich was shy with him, suspected him of evil intentions, and openly expressed his animosity, but then he got used to him and changed his cutting manner to a condescendingly ironic one.

The rumor soon spread through the hospital that Dr. Andrei Yefimych had begun visiting Ward No. 6. No one, neither his assistant, nor Nikita, nor the nurses, could understand why he went there, why he sat there for hours at a time, what he talked about, why he did not make any prescriptions. His behavior seemed strange. Mikhail Averyanych often did not find him at home, something that had never happened before, and Daryushka was very confused, because the doctor no longer drank his beer at a certain time and occasionally was even late for dinner.

Once—this was already at the end of June—Dr. Khobotov came to see Andrei Yefimych on some business; not finding him at home, he went to look for him in the yard; there he was told that the old doctor had gone to visit the mental patients. Khobotov went into the annex and, stopping in the front hall, heard the following conversation:

"We'll never see eye to eye, and you won't succeed in converting me to your faith," Ivan Dmitrich was saying vexedly. "You're totally unacquainted with reality, and you've never suffered, but, like a leech, have only fed on the sufferings of others, while I have suffered constantly from the day of my birth to this very day. Therefore I tell you frankly that I consider myself superior to you and more competent in all respects. It's not for you to teach me."

"I make no pretense of converting you to my faith," Andrei Yefimych said softly, regretting that the other refused to understand him. "And that is not the point, my friend. The point is not that you have suffered and I have not. Sufferings and joys are transient; let's drop them, with God's blessing. The point is that you and I think; we see in each other people who are able to think and reason, and that makes for solidarity between us, however different our views may be. If you knew, my friend, how tired I am of the general madness, giftlessness, obtuseness, and with what joy I talk with you each time! You're an intelligent man, and I delight in you."

Khobotov opened the door an inch and peeked into the room. Dr. Andrei Yefimych and Ivan Dmitrich in his nightcap were sitting side by side on the bed. The madman grimaced, twitched, and convulsively wrapped his robe around him, while the doctor sat motionless, his head bowed, his face red, helpless, and sad. Khobotov shrugged, grinned, and exchanged glances with Nikita. Nikita also shrugged.

The next day Khobotov came to the annex together with the assistant doctor. The two stood in the front hall and eavesdropped.

"It seems our grandpa's gone completely loony," said Khobotov, leaving the annex.

"God have mercy on us sinners!" sighed the beauteous Sergei Sergeich, carefully sidestepping the puddles to avoid muddying his brightly polished boots. "I confess, my esteemed Evgeny Fyodorych, I've long been expecting that!"

XII

After that Andrei Yefimych began to notice a certain mysteriousness around him. The peasants, the nurses, and the patients, when they met him, glanced at him inquisitively and then whispered. The little girl Masha, the superintendent's daughter, whom he enjoyed meeting in the hospital garden, now, when he came up to her with a smile to pat her on the head, for some reason ran away from him. The postmaster, Mikhail Averyanych, listening to him, no longer said: "Quite right," but muttered in inexplicable embarrassment: "Yes, yes, yes . . ." and looked at him wistfully and sadly. For some reason he began advising his friend to give up vodka and beer, but, being a delicate man, spoke not directly but in hints, telling now about a certain battalion commander, an excellent man, now about a regimental priest, a nice fellow, both of whom drank themselves sick, but when they stopped drinking became completely well. Two or three times Andrei Yefimych's colleague Khobotov came to see him; he, too, advised him to give up alcohol and, for no apparent reason, recommended that he take potassium bromide.

In August Andrei Yefimych received a letter from the mayor with a request that he kindly come on a very important matter. Arriving at the town hall at the appointed time, Andrei Yefimych found there the military commander, the inspector of the district high school, a member of the town council, Khobotov, and yet another stout, blond gentleman, who was introduced to him as a doctor. This doctor, who had a Polish name that was very hard to pronounce, lived on a stud farm twenty miles away and was just passing through town.

"Here's a little application along your lines, sir," the member of the council addressed Andrei Yefimych, after they had all exchanged greetings and sat down at the table. "Evgeny Fyodorych says here that there's not enough room for the dispensary in the main building, and that it ought to be transferred to one of the annexes. That's all right, of course, the transfer is possible, but the main concern is that the annex will need renovation."

"Yes, it won't do without renovation," Andrei Yefimych said, after some reflection. "If, for example, we decide to fit out the corner annex as a dispensary, we'll need a minimum of five hundred roubles. An unproductive expense."

A short silence ensued.

"I already had the honor of reporting ten years ago," Andrei Yefimych went on in a low voice, "that this hospital in its present state is a luxury beyond the town's means. It was built in the forties, but the means were different then. The town spends too much on unnecessary buildings and superfluous jobs. I think that with a different system it would be possible to run two model hospitals on the same money."

"Then let's set up a different system!" the member of the council said briskly.

"As I've already had the honor of reporting, the medical area should be transferred to the jurisdiction of the zemstvo."

"Yes, transfer the money to the zemstvo, and let them steal it," the blond doctor laughed.

"That's just what they'll do," said the council member, and he also laughed.

Andrei Yefimych gave the blond doctor a dull and listless look and said:

"We must be fair."

Another silence ensued. Tea was served. The military commander, very embarrassed for some reason, touched Andrei Yefimych's hand across the table and said:

"You've quite forgotten us, doctor. You're a monk, anyhow: you don't play cards, you don't like women. You're bored with our sort."

Everybody began talking about how boring it was for a decent man to live in this town. No theater, no music, and at the last club dance there were some twenty ladies and only two gentlemen. The young people do not dance but spend all their time crowding around the buffet or playing cards. Slowly and softly, without looking at anyone, Andrei Yefimych began to say how regrettable, how deeply regrettable, it was that the townspeople put their life's energy, their hearts and minds, into playing cards or gossiping, and neither can nor wish to spend time in interesting conversation or reading, to enjoy the delights furnished by the mind. The mind alone is interesting and remarkable, while the rest is petty and base. Khobotov listened attentively to his colleague and suddenly asked:

"Andrei Yefimych, what is the date today?"

Having received an answer, he and the blond doctor, in the tone of examiners aware of their incompetence, began to ask Andrei Yefimych what day it was, how many days there were in a year, and whether it was true that a remarkable prophet was living in Ward No. 6.

In answer to the last question, Andrei Yefimych blushed and said:

"Yes, he's ill, but he's an interesting young man."

They did not ask him any more questions.

As he was putting his coat on in the front hall, the military governor placed his hand on his shoulder and said with a sigh:

"It's time we old men had a rest!"

On leaving the town hall, Andrei Yefimych realized that this had been a commission appointed to verify his mental abilities. He recalled the questions he had been asked, blushed, and now, for some reason, for the first time in his life felt bitterly sorry for medicine.

"My God," he thought, remembering how the doctors had just tested him, "they took courses in psychiatry so recently, passed examinations—why this total ignorance? They have no idea what psychiatry is!"

And for the first time in his life he felt insulted and angry.

That same evening Mikhail Averyanych came to see him.

Without any greeting, the postmaster went up to him, took him by both hands, and said in a worried voice:

"My dear friend, prove to me that you believe in my genuine sympathy and consider me your friend . . . My friend!" and stopping Andrei Yefimych from speaking, he went on worriedly: "I love you for your education and nobility of soul. Listen to me, my dear. The rules of science demand that the doctors conceal the truth from you, but I, being a military man, come straight out with it: you're not well! Forgive me, my dear, but it's true, everybody around you noticed it long ago. Dr. Evgeny Fyodorych has just told me that for the sake of your health you need rest and diversion. Absolutely right! Excellent! In a few days I'll be taking a leave, to go and sniff a different air. Prove to me that you're my friend, come with me! Come along, we'll dust off the old days."

"I feel perfectly well," Andrei Yefimych said, after thinking a little. "I can't go. Allow me to prove my friendship for you in some other way."

To go somewhere, for no known reason, without books, without Daryushka, without beer, to sharply disrupt an order of life established for twenty years—this idea at first seemed wild and fantastic to him. But he recalled the conversation he had had in the town hall, and the painful mood he had experienced as he returned home, and the thought of a brief absence from this town, where stupid people considered him mad, appealed to him.

"And where, in fact, do you intend to go?" he asked.

"To Moscow, to Petersburg, to Warsaw . . . I spent the five happiest years of my life in Warsaw. What an amazing city! Let's go, my friend!"

XIII

A week later it was suggested to Andrei Yefimych that he get some rest—that is, retire—which suggestion he met with indifference, and a week after that he and Mikhail Averyanych were sitting in a stagecoach heading for the nearest railway station. The days were cool, clear, with blue sky and a transparent view. They made the hundred and fifty miles to the railway station in two days, stopping twice for the night. When the tea at the posting stations was served in poorly washed glasses, or the harnessing of the horses took too long, Mikhail Averyanych turned purple, shook all over, and shouted: "Silence! no argument!" And sitting in the coach, he talked non-stop about his travels around the Caucasus and the Kingdom of Poland. So many adventures, such encounters! He spoke loudly and made such astonished eyes that one might have thought he was lying. Besides, as he talked, he breathed into Andrei Yefimych's face and guffawed in his ear. This bothered the doctor and interfered with his thinking and concentration.

On the train they traveled third class for economy, in a non-smoking car. Half the people were of the clean sort. Mikhail Averyanych soon made everyone's acquaintance and, going from seat to seat, said loudly that one ought not to travel by these outrageous railways. Cheating everywhere! No comparison with riding a horse: you zoom through sixty miles in a day and afterwards feel healthy and fresh. And our crop failures were caused by the draining of the Pinsk marshes. Generally, there were terrible disorders. He got excited, spoke loudly, and did not let others speak. This endless babble interspersed with loud guffaws and expressive gestures wearied Andrei Yefimych.

"Which of us is the madman?" he thought with vexation. "Is it I, who try not to trouble the passengers with anything, or this egoist, who thinks he's the most intelligent and interesting man here and so won't leave anyone in peace?"

In Moscow Mikhail Averyanych donned a military jacket without epaulettes and trousers with red piping. He went out in a military cap and greatcoat, and soldiers saluted him. Andrei Yefimych now thought that this was a man who, of the grand manners he once possessed, had squandered all the good and kept only the bad. He liked to be waited on, even when it was quite unnecessary. A box of matches would be lying before him on the table, and he would see it, yet he would call for a servant to hand him matches; he was not embarrassed to walk about in his underwear in front of the maid; all manservants without distinction, even the old ones, he addressed familiarly, and, getting angry, dubbed them blockheads and fools. It seemed to Andrei Yefimych that this was grand, but vile.

Before anything else, Mikhail Averyanych took his friend to see the Iverskaya icon. He prayed ardently, bowing to the ground and with tears, and when he finished, sighed deeply and said:

"Even if you don't believe, you feel somehow more at ease once you've prayed. Kiss it, my dear."

Andrei Yefimych became embarrassed and kissed the icon, while Mikhail Averyanych pursed his lips and, nodding his head, prayed in a whisper, tears coming to his eyes again. Then they went to the Kremlin and there looked at the Tsar-cannon and the Tsar-bell and even touched them with their fingers, admired the view of Zamoskvorechye, visited the Cathedral of Christ the Savior and the Rumiantsev Museum.[16]

They had dinner at Testov's. Mikhail Averyanych spent a long time studying the menu, stroking his side-whiskers, and said in the tone of a gourmand who feels in a restaurant as if he were at home:

"Let's see what you can offer us to eat today, my angel!"

XIV

The doctor walked, looked, ate, drank, but had only one feeling: vexation with Mikhail Averyanych. He wanted to have a rest from his friend, to leave him, to hide, but the friend considered it his duty not to let him go a step away and to provide him with as many diversions as possible. When there was nothing to look at, he diverted him with talk. Andrei Yefimych held out for two days, but on the third he announced to his friend that he was sick and wanted to stay home all day. The friend said that in that case he, too, would stay home. Indeed, one had to rest or one's legs would fall off. Andrei Yefimych lay on the sofa, face to the wall, and with clenched teeth listened to his friend hotly insisting that France was certain to defeat Germany sooner or later, that there were a great many swindlers in Moscow, and that one cannot judge a horse by its color. The doctor had a buzzing in his ears, his heart pounded, but out of delicacy he dared not ask his friend to be quiet. Fortunately, Mikhail Averyanych got bored sitting in the hotel room, and after dinner he went out for a stroll.

Left alone, Andrei Yefimych gave himself up to a feeling of relief. How pleasant to lie motionless on the sofa and realize that you are alone in the room! True happiness is impossible without solitude. The fallen angel probably betrayed God because he longed for solitude, which angels do not know. Andrei Yefimych wanted to think about what he had seen and heard in the last few days, but he could not get Mikhail Averyanych out of his head.

"He took a leave and came with me out of friendship, out of

magnanimity," the doctor thought with vexation. "There's nothing worse than this friendly solicitude. It seems he's a kind, magnanimous, and merry fellow, and yet he's a bore. An insufferable bore. Just as there are people who always say only nice and intelligent things, yet you can sense that they're quite obtuse."

In the days that followed, Andrei Yefimych gave himself out as ill and never left the room. He lay facing the back of the sofa and languished while his friend amused him with conversation, or rested while his friend was absent. He was annoyed with himself for having come along and with his friend for growing more talkative and casual every day; he simply could not manage to attune his thoughts to anything serious and lofty.

"The reality Ivan Dmitrich spoke about is getting to me," he thought, angry at his own pettiness. "However, it's nonsense . . . I'll go home and everything will be as before . . ."

In Petersburg it was the same: he spent whole days without leaving the hotel room, lay on the sofa, and got up only to have some beer.

Mikhail Averyanych kept urging him to go to Warsaw.

"My dear, why should I go there?" Andrei Yefimych said in an imploring tone. "Go by yourself and let me go home! I beg you!"

"Not for anything!" protested Mikhail Averyanych. "It's an amazing city. I spent the five happiest years of my life in it."

Andrei Yefimych did not have enough character to stand up for himself and, sick at heart, went to Warsaw. There he never left the hotel room, lay on the sofa, angry with himself, with his friend, and with the servants who stubbornly refused to understand Russian, while Mikhail Averyanych, hale, hearty, and cheerful as ever, went around the city from morning till evening, looking up his old acquaintances. Several times he stayed away all night. After one such night, spent who knows where, he came home early in the morning, greatly agitated, red-faced, and disheveled. He paced up and down the room for a long time, muttering something to himself, then stopped and said:

"Honor before all!"

After pacing a little more, he clutched his head and said in a tragic voice:

"Yes, honor before all! Cursed be the moment I first thought of coming to this Babylon! My dear," he turned to the doctor, "despise me: I lost at cards! Give me five hundred roubles!"

Andrei Yefimych counted out five hundred roubles and silently handed them to his friend. The man, still crimson with shame and wrath, uttered some needless oath incoherently, put his cap on his head, and went out. Returning about two hours later, he collapsed into an armchair, sighed loudly, and said:

"My honor is saved! Let's go, my friend. I don't want to stay a minute longer in this cursed city. Crooks! Austrian spies!"

When the friends returned to their town, it was already November and the streets were deep in snow. Andrei Yefimych's post had been taken over by Dr. Khobotov. He was still living in his old apartment, waiting for Andrei Yefimych to come and vacate the hospital apartment. The homely woman whom he called his cook was already living in one of the annexes.

New hospital rumors went around town. It was said that the homely woman had quarreled with the superintendent, and that the man had supposedly crawled on his knees before her, begging forgiveness.

The first day after his arrival, Andrei Yefimych had to find himself an apartment.

"My friend," the postmaster said to him timidly, "forgive my indiscreet question: what means do you have at your disposal?"

Andrei Yefimych silently counted his money and said:

"Eighty-six roubles."

"That's not what I'm asking," Mikhail Averyanych said in embarrassment, not understanding the doctor. "I'm asking what means you have in general."

"But I told you: eighty-six roubles . . . That's all I have."

Mikhail Averyanych considered the doctor an honest and noble man, but even so he suspected him of having a capital of some twenty thousand at least. Learning now that Andrei Yefimych was destitute, that he had nothing to live on, he suddenly wept for some reason and embraced his friend.

XV

Andrei Yefimych lived in the little three-windowed house of the tradeswoman Belov. There were only three rooms in this little house, not counting the kitchen. The doctor occupied the two with windows on the street, and in the third and the kitchen lived

Daryushka, the tradeswoman, and her three children. Sometimes the landlady's lover came to spend the night with her, a drunken lout who got violent during the night and terrified the children and Daryushka. When he came, settled himself in the kitchen, and started demanding vodka, everybody felt very crowded, and out of pity the doctor would take the crying children to his rooms and bed them down on the floor, and this gave him great pleasure.

He got up at eight o'clock, as formerly, and after tea sat down to read his old books and magazines. He now had no money for new ones. Either because the books were old, or perhaps because of the change of circumstances, reading wearied him and no longer interested him deeply. So as not to spend his time in idleness, he made a detailed catalogue of his books and glued labels to their spines, and this mechanical, painstaking work seemed to him more interesting than reading. This monotonous, painstaking work lulled his mind in some incomprehensible way, he did not think of anything, and the time passed quickly. He even found it interesting to sit in the kitchen and peel potatoes with Daryushka or sort buckwheat. On Saturdays and Sundays he went to church. Standing by the wall, eyes closed, he listened to the singing and thought about his father, his mother, the university, religion; he felt peaceful, sad, and afterwards, leaving the church, was sorry the service had ended so soon.

Twice he went to the hospital to see Ivan Dmitrich and talk with him. But both times Ivan Dmitrich was unusually upset and angry; he begged to be left alone, having long since grown weary of empty chatter, and for all his sufferings he asked only one reward of cursed, mean people—solitary confinement. Was even that to be denied him? Both times, when Andrei Yefimych took leave of him and wished him a good night, he snarled and said:

"Go to the devil!"

And now Andrei Yefimych did not know whether he should go a third time or not. But he wanted to go.

Formerly, in the time after dinner, Andrei Yefimych had paced his rooms and reflected, but now he spent the time between dinner and evening tea lying on the sofa, face to the back, giving himself up to petty thoughts, which he was unable to fight off. He felt offended that for his more than twenty years of service he had been given neither a pension nor a one-time payment. True, he had served dishonestly, but everyone who served got a pension, whether

they were honest or not. Contemporary justice consisted in grant-
ing rank, decorations, and pensions not to moral qualities or abilities but to service in general, however it was performed. Why
should he be the only exception? He had no money at all. He was
ashamed to pass the grocery shop and look at the shopkeeper. He
had already run up a bill of thirty-two roubles for beer. He also
owed money to the tradeswoman Belov. Daryushka sold old clothes
and books on the sly and lied to the landlady that the doctor was
soon to receive a very large sum of money.

He was angry with himself for having spent the thousand roubles he had saved on a trip. How useful that thousand would have
been to him now! He was vexed that people would not leave him
alone. Khobotov considered it his duty to visit his sick colleague occasionally. Everything about him disgusted Andrei Yefimych: his
well-fed face, and his bad, condescending tone, and the word "colleague," and his high boots; most disgusting was that he considered
it his duty to treat Andrei Yefimych and thought that he was indeed
treating him. On each of his visits he brought a bottle of potassium
bromide and rhubarb pills.

Mikhail Averyanych also considered it his duty to visit his friend
and divert him. He always entered Andrei Yefimych's with affected
nonchalance and a forced guffaw and began assuring him that he
looked very well today and, thank God, things were improving,
from which it could be concluded that he considered his friend's
condition hopeless. He had not yet paid back his Warsaw debt and
was weighed down by heavy shame, felt tense, and therefore tried
to guffaw more loudly and talk more amusingly. His jokes and stories now seemed endless and were a torment both to Andrei
Yefimych and for himself.

In his presence Andrei Yefimych usually lay on the sofa with his
face to the wall and listened with clenched teeth; layers of scum settled on his soul, and after each visit from his friend he felt this scum
rising higher, as if reaching to his throat.

To stifle his petty feelings, he hastened to reflect that he himself,
and Khobotov, and Mikhail Averyanych, must die sooner or later,
without leaving even a trace on nature. If one should imagine some
spirit, a million years from now, flying through space past the earth,
that spirit would see only clay and bare cliffs. Everything—including culture and moral law—would have perished, and no burdock

would even be growing.[17] What, then, was this shame before the shopkeeper, the worthless Khobotov, the painful friendship of Mikhail Averyanych? It was all nonsense and trifles.

But such reasoning no longer helped. As soon as he imagined the earth a million years from now, Khobotov appeared in high boots from behind a bare cliff, or else the forcedly laughing Mikhail Averyanych, and he even heard his shamefaced whisper: "I'll pay back the Warsaw debt one of these days, my dear . . . Without fail."

XVI

Once Mikhail Averyanych came after dinner, when Andrei Yefimych was lying on the sofa. It so happened that Khobotov also arrived at the same time with the potassium bromide. Andrei Yefimych got up heavily, sat on the sofa, and propped himself with both hands.

"And today, my dear," Mikhail Averyanych began, "your color has much improved over yesterday. Well done, by God! Well done!"

"It's high time, high time you got better, colleague," Khobotov said, yawning. "You must be tired of this flim-flam yourself."

"We'll get better," Mikhail Averyanych said cheerfully. "We'll live another hundred years! Yes, sir!"

"Hundred or no hundred, there's enough in him for twenty," Khobotov reassured. "Never mind, never mind, colleague, don't be so glum . . . Stop blowing smoke."

"We'll still show ourselves!" Mikhail Averyanych guffawed and patted his friend's knee. "We'll show ourselves! Next summer, God willing, we'll take a swing through the Caucasus and cover it all on horseback—hup! hup! hup! And when we come back from the Caucasus, for all I know, we'll dance at a wedding." Mikhail Averyanych winked slyly. "We'll get you married, dear friend . . . married . . ."

Andrei Yefimych suddenly felt the scum rise to his throat; his heart was pounding terribly.

"This is all so banal!" he said, getting up quickly and going to the window. "Don't you understand that you're speaking in banalities?"

He wanted to go on gently and politely, but against his will suddenly clenched his fists and raised them above his head.

"Leave me alone!" he shouted in a voice not his own, turning purple and trembling all over. "Get out! Get out, both of you!"

Mikhail Averyanych and Khobotov stood up and stared at him first in bewilderment, then in fear.

"Get out, both of you!" Andrei Yefimych went on shouting. "Obtuse people! Stupid people! I need neither your friendship nor your medicine, obtuse man! Banality! Filth!"

Khobotov and Mikhail Averyanych, exchanging perplexed looks, backed their way to the door and went out into the front hall. Andrei Yefimych seized the bottle of potassium bromide and hurled it after them; the bottle smashed jingling on the threshold.

"Go to the devil!" he shouted in a tearful voice, running out to the front hall. "To the devil!"

After his visitors left, Andrei Yefimych, trembling as in a fever, lay down on the sofa and for a long time went on repeating:

"Obtuse people! Stupid people!"

When he calmed down, it occurred to him first of all that poor Mikhail Averyanych must now be terribly ashamed and dispirited and that all this was terrible. Nothing like it had ever happened before. Where were his intelligence and tact? Where were his comprehension of things and his philosophical indifference?

The doctor was unable to sleep all night from shame and vexation with himself, and in the morning, around ten o'clock, he went to the post office and apologized to the postmaster.

"We'll forget what happened," the moved Mikhail Averyanych said with a sigh, firmly pressing his hand. "Let bygones be bygones. Lyubavkin!" he suddenly shouted so loudly that all the postal clerks and clients jumped. "Fetch a chair! And you wait!" he shouted at a peasant woman who was passing him a certified letter through the grille. "Can't you see I'm busy? We'll forget the bygones," he went on tenderly, addressing Andrei Yefimych. "Sit down, my dear, I humbly beg you."

He patted his knees in silence for a moment and then said:

"It never occurred to me to be offended with you. Illness is nobody's friend, I realize. Your fit yesterday frightened me and the doctor, and we talked about you for a long time afterwards. My dear friend, why don't you want to attend seriously to your illness? This can't go on! Excuse my friendly candor," Mikhail Averyanych whispered, "but you live in the most unfavorable circumstances: it's crowded, dirty, nobody looks after you, there's no money for treatment . . . My dear friend, the doctor and I beg you with all our hearts to heed our advice: go to the hospital! The food there is wholesome, they'll look after you and treat you. Evgeny Fyodorovich may be in *mauvais ton*,[18] just between us, but he's well-informed and totally reliable. He gave me his word he'd look after you."

Andrei Yefimych was touched by this genuine concern and by the tears that suddenly glistened on the postmaster's cheeks.

"My esteemed friend, don't believe it!" he whispered, placing his hand on his heart. "Don't believe them! It's not true! My only illness is that in twenty years I've found only one intelligent man in the whole town, and he's mad. There is no illness at all, I simply got into a magic circle that I can't get out of. It makes no difference to me, I'm ready for everything."

"Go to the hospital, my dear."

"Or to the pit—it makes no difference to me."

"Give me your word, my dearest friend, that you'll obey Evgeny Fyodorych in all things."

"If you please, I give my word. But I repeat, my esteemed friend, I got into a magic circle. Now everything, even the genuine sympathy of my friends, leads to one thing—my perdition. I'm perishing, and I have enough courage to realize it."

"You'll get well, my friend."

"Why say that?" Andrei Yefimych said vexedly. "It's a rare man who doesn't experience the same thing towards the end of his life as I am experiencing now. When you're told that you have something like a bad kidney or an enlarged heart, and you start getting treated, or that you're a madman or a criminal, that is, in short, when people suddenly pay attention to you, then you should know that you've gotten into a magic circle and you'll never get out of it. If you try to get out, you'll get more lost. Give up, because no human effort can save you. So it seems to me."

Meanwhile people were crowding to the grille. Andrei Yefimych, not wishing to hinder anyone, got up and began to take his leave. Mikhail Averyanych once again asked him for his word of honor and saw him to the front door.

That same day, before evening, Andrei Yefimych received an unexpected visit from Khobotov, in his short jacket and high boots, who said, as if nothing had happened the day before:

"I'm here on business, colleague. I've come to ask you if you'd like to join me in a consultation. Eh?"

Thinking that Khobotov wanted to divert him with a stroll, or indeed give him a chance to earn some money, Andrei Yefimych put on his coat and went out with him. He was glad of the chance to smooth over his fault of the day before and make peace, and in his heart was grateful to Khobotov, who did not utter a peep about the day before and was obviously sparing him. He would hardly have expected such delicacy from this uncultivated man.

"Where's your patient?" asked Andrei Yefimych.

"In the hospital. I've been wanting to show you for a long time . . . A most interesting case."

They went into the hospital yard and, going around the main building, made their way to the annex where the insane were housed. And all this, for some reason, in silence. When they went into the annex, Nikita jumped up as usual and stood at attention.

"One of them has developed a lung complication," Khobotov said in a low voice, as he and Andrei Yefimych went into the ward. "Wait here, I'll be back at once. I must get my stethoscope."

And he went out.

XVII

It was twilight. Ivan Dmitrich lay on his bed, his face in the pillow; the paralytic sat motionless, weeping softly and moving his lips. The fat peasant and the former sorter were asleep. It was quiet.

Andrei Yefimych sat down on Ivan Dmitrich's bed and waited. But about half an hour went by, and instead of Khobotov, Nikita came into the ward carrying a hospital robe, someone's underwear and slippers.

"Please put these on, Your Honor," he said softly. "Here's your little bed, if you please," he added, pointing to an empty bed, obviously brought in recently. "Never mind, God willing, you'll get well."

Andrei Yefimych understood everything. Without saying a word, he went over to the bed Nikita had pointed to and sat down; seeing that Nikita was standing and waiting, he undressed completely and felt embarrassed. Then he put on the hospital clothes.

The drawers were very short, the shirt long, and the robe smelled of smoked fish.

"You'll get well, God willing," Nikita repeated.

He gathered up Andrei Yefimych's clothes, went out, and closed the door behind him.

"It makes no difference . . ." thought Andrei Yefimych, shyly wrapping himself in the robe, and feeling that his new costume made him look like a prisoner. "It makes no difference . . . no difference whether it's a tailcoat, a uniform, or this robe . . ."

But what about his watch? And the notebook in the side pocket? And the cigarettes? Where had Nikita taken his clothes? Now, perhaps, he would not put on his trousers, waistcoat, and shoes till his dying day. All this was somehow strange and even incomprehensible at first. Andrei Yefimych was still convinced that there was no difference between the house of the tradeswoman Belov and Ward No. 6, and that everything in this world was nonsense and vanity of vanities, and yet his hands shook, his feet were cold, and he felt eerie at the thought that Ivan Dmitrich would soon get up and see him in the robe. He stood up, paced a little, and sat down.

Now he had been sitting for half an hour, an hour, and he was sick of it to the point of anguish. Could one really live here for a day, a week, and even years, like these people? Well, so he sat, paced, and sat down again; he could go and look out the window, and again pace up and down. And then what? Go on sitting this way all the time, like an idol, and thinking? No, that was hardly possible.

Andrei Yefimych lay down, but got up at once, wiped the cold sweat from his forehead with his sleeve, and felt that his whole face smelled of smoked fish. He paced again.

"This is some sort of misunderstanding . . ." he said, spreading his arms in perplexity. "It must be explained, there's a misunderstanding here . . ."

Just then Ivan Dmitrich woke up. He sat up and propped his cheeks on his fists. He spat. Then he glanced lazily at the doctor and for the first moment apparently understood nothing; but soon his sleepy face turned malicious and jeering.

"Aha, so they've stuck you in here, too, my dear!" he said in a voice hoarse from sleep, squinting one eye. "Delighted. You used to suck people's blood, now they'll suck yours. Excellent!"

"This is some sort of misunderstanding . . ." said Andrei

Yefimych, frightened by Ivan Dmitrich's words; he shrugged and repeated: "A misunderstanding of some sort . . ."

Ivan Dmitrich spat again and lay down.

"Cursed life!" he growled. "And what's so bitter and offensive is
that this life will end not with a reward for suffering, not with an
apotheosis, as in the opera, but with death; peasants will come and
drag your dead body by the arms and legs to the basement. Brr!
Well, never mind . . . But in the other world it will be our turn to
celebrate . . . I'll come from the other world as a ghost and scare
these vipers. I'll give them all gray hair."

Moiseika came back and, seeing the doctor, held out his hand.

"Give me a little kopeck!" he said.

XVIII

Andrei Yefimych walked over to the window and looked out at the
field. It was getting dark, and on the horizon to the right a cold,
crimson moon was rising. Not far from the hospital fence, no more
than two hundred yards away, stood a tall white building surrounded by a stone wall. This was the prison.

"Here is reality!" thought Andrei Yefimych, and he felt frightened.

The moon was frightening, and the prison, and the nails on the
fence, and the distant flame of the bone-burning factory. He heard
a sigh behind him. Andrei Yefimych turned around and saw a man
with stars and decorations gleaming on his chest, who smiled and
slyly winked his eye. This, too, was frightening.

Andrei Yefimych assured himself that there was nothing special
about the moon or the prison, and that mentally sound people also
wore decorations, and that in time everything would rot and turn
to clay, but despair suddenly overwhelmed him, he seized the grille
with both hands and shook it with all his might. The strong grille
did not yield.

Then, not to feel so frightened, he went to Ivan Dmitrich's bed
and sat down.

"I've lost heart, my dear," he murmured, trembling and wiping
off the cold sweat. "Lost heart."

"Try philosophizing," Ivan Dmitrich said jeeringly.

"My God, my God . . . Yes, yes . . . You once said there's no philosophy in Russia, yet everybody philosophizes, even little folk. But little folk's philosophizing doesn't harm anyone," Andrei Yefimych said, sounding as if he wanted to weep and awaken pity. "Why, then, this gleeful laughter, my dear? And how can little folk help philosophizing, if they're not content? An intelligent, educated, proud, freedom-loving man, the likeness of God,[19] has no other recourse than to work as a doctor in a dirty, stupid little town, and deal all his life with cupping glasses, leeches, and mustard plasters! Charlatanism, narrow-mindedness, banality! Oh, my God!"

"You're pouring out nonsense. If you loathe being a doctor, you should have become a government minister."

"Impossible, it's all impossible. We're weak, my dear . . . I used to be indifferent, I reasoned cheerfully and sensibly, but life had only to touch me rudely and I lost heart . . . prostration . . . We're weak, we're trash . . . And you, too, my dear. You're intelligent, noble, you drank in good impulses with your mother's milk, but as soon as you entered into life, you got tired and fell ill . . . Weak, weak!"

Something persistent, apart from fear and a feeling of offense, oppressed Andrei Yefimych all the while as evening drew on. Finally, he realized that he wanted to drink some beer and smoke.

"I'm getting out of here, my dear," he said. "I'll tell them to bring a light here . . . I can't take this . . . I'm not able . . ."

Andrei Yefimych went to the door and opened it, but Nikita immediately jumped up and barred his way.

"Where are you going? You can't, you can't!" he said. "It's bedtime!"

"But I'll only go out for a minute to stroll in the yard!" said Andrei Yefimych, quite dumbstruck.

"You can't, you can't, it's against orders. You know it yourself."

Nikita slammed the door and leaned his back against it.

"But if I go out, what's that to anyone?" Andrei Yefimych asked, shrugging his shoulders. "I don't understand! Nikita, I have to go out!" he said in a quavering voice. "I must!"

"Don't start any disorder, it's not good!" Nikita said admonishingly.

"What the devil is all this!" Ivan Dmitrich suddenly shouted and jumped up. "What right does he have not to let you out? How dare they keep us here? I believe the law clearly states that no one can be deprived of freedom without a trial! This is coercion! Tyranny!"

"Of course it's tyranny!" said Andrei Yefimych, encouraged by Ivan Dmitrich's shout. "I must go out, I have to! He has no right. Let me out, I tell you!"

"Do you hear, you dumb brute?" shouted Ivan Dmitrich, and he banged on the door with his fist. "Open up, or I'll break the door down! Butcher!"

"Open up!" cried Andrei Yefimych, trembling all over. "I demand it!"

"Keep talking!" Nikita answered from outside the door. "Keep talking!"

"At least call Evgeny Fyodorych here! Tell him I ask him kindly . . . for a minute!"

"He'll come himself tomorrow."

"They'll never let us out!" Ivan Dmitrich went on meanwhile. "They'll make us rot here! O Lord, can it be there's no hell in the other world and these scoundrels will be forgiven? Where is the justice? Open up, scoundrel, I'm suffocating!" he shouted in a hoarse voice and leaned his weight against the door. "I'll smash my head! Murderers!"

Nikita quickly opened the door, rudely shoved Andrei Yefimych aside with his hands and knee, then swung and hit him in the face with his fist. Andrei Yefimych felt as if a huge salt wave had broken over him and was pulling him towards the bed; in fact, there was a salt taste in his mouth: his teeth were probably bleeding. He waved his arms as if trying to swim and got hold of someone's bed, and just then he felt Nikita hit him twice in the back.

Ivan Dmitrich gave a loud cry. He, too, must have been beaten.

Then all was quiet. Thin moonlight came through the grille, and a shadow resembling a net lay on the floor. It was frightening. Andrei Yefimych lay there with bated breath: he waited in terror to be hit again. It was as if someone had taken a sickle, plunged it into him, and twisted it several times in his chest and guts. He bit his pillow in pain and clenched his teeth, and suddenly, amidst the chaos, a dreadful, unbearable thought flashed clearly in his head, that exactly the same pain must have been felt day after day, for years, by these people who now looked like black shadows in the moonlight. How could it happen that in the course of more than twenty years he had not known and had not wanted to know it? He had not known, he had had no notion of pain, and therefore was not to blame, but his conscience, as rough and intractable as

Nikita, made him go cold from head to foot. He jumped up, wanted to shout with all his might and run quickly to kill Nikita, then Khobotov, the superintendent, and the assistant doctor, then himself, but no sound came from his chest and his legs would not obey him; suffocating, he tore at the robe and shirt on his chest, ripped them, and collapsed unconscious on his bed.

XIX

The next morning his head ached, there was a ringing in his ears, and his whole body felt sick. Recalling his weakness yesterday, he was not ashamed. He had been fainthearted yesterday, afraid even of the moon, had sincerely uttered feelings and thoughts he had previously not suspected were in him. For instance, thoughts about the discontent of the philosophizing little folk. But now it made no difference to him.

He did not eat or drink, lay motionless and was silent.

"It makes no difference to me," he thought, when he was asked questions. "I won't answer . . . It makes no difference to me."

After dinner Mikhail Averyanych came and brought a quarter of a pound of tea and a pound of fruit jellies. Daryushka also came and stood by his bed for a whole hour with a look of dumb grief on her face. Doctor Khobotov visited him, too. He brought a bottle of potassium bromide and told Nikita to fumigate the ward with something.

Towards evening Andrei Yefimych died of apoplexy. First he felt violent chills and nausea; something disgusting, which seemed to pervade his whole body, even his fingers, welled up from his stomach to his head and flooded his eyes and ears. Everything turned green before him. Andrei Yefimych understood that his end had come and remembered that Ivan Dmitrich, Mikhail Averyanych, and millions of people believed in immortality. And what if it was so? But he did not want immortality, and he thought of it for only a moment. A herd of deer, extraordinarily beautiful and graceful, which he had read about the day before, ran past him; then a peasant woman reached out to him with a certified letter . . . Mikhail Averyanych said something. Then everything vanished and Andrei Yefimych lost consciousness forever.

Peasants came, picked him up by the arms and legs, and carried him to the chapel. He lay there on a table, his eyes open, and the moon shone on him at night. In the morning Sergei Sergeich came, prayed piously before the crucifix, and closed his former superior's eyes.

The following day Andrei Yefimych was buried. Only Mikhail Averyanych and Daryushka attended the funeral.

NOVEMBER 1892

The Black Monk

I

Andrei Vassilyich Kovrin, master of arts, was overworked and his nerves were upset. He was not being treated, but once in passing, over a bottle of wine, he talked about it with a doctor friend, who advised him to spend the spring and summer in the country. Quite opportunely, a long letter also came from Tanya Pesotsky, inviting him to come to Borisovka and stay for a while. And he decided that he did in fact need to get away.

First—this was in April—he went to his own place, his family estate Kovrinka, and there spent three weeks in solitude; then, having waited for good roads, he set out by carriage to visit his former guardian and tutor Pesotsky, a horticulturist well known in Russia. From Kovrinka to Borisovka, where the Pesotskys lived, was no more than fifty miles, and driving on a soft springtime road in a comfortable, well-sprung carriage was a true pleasure.

Pesotsky's house was enormous, with columns, with lions whose plaster was peeling off, and with a tailcoated lackey at the entrance. The old park, gloomy and severe, laid out in the English manner, spread over more than half a mile from the house to the river and ended at a sheer, steep, clayey bank on which pine trees grew, their bared roots looking like shaggy paws; water glistened desolately below, snipe flitted about with a pitiful peeping, and the mood there always made you want to sit down and write a ballad. But near the house, in the yard and gardens, which together with the nursery took up some eighty acres, it was cheerful and exhilarating even in bad weather. Kovrin had never seen anywhere else such amazing roses, lilies, camellias, such tulips of every possible color, beginning with bright white and ending with sooty black, nor such a wealth of flowers in general, as in Pesotsky's garden. Spring was only just beginning, and the real luxuriance of flowers was still hidden in the hothouse, yet what blossomed along the walks and here and there in the flower beds was enough so that, strolling in the garden, you felt yourself in a kingdom of tender colors, especially in the early hours when dew sparkled on every petal.

What formed the decorative part of the gardens, and which Pesotsky himself scornfully referred to as trifles, had made a fairy-tale impression on Kovrin when he was a child. What whims, refined monstrosities, and mockeries of nature there were here! There were espaliered fruit trees, a pear tree that had the form of a Lombardy poplar, spherical oaks and lindens, an umbrella-shaped apple tree, arches, monograms, candelabras, and even an 1862 of plum trees—representing the year in which Pesotsky first took up horticulture. You would meet beautiful, shapely trees, their trunks straight and strong as palms, and only on closer inspection would you discover that they were gooseberry or currant bushes. But what was most cheerful about the gardens and gave them an animated look, was the constant movement. From early morning till evening people with wheelbarrows, hoes, and watering cans were milling around the trees, the bushes, the walks and flower beds . . .

Kovrin arrived at the Pesotskys in the evening, past nine o'clock. He found Tanya and her father, Yegor Semyonych, greatly alarmed. The thermometer and the clear, starry sky foretold frost by morning, and meanwhile the gardener, Ivan Karlych, had gone to town, and there was no one they could count on. Over supper they talked only of the morning frost, and it was decided that Tanya would not go to bed and after midnight would make the rounds of the gardens to see if all was in order, and that Yegor Semyonych would get up at three or even earlier.

Kovrin sat with Tanya all evening and after midnight went to the gardens with her. It was cold. Outside there was already a strong smell of smoke. In the big orchard, which was called commercial and which brought Yegor Semyonych several thousand a year in net income, thick, black, pungent smoke covered the ground and, enveloping the trees, saved those thousands from the frost. The trees here stood in a checkerboard pattern, their rows straight and regular as ranks of soldiers, and this strict, pedantic regularity and the fact that all the trees were of the same height and had perfectly uniform crowns and trunks, made the picture monotonous and even dull. Kovrin and Tanya walked along the rows, where fires of dung, straw, and assorted refuse smoldered, and occasionally met workers, who wandered through the smoke like shades. Only the cherries, plums, and some varieties of apple were in bloom, yet the entire orchard was drowned in smoke, and it was only near the nursery that Kovrin could draw a deep breath.

"When I was still a child I used to sneeze from the smoke here," he said, shrugging his shoulders, "but to this day I don't understand why smoke protects against frost."

"Smoke takes the place of clouds, when there aren't any . . ." replied Tanya.

"And what are clouds needed for?"

"When the weather's gray and overcast, there are no morning frosts."

"So that's it!"

He laughed and took her by the hand. Her broad, very serious, chilled face, with its narrow, dark eyebrows, the upturned collar of her coat, which prevented her from moving her head freely, and she herself, lean, trim, her dress tucked up on account of the dew, moved him to tenderness.

"Lord, she's already grown up!" he said. "When I left here the last time, five years ago, you were still a child. You were so skinny and long-legged, you went bare-headed, dressed in short skirts, and to tease you I called you a stork . . . What time can do!"

"Yes, five years!" Tanya sighed. "A lot of water has flowed under the bridge. Tell me, Andryusha, in all conscience," she began animatedly, looking into his face, "have you grown unaccustomed to us? Though why do I ask? You're a man, you live your own interesting life, you're important . . . Estrangement is so natural! But, however it may be, Andryusha, I'd like you to consider us your own. We have a right to that."

"I do, Tanya."

"Word of honor?"

"Yes, word of honor."

"You were surprised today that we have so many photographs of you. But you know my father adores you. I sometimes think he loves you more than he does me. He's proud of you. You're a learned, extraordinary man, you've made a brilliant career, and he's sure you've turned out like this because he brought you up. I don't prevent him from thinking so. Let him."

Dawn was already breaking, and this was especially noticeable from the distinctness with which the billows of smoke and the crowns of the trees stood out in the air. Nightingales were singing, and the calling of quails came from the fields.

"Anyhow, it's time for bed," said Tanya. "And it's cold." She took him under the arm. "Thank you for coming, Andryusha. We have uninteresting acquaintances, and few of them at that. All we have is orchard, orchard, orchard—and nothing more. Full-stock, half-stock," she laughed, "pippin, rennet, borovinka, budding, graft-ing . . . All, all our life has gone into the orchard, I never even dream of anything but apple and pear trees. Of course, it's good and useful, but sometimes one wants something else for diversity. I remember how you used to come to us for vacations, or just so, and the house felt somehow more fresh and bright, as if the dust covers had been taken off the furniture and lamps. I was a little girl then and yet I understood."

She spoke for a long time and with great feeling. For some rea-son it occurred to him that he might become attached to this small, weak, loquacious being, get carried away, and fall in love—in their situation it was so possible and natural! This thought moved and amused him, he bent down to the sweet, preoccupied face and sang softly:

"Onegin, I will not conceal it,
    Madly do I love Tatiana . . ." [1]

When they came home, Yegor Semyonych was already up. Kovrin was not sleepy, he got to talking with the old man and went back to the gardens with him. Yegor Semyonych was tall, broad-shouldered, big-bellied, and suffered from shortness of breath, but he always walked so quickly that it was hard to keep up with him. He had an extremely preoccupied air, was always hurrying some-where, and with a look implying that if he were even one minute late, all would be lost!

"Here's something, my boy . . ." he began, pausing to catch his breath. "On the surface of the ground, as you see, it's freezing, but if you raise the thermometer on a stick four yards above ground, it's warm . . . Why is that?"

"I really don't know," Kovrin said, laughing.

"Hm . . . One can't know everything, of course . . . However vast the mind, not everything will find room in it. Philosophy is more in your line?"

"Yes. I teach psychology, but I'm generally concerned with philosophy."

"And it doesn't bore you?"

"On the contrary, it's all I live for."

"Well, God be with you . . ." Yegor Semyonych said, stroking his side-whiskers thoughtfully. "God be with you . . . I'm very glad . . . very glad for you, my boy . . ."

But suddenly he cocked an ear and, making a terrible face, ran off and soon disappeared behind the trees into the clouds of smoke.

"Who tied a horse to that apple tree?" his desperate, heartrending cry was heard. "What scoundrel and villain dared to tie a horse to that apple tree? My God, my God! Befouled, begrimed, besmutted, bedeviled! The orchard's lost! The orchard's ruined! My God!"

When he came back to Kovrin, his face was exhausted, offended.

"What can you do with these confounded people?" he said in a tearful voice, spreading his arms. "Styopka brought a load of manure during the night and tied his horse to an apple tree! The scoundrel wrapped the reins so tightly around it that the bark wore through in three places. Imagine! I tell him, and the dimwit just stands there blinking his eyes! Hanging's too good for him!"

Having calmed down, he embraced Kovrin and kissed him on the cheek.

"Well, God be with you . . . God be with you . . ." he muttered. "I'm very glad you've come. I can't tell you how glad . . . Thank you."

Then at the same quick pace and with a preoccupied air he went around all the gardens and showed his former ward the conservatories, hothouses, potting sheds, and his two apiaries, which he called the wonder of our century.

As they walked about, the sun rose and brightly lit up the gardens. It became warm. Anticipating a clear, long, happy day, Kovrin remembered that it was still only the beginning of May and the whole summer still lay ahead, just as clear, long, and happy, and suddenly a joyful young feeling stirred in his breast, such as he had experienced in childhood running about in these gardens. And he embraced the old man and kissed him tenderly. They were both moved. They went in and sat down to tea from old porcelain cups, with cream, with rich, buttery rolls—and these small things again reminded Kovrin of his childhood and youth. The beautiful present and the awakening impressions of the past flowed together in him; they made his soul feel crowded but good.

He waited till Tanya woke up and had his coffee with her, strolled a little, then went to his room and sat down to work. He read attentively, took notes, and occasionally raised his eyes to look at the open windows or the fresh flowers, still wet with dew, that stood in vases on the table, then lowered them to the book again, and it seemed to him that every fiber of him was thrilling and frolicking with pleasure.

II

In the country he went on leading the same nervous and restless life as in the city. He read and wrote a great deal, studied Italian, and while strolling thought with pleasure that he would soon sit down to work again. He slept so little that everyone was amazed; if he inadvertently dozed off for half an hour in the afternoon, he would not sleep all night afterwards, and following the sleepless night would feel himself as brisk and cheerful as if nothing had happened.

He talked a lot, drank wine, and smoked expensive cigars. Often, if not every day, neighboring young ladies visited the Pesotskys, sang and played the piano with Tanya; occasionally a young man came, a neighbor, who was a good violinist. Kovrin listened eagerly to the music and singing, and it filled him with languor, which manifested itself physically in the closing of his eyes and the drooping of his head to one side.

Once after evening tea he was sitting on the balcony reading. In the drawing room, just then, Tanya—a soprano, one of her friends—a contralto, and the young man with the violin were rehearsing the famous serenade of Braga.[2] Kovrin listened to the words—they were in Russian—and was quite unable to understand their meaning. Finally he put his book down and, listening attentively, understood: a girl with a morbid imagination heard some sort of mysterious sounds in the garden at night, so beautiful and strange that she could only take them for a sacred harmony, which we mortals were unable to understand and which therefore flew back to heaven. Kovrin's eyes began to close. He got up and strolled languidly through the drawing room, then through the reception hall. When the singing stopped, he took Tanya under the arm and walked out to the balcony with her.

"Ever since this morning I've been thinking about a certain legend," he said. "I don't remember whether I read it or heard it somewhere, but the legend is somehow strange, incongruous. In the first place, it's not distinguished by its clarity. A thousand years ago a monk, dressed in black, was walking in the desert somewhere in Syria or Arabia . . . Several miles from the place where he was walking, some fishermen saw another black monk moving slowly over the surface of a lake. This second monk was a mirage. Now forget all the laws of optics, which the legend seems not to recognize, and listen further. The mirage produced another mirage, and that one a third, so that the image of the black monk began to be transmitted endlessly from one layer of the atmosphere to another. He was seen now in Africa, now in Spain, now in India, now in the Far North . . . Finally he left the limits of the earth's atmosphere and is now wandering all over the universe, never getting into conditions that might enable him to fade away. Perhaps he can now be seen somewhere on Mars or on some star in the Southern Cross. But, my dear, the very essence, the crux, of the legend is that exactly a thousand years after the monk walked in the desert, the mirage will enter the earth's atmosphere again and show itself to people. And the thousand years are now supposedly at an end . . . According to the legend, we ought to expect the black monk any day now."

"A strange mirage," said Tanya, who did not like the legend.

"But the most amazing thing," laughed Kovrin, "is that I'm quite unable to remember how this legend came into my head. Did I read it? Hear it? Or maybe I dreamed of the black monk? I swear to God, I don't remember. But I'm taken by this legend. I've been thinking about it all day today."

Letting Tanya go back to her guests, he left the house and strolled pensively among the flower beds. The sun was setting. The flowers had just been watered and gave off a damp, irritating smell. There was singing in the house again, and from a distance the violin gave the impression of a human voice. Straining his mind to recall where he had heard or read the legend, Kovrin went unhurriedly towards the park and without noticing it came to the river.

Following the path that ran down the steep bank past the bared roots, he descended to the water, disturbing some snipe and scaring away two ducks. The last rays of the setting sun still glowed on the gloomy pines, but there was already real evening on the surface of the river. Kovrin crossed the river on some planks. Before him now lay a wide field covered with young, not yet flowering rye. No human dwelling, no living soul in the distance, and it seemed that the path, if one followed it, would lead you to that unknown, mysterious place where the sun had just gone down, and where the sunset flamed so vastly and majestically.

"How spacious, free, and quiet it is here!" thought Kovrin, walking along the path. "It seems the whole world is looking at me, hiding and waiting for me to understand it . . ."

But now waves passed over the rye, and a light evening breeze gently touched his bare head. A moment later there was another gust of wind, stronger now—the rye rustled, and the muted murmur of the pines came from behind him. Kovrin stopped in amazement. On the horizon, looking like a whirlwind or a tornado, a tall black pillar rose from the earth to the sky. Its contours were indistinct, but from the very first moment it was evident that it was not standing in place but moving at terrific speed, moving precisely there, straight at Kovrin, and the nearer it drew, the smaller and clearer it became. Kovrin rushed to one side, into the rye, to make way for it, and he barely had time to do so . . .

A monk dressed in black, with gray hair and black eyebrows, his arms crossed on his chest, raced past . . . His bare feet did not touch the ground. He was already some twenty feet past Kovrin when he looked back at him, nodded and smiled at him tenderly and at the same time slyly. But what a pale, terribly pale, thin face! Beginning to grow again, he flew across the river, noiselessly struck against the clayey bank and the pines, and, passing through them, vanished like smoke.

"Well, so you see . . ." Kovrin muttered. "It means the legend is true."

Without trying to explain the strange event to himself, pleased merely at having seen not only the black clothes but even the face and eyes of the monk so closely and clearly, feeling pleasantly excited, he returned home.

In the park and garden people were calmly walking, there was music in the house—it meant that he alone had seen the monk. He had a great desire to tell Tanya and Yegor Semyonych everything, but he realized that they would probably consider his words raving, and that would frighten them; it was better to keep quiet. He laughed loudly, sang, danced a mazurka, had a merry time, and everybody, the guests and Tanya, found that his face was somehow especially radiant and inspired that day, and that he was very interesting.

III

After supper, when the guests had gone, he went to his room and lay down on the sofa: he wanted to think about the monk. But a moment later Tanya came in.

"Here, Andryusha, read my father's articles," she said, handing him a stack of booklets and offprints. "Wonderful articles. He's an excellent writer."

"Excellent, really!" said Yegor Semyonych, coming in after her and laughing forcedly; he was embarrassed. "Don't listen to her, please, don't read them! However, if you want to fall asleep, then by all means read them: a wonderful soporific."

"In my opinion, they are splendid articles," Tanya said with great conviction. "Read them, Andryusha, and persuade papa to write more often. He could write a complete course in horticulture."

Yegor Semyonych gave a strained chuckle, blushed, and began repeating the phrases that bashful authors usually say. Finally he began to give in.

"In that case, read the article by Gaucher first, and then these little Russian articles," he murmured, fumbling over the booklets with trembling hands, "otherwise you won't understand. Before reading my objections, you should know what I'm objecting to. It's nonsense, however . . . boring. Anyway, I believe it's time for bed."

Tanya left. Yegor Semyonych sat next to Kovrin on the sofa and sighed deeply.

"Yes, my dear boy . . ." he began, after some silence. "Yes, my gentle master of arts. So I, too, write articles and take part in exhibitions and win medals . . . They say Pesotsky's apples are as big as your head, and Pesotsky, they say, has made a fortune on his orchard. In short, Kochubey is rich and famous.[3] But, you may ask, why all this? The orchard is indeed beautiful, exemplary . . . It's not an orchard, it's a whole institution of great national significance, because it is, so to speak, a step into a new era of the Russian economy and Russian industry. But why? With what aim?"

"The work speaks for itself."

"That's not what I mean. I want to ask: what will happen to the orchard when I die? Without me it won't hold out the way it is now for even a month. The whole secret of success is not that it's a big orchard and there are lots of workers, but that I love doing it—you understand?—love it maybe more than my own self. Look at me: I do everything myself. I work from morning till night. I do all the budding myself, all the pruning, all the planting, I do everything myself. When somebody helps me, I get jealous and irritated to the point of rudeness. The whole secret is in love, that is, in the master's keen eye, and the master's hands, and in that feeling when you go for an hour's visit somewhere, and you sit there, but your heart is uneasy, you're not yourself: you're afraid something may happen in the orchard. And when I die, who will look after it? Who'll do the work? The gardener? The hired hands? Yes? I'll tell you this, my gentle friend: the first enemy in our work isn't the hare, or the cockchafer, or the frost, but the outsider."

"And Tanya?" asked Kovrin, laughing. "It can't be that she's worse than a hare. She loves and understands the work."

"Yes, she loves and understands it. If she gets the orchard after my death and becomes its manager, then one certainly could wish for nothing better. Well, but if, God forbid, she should marry?" Yegor Semyonych whispered and looked fearfully at Kovrin. "There's the thing! She'll marry, start having children, there'll be no time to think about the orchard. What I fear most is that she'll marry some fine fellow, and he'll turn greedy and lease the orchard to some market women, and everything will go to hell in the very first year! In our work, women are the scourge of God!"

Yegor Semyonych sighed and was silent for a time.

"Maybe it's egoism, but I'll tell you frankly: I don't want Tanya to get married. I'm afraid! There's a fop with a fiddle who comes here and scrapes away; I know Tanya won't marry him, I know it very well, but I hate the sight of him! Generally, my boy, I'm a great eccentric. I admit it."

Yegor Semyonych got up and paced the room in agitation, and it was evident that he wanted to say something very important, but could not decide to do it.

"I love you dearly and I'll speak frankly with you," he finally decided, thrusting his hands into his pockets. "My attitude to certain ticklish questions is simple, I say straight out what I think, and I can't stand so-called hidden thoughts. I'll say straight out: you are the only man to whom I would not be afraid to marry my daughter. You're intelligent, and a man of heart, and you wouldn't let my beloved work perish. And the main reason is—I love you like a son . . . and I'm proud of you. If you and Tanya should somehow have a romance, then—why, I'd be very glad and even happy. I say it straight out, without mincing, as an honest man."

Kovrin laughed. Yegor Semyonych opened the door to go out, but stopped on the threshold.

"If you and Tanya had a son, I'd make a horticulturist of him," he said, pondering. "However, that is but vain dreaming . . . Good night."

Left alone, Kovrin lay down more comfortably and began on the articles. One was entitled "On Intermediate Crops," another "A Few Words Concerning the Note by Mr. Z. on Turning Over the Soil for a New Garden," a third "More on Budding with Dormant Eyes," and the rest were in the same vein. But what an uneasy, uneven tone, what nervous, almost morbid defiance! Here was an article with what one would think was the most peaceable title and indifferent content: the subject was the Russian Antonov apple tree. Yet Yegor Semyonych began it with *audiatur altera pars* and ended with *sapienti sat*,[4] and between these two pronouncements there was a whole fountain of venomous words of all sorts addressed to "the learned ignorance of our patented Messers the Horticulturists who observe nature from the height of their lecterns," or to M. Gaucher, "whose success was created by amateurs and dilettantes," followed by an inappropriately forced and insincere regret that it was no longer possible to give peasants a birching for stealing fruit and breaking the trees while they are at it.

"This is beautiful, sweet, and healthy work, but here, too, there are passions and war," thought Kovrin. "It must be that everywhere and in all occupations, people with ideas are nervous and marked by high sensitivity. It probably has to be that way."

He thought of Tanya, who loved Yegor Semyonych's articles so much. Small of stature, pale, so skinny that you could see her collarbones; her eyes wide open, dark, intelligent, always peering somewhere and seeking something; her gait like her father's— small, hurried steps. She talks a lot, likes to argue, and accompanies every phrase, even the most insignificant, with expressive looks and gestures. She must be nervous in the highest degree.

Kovrin began to read further, but understood nothing and dropped it. The pleasant excitement, the same with which he had danced the mazurka and listened to the music earlier, now oppressed him and evoked a great many thoughts. He got up and began pacing the room, thinking about the black monk. It occurred to him that if he alone had seen this strange, supernatural monk, it meant that he was ill and had gone as far as hallucinations. This thought alarmed him, but not for long.

"But I'm quite well, and I do no one any harm, so there's nothing bad in my hallucination," he thought and felt good again.

He sat down on the sofa and put his head in his hands, holding back the incomprehensible joy that filled his whole being, then he paced about again and sat down to work. But the thoughts he read in the book did not satisfy him. He wanted something gigantic, boundless, staggering. Towards morning he undressed and reluctantly went to bed: he did have to sleep!

When he heard the footsteps of Yegor Semyonych leaving for the gardens, Kovrin rang the bell and told the servant to bring some wine. He drank several glasses of Lafite with pleasure, then pulled the blanket over his head; his consciousness went dim, and he fell asleep.

IV

Yegor Semyonych and Tanya often quarreled and said unpleasant things to each other.

One morning they had a squabble over something. Tanya began to cry and went to her room. She did not come out for dinner or for tea. Yegor Semyonych first went about all pompous, puffed up, as if wishing to make it known that for him the interests of justice and order were higher than anything in the world, but soon his character failed him and he lost his spirits. He wandered sadly through the park and kept sighing: "Ah, my God, my God!"—and did not eat a single crumb at dinner. Finally, guilty, suffering remorse, he knocked on the locked door and timidly called:

"Tanya! Tanya!"

And in answer to him a weak voice, exhausted from tears and at the same time resolute, came from behind the door:

"Leave me alone, I beg you."

The suffering of the masters affected the entire household, even the people who worked in the garden. Kovrin was immersed in his interesting work, but in the end he, too, felt dull and awkward. To disperse the general bad mood somehow, he decided to intervene and before evening knocked on Tanya's door. He was admitted.

"Aie, aie, what a shame!" he began jokingly, looking in surprise at Tanya's tear-stained, mournful face, covered with red spots. "Can it be so serious? Aie, aie!"

"But if you only knew how he torments me!" she said, and tears, bitter, abundant tears, poured from her big eyes. "He wears me out!" she went on, wringing her hands. "I didn't say anything to him . . . not anything . . . I just said there was no need to keep . . . extra workers, if . . . if it's possible to hire day laborers whenever we like. The . . . the workers have already spent a whole week doing nothing . . . I . . . I just said it, and he began to shout and said . . . a lot of insulting . . . deeply offensive things to me. What for?"

"Come, come," said Kovrin, straightening her hair. "You've quarreled, cried, and enough. You mustn't be angry for so long, it's not nice . . . especially since he loves you no end."

"He's ruined my . . . my whole life," Tanya went on, sobbing. "All I hear is insults and offense. He considers me useless in his house. So, then? He's right. I'll leave here tomorrow, get hired as a telegraph girl . . . Let him . . ."

"Well, well, well . . . Don't cry, Tanya. Don't cry, my dear . . . You're both hot-tempered, irritable, you're both to blame. Come, I'll make peace between you."

Kovrin spoke tenderly and persuasively, and she went on crying, her shoulders shaking and her hands clenched, as if some terrible misfortune had actually befallen her. He felt the more sorry for her because, though her grief was not serious, she suffered deeply. What trifles sufficed to make this being unhappy for a whole day, and perhaps even all her life! As he comforted Tanya, Kovrin was thinking that, apart from this girl and her father, there were no people to be found in the whole world who loved him like their own, like family; that if it were not for these two persons, he, who had lost his father and mother in early childhood, might have died without knowing genuine tenderness and that naïve, unreasoning love which one feels only for very close blood relations. And he felt that the nerves of this crying, shaking girl responded, like iron to a magnet, to his own half-sick, frayed nerves. He never could have loved a healthy, strong, red-cheeked woman, but pale, weak, unhappy Tanya he liked very much.

And he gladly stroked her hair and shoulders, pressed her hands and wiped her tears . . . Finally she stopped crying. She went on for a long time complaining about her father and her difficult, unbearable life in this house, imploring Kovrin to put himself in her place; then she gradually began to smile and sigh about God having given her such a bad character, in the end burst into loud laughter, called herself a fool, and ran out of the room.

When Kovrin went out to the garden a little later, Yegor Semyonych and Tanya were strolling side by side along the walk, as if nothing had happened, and they were both eating black bread and salt, because they were both hungry.

V

Pleased that he had succeeded so well in the role of peacemaker, Kovrin went into the park. As he sat on a bench and reflected, he heard the rattle of carriages and women's laughter—that was guests arriving. When the evening shadows began to lengthen in the garden, he vaguely heard the sounds of a violin and voices singing, and that reminded him of the black monk. Where, in what country or on what planet, was that optical incongruity racing about now?

No sooner had he remembered the legend and pictured in his imagination the dark phantom he had seen in the rye field, than there stepped from behind a pine tree just opposite him, inaudibly, without the slightest rustle, a man of average height, with a bare, gray head, all in dark clothes and barefoot, looking like a beggar, and his black eyebrows stood out sharply on his pale, deathly face. Nodding his head affably, this beggar or wanderer noiselessly approached the bench and sat down, and Kovrin recognized him as the black monk. For a moment the two looked at each other—Kovrin with amazement, and the monk tenderly and, as before, a little slyly, with the expression of one who keeps his own counsel.

"But you are a mirage," said Kovrin. "Why are you here and sitting in one place? It doesn't agree with the legend."

"That makes no difference," the monk answered after a moment, in a low voice, turning his face to him. "The legend, the mirage, and I—it is all a product of your excited imagination. I am a phantom."

"So you don't exist?" asked Kovrin.

"Think as you like," said the monk, and he smiled faintly. "I exist in your imagination, and your imagination is part of nature, which means that I, too, exist in nature."

"You have a very old, intelligent, and highly expressive face, as if you really have lived more than a thousand years," said Kovrin. "I didn't know that my imagination was capable of creating such phenomena. But why are you looking at me with such rapture? Do you like me?"

"Yes. You are one of the few who are justly called the chosen of God. You serve the eternal truth. Your thoughts and intentions, your astonishing science and your whole life bear a divine, heavenly imprint, because they are devoted to the reasonable and the beautiful—that is, to what is eternal."

"You said: the eternal truth . . . But can people attain to eternal truth and do they need it, if there is no eternal life?"

"There is eternal life," said the monk.

"You believe in people's immortality?"

"Yes, of course. A great, magnificent future awaits you people. And the more like you there are on earth, the sooner that future will be realized. Without you servants of the higher principle, who live consciously and freely, mankind would be insignificant; developing in natural order, it would wait a long time for the end of its earthly history. But you will lead it into the kingdom of eternal truth several thousand years earlier—and in that lies your high worth. You incarnate in yourselves the blessing of God that rests upon people."

"And what is the goal of eternal life?" asked Kovrin.

"The same as of any life—enjoyment. True enjoyment is in

knowledge, and eternal life will provide countless and inexhaustible sources for knowledge, and in that sense it is said: 'In my Father's house are many mansions.' "[5]

"If you only knew how nice it is to listen to you!" said Kovrin, rubbing his hands with pleasure.

"I'm very glad."

"But I know: when you leave, I'll be troubled by the question of your essence. You're a phantom, a hallucination. Meaning that I'm mentally ill, abnormal?"

"Suppose you are. What is so troubling? You're ill because you worked beyond your strength and got tired, and that means you sacrificed your health to an idea, and the time is near when you will also give your life to it. What could be better? That is generally what all noble natures, endowed from on high, strive for."

"If I know that I am mentally ill, then can I believe myself?"

"And how do you know that people of genius, whom the whole world believes, did not also see phantoms? Learned men now say that genius is akin to madness. My friend, only the ordinary herd people are healthy and normal. Reflections on this nervous age, fatigue, degeneracy, and so on, can seriously worry only those who see the goal of life in the present, that is, herd people."

"The Romans said: *mens sana in corpore sano.*"[6]

"Not everything that the Romans or Greeks said was true. An exalted state, excitement, ecstasy—all that distinguishes the prophets, the poets, the martyrs for an idea, from ordinary people—runs counter to the animal side of man, that is, to his physical health. I repeat: if you want to be healthy and normal, join the herd."

"Strange, you're repeating what often goes through my own head," said Kovrin. "It's as if you had spied and eavesdropped on my innermost thoughts. But let's not talk about me. What do you mean by eternal truth?"

The monk did not reply. Kovrin looked at him and could not make out his face: his features were dim and blurred. Then the monk's head and hands began to disappear; his body mingled with the bench and the evening twilight, and he vanished completely.

"The hallucination is over!" said Kovrin, and he laughed. "Too bad."

He went back to the house cheerful and happy. The little that the black monk had said to him had flattered not his vanity but his whole soul, his whole being. To be a chosen one, to serve the eternal truth, to stand in the ranks of those who will make mankind worthy of the Kingdom of God several thousand years earlier, that is, deliver people from several thousand extra years of struggle, sin, and suffering, to give everything to that idea—youth, strength, health, to be ready to die for the common good—what a lofty, what a happy fate! His past, pure, chaste, filled with toil, raced through his memory, he remembered all that he had studied and what he taught others, and he decided that there was no exaggeration in the monk's words.

Tanya came walking towards him through the park. She was wearing a different dress.

"You're here?" she said. "And we've been looking and looking for you . . . But what's the matter?" she said in surprise, seeing his rapturous, radiant face and his eyes brimming with tears. "You're so strange, Andryusha."

"I'm contented, Tanya," said Kovrin, placing his hands on her shoulders. "I'm more than contented, I'm happy! Tanya, dear Tanya, you're an extremely sympathetic being. Dear Tanya, I'm so glad, so glad!"

He warmly kissed both her hands and went on:

"I've just lived through some bright, wondrous, unearthly moments. But I can't tell you everything, because you'll call me mad or you won't believe me. Let's talk about you. Dear, nice Tanya! I love you and I'm used to loving you. To have you near, to meet you a dozen times a day, has become a necessity for my soul. I don't know how I'll do without you when I go back home."

"Well!" Tanya laughed. "You'll forget us in two days. We're little people, and you're a great man."

"No, let's talk seriously!" he said. "I'll take you with me, Tanya. Yes? Will you go with me? Do you want to be mine?"

"Well!" said Tanya, and again she wanted to laugh, but the laughter did not come out, and red spots appeared on her face.

She started breathing fast, and quickly went, not towards the house, but further into the park.

"I wasn't thinking of that . . . I wasn't!" she said, clasping her hands as if in despair.

And Kovrin followed her, saying with the same radiant, rapturous face:

"I want a love that will capture the whole of me, and only you, Tanya, can give me that love. I'm happy! Happy!"

She was stunned, she bent, shrank, and seemed to grow ten years older, but he found her lovely and expressed his rapture aloud: "How beautiful she is!"

VI

On learning from Kovrin not only that the romance was under way, but that there was even to be a wedding, Yegor Semyonych paced up and down for a long time, trying to conceal his agitation. His hands began to tremble, his neck swelled and turned purple, he ordered his racing droshky harnessed and drove off somewhere. Tanya, seeing how he whipped up the horse and how far down, almost to the ears, he had pulled his cap, understood his mood, locked herself in her room, and cried all day.

The peaches and plums were already ripe in the conservatory; the packing and sending of these delicate and capricious goods to Moscow called for much attention, work, and trouble. The summer being very hot and dry, it was necessary to water every tree, which took a lot of time and labor, and besides that multitudes of caterpillars appeared, which the workers, and even Yegor Semyonych and Tanya, squashed in their fingers, to Kovrin's great disgust. With all that it was necessary to receive the fall orders for fruit and trees and carry on a vast correspondence. And at the busiest time, when nobody seemed to have a single free moment, the time came for work in the fields, which took half the workers from the gardens; Yegor Semyonych, deeply tanned, worn out, angry, galloped off now to the gardens, now to the fields, and shouted that he was being torn to pieces and that he was going to put a bullet through his head.

And on top of that there was the bustling over the trousseau, something to which the Pesotskys attached great importance; the snick of scissors, the rattle of sewing machines, the burning smell of irons, the fussiness of the dressmaker, a nervous, easily offended lady, made everyone in the house dizzy. And, as if by design, guests came every day, who had to be entertained, fed, and even put up overnight. But all this hard labor passed unobserved, as in a fog. Tanya felt as if love and happiness had caught her unawares, though for some reason she had been certain since the age of fourteen that Kovrin would marry precisely her. She was amazed, perplexed, did not believe herself . . . Sometimes she would be flooded with such joy that she wanted to fly up to the clouds and there pray to God, but then she would suddenly remember that in August she had to part with her own nest and leave her father, or else the thought would come, God knows from where, that she was insignificant, small, and unworthy of such a great man as Kovrin—and she would go to her room, lock herself in, and weep bitterly for several hours. When guests came, she would suddenly think that Kovrin was remarkably handsome and that all the women were in love with him and envied her, and her soul would be filled with rapture and pride, as if she had conquered the whole world, but he had only to smile affably to some young lady, and she would tremble with jealousy, go to her room, and—tears again. These new feelings took complete possession of her, she helped her father mechanically, and did not notice the peaches, or the caterpillars, or the workers, or how quickly the time raced by.

Almost the same thing happened with Yegor Semyonych. He worked from morning till night, was always hurrying somewhere, lost patience, became irritated, but all as if in some magical half dream. It was now as if two persons were sitting in him: one was the real Yegor Semyonych, who, listening to the gardener, Ivan Karlych, reporting some disorders to him, became indignant and clutched his head in despair, and the other not the real one, as if half drunk, who would suddenly break off the business conversation in mid-sentence, touch the gardener's shoulder, and begin to murmur:

"Whatever you say, blood means a lot. His mother was a most amazing, noble, intelligent woman. It was a pleasure to look at her face, as kind, bright, and pure as an angel's. She made wonderful drawings, wrote verses, spoke five foreign languages, sang . . . The poor thing died of consumption, may she rest in peace."

The unreal Yegor Semyonych sighed and, after a pause, went on:

"When he was a little boy and growing up in my house, he had the same angelic face, bright and good. His eyes, his movements, and his conversation were gentle and graceful, like his mother's. And his intelligence? He always amazed us with his intelligence. Let me tell you, he's not a master of arts for nothing. Not for nothing. Wait and see, Ivan Karlych, what becomes of him in ten years. He'll be unapproachable!"

But here the real Yegor Semyonych would recollect himself, make a terrible face, clutch his head, and shout:

"Devils! Besmutted, bemangled, begrimed! The orchard's lost! The orchard's ruined!"

And Kovrin worked with his former zeal and did not notice the turmoil. Love only added fuel to the fire. After each meeting with Tanya, he went to his room, happy, rapturous, and with the same passion with which he had just kissed Tanya and declared his love to her, got down to his book or manuscript. What the black monk had said about the chosen of God, the eternal truth, the magnificent future of mankind, and so on, endowed his work with a special, extraordinary importance and filled his soul with pride, with an awareness of his own loftiness. He met the black monk once or twice a week, in the park or in the house, and had long talks with him, but that did not alarm him; on the contrary, it delighted him, because he was now firmly convinced that such visions came only to chosen, outstanding people who devoted themselves to the service of the idea.

Once the monk came during dinner and sat by the window in the dining room. Kovrin was glad and very adroitly started a conversation with Yegor Semyonych and Tanya about something that would interest the monk; the black visitor listened and nodded affably, and Yegor Semyonych and Tanya also listened and smiled cheerfully, not suspecting that Kovrin was not talking to them but to his hallucination.

The Dormition fast[7] arrived unnoticed, and soon after it the day of the wedding, which, at the insistence of Yegor Semyonych, was celebrated "with a smash," that is, with senseless revelry that went on for two days and nights. The eating and drinking ran to about three thousand roubles, but the bad hired music, the loud toasting, and the rushing about of servants made it impossible to appreciate the taste of the expensive wines and the extraordinary delicacies ordered from Moscow.

VII

Once on one of the long winter nights Kovrin was lying in bed reading a French novel. Poor Tanya, who had headaches in the evenings from being unused to city life, had long been asleep and occasionally in her sleep murmured some incoherent phrases.

The clock struck three. Kovrin put out the candle and lay down; for a long time he lay with closed eyes but could not sleep, because, as it seemed to him, the room was very hot and Tanya was murmuring. At four-thirty he lit the candle again and this time saw the black monk, who was sitting in the armchair near the bed.

"Hello," said the monk and, after some silence, he asked: "What are you thinking about now?"

"About fame," replied Kovrin. "In the French novel I've just been reading, there is a man, a young scholar, who does foolish things and pines away from a longing for fame. This longing for fame is incomprehensible to me."

"Because you're intelligent. You look upon fame with indifference, as upon a plaything that does not interest you."

"Yes, that's true."

"Celebrity has no charm for you. Is it flattering, or amusing, or instructive to have your name carved on a tombstone and then have time erase the inscription along with the gilding? Fortunately, though, there are too many of you for weak human memory to be able to preserve your names."

"Agreed," said Kovrin. "And why remember them? But let's talk about something else. About happiness, for instance. What is happiness?"

When the clock struck five, he was sitting on his bed, his feet hanging down on the rug, and, addressing the monk, was saying:

"In ancient times one happy man finally became frightened of his happiness—so great it was!—and, to appease the gods, sacrificed his favorite ring to them. You know? I, too, like Polycrates,[8] am beginning to worry a little about my happiness. It seems strange to me that I experience nothing but joy from morning till evening. It fills the whole of me and stifles all my other feelings. I don't know what sadness, sorrow, or boredom is. I'm not asleep now, I have insomnia, but I'm not bored. I say it seriously: I'm beginning to be puzzled."

"But why?" The monk was amazed. "Is joy a supernatural feeling? Should it not be the normal state of man? The higher man is in his mental and moral development, the freer he is, the greater the pleasure that life affords him. Socrates, Diogenes, and Marcus Aurelius experienced joy, not sorrow. And the Apostle says: 'Rejoice evermore.'[9] Rejoice, then, and be happy."

"And what if the gods suddenly get angry?" Kovrin joked and laughed. "If they take my comfort from me and make me suffer cold and hunger, it will hardly be to my liking."

Tanya had awakened meanwhile and was looking at her husband with amazement and horror. He was addressing the armchair, gesticulating and laughing: his eyes shone, and there was something strange in his laughter.

"Andryusha, who are you talking to?" she asked, seizing the arm he had stretched out to the monk. "Andryusha! Who?"

"Eh? Who?" Kovrin was embarrassed. "To him . . . He's sitting there," he said, pointing to the black monk.

"No one is there . . . no one! Andryusha, you're ill!"

Tanya embraced her husband and pressed herself to him, as if protecting him from visions, and she covered his eyes with her hand.

"You're ill!" she began to sob, trembling all over. "Forgive me, my sweet, my dear, but I've long noticed that your soul is troubled by something . . . You're mentally ill, Andryusha . . ."

Her trembling communicated itself to him. He glanced once more at the chair, which was now empty, suddenly felt a weakness in his arms and legs, became frightened, and began to dress.

"It's nothing, Tanya, nothing . . ." he murmured, trembling. "In fact, I am a bit unwell . . . it's time I admitted it."

"I've long noticed it . . . and papa has noticed it," she said, trying to hold back her sobs. "You talk to yourself, smile somehow strangely . . . don't sleep. Oh, my God, my God, save us!" she said in horror. "But don't be afraid, Andryusha, don't be afraid, for God's sake, don't be afraid . . ."

She, too, began to dress. Only now, looking at her, did Kovrin realize all the danger of his situation, realize what the black monk and his conversations with him meant. It was clear to him now that he was mad.

They both got dressed, not knowing why themselves, and went to the drawing room: she first, and he after her. There, already awakened by the sobbing, in a dressing gown and with a candle in his hand, stood Yegor Semyonych, who was visiting them.

"Don't be afraid, Andryusha," Tanya was saying, trembling as if in fever, "don't be afraid . . . Papa, it will go away . . . it will all go away . . ."

Kovrin was too agitated to speak. He wanted to say to his father-in-law, in a jocular tone: "Congratulate me, I think I've lost my mind," but he only moved his lips and smiled bitterly.

At nine o'clock in the morning they put a coat on him, then a fur coat, then wrapped him in a shawl, and drove him in a carriage to the doctor's. He started treatment.

VIII

Summer came again, and the doctor ordered him to go to the country. Kovrin was well by then, had stopped seeing the black monk, and it only remained for him to restore his physical strength. Living with his father-in-law in the country, he drank a lot of milk, worked only two hours a day, did not drink wine and did not smoke.

On the eve of St. Elijah's day,[10] the vigil was served at home. When the subdeacon handed the censer to the priest, the vast old hall began to smell like a cemetery, and Kovrin felt bored. He went out to the garden. Not noticing the luxuriant flowers, he strolled through the garden, sat on a bench for a while, then wandered into the park; coming to the river, he went down and stood lost in thought, gazing at the water. The gloomy pines with their shaggy roots, which had seen him there last year so young, joyful and lively, now did not whisper but stood motionless, mute, as if they did not recognize him. And indeed his head was cropped, his long, beautiful hair was gone, his pace was sluggish, his face, compared to last year, had grown fuller and more pale.

He crossed the planks to the other side. Where there had been rye the previous year, reaped oats now lay in rows. The sun had already set, and a broad red glow blazed on the horizon, forecasting windy weather for the next day. It was still. Peering in the direction where the black monk had first appeared the year before, Kovrin stood for some twenty minutes till the sunset began to fade . . .

When he returned home, sluggish, dissatisfied, the vigil was over. Yegor Semyonych and Tanya were sitting on the steps of the terrace having tea. They were talking about something, but on seeing Kovrin they suddenly fell silent, and by their faces he concluded that the talk had been about him.

"I think it's time for your milk," Tanya said to her husband.

"No, it's not . . ." he said, sitting on the lowest step. "Drink it yourself. I don't want to."

Tanya exchanged worried glances with her father and said in a guilty voice:

"You've noticed yourself that milk is good for you."

"Yes, very good!" Kovrin grinned. "My congratulations: since Friday I've gained another pound." He clutched his head tightly with his hands and said in anguish: "Why, why did you have me treated? Bromides, inactivity, warm baths, supervision, fainthearted fear over every mouthful, every step—it will all finally drive me to idiocy. I was losing my mind, I had megalomania, but I was gay, lively, and even happy, I was interesting and original. Now I've become more solid and reasonable, but as a result I'm just like everybody else: I'm a mediocrity, I'm bored with life . . . Oh, how cruel you've been to me! I had hallucinations, but did that harm anybody? I ask you, did it harm anybody?"

"God knows what you're saying!" Yegor Semyonych sighed. "It's even boring to listen."

"Don't listen, then."

The presence of people, especially of Yegor Semyonych, now irritated Kovrin, and he answered him drily, coldly, and even rudely, and never looked at him otherwise than with mockery and hatred, and Yegor Semyonych felt embarrassed and coughed guiltily, though he did not feel guilty of anything. Not understanding why their sweet, cordial relations had changed so abruptly, Tanya pressed herself to her father and peered anxiously into his eyes; she wanted to understand and could not, and it was only clear to her that their relations were getting worse and worse each day, that her father had aged very much recently, and her husband had become irritable, capricious, cranky, and uninteresting. She could no longer laugh and sing, ate nothing at dinner, did not sleep all night, expecting something terrible, and was so worn out that she once lay in a faint from dinner till evening. During the vigil it had seemed to her that her father wept, and now, as the three of them sat on the terrace, she tried not to think about it.

"How lucky Buddha and Mohammed and Shakespeare were that their kind relations and doctors did not treat them for ecstasy and inspiration!" said Kovrin. "If Mohammed had taken potassium bromide for his nerves, worked only two hours a day, and drunk milk, there would have been as little left after this remarkable man as after his dog. Doctors and kind relations will finally make it so that mankind will grow dull, mediocrity will be considered genius, and civilization will die out. If you only knew," Kovrin said with vexation, "how grateful I am to you!"

He felt extremely irritated and, to avoid saying something excessive, quickly got up and went into the house. It was quiet, and the scent of nicotiana and jalap came through the open windows from the garden. Moonlight lay in green patches on the floor and on the grand piano in the vast dark hall. Kovrin recalled the raptures of last summer, when there had been the same smell of jalap and moonlight shining in the windows. To bring back last year's mood, he went quickly to his study, lit a strong cigar, and told the servant to bring wine. But the cigar was bitter and disgusting in his mouth, and the wine did not taste the same as last year. That was what it meant to lose the habit! The cigar and two sips of wine made him dizzy, and his heart started pounding so that he had to take potassium bromide.

Before going to bed, Tanya said to him:

"My father adores you. You're angry with him for something, and it's killing him. Look: he's aging not by the day but by the hour. I beg you, Andryusha, for God's sake, for the sake of your late father, for the sake of my own peace, be nice to him!"

"I can't and won't."

"But why?" asked Tanya, beginning to tremble all over. "Explain to me, why?"

"Because I find him unsympathetic, that's all," Kovrin said carelessly and shrugged his shoulders. "But let's not talk about him, he's your father."

"I can't, I can't understand!" said Tanya, pressing her temples and staring at a single point. "Something inconceivable, something terrible is happening in our home. You've changed, you're no longer yourself . . . You, an intelligent, extraordinary man, become irritated over trifles, get into squabbles . . . You become upset over such small things that I'm sometimes astonished and can't believe it's really you. Well, well, don't be angry, don't be angry," she went on, frightened at her own words and kissing his hands. "You're intelligent, kind, noble. You'll be fair to my father. He's so good!"

"He's not good, he's good-natured. Vaudeville uncles like your father, with well-fed, good-natured physiognomies, extremely hospitable and whimsical, used to touch me and make me laugh in stories and vaudevilles, and in life, but now I find them repulsive. They're egoists to the marrow of their bones. What I find most repulsive is their well-fed look and that visceral, purely bullish or boarish optimism."

Tanya sat down on the bed and lay her head on the pillow.

"This is torture," she said, and it was clear from her voice that she was extremely tired and had difficulty speaking. "Not one peaceful moment since winter . . . My God, this is terrible! I'm suffering . . ."

"Yes, of course, I'm Herod and you and your dear papa are Egyptian infants.[11] Of course!"

His face seemed ugly and unpleasant to Tanya. Hatred and a mocking expression did not become him. She had noticed even earlier that his face now lacked something, as if, since he cut his hair, his face had also changed. She wanted to say something offensive to him, but she caught herself at once feeling animosity, became frightened, and left the bedroom.

IX

Kovrin was awarded his own chair. The inaugural lecture was scheduled for the second of December, and the announcement was posted in the university corridor. But on the scheduled day he informed the director of studies by telegram that the lecture would not be delivered on account of illness.

He was bleeding from the throat. He had been spitting blood, but about twice a month he bled profusely, and then he became extremely weak and fell into somnolence. The illness did not frighten him very much, because he knew that his late mother had lived for ten years or even longer with the same illness; and the doctors assured him that it was not dangerous and merely advised him not to worry, to lead a regular life, and to talk less.

In January the lecture failed to take place for the same reason, and in February it was too late to begin the course. It had to be postponed until the next year.

He now lived not with Tanya but with another woman, who was two years older than he and looked after him like a child. His state of mind was placid, submissive; he willingly obeyed, and when Varvara Nikolaevna—that was his friend's name—decided to take him to the Crimea, he agreed, though he had a presentiment that nothing good would come of this trip.

They arrived in Sebastopol in the evening and stayed at a hotel to get some rest and go on to Yalta the following day. They were both weary from traveling. Varvara Nikolaevna had tea, went to bed, and soon fell asleep. But Kovrin did not go to bed. At home, an hour before they left for the station, he had received a letter from Tanya and had been unable to bring himself to open it. It was now lying in his side pocket, and the thought of it troubled him unpleasantly. Frankly, at the bottom of his heart, he now considered his marriage to Tanya a mistake, was content to be finally separated from her, and the memory of this woman who in the end had turned into a living skeleton and in whom everything seemed to have died except for the big, intently peering, intelligent eyes, the memory of her called up in him only pity and vexation with himself. The handwriting on the envelope reminded him of how cruel and unfair he had been two years ago, how he had vented his inner emptiness, boredom, solitude, and dissatisfaction with life on totally blameless people. He incidentally remembered how one day he had torn his dissertation and all the articles he had written during his illness into little pieces and thrown them out the window, and how the scraps, flying with the wind, had caught on trees and flowers; in every line he had seen strange, totally unfounded claims, light-minded defiance, impudence, megalomania, and it had made the same impression on him as if he were reading a description of his own vices; but when the last notebook had been torn up and sent flying out the window, he had suddenly felt bitter and vexed for some reason, had gone to his wife and told her a lot of unpleasant things. My God, how he had tormented her! Once, wishing to cause her pain, he had told her that her father had played an unflattering role in their romance, because he had asked him to marry her; Yegor Semyonych had accidentally overheard it, rushed into the room, and, unable to utter a single word from despair, only shifted from one foot to the other and moaned somehow strangely, as if he had lost the power of speech, and Tanya, looking at her father, had cried out in a heartrending voice and fainted. It was hideous.

All this rose up in his memory as he looked at the familiar handwriting. Kovrin went out on the balcony; the weather was still and warm, and there was a smell of the sea. The beautiful bay reflected the moon and the lights and had a color for which it was difficult to find a name. It was a gentle and soft combination of blue and green; in places the water resembled blue vitriol in color, and in places the bay seemed filled with condensed moonlight instead of water, and overall what a harmony of colors, what a peaceful, calm, and lofty feeling!

On the lower floor, under the balcony, the windows were probably open, because women's voices and laughter could be heard distinctly. A party was evidently going on there.

Kovrin forced himself to open the letter and, going into his room, read:

"My father has just died. I owe that to you, because you killed him. Our orchard is perishing, strangers have already taken it over, which is precisely what my poor father feared would happen. I owe that to you as well. I hate you with all my heart and wish you to perish soon. Oh, how I suffer! My soul burns with unbearable pain . . . May you be cursed! I took you for an extraordinary man, a genius, I loved you, but you turned out to be mad . . ."

Kovrin could read no further, tore up the letter, and dropped it. An anxiety that resembled fear came over him. Behind the screen Varvara Nikolaevna lay asleep, and he could hear her breathing; from the lower floor came women's voices and laughter, yet he had the feeling that apart from him there was not a single living soul in the whole hotel. That the unfortunate, grief-stricken Tanya had cursed him in her letter and wished him to perish, gave him an eerie feeling, and he kept glancing at the door, as if fearing that the unknown power which in some two years had wrought such destruction in his life and the lives of his relations, might come into the room and again take control of him.

He knew from experience that when his nerves acted up, the best remedy for it was work. He had to sit down at the table and make himself concentrate on some thought, whatever the cost. He took a notebook from his red briefcase in which he had jotted down the synopsis of a small compilatory work he had thought up in case he found it boring in the Crimea with nothing to do. He sat down at the table and began working on this synopsis, and it seemed to him that his peaceful, submissive, indifferent mood was returning. The notebook with the synopsis even led him to reflect on worldly vanity. He thought of the high toll life takes for the insignificant or very ordinary blessings it bestows on man. For instance, to have a chair by the time you are forty, to be an ordinary professor, to explain ordinary thoughts, and other people's at that, in sluggish, boring, heavy language—in short, to attain the position of a mediocre scholar—he, Kovrin, had had to study for fifteen years, to work day and night, to suffer a grave mental illness, to live through an unsuccessful marriage, and to do all sorts of stupid and unfair things, which it would be more pleasant not to remember. Kovrin clearly recognized now that he was a mediocrity, and he willingly accepted it, because, in his opinion, each man should be content with what he is.

The synopsis might have calmed him down completely, but the torn-up letter lay white on the floor and disturbed his concentration. He got up from the table, picked up the scraps of the letter, and threw them out the window, but a light breeze was blowing from the sea, and the scraps scattered over the windowsill. Again an anxiety that resembled fear came over him, and it began to seem as if, apart from him, there was not a single soul in the whole hotel . . . He went out on the balcony. The bay, as if alive, looked at him with a multitude of blue, aquamarine, turquoise, and fiery eyes and beckoned to him. It was indeed hot and stifling, and it would have done no harm to go for a swim.

Suddenly on the lower floor, under the balcony, a violin started playing and two tender women's voices began to sing. It was something familiar. The romance they were singing below spoke of some girl with a morbid imagination, who heard mysterious sounds in the garden at night and decided that it was a sacred harmony incomprehensible to us mortals . . . Kovrin's breath was taken away, and his heart was wrung with sorrow, and a wonderful, sweet joy, such as he had long forgotten, trembled in his breast.

A black, tall pillar, resembling a whirlwind or a tornado, appeared on the far shore of the bay. With terrific speed it moved across the bay in the direction of the hotel, growing ever smaller and darker, and Kovrin barely had time to step aside and let it pass . . . A monk with a bare, gray head and black eyebrows, barefoot, his arms crossed on his chest, raced by and stopped in the middle of the room.

"Why didn't you believe me?" he asked reproachfully, looking tenderly at Kovrin. "If you had believed me then, when I said you were a genius, you would not have spent these two years so sadly and meagerly."

Kovrin now believed that he was chosen of God and a genius, he vividly recalled all his old conversations with the black monk and wanted to speak, but blood flowed from his throat straight on to his chest, and he, not knowing what to do, moved his hands over his chest, and his cuffs became wet with blood. He wanted to call Varvara Nikolaevna, who was sleeping behind the screen, made an effort and said:

"Tanya!"

He fell to the floor and, propping himself on his arms, again called:

"Tanya!"

He called out to Tanya, called out to the big garden with its luxuriant flowers sprinkled with dew, called out to the park, the pines with their shaggy roots, the field of rye, his wonderful science, his youth, courage, joy, called out to life that was so beautiful. He saw a big pool of blood on the floor by his face, and could no longer utter a single word from weakness, but an inexpressible, boundless happiness filled his whole being. Below, under the balcony, they were playing the serenade, and the black monk was whispering to him that he was a genius and was dying only because his weak human body had lost its equilibrium and could no longer serve as a container for genius.

When Varvara Nikolaevna woke up and came from behind the screen, Kovrin was already dead, and a blissful smile was frozen on his face.

JANUARY 1894

ROTHSCHILD'S FIDDLE

The town was small, worse than a village, and in it lived almost none but old people, who died so rarely it was even annoying. And in the hospital and jail there was very little demand for coffins. In short, business was bad. If Yakov Ivanov had been a coffin-maker in the provincial capital, he would most likely have had a house of his own and been called Yakov Matveich; but in this wretched little town he was simply called Yakov, his street nickname for some reason was "Bronzy," and he lived a poor life, like a simple peasant, in a little old cottage with only one room, and that room housed himself, Marfa, the stove, the double bed, the coffins, the workbench, and all his chattels.

Yakov made good, sturdy coffins. For peasants and tradesmen he made them his own size and was never once mistaken, because no one anywhere, not even in the jail, was taller or stronger than he, though he was now seventy years old. For gentlefolk and women he worked to measure, and for that he used an iron ruler. He accepted orders for children's coffins very reluctantly, and made them straight off without measurements, scornfully, and, taking the money for his work, would say each time:

"I confess, I don't like messing with trifles."

Besides his craft, he also earned a little money playing the fiddle. There was a Jewish orchestra in town that usually played at weddings, conducted by the tinsmith Moisei Ilyich Shakhkes, who took more than half the proceeds for himself. Since Yakov played the fiddle very well, especially Russian songs, Shakhkes sometimes invited him to join the orchestra for fifty kopecks a day, not counting gifts from the guests. When Bronzy sat in the orchestra, his face first of all sweated and turned purple; it was hot, the smell of garlic was stifling, the fiddle screeched, the double bass croaked just by his right ear, and by his left wept the flute, played by a skinny, red-headed Jew with a whole network of red and blue veins on his face, who bore the name of the famous rich man Rothschild. And this cursed Jew managed to play even the merriest things plaintively. For no apparent reason, Yakov gradually began to be filled with hatred and contempt for the Jews, and especially for Rothschild; he started picking on him, abusing him with bad words, and once was even about to give him a beating, and Rothschild got offended and, looking at him fiercely, said:

"If not for respecting your talent, I'd be chucking you out the window long ago."

Then he wept. And so Bronzy was not invited to join the orchestra very often, only in cases of extreme need, when one of the Jews was absent.

Yakov was never in good spirits, because he always had to suffer terrible losses. For instance, it was sinful to work on Sundays and holidays, Monday was an unlucky day, and as a result in one year there was a total of about two hundred days when he had, willy-nilly, to sit with folded arms. And what a loss that was! If anyone in town celebrated a wedding without music, or if Shakhkes did not invite Yakov, that, too, was a loss. The police inspector had been sick and pining away for two years, and Yakov had been waiting impatiently for him to die, but the inspector went to the provincial capital for treatment, and up and died there. That was a loss for you, ten roubles at the very least, because he would have had to make him an expensive coffin, with silk brocade. The thought of these losses bothered Yakov especially at night; he used to place the fiddle beside him on the bed, and when all sorts of nonsense started coming into his head, he would touch the strings, the fiddle would go twang in the darkness, and he would feel better.

On the sixth of May of the previous year, Marfa suddenly fell ill. The old woman breathed heavily, drank a lot of water, and staggered about, but all the same she stoked the stove in the morning and even went to fetch water. Towards evening she took to her bed. Yakov spent the whole day playing his fiddle; when it got completely dark, he took the notebook in which he recorded his losses daily, and out of boredom began adding up the yearly total. It came to over a thousand roubles. This astounded him so much that he flung the abacus to the floor and stamped his feet. Then he picked up the abacus, again clicked away for a long time, and sighed deeply and tensely. His face was purple and wet with sweat. He thought that if he could have put that lost thousand roubles in the bank, he would have earned at least forty roubles a year in interest. And therefore those forty roubles were also a loss. In short, wherever you turned, there was nothing but losses everywhere.

"Yakov!" Marfa called out unexpectedly. "I'm dying."

He turned to look at his wife. Her face, rosy with fever, was unusually serene and joyful. Bronzy, who was used to seeing her face always pale, timid, and unhappy, was now dismayed. It looked as if she was indeed dying, and was glad to be leaving that cottage, the coffins, and Yakov finally and forever . . . She was gazing at the ceiling and moving her lips, and her expression was happy, as if she could see death, her deliverer, and was whispering to him.

Day was already breaking, and the glow of early dawn appeared in the window. Looking at the old woman, Yakov for some reason recalled that in all their life, it seemed, he had never once been gentle with her, or sorry for her, had never once thought of buying her a little shawl or bringing her something sweet from a wedding, but had only yelled at her, scolded her for their losses, threatened her with his fists; true, he had never beaten her, but he had frightened her, and each time she was frozen with fear. Yes, he had told her not to drink tea, because expenses were high as it was, and she had drunk only hot water. And he understood why she had such a strange, joyful face now, and it gave him an eerie feeling.

Having waited for morning, he borrowed a neighbor's horse and took Marfa to the clinic. There were not many patients, and he did not have to wait long, only about three hours. To his great satisfaction, the patients were being received not by the doctor, who was ill himself, but by the doctor's assistant, Maxim Nikolaich, an old man, of whom everyone in town said that, though he was a drunkard and a brawler, he understood more than the doctor.

"Good day to you," said Yakov, leading his old woman into the receiving room. "Excuse us, Maxim Nikolaich, for troubling you with our trifling affairs. Here, you'll kindly see, my object has taken sick. My life's companion, as they say, excuse the expression . . ."

Knitting his gray eyebrows and stroking his side-whiskers, the assistant doctor began to examine the old woman, and she sat there on the stool, hunched up and skinny, sharp-nosed, her mouth open, in profile resembling a thirsty bird.

"Mm, yes . . . So . . ." the assistant said slowly and sighed. "Influenza, and maybe ague. There's typhus going around town. So? The old woman has lived, thank God . . . How old is she?"

"One year short of seventy, Maxim Nikolaich."

"So? The old woman has lived. Enough and to spare."

"There, of course, you've made a correct observation, Maxim Nikolaich," said Yakov, smiling out of politeness, "and we're heartily grateful for your agreeableness, but—permit me the expression—every insect wants to live."

"What else is new!" the assistant said, sounding as if it depended on him whether the old woman was to live or die. "Now then, my good man, you put a cold compress on her head and give her these powders twice a day. And with that—bye-bye, bonzhur."

From the expression of his face Yakov could see that things were bad and that no powders would help; it was clear to him now that Marfa would die very soon, if not today then tomorrow. He gave the assistant a slight nudge in the arm, winked at him, and said in a low voice:

"Maybe try cupping glasses,[1] Maxim Nikolaich."

"No time, no time, my good man. Take your old woman and God speed you. Bye-bye."

"Do us a kindness," Yakov implored. "You know yourself that if she had, say, a stomachache or something else inside, well, then it would be powders and drops, but she's got a cold! The first thing with a cold is to let blood, Maxim Nikolaich."

But the assistant doctor was already calling for the next patient, and a peasant woman with a boy was coming into the receiving room.

"Go, go . . ." he said to Yakov, frowning. "Don't blow smoke."

"In that case at least apply leeches to her! I'll pray to God eternally for you!"

The assistant doctor blew up and shouted:

"Just won't stop talking! B-blockhead . . ."

Yakov also blew up and turned all purple, but he did not say a word, he took Marfa under the arm and led her out of the receiving room. Only when they were getting into the cart did he give the clinic a stern and derisive look and say: "Got yourselves nicely planted there, play-actors! You'd be sure to cup a rich man, but you won't even spare a poor man a leech! Herods!"

When they came home, Marfa went into the cottage and stood for ten minutes holding on to the stove. She thought that if she lay down Yakov would start talking about losses and scold her for lying down all the time and not wanting to work. And Yakov gazed dully at her and remembered that tomorrow was St. John the Theologian's, and the next day St. Nicholas the Wonderworker's,[2] then Sunday, then Monday—the unlucky day. He would not be able to work for four days, and Marfa was sure to die on one of them; meaning that the coffin had to be made today. He took his iron ruler, went over to the old woman and measured her. Then she lay down, and he crossed himself and started making the coffin.

When the work was done, Bronzy put on his spectacles and wrote in his notebook:

"Coffin for Marfa Ivanov—2 roubles, 40 kopecks."

And sighed. The old woman lay silent all the while with her eyes closed. But in the evening, when it grew dark, she suddenly called to the old man.

"Remember, Yakov?" she asked, looking at him joyfully. "Remember, fifty years ago God gave us a little baby with a blond little head? You and I used to sit by the river then and sing songs . . . under the pussywillow." And with a bitter smile she added: "The little girl died."

Yakov strained his memory, but simply could not remember either the baby or the pussywillow.

"You're imagining it," he said.

The priest came, gave her communion and anointed her with oil. Then Marfa began to murmur something incoherent, and towards morning she passed away.

Some old neighbor women washed her and dressed her and put her in the coffin. To avoid paying extra to the reader, Yakov read the Psalter himself, and they did not charge him for the grave either, because the cemetery caretaker was his chum. Four peasants carried the coffin to the cemetery, not for money but out of respect. Old women, beggars, and two holy fools followed the coffin, passersby crossed themselves piously . . . And Yakov was very pleased that it was all so honorable, decent, and cheap, and no offense to anyone. Bidding his last farewell to Marfa, he touched the coffin with his hand and thought, "Fine work!"

But on his way back from the cemetery, he was overcome by intense anguish. Something was wrong with him: his breath was hot and heavy, his legs were weak, he felt thirsty. And then all sorts of thoughts began coming into his head. He recalled again that in his whole life he had never once pitied Marfa or been gentle with her. The fifty-two years that they had lived in the same cottage had dragged on and on, yet it turned out somehow that in all that time he had never thought of her, never paid attention to her, as if she were a cat or a dog. And yet every day she had stoked the stove, cooked and baked, fetched water, chopped wood, slept in the same bed with him, and when he came home drunk from weddings, she reverently hung his fiddle on the wall each time and put him to bed, and all that in silence, with a timid, solicitous look.

Rothschild came towards Yakov, smiling and bowing.

"And I've been looking for you, uncle!" he said. "Moisei Ilyich greets you and tells you to come to him right away."

Yakov could not be bothered with that. He wanted to weep.

"Let me be!" he said and walked on.

"But how is this possible?" Rothschild became all alarmed and ran ahead of him. "Moisei Ilyich will be upset! He said right away."

Yakov found it disgusting that the Jew was out of breath, kept blinking, and had so many red freckles. And it was repulsive to look at his green frock coat with its dark patches and at his whole fragile, delicate figure.

"What are you bothering me for, you piece of garlic?" Yakov shouted. "Leave me alone!"

The Jew got angry and also shouted:

"But you please calm down, or I'm sending you flying over the fence!"

"Out of my sight!" Yakov bellowed and rushed at him with his fists. "These mangy Yids won't let a man live!"

Rothschild went dead with fear, cowered, and waved his arms over his head as if protecting himself from blows, then jumped up and ran away as fast as he could. He hopped as he ran, clasped his hands, and you could see his long, skinny back twitch. The street urchins, glad of the chance, ran after him, shouting: "Yid! Yid!" The dogs also chased him, barking. Somebody guffawed, then whistled, the dogs barked louder and more in unison . . . Then one of the dogs must have bitten Rothschild, because there was a desperate cry of pain.

Yakov walked about the common, then, skirting the town, went wherever his feet took him, and the urchins shouted: "There goes Bronzy! There goes Bronzy!" And here was the river. Snipe flitted about and peeped, ducks quacked. The sun was very hot, and the water was so dazzling it was painful to look at. Yakov strolled down the path along the bank, saw a fat, red-cheeked lady come out of a bathing house, and thought: "Some otter you are!" Not far from the bathing house boys were catching crayfish with meat for bait; seeing him, they started shouting maliciously: "Bronzy! Bronzy!" And here was an old spreading pussywillow with an enormous hole and crows' nests in its branches . . . And suddenly in Yakov's memory there appeared, as if alive, the blond-headed little baby and the pussywillow Marfa had spoken of. Yes, it was the same pussywillow, green, quiet, sad . . . How aged it was, poor thing!

He sat down under it and began to recall. On the far bank, where there was now a water meadow, a big birch grove had once stood, and back then that bare hill visible on the horizon had been covered by the blue mass of an age-old pine forest. Wooden barges had navigated the river. And now everything was level and smooth, and only one birch tree stood on the far shore, young and shapely as a squire's daughter, and there were only ducks and geese on the river, and it did not look as if there had ever been barges here. It even seemed as if the geese had grown fewer compared with former times. Yakov closed his eyes, and huge flocks of white geese rushed towards each other in his imagination.

He was puzzled how it had turned out that in the last forty or fifty years of his life he had never gone to the river, or, if he had, that he had paid no attention to it. It was a big river, not some trifling thing; fishing could be organized on it, and the fish could be sold to merchants, officials, and the barman at the train station, and the money could be put in the bank; you could go by boat from farmstead to farmstead and play the fiddle, and people of all ranks would pay you for it; you could try towing barges again—it was better than making coffins; finally, you could raise geese, kill them, and send them to Moscow in the winter; most likely you would get as much as ten roubles a year for the down alone. But he had missed it, he had done none of it. What losses! Ah, what losses!

And if he had done all of it together—caught the fish, and played the fiddle, and towed the barges, and slaughtered the geese—what capital it would have produced! But none of it had happened even in dreams, his life had gone by without benefit, without any enjoyment, had gone for nought, for a pinch of snuff; there was nothing left ahead, and looking back there was nothing but losses, and such terrible losses it made you shudder. And why could man not live so that there would not be all this waste and loss? Why, you might ask, had the birch grove and the pine forest been cut down? Why was the common left unused? Why did people always do exactly what they should not do? Why had Yakov spent his whole life abusing people, growling at them, threatening them with his fists, and offending his wife, and, you might ask, what need had there been to frighten and insult the Jew earlier that day? Generally, why did people interfere with each other's lives? It made for such losses! Such terrible losses! If there were no hatred and malice, people would be of enormous benefit to each other.

That evening and night he imagined the baby, the pussywillow, the fish, the slaughtered geese, and Marfa, looking in profile like a thirsty bird, and Rothschild's pale, pitiful face, and some sort of mugs getting at him from all sides and muttering about losses. He tossed and turned and got out of bed five times to play his fiddle.

In the morning he forced himself to get up and go to the clinic. The same Maxim Nikolaich told him to put cold compresses on his head, gave him some powders, and, by his tone and the look on his face, Yakov understood that things were bad and no powder would help. Going home afterwards, he reflected that death would only be a benefit: no need to eat or drink, or pay taxes, or offend people, and since a man lies in the grave not one year but hundreds and thousands of years, if you added it up, the benefit was enormous. Life was to a man's loss, but death was to his benefit. This reflection was, of course, correct, but all the same it was bitter and offensive: why was the world ordered so strangely that life, which is given man only once, goes by without any benefit?

He was not sorry to die, but when he saw his fiddle at home, his heart was wrung and he did feel sorry. He could not take the fiddle with him to the grave, and it would now be orphaned, and the same thing would happen to it as to the birch grove and the pine forest. Everything in this world perished and would go on perishing! Yakov went out of the cottage and sat on the step, clutching the fiddle to his breast. Thinking about this perishing life of loss, he began to play, himself not knowing what, but it came out plaintive and moving, and tears flowed down his cheeks. And the harder he thought, the sadder the fiddle sang.

The latch creaked once or twice, and Rothschild appeared in the gateway. He bravely crossed half the yard, but seeing Yakov he suddenly stopped, became all shrunken, and, probably out of fear, began to make signs with his hands as if he wanted to show what time it was with his fingers.

"Come on, it's all right," Yakov said gently and beckoned to him. "Come on!"

Looking mistrustful and afraid, Rothschild began to approach and stopped six feet away from him.

"But you kindly don't beat me!" he said, cowering. "Moisei Ilyich is sending me again. 'Don't be afraid,' he says, 'go to Yakov again and tell him I say it's impossible to do without him. There's a wedding Wednesday . . . ' Ye-e-es! Mister Shapovalov is marrying his daughter to a good mensch. And, oi, what a rich wedding it's going to be!" the Jew added and squinted one eye.

"Can't do it . . ." said Yakov, breathing heavily. "I've taken sick, brother."

And he started playing again, and tears poured from his eyes on to the fiddle. Rothschild listened attentively, standing sideways to him, his arms crossed on his chest. The frightened, puzzled look on his face gradually changed to a mournful and suffering one, he rolled up his eyes as if experiencing some painful ecstasy and said: "Weh-h-h! . . ." And tears flowed slowly down his cheeks and dripped onto the green frock coat.

And afterwards Yakov lay all day and grieved. When the priest, confessing him that evening, asked if he had any particular sins on his mind, he strained his fading memory, again recalled Marfa's unhappy face and the desperate cry of the Jew bitten by a dog, and said barely audibly:

"Give the fiddle to Rothschild."

"Very well," said the priest.

And now everybody in town asks: where did Rothschild get such a good fiddle? Did he buy it, or steal it, or maybe take it in pawn? He has long abandoned his flute and now only plays the fiddle. The same plaintive sounds pour from under his bow as in former times from his flute, but when he tries to repeat what Yakov had played as he sat on the step, what comes out is so dreary and mournful that his listeners weep, and he himself finally rolls up his eyes and says: "Weh-h-h! . . ." And this new song is liked so much in town that merchants and officials constantly send for Rothschild and make him play it dozens of times.

FEBRUARY 1894

THE STUDENT

At first the weather was fine, still. Blackbirds called, and in the nearby swamp something alive hooted plaintively, as if blowing into an empty bottle. A woodcock chirred by, and a shot rang out boomingly and merrily in the spring air. But when the forest grew dark, an unwelcome east wind blew up, cold and piercing, and everything fell silent. Needles of ice reached over the puddles, and the forest became inhospitable, forsaken, desolate. It felt like winter.

Ivan Velikopolsky, a seminary student, son of a verger, was coming home from fowling along a path that went all the way across a water meadow. His fingers were numb, and his face was burned by the wind. It seemed to him that this sudden onset of cold violated the order and harmony of everything, that nature herself felt dismayed, and therefore the evening darkness fell more quickly than it should. It was deserted around him and somehow especially gloomy. Only by the widows' gardens near the river was there a light burning; but far around and where the village lay, some two miles off, everything was completely drowned in the cold evening darkness. The student remembered that, when he left the house, his mother was sitting on the floor in the front hall, barefoot, polishing the samovar, and his father was lying on the stove and coughing; because it was Good Friday there was no cooking in the house,[1] and he was painfully hungry. And now, hunching up from the cold, the student thought how exactly the same wind had blown in the time of Rurik, and of Ioann the Terrible, and of Peter,[2] and in their time there had been the same savage poverty and hunger; the same leaky thatched roofs, ignorance and anguish, the same surrounding emptiness and darkness, the sense of oppression—all these horrors had been, and were, and would be, and when another thousand years had passed, life would be no better. And he did not want to go home.

The gardens were called the widows' because they were kept by two widows, a mother and daughter. The fire burned hotly, with a crackle, throwing light far around over the ploughed soil. The widow Vasilisa, a tall, plump old woman in a man's coat, stood by and gazed pensively at the fire; her daughter Lukerya, small, pock-marked, with a slightly stupid face, was sitting on the ground washing the pot and spoons. Evidently they had only just finished supper. Male voices were heard; it was local laborers watering their horses at the river.

"Well, here's winter back again," said the student, approaching the fire. "Good evening!"

Vasilisa gave a start, but recognized him at once and smiled affably.

"I didn't recognize you. God bless you," she said, "you'll be a rich man."[3]

They talked. Vasilisa had been around, had once served gentlefolk as a wet nurse, then as a nanny, and her speech was delicate, and the gentle, dignified smile never left her face; her daughter Lukerya, a village woman, beaten down by her husband, only squinted at the student and kept silent, and her expression was strange, like that of a deaf-mute.

"In the same way the apostle Peter warmed himself by a fire on a cold night," said the student, holding his hands out to the flames. "So it was cold then, too. Ah, what a dreadful night that was, granny! An exceedingly long, dreary night!"

He looked around at the darkness, shook his head convulsively, and asked:

"I expect you've been to the Twelve Gospels?"[4]

"I have," replied Vasilisa.

"At the time of the Last Supper, you remember, Peter said to Jesus: 'I am ready to go with you, both into prison and to death.' And the Lord said to him: 'I tell you, Peter, the cock will not crow this day, before you deny three times that you know me.' After the supper, Jesus was praying in the garden, sorrowful unto death, and poor Peter was worn out in his soul, he grew weak, his eyes were heavy, and he could not fight off his sleepiness. He slept. Then that same night, as you heard, Judas kissed Jesus and betrayed him to the executioners. He was bound and led to the high priest, and was beaten, and Peter, exhausted, suffering in sorrow and anguish, you see, not having had enough sleep, sensing that something terrible was about to happen on earth, followed after him . . . He loved Jesus passionately, to distraction, and now from afar he saw how they beat him . . ."

Lukerya abandoned the spoons and turned her fixed gaze on the student.

"They came to the high priest," he went on, "Jesus was questioned, and the servants meanwhile made a fire in the courtyard, because it was cold, and they warmed themselves. Peter stood by the fire with them and also warmed himself, as I'm doing now. A woman saw him and said: 'This man was also with Jesus,' meaning that he, too, should be taken and questioned. And all the servants who were by the fire must have looked at him suspiciously and sternly, because he became confused and said: 'I do not know the man.' A little later someone again recognized him as one of Jesus' disciples and said: 'You are one of them.' But he denied it again. And a third time someone turned to him: 'Did I not see you today in the garden with him?' A third time he denied it. And right after that the cock crowed, and Peter, looking at Jesus from afar, remembered the word he had said to him at the supper . . . Remembered, recovered, went out of the courtyard, and wept bitterly. The Gospel says: 'And he went out, and wept bitterly.' I picture it: a very, very silent and dark garden, and, barely heard in the silence, a muffled sobbing . . ."

The student sighed and fell to thinking. Still smiling, Vasilisa suddenly choked, and big, abundant tears rolled down her cheeks. She shielded her face from the fire with her sleeve, as if ashamed of her tears, and Lukerya, gazing fixedly at the student, flushed, and her expression became heavy, strained, as in someone who is trying to suppress intense pain.

The laborers were coming back from the river, and one of them, on horseback, was already close, and the light of the fire wavered on him. The student wished the widows good night and went on. And again it was dark, and his hands were cold. A cruel wind was blowing, and winter was indeed coming back, and it did not seem that in two days it would be Easter.

Now the student was thinking about Vasilisa: if she wept, it meant that everything that had happened with Peter on that dreadful night had some relation to her . . .

He looked back. The solitary fire flickered peacefully in the darkness, and the people around it could no longer be seen. The student thought again that if Vasilisa wept and her daughter was troubled, then obviously what he had just told them, something that had taken place nineteen centuries ago, had a relation to the present—to both women, and probably to this desolate village, to himself, to all people. If the old woman wept, it was not because he was able to tell it movingly, but because Peter was close to her and she was interested with her whole being in what had happened in Peter's soul.

And joy suddenly stirred in his soul, and he even stopped for a moment to catch his breath. The past, he thought, is connected with the present in an unbroken chain of events flowing one out of the other. And it seemed to him that he had just seen both ends of that chain: he touched one end, and the other moved.

And when he crossed the river on the ferry, and then, going up the hill, looked at his native village and to the west, where a narrow strip of cold, crimson sunset shone, he kept thinking how the truth and beauty that had guided human life there in the garden and in the high priest's courtyard, went on unbroken to this day and evidently had always been the main thing in human life and generally on earth; and a feeling of youth, health, strength—he was only twenty-two—and an inexpressibly sweet anticipation of happiness, an unknown, mysterious happiness, gradually came over him, and life seemed to him delightful, wondrous, and filled with lofty meaning.

APRIL 1894

ANNA ON THE NECK

I

After the wedding there was not even a light snack; the newly-weds drank a glass, changed their clothes, and went to the station. Instead of a gay wedding ball and dinner, instead of music and dancing—a two-hundred-mile pilgrimage.[1] Many approved of it, saying that Modest Alexeich was of high rank and no longer young, and a noisy wedding might perhaps not seem quite proper; and then, too, it was boring to listen to music, when a fifty-two-year-old official married a girl barely over eighteen. It was also said that Modest Alexeich, as a man of principle, undertook this trip to the monastery, essentially, to let his young wife know that in marriage, too, he gave first place to religion and morality.

The newlyweds were seen off. A crowd of colleagues and relatives stood with glasses, waiting to shout "hurrah" as the train left, and Pyotr Leontyich, the father of the bride, in a top hat and a schoolmaster's tailcoat, already drunk and very pale, kept holding out his glass towards the window and saying imploringly:

"Anyuta! Anya! Anya, just one word!"

Anya leaned out the window towards him, and he whispered something to her, breathing winy fumes on her, blowing in her ear—she understood none of it—and made a cross over her face, breast, hands; his breath trembled and tears glistened in his eyes. And Anya's brothers, Petya and Andryusha, both high-school students, pulled him from behind by the tailcoat and whispered in embarrassment:

"Papa, that will do . . . Papa, you mustn't . . ."

When the train set off, Anya saw her father run a little way after their car, staggering and spilling his wine, and what a pathetic, kind, and guilty face he had.

"Hur-ra-a-ah!" he shouted.

The newlyweds were left alone. Modest Alexeich looked around the compartment, put their things on the racks, and sat down opposite his young wife, smiling. He was an official of average height, rather stout, plump, very well fed, with long side-whiskers and no mustache, and his clean-shaven, round, sharply outlined chin resembled a heel. What most characterized his face was the missing mustache, that freshly shaven, bare space which gradually turned into fat cheeks quivering like jelly. His bearing was dignified, his movements were not quick, his manners were gentle.

"I can't help recalling one circumstance now," he said, smiling. "Five years ago, when Kosorotov got the Order of St. Anna second degree[2] and went to say thank you, His Excellency expressed himself thus: 'So now you have three Annas: one in your buttonhole and two on your neck.' And I should mention that at that time Kosorotov's wife had just come back to him, a shrewish and frivolous person whose name was Anna. I hope that when I get the Anna second degree, His Excellency will have no reason to say the same to me."

He smiled with his little eyes. And she also smiled, troubled by the thought that this man might at any moment kiss her with his full, moist lips, and she no longer had the right to deny him that. The soft movements of his plump body frightened her, she felt afraid and squeamish. He got up, unhurriedly removed his decoration from his neck, took off his tailcoat and waistcoat, and put on his dressing gown.

"There," he said, sitting down beside Anya.

She recalled how painful the wedding ceremony had been, when it had seemed to her that the priest, the guests, and all the people in the church were looking at her sorrowfully: why, why was she, such a sweet, nice girl, marrying this middle-aged, uninteresting gentleman? That morning she had still been delighted that everything was turning out so well, but during the wedding, and now on the train, she felt guilty, deceived, and ridiculous. Here she had married a rich man, yet she still had no money, the wedding dress had been made on a loan, and when her father and brothers were seeing her off today, she could tell by their faces that they did not have a kopeck. Would they have any supper tonight? And tomorrow? And for some reason it seemed to her that her father and the boys were now sitting there without her, hungry and feeling exactly the same anguish as they had the first evening after their mother's funeral.

"Oh, how unhappy I am!" she thought. "Why am I so unhappy?"

With the awkwardness of a dignified man unused to dealing with women, Modest Alexeich touched her waist and patted her shoulder, while she thought about money, about her mother and her death. When her mother died, her father, Pyotr Leontyich, a teacher of penmanship and drawing in the high school, took to drinking, and they fell into want; the boys had no boots or galoshes, the father kept being dragged before the justice of the peace, the bailiff came to make an inventory of the furniture . . . Such shame! Anya had to look after the drunken father, darn her brothers' socks, go to the market, and when people praised her beauty, youth, and gracious manners, it seemed to her that the whole world could see that her hat was cheap and the holes in her shoes were daubed over with ink. And during the nights, there were tears and the persistent, troubling thought that her father would very soon be dismissed from the school on account of his weakness, that he would not survive it and would also die, as her mother had died. But then their lady acquaintances got busy and began looking for a good man for Anya. Soon they came up with this same Modest Alexeich, neither young nor handsome, but with money. He had a hundred thousand in the bank and also a family estate that he leased. He was a man of principle and in good standing with His Excellency; it would be nothing for him, as Anya was told, to take a note from His Excellency to the principal of the school and even to the superintendent, to keep Pyotr Leontyich from being dismissed . . .

As she recalled these details, she suddenly heard music bursting through the window with the noise of voices. The train had stopped at a small station. Beyond the platform, in the crowd, an accordion and a cheap, shrill fiddle were playing briskly, and from beyond the tall birches and poplars, from beyond the dachas bathed in moonlight, came the sounds of a military band: they must have been having an evening dance. Summer residents and city-dwellers, who came there in good weather to breathe the clean air, strolled along the platform. Artynov was also there, the owner of this whole summer colony, a rich man, tall, stout, dark-haired, with an Armenian-looking face, protruding eyes, and a strange costume. He was wearing a shirt unbuttoned on the chest and high boots with spurs; a black cloak hung from his shoulders, dragging on the ground like a train. Two Borzoi hounds, their sharp muzzles lowered, followed after him.

Anya's eyes still glistened with tears, but she was no longer thinking about her mother, or money, or her wedding, but was shaking hands with some high-school students and officers she knew, laughing merrily and saying quickly:

"Hello! How are you?"

She went out to the end of the corridor, into the moonlight, and stood in such a way as to be fully visible in her magnificent new dress and hat.

"Why have we stopped here?" she asked.

"There's a sidetrack here," came the answer, "we're expecting the mail train."

Noticing that Artynov was looking at her, she narrowed her eyes coquettishly and began speaking loudly in French, and because her own voice sounded so pretty, and there was music, and the moon was reflected in the pond, and because Artynov, that notorious Don Juan and prankster, was looking at her greedily and with curiosity, and because everyone felt merry, she was suddenly filled with joy, and when the train started, and her officer acquaintances touched their visors in farewell, she was already humming the strains of a polka that the military band, banging away somewhere beyond the trees, sent after her; and she went back to her compartment feeling as if she had been convinced at the station that she would certainly be happy, no matter what.

The newlyweds spent two days at the monastery and then returned to town. They lived in a government apartment. When Modest Alexeich went to work, Anya played the piano, or wept from boredom, or lay on the couch and read novels and looked through fashion magazines. At dinner Modest Alexeich ate a great deal and talked about politics, about appointments, transfers, and bonuses, and that one had to work, that family life was not a pleasure but a duty, that a penny saved was a penny earned, and that he considered religion and morality the highest things in the world. And, gripping the knife in his fist like a sword, he said:

"Every man must have his responsibilities!"

And Anya listened to him, afraid and unable to eat, and usually left the table hungry. After dinner her husband rested and snored loudly, and she went to see her family. Her father and the boys looked at her somehow peculiarly, as if, just before she came, they had been denouncing her for marrying for the sake of money a dull, boring man whom she did not love; her rustling dress, her bracelets and ladylike look in general, embarrassed and offended them; in her presence they felt slightly abashed and did not know what to talk about; but still they loved her as before and had not yet grown accustomed to eating without her. She sat down with them and ate shchi, kasha,[3] and potatoes fried in mutton fat, which smelled like candles. With a trembling hand, Pyotr Leontyich poured from a decanter and drank quickly, greedily, with disgust, then drank another glass, then a third . . . Petya and Andryusha, thin, pale boys with big eyes, took the decanter away and said in perplexity:

"You mustn't, papa . . . That's enough, papa . . ."

And Anya was also worried and begged him not to drink any more, and he suddenly flared up and banged his fist on the table.

"I won't let anyone supervise me!" he cried. "Mere infants! I'll throw you all out!"

But there was weakness and kindness in his voice, and no one was afraid of him. After dinner he usually got dressed up; pale, with razor nicks on his chin, stretching his skinny neck, he spent half an hour standing in front of the mirror preening himself, brushing his hair, twirling his black mustache, spraying himself with scent, knotting his tie, then put on his gloves and top hat and went to give private lessons. But if it was a feast day, he stayed home and painted or played the harmonium, which hissed and roared; he tried to squeeze whole, harmonious sounds out of it and sang along, or else said gruffly to the boys:

"Scoundrels! Blackguards! You've ruined the instrument!"

In the evenings Anya's husband played cards with his colleagues, who lived under the same roof with him in the government building. During cards the wives of the officials got together, ugly, tastelessly dressed, coarse as kitchen maids, and gossip would begin, as ugly and tasteless as the wives themselves. Occasionally, Modest

Alexeich took Anya to the theater. In the intermissions he never allowed her to go a step away from him, and walked, holding her under the arm, in the corridor and foyer. When he greeted someone, he would immediately whisper to Anya: "State councillor . . . received by His Excellency" or: "Wealthy . . . owns a house . . ." When they passed the buffet, Anya always wanted very much to eat something sweet; she loved chocolate and apple tarts, but she had no money and was embarrassed to ask her husband. He would take a pear, finger it, and ask hesitantly:

"How much?"

"Twenty-five kopecks."

"Really!" he would say and put the pear back, but since it was awkward to leave the buffet without buying anything, he would ask for seltzer water and drink the whole bottle himself, and tears would come to his eyes, and Anya hated him at those moments.

Or else, blushing all over, he would say:

"Bow to this old lady!"

"But I don't know her."

"Never mind. She's the wife of the chief treasurer! Bow to her, I tell you!" he murmured insistently. "Your head won't fall off."

Anya bowed, and indeed her head did not fall off, but it was painful. She did everything her husband wanted and was angry with herself for having been deceived like a perfect little fool. She had married him only for money, and yet she now had less money than before her marriage. Formerly, her father at least used to give her twenty kopecks, but now she did not have a cent. She could not take money secretly or ask for it, she was afraid of her husband and trembled before him. It seemed to her that she had borne a fear of this man in her soul for a long time. In childhood the most imposing and terrible power for her, which came like a storm cloud or a locomotive ready to crush her, was her school principal; another such power, which they always talked about in the family, and which they feared for some reason, was His Excellency; and there were also some dozen powers of a lesser sort, among them stern, implacable schoolmasters who shaved their mustaches, and now, finally, there was Modest Alexeich, a man of principle, who even looked like a director. And in Anya's imagination all these powers blended into one, and in the shape of one terrible, enormous polar bear came down upon the weak and guilty, like her father, and she was afraid to say anything in protest, and she forced herself to smile and show feigned pleasure when she was crudely caressed and defiled with embraces that terrified her.

Only once did Pyotr Leontyich dare to ask for a loan of fifty roubles to pay some very unpleasant debt, but what a torment it was!

"Very well, I'll give you a loan," said Modest Alexeich, after some thought, "but I warn you that I will not assist you any more until you stop drinking. For a man in government service, such weakness is a disgrace. I cannot but remind you of the commonly known fact that many capable people have been ruined by this passion, whereas, if they had been temperate, they might in time have become high-ranking people."

And lengthy periods followed: "inasmuch as . . . ," "considering the fact that . . . ," "in view of the aforementioned . . . ," while poor Pyotr Leontyich suffered humiliation and felt a strong desire for a drink.

And when the boys came to visit Anya, usually wearing torn boots and shabby trousers, they also had to listen to admonishments.

"Every man must have his responsibilities!" Modest Alexeich said to them.

But he gave no money. Instead, he gave Anya rings, bracelets, brooches, saying it was good to keep these things for an unlucky day. And he often unlocked her chest of drawers and checked that all the things were there.

II

Meanwhile winter came. Long before Christmas the local paper announced that the customary winter ball "would this year take place" on December 29th, at the Assembly of the Nobility. Every evening, after cards, Modest Alexeich, agitated, whispered with the officials' wives, glanced worriedly at Anya, and afterwards paced the room for a long time, pondering something. Finally, late one evening, he stopped in front of Anya and said:

"You must have a ball gown made for you. Understand? Only please get advice from Marya Grigoryevna and Natalya Kuzminishna."

And he gave her a hundred roubles. She took it; but, in ordering her ball gown, she did not get anyone's advice, but only talked it over with her father and tried to imagine how her mother would have dressed for the ball. Her late mother had always dressed in the latest fashion and had always fussed over Anya, dressed her as elegantly as a doll, and taught her to speak French and dance the mazurka superbly (before her marriage she had worked as a governess for five years). Like her mother, Anya was able to make a new dress out of an old one, to clean her gloves with benzine, to rent *bijoux*, and, like her mother, she knew how to narrow her eyes, roll her *r*'s, assume beautiful poses, become enraptured when necessary, gaze sorrowfully and mysteriously. And from her father she had inherited her dark hair and eyes, her nervousness, and that manner of always preening herself.

When Modest Alexeich came into her room, without his frock coat, a half hour before going to the ball, in order to put his decoration on his neck in front of her pier glass, he was enchanted by the beauty and splendor of her fresh, airy costume, brushed out his side-whiskers smugly, and said:

"So that's how you are . . . that's how you are! Anyuta!" he went on, suddenly falling into a solemn tone. "I've made your happiness, and today you can make mine. I beg you to get yourself introduced to His Excellency's wife! For God's sake! Through her I may get the post of senior aide!"

They went to the ball. Here was the Assembly of the Nobility and the main entrance with its doorkeeper. The front hall with its cloakroom, fur coats, scurrying servants, and ladies in décolleté, shielding themselves from the drafty wind with fans. It smelled of gaslights and soldiers. When Anya, going up the stairs on her husband's arm, heard the music and saw her whole figure in an enormous mirror under the light of many lamps, joy awoke in her soul and with it the same presentiment of happiness she had felt on that moonlit evening at the little station. She walked proudly, self-confidently, for the first time feeling herself not a girl but a lady, and inadvertently copying the gait and manner of her late mother. And for the first time she felt herself rich and free. Even the presence of her husband did not hamper her, because, as she crossed the threshold of the Assembly, she already guessed instinctively that the proximity of an old husband was not humiliating to her in the least, but, on the contrary, placed upon her the stamp of piquant mysteriousness that men like so much. In the big hall the orchestra thundered and the dancing began. After her government apartment, caught up in impressions of light, colors, music, noise, Anya passed her gaze over the hall and thought: "Ah, how good!" and at once made out all her acquaintances in the crowd, everyone she had met earlier at soirées or promenades, all those officers, teachers, lawyers, officials, landowners, His Excellency, Artynov, and the high-society ladies, decked out, extremely décolleté, the beautiful and the ugly, who had already taken up their posts in the little booths and pavilions in order to start the charity bazaar for the benefit of the poor. An immense officer with epaulettes—she had met him in Staro-Kievsky Street when she was a schoolgirl and no longer remembered his last name—appeared as if from out of the ground and invited her for the waltz, and she flew away from her husband, and it seemed to her as if she were sailing in a boat through a heavy storm, and her husband had stayed far behind on the shore . . . She danced with passion, with enthusiasm, the waltz, the polka, the quadrille, passing from hand to hand, dazed by the music and noise, mixing Russian with French, rolling her *r*'s, laughing, and not thinking of her husband, or anyone, or anything. She was a success with men, that was clear and could not have been otherwise, she was breathless with excitement, she convulsively clutched her fan and wanted to drink. Her father, Pyotr Leontyich, in a wrinkled tailcoat that smelled of benzine, came up to her, offering her a dish of red ice cream.

"You're charming today," he said, looking at her with delight, "and never have I regretted so much that you rushed into marriage . . . Why? I know you did it for us, but . . ." With trembling hands he took out a small wad of money and said: "Today I was paid for my lessons and can repay my debt to your husband."

She put the dish in his hands and, carried off by someone, flew far away, and over her partner's shoulder she caught a glimpse of her father gliding across the parquet floor, putting his arms around a lady, and racing through the hall with her.

"He's so sweet when he's sober!" she thought.

She danced the mazurka with the same immense officer; he stepped gravely and heavily, like a uniformed side of beef, moved his shoulders and chest, barely stamped his feet—he was terribly reluctant to dance, and she fluttered around him, teasing him with her beauty, with her open neck; her eyes burned with provocation, her movements were passionate, while he became ever more indifferent and held his arms out to her benevolently, like a king.

"Bravo, bravo! . . ." came from the public.

But the immense officer gradually loosened up; he became lively, excited, and, yielding now to the enchantment, waxed enthusiastic and moved lightly, youthfully, while she only shifted her shoulders and glanced at him slyly, as if she were a queen and he her slave, and it seemed to her just then that everyone in the hall was looking at them, that all these people were thrilled and envied them. The immense officer had barely managed to thank her, when the public suddenly parted and the men straightened up somehow strangely, their arms at their sides . . . Walking towards her was His Excellency, in a tailcoat with two stars. Yes, His Excellency was walking precisely towards her, because he was looking straight at her with a saccharine smile and at the same time munching his lips, something he always did at the sight of pretty women.

"Delighted, delighted . . ." he began. "I'll order your husband put under arrest for concealing such a treasure from us till today. I've come on an errand from my wife," he went on, offering her his arm. "You must help us . . . Mm, yes . . . We should give you a prize for beauty . . . as in America . . . Mm, yes . . . The Americans . . . My wife is waiting impatiently for you."

He brought her to a booth, to an elderly lady, the lower part of whose face was so incongruously large that it seemed as if she were holding a big stone in her mouth.

"Help us," she said through her nose, in a sing-song voice. "All the pretty women are working at the charity bazaar, and you alone are having fun for some reason. Why don't you want to help us?"

She left, and Anya took her place by the silver samovar and cups. A brisk trade began at once. Anya took no less than a rouble per cup of tea, and she made the immense officer drink three cups. Artynov came up; the rich man with the prominent eyes, who suffered from shortness of breath, was no longer in the strange costume in which Anya had seen him that summer, but was wearing a tailcoat like everyone else. Not tearing his eyes from Anya, he drank a glass of champagne and paid a hundred roubles for it, then drank tea and gave another hundred—and all that in silence, suffering from asthma . . . Anya called customers over and took their money, now deeply convinced that her smiles and looks gave these people nothing but the greatest pleasure. She already understood that she had been created solely for this noisy, brilliant, laughing life with its music, dancing, and admirers, and her long-standing fear before the power that was coming down on her and threatening to crush her, seemed ridiculous to her; she was no longer afraid of anyone and only regretted that her mother was not there to rejoice with her now over her successes.

Pyotr Leontyich, pale but still keeping firmly on his feet, came up to the booth and asked for a glass of cognac. Anya blushed, expecting him to say something inappropriate (she was already ashamed of having such a poor, such an ordinary father), but he drank up, peeled off ten roubles from his little wad, and sedately walked away without saying a word. A little later she saw him stepping out the *grand rond* with a partner, and this time he staggered and shouted something, to the great embarrassment of his lady, and Anya remembered how three years ago he had staggered and shouted in the same way at a ball, and it had ended with a policeman taking him home to bed, and next day the director had threatened to dismiss him from his work. How untimely this memory was!

When the samovars went out in the booths and the weary benefactresses handed their receipts over to the elderly woman with the stone in her mouth, Artynov led Anya by the arm to the big hall, where supper was laid out for all the participants in the charity bazaar. There were about twenty people at the table, not more, but it was very noisy. His Excellency gave the toast: "In this magnificent dining room it would be appropriate to drink to the prosperity of the cheap eateries that were the object of today's bazaar." A brigadier general suggested that they drink "to the power before which even the artillery quails," and everybody began clinking with the ladies. There was great, great merriment!

When Anya was taken home, day was already breaking and the cooks were going to market. Joyful, drunk, filled with new impressions, exhausted, she undressed, collapsed on her bed, and fell asleep at once . . .

Past one o'clock in the afternoon her maid awakened her and reported that Mr. Artynov had come to visit. She dressed quickly and went to the drawing room. Soon after Artynov, His Excellency came to thank her for taking part in the charity bazaar. Munching and looking at her with saccharine eyes, he kissed her hand, asked her permission to come again, and left, while she stood in the middle of the drawing room, amazed, enchanted, unable to believe that the change in her life, an astonishing change, had taken place so soon; and just then her husband, Modest Alexeich, came in . . . And he stood before her now with the same ingratiating, sweet, slavishly deferential expression she was accustomed to seeing him have in the presence of the strong and distinguished; and with rapture, with indignation, with scorn, confident now that nothing would happen to her for it, she said, pronouncing each word distinctly:

"Get out, blockhead!"

After that Anya never had a single free day, for she participated now in a picnic, now in a promenade, now in a performance. She came home each day towards morning and lay on the floor in the drawing room, and then touchingly told everyone how she had slept under the flowers. She needed a great deal of money, but she was no longer afraid of Modest Alexeich and spent his money as if it were her own; she did not ask, did not demand, but merely sent him the bills or notes: "Pay the bearer 200 r.," or "100 r. payable at once."

At Easter Modest Alexeich received the Anna second degree. When he went to say thank you, His Excellency laid aside his newspaper and settled deeper into his armchair.

"So now you have three Annas," he said, examining his white hands with their pink nails, "one in the buttonhole and two on your neck."

Modest Alexeich put two fingers to his lips as a precaution against laughing out loud, and said:

"It now only remains to wait for a little Vladimir to come into the world. I make so bold as to ask Your Excellency to be the godfather."

He was alluding to the Vladimir fourth degree,[4] and was already imagining himself telling everywhere about this pun, so fortunate in its resourcefulness and boldness, and he wanted to say something else equally fortunate, but His Excellency again immersed himself in his newspaper and nodded his head . . .

And Anya kept riding about in troikas, went hunting with Artynov, acted in one-act plays, had suppers, and visited her family more and more rarely. They now dined by themselves. Pyotr Leontyich drank more than ever, they had no money, and the harmonium had long since been sold to pay a debt. Now the boys never let him go out alone and watched him lest he fall down; and when they met Anya in Staro-Kievsky Street in a coach and pair with an outrunner, and Artynov on the box instead of a driver, Pyotr Leontyich took off his top hat and was about to shout something, but Petya and Andryusha held him by the arms and said imploringly:

"You mustn't, papa . . . That will do, papa . . ."

OCTOBER 1895

The House with the Mezzanine

An Artist's Story

I

This was six or seven years ago, when I was living in one of the districts of T—— province, on the estate of the landowner Belokurov, a young man who got up very early, went about in a vest, drank beer in the evenings, and kept complaining to me that he met with no sympathy anywhere or from anyone. He lived in a cottage in the garden, and I in the old mansion, in a huge hall with columns, where there was no furniture except a wide sofa on which I slept and a table on which I played patience. Here, even in calm weather, something always howled in the old Amosov stoves,[1] but during a thunderstorm the whole house trembled and seemed to crack to pieces, and it was a little frightening, especially at night, when all ten big windows were suddenly lit up by lightning.

Condemned by fate to permanent idleness, I was doing decidedly nothing. I spent whole hours looking out my windows at the sky, the birds, the avenues, read everything that came in the mail, slept. Sometimes I left the house and wandered about somewhere till late in the evening.

Once, returning home, I accidentally wandered onto an unfamiliar estate. The sun was already hiding, and evening shadows stretched across the flowering rye. Two rows of old, closely planted, very tall fir trees stood like two solid walls, forming a beautiful, gloomy avenue. I easily climbed the fence and went down this avenue, slipping on the fir needles that lay inches-thick on the ground. It was quiet, dark, and only high in the treetops did a bright golden light tremble here and there and play iridescently on the spiderwebs. There was a strong, almost stifling, smell of fir needles. Then I turned down a long linden avenue. Here, too, there was old age and desolation; last year's leaves rustled sorrowfully under my feet, and shadows hid in the twilight between the trees. To the right, in an old orchard, an oriole sang reluctantly, in a weak voice—it must have been a little old lady, too. But now the lindens also ended; I passed a white house with a terrace and a mezzanine, and before me there unexpectedly opened up a view of the manor yard and a wide pond with a bathing house, a stand of green willows, a village on the other side, with a tall, slender belfry, the cross of which blazed, reflecting the setting sun. For a moment I felt the enchantment of something dear and very familiar, as if I had already seen this same panorama sometime in my childhood.

And by the white stone gateway that led from the yard into the fields, by the sturdy old gates with their lions, stood two girls. One of them, the elder, slender, pale, very beautiful, with a whole mass of chestnut hair on her head, with a small, stubborn mouth, had a stern expression and barely paid any attention to me; the other, still very young—she was seventeen or eighteen years old, not more—also slender and pale, with a big mouth and big eyes, looked at me in surprise as I passed by, said something in English, and became embarrassed, and it seemed to me that these two sweet faces had also been long familiar to me. And I returned home feeling as if I had had a good dream.

Soon after that, around noon one day, as Belokurov and I were strolling near the house, a spring carriage, swishing through the grass, unexpectedly drove into the yard, with one of those girls sitting in it. It was the older one. She had come with a subscription list, seeking aid for the victims of a fire. Without looking at us, she told us very seriously and in detail how many houses had burned down in the village of Siyanovo, how many men, women, and children had been left without a roof, and what the committee for the victims, of which she was now a member, intended to undertake as a first step. After having us sign it, she put the list away and at once began taking her leave.

"You've quite forgotten us, Pyotr Petrovich," she said to Belokurov, giving him her hand. "Come over, and if Monsieur X" (she said my name) "wishes to have a look at how some admirers of his talent live, and is so good as to visit us, mama and I will be very glad."

I bowed.

When she left, Pyotr Petrovich told me the story. This girl, in his words, was from a good family, her name was Lydia Volchaninova, and the estate she lived on with her mother and sister was called Shelkovka, the same as the one across the pond. Her father had once occupied a prominent position in Moscow and had died with the rank of privy councillor. Although they were well off, the Volchaninovs lived permanently in the country, summer and winter, and Lydia was a teacher in a zemstvo[2] school in her own Shelkovka and earned twenty-five roubles a month. She spent only this money on herself and was proud to be living at her own expense.

"An interesting family," said Belokurov. "We might go and see them sometime. They'd be very glad to have you."

After dinner once, on a feast day, we remembered the Volchaninovs and went to visit them in Shelkovka. They, the mother and both daughters, were at home. The mother, Ekaterina Pavlovna, evidently beautiful once but now flabby beyond her years, suffering from shortness of breath, sad, distracted, tried to engage me in a conversation about painting. Having learned from her daughter that I might visit Shelkovka, she had hastily recalled two or three landscapes of mine that she had seen at exhibitions in Moscow, and now asked me what I had meant to express in them. Lydia, or Lida, as they called her at home, talked more with Belokurov than with me. Serious, unsmiling, she asked him why he did not serve in the zemstvo and why he had never yet come to a single zemstvo meeting.

"It's not good, Pyotr Petrovich," she said reproachfully. "It's not good. It's a shame."

"True, Lida, true," her mother agreed. "It's not good."

"Our whole district is in the hands of Balagin," Lida went on, turning to me. "He himself is the chairman of the board, and he's given all the posts in the district to his nephews and sons-in-law and does whatever he likes. We must fight. The young people should form a strong party, but you see what kind of young people we have. It's a shame, Pyotr Petrovich!"

While we talked about the zemstvo, the younger sister, Zhenya, was silent. She did not take part in serious conversations, the family did not consider her grown up yet, and called her Missyus, like a little girl, because that was what she had called *Miss,* her governess, as a child. She kept looking at me with curiosity, and when I glanced through the photograph album, she explained to me: "That's my uncle . . . That's my godfather," and moved her little finger over the portraits, and at that moment she touched me childishly with her shoulder, and I could see close-up her weak, undeveloped breast, her slender shoulders, her braid, and her thin body, tightly bound with a sash.

We played croquet and lawn tennis, strolled about the garden, had tea, and then a long supper. After the enormous, empty hall with columns, I felt somehow ill at ease in this small, cozy house in which there were no oleographs on the walls and the servants were addressed formally, and everything seemed young and pure to me, owing to the presence of Lida and Missyus, and everything breathed respectability. Over supper Lida again talked with Belokurov about the zemstvo, about Balagin, about the school libraries. She was a lively, sincere girl, with deep convictions, and it was interesting to listen to her, though she talked a lot and loudly—perhaps because she was used to talking at school. On the other hand, my Pyotr Petrovich, who from his student days had kept the manner of turning every conversation into an argument, spoke dully, listlessly, and at length, with the obvious wish of appearing to be an intelligent and progressive man. Gesticulating, he overturned the sauceboat with his sleeve, and a big puddle formed on the tablecloth, but, except for me, no one seemed to notice it.

When we returned home, it was dark and still.

"Good manners doesn't mean not spilling sauce on the tablecloth, but not noticing when someone else does," said Belokurov, and he sighed. "Yes, a wonderful, intellectual family. I've lost touch with good people, indeed I have! I'm always busy, busy, busy!"

He talked of how much one had to work if one wanted to be a model farmer. And I thought: what a sluggish and lazy fellow he is! When he talked about something serious, he drawled and strained, "E-e-eh," and he worked the same way as he talked—slow, always late, missing all deadlines. I had little faith in his business abilities, if only because when I asked him to mail some letters for me, he carried them around in his pockets for weeks.

"The hardest thing of all," he muttered, walking beside me, "the hardest thing of all is to work and get no sympathy from anybody. No sympathy at all!"

II

I began to visit the Volchaninovs. Usually I sat on the bottom step of the terrace; dissatisfaction with myself oppressed me, I felt sorry for my life, which was passing so quickly and uninterestingly, and I kept thinking how good it would be to tear this heart, which had grown so heavy, out of my breast. And all the while there would be talking on the terrace, one could hear the rustling of dresses and the leafing-through of books. I soon became accustomed to Lida's receiving sick people in the afternoon, handing out books, and often leaving for the village, bare-headed[3] under her parasol, and in the evening talking loudly about the zemstvo and schools. This slender, beautiful, invariably severe girl, with her small, gracefully outlined mouth, would turn to me whenever a practical conversation began, and say drily:

"This is of no interest to you."

She did not find me sympathetic. She disliked me because I was a landscape painter and did not portray the needs of the people in my pictures, and because I was, as it seemed to her, indifferent to what she so strongly believed in. I remember once riding along the shore of Baikal and meeting a Buryat[4] girl in a shirt and blue dungaree trousers, on horseback; I asked her if she would sell me her pipe, and as we spoke, she looked scornfully at my European face and my hat, and after a minute got sick of talking to me, whooped, and galloped off. In the same way, Lida scorned the alien in me. She did not express her indisposition towards me in any external way, but I sensed it and, sitting on the bottom step of the terrace, felt annoyed and said that to treat peasants without being a doctor was to deceive them and that it was easy to be philanthropic when one owned five thousand acres.

But her sister, Missyus, had no cares and spent her life in total idleness, as I did. When she got up in the morning, she at once took a book and started reading, sitting on the terrace in a deep armchair, so that her little feet barely touched the ground, or she hid herself with a book in the linden avenue, or went out the gates into the fields. She read for the whole day, peering greedily into her book, and only because her eyes sometimes became tired, dazed, and her face very pale, could you guess that this reading wearied her brain. When I came, she would blush slightly on seeing me, put her book down, and, looking into my face with her big eyes, tell me excitedly about things that had happened: for instance, that there had been a chimney fire in the servants' quarters or that some worker had caught a big fish in the pond. On weekdays she usually went about in a pale blouse and a dark blue skirt. We took walks together, picked cherries for preserves, went for boat rides, and when she jumped up to reach a cherry, or handled the oars, her thin, weak arms showed through her loose sleeves. Or else I would paint a study, and she would stand beside me and watch with admiration.

One Sunday at the end of July I came to the Volchaninovs' in the morning, around nine o'clock. I walked through the park, keeping away from the house, and looked for mushrooms, which were very numerous that summer, and marked the places, in order to pick them later with Zhenya. A warm breeze was blowing. I saw Zhenya and her mother, both in pale festive dresses, walking from church to the house, and Zhenya keeping her hat from blowing off in the wind. Then I heard them having tea on the terrace.

For a carefree man like me, seeking to justify his constant idleness, these festive summer mornings on our country estates have always been extremely attractive. When a green garden, still moist with dew, shines all over in the sun and looks happy, when there is a smell of mignonette and oleander around the house, the young people have just come back from church and are having tea in the garden, and when everyone is so nicely dressed and cheerful, and when you know that all these healthy, well-fed, handsome people will do nothing all day long, then you want all of life to be like that. And now I was thinking the same thing and walking in the garden, ready to walk that way, idly and aimlessly, all day, all summer.

Zhenya came with a basket; she looked as if she knew or anticipated that she would find me in the garden. We picked mushrooms and talked, and when she asked about something, she went ahead so as to see my face.

"Yesterday a miracle took place in our village," she said. "Lame Pelageya was sick for a whole year, no doctors or medicines helped her, but yesterday an old woman whispered something and it went away."

"That's no matter," I said. "We shouldn't look for miracles only around sick people and old women. Isn't health a miracle? And life itself? Whatever is incomprehensible is a miracle."

"Aren't you afraid of what's incomprehensible?"

"No. I approach phenomena that I don't understand with good cheer and don't give in to them. I'm above them. Man should be aware that he is above lions, tigers, stars, above everything in nature, even above what is incomprehensible and seems miraculous, otherwise he's not a man but a mouse afraid of everything."

Zhenya thought that, being an artist, I knew a lot and could make right guesses about what I did not know. She would have liked me to lead her into the region of the eternal and the beautiful, that higher world where, in her opinion, I was at home, and she talked to me about God, about eternal life, about the miraculous. And, unable to conceive that I and my imagination would perish forever after death, I replied: "Yes, people are immortal," "Yes, eternal life awaits us." And she listened, believed, and did not ask for proofs.

As we walked towards the house, she suddenly stopped and said:

"Our Lida is a remarkable person. Isn't it so? I love her dearly and could sacrifice my life for her at any moment. But tell me," Zhenya touched my sleeve with her finger, "tell me, why do you argue with her all the time? Why are you annoyed?"

"Because she's wrong."

Zhenya shook her head, and tears came to her eyes.

"It's so incomprehensible!" she said.

At that moment Lida had just returned from somewhere and, standing by the porch with a whip in her hand, trim, beautiful, lit by the sun, was giving orders to a workman. Hurrying and talking loudly, she received two or three patients, then, with a busy, preoccupied air, she went through the rooms, opening first one cupboard, then another, and went up to the mezzanine; they spent a long time looking for her and calling her to dinner, and she came when we had already finished the soup. For some reason I remember and love all these little details, and I remember that whole day vividly, though nothing special happened. After dinner Zhenya read, lying in a deep armchair, and I sat on the bottom step of the terrace. We were silent. The whole sky clouded over, and a fine, light rain began to drizzle. It was hot, the wind had died down long ago, and it seemed the day would never end. Ekaterina Pavlovna came out to us on the terrace, sleepy, holding a fan.

"Oh, mama," said Zhenya, kissing her hand, "it's not good for you to sleep in the afternoon."

They adored each other. Whenever one went to the garden, the other would stand on the terrace and, looking at the trees, call: "Hallo-o-o, Zhenya!" or "Mamochka, where are you?" They always prayed together, and both had the same beliefs and understood each other very well even when they were silent. And their attitude towards people was the same. Ekaterina Pavlovna, too, soon became accustomed and attached to me, and when I did not appear for two or three days, she would send to find out if I was well. She, too, looked at my studies with admiration, and, as loquaciously and candidly as Missyus, told me about things that had happened and often entrusted me with her domestic secrets.

She stood in awe of her elder daughter. Lida was never tender, she spoke only about serious things; she lived her own separate life and for her mother and sister was as sacred and slightly mysterious a personage as an admiral who always remains in his cabin is for his sailors.

"Our Lida is a remarkable person," the mother often said. "Isn't it so?"

And now, as the rain drizzled, we talked of Lida.

"She's a remarkable person," the mother said and added in a conspiratorial half-whisper, looking around fearfully: "It would be hard to find the like of her anywhere, though, you know, I'm beginning to worry a little. School, first-aid kits, books—it's all very good, but why go to extremes? She's nearly twenty-four, it's time she thought seriously about herself. With all these books and first-aid kits, she won't see how life is passing by . . . She should marry."

Zhenya, pale from reading, her hair disheveled, raised her head and, looking at her mother, said as if to herself:

"Mamochka, it all depends on God's will!"

And again she immersed herself in reading.

Belokurov came in a vest and an embroidered shirt. We played croquet and lawn tennis, then, when it grew dark, had a long supper, and Lida again talked about schools and about Balagin, who had the whole district in his hands. Leaving the Volchaninovs' that evening, I went away with the impression of a very long, idle day, and the sad awareness that everything in this world, however long, comes to an end. Zhenya accompanied us to the gate, and perhaps because she had spent the whole day with me from morning till evening, I felt that without her I was somehow dull and that this whole dear family was close to me; and for the first time all summer I wanted to paint.

"Tell me, why is your life so dull, so colorless?" I asked Belokurov, walking home with him. "My life is dull, heavy, monotonous, because I'm an artist, a strange man, from my youth I've been chafed by jealousy, dissatisfaction with myself, lack of faith in what I'm doing, I'm always poor, I'm a vagabond, but you, you're a healthy, normal person, a landowner, a squire—why do you live so uninterestingly, why do you take so little from life? Why, for instance, haven't you fallen in love with Lida or Zhenya yet?"

"You forget that I love another woman," Belokurov replied.

He was speaking of his friend, Lyubov Ivanovna, who lived with him in the cottage. Every day I saw this lady, very stout, plump, imposing, like a well-fed goose, strolling in the garden, in a Russian costume with beads, always under a parasol, and a serving girl kept calling her, now to eat, now to have tea. Some three years before she had rented one of the cottages as a dacha and had simply gone on living at Belokurov's, apparently forever. She was a good ten years older than he and ruled him so strictly that, whenever he went away from the house, he had to ask her permission. She sobbed frequently in a male voice, and then I would send word that unless she stopped I would give up my lodgings, and she would stop.

When we came home, Belokurov sat on the sofa and frowned pensively, and I began pacing the hall, feeling a quiet excitement, as if I were in love. I wanted to talk about the Volchaninovs.

"Lida can only fall in love with a zemstvo activist, whose passions are the same as hers—hospitals and schools," I said. "Oh, for the sake of such a girl you could not only join the zemstvo, but even wear out a pair of iron shoes, as in the old tale.[5] And Missyus? How lovely this Missyus is!"

Belokurov, with his drawn out "E-e-eh," began talking at length about the disease of the age—pessimism. He spoke confidently and in such a tone as if I were arguing with him. Hundreds of miles of deserted, monotonous, scorched steppe cannot produce such gloom as one man when he sits and talks and nobody knows when he will leave.

"The point isn't pessimism or optimism," I said irritably, "but that ninety-nine people out of a hundred are witless."

Belokurov took it personally, became offended, and left.

III

"The prince is visiting in Malozyomovo and sends you his greetings," Lida was saying to her mother, having returned from somewhere and taking off her gloves. "He tells many interesting things . . . He promises to raise the question of a dispensary in Malozyomovo again in the provincial assembly, but he says there's little hope." And turning to me, she said: "Excuse me, I keep forgetting that this cannot be of interest to you."

I felt annoyed.

"Why not?" I asked and shrugged my shoulders. "You have no wish to know my opinion, but I assure you the question is of lively interest to me."

"It is?"

"Yes, it is. In my opinion there's no need at all for a dispensary in Malozyomovo."

My annoyance communicated itself to her; she looked at me, narrowing her eyes, and asked:

"What do they need? Landscapes?"

"No need for landscapes either. They don't need anything."

She finished taking off her gloves and opened a newspaper that had just been brought from the post office; after a minute she said softly, obviously restraining herself:

"Last week Anna died in childbirth. If there had been a dispensary nearby, she would still be alive. And it seems to me that gentleman landscape painters ought to have some sort of convictions in that regard."

"I have very definite convictions in that regard, I assure you," I replied, but she shielded herself from me with the newspaper as if she did not wish to listen. "In my opinion, dispensaries, schools, libraries, first-aid kits, under the existing conditions, only serve enslavement. The people are fettered with a great chain, and you don't cut the chain, you merely add new links to it—there's my conviction for you."

She raised her eyes to me and smiled derisively, while I went on trying to grasp my main thought:

"What matters is not that Anna died in childbirth, but that all these Annas, Mavras, Pelageyas bend their backs from early morning till dark, get sick from overwork, tremble all their lives for their hungry and sick children, fear death and sickness all their lives, get treated all their lives, fade early, age early, and die in dirt and stench; their children grow up and start the same tune, and so hundreds of years go by, and billions of people live worse than animals—only for the sake of a crust of bread, knowing constant fear. The whole horror of their situation is that they have no time to think of their souls, no time to remember their image and likeness;[6] hunger, cold, animal fear, a mass of work, like a snowslide, bar all the paths to spiritual activity, to what precisely distinguishes man from animal and is the only thing worth living for. You come to their aid with hospitals and schools, but that doesn't free them from bondage, but, on the contrary, enslaves them still more, because, by introducing new prejudices in their life, you increase the number of their needs, not to mention that they must pay the zemstvo for their little pills and primers, and that means bending their backs even more."

"I won't argue with you," said Lida, lowering the newspaper. "I've already heard it all. I'll tell you just one thing: it's impossible to sit with folded arms. True, we're not saving mankind, and maybe we're mistaken in many ways, but we do what we can, and we're right. The highest and holiest task for a cultured person is to serve his neighbor, and we try to serve as we can. You don't like it, but one can't please everyone."

"True, Lida, true," said the mother.

She was always timid in Lida's presence, and kept glancing at her anxiously when she spoke, afraid of saying something unnecessary or inappropriate, and she never contradicted her, but always agreed—true, Lida, true.

"Dispensaries, peasant literacy, books with pathetic precepts and jokes cannot diminish either ignorance or mortality, any more than the light from your windows can illuminate this huge garden," I said. "You give nothing with your interference in these people's lives, you only create new needs, new pretexts for work."

"Ah, my God, but something must be done!" Lida said with vexation, and from her tone it was clear that she considered my arguments worthless and despised them.

"The people must be freed from heavy physical labor," I said. "Their yoke must be lightened, they must be given a respite, so that they don't spend their whole lives at the stove, the washtub, and in the fields, but also have time to think about their souls, about God, to give wider scope to their spiritual capacities. Every man's calling lies in spiritual activity—in a constant search for truth and the meaning of life. Make it so that crude, brutish labor is not necessary for them, let them feel themselves free, and then you'll see what a mockery these books and first-aid kits essentially are. Once a man is conscious of his true calling, he can be satisfied only by religion, the sciences, the arts, and not these trifles."

"Free them from labor!" Lida grinned. "Is that really possible?"

"Yes. Take a share of their work on yourself. If all of us, city and country dwellers, all of us without exception, agreed to divide up the work expended by mankind in general to satisfy its physical needs, the portion for each of us might be no more than two or three hours a day. Imagine that all of us, rich and poor, work only three hours a day, and the rest of our time is left free. Imagine, too, that in order to depend still less on our bodies and to work less, we invent machines to work for us, and try to reduce the number of our needs to the minimum. We train ourselves and our children not to fear hunger and cold, so that we don't constantly tremble for their health as Anna, Mavra, and Pelageya do. Imagine that we don't get treated, don't keep pharmacies, tobacco factories, distilleries—what a lot of free time we'd have in the end! All of us together would devote this leisure to the arts and sciences. As peasants sometimes get together to mend a road, so all of us together would seek truth and the meaning of life, and—I'm certain of it—the truth would be discovered very soon, man would be delivered from this constant, tormenting, oppressive fear, and even from death itself."

"You contradict yourself, however," said Lida. "You say science, science, yet you reject literacy."

"Literacy, when a man can only use it to read pothouse signboards and occasional books that he doesn't understand—such literacy has been with us since the time of Rurik, Gogol's Petrushka[7] has been reading for a long time, and yet the village remains to this day what it was under Rurik. What we need is not literacy, but the freedom to give wide scope to our spiritual capacities. We need not schools but universities."

"You reject medicine as well."

"Yes. It would be needed only for the study of illnesses as phenomena of nature, not for their treatment. If we're to treat something, it should be not illnesses but their causes. Remove the main cause—physical work—and there will be no illnesses. I don't recognize the science of treatment," I went on excitedly. "The arts and sciences, when genuine, aspire not to temporary, not to specific purposes, but to the eternal and the general—they seek truth and the meaning of life, they seek God, the soul, and when they're harnessed to the needs and evils of the day, to first-aid kits and libraries, they only complicate and clutter life. We have lots of doctors, pharmacists, lawyers, there are lots of literate people, but no biologists, mathematicians, philosophers, poets. All our intelligence, all our inner energies have gone to satisfying temporary, passing needs . . . Among scientists, writers, and artists, work is at the boil, the comforts of life increase every day thanks to them, bodily needs multiply, and yet the truth is still far off, and man still remains the most predatory and slovenly of animals, and the tendency in the majority of mankind is towards degeneration and the permanent loss of all vitality. In such conditions an artist's life has no meaning, and the more talented he is, the more strange and incomprehensible his role, since it turns out that, in reality, he is working for the amusement of a predatory, slovenly animal and supporting the existing order of things. But I don't want to work and will not . . . Nothing's any use, let the earth go to hell and gone!"

"Missyuska, leave us," Lida said to her sister, obviously finding my words harmful for such a young girl.

Zhenya looked sadly at her sister and mother and left.

"Such nice things are commonly said when one wants to justify one's indifference," said Lida. "To reject hospitals and schools is easier than to treat or teach people."

"True, Lida, true," the mother agreed.

"You threaten to stop working," Lida went on. "Obviously you value your works highly. But let's stop arguing, we'll never see eye to eye, because I place the least perfect of all little libraries and first-aid kits, which you've just spoken of with such scorn, above all the landscape paintings in the world." And straightaway, turning to her mother, she began in a completely different tone: "The prince has lost a lot of weight and is greatly changed since he visited us. They sent him to Vichy."[8]

She told her mother about the prince, so as not to speak with me. Her face was burning, and to conceal her agitation, she bent low to the table, as if she were nearsighted, pretending to read the newspaper. My presence was disagreeable. I said good-night and went home.

IV

Outside it was quiet; the village on the other side of the pond was already asleep, there was not a single light to be seen, and only the pale reflections of stars shone faintly on the pond. By the gate with the lions Zhenya stood motionless, waiting to see me off.

"Everyone's asleep in the village," I said to her, trying to make out her face in the darkness, and I saw her dark, sorrowful eyes directed at me. "The tavernkeeper and the horse thieves are sleeping peacefully, and we respectable people annoy each other and argue."

It was a sad August night—sad because autumn was already in the air; covered by a purple cloud, the moon was rising, barely lighting up the road and the dark fields of winter wheat on either side. There were lots of falling stars. Zhenya walked down the road beside me, trying not to look at the sky, so as not to see the falling stars, which for some reason frightened her.

"I think you're right," she said, shivering from the night's dampness. "If all people together could give themselves to spiritual activity, they would soon know everything."

"Of course. We are higher beings, and if we were really conscious of the whole power of human genius and lived only for higher purposes, then in the end we would become like gods. But that will never be—mankind will degenerate, and there won't be any trace of genius left."

When the gates could no longer be seen, Zhenya stopped and hastily pressed my hand.

"Good night," she said, shivering; her shoulders were covered only by a little blouse, and she hunched up from the cold. "Come tomorrow."

The thought that I would be left alone, annoyed, dissatisfied with myself and with other people, gave me an eerie feeling; and now I myself tried not to look at the falling stars.

"Spend another moment with me," I said. "I beg you."

I loved Zhenya. It must be that I loved her for meeting me and seeing me off, for looking at me tenderly and with admiration. How touchingly beautiful her pale face was, her slender neck, her slender arms, her frailty, her idleness, her books! And her intelligence? I suspected that she was of uncommon intelligence, I admired the breadth of her views, perhaps because she thought differently from the severe and beautiful Lida, who did not like me. Zhenya liked me as an artist, I had won her heart with my talent, I passionately wanted to paint for her alone, and I dreamed of her as my little queen who, together with me, would one day possess these trees, fields, mists, the dawn, this nature, wonderful, enchanting, but in the midst of which I had till then felt myself hopelessly lonely and useless.

"Stay another moment," I asked. "I implore you."

I took off my coat and covered her chilled shoulders; she, afraid of looking ridiculous and unattractive in a man's coat, laughed and threw it off, and at that moment I embraced her and began to shower kisses on her face, shoulders, hands.

"Till tomorrow!" she whispered, and cautiously, as if afraid of breaking the silence of the night, embraced me. "We have no secrets from each other, I must tell mama and my sister everything at once . . . It's so scary! Mama's nothing, mama likes you, but Lida!"

She ran towards the gates.

"Good-bye!" she called.

And then for about two minutes I listened to her running. I had no wish to go home, nor any reason to go there. I stood for a while in thought and quietly trudged back, to look again at the house where she lived, a dear, naïve old house, which seemed to look at me with the windows of its mezzanine as if with eyes, and to understand everything. I went past the terrace, sat down on a bench by the tennis court, in the darkness under an old elm, and looked at the house from there. In the windows of the mezzanine, where Missyus lived, there was a flash of bright light, then a peaceful green—the lamp had been covered with a shade. Shadows moved about . . . I was filled with tenderness, quietude, and satisfaction with myself—satisfaction that I could be carried away and fall in love—and at the same time I felt discomfort at the thought that just then, a few steps away from me, in one of the rooms of that house, lived Lida, who did not like, and perhaps hated, me. I sat and kept waiting, in case Zhenya came out, listening, and it seemed to me that there was talking in the mezzanine.

About an hour passed. The green light went out, and the shadows could no longer be seen. The moon had risen high over the house, lighting up the sleeping garden, the paths; the dahlias and roses in the flower garden in front of the house were clearly visible and seemed to be all of the same color. It was getting very cold. I left the garden, picked up my coat on the road, and unhurriedly plodded home.

When I came to the Volchaninovs' the next day after dinner, the glass door to the garden was wide open. I sat on the terrace, expecting that Zhenya would appear at any moment on the tennis court beyond the flower garden, or on one of the paths, or that her voice would come from inside; then I went to the drawing room, the dining room. There was not a soul. From the dining room I walked down the long corridor to the front hall, then back. There were several doors in the corridor, and behind one of them Lida's voice rang out.

"To a crow somewhere . . . God . . ." she said loudly and slowly, probably dictating. "God sent a piece of cheese . . . To a crow . . . somewhere . . . ⁹ Who's there?" she suddenly called out, hearing my footsteps.

"It's me."

"Ah! Excuse me, I can't come right now, I'm busy with Dasha."

"Is Ekaterina Pavlovna in the garden?"

"No, she and my sister left this morning to visit our aunt in Penza province. And in the winter they will probably go abroad . . ." she added after a pause. "To a crow somewhere . . . God sent a pie-e-ece of che-e-ese . . . Have you written that?"

I went out to the front hall and, not thinking of anything, stood and looked from there at the pond and the village, and the words came to me:

"A piece of cheese . . . To a crow somewhere God sent a piece of cheese . . ."

And I left the estate by the same road I had come there on the first time, only in reverse: from the yard to the garden, past the house, then down the linden avenue . . . There a boy caught up with me and gave me a note. "I told my sister everything, and she demands that I part with you," I read. "It is beyond me to upset her by my disobedience. Forgive me, and God grant you happiness. If you only knew how bitterly mama and I are weeping!"

Then the dark avenue of firs, the collapsed fence . . . In the field where rye was flowering then and quail were calling, cows and hobbled horses now wandered. Here and there on the hills the winter wheat showed bright green. A sober, everyday mood came over me, and I felt ashamed of everything I had said at the Volchaninovs, and bored with life, as before. I went home, packed, and left that evening for Petersburg.

I never saw the Volchaninovs again. Recently, going to the Crimea, I met Belokurov on the train. As usual, he was wearing his vest and embroidered shirt, and when I asked how he was getting along, he said: "By your prayers." We got to talking. He had sold his estate and bought another, a smaller one, in Lyubov Ivanovna's name. Of the Volchaninovs he said little. Lida, according to him, was still living at Shelkovka and teaching children in the school; she had gradually succeeded in gathering a circle of people sympathetic to her, who had formed themselves into a strong party and, at the last zemstvo elections, had "ousted" Balagin, who till then had had the whole district in his hands. Of Zhenya, Belokurov told me only that she was not living at home and he did not know where she was.

I am beginning to forget about the house with the mezzanine, and only rarely, while painting or reading, will I suddenly recall, as if at random, now the green light in the window, now the sound of my own footsteps in the fields at night, as I, in love, made my way home, rubbing my hands from the cold. And still more rarely, at moments when solitude weighs on me and I feel sad, I dimly remember, and for some reason I am gradually beginning to think that I, too, am remembered, waited for, and that we will meet . . .

Missyus, where are you?

APRIL 1896

The Man in a Case

At the very edge of the village of Mironositskoe, in the headman Prokofy's shed, some belated hunters had settled down for the night. There were only two of them: the veterinarian Ivan Ivanych and the high-school teacher Burkin. Ivan Ivanych had a rather strange double surname—Chimsha-Himalaysky—which did not go with him at all, and throughout the province he was known simply by his first name and patronymic; he lived on a stud farm near town and had gone hunting now to get a breath of fresh air. The high-school teacher Burkin visited Count P. every summer and had long been a familiar man in those parts.

They were not asleep. Ivan Ivanych, a tall, lean old man with a long mustache, sat outside by the entrance and smoked his pipe; the moon shone on him. Burkin lay inside on the hay, and could not be seen in the darkness.

They told various stories. Among other things they talked about the headman's wife, Mavra, a healthy woman and not stupid—that she had never gone anywhere outside her native village, had never seen a town or a railroad, and for the last ten years had always sat behind the stove and went outside only at night.

"What's surprising about that!" said Burkin. "There are not a few naturally solitary people in this world, who try to hide in their shells like hermit crabs or snails. Maybe what we have here is the phenomenon of atavism, a return to the time when man's ancestors were not yet social animals and lived solitarily in their dens, or maybe it's simply one of the varieties of human character—who knows? I'm not a natural scientist, and it's not my business to touch on such questions; I only want to say that people like Mavra are not a rare phenomenon. No need to look far, about two months ago a certain Belikov died in our town, a teacher of Greek, my colleague. You've heard of him, of course. He was remarkable for always going out, even in the finest weather, in galoshes and with an umbrella, and unfailingly wearing a warm, padded coat. His umbrella had a cover, and his watch a cover of gray suede, and when he took out his penknife to sharpen a pencil, the penknife, too, had a little cover; and his face also seemed to have a cover over it, because he always hid it behind his turned-up collar. He wore dark glasses, a quilted jacket, stopped his ears with cotton, and whenever he took a cab, ordered the top put up. In short, the man showed a constant and insuperable impulse to envelop himself, to create a case for himself, so to speak, that would isolate him, protect him from outside influences. Reality irritated him, frightened him, kept him in constant anxiety, and, maybe in order to justify his timidity, his aversion to the present, he always praised the past and what had never been; the ancient languages he taught were for him essentially the same galoshes and umbrella, in which he hid from real life.

" 'Oh, how sonorous, how beautiful the Greek language is!' he used to say, with a sweet expression; and, as if to prove his words, he would narrow his eyes and, raising a forefinger, pronounce: 'Anthropos!'

"And Belikov tried to hide his thoughts in a case as well. The only things that were clear for him were circulars and newspaper articles in which something was forbidden. When a circular forbade the schoolboys to go out after nine o'clock in the evening, or some article forbade carnal love, he found that clear, definite; it's forbidden, and—basta! But the permitting, the authorizing of something always concealed an element of dubiousness for him, something vague and not quite spoken. When a dramatic circle, a reading room or tearoom was permitted in town, he would shake his head and say softly:

" 'That's very well, of course, it's all splendid, but something may come of it.'

"Any sort of violation, deviation, departure from the rules threw him into dejection, though you might wonder what business it was of his. If some colleague of his was late for prayers, or rumor reached him of some schoolboy prank, or a mistress from the girls' school was seen late at night with an officer, he would become very worried and keep saying that something might come of it. And at faculty meetings he simply oppressed us with his prudence, suspiciousness, and purely case-like reasonings about how the students in the boys' and girls' high schools behave badly, they're very noisy in class—ah, what if it gets to the authorities, ah, something may come of it—and if we expel Petrov from the second grade and Yegorov from the fourth, it would be a very good thing. And what then? With his sighing, his whining, his dark glasses on his pale little face—you know, a little face, like a weasel's—he crushed us all, and we gave in, lowered Petrov's and Yegorov's marks for conduct, locked them up, and finally expelled them both. He had a strange habit—of visiting our apartments. He would call on a teacher, sit down, and say nothing, as if he were spying something out. He would sit like that, silently, for an hour or two, and then leave. He called it 'maintaining good relations with his colleagues,' and it was obviously painful for him to come to us and sit, and he came only because he considered it his comradely duty. We teachers were afraid of him. And even the director was afraid. Figure, our teachers were all profoundly respectable, thinking people, brought up on Turgenev and Shchedrin,[1] yet this little man, who always went about in galoshes and with an umbrella, held the whole school in his hands for as long as fifteen years! School, nothing! The whole town! Our ladies refused to arrange home dramatic performances on Saturdays for fear he might find out; and the clergy were embarrassed to eat non-lenten fare and play cards in his presence. During the last ten or fifteen years, under the influence of people like Belikov, our town developed a fear of everything. A fear of talking loudly, of sending letters, of making acquaintances, reading books, helping the poor, teaching reading and writing . . ."

Ivan Ivanych, wishing to say something, coughed, but first lit his pipe, looked at the moon, and only then said measuredly:

"Yes. Thinking people, respectable, reading Shchedrin and Turgenev, and all sorts of Buckles[2] and so on, and yet they gave in and endured . . . There you have it."

"Belikov lived in the same house I did," Burkin went on, "on the same floor, his door faced mine, we saw each other often, and I knew his home life. At home it was the same story: dressing gown, nightcap, shutters, latches, a whole array of restrictions, limitations, and—ah, something may come of it! Lenten fare isn't good for you, and non-lenten food is forbidden, because people might say Belikov didn't observe the fasts,[3] so he ate pike-perch fried in butter—not lenten food, but you couldn't say it was non-lenten. He didn't keep a serving woman for fear people might think ill of him, but he kept a cook, Afanasy, an old man of about sixty, drunk and half-crazy, who had served as an orderly and was able to slap a meal together. This Afanasy usually stood by the door, his arms crossed, and always muttered one and the same thing with a deep sigh:

" 'There's a lot of *them* around nowadays!'

"Belikov's bedroom was small, like a box, and the bed had a canopy over it. Lying down to sleep, he would cover his head with a blanket; it was hot, stuffy, the wind knocked at the closed doors, the stove howled; sighs came from the kitchen, sinister sighs . . .

"And he was afraid under his blanket. He feared that something might happen, that Afanasy might put a knife in him, that thieves might come, and then all night he would have troubled dreams, and in the morning, when he and I walked to school together, he would be dull, pale, and you could see that the crowded school he was going to was frightening, contrary to his whole being, and that for him, a naturally solitary man, walking beside me was very painful.

" 'It's too noisy in our classrooms,' he would say, as if trying to find an explanation for his painful feeling. 'I've never seen the like.'

"And this teacher of Greek, this man in a case, if you can imagine it, nearly got married."

Ivan Ivanych quickly glanced into the shed and said:

"You're joking!"

"Yes, he nearly got married, strange as it sounds. A new teacher of history and geography was appointed to us, a certain Kovalenko, Mikhail Savvich, a Ukrainian. He didn't come alone, but with his sister Varenka. He was young, tall, swarthy, with enormous hands, and by the looks of him you could see he had a bass voice, and in fact he boomed like a barrel: boo, boo, boo . . . And she was no longer young, about thirty, but also tall, trim, dark-browed, red-cheeked—in short, not a girl but a sugarplum—and so saucy and loud, and she sang Ukrainian romances and laughed all the time. At the least thing she'd burst into peals of laughter: ha, ha, ha! Our first real acquaintance with the Kovalenkos came, I remember, at the director's name-day party. Amidst the stern, tensely dull pedagogues, who even came to name-day parties out of duty, we suddenly see: a new Aphrodite rising from the foam. She walks about, arms akimbo, laughs, sings, dances . . . She sang 'The Winds Waft' with feeling, then another romance, and another, and charmed us all—all, even Belikov. He sat down beside her and said with a sweet smile:

" 'The Ukrainian language, in its softness and pleasing sonority, is reminiscent of the ancient Greek.'

"This flattered her, and she began telling him, with feeling and conviction, that she had a farmstead in the Gadyach district, that her dear mama lived on that farmstead, and they had such pears there, such melons, such squash! In the Ukraine pumpkins are called squash, and squash are called gourds, and they make borscht out of them with little red peppers and little blue eggplants, 'so tasty, so tasty, it's simply—awful!'

"We listened and listened, and suddenly the same thought occurred to us all.

" 'It would be nice to get them married,' the director's wife said to me softly.

"We all remembered for some reason that our Belikov wasn't married, and now it seemed strange to us that we had somehow never noticed, had completely lost sight of such an important detail of his life. What generally was his attitude towards women, and how did he resolve this essential question for himself? Earlier that hadn't interested us at all; maybe we hadn't even admitted the thought that a man who wore galoshes in all weather and slept under a canopy was able to love.

" 'He's well over forty, and she's thirty . . .' the director's wife clarified her thought. 'I think she'd accept him.'

"So many things are done in our provinces out of boredom, so much that's unnecessary, absurd! That's because what's necessary doesn't get done at all. Well, so why did we suddenly have to marry off this Belikov, whom it was even impossible to imagine married? The director's wife, the inspector's wife, and our lady teachers all livened up, even became prettier, as if they suddenly saw some purpose in life. The director's wife reserved a box in the theater, and we looked—there was Varenka sitting in her box with a fan, radiant, happy, and beside her Belikov, small, hunched up, as if they'd pulled him out of his house with pliers. I gave a party and the ladies demanded that I invite Belikov and Varenka without fail. In short, the machine got going. It turned out that Varenka wouldn't have minded getting married. Her life with her brother was not so happy, all they could do was argue and quarrel the whole day long. Here's a scene for you: Kovalenko goes walking down the street, a tall, hefty hulk in an embroidered shirt, his forelock falling over his forehead from under his cap; a pile of books in one hand, a thick, knotty stick in the other. Behind him comes his sister, also with books.

" 'But Mikhailik, you haven't read this one!' she protests loudly. 'I'm telling you, I swear, you haven't read it at all!'

" 'And I tell you I have!' shouts Kovalenko, rapping his stick on the sidewalk.

" 'Ah, my God, Minchik! Why are you getting angry, we're having a conversation of principle.'

" 'And I tell you I've read it!' Kovalenko shouts still louder.

"And at home, whenever an outsider comes, there's some spat. Such a life was probably boring, she wanted a corner of her own, and age was also a consideration; there was no time for choosing, she'd marry anybody, even the teacher of Greek. And to tell the truth, for the majority of our young ladies, it didn't matter whom they married, as long as they got married. Be that as it may, Varenka began to show our Belikov a marked benevolence.

"And Belikov? He called on Kovalenko just as he did on us. He'd come to him and say nothing. He'd say nothing, and Varenka would sing 'The Winds Waft' for him, or look at him pensively with her dark eyes, or suddenly dissolve:

" 'Ha, ha, ha!'

"In amorous matters, especially in marriage, insinuation plays a major role. Everybody—his colleagues and the ladies—started assuring Belikov that he must marry, that there was nothing left for him in life but to marry; we all congratulated him and with important faces uttered various banalities, such as that marriage was a serious step; besides, Varenka was interesting and not bad-looking, she was the daughter of a state councillor and owned a farmstead, and, above all, she was the first woman who had treated him gently, cordially—his head got in a whirl, and he decided that he really did have to marry."

"That was the time to take away his galoshes and umbrella," said Ivan Ivanych.

"Imagine, that turned out to be impossible. He put Varenka's portrait on his desk and kept coming to me and talking about

Varenka, about family life, about marriage being a serious step, he visited the Kovalenkos frequently, but he didn't change his way of life in the least. Even the opposite, the decision to marry affected him somehow morbidly, he lost weight, grew pale, and seemed to withdraw further into his case.

" 'I like Varvara Savvishna,' he said to me with a faint, crooked little smile, 'and I know that every man needs to marry, but . . . you know, all this has happened somehow suddenly . . . I have to think.'

" 'What's there to think about?' I say to him. 'Marry her, and that's that.'

" 'No, marriage is a serious step, I must first weigh my future duties, responsibilities . . . or something may come of it later. It bothers me so much that I've now stopped sleeping at night. And, I confess, I'm afraid: she and her brother have some strange way of thinking, they reason, you know, somehow strangely, and her character is very sprightly. I'll get married and then, for all I know, wind up in some kind of trouble.'

"And he didn't propose, he kept postponing it, to the great vexation of the director's wife and our other ladies; he kept weighing his future duties and responsibilities and meanwhile went strolling with Varenka almost every day, perhaps thinking it was necessary in his position, and came to me to talk about family life. And, in all probability, he would have proposed in the end, and one of those needless, stupid marriages would have taken place, such as take place here by the thousand out of boredom and idleness, if a *kolossalische Scandal* had not suddenly occurred. It must be said that Varenka's brother, Kovalenko, had hated Belikov from the first day of their acquaintance and could not bear him.

" 'I don't understand,' he said to us, shrugging his shoulders, 'I don't understand how you stomach that snitcher, that vile mug! Eh, gentlemen, how can you live here? The atmosphere is nasty, stifling. Are you pedagogues, teachers? No, you're rank-grabbers, your school isn't a temple of knowledge, it's an office of public order, and there's a sour stink to it, like in a sentry's box. No, brothers, I'll live with you a little longer and then go back to my farmstead to catch crayfish and teach little Ukrainians. I'll leave you, and you can stay here with your Judas till he bursts.'

"Or else he'd laugh, laugh himself to tears, now in a bass, now in a thin, squeaky voice, and ask me, spreading his hands:

" 'Why is he sitting with me? What does he want? He sits and looks.'

"He even gave Belikov the name of 'the bloodsucker, alias the spider.' And, to be sure, we avoided talking to him about his sister Varenka marrying 'alias the spider.' And once when the director's wife hinted to him that it would be nice to have his sister settle down with such a solid, well-respected man as Belikov, he scowled and said gruffly:

" 'It's none of my business. She can even marry a viper, I don't like interfering in other people's affairs.'

"Now hear what happened next. Some prankster drew a caricature: Belikov walking in his galoshes, with his tucked-in trousers, under an umbrella, and Varenka arm-in-arm with him; the caption underneath: 'Anthropos in love.' The expression was really caught remarkably well. The artist must have worked more than one night, because all the teachers in the boys' and girls' schools, the seminary teachers, the officials—everybody got a copy. Belikov got one, too. The caricature made a most painful impression on him.

"We're leaving the house together—it was the first of May, a Sunday, and all of us, teachers and students, had arranged to meet by the school and then go on foot together to the woods outside town—we're leaving the house, and he's green, dark as a cloud.

" 'What bad, wicked people there are!' he said, and his lips trembled.

"I even felt sorry for him. We're walking along and suddenly, if you can imagine, Kovalenko rides by on a bicycle, followed by Varenka, also on a bicycle, red, tired, but cheerful, joyful.

" 'And we're going on ahead!' she cries. 'The weather's so fine, so fine, it's simply awful!'

"And they both vanished. My Belikov turned from green to white and froze. He stopped and stared at me . . .

" 'Excuse me, but what is that?' he asked. 'Or maybe my eyes are deceiving me? Is it proper for schoolmasters and women to ride bicycles?'

" 'What's improper about it?' I said. 'They can ride as much as they like.'

" 'But how is this possible?' he cried, amazed at my calmness. 'What are you saying?!'

"He was so struck that he refused to go any further and turned back home.

"The next day he kept rubbing his hands nervously and twitching all the time, and you could see from his face that he wasn't well. And he left class, which happened to him for the first time in his life. And he ate no dinner. Towards evening he got dressed warmly, though it was quite summery outside, and trudged to the Kovalenkos. Varenka was not at home, he found only her brother.

" 'Kindly sit down,' Kovalenko said coldly and scowled; his face was sleepy, he had just finished his after-dinner nap and was in a very bad humor.

"Belikov sat silently for some ten minutes and then began:

" 'I've come to you to ease my soul. I'm very, very distressed. Some lampoonist has portrayed me and another person close to us both in a ridiculous way. I consider it my duty to assure you that I have nothing to do with it . . . I never gave any pretext for such mockery—on the contrary, I've always behaved as a perfectly decent man.'

"Kovalenko sat pouting and said nothing. Belikov waited a little and went on softly, in a mournful voice:

" 'And I have something else to tell you. I have been teaching for a long time, while you are just beginning, and I consider it my duty, as an older colleague, to warn you. You ride a bicycle, and that is an amusement absolutely improper for a teacher of youth.'

" 'Why so?' Kovalenko asked in a bass voice.

" 'But is there anything here that needs more explaining, Mikhail Savvich, is there anything that isn't clear? If the teacher rides on a bicycle, what remains for the students? It remains only for them to walk on their heads! And since it is not permitted by the circulars, you cannot do it. I was horrified yesterday! When I saw your sister, my eyes went dim. A woman or a girl on a bicycle—it's awful!'

" 'What exactly do you want?'

" 'I want just one thing—to warn you, Mikhail Savvich. You are a young man, you have a future ahead of you, you must behave very, very carefully, yet you are negligent, oh, so negligent! You go around in an embroidered shirt, you're always outside with some sort of books, and now there's also the bicycle. The director will find out that you and your sister ride bicycles, then it will reach the superintendent . . . What's the good of it?'

" 'That my sister and I ride bicycles is nobody's business!' Kovalenko said and turned purple. 'And if anybody meddles in my domestic and family affairs, I'll send him to all the devils in hell.'

"Belikov paled and got up.

" 'If you talk with me in such a tone, I cannot go on,' he said. 'And I beg you never to speak like that in my presence about our superiors. You must treat the authorities with respect.'

" 'Did I say anything bad about the authorities?' Kovalenko asked, looking at him spitefully. 'Kindly leave me in peace. I'm an honest man and have no wish to talk with gentlemen like you. I don't like snitchers.'

"Belikov fussed about nervously and quickly began to dress, with a look of horror on his face. It was the first time in his life that he'd heard such rude things.

" 'You may say whatever you like,' he said, as he went out from the front hall to the landing. 'Only I must warn you: someone may have heard us, and, since our conversation might be misunderstood and something might come of it, I will have to report the content of our conversation to the director . . . in its main features. It is my duty to do so.'

" 'Report? Go on, report!'

"Kovalenko seized him from behind by the collar and shoved, and Belikov went tumbling down the stairs, his galoshes clunking. The stairs were high and steep, but he reached the bottom safely, got up, and felt his nose: were his glasses broken? But just as he was tumbling down the stairs, Varenka came in and there were two ladies with her; they stood below and watched—and for Belikov this was the most terrible thing of all. It would have been better, he thought, to break his neck and both legs than to become a laughingstock: now the whole town would know, it would reach the director, the superintendent—ah, something might come of it!—there would be a new caricature, and the upshot of it all would be that he would be ordered to resign . . .

"When he got up, Varenka recognized him and, looking at his ridiculous face, his crumpled overcoat, his galoshes, not understanding what it was about, and supposing he had fallen accidentally, could not help herself and laughed for the whole house to hear:

" 'Ha, ha, ha!'

"And this rolling, pealing 'ha, ha, ha!' put an end to everything: both the engagement and the earthly existence of Belikov. He did not hear what Varenka said, nor did he see anything. Returning home, he first of all removed the portrait from the desk, and then he lay down and never got up again.

"Three days later Afanasy came to me and asked if he ought to send for the doctor, because, he said, something was wrong with his master. I went to see Belikov. He lay under the canopy, covered with a blanket, and said nothing; you ask him, and he just says yes or no—and not another sound. He lies there, and Afanasy walks around, gloomy, scowling, and sighs deeply; and he reeks of vodka like a tavern.

"A month later Belikov died. We all went to his burial, that is, both schools and the seminary. Now, lying in the coffin, his expression was meek, pleasant, even cheerful, as if he were glad that he had finally been put in a case he would never have to leave. Yes, he had attained his ideal! And, as if in his honor, the weather during the burial was gray, rainy, and we were all in galoshes and carrying umbrellas. Varenka was also at the burial, and she wept a little when the coffin was lowered into the grave. I've noticed that Ukrainian girls only weep or laugh, they have no in-between state.

"I confess, burying people like Belikov is a great pleasure. As we came back from the cemetery, we had modest, lenten physiognomies; nobody wanted to show this feeling of pleasure—a feeling like that experienced long, long ago, in childhood, when the grown-ups went away and we could spend an hour or two running around in the garden, relishing our full freedom. Ah, freedom, freedom! Even a hint, even a faint hope of it lends the soul wings, isn't that so?

"We came back from the cemetery in good spirits. But no more than a week went by, and life flowed on as before, the same grim, wearisome, witless life, not forbidden by the circulars, yet not fully permitted. Things didn't get any better. And, indeed, we had buried Belikov, but how many more men in cases there still are, and how many more there will be!"

"Right you are," said Ivan Ivanych, and he lit his pipe.

"How many more there will be!" Burkin repeated.

The schoolteacher came out of the shed. He was a short man, fat, completely bald, with a black beard almost down to his waist. Two dogs came out with him.

"What a moon!" he said, looking up.

It was already midnight. To the right the whole village was visible, the long street stretching into the distance a good three miles. Everything was sunk in a hushed, deep sleep; not a movement, not a sound, it was hard to believe that nature could be so hushed.

When you see a wide village street on a moonlit night, with its cottages, haystacks, sleeping willows, your own soul becomes hushed; in that peace, hiding from toil, care, and grief in the shadows of the night, it turns meek, mournful, beautiful, and it seems that the stars, too, look down on it tenderly and with feeling, and that there is no more evil on earth, and all is well. Fields spread out to the left from the edge of the village; they were visible as far as the horizon, and across the whole breadth of those fields, flooded with moonlight, there was also no movement or sound.

"Right you are," Ivan Ivanych repeated. "And that we live in town, stifled, crowded, writing useless papers, playing cards—isn't that a case? And that we spend our lives among do-nothings, pettifoggers, stupid, idle women, that we say and hear all kinds of nonsense—isn't that a case? Here, if you like, I'll tell you an instructive story."

"No, it's time to sleep," said Burkin. "Good night."

They both went into the shed and lay down in the hay. And they had both already covered themselves and dozed off when light footsteps were heard: tap, tap . . . Someone was walking near the shed; walked and then stopped, and after a moment again: tap, tap . . . The dogs growled.

"That's Mavra out walking," said Burkin.

The steps died away.

"To see and hear people lie," said Ivan Ivanych, turning over on the other side, "and to be called a fool yourself for putting up with the lie; to endure insults, humiliations, not daring to say openly that you're on the side of honest, free people, and to have to lie yourself, to smile, and all that for a crust of bread, a warm corner, some little rank that's not worth a penny—no, it's impossible to live like that any longer!"

"Well, that's from another opera, Ivan Ivanych," said the teacher. "Let's get some sleep."

And ten minutes later Burkin was asleep. But Ivan Ivanych kept tossing from side to side and sighing. Then he got up, went out again, sat by the doorway, and lit his pipe.

JULY 1898

GOOSEBERRIES

Since early morning the whole sky had been covered with dark clouds; it was not hot, but still and dull, as usual on gray, bleak days, when clouds hang over the fields for a long time, you wait for rain, but it does not come. The veterinarian Ivan Ivanych and the high-school teacher Burkin were tired of walking, and the fields seemed endless to them. Far ahead the windmills of the village of Mironositskoe were barely visible, to the right a line of hills stretched away and then disappeared far beyond the village, and they both knew that this was the bank of the river, with meadows, green willows, country houses, and if you stood on one of the hills, from there you could see equally vast fields, telegraph poles, and the train, which in the distance looked like a crawling caterpillar, and in clear weather you could even see the town. Now, in the still weather, when all nature seemed meek and pensive, Ivan Ivanych and Burkin were imbued with love for these fields, and both thought how great, how beautiful this land was.

"Last time, when we were in the headman Prokofy's shed," said Burkin, "you were going to tell some story."

"Yes, I wanted to tell about my brother."

Ivan Ivanych gave a long sigh and lit his pipe, so as to begin the story, but just then it started to rain. And about five minutes later a hard rain was pouring down and there was no telling when it would end. Ivan Ivanych and Burkin stopped and considered; the dogs, already wet, stood with their tails between their legs, looking at them tenderly.

"We'll have to take cover somewhere," said Burkin. "Let's go to Alekhin's. It's nearby."

"All right."

They turned aside and went on walking over the mowed fields, now straight, now bearing to the right, until they came to the road. Soon poplars appeared, a garden, then the red roofs of the barns; the river sparkled, and the view opened onto a wide pond with a mill and a white bathing house. This was Sofyino, where Alekhin lived.

The mill was working, drowning out the noise of the rain; the dam shook. Here by the carts stood wet horses, hanging their heads, and people walked about, their heads covered with sacks. It was damp, muddy, unwelcoming, and the pond looked cold, malevolent. Ivan Ivanych and Burkin felt thoroughly wet, dirty and uncomfortable, their feet were weighed down with mud, and when, after crossing the dam, they went up toward the master's barns, they were silent, as if angry with each other.

In one of the barns a winnowing machine was clattering; the door was open, and dust was pouring out of it. On the threshold stood Alekhin himself, a man of about forty, tall, stout, with long hair, looking more like a professor or an artist than a landowner. He was wearing a white, long-unwashed shirt with a braided belt, drawers instead of trousers, and his boots were also caked with mud and straw. His nose and eyes were black with dust. He recognized Ivan Ivanych and Burkin and was apparently very glad.

"Please go to the house, gentlemen," he said, smiling. "I'll be with you in a moment."

It was a big, two-storied house. Alekhin lived downstairs, in two vaulted rooms with small windows, where the stewards once lived; the furnishings here were simple, and it smelled of rye bread, cheap vodka, and harness. He rarely went upstairs to the formal rooms, only when he received guests. Ivan Ivanych and Burkin were met inside by a maid, a young woman of such beauty that they both stopped at once and looked at each other.

"You can't imagine how glad I am to see you, gentlemen," Alekhin said, coming into the front hall with them. "Quite unexpected! Pelageya," he turned to the maid, "give the guests something to change into. And, incidentally, I'll change, too. Only first I must go and bathe—I don't think I've bathed since spring. Why not come to the bathing house, gentlemen, while things are made ready here."

The beautiful Pelageya, such a delicate girl and with such a soft look, brought towels and soap, and Alekhin went with his guests to the bathing house.

"Yes, I haven't bathed for a long time," he said, undressing. "My bathing house is nice, as you see, my father built it, but I somehow never have time to bathe."

He sat down on the step, soaped his long hair and neck, and the water around him turned brown.

"Yes, I declare . . ." said Ivan Ivanych, looking significantly at his head.

"I haven't bathed for a long time . . ." Alekhin repeated bashfully and soaped himself once more, and the water around him turned dark blue, like ink.

Ivan Ivanych went outside, threw himself noisily into the water and swam under the rain, swinging his arms widely, and he made waves, and the white lilies swayed on the waves; he reached the middle of the pond and dove, and a moment later appeared in another place and swam further, and kept diving, trying to reach the bottom. "Ah, my God . . ." he repeated delightedly. "Ah, my God . . ." He swam as far as the mill, talked about something with the peasants there and turned back, and in the middle of the pond lay face up to the rain. Burkin and Alekhin were already dressed and ready to go, but he kept swimming and diving.

"Ah, my God . . ." he repeated. "Ah, Lord have mercy."

"That's enough!" Burkin shouted to him.

They went back to the house. And only when the lamp was lit in the big drawing room upstairs, and Burkin and Ivan Ivanych, in silk dressing gowns and warm slippers, were sitting in armchairs, and Alekhin himself, washed, combed, in a new frock coat, was pacing about the drawing room, obviously enjoying the feeling of warmth, cleanness, dry clothes, light shoes, and when the beautiful Pelageya, stepping noiselessly over the carpet and smiling softly, served the tray with tea and preserves, only then did Ivan Ivanych begin his story, and it seemed that not only Burkin and Alekhin, but also the old and young ladies, and the military men, who gazed calmly and sternly from their gilded frames, listened to him.

"We're two brothers," he began, "I'm Ivan Ivanych, and he's

Nikolai Ivanych, some two years younger. I went in for studying and became a veterinarian, while Nikolai sat in a government office from the age of nineteen. Our father, Chimsha-Himalaysky, was a cantonist,[1] but he earned officer's rank in the service and left us hereditary nobility and a small estate. After his death, the estate went to pay debts, but, be that as it may, we spent our childhood in the freedom of the countryside. Just like peasant children, we spent days and nights in the fields, in the woods, tending horses, stripping bast,[2] fishing, and all the rest . . . And you know that anyone who at least once in his life has caught a perch or seen blackbirds migrating in the fall, when they rush in flocks over the village on clear, cool days, is no longer a townsman, and will be drawn towards freedom till his dying day. My brother languished in the office. Years passed, and he was still sitting in the same place, writing the same papers and thinking about the same thing—how to get to the country. And this languishing slowly formed itself into a definite desire, the dream of buying himself a small country place somewhere on the bank of a river or a lake.

"He was a kind, meek man, and I loved him, but I never sympathized with this desire to lock himself up for life in his own country place. It's a common saying that a man needs only six feet of earth. But it's a corpse that needs six feet, not a man. And they also say now that if our intelligentsia is drawn to the soil and longs for country places, it's a good thing. But these country places are the same six feet of earth. To leave town, quit the struggle and noise of life, go and hide in your country place, isn't life, it's egoism, laziness, it's a sort of monasticism, but a monasticism without spiritual endeavor. Man needs, not six feet of earth, not a country place, but the whole earth, the whole of nature, where he can express at liberty all the properties and particularities of his free spirit.

"My brother Nikolai, sitting in his office, dreamed of how he would eat his own shchi, the savory smell of which would fill the whole yard, eat on the green grass, sleep in the sun, spend whole hours sitting outside the gate on a bench, gazing at the fields and woods. Books on agriculture and all sorts of almanac wisdom were his joy, his favorite spiritual nourishment; he liked to read newspapers, too, but only the advertisements about the sale of so many acres of field and meadow, with a country house, a river and a garden, a mill and a mill pond. And in his head he pictured garden paths, flowers, fruit, birdhouses, carp in the pond—you know, all that stuff. These imaginary pictures differed, depending on the advertisements he came upon, but for some reason gooseberries were unfailingly present in each of them. He was unable to imagine a single country place, a single poetic corner, that was without gooseberries.

" 'Country life has its conveniences,' he used to say. 'You sit on the balcony drinking tea, and your ducks swim in the pond, and it smells so good, and . . . and the gooseberries are growing.'

"He'd draw the plan of his estate, and each time it came out the same: a) the master's house, b) the servants' quarters, c) the kitchen garden, d) the gooseberries. He lived frugally: ate little, drank little, dressed God knows how, like a beggar, and kept saving money and putting it in the bank. He was terribly stingy. It was painful for me to see, and I used to give him money, and send him something on holidays, but he put that away, too. Once a man gets himself an idea, there's nothing to be done.

"Years went by, he was transferred to another province, he was already over forty, and he went on reading the advertisements in the newspapers and saving money. Then I heard he got married. Still with the same purpose of buying himself a country place with gooseberries, he married an ugly old widow for whom he felt nothing, only because she had a little money. He was tightfisted with her, too, kept her hungry, and put her money in the bank under his name. Earlier she had been married to the postmaster and had become used to pies and liqueurs, but with her second husband she didn't even have enough black bread; she began to pine away from such a life, and about three years later she gave up her soul to God. And, of course, my brother never thought for a moment that he was guilty of her death. Money, like vodka, does strange things to a man. A merchant was dying in our town. Before he died, he asked to be served a dish of honey and ate all his money and lottery tickets with it, so that nobody would get them. Once I was inspecting cattle at the station, and just then one of the dealers fell under a locomotive and his foot was cut off. We carried him to the hospital, blood was pouring out—a horrible business—and he kept asking us to find his foot and worrying: in the boot on his cut-off foot there were twenty roubles he didn't want to lose."

"That's from another opera," said Burkin.

"After his wife's death," Ivan Ivanych went on, having reflected for half a minute, "my brother began looking for an estate to buy.

Of course, you can look for five years and in the end make a mistake and not buy what you were dreaming of at all. Brother Nikolai bought, through an agent, by a transfer of mortgage, three hundred acres with a master's house, servants' quarters, a park, but no orchard, or gooseberries, or ponds with ducks; there was a river, but the water in it was coffee-colored, because there was a brick factory on one side of the estate and a bone-burning factory on the other. But my brother Nikolai Ivanych didn't lament over it; he ordered twenty gooseberry bushes, planted them, sat down and began living like a landowner.

"Last year I went to visit him. I'll go, I thought, and see how things are there. In his letters my brother called his estate: the Chumbaroklov plot, alias Himalayskoe. I arrived in 'alias Himalayskoe' past noon. It was hot. Ditches, fences, hedges, lines of fir trees everywhere—I didn't know how to get into the courtyard, where to put the horse. I walked toward the house, and a ginger dog met me, fat, looking like a pig. It would have liked to bark, but was too lazy. The cook came out of the kitchen, barefoot, fat, also looking like a pig, and said that the master was resting after dinner. I went into my brother's room, he was sitting in bed, his knees covered with a blanket; he had grown old, fat, flabby; his cheeks, nose, and lips thrust forward—he looked as if he were about to grunt into the blanket.

"We embraced and wept with joy and with the sad thought that we had been young once, and were now both gray-haired, and it was time to die. He got dressed and took me around to view his estate.

" 'Well, how are you getting on here?' I asked.

" 'Oh, all right, thank God, I live well.'

"He was no longer a timid and wretched little official, but a real landowner, a squire. He had settled in here, grown accustomed to it, relished it; he ate a lot, washed in a bathhouse, gained weight, was already at law with the commune and both factories, and was very offended when the peasants didn't call him 'Your Honor.' He took solid, squirely care of his soul, and did good deeds not simply but imposingly. And what were they? He treated the peasants for all ailments with soda and castor oil, and on his name day held a thanksgiving prayer service in the middle of the village, and then stood them all to a half-bucket of vodka, thinking it necessary. Ah, these horrible half-buckets! Today the fat landowner drags the peasant to the head of the zemstvo for poaching, and tomorrow, for the holiday, he treats them to a half-bucket, and they drink and shout 'hurrah,' and bow down drunk before him. A change of life for the better, good eating, idleness, develop the most insolent conceit in a Russian. Nikolai Ivanych, who, while in the government office, was afraid to have his own views even for himself personally, now uttered nothing but truths, and in the tone of a government minister: 'Education is necessary, but for the people it is premature,' 'Corporal punishment is generally bad, but on certain occasions it is useful and indispensable.'

" 'I know the people and know how to handle them,' he said. 'The people like me. I have only to move a finger, and the people do whatever I want.'

"And, note, it was all said with a kindly, intelligent smile. He repeated twenty times: 'We, the nobility,' 'I, as a nobleman'—obviously he no longer remembered that our grandfather was a peasant and our father a soldier. Even our family name, Chimsha-Himalaysky, which is essentially incongruous, now seemed sonorous, noble, and highly agreeable to him.

"But the point was not in him, but in myself. I want to tell you what a change took place in me during the few hours I spent at his place. In the evening, while we were having tea, the cook served a full plate of gooseberries. They weren't bought, they were his own gooseberries, the first picked since the bushes were planted. Nikolai Ivanych laughed and gazed silently at the gooseberries for a moment with tears in his eyes—he couldn't speak for excitement; then he put one berry in his mouth, glanced at me with the triumph of a child who has finally gotten his favorite toy, and said:

" 'How delicious!'

"And he ate greedily and kept repeating:

" 'Ah, how delicious! Try them!'

"They were tough and sour, but as Pushkin said, 'Dearer to us than a host of truths is an exalting illusion.'[3] I saw a happy man, whose cherished dream had so obviously come true, who had attained his goal in life, had gotten what he wanted, who was content with his fate and with himself. For some reason there had always been something sad mixed with my thoughts about human happiness, but now, at the sight of a happy man, I was overcome by an oppressive feeling close to despair. It was especially oppressive during the night. My bed was made up in the room next to my brother's bedroom, and I could hear that he was not asleep and that he kept getting up and going to the plate of gooseberries and taking a berry. I thought: there are, in fact, so many contented, happy people! What an overwhelming force! Just look at this life: the insolence and idleness of the strong, the ignorance and brutishness of the weak, impossible poverty all around us, overcrowding, degeneracy, drunkenness, hypocrisy, lies . . . Yet in all the houses and streets it's quiet, peaceful; of the fifty thousand people who live in town there is not one who would cry out or become loudly indignant. We see those who go to the market to buy food, eat during the day, sleep during the night, who talk their nonsense, get married, grow old, complacently drag their dead to the cemetery; but we don't see or hear those who suffer, and the horrors of life go on somewhere behind the scenes. Everything is quiet, peaceful, and only mute statistics protest: so many gone mad, so many buckets drunk, so many children dead of malnutrition . . . And this order is obviously necessary; obviously the happy man feels good only because the unhappy bear their burden silently, and without that silence happiness would be impossible. It's a general hypnosis. At the door of every contented, happy man somebody should stand with a little hammer, constantly tapping, to remind him that unhappy people exist, that however happy he may be, sooner or later life will show him its claws, some calamity will befall him—illness, poverty, loss—and nobody will hear or see, just as he doesn't hear or see others now. But there is nobody with a little hammer, the happy man lives on, and the petty cares of life stir him only slightly, as wind stirs an aspen—and everything is fine.

"That night I understood that I, too, was content and happy," Ivan Ivanych continued, getting up. "Over dinner or out hunting, I, too, gave lessons in how to live, how to believe, how to govern the people. I, too, said that knowledge is light, that education is necessary, but that for simple people literacy is enough for now. Freedom is good, I said, it's like air, we can't do without it, but we must wait. Yes, that was what I said, but now I ask: wait in the name of what?" Ivan Ivanych asked, looking angrily at Burkin. "Wait in the name of what, I ask you? In the name of what considerations? They tell me that it can't be done all at once, that every idea is realized gradually, in due time. But who says that? Where are the proofs that it's so? You refer to the natural order of things, to the lawfulness of phenomena, but is there order and lawfulness in the fact that I, a living and thinking man, must stand at a ditch and wait until it gets overgrown or silted up, when I could perhaps jump over it or build a bridge across it? And, again, wait in the name of what? Wait, when you haven't the strength to live, and yet you must live and want to live!

"I left my brother's early the next morning, and since then it has become unbearable for me to live in town. I'm oppressed by the peace and quiet, I'm afraid to look in the windows, because there's no more painful spectacle for me now than a happy family sitting around a table and drinking tea. I'm old and not fit for struggle, I'm not even capable of hatred. I only grieve inwardly, become irritated, vexed, my head burns at night from a flood of thoughts, and I can't sleep . . . Ah, if only I were young!"

Ivan Ivanych paced the room in agitation and repeated:

"If only I were young!"

He suddenly went up to Alekhin and began pressing him by one hand, then the other.

"Pavel Konstantinych!" he said in an entreating voice, "don't settle in, don't let yourself fall asleep! As long as you're young, strong, energetic, don't weary of doing good! There is no happiness and there shouldn't be, and if there is any meaning and purpose in life, then that meaning and purpose are not at all in our happiness, but in something more intelligent and great. Do good!"

And Ivan Ivanych said all this with a pitiful, pleading smile, as if he were asking personally for himself.

Then all three sat in armchairs at different ends of the drawing room and were silent. Ivan Ivanych's story satisfied neither Burkin nor Alekhin. With generals and ladies gazing from gilded frames, looking alive in the twilight, it was boring to hear a story about a wretched official who ate gooseberries. For some reason they would have preferred to speak and hear about fine people, about women. And the fact that they were sitting in a drawing room where everything—the covered chandelier, the armchairs, the carpets under their feet—said that here those very people now gazing from the frames had once walked, sat, drunk tea, and that the beautiful Pelageya now walked noiselessly here, was better than any story.

Alekhin had a strong desire to sleep; farming got him up early, before three in the morning, and his eyes kept closing, but he was afraid that the guests would start telling something interesting without him, and he would not leave. Whether what Ivan Ivanych had said was intelligent or correct, he did not try to figure out; his guests were not talking of grain, or hay, or tar, but about something that had no direct bearing on his life, and he was glad and wanted them to go on . . .

"However, it's time for bed," said Burkin, getting up. "Allow me to wish you good-night."

Alekhin took leave of them and went to his room below, while the guests stayed upstairs. They were both put for the night in a big room with two old, carved wooden beds in it, and with an ivory crucifix in the corner. Their beds, wide and cool, made up by the beautiful Pelageya, smelled pleasantly of fresh linen.

Ivan Ivanych silently undressed and lay down.

"Lord, forgive us sinners!" he said, and pulled the covers over his head.

His pipe, left on the table, smelled strongly of stale tobacco, and Burkin lay awake for a long time and still could not figure out where that heavy odor was coming from.

Rain beat on the windows all night.

AUGUST 1898

A MEDICAL CASE

A professor received a telegram from the Lialikovs' factory asking
him to come quickly. The daughter of a certain Mrs. Lialikov,
apparently the owner of the factory, was sick—nothing more could
be understood from the long, witlessly composed telegram. The
professor did not go himself, but sent his intern Korolev in his
place.

He had to go two stations away from Moscow and then some
three miles by carriage. A troika was sent to the station to pick
Korolev up; the driver wore a hat with a peacock feather, and to all
questions responded with a loud military "No, sir!" or "Yes, sir!" It
was Saturday evening, the sun was setting. Crowds of workers came
walking from the factory to the station and bowed to the horses
that were bringing Korolev. And he was enchanted by the evening,
and the country houses and dachas along the way, and the birches,
and that quiet mood all around, when it seemed that, together with
the workers, the fields, the woods, and the sun were preparing to
rest on the eve of the holy day—to rest and perhaps to pray . . .

He was born and grew up in Moscow, did not know the countryside and had never been interested in factories or visited them.
But he had chanced to read about factories and to visit factory
owners and talk with them; and when he saw some factory in the
distance or up close, he thought each time of how quiet and peaceful everything was outside, and how inside there must be the impenetrable ignorance and obtuse egoism of the owners, the tedious,

unhealthy labor of the workers, squabbles, vodka, vermin. And now, as the workers deferentially and timorously stepped aside before the carriage, in their faces, caps, and gait he could discern physical uncleanness, drunkenness, nervousness, perplexity.

They drove through the factory gates. On both sides flashed workers' cottages, women's faces, linen and blankets on the porches. "Watch out!" cried the driver, not reining in the horses. Then came a wide yard with no grass, and in it five huge buildings with smokestacks, standing separate from each other, warehouses, barracks, and over everything lay some sort of gray coating, as of dust. Here and there, like oases in the desert, were pathetic little gardens and the green or red roofs of the houses where the management lived. The driver suddenly reined in the horses, and the carriage stopped at a house newly painted gray; there was a front garden with dust-covered lilacs, and a strong smell of paint on the yellow porch.

"Come in, doctor," women's voices said from the hall and the front room, followed by sighs and whispers. "Come in, we've been waiting . . . it's very bad. Come in here."

Mrs. Lialikov, a stout, elderly lady in a black silk dress with fashionable sleeves, but, judging by her face, a simple and illiterate one, looked at the doctor with anxiety and hesitated, not daring to offer him her hand. Beside her stood a person with short hair and a pince-nez, in a bright multicolored blouse, skinny and no longer young. The servants called her Christina Dmitrievna, and Korolev figured that she was a governess. It was probably she, as the most educated person in the house, who had been charged with meeting and receiving the doctor, because she at once began hastily explaining the causes of the illness in minute, nagging detail, but without saying who was ill or what was the matter.

The doctor and the governess sat and talked, while the mistress stood motionless by the door, waiting. Korolev understood from the conversation that the ill person was Liza, a girl of twenty, Mrs. Lialikov's only daughter, the heiress; she had long been ill and had been treated by various doctors, and during the past night, from evening till morning, she had had such a pounding of the heart that no one in the house had slept for fear she might die.

"She's been sickly, you might say, from childhood," Christina Dmitrievna went on recounting in a sing-song voice, wiping her lips with her hand now and then. "The doctors say it's nerves, but when she was little, the doctors drove her scrofula inside, so I think it might come from that."

They went to see the patient. Quite grown-up, big, tall, but not pretty, resembling her mother, with the same small eyes and broad, overly developed lower face, her hair undone, the blanket drawn up to her chin, she gave Korolev the impression at first of a wretched, woebegone creature who had been taken in and given shelter here out of pity, and it was hard to believe that she was the heiress to five huge buildings.

"And so," Korolev began, "we've come to take care of you. How do you do."

He introduced himself and shook her hand—a big, cold, uncomely hand. She sat up and, obviously long accustomed to doctors, not caring that her shoulders and breast were uncovered, allowed herself to be auscultated.

"My heart pounds," she said. "All last night, it was so terrible . . . I nearly died of fright! Give me something for it!"

"I will, I will! Calm down."

Korolev examined her and shrugged his shoulders.

"Nothing's wrong with your heart," he said, "everything's well, everything's in order. Your nerves are probably acting up a bit, but that's not unusual. I assume the attack is over now. Lie down and sleep."

Just then a lamp was brought into the bedroom. The sick girl squinted at the light and suddenly clutched her head with her hands and burst into tears. And the impression of a woebegone and uncomely creature suddenly vanished, and Korolev no longer noticed either the small eyes or the coarsely developed lower face; he saw a soft, suffering look, which was both reasonable and touching, and the whole of her seemed shapely to him, feminine, simple, and he would have liked to comfort her now, not with medications, not with advice, but with a simple, tender word. Her mother embraced her head and pressed it to her. There was so much despair, so much grief in the old woman's face! She, the mother, had nourished and raised her daughter, sparing nothing, had given her whole life to teaching her French, dancing, music, had invited dozens of tutors, the best doctors, had kept a governess, and now she could not understand where these tears came from, why so much torment, could not understand and was at a loss, had a guilty, anxious, despairing look, as if she had missed something else very important, had failed to do something else, to invite someone else, but whom—she did not know.

"Lizanka, again . . . again," she said, pressing her daughter to her. "My dear, my darling, my child, what's wrong? Have pity on me, tell me."

They both wept bitterly. Korolev sat on the edge of the bed and took Liza's hand.

"Come, is it worth crying?" he said tenderly. "There's nothing in the world that merits these tears. Let's not cry, now, there's no need to . . ."

And he thought to himself:

"It's time she was married . . ."

"Our factory doctor gave her potassium bromide," said the governess, "but I've noticed that it makes her even worse. I think, if it's for her heart, it should be those drops . . . I forget what they're called . . . Convallarin, or whatever."

And again there followed all sorts of details. She interrupted the doctor, prevented him from speaking; zeal was written all over her face, as if she assumed that, being the best-educated woman in the house, she had to engage the doctor in ceaseless conversation and about nothing but medicine.

Korolev became bored.

"I don't find anything in particular," he said, coming out of the bedroom and addressing the mother. "Since the factory doctor has been treating your daughter, let him continue. So far the treatment has been correct, and I see no need to change doctors. Why change? It's an ordinary illness, nothing serious . . ."

He spoke unhurriedly, putting on his gloves, while Mrs. Lialikov stood motionless and looked at him with tear-filled eyes.

"It's half an hour till the ten o'clock train," he said. "I hope I won't be late."

"Can't you stay with us?" she asked, and tears poured down her cheeks again. "It's a shame to trouble you, but be so kind . . . for God's sake," she went on in a low voice, glancing at the door, "stay with us overnight. She's my only . . . my only daughter . . . She frightened us last night, I can't get over it . . . Don't leave, for God's sake . . ."

He was about to tell her that he had much work in Moscow, that his family was waiting for him at home; it was hard for him to spend the whole evening and night needlessly in a strange house, but he looked at her face, sighed, and silently began taking off his gloves.

All the lamps and candles were lighted for him in the reception room and the drawing room. He sat at the grand piano and leafed through the scores, then examined the paintings on the walls, the portraits. The paintings, done in oils, with gilded frames, were views of the Crimea, a stormy sea with a little boat, a Catholic monk with a wineglass, and all of them dry, slick, giftless . . . Not a single handsome, interesting face among the portraits, everywhere wide cheekbones, astonished eyes; Lialikov, Liza's father, had a narrow forehead and a self-satisfied face, the uniform hung like a sack on his big, plebeian body, on his chest he had a medal and the badge of the Red Cross. The culture was poor, the luxury accidental, unconscious, ill at ease, like his uniform; the gleam of the floors was annoying, the chandelier was annoying, and for some reason brought to mind the story of the merchant who went to the bathhouse with a medal on his neck . . .

From the front hall came a whispering, someone quietly snored. And suddenly sharp, abrupt, metallic noises came from outside, such as Korolev had never heard before and could not understand now; they echoed strangely and unpleasantly in his soul.

"I don't think I'd ever stay and live here for anything . . ." he thought, and again took up the scores.

"Doctor, come and have a bite to eat!" the governess called in a low voice.

He went to supper. The table was big, well furnished with food and wines, but only two people sat down: himself and Christina Dmitrievna. She drank Madeira, ate quickly, and talked, looking at him through her pince-nez:

"The workers are very pleased with us. We have theatricals at the factory every winter, the workers themselves act in them, and there are magic-lantern lectures, a magnificent tearoom, and whatever you like. They're very devoted to us, and when they learned that Lizanka was worse, they held a prayer service for her. They're uneducated, and yet they, too, have feelings."

"It looks as if you have no men in the house," said Korolev.

"Not one. Pyotr Nikanorych died a year and a half ago, and we were left by ourselves. So there's just the three of us. In the summer we live here, and in the winter in Moscow, on Polianka Street. I've been with them for eleven years now. Like one of the family."

For supper they were served sterlet, chicken cutlets, and fruit compote; the wines were expensive, French.

"Please, doctor, no ceremony," said Christina Dmitrievna, eating and wiping her mouth with her fist, and it was obvious that her life there was fully to her satisfaction. "Please eat."

After dinner the doctor was taken to a room where a bed had been made for him. But he did not want to sleep, it was stuffy and the room smelled of paint; he put his coat on and went out.

It was cool outside; dawn was already breaking,[1] and in the damp air all five buildings with their tall smokestacks, the barracks and warehouses were clearly outlined. Since it was Sunday, no one was working, the windows were dark, and only in one of the buildings was a furnace still burning; the two windows were crimson and, along with smoke, fire occasionally came from the smokestack. Further away, beyond the yard, frogs were croaking and a nightingale sang.

Looking at the buildings and at the barracks where the workers slept, he again thought what he always thought when he saw factories. There may be theatricals for the workers, magic lanterns, factory doctors, various improvements, but even so the workers he had met that day on his way from the station did not look different in any way from the workers he had seen back in his childhood, when there were no factory theatricals or improvements. As a physician, he could make correct judgments about chronic ailments the fundamental cause of which was incomprehensible and incurable, and he looked at factories as a misunderstanding the cause of which was also obscure and irremediable, and while he did not consider all the improvements in the workers' lives superfluous, he saw them as the equivalent of treating an incurable illness.

"This is a misunderstanding, of course . . ." he thought, looking at the crimson windows. "Fifteen hundred, two thousand factory hands work without rest, in unhealthy conditions, producing poor-quality calico, starving, and only occasionally sobering up from this nightmare in a pothouse; a hundred men supervise the work, and the whole life of those hundred men goes into levying fines, pouring out abuse, being unjust, and only the two or three so-called owners enjoy the profits, though they don't work at all and scorn poor-quality calico. But what profits, and how do they enjoy them? Mrs. Lialikov and her daughter are unhappy, it's a pity to look at them, only Christina Dmitrievna, a rather stupid old maid in a pince-nez, lives to her full satisfaction. And so it turns out that all five of these buildings work, and poor-quality calico is sold on the Eastern markets, only so that Christina Dmitrievna can eat sterlet and drink Madeira."

Strange sounds suddenly rang out, the same that Korolev had heard before supper. Near one of the buildings someone banged on a metal bar, banged and stopped the sound at once, so that what came out were short, sharp, impure sounds, like "derr . . . derr . . . derr . . ." Then a half minute of silence, and then sounds rang out by another building, as sharp and unpleasant, but lower now, more bass—"drinn . . . drinn . . . drinn . . ." Eleven times. Evidently this was the watchman banging out eleven o'clock.

From near another building came a "zhak . . . zhak . . . zhak . . ." And so on near all the buildings and then beyond the barracks and the gates. And in the silence of the night it seemed as if these sounds were being produced by the crimson-eyed monster, the devil himself, who ruled here over both owners and workers and deceived the ones like the others.

Korolev went out of the yard to the fields.

"Who goes there?" a coarse voice called to him by the gates.

"Just like a prison . . ." he thought and did not answer.

Here the nightingales and frogs could be heard better, you could feel the May night. The noise of a train came from the station; sleepy cocks crowed somewhere, but even so the night was still, the world slept peacefully. In the field, not far from the factory, a house-frame stood, with building materials piled by it. Korolev sat on some planks and went on thinking:

"Nobody feels good here except the governess, and the factory works for her satisfaction. But it just seems so, she's only a straw man here. The main one that everything here is done for is—the devil."

And he thought about the devil, in whom he did not believe, and kept glancing back at the two windows gleaming with fire. It seemed to him that the devil himself was gazing at him through those crimson eyes, the unknown power that created the relations between strong and weak, the grave mistake that now could in no way be set right. It had to be that the strong hinder the life of the weak, such was the law of nature, but this thought could be clearly and easily formulated only in a newspaper article or a textbook, while in the mishmash that is everyday life, in the tangle of all the trifles of which human relations are woven, it was not a law but a logical incongruity, when strong and weak alike fell victim to their mutual relations, inadvertently obeying some controlling power, unknown, extraneous to life, alien to man. So thought Korolev as he sat on the planks, and the feeling gradually came over him that this unknown, mysterious power was in fact close by and watching. Meanwhile the east grew paler, the time passed quickly. Against the gray background of the dawn, with not a soul around, as if everything had died out, the five buildings and smokestacks had a peculiar look, different from in the daytime; the steam engines, electricity, telephones inside them left one's mind, and one somehow kept thinking of pile-dwellings, of the Stone Age, one sensed the presence of crude, unconscious power . . .

And again came the banging:

"Derr . . . derr . . . derr . . . derr . . ."

Twelve times. Then stillness, half a minute of stillness, and from the other end of the yard came:

"Drinn . . . drinn . . . drinn . . ."

"Terribly unpleasant!" thought Korolev.

"Zhak . . . zhak . . ." came from a third place, abruptly, sharply, as if in vexation, "zhak . . . zhak . . ."

And it took them about four minutes to strike twelve. Then it was still; and again the impression was as if everything around had died out.

Korolev sat a while longer and then went back to the house, but he did not go to bed for a long time. There was whispering in the neighboring rooms, a shuffling of slippers and bare feet.

"Is she having another fit?" thought Korolev.

He went to have a look at the patient. It was already quite light in the rooms, and on the walls and floor of the reception room sunlight trembled faintly, having broken through the morning mist. The door to Liza's room was open, and she was sitting in an armchair by the bed, in a robe, a shawl around her shoulders, her hair undone. The window blinds were drawn.

"How are you feeling?" asked Korolev.

"Well, thank you."

He took her pulse, then straightened the hair that had fallen across her forehead.

"You're not asleep," he said. "The weather is wonderful outside, it's spring, the nightingales are singing, and you sit in the dark and brood on something."

She listened and looked into his face; her eyes were sad, intelligent, and it was clear that she wanted to say something to him.

"Does this happen to you often?" he asked.

She moved her lips and answered:

"Often. I feel oppressed almost every night."

Just then the watchmen in the yard began striking two: "Derr . . . derr . . ." and she gave a start.

"Does this rapping upset you?" he asked.

"I don't know. Everything here upsets me," she said, and thought a little. "Everything. I hear sympathy in your voice, at the first sight of you I thought for some reason that I could talk with you about everything."

"Please do talk."

"I want to tell you my opinion. It seems to me that I'm not ill, but I'm upset and afraid because that's how it should be and it can't be otherwise. Even the healthiest person can't help being upset if, for instance, a robber is prowling under his windows. I've been treated often," she went on, looking into her lap and smiling bashfully. "I'm very grateful, of course, and I don't deny the benefits of the treatment, but I'd like to talk, not to a doctor, but to someone close to me, a friend who would understand me, who could convince me that I'm either right or wrong."

"You don't have any friends?" asked Korolev.

"I'm lonely. I have my mother, I love her, but still I'm lonely. Life has worked out this way . . . Lonely people read a lot, but talk little and hear little, life is mysterious for them; they're mystics and often see the devil where he's not. Lermontov's Tamara was lonely and saw the devil."[2]

"And you read a lot?"

"Yes. My time is all free, from morning till evening. During the day I read, but in the night my head is empty, there are some sort of shadows instead of thoughts."

"Do you see things at night?" asked Korolev.

"No, but I feel . . ."

Again she smiled and raised her eyes to the doctor, and looked at him so sadly, so intelligently; and it seemed to him that she trusted him, wanted to talk openly with him, and that she thought as he did. But she was silent, perhaps waiting for him to speak.

And he knew what to tell her. It was clear to him that she ought quickly to leave those five buildings and the million, if she had it, to leave that devil who watched at night; it was also clear to him that she herself thought so, too, and was only waiting for someone she trusted to confirm it.

But he did not know how to say it. How? It was mortifying to ask condemned people what they were condemned for; just as it was awkward to ask very rich people what they needed so much money for, why they disposed of their wealth so badly, why they would not abandon it, even when they could see it was to their own misfortune; and if such a conversation began, it usually turned out to be embarrassing, awkward, long.

"How to say it?" pondered Korolev. "And need I say it?"

And he said what he wanted to say, not directly, but in a round-about way:

"You're not content in your position as a factory owner and a rich heiress, you don't believe in your right to it, and now you can't sleep, which, of course, is certainly better than if you were content, slept soundly, and thought everything was fine. Your insomnia is respectable; in any event, it's a good sign. In fact, for our parents such a conversation as we're having now would have been unthinkable; they didn't talk at night, they slept soundly, but we, our generation, sleep badly, are anguished, talk a lot, and keep trying to decide if we're right or not. But for our children or grandchildren this question—whether they're right or not—will be decided. They'll see better than we do. Life will be good in fifty years or so, it's only a pity we won't make it that far. It would be interesting to have a look."

"And what will the children and grandchildren do?" asked Liza.

"I don't know . . . They'll probably drop it all and leave."

"For where?"

"Where? . . . Why, wherever they like," said Korolev, and he laughed. "As if there weren't lots of places a good, intelligent person can go."

He glanced at his watch.

"The sun is up, however," he said. "It's time you slept. Get undressed and have a good sleep. I'm very glad to have met you," he went on, pressing her hand. "You are a nice, interesting person. Good night!"

He went to his room and slept.

Next morning, when the carriage drove up, everybody came out on the porch to see him off. Liza was festive in a white dress, with a flower in her hair, pale, languid; she looked at him, as yesterday, sadly and intelligently, smiled, talked, and all with an expression as if she would have liked to say something special, important—to him alone. One could hear the larks singing, the church bells ringing. The windows of the factory shone merrily, and, driving through the yard and then on the way to the station, Korolev no longer remembered the workers, or the pile-dwellings, or the devil, but thought about the time, perhaps close at hand, when life would be as bright and joyful as this quiet Sunday morning; and he thought about how nice it was, on such a morning, in springtime, to ride in a good carriage with a troika and feel the warmth of the sun.

DECEMBER 1898

THE DARLING

Olenka, daughter of the retired collegiate assessor Plemyannikov, was sitting on the back porch in her courtyard, deep in thought. It was hot, the flies were naggingly persistent, and it was so pleasant to think that it would soon be evening. Dark rain clouds were gathering from the east, and an occasional breath of moisture came from there.

Kukin, an entrepreneur and owner of the Tivoli amusement garden, who lodged there in the yard, in the wing, was standing in the middle of the yard and looking at the sky.

"Again!" he said in despair. "Again it's going to rain! Every day it rains, every day—as if on purpose! It's a noose! It's bankruptcy! Every day terrible losses!"

He clasped his hands and went on, addressing Olenka:

"There's our life for you, Olga Semyonovna. It could make you weep! You work, you do your utmost, you suffer, you don't sleep, thinking how to do your best—and what then? On the one hand, the public is ignorant, savage. I give them the very best in operetta, fairy pageants, excellent music-hall singers, but is that what they want? Do they understand anything about it? They want buffoonery! Give them banality! On the other hand, look at the weather. It rains almost every evening. It started on the tenth of May, and it's gone on nonstop all of May and June—simply awful! The public doesn't come, but don't I pay the rent? Don't I pay the artists?"

The next day towards evening the clouds gathered again, and Kukin said, laughing hysterically:

"Well, so? Let it rain! Let the whole garden be flooded out, and me along with it! Let me not have any happiness either in this world or in the next! Let the artists sue me! What, sue? Hard labor in Siberia! The scaffold! Ha, ha, ha!"

And the third day it was the same . . .

Olenka listened to Kukin silently, seriously, and tears occasionally came to her eyes. In the end, Kukin's misfortunes touched her, and she fell in love with him. He was small, skinny, with a yellow face and brushed-up temples; he spoke in a thin little tenor and when he spoke, his mouth went askew; and despair was always written on his face, but even so he aroused deep, true feeling in her. She forever loved someone, and could not live without it. Earlier she had loved her father, who now sat ill, in a dark room, in an armchair, and breathed heavily; she had loved her aunt, who occasionally, once or twice a year, had come from Briansk; and earlier still, while in high school, she had loved her French teacher. She was a quiet, good-natured, pitiful young lady, with meek, soft eyes, and very healthy. Looking at her plump pink cheeks, at her soft white neck with its dark birthmark, at the kind, naïve smile her face bore when she listened to something pleasant, men thought: "Yes, not bad at all . . ." and also smiled, and lady visitors could not refrain from seizing her hand in the middle of the conversation and saying, in a burst of pleasure:

"You darling!"

The house, which she had lived in since the day she was born, and which had been put in her name in the will, stood at the edge of town, in the Gypsy quarter, not far from the Tivoli garden; in the evening and at night she could hear music playing in the garden; rockets burst and crackled, and it seemed to her that it was Kukin wrestling with his fate and taking by storm his chief enemy—the indifferent public; her heart sank with sweetness, she did not feel sleepy at all, and when he came home towards morning, she tapped softly on her bedroom window and, showing him only her face and one shoulder through the curtains, smiled tenderly . . .

He proposed, and they were married. And when he had a proper look at her neck and her plump, healthy shoulders, he clasped his hands and said:

"You darling!"

He was happy, but since it rained on the day of the wedding and later that night, the look of despair never left his face.

After the wedding they had a good life. She sat in his box office, looked after things in the garden, recorded the expenses, handed out the pay, and her pink cheeks and sweet, naïve, radiant-looking smile flashed now in the box-office window, now backstage, now in the buffet. And she told her acquaintances that the most remarkable, the most important and necessary thing in the world was the theater, and that only in the theater could one find true pleasure and become educated and humane.

"But does the public understand that?" she said. "They want buffoonery! Yesterday we showed *Faust Inside Out,* and nearly all the boxes were empty, but if Vanechka and I produced some sort of banality, believe me, the theater would be packed. Tomorrow Vanechka and I are showing *Orpheus in the Underworld.*[1] Do come."

And whatever Kukin said about the theater and actors, she repeated. She despised the public just as he did, for its ignorance and indifference to art; she interfered at rehearsals, corrected the actors, looked after the conduct of the musicians, and when the local newspaper spoke disapprovingly of the theater, she wept, and then went to the editorial offices for an explanation.

The actors loved her and called her "Vanechka and I" and "the darling." She felt sorry for them and would lend them small sums of money, and if they happened to cheat her, she merely wept quietly, but did not complain to her husband.

In the winter they also had a good life. They rented the town theater for the whole winter and leased it for short terms, now to a Ukrainian troupe, now to a conjuror, now to local amateurs. Olenka gained weight and was all radiant with contentment, while Kukin grew skinnier and yellower and complained about terrible losses, though business was not bad all winter. He coughed at night, and she gave him raspberry and linden-blossom infusions, rubbed him with eau de cologne, and wrapped him in her soft shawls.

"Aren't you my sweetie!" she said with complete sincerity, smoothing his hair. "Aren't you my pretty one!"

During Lent he went to Moscow to recruit a company, and without him she could not sleep, but sat all night at the window and looked at the stars. And during that time she compared herself to the hens, who also do not sleep all night and feel anxious when the cock is not in the chicken coop. Kukin was detained in Moscow and wrote that he would come for Easter, and in his letters gave orders concerning the Tivoli. But on the eve of Holy Monday, late at night, there suddenly came a sinister knocking at the gate; someone banged on the wicket as on a barrel: boom! boom! boom! The sleepy cook, splashing barefoot through the puddles, ran to open.

"Open up, please!" someone outside the gates said in a muted bass. "There's a telegram for you!"

Olenka had received telegrams from her husband before, but now for some reason she went numb. With trembling hands she opened the telegram and read:

"Ivan Petrovich died unexpectedly today mirst awaiting orders huneral Tuesday."

That was how it was written in the telegram—"huneral" and also the incomprehensible word "mirst." It was signed by the director of the operetta troupe.

"My little dove!" wept Olenka. "My sweet Vanechka, my little dove! Why did I meet you? Why did I know and love you? How could you go and leave your poor Olenka, poor, wretched me? . . ."

Kukin was buried on Tuesday, in Moscow, at the Vagankovo cemetery; Olenka came back on Wednesday, and as soon as she entered her room, she collapsed on the bed and wept so loudly that it could be heard in the street and the neighboring courtyards.

"The darling!" said the neighbor women, crossing themselves. "Darling Olga Semyonovna, the dear heart, how she grieves!"

Three months later Olenka was returning from church one day, sad, in deep mourning. One of her neighbors, Vassily Andreich Pustovalov, manager of the merchant Babakaev's lumberyard, happened to be walking beside her, also returning from church. He was wearing a straw hat and a white waistcoat with a gold chain, and looked more like a landowner than a dealer.

"There is order in all things, Olga Semyonovna," he said gravely, with sympathy in his voice, "and if one of our relations dies, it means that it's God's will, and in that case we must recollect ourselves and bear it with submission."

Having accompanied Olenka to the gate, he said good-bye and went on. After that she heard his grave voice all day, and the moment she closed her eyes, she pictured his dark beard. She liked him very much. And apparently she had also made an impression on him, because shortly afterwards an elderly lady with whom she was barely acquainted came to have coffee with her, and had only just sat down at the table when she immediately began talking about Pustovalov, what a good, solid man he was, and how any bride would be pleased to marry him. Three days later Pustovalov himself came for a visit; he did not stay long, about ten minutes, and spoke little, but Olenka fell in love with him, so much so that she did not sleep all night and burned as in a fever, and in the morning sent for the elderly lady. The match was soon made, after which came the wedding.

Pustovalov and Olenka, once they were married, had a good life. He usually sat in the lumberyard till dinnertime, then left on business and was replaced by Olenka, who sat in the office till evening and there kept the accounts and filled orders.

"Nowadays the price of lumber goes up twenty percent a year," she would say to customers and acquaintances. "Gracious, before we dealt in local lumber, and now every year Vasechka has to go for lumber to Mogilev province. And the taxes!" she said, covering both cheeks with her hands in horror. "The taxes!"

It seemed to her that she had been dealing in lumber for a very, very long time, that lumber was the most important and necessary thing in life, and for her there was something dear and touching in the sound of the words beam, post, board, plank, batten, slat, lath, slab . . . At night, when she slept, she dreamed of whole mountains of boards and planks, of long, endless lines of carts carrying lumber somewhere far out of town; she dreamed of a whole regiment of ten-yard-long, ten-inch-thick logs marching upended against the lumberyard, of beams, posts, and slabs striking together, making the ringing sound of dry wood, all falling and rising up again, piling upon each other. Olenka cried out in her sleep, and Pustovalov said tenderly to her:

"Olenka, dear, what's the matter? Cross yourself!"

Whatever her husband thought, she thought, too. If he thought the room was hot or business was slow, she thought the same. Her husband did not like entertainment of any sort and stayed at home on Sundays, and so did she.

"You're always at home or in the office," her acquaintances said. "You should go to the theater, darling, or to the circus."

"Vasechka and I have no time for going to theaters," she replied gravely. "We're working people, we can't be bothered with trifles. What's the good of these theaters?"

On Saturdays she and Pustovalov went to the evening vigil, on Sundays to the early liturgy, and returning from church, they walked side by side, looking moved, a nice smell came from both of them, and her silk dress rustled pleasantly; and at home they had tea with fancy bread and various preserves, and then ate pastry. Each day at noon, in the yard and in the street outside the gates, there was a savory smell of borscht and roast lamb or duck, or, on fast days, of fish, and one could not pass the gate without feeling hungry. The samovar was always boiling in the office, and customers were treated to tea and bagels. Once a week the spouses went to the baths and came back side by side, both bright red.

"Still, we have a good life," Olenka said to her acquaintances, "thank God. God grant everyone a life like Vasechka's and mine."

When Pustovalov left for Mogilev province to buy lumber, she missed him very much and at night did not sleep but wept. Sometimes in the evening the regimental veterinarian Smirnin, a young man who was renting her wing, came to visit her. He told her some story or played cards with her, and that diverted her. Especially interesting were his stories about his own family life; he was married and had a son, but he was separated from his wife, because she had been unfaithful to him, and now he hated her and sent her forty roubles every month for his son's keep. And, listening to that, Olenka sighed and shook her head, and felt sorry for him.

"Well, God save you," she said, seeing him to the stairs with a candle as he took his leave. "Thank you for sharing my boredom, God grant you good health, and may the Queen of Heaven . . ."

And she always spoke so gravely, so sensibly, imitating her husband; the veterinarian was already disappearing through the door below when she called out to him and said:

"You know, Vladimir Platonych, you ought to make peace with your wife. Forgive her, if only for your son's sake! . . . The boy must understand everything."

And when Pustovalov came back, she told him in a low voice about the veterinarian and his unhappy family life, and they both sighed and shook their heads, and talked about the boy, who probably missed his father, and then, by some strange train of thought, they both stood before the icons, bowed to the ground, and prayed to God to send them children.

And so the Pustovalovs lived quietly and placidly, in love and perfect harmony, for six years. Then one winter day Vassily Andreich, after drinking hot tea in the lumberyard, went out to deliver some lumber, caught cold, and fell ill. He was treated by the best doctors, but the disease took its toll, and after four months of illness, he died. And Olenka was widowed again.

"Why did you go and leave me, my little dove?" she wept, having buried her husband. "How am I to live without you now, wretched and unhappy as I am? Good people, have pity on me, an orphan . . ."

She went about in a black dress with weepers, and forever gave up wearing a hat and gloves, rarely left the house, except to go to church or visit her husband's grave, and lived at home like a nun. And only when six months had passed did she remove the weepers and begin opening the shutters of her windows. Occasionally she was seen in the morning, going to market for provisions with her cook, but how she lived now and what went on in her house could only be guessed. Guessed, for instance, from the fact that she was seen having tea in the garden with the veterinarian, while he read the newspaper aloud to her, or that, on meeting a lady of her acquaintance in the post office, she said:

"There's no proper veterinarian supervision in our town, and that results in many diseases. You keep hearing of people getting sick from milk or catching infections from horses and cows. In fact, the health of domestic animals needs as much care as the health of people."

She repeated the veterinarian's thoughts, and was now of the same opinion as he about everything. It was clear that she could not live without an attachment even for one year, and had found her new happiness in her own wing. Another woman would have been condemned for it, but no one could think ill of Olenka, and everything was so clear in her life. She and the veterinarian told no one about the change that had occurred in their relations and tried to conceal it, but they did not succeed, because Olenka could not keep a secret. When he had guests, his colleagues from the regiment, she would start talking about cattle plague, or pearl disease, or the town slaughterhouses, while she poured the tea or served supper, and he would be terribly embarrassed and, when the guests left, would seize her by the arm and hiss angrily:

"I asked you not to talk about things you don't understand! When we veterinarians are talking among ourselves, please don't interfere. It's tedious, finally!"

But she would look at him in amazement and alarm and ask:

"Volodechka, what then am I to talk about?"

And with tears in her eyes she would embrace him, beg him not to be angry, and they would both be happy.

However, this happiness did not last long. The veterinarian left with his regiment, left forever, because his regiment was transferred to somewhere very far away, almost to Siberia. And Olenka was left alone.

Now she was completely alone. Her father had died long ago; his armchair was lying in the attic, dusty, one leg missing. She lost weight and lost her looks, and those who met her in the street no longer looked at her as before and no longer smiled at her; obviously, the best years were already past, left behind, and now some new life was beginning, unknown, of which it was better not to think. In the evenings Olenka sat on the back porch, and could hear music playing in the Tivoli and rockets bursting, but that called up no thoughts in her. She gazed indifferently at her empty courtyard, thought of nothing, wanted nothing, and later, when night fell, went to sleep and dreamed of her empty courtyard. She ate and drank as if against her will.

But chiefly, which was worst of all, she no longer had any opinions. She saw the objects around her and was aware of all that went on around her, but she was unable to form an opinion about anything and did not know what to talk about. And how terrible it was to have no opinions! You see, for instance, that a bottle is standing there, or that it is raining, or that a peasant is driving a cart, but why the bottle, the rain, or the peasant are there, what sense they make, you cannot say and even for a thousand roubles you could not say anything. With Kukin and Pustovalov, and later with the veterinarian, Olenka had been able to explain everything and give her opinion on anything you like, but now in her thoughts and in her heart there was the same emptiness as in her courtyard. And it felt as eerie and bitter as if she had eaten wormwood.

The town was gradually expanding on all sides; the Gypsy quarter was already called a street, and houses grew up and many lanes appeared where the Tivoli garden and the lumberyard used to be. How quickly time flies! Olenka's house darkened, the roof rusted, the shed slumped, and the whole courtyard was overgrown with weeds and prickly nettles. Olenka herself aged and lost her looks. In summer she sits on her porch, and as usual in her soul it is empty, and tedious, and smells of wormwood, and in winter she sits at the window and looks at the snow. There is a breath of spring, the ringing of the cathedral bells is borne on the wind, and suddenly a flood of memories from the past comes, her heart is sweetly wrung, and abundant tears flow from her eyes, but this lasts only a minute, and then again there is emptiness, and she does not know why she is alive. The little black cat Bryska rubs against her and purrs softly, but Olenka is not touched by the cat's tenderness. Is that what she needs? She needs such love as would seize her whole being, her whole soul and mind, would give her thoughts, a direction in life, would warm her aging blood. And she shakes the black Bryska off her lap and says to her in vexation:

"Go, go . . . You've no business here!"

And so it went, day after day, year after year—and not one joy, and no opinions of any sort. Whatever the cook Mavra said was good enough.

One hot July day, towards evening, when the town herd was being driven down the street and the whole yard was filled with clouds of dust, someone suddenly knocked at the gate. Olenka herself went to open, looked, and was dumbstruck: outside the gate stood the veterinarian Smirnin, gray-haired now and in civilian dress. She suddenly remembered everything, could not help herself, burst into tears, and laid her head on his chest without saying a word, and was so shaken that she did not notice how they both went into the house then, how they sat down to tea.

"My little dove!" she murmured, trembling with joy. "Vladimir Platonych! Where did God bring you from?"

"I want to settle here for good," he told her. "I've retired and am here to try my luck on my own, to live a sedentary life. And it's time my son went to school. He's a big boy. You know, I made peace with my wife."

"Where is she?" asked Olenka.

"She's in the hotel with my son, and I'm going around looking for lodgings."

"Lord, dear heart, take my house! Isn't that lodgings? Oh, Lord, I won't even take anything from you," Olenka became excited and again began to cry. "Live here, and I'll be content with the wing. Lord, what joy!"

The next day the roof of the house was being painted and the walls whitewashed, and Olenka, arms akimbo, strode about the yard giving orders. The former smile lit up on her face, and she became all alive, fresh, as if she had awakened after a long sleep. The veterinarian's wife came, a thin, plain lady with short hair and a capricious expression, and with her came Sasha, small for his years (he was going on ten), plump, with bright blue eyes and dimples on his cheeks. And as soon as the boy came into the yard, he ran after the cat, and immediately his merry, joyful laughter rang out.

"Auntie, is that your cat?" he asked Olenka. "When she has kittens, please give us one. Mama's very afraid of mice."

Olenka talked with him, gave him tea, and the heart in her breast suddenly warmed and was wrung sweetly, as if this boy were her own son. And when he sat in the dining room that evening repeating his lessons, she looked at him with tenderness and pity and whispered:

"My little dove, my handsome one . . . My little child, you came out so smart, so fair!"

"An island," he read, "is a piece of dry land surrounded on all sides by water."

"An island is a piece of dry land . . ." she repeated, and this was the first opinion she uttered with conviction after so many years of silence and emptiness in her thoughts.

And she had her own opinions now and over dinner talked with Sasha's parents about how difficult it was for children to study in school, but that all the same classical education was better than modern, because after school all paths are open: if you wish, you can be a doctor, if you wish, an engineer.

Sasha started going to school. His mother went to Kharkov to visit her sister and did not come back; his father went somewhere every day to inspect the herds, and sometimes was away from home for three days, and it seemed to Olenka that Sasha was completely abandoned, that he was not wanted in the house, that he was starving to death; and she moved him to her wing and set him up in a little room there.

And for six months now Sasha has been living with her in the wing. Each morning Olenka goes into his room; he is fast asleep, his hand under his cheek, breathing lightly. She is sorry to wake him up.

"Sashenka," she says sadly, "get up, dear heart! It's time for school."

He gets up, dresses, says his prayers, then sits down to tea. He drinks three cups of tea and eats two big bagels and half a French roll with butter. He has not quite recovered from sleep and is therefore cross.

"You haven't learned your fable well, Sashenka," says Olenka, looking at him as if she were seeing him off on a long journey. "You worry me so. You must do your best, dear heart, study . . . Listen to your teachers."

"Oh, leave me alone, please!" says Sasha.

Then he marches down the street to school, a little boy, but in a big visored cap, with a satchel on his back. Olenka noiselessly follows him.

"Sashenka-a!" she calls.

He turns around, and she puts a date or a caramel in his hand. When they turn down the lane where his school is, he gets embarrassed that this tall, stout woman is following after him; he turns around and says:

"Go home, auntie, I can get there myself now."

She stops and looks after him without blinking, until he disappears through the doors of the school. Ah, how she loves him! Of all her former attachments, none was so deep, never before had her soul submitted so selflessly, so disinterestedly, and with such delight as now, when the maternal feeling burned in her more and more. For this boy who was not her own, for the dimples on his cheeks, for his visored cap, she would give her whole life, give it joyfully, with tears of tenderness. Why? Who knows why?

Having seen Sasha off to school, she slowly returns home, so content, so calm, so full of love; her face, which has grown younger in the last six months, smiles and beams; meeting her, looking at her, people feel pleasure and say to her:

"Good morning, darling Olga Semyonovna! How are you, darling?"

"School studies are getting difficult nowadays," she says at the market. "It's no joke, yesterday they gave the first-year students a fable to learn by heart, and a Latin translation, and a problem . . . It's hard for a little boy!"

And she starts talking about teachers, lessons, textbooks—saying all the same things that Sasha says about them.

Between two and three they have dinner together, in the evening they do his homework together and weep. As she puts him to bed, she spends a long time making the cross over him and whispering a prayer. Then, going to sleep, she dreams of the far-off, misty future when Sasha has finished his studies, has become a doctor or an engineer, has his own big house, horses, a carriage, gets married, has children . . . She falls asleep and keeps thinking about the same thing, and from her closed eyes tears flow down her cheeks. And the little black cat lies beside her and purrs:

"Purr . . . purr . . . purr . . ."

Suddenly there is a loud knocking at the gate. Olenka wakes up, breathless with fear; her heart pounds hard. Half a minute goes by and there is more knocking.

"It's a telegram from Kharkov," she thinks, beginning to tremble all over. "Sasha's mother wants him in Kharkov . . . Oh, Lord!"

She is in despair; her head, her feet, her arms go numb, and it seems that no one in the whole world is unhappier than she. But another minute goes by, she hears voices: it is the veterinarian coming home from the club.

"Well, thank God," she thinks.

The weight gradually lifts from her heart, she feels light again; she lies down and thinks about Sasha, who is fast asleep in the next room and occasionally murmurs deliriously:

"I'll sh-show you! Get out! No fighting!"

JANUARY 1899

On Official Business

The acting coroner and the district doctor were driving to the village of Syrnya for an autopsy. On the way they were caught in a blizzard, wandered in circles for a long time, and reached the place not at noon, as they had wanted, but only towards evening, when it was already dark. They put up for the night in the zemstvo[1] cottage. And right there in the zemstvo cottage, as it happened, also lay the corpse, the corpse of the zemstvo insurance agent Lesnitsky, who had come to Syrnya three days earlier and, having settled in the zemstvo cottage and ordered a samovar, had shot himself, quite unexpectedly for everyone; and the circumstance that he had put an end to his life somehow strangely, over the samovar, with food laid out on the table, gave many the occasion to suspect murder; an autopsy became necessary.

The doctor and the coroner stamped their feet in the front hall, shaking off the snow, and the beadle Ilya Loshadin, an old man, stood beside them holding a tin lamp and lighted the place for them. There was a strong smell of kerosene.

"Who are you?" asked the doctor.

"The biddle . . ." answered the beadle.

He also signed it that way at the post office: the biddle.

"And where are the witnesses?"

"Must've gone to have tea, Your Honor."

To the right was the clean room, the "visiting" or master's room, to the left the black room, with a big stove and a stove bench. The doctor and the coroner, followed by the beadle holding the lamp above his head, went into the clean room. There on the floor, by the legs of the table, the long body lay motionless, covered with a white sheet. Besides the white sheet, a pair of new rubber galoshes was clearly visible in the weak light of the lamp, and everything there was disturbing, eerie: the dark walls, and the silence, and the galoshes, and the immobility of the dead body. On the table was a samovar, long cold, and around it were some packets, probably of food.

"To shoot oneself in a zemstvo cottage—how tactless!" said the doctor. "If you're so eager to put a bullet in your head, shoot yourself at home, somewhere in the barn."

Just as he was, in his hat, fur coat, and felt boots, he lowered himself onto the bench; his companion, the coroner, sat down facing him.

"These hysterical and neurasthenic types are great egoists," the doctor went on bitterly. "When a neurasthenic sleeps in the same room with you, he rustles his newspaper; when he dines with you, he makes a scene with his wife, not embarrassed by your presence; and when he decides to shoot himself, he goes and shoots himself in some village, in a zemstvo cottage, to cause more trouble for everybody. In all circumstances of life, these gentlemen think only of themselves. Only of themselves! That's why the old folks dislike this 'nervous age' of ours so much."

"The old folks dislike all sorts of things," said the coroner, yawning. "Go and point out to these old folk the difference between former and present-day suicides. The former so-called respectable man shot himself because he'd embezzled government funds, the present-day one because he's sick of life, in anguish . . . Which is better?"

"Sick of life, in anguish, but you must agree, he might have shot himself somewhere else than in a zemstvo cottage."

"Such a dire thing," the beadle began to say, "a dire thing—sheer punishment. Folks are very upset, Your Honor, it's the third night they haven't slept. The kids are crying. The cows need milking, but the women won't go to the barn, they're afraid . . . lest the master appear to them in the dark. Sure, they're foolish women, but even some of the men are afraid. Once night comes, they won't go past the cottage singly, but always in a bunch. And the witnesses, too . . ."

Dr. Starchenko, a middle-aged man with a dark beard and spectacles, and the coroner Lyzhin, blond, still young, who had finished his studies only two years before and looked more like a student than an official, sat silently, pondering. They were vexed at being late. They now had to wait till morning, stay there overnight, though it was not yet six, and they were faced with a long evening, then the long, dark night, boredom, uncomfortable beds, cockroaches, the morning cold; and, listening to the blizzard howling in the chimney and in the loft, they both thought how all this was unlike the life they would have wished for themselves and had once dreamed of, and how far they both were from their peers, who were now walking the well-lit city streets, heedless of the bad weather, or were about to go to the theater, or were sitting in their studies over a book. Oh, how dearly they would have paid now just to stroll down Nevsky Prospect, or Petrovka Street in Moscow, to hear some decent singing, to sit for an hour or two in a restaurant . . .

"Hoo-o-o!" sang the blizzard in the loft, and something outside slammed spitefully, probably the signboard on the zemstvo cottage. "Hoo-o-o!"

"Do as you like, but I have no wish to stay here," Starchenko said, getting up. "It's not six yet, too early for bed, I'll go somewhere. Von Taunitz lives nearby, only a couple of miles from Syrnya. I'll go to his place and spend the evening. Beadle, go and tell the coachman not to unharness. What about you?" he asked Lyzhin.

"I don't know. I'll go to bed, most likely."

The doctor wrapped his coat around him and went out. One could hear him talking to the coachman and the little bells jingling on the chilled horses. He drove off.

"It's not right for you to spend the night here, sir," said the beadle. "Go to the other side. It's not clean there, but for one night it won't matter. I'll fetch a samovar from the peasants and get it going, and after that I'll pile up some hay for you, and you can sleep, Your Honor, with God's help."

A short time later the coroner was sitting in the black side, at a table, drinking tea, while the beadle Loshadin stood by the door and talked. He was an old man, over sixty, not tall, very thin, bent over, white-haired, a naïve smile on his face, his eyes tearful, his lips constantly smacking as if he were sucking candy. He wore a short coat and felt boots, and never let the stick out of his hands. The coroner's youth evidently aroused pity in him, and that may have been why he addressed him familiarly.

"The headman, Fyodor Makarych, told me to report to him as soon as the police officer or coroner came," he said. "So, in that case, I'll have to go now . . . It's three miles to town, there's a blizzard, a terrible lot of snow has piled up, I may not make it before midnight. Listen to that howling."

"I don't need the headman," said Lyzhin. "There's nothing for him to do here."

He gave the old man a curious glance and asked:

"Tell me, grandpa, how many years have you been going around as a beadle?"

"How many? Thirty years now. I started about five years after the freeing,[2] so you can count it up. Since then I've gone around every day. People have holidays, and I go around. It's Easter, the bells are ringing, Christ is risen, and I'm there with my bag. To the treasury, to the post office, to the police chief's house, to a zemstvo member, to the tax inspector, to the council, to the gentry, to the peasants, to all Orthodox Christians. I carry packages, summonses, writs, letters, various forms, reports, and nowadays, my good sir, Your Honor, they've started having these forms for putting down numbers—yellow, white, red—and every landowner, or priest, or rich peasant has to report without fail some ten times a year on how much he sowed and reaped, how many bushels or sacks of rye, how much oats and hay, and what the weather was like, and what kinds of bugs there were. They can write whatever they want, of course, it's just a formality, but I have to go and hand out the papers, and then go again and collect them. There's no point, for instance, in gutting this gentleman here, you know yourself it's useless, you're just getting your hands dirty, but you took the trouble and came, Your Honor, because it's a formality; there's no help for it. For thirty years I've been going around on formalities. In summer it's all right, warm, dry, but in winter or autumn it's no good. I've drowned, frozen—everything's happened. And bad people took my bag from me in the woods, and beat me up, and I was put on trial . . ."

"For what?"

"Swindling."

"What kind of swindling?"

"The clerk Khrisanf Grigoryev sold somebody else's lumber to a contractor—cheated him, that is. I was there when the deal was made, they sent me to the tavern for vodka; well, the clerk didn't share with me, didn't even offer me a glass, but since, poor as I am, I was seen as an unreliable, worthless man, we both went to trial; he was put in jail, but I, thank God, was justified in all my rights. They read some paper in court. And they were all in uniforms. There in the court. I'll tell you what, Your Honor, for a man who's not used to it, this work is a sheer disaster—God forbid—but for me it's all right. My legs even hurt when I don't walk. And it's worse for me to stay home. In the office in my village it's nothing but light the clerk's fire, fetch the clerk's water, polish the clerk's boots."

"And how much are you paid?" asked Lyzhin.

"Eighty-four roubles a year."

"You probably make a little something on the side, don't you?"

"What little something? Gentlemen rarely give tips nowadays. Gentlemen are strict these days, they keep getting offended. You bring him a paper—he gets offended. You take your hat off before him—he gets offended. 'You came in by the wrong entrance,' he says, 'you're a drunkard,' he says, 'you stink of onions, you're a blockhead, a son of a bitch.' Some are kind, of course, but you can't expect anything from them, they just make fun of you with all sorts of nicknames. Mr. Altukhin, for instance. He's kind and sober, and sensible enough, but when he sees me he shouts, and doesn't know what himself. He's given me this nickname. Hey, he says, you . . .'"

The beadle mumbled some word, but so softly that it was impossible to make it out.

"How's that?" asked Lyzhin. "Repeat it."

"Administration!" the beadle repeated loudly. "He's been calling me that for a long time, some six years. Greetings, administration! But let him, I don't mind, God bless him. Some lady may happen to send me out a glass of vodka and a piece of pie, so then I drink to her health. It's mostly peasants that tip me; peasants have heart, they're more god-fearing; they give me bread, or cabbage soup, or sometimes even a drink. The elders treat me to tea in the tavern. Right now the witnesses have gone for tea. 'Loshadin,' they said, 'you stay here and watch for us,' and they gave me a kopeck each. They're scared because they're not used to it. And yesterday they gave me fifteen kopecks and treated me to a little glass."

"And you're not afraid?"

"I am, sir, but it's part of the work—the job, there's no getting away from it. In the summer I was taking a prisoner to town, and he starts hitting me—whack! whack! whack! All fields and forest around—nowhere to run to. It's the same here. I remember Mr. Lesnitsky when he was just so high, and I knew his father and mother. I'm from the village of Nedoshchotovo, and the Lesnitsky family is no more than half a mile from us, maybe less, we have a common boundary. And old Mr. Lesnitsky had a maiden sister, a god-fearing and merciful lady. Remember, O Lord, the soul of your servant Yulia, of eternal memory. She never got married, and before she died, she divided up all her property; she left two hundred and fifty acres to the monastery and five hundred to us, the peasant community of the village of Nedoshchotovo, for the memory of her soul. But her brother, the squire, hid the paper, burned it in the stove, they say, and took all the land for himself. Meaning he hoped to profit from it, but—no, hold on, brother, you can't live by injustice in the world. The squire didn't go to confession for some twenty years after that, he kept away from church, meaning he died without confession, just popped. He was fat as could be. Just popped open. After that the young squire—Seryozha, that is—had it all taken from him for debts, all there was. Well, he didn't get far in his studies, couldn't do anything, so his uncle, the chairman of the zemstvo council, thought, 'Why don't I take Seryozha to work for me as an agent, he can insure people, it's not complicated.' But the young squire was a proud man, he would have liked a broader life, fancier, with more freedom, he resented having to drive around the area in a little cart and talk to peasants; he always went about looking at the ground, looking and saying nothing; you'd shout, 'Sergei Sergeich!' right by his ear, and he'd turn and say, 'Eh?' and look at the ground again. And now, see, he's laid hands on himself. It makes no sense, Your Honor, it's not right. Merciful God, you can't tell what's happening in the world. Say your father was rich and you're poor—that's too bad, of course, but you have to get used to it. I, too, had a good life, Your Honor, I had two horses, three cows, some twenty head of sheep, but the time came when I was left with nothing but a little bag, and it's not mine at that, it comes with the job, and now, in our Nedoshchotovo, my house is the worst of all, truth to tell. Four lackeys had Moky, now Moky's a lackey. Four workers had Burkin, now Burkin's a worker."

"What made you so poor?" asked the coroner.

"My sons are hard drinkers. They drink so hard, so hard, I can't tell you, you wouldn't believe me."

Lyzhin listened and thought that while he, Lyzhin, would sooner or later go back to Moscow, this old man would stay here forever and keep on walking and walking; and how many of these old men he would meet in his life, tattered, disheveled, "worthless," in whose hearts a fifteen-kopeck piece, a glass of vodka, and the profound belief that you cannot live by injustice in this world were somehow welded fast together. Then he became bored with listening and ordered some hay brought for his bed. There was an iron bed with a pillow and blanket in the visitors' side, and it could have been brought over, but the deceased had been lying next to it for almost three days (had, perhaps, sat on it before he died), and now it would be unpleasant to sleep on it . . .

"It's only seven-thirty," thought Lyzhin, glancing at his watch. "How terrible!"

He did not want to sleep, but having nothing to do and needing to pass the time somehow, he lay down and covered himself with a plaid. Loshadin, as he cleared the dishes away, came in and out several times, smacking his lips and sighing, kept shuffling about by the table, finally took his lamp and left; and, looking at his long gray hair and bent body from behind, Lyzhin thought: "Just like a sorcerer in the opera."

It grew dark. There must have been a moon behind the clouds, because the windows and the snow on the window frames were clearly visible.

"Hoo-o-o!" sang the blizzard. "Hoo-o-o!"

"Oh, Lo-o-ord!" a woman howled in the loft, or so it seemed. "Oh, my Lo-o-ord!"

"Bang!" Something hit the wall outside. "Crash!"

The coroner listened: there was no woman, it was the wind howling. He was chilly and covered himself with his coat as well, on top of the plaid. While he was making himself warm, he thought of how all this—the blizzard, and the cottage, and the old man, and the dead body lying in the next room—how all this was far from the life he wanted for himself, and how foreign it all was to him, how petty and uninteresting. If this man had killed himself in Moscow or somewhere near Moscow, and he were conducting the investigation there, it would be interesting, important, and perhaps even frightening to sleep next to the corpse; but here, a thousand miles from Moscow, all this seemed to appear in a different light, all this was not life, not people, but something that existed only "on formality," as Loshadin had said, all this would leave not the slightest trace in his memory and would be forgotten as soon as he, Lyzhin, left Syrnya. The motherland, the true Russia, was Moscow, Petersburg, and this was a province, a colony; when you dream of playing a role, of being popular, of being, for instance, an investigator in cases of special importance or a prosecutor for the district court, of being a social lion, you inevitably think of Moscow. To live means to live in Moscow, whereas here you wanted nothing, easily became reconciled with your inconspicuous role, and hoped for only one thing from life—to leave, to leave soon. And Lyzhin mentally raced about the Moscow streets, entered familiar houses, saw his family, his friends, and his heart was wrung sweetly at the thought that he was now twenty-six years old, and if he escaped from here and got to Moscow in five or ten years, even then it would not be too late and there would still be a whole life ahead of him. And as he fell into oblivion, when his thoughts were already becoming confused, he imagined the long corridors of the Moscow court, himself giving a speech, his sisters, an orchestra which for some reason kept howling:

"Hoo-o-o! Hoo-o-o!"

"Bang! Crash!" came again. "Bang!"

And he suddenly remembered how once in the zemstvo office, when he was talking with an accountant, a gentleman came over to the desk, dark-eyed, dark-haired, thin, pale; he had an unpleasant look in his eyes, as people do when they have taken a long after-dinner nap, and it spoiled his fine, intelligent profile; and the high boots he wore were unbecoming and seemed crude on him. The accountant introduced him: "This is our zemstvo agent."

"So that was Lesnitsky . . . this same one . . ." Lyzhin now realized.

He remembered Lesnitsky's soft voice, pictured his way of walking, and it seemed to him that someone was now walking around him, walking in the same way as Lesnitsky.

He suddenly became frightened, his head felt cold.

"Who's there?" he asked in alarm.

"The biddle."

"What do you want here?"

"To ask your permission, Your Honor. Earlier you said there was no need for the headman, but I'm afraid he may get angry. He told me to come. So maybe I'll go."

"Ah, you! I'm sick of it . . ." Lyzhin said in vexation and covered himself up again.

"He may get angry . . . I'll go, Your Honor, you have a good stay."

And Loshadin left. There was coughing and half-whispered talk in the front hall. The witnesses must have come back.

"Tomorrow we'll let the poor fellows go home earlier . . ." thought the coroner. "We'll start the autopsy as soon as it's light."

He was beginning to doze off when suddenly there came someone's steps again, not timid this time, but quick, loud. The slamming of a door, voices, the scrape of a match . . .

"Are you asleep? Are you asleep?" Dr. Starchenko asked hurriedly and angrily, lighting one match after another; he was all covered with snow, and gave off cold. "Are you asleep? Get up, let's go to von Taunitz. He's sent horses to fetch you. Let's go, you'll at least get supper there, and sleep like a human being. You see, I came for you myself. The horses are excellent, we'll be there in twenty minutes."

"And what time is it now?"

"A quarter past ten."

Sleepy and displeased, Lyzhin put on his boots, fur coat, hat, and hood, and went outside with the doctor. It was not too freezing, but a strong, piercing wind was blowing, driving billows of snow down the street, which looked as if they were fleeing in terror; high drifts were already piled up by the fence and near the porches. The doctor and the coroner got into the sleigh, and the white driver leaned over them to button up the flap. They both felt hot.

"Drive!"

They went through the village. "Turning up fluffy furrows . . ."[3] the coroner thought listlessly, watching the outrunner working his legs. There were lights in all the cottages, as on the eve of a great feast: the peasants had not gone to bed for fear of the dead man. The driver was glumly silent; he must have grown bored standing by the zemstvo cottage, and now was also thinking of the dead man.

"When they learned at Taunitz's that you were spending the night in the cottage," said Starchenko, "they all fell on me for not bringing you along."

As they drove out of the village, at a bend, the driver suddenly shouted at the top of his lungs:

"Clear the way!"

Some man flashed by; he had stepped off the road and was standing knee-deep in the snow, looking at the troika; the coroner saw the crook-topped stick, the beard, the bag at his side, and it seemed to him that it was Loshadin, and it even seemed to him that he was smiling. He flashed by and disappeared.

The road first ran along the edge of the forest, then down the wide forest cutting; old pines flashed by, and young birches, and tall, young gnarled oaks, standing solitarily in the recently cleared openings, but soon everything in the air became confused in the billows of snow; the driver claimed he could see the forest, but the coroner could see nothing but the outrunner. The wind blew in their backs.

Suddenly the horses stopped.

"Well, what now?" Starchenko asked crossly.

The driver silently got down from the box and began running around the sleigh, stepping on his heels; he made wider and wider circles, moving further and further from the sleigh, and it looked as if he were dancing; finally he came back and began turning to the right.

"Have you lost the way, or what?" asked Starchenko.

"Never mi-i-ind . . ."

Here was some little village with not a single light. Again the forest, the fields, again they lost the way, and the driver got down from the box and danced. The troika raced down a dark avenue, raced quickly, and the excited outrunner kicked the front of the sleigh. Here the trees made a hollow, frightening noise, it was pitch-dark, as if they were racing into some sort of abyss, and suddenly their eyes were dazzled by the bright light of a front entrance and windows, they heard loud, good-natured barking, voices . . . They had arrived.

While they were taking off their coats and boots downstairs, someone upstairs was playing *Un petit verre de Cliquot*[4] on the piano, and the stamping of children's feet could be heard. The visitors were immediately enveloped in warmth, the smell of an old manor house, where, whatever the weather outside, life is so warm, clean, comfortable.

"That's splendid," said von Taunitz, a fat man with an incredibly thick neck and side-whiskers, shaking the coroner's hand. "That's splendid. Welcome to my house, I'm very glad to meet you. You and I are almost colleagues. I was once the assistant prosecutor, but not for long, only two years; I came here to look after the estate and I've grown old on the place. An old coot, in short. Welcome," he went on, obviously controlling his voice so as not to speak loudly; he and the guests were going upstairs. "I have no wife, she died, but here, let me introduce my daughters." And turning around, he shouted downstairs in a thunderous voice: "Tell Ignat there to have the horses ready by eight o'clock!"

In the reception room were his four daughters, young, pretty girls, all in gray dresses and with their hair done in the same way, and their cousin with children, also a young and interesting woman. Starchenko, who was acquainted with them, immediately started asking them to sing something, and two of the girls spent a long time assuring him that they could not sing and that they had no music, then the cousin sat down at the piano and in trembling voices they sang a duet from *The Queen of Spades.*[5] *Un petit verre de Cliquot* was played again, and the children started hopping, stamping their feet in time with the music. Starchenko started hopping, too. Everybody laughed.

Then the children said good-night before going to bed. The coroner laughed, danced a quadrille, courted the girls, and thought to himself: was all that not a dream? The black side of the zemstvo cottage, the pile of hay in the corner, the rustling of cockroaches, the revolting, beggarly furnishings, the voices of the witnesses, the wind, the blizzard, the danger of losing the way, and suddenly these magnificent, bright rooms, the sounds of the piano, beautiful girls, curly-headed children, merry, happy laughter—it seemed to him like a fairy-tale transformation; and it was incredible that such transformations could take place in the space of some two miles, in one hour. And dull thoughts spoiled his merriment, and he kept thinking that this was not life around him, but scraps of life, fragments, that everything here was accidental, it was impossible to draw any conclusions; and he even felt sorry for these girls who lived and would end their lives here in this backwoods, in the provinces, far from any cultivated milieu where nothing was accidental, everything made sense, was right, and where every suicide, for example, could be understood and one could explain why and what its significance was in the general course of life. He supposed that if the life hereabouts, in this backwater, was incomprehensible to him and if he did not see it, that meant that it was not there at all.

Over dinner the conversation turned to Lesnitsky.

"He left a wife and child," said Starchenko. "I would forbid neurasthenics and generally people whose nervous system is in disorder to get married; I would deprive them of the right and opportunity to breed more of their kind. To bring children with nervous ailments into the world is a crime."

"An unfortunate young man," said von Taunitz, quietly sighing and shaking his head. "How much one must think and suffer before finally taking one's own life . . . a young life. Such misfortunes can happen in any family, and that is terrible. It's hard to endure it, unbearable . . ."

And all the girls listened silently, with serious faces, looking at their father. Lyzhin felt that, for his part, he also ought to say something, but he could not think of anything, and said only:

"Yes, suicide is an undesirable phenomenon."

He slept in a warm room, in a soft bed, covered by a fine, fresh sheet and a blanket, but for some reason he did not feel comfortable; perhaps it was because the doctor and von Taunitz spent a long time talking in the neighboring room, and above the ceiling and in the stove the blizzard made the same noise as in the zemstvo cottage, and howled just as pitifully:

"Hoo-o-o!"

Taunitz's wife had died two years ago, and he was still not reconciled to it, and whatever the talk was about, he always came back to his wife; and there was nothing of the prosecutor left in him.

"Can it be that I, too, will reach such a state some day?" thought Lyzhin as he was falling asleep, hearing the man's restrained, as if orphaned, voice through the wall.

The coroner slept restlessly. It was hot, uncomfortable, and it seemed to him in his sleep that he was not in Taunitz's house and not in a soft, clean bed, but still in the zemstvo cottage, on hay, hearing the witnesses talking in half-whispers; it seemed to him that Lesnitsky was nearby, fifteen steps away. Again in his sleep he remembered the zemstvo agent, dark-haired, pale, in tall, dusty boots, coming up to the accountant's desk. "This is our zemstvo agent . . ." Then he imagined Lesnitsky and the beadle Loshadin walking over the snow in the fields, side by side, holding each other up; the blizzard whirled above them, the wind blew in their backs, and they walked on and sang:

"We walk, walk, walk."

The old man looked like a sorcerer in the opera, and they were both indeed singing, as if in the theater:

"We walk, walk, walk . . . You live in warmth, in brightness, in softness, and we walk through the freezing cold, through the blizzard, over the deep snow . . . We know no rest, we know no joy . . . We bear the whole burden of this life, both ours and yours, on ourselves . . . Hoo-o-o! We walk, walk, walk . . ."

Lyzhin awoke and sat up in bed. What a disturbing, unpleasant dream! And why were the agent and the beadle together in his dream? What nonsense! And now, when Lyzhin's heart was pounding hard, and he sat in bed holding his head in his hands, it seemed to him this insurance agent and the beadle really had something in common in life. Had they not gone side by side in life, too, holding on to each other? Some invisible but significant and necessary connection existed between the two men, even between them and Taunitz, and between everyone, everyone; in this life, even in the most desolate backwater, nothing was accidental, everything was filled with one common thought, everything had one soul, one purpose, and to understand it, it was not enough to think, not enough to reason, one probably had to have the gift of penetrating into life, a gift which apparently was not given to everyone. And the unfortunate, overstrained "neurasthenic," as the doctor called him, who had killed himself, and the old peasant, who every day of his life had been going from one man to another, were accidents, scraps of life, for someone who considered his own existence accidental, but were parts of one wonderful and reasonable organism for someone who considered his own life, too, a part of this common thing and was aware of it. So thought Lyzhin, and this had long been his secret thought, and only now did it unfold broadly and clearly in his mind.

He lay down and began to fall asleep; and suddenly they were walking together and singing again:

"We walk, walk, walk . . . We take what's hardest and bitterest from life, and leave you what's easy and joyful, and you, sitting over your supper, can reason coolly and soberly about why we suffer and perish, and why we're not as healthy and contented as you."

What they sang had occurred to him before, but this thought had somehow sat behind other thoughts in his head and flashed timidly, like a distant lantern in misty weather. And he felt that this suicide and the peasant's grievances lay on his conscience, too; to be reconciled with the fact that these people, submissive to their lot, heaped on themselves what was heaviest and darkest in life—how terrible it was! To be reconciled with that, and to wish for oneself a bright, boisterous life among happy, contented people, and to dream constantly of such a life, meant to dream of new suicides by overworked, careworn people, or by weak, neglected people, whom one sometimes talked about with vexation or mockery over dinner, but whom one did not go to help . . . And again:

"We walk, walk, walk . . ."

As if someone were beating on his temples with a hammer.

In the morning he woke up early, with a headache, roused by noise; in the neighboring room von Taunitz was saying loudly to the doctor:

"You can't go now. Look what it's doing outside. Don't argue, just ask the driver: he won't take you in such weather even for a million roubles."

"But it's only two miles," the doctor said in a pleading voice.

"Even if it was half a mile. When you can't, you can't. The moment you go out the gate, it will be sheer hell, you'll instantly lose your way. Say what you like, I won't let you go for anything."

"It's sure to quiet down towards evening," said the peasant who was lighting the stove.

And the doctor in the neighboring room started talking about the influence of the harshness of nature on the Russian character, about the long winters which, by restricting freedom of movement, hampered people's mental growth, and Lyzhin listened vexedly to these arguments, looked out the windows at the snowdrifts heaped up by the fence, looked at the white dust that filled all visible space, at the trees bending desperately to the right, then to the left, listened to the howling and banging, and thought gloomily:

"Well, what sort of moral can be drawn here? It's a blizzard, that's all . . ."

At noon they had lunch, then wandered aimlessly about the house, going up to the windows.

"And Lesnitsky's lying there," thought Lyzhin, gazing at the whirls of snow spinning furiously over the drifts. "Lesnitsky's lying there, the witnesses are waiting . . ."

They talked of the weather, saying that a blizzard usually lasts two days, rarely longer. At six o'clock they had dinner, then played cards, sang, danced, ended with supper. The day was over, they went to bed.

Between night and morning everything quieted down. When they got up and looked out the windows, the bare willows with their weakly hanging branches stood perfectly motionless, it was gray, still, as if nature were now ashamed of her rioting, of the insane nights and the free rein she had given to her passions. The horses, harnessed in a line, had been waiting by the porch since five o'clock in the morning. When it was fully light, the doctor and the coroner put on their coats and boots, and, after taking leave of their host, went out.

At the porch, beside the driver, stood their acquaintance, the biddle Ilya Loshadin, hatless, with an old leather bag over his shoulder, all covered with snow; and his face was red, wet with sweat. The servant who came out to help the guests into the sleigh and cover their legs gave him a stern look and said:

"What are you standing here for, you old devil? Away with you!"

"Your Honor, folks are worried . . ." Loshadin began, with a naïve smile all over his face, obviously pleased to see the ones he had been waiting for so long. "Folks are very worried, the kids are crying . . . We thought you'd gone back to town, Your Honor. For God's sake, take pity on us, dear benefactors . . ."

The doctor and the coroner said nothing, got into the sleigh, and drove to Syrnya.

JANUARY 1899

The Lady with the Little Dog

I

The talk was that a new face had appeared on the embankment: a lady with a little dog. Dmitri Dmitrich Gurov, who had already spent two weeks in Yalta and was used to it, also began to take an interest in new faces. Sitting in a pavilion at Vernet's, he saw a young woman, not very tall, blond, in a beret, walking along the embankment; behind her ran a white spitz.

And after that he met her several times a day in the town garden or in the square. She went strolling alone, in the same beret, with the white spitz; nobody knew who she was, and they called her simply "the lady with the little dog."

"If she's here with no husband or friends," Gurov reflected, "it wouldn't be a bad idea to make her acquaintance."

He was not yet forty, but he had a twelve-year-old daughter and two sons in school. He had married young, while still a second-year student, and now his wife seemed half again his age. She was a tall woman with dark eyebrows, erect, imposing, dignified, and a thinking person, as she called herself. She read a great deal, used the new orthography, called her husband not Dmitri but Dimitri, but he secretly considered her none too bright, narrow-minded, graceless, was afraid of her, and disliked being at home. He had begun to be unfaithful to her long ago, was unfaithful often, and, probably for that reason, almost always spoke ill of women, and when they were discussed in his presence, he would say of them:

"An inferior race!"

It seemed to him that he had been taught enough by bitter experience to call them anything he liked, and yet he could not have lived without the "inferior race" even for two days. In the company of men he was bored, ill at ease, with them he was taciturn and cold, but when he was among women, he felt himself free and knew what to talk about with them and how to behave; and he was at ease even being silent with them. In his appearance, in his character, in his whole nature there was something attractive and elusive that disposed women towards him and enticed them; he knew that, and he himself was attracted to them by some force.

Repeated experience, and bitter experience indeed, had long since taught him that every intimacy, which in the beginning lends life such pleasant diversity and presents itself as a nice and light adventure, inevitably, with decent people—especially irresolute Muscovites, who are slow starters—grows into a major task, extremely complicated, and the situation finally becomes burdensome. But at every new meeting with an interesting woman, this experience somehow slipped from his memory, and he wanted to live, and everything seemed quite simple and amusing.

And so one time, towards evening, he was having dinner in the garden, and the lady in the beret came over unhurriedly to take the table next to his. Her expression, her walk, her dress, her hair told him that she belonged to decent society, was married, in Yalta for the first time, and alone, and that she was bored here . . . In the stories about the impurity of local morals there was much untruth, he despised them and knew that these stories were mostly invented by people who would eagerly have sinned themselves had they known how; but when the lady sat down at the next table, three steps away from him, he remembered those stories of easy conquests, of trips to the mountains, and the tempting thought of a quick, fleeting liaison, a romance with an unknown woman, of whose very name you are ignorant, suddenly took possession of him.

He gently called the spitz, and when the dog came over, he shook his finger at it. The spitz growled. Gurov shook his finger again.

The lady glanced at him and immediately lowered her eyes.

"He doesn't bite," she said and blushed.

"May I give him a bone?" and, when she nodded in the affirmative, he asked affably: "Have you been in Yalta long?"

"About five days."

"And I'm already dragging through my second week here."

They were silent for a while.

"The time passes quickly, and yet it's so boring here!" she said without looking at him.

"It's merely the accepted thing to say it's boring here. The ordinary man lives somewhere in his Belevo or Zhizdra and isn't bored, then he comes here: 'Ah, how boring! Ah, how dusty!' You'd think he came from Granada."

She laughed. Then they went on eating in silence, like strangers; but after dinner they walked off together—and a light, bantering conversation began, of free, contented people, who do not care where they go or what they talk about. They strolled and talked of how strange the light was on the sea; the water was of a lilac color, so soft and warm, and over it the moon cast a golden strip. They talked of how sultry it was after the hot day. Gurov told her he was a Muscovite, a philologist by education, but worked in a bank; had once been preparing to sing in an opera company, but had dropped it, owned two houses in Moscow . . . And from her he learned that she grew up in Petersburg, but was married in S., where she had now been living for two years, that she would be staying in Yalta for about a month, and that her husband might come to fetch her, because he also wanted to get some rest. She was quite unable to explain where her husband served—in the provincial administration or the zemstvo council—and she herself found that funny. And Gurov also learned that her name was Anna Sergeevna.

Afterwards, in his hotel room, he thought about her, that tomorrow she would probably meet him again. It had to be so. Going to bed, he recalled that still quite recently she had been a schoolgirl, had studied just as his daughter was studying now, recalled how much timorousness and angularity there was in her laughter, her conversation with a stranger—it must have been the first time in her life that she was alone in such a situation, when she was followed, looked at, and spoken to with only one secret purpose, which she could not fail to guess. He recalled her slender, weak neck, her beautiful gray eyes.

"There's something pathetic in her all the same," he thought and began to fall asleep.

II

A week had passed since they became acquainted. It was Sunday. Inside it was stuffy, but outside the dust flew in whirls, hats blew off. They felt thirsty all day, and Gurov often stopped at the pavilion, offering Anna Sergeevna now a soft drink, now ice cream. There was no escape.

In the evening when it relented a little, they went to the jetty to watch the steamer come in. There were many strollers on the pier; they had come to meet people, they were holding bouquets. And here two particularities of the smartly dressed Yalta crowd distinctly struck one's eye: the elderly ladies were dressed like young ones, and there were many generals.

Owing to the roughness of the sea, the steamer arrived late, when the sun had already gone down, and it was a long time turning before it tied up. Anna Sergeevna looked at the ship and the passengers through her lorgnette, as if searching for acquaintances, and when she turned to Gurov, her eyes shone. She talked a lot, and her questions were abrupt, and she herself immediately forgot what she had asked; then she lost her lorgnette in the crowd.

The smartly dressed crowd was dispersing, the faces could no longer be seen, the wind had died down completely, and Gurov and Anna Sergeevna stood as if they were expecting someone else to get off the steamer. Anna Sergeevna was silent now and smelled the flowers, not looking at Gurov.

"The weather's improved towards evening," he said. "Where shall we go now? Shall we take a drive somewhere?"

She made no answer.

Then he looked at her intently and suddenly embraced her and kissed her on the lips, and he was showered with the fragrance and moisture of the flowers, and at once looked around timorously—had anyone seen them?

"Let's go to your place . . ." he said softly.

And they both walked quickly.

Her hotel room was stuffy and smelled of the perfumes she had bought in a Japanese shop. Gurov, looking at her now, thought: "What meetings there are in life!" From the past he had kept the memory of carefree, good-natured women, cheerful with love, grateful to him for their happiness, however brief; and of women—

his wife, for example—who loved without sincerity, with superfluous talk, affectedly, with hysteria, with an expression as if it were
not love, not passion, but something more significant; and of those
two or three very beautiful, cold ones, in whose faces a predatory
expression would suddenly flash, a stubborn wish to take, to snatch
from life more than it could give, and these were women not in
their first youth, capricious, unreasonable, domineering, unintelli-
gent, and when Gurov cooled towards them, their beauty aroused
hatred in him, and the lace of their underwear seemed to him like
scales.

But here was all the timorousness and angularity of inexperienced youth, a feeling of awkwardness, and an impression of bewilderment, as if someone had suddenly knocked at the door. Anna
Sergeevna, the "lady with the little dog," somehow took a special,
very serious attitude towards what had happened, as if it were her
fall—so it seemed, and that was strange and inopportune. Her features drooped and faded, and her long hair hung down sadly on
both sides of her face, she sat pondering in a dejected pose, like the
sinful woman in an old painting.

"It's not good," she said. "You'll be the first not to respect me
now."

There was a watermelon on the table in the hotel room. Gurov
cut himself a slice and unhurriedly began to eat it. At least half an
hour passed in silence.

Anna Sergeevna was touching, she had about her a breath of the
purity of a proper, naïve, little-experienced woman; the solitary
candle burning on the table barely lit up her face, but it was clear
that her heart was uneasy.

"Why should I stop respecting you?" asked Gurov. "You don't
know what you're saying yourself."

"God forgive me!" she said, and her eyes filled with tears. "This
is terrible."

"It's like you're justifying yourself."

"How can I justify myself? I'm a bad, low woman, I despise myself and am not even thinking of any justification. It's not my husband I've deceived, but my own self! And not only now, I've been
deceiving myself for a long time. My husband may be an honest
and good man, but he's a lackey! I don't know what he does there,
how he serves, I only know that he's a lackey. I married him when I
was twenty, I was tormented by curiosity, I wanted something bet-

ter. I told myself there must be a different life. I wanted to live! To live and live . . . I was burning with curiosity . . . you won't understand it, but I swear to God that I couldn't control myself any longer, something was happening to me, I couldn't restrain myself, I told my husband I was ill and came here . . . And here I go about as if in a daze, as if I'm out of my mind . . . and now I've become a trite, trashy woman, whom anyone can despise."

Gurov was bored listening, he was annoyed by the naïve tone, by this repentance, so unexpected and out of place; had it not been for the tears in her eyes, one might have thought she was joking or playing a role.

"I don't understand," he said softly, "what is it you want?"

She hid her face on his chest and pressed herself to him.

"Believe me, believe me, I beg you . . ." she said. "I love an honest, pure life, sin is vile to me, I myself don't know what I'm doing. Simple people say, 'The unclean one beguiled me.' And now I can say of myself that the unclean one has beguiled me."

"Enough, enough . . ." he muttered.

He looked into her fixed, frightened eyes, kissed her, spoke softly and tenderly, and she gradually calmed down, and her gaiety returned. They both began to laugh.

Later, when they went out, there was not a soul on the embankment, the town with its cypresses looked completely dead, but the sea still beat noisily against the shore; one barge was rocking on the waves, and the lantern on it glimmered sleepily.

They found a cab and drove to Oreanda.

"I just learned your last name downstairs in the lobby: it was written on the board—von Dideritz," said Gurov. "Is your husband German?"

"No, his grandfather was German, I think, but he himself is Orthodox."[1]

In Oreanda they sat on a bench not far from the church, looked down on the sea, and were silent. Yalta was barely visible through the morning mist, white clouds stood motionless on the mountaintops. The leaves of the trees did not stir, cicadas called, and the monotonous, dull noise of the sea, coming from below, spoke of the peace, of the eternal sleep that awaits us. So it had sounded below when neither Yalta nor Oreanda were there, so it sounded now and would go on sounding with the same dull indifference when we are no longer here. And in this constancy, in this utter indifference to the life and death of each of us, there perhaps lies hidden the pledge of our eternal salvation, the unceasing movement of life on earth, of unceasing perfection. Sitting beside the young woman, who looked so beautiful in the dawn, appeased and enchanted by the view of this magical décor—sea, mountains, clouds, the open sky—Gurov reflected that, essentially, if you thought of it, everything was beautiful in this world, everything except for what we ourselves think and do when we forget the higher goals of being and our human dignity.

Some man came up—it must have been a watchman—looked at them, and went away. And this detail seemed such a mysterious thing, and also beautiful. The steamer from Feodosia could be seen approaching in the glow of the early dawn, its lights out.

"There's dew on the grass," said Anna Sergeevna after a silence.

"Yes. It's time to go home."

They went back to town.

After that they met on the embankment every noon, had lunch together, dined, strolled, admired the sea. She complained that she slept poorly and that her heart beat anxiously, kept asking the same questions, troubled now by jealousy, now by fear that he did not respect her enough. And often on the square or in the garden, when there was no one near them, he would suddenly draw her to him and kiss her passionately. Their complete idleness, those kisses in broad daylight, with a furtive look around and the fear that someone might see them, the heat, the smell of the sea, and the constant flashing before their eyes of idle, smartly dressed, well-fed people, seemed to transform him; he repeatedly told Anna Sergeevna how beautiful she was, and how seductive, was impatiently passionate, never left her side, while she often brooded and kept asking him to admit that he did not respect her, did not love her at all, and saw in her only a trite woman. Late almost every evening they went somewhere out of town, to Oreanda or the cascade; these outings were successful, their impressions each time were beautiful, majestic.

They were expecting her husband to arrive. But a letter came from him in which he said that his eyes hurt and begged his wife to come home quickly. Anna Sergeevna began to hurry.

"It's good that I'm leaving," she said to Gurov. "It's fate itself."

She went by carriage, and he accompanied her. They drove for a whole day. When she had taken her seat in the express train and the second bell had rung, she said:

"Let me have one more look at you . . . One more look. There."
She did not cry, but was sad, as if ill, and her face trembled.

"I'll think of you . . . remember you," she said. "God be with you. Don't think ill of me. We're saying good-bye forever, it must be so, because we should never have met. Well, God be with you."

The train left quickly, its lights soon disappeared, and a moment later the noise could no longer be heard, as if everything were conspiring on purpose to put a speedy end to this sweet oblivion, this madness. And, left alone on the platform and gazing into the dark distance, Gurov listened to the chirring of the grasshoppers and the hum of the telegraph wires with a feeling as if he had just woken up. And he thought that now there was one more affair or adventure in his life, and it, too, was now over, and all that was left was the memory . . . He was touched, saddened, and felt some slight remorse; this young woman whom he was never to see again had not been happy with him; he had been affectionate with her, and sincere, but all the same, in his treatment of her, in his tone and caresses, there had been a slight shade of mockery, the somewhat coarse arrogance of a happy man, who was, moreover, almost twice her age. She had all the while called him kind, extraordinary, lofty; obviously, he had appeared to her not as he was in reality, and therefore he had involuntarily deceived her . . .

Here at the station there was already a breath of autumn, the wind was cool.

"It's time I headed north, too," thought Gurov, leaving the platform. "High time!"

III

At home in Moscow everything was already wintry, the stoves were heated, and in the morning, when the children were getting ready for school and drinking their tea, it was dark, and the nanny would light a lamp for a short time. The frosts had already set in. When the first snow falls, on the first day of riding in sleighs, it is pleasant to see the white ground, the white roofs; one's breath feels soft and pleasant, and in those moments one remembers one's youth. The old lindens and birches, white with hoarfrost, have a good-natured look, they are nearer one's heart than cypresses and palms, and near them one no longer wants to think of mountains and the sea.

Gurov was a Muscovite. He returned to Moscow on a fine, frosty day, and when he put on his fur coat and warm gloves and strolled down Petrovka, and when on Saturday evening he heard the bells ringing, his recent trip and the places he had visited lost all their charm for him. He gradually became immersed in Moscow life, now greedily read three newspapers a day and said that he never read the Moscow newspapers on principle. He was drawn to restaurants, clubs, to dinner parties, celebrations, and felt flattered that he had famous lawyers and actors among his clients, and that at the Doctors' Club he played cards with a professor. He could eat a whole portion of selyanka from the pan[2] . . .

A month would pass and Anna Sergeevna, as it seemed to him, would be covered by mist in his memory and would only appear to him in dreams with a touching smile, as other women did. But more than a month passed, deep winter came, and yet everything was as clear in his memory as if he had parted with Anna Sergeevna only the day before. And the memories burned brighter and brighter. Whether from the voices of his children doing their homework, which reached him in his study in the evening quiet, or from hearing a romance, or an organ in a restaurant, or the blizzard howling in the chimney, everything would suddenly rise up in his memory: what had happened on the jetty, and the early morning with mist on the mountains, and the steamer from Feodosia, and the kisses. He would pace the room for a long time, and remember, and smile, and then his memories would turn to reveries, and in his imagination the past would mingle with what was still to be. Anna Sergeevna was not a dream, she followed him everywhere like a shadow and watched him. Closing his eyes, he saw her as if alive, and she seemed younger, more beautiful, more tender than she was; and he also seemed better to himself than he had been then, in Yalta. In the evenings she gazed at him from the bookcase, the fireplace, the corner, he could hear her breathing, the gentle rustle of her skirts. In the street he followed women with his eyes, looking for one who resembled her . . .

And he was tormented now by a strong desire to tell someone his memories. But at home it was impossible to talk of his love, and away from home there was no one to talk with. Certainly not among his tenants nor at the bank. And what was there to say? Had he been in love then? Was there anything beautiful, poetic, or instructive, or merely interesting, in his relations with Anna

Sergeevna? And he found himself speaking vaguely of love, of women, and no one could guess what it was about, and only his wife raised her dark eyebrows and said:

"You know, Dimitri, the role of fop doesn't suit you at all."

One night, as he was leaving the Doctors' Club together with his partner, an official, he could not help himself and said:

"If you only knew what a charming woman I met in Yalta!"

The official got into a sleigh and drove off, but suddenly turned around and called out:

"Dmitri Dmitrich!"

"What?"

"You were right earlier: the sturgeon was a bit off!"

Those words, so very ordinary, for some reason suddenly made Gurov indignant, struck him as humiliating, impure. Such savage manners, such faces! These senseless nights, and such uninteresting, unremarkable days! Frenzied card-playing, gluttony, drunkenness, constant talk about the same thing. Useless matters and conversations about the same thing took for their share the best part of one's time, the best of one's powers, and what was left in the end was some sort of curtailed, wingless life, some sort of nonsense, and it was impossible to get away or flee, as if you were sitting in a madhouse or a prison camp!

Gurov did not sleep all night and felt indignant, and as a result had a headache all the next day. And the following nights he slept poorly, sitting up in bed all the time and thinking, or pacing up and down. He was sick of the children, sick of the bank, did not want to go anywhere or talk about anything.

In December, during the holidays, he got ready to travel and told his wife he was leaving for Petersburg to solicit for a certain young man—and went to S. Why? He did not know very well himself. He wanted to see Anna Sergeevna and talk with her, to arrange a meeting, if he could.

He arrived at S. in the morning and took the best room in the hotel, where the whole floor was covered with gray army flannel and there was an inkstand on the table, gray with dust, with a horseback rider, who held his hat in his raised hand, but whose head was broken off. The hall porter gave him the necessary information: von Dideritz lives in his own house on Staro-Goncharnaya Street, not far from the hotel; he has a good life, is wealthy, keeps his own horses, everybody in town knows him. The porter pronounced it "Dridiritz."

Gurov walked unhurriedly to Staro-Goncharnaya Street, found the house. Just opposite the house stretched a fence, long, gray, with spikes.

"You could flee from such a fence," thought Gurov, looking now at the windows, now at the fence.

He reflected: today was not a workday, and the husband was probably at home. And anyhow it would be tactless to go in and cause embarrassment. If he sent a message, it might fall into the husband's hands, and that would ruin everything. It would be best to trust to chance. And he kept pacing up and down the street and near the fence and waited for his chance. He saw a beggar go in the gates and saw the dogs attack him, then, an hour later, he heard someone playing a piano, and the sounds reached him faintly, indistinctly. It must have been Anna Sergeevna playing. The front door suddenly opened and some old woman came out, the familiar white spitz running after her. Gurov wanted to call the dog, but his heart suddenly throbbed, and in his excitement he was unable to remember the spitz's name.

He paced up and down, and hated the gray fence more and more, and now he thought with vexation that Anna Sergeevna had forgotten him, and was perhaps amusing herself with another man, and that that was so natural in the situation of a young woman who had to look at this cursed fence from morning till evening. He went back to his hotel room and sat on the sofa for a long time, not knowing what to do, then had dinner, then took a long nap.

"How stupid and upsetting this all is," he thought, when he woke up and looked at the dark windows: it was already evening. "So I've had my sleep. Now what am I to do for the night?"

He sat on the bed, which was covered with a cheap, gray, hospital-like blanket, and taunted himself in vexation:

"Here's the lady with the little dog for you . . . Here's an adventure for you . . . Yes, here you sit."

That morning, at the train station, a poster with very big lettering had caught his eye: it was the opening night of *The Geisha*. He remembered it and went to the theater.

"It's very likely that she goes to opening nights," he thought.

The theater was full. And here, too, as in all provincial theaters

generally, a haze hung over the chandeliers, the gallery stirred noisily; the local dandies stood in the front row before the performance
started, their hands behind their backs; and here, too, in the governor's box, the governor's daughter sat in front, wearing a boa, while
the governor himself modestly hid behind the portière, and only
his hands could be seen; the curtain swayed, the orchestra spent a
long time tuning up. All the while the public came in and took
their seats, Gurov kept searching greedily with his eyes.

Anna Sergeevna came in. She sat in the third row, and when
Gurov looked at her, his heart was wrung, and he realized clearly
that there was now no person closer, dearer, or more important for
him in the whole world; this small woman, lost in the provincial
crowd, not remarkable for anything, with a vulgar lorgnette in her
hand, now filled his whole life, was his grief, his joy, the only happiness he now wished for himself; and to the sounds of the bad orchestra, with its trashy local violins, he thought how beautiful she
was. He thought and dreamed.

A man came in with Anna Sergeevna and sat down next to her, a
young man with little side-whiskers, very tall, stooping; he nodded
his head at every step, and it seemed he was perpetually bowing.
This was probably her husband, whom she, in an outburst of bitter
feeling that time in Yalta, had called a lackey. And indeed, in his
long figure, his side-whiskers, his little bald spot, there was something of lackeyish modesty; he had a sweet smile, and the badge of
some learned society gleamed in his buttonhole, like the badge of a
lackey.

During the first intermission the husband went to smoke; she remained in her seat. Gurov, who was also sitting in the stalls, went
up to her and said in a trembling voice and with a forced smile:

"How do you do?"

She looked at him and paled, then looked again in horror, not
believing her eyes, and tightly clutched her fan and lorgnette in her
hand, obviously struggling with herself to keep from fainting. Both
were silent. She sat, he stood, alarmed at her confusion, not ventur-
ing to sit down next to her. The tuning-up violins and flutes sang
out, it suddenly became frightening, it seemed that people were
gazing at them from all the boxes. But then she got up and quickly
walked to the exit, he followed her, and they both went confusedly
through corridors and stairways, going up, then down, and the uni-

forms of the courts, the schools, and the imperial estates flashed before them, all with badges; ladies flashed by, fur coats on hangers, a drafty wind blew, drenching them with the smell of cigar stubs. And Gurov, whose heart was pounding, thought: "Oh, Lord! Why these people, this orchestra . . ."

And just then he suddenly recalled how, at the station in the evening after he had seen Anna Sergeevna off, he had said to himself that everything was over and they would never see each other again. But how far it still was from being over!

On a narrow, dark stairway with the sign "To the Amphitheater," she stopped.

"How you frightened me!" she said, breathing heavily, still pale, stunned. "Oh, how you frightened me! I'm barely alive. Why did you come? Why?"

"But understand, Anna, understand . . ." he said in a low voice, hurrying. "I beg you to understand . . ."

She looked at him with fear, with entreaty, with love, looked at him intently, the better to keep his features in her memory.

"I've been suffering so!" she went on, not listening to him. "I think only of you all the time, I've lived by my thoughts of you. And I've tried to forget, to forget, but why, why did you come?"

Further up, on the landing, two high-school boys were smoking and looking down, but Gurov did not care, he drew Anna Sergeevna to him and began kissing her face, her cheeks, her hands.

"What are you doing, what are you doing!" she repeated in horror, pushing him away from her. "We've both lost our minds. Leave today, leave at once . . . I adjure you by all that's holy, I implore you . . . Somebody's coming!"

Someone was climbing the stairs.

"You must leave . . ." Anna Sergeevna went on in a whisper. "Do you hear, Dmitri Dmitrich? I'll come to you in Moscow. I've never been happy, I'm unhappy now, and I'll never, never be happy, never! Don't make me suffer still more! I swear I'll come to Moscow. But we must part now! My dear one, my good one, my darling, we must part!"

She pressed his hand and quickly began going downstairs, turning back to look at him, and it was clear from her eyes that she was indeed not happy . . . Gurov stood for a little while, listened, then, when everything was quiet, found his coat and left the theater.

IV

And Anna Sergeevna began coming to see him in Moscow. Once every two or three months she left S., and told her husband she was going to consult a professor about her female disorder—and her husband did and did not believe her. Arriving in Moscow, she stayed at the Slavyansky Bazaar[3] and at once sent a man in a red hat to Gurov. Gurov came to see her, and nobody in Moscow knew of it.

Once he was going to see her in that way on a winter morning (the messenger had come the previous evening but had not found him in). With him was his daughter, whom he wanted to see off to school, which was on the way. Big, wet snow was falling.

"It's now three degrees above freezing, and yet it's snowing," Gurov said to his daughter. "But it's warm only near the surface of the earth, while in the upper layers of the atmosphere the temperature is quite different."

"And why is there no thunder in winter, papa?"

He explained that, too. He spoke and thought that here he was going to a rendezvous, and not a single soul knew of it or probably would ever know. He had two lives: an apparent one, seen and known by all who needed it, filled with conventional truth and conventional deceit, which perfectly resembled the lives of his acquaintances and friends, and another that went on in secret. And by some strange coincidence, perhaps an accidental one, everything that he found important, interesting, necessary, in which he was sincere and did not deceive himself, which constituted the core of his life, occurred in secret from others, while everything that made up his lie, his shell, in which he hid in order to conceal the truth—for instance, his work at the bank, his arguments at the club, his "inferior race," his attending official celebrations with his wife—all this was in full view. And he judged others by himself, did not believe what he saw, and always supposed that every man led his own real and very interesting life under the cover of secrecy, as under the cover of night. Every personal existence was upheld by a secret, and it was perhaps partly for that reason that every cultivated man took such anxious care that his personal secret should be respected.

After taking his daughter to school, Gurov went to the Slavyansky Bazaar. He took his fur coat off downstairs, went up, and knocked softly at the door. Anna Sergeevna, wearing his favorite gray dress, tired from the trip and the expectation, had been waiting for him since the previous evening; she was pale, looked at him and did not smile, and he had barely come in when she was already leaning on his chest. Their kiss was long, lingering, as if they had not seen each other for two years.

"Well, how is your life there?" he asked. "What's new?"

"Wait, I'll tell you . . . I can't."

She could not speak because she was crying. She turned away from him and pressed a handkerchief to her eyes.

"Well, let her cry a little, and meanwhile I'll sit down," he thought, and sat down in an armchair.

Then he rang and ordered tea; and then, while he drank tea, she went on standing with her face turned to the window . . . She was crying from anxiety, from a sorrowful awareness that their life had turned out so sadly; they only saw each other in secret, they hid from people like thieves! Was their life not broken?

"Well, stop now," he said.

For him it was obvious that this love of theirs would not end soon, that there was no knowing when. Anna Sergeevna's attachment to him grew ever stronger, she adored him, and it would have been unthinkable to tell her that it all really had to end at some point; and she would not have believed it.

He went up to her and took her by the shoulders to caress her, to make a joke, and at that moment he saw himself in the mirror.

His head was beginning to turn gray. And it seemed strange to him that he had aged so much in those last years, had lost so much of his good looks. The shoulders on which his hands lay were warm and trembled. He felt compassion for this life, still so warm and beautiful, but probably already near the point where it would begin to fade and wither, like his own life. Why did she love him so? Women had always taken him to be other than he was, and they had loved in him, not himself, but a man their imagination had created, whom they had greedily sought all their lives; and then, when they had noticed their mistake, they had still loved him. And not one of them had been happy with him. Time passed, he met women, became intimate, parted, but not once did he love; there was anything else, but not love.

And only now, when his head was gray, had he really fallen in love as one ought to—for the first time in his life.

He and Anna Sergeevna loved each other like very close, dear people, like husband and wife, like tender friends; it seemed to them that fate itself had destined them for each other, and they could not understand why he had a wife and she a husband; and it was as if they were two birds of passage, a male and a female, who had been caught and forced to live in separate cages. They had forgiven each other the things they were ashamed of in the past, they forgave everything in the present, and they felt that this love of theirs had changed them both.

Formerly, in sad moments, he had calmed himself with all sorts of arguments, whatever had come into his head, but now he did not care about any arguments, he felt deep compassion, he wanted to be sincere, tender . . .

"Stop, my good one," he said, "you've had your cry—and enough . . . Let's talk now, we'll think up something."

Then they had a long discussion, talked about how to rid themselves of the need for hiding, for deception, for living in different towns and not seeing each other for long periods. How could they free themselves from these unbearable bonds?

"How? How?" he asked, clutching his head. "How?"

And it seemed that, just a little more—and the solution would be found, and then a new, beautiful life would begin; and it was clear to both of them that the end was still far, far off, and that the most complicated and difficult part was just beginning.

DECEMBER 1899

At Christmastime

I

"What'll I write?" asked Yegor, and he dipped the pen.

Vasilisa had not seen her daughter for four years now. After the wedding, her daughter Yefimia had left for Petersburg with her husband, had sent two letters, and then seemed to have dropped from sight: not a sound, not a breath. And whether the old woman was milking the cow at dawn, or lighting the stove, or dozing at night, she kept thinking of one thing: how was Yefimia, was she alive? She would have liked to write a letter, but the old man did not know how to write, and there was nobody to ask.

But now Christmastime had come, and Vasilisa could not help herself and went to Yegor, the tavernkeeper's brother, who, once he came home from the army, just stayed around the tavern all the time and did nothing; they said he was good at writing letters, if you paid him properly. Vasilisa spoke with the cook in the tavern, then with the tavernkeeper, then with Yegor himself. They agreed on fifteen kopecks.

And now—this was in the tavern, in the kitchen, the day after the feast—Yegor was sitting at the table and holding the pen in his hand. Vasilisa stood before him, deep in thought, with an expression of care and grief on her face. Her old man, Pyotr, very thin, tall, with a tanned bald spot, had come with her; he stood and gazed fixedly ahead of him, like a blind man. Pork was being fried in a pan on the stove; it hissed and spat and even seemed to say "flu-flu-flu." It was stuffy.

"What'll I write?" Yegor asked again.

"Wait!" said Vasilisa, looking at him angrily and suspiciously. "Don't rush me! You're not writing for free, you're getting money for it! Well, so write. To our gentle son-in-law, Andrei Khrisanfych, and our beloved only daughter, Yefimia Petrovna, we send with our love a low bow and our parental blessing forever inviolable."

"Got it. Keep shooting."

"And we also wish you a happy feast of the Nativity of Christ, we are alive and well and wish you the same from the Lord . . . the Heavenly King."

Vasilisa pondered and exchanged glances with the old man.

"And wish you the same from the Lord . . . the Heavenly King . . ." she repeated and began to cry.

She could not say anything more. And before, when she used to lie thinking at night, it had seemed to her that even ten letters would not have held everything. Since her daughter had left with her husband much water had flowed under the bridge, the old people had lived like orphans and sighed deeply at night, as if they had buried their daughter. And so many things had happened in the village during that time, so many weddings, so many deaths. Such long winters! Such long nights!

"It's hot!" said Yegor, unbuttoning his waistcoat. "Must be a hundred degrees. What else?" he asked.

The old people were silent.

"What does your son-in-law do?" asked Yegor.

"He used to be a soldier, my dear, you know that," the old man answered in a weak voice. "He came home from the army the same time you did. He was a soldier, and so now he's in Petersburg, in some water-curing institution. The doctor treats his patients with water. So he's doorkeeper at the doctor's."

"It's written here . . ." the old woman said, taking a letter out of her handkerchief. "We got it from Yefimia, God knows how long ago. Maybe they're no longer in this world."

Yegor thought a little and began writing quickly.

"In this present time," he wrote, "since your fate has destinned you out for a Military Cureer, we advise You to open the Code of Disciplinery Measures and the Criminal Laws of the Department of War and You will perceive in the said Law the civilizaytion of the Ranks of the Department of War."

He was writing and reading aloud what he had written, and Vasilisa reflected that they ought to write about the want of the past year, when they had not had grain enough to last even till Christmastime, and they had been forced to sell the cow. They ought to ask for some money, to write and say that the old man was often sick and probably would soon give up his soul to God . . . But how to put it into words? What to say first and what after?

"Pay atention," Yegor went on writing, "to Volume 5 of the Military Decrees. Soldier is a commun noun, a Well-nown one. The Soldier is called the Farmost General and the leest Private . . ."

The old man moved his lips and said quietly:

"It wouldn't be a bad thing to see the grandchildren."

"What grandchildren?" asked the old woman, and she gave him an angry look. "Maybe there aren't any!"

"No grandchildren? And maybe there are. Who knows!"

"And thereby You can judge," Yegor was rushing along, "who is the Forin enemy and who is the Inturnal one. Our Farmost Inturnal Enemy is: Bacchus."

The pen scratched away, making flourishes that looked like fish hooks on the paper. Yegor hurried and re-read every line several times. He was sitting on a stool, his legs spread wide under the table, well-fed, stalwart, beefy-faced, ruddy-necked. This was vulgarity itself, crude, arrogant, invincible, proud of having been born and raised in a tavern, and Vasilisa understood very well that this was vulgarity, but she could not put it into words, and only glared angrily and suspiciously at Yegor. His voice, his incomprehensible words, the heat and stuffiness gave her a headache, confused her thoughts, and she did not say or think anything more, but only waited until he finished his scratching. But the old man looked on with complete trust. He trusted both in the old woman who had brought him there and in Yegor; and earlier, when he had mentioned the water-curing institution, his face had shown clearly that he trusted both in the institution and in the curative power of water.

When he finished writing, Yegor stood up and read out the whole letter from the beginning. The old man did not understand it, but he nodded his head trustfully.

"Nice job, smooth . . ." he said. "God bless you. Nice job . . ."

They put three five-kopeck pieces on the table and left the tavern; the old man looked straight ahead of him fixedly, like a blind man, and complete trust was written on his face, but Vasilisa shook her fist at the dog as they left the tavern, and said angrily:

"Ugh, you pest!"

The old woman did not sleep all night, troubled by thoughts, but she got up at dawn, said her prayers, and went to the station to mail the letter.

The station was seven miles away.

II

The water-curing clinic of Dr. B. O. Moselweiser was open on New Year's Day, just as on ordinary days, only the doorkeeper Andrei Khrisanfych was wearing a uniform with new galloons, his boots shone somehow specially, and he wished everyone who came in a Happy New Year.

It was morning. Andrei Khrisanfych stood by the door and read a newspaper. At exactly ten o'clock a general came in, a familiar figure, one of the regular clients, and after him the postman. Andrei Khrisanfych helped the general out of his overcoat and said:

"Happy New Year, Your Excellency!"

"Thank you, my good man. And the same to you."

And, going up the stairs, the general nodded towards a door and asked (he asked every day and then forgot each time):

"What's in this room?"

"That is the massage room, Your Excellency!"

When the general's steps died away, Andrei Khrisanfych looked through the mail and found a letter addressed to him. He opened it, read a few lines, then, while looking into his newspaper, went unhurriedly to his room, which was right there, downstairs, at the end of the corridor. His wife Yefimia was sitting on the bed nursing a baby; another child, the eldest, stood beside her, resting his curly head on her lap, and the third was asleep on the bed.

Going into his little room, Andrei handed the letter to his wife and said:

"Must be from the village."

Then he went out, without taking his eyes off the newspaper, and stopped in the corridor not far from his door. He could hear Yefimia reading the first lines in a trembling voice. She read and could not go on; those lines were enough for her, she dissolved in tears and, embracing her eldest boy and kissing him, began to talk, and it was impossible to tell whether she was crying or laughing.

"It's from grandma and grandpa . . ." she said. "From the village . . . Queen of Heaven, saints above. There's snow there now, up to the roofs . . . the trees are all white. Children on tiny sleds . . . And dear, bald-headed grandpa on the stove . . . and the little yellow dog . . . My dear darlings!"

Andrei Khrisanfych, listening to that, remembered that his wife had given him letters three or four times, asking him to send them to the village, but some important business had prevented him: he had not sent the letters and they had gotten lost somewhere.

"There are little hares running in the field," Yefimia went on chanting, bathed in tears, kissing her boy. "Grandpa is quiet, kind, grandma is kind, too, pitiful. It's a soulful life in the village, a god-fearing life . . . And there's a church there, the peasants sing in the choir. Queen of Heaven, our mother and helper, take us away from here!"

Andrei Khrisanfych went back to his little room to smoke until someone came, and Yefimia suddenly fell silent, quieted down, and wiped her eyes, and only her lips quivered. She was very afraid of him, oh, how afraid! She trembled, she was terrified by his step, his glance; she did not dare say a single word in his presence.

Andrei Khrisanfych lit a cigarette, but just then there came a ring from upstairs. He put the cigarette out and, making a very serious face, ran to his front door.

The general was coming down, pink and fresh after his bath.

"And what's in this room?" he asked, pointing to a door.

Andrei Khrisanfych drew himself to attention and said loudly: "Charcot showers,[1] Your Excellency!"

JANUARY 1900

In the Ravine

I

The village of Ukleyevo lay in a ravine, so that from the highway and the railroad station all you could see was the belfry and the smokestacks of the cotton mills. When passersby asked what village it was, they would be told:

"The one where the verger ate all the caviar at the funeral."

Once, at the memorial dinner for the factory-owner Kostiukov, the old verger spotted black caviar among the hors d'oeuvres and greedily began to eat it; they pushed him, pulled him by the sleeve, but he was as if frozen with pleasure; he felt nothing and simply ate. He ate all the caviar, and there were about four pounds of it in the jar. And much time had passed since then, the verger was long dead, but the caviar was still remembered. Either the life there was so poor, or the people were unable to notice anything except this unimportant event that had happened ten years ago, but nothing else was ever told about the village of Ukleyevo.

It was a place of ever-present fever, and there was swampy mud even in summer, especially under the fences, over which old pussy-willows hung, casting broad shadows. There was always a smell of factory waste and the acetic acid used in the treatment of the cotton. The factories—three cotton mills and one tannery—were situated not in the village itself but on the outskirts and further away. They were small factories, and in all employed about four hundred workers, not more. The water in the river often stank on account of the tannery; the waste contaminated the meadows, the peasants' cattle suffered from anthrax, and the factory was ordered closed. It was considered closed, but went on working secretly, with the knowledge of the district police officer and the district doctor, to each of whom the owner paid ten roubles a month. There were only two decent houses in the whole village, brick, with iron roofs: one housed the rural administration; in the other, a two-story house just opposite the church, lived Grigory Petrovich Tsybukin, a tradesman from Epifanyevo.

Grigory kept a grocery store, but that was only for appearances; in reality he traded in vodka, cattle, leather, grain, pigs, traded in whatever there was, and when, for instance, there was a demand abroad for magpie feathers for ladies' hats, he made thirty kopecks a pair; he bought up woodlots for cutting, lent money on interest, was generally a shrewd old man.

He had two sons. The elder, Anisim, served with the police, in the criminal investigation department, and was rarely at home. The younger, Stepan, went into trading and helped his father, but no real help was expected of him, because he was of weak health and deaf; his wife Aksinya, a beautiful, shapely woman, who went about on Sundays in a hat and with a parasol, got up early, went to bed late, and, with her skirts held up and her keys jangling, raced about all day long, now to the barn, now to the cellar, now to the shop, and old Tsybukin watched her merrily, his eyes glowed, and at such moments he regretted that it was not the elder son who had married her but the younger, the deaf one, who obviously had little understanding of feminine beauty.

The old man had always had an inclination for family life, and he loved his family more than anything in the world, especially his elder son, the detective, and his daughter-in-law. Aksinya had no sooner married the deaf son than she showed an extraordinary business sense and knew at once who could be given credit and who could not, kept the keys herself, not trusting them even to her husband, clicked on the abacus, looked horses in the teeth like a peasant, and was forever laughing or shouting; and, no matter what she did or said, the old man only went soft and murmured:

"Ah, what a daughter-in-law! What a beauty . . ."

He was a widower, but a year after his son's wedding he could no longer stand it and got married himself. Twenty miles from

Ukleyevo a girl was found for him, Varvara Nikolaevna, from a good family, no longer young, but beautiful, imposing. As soon as she settled in the little upstairs room, everything brightened in the house, as if new glass had been put in the windows. The icon lamps were lit, the tables were covered with snow-white tablecloths, red-eyed flowers appeared on the windowsills and in the front garden, and at dinner they no longer ate from one bowl, but a plate was set in front of each person. Varvara Nikolaevna smiled pleasantly and gently, and it seemed as if everything in the house were smiling. Beggars, wayfarers, and pilgrims began coming into the yard, something that had never happened before; the plaintive, sing-song voices of Ukleyevo peasant women and the guilty coughing of weak, wasted men dismissed from the factories for drunkenness, were heard under the windows. Varvara Nikolaevna helped out with money, bread, old clothes, and later, once she felt at home, also began pilfering from the shop. Once the deaf son saw her take two packets of tea, and that puzzled him.

"Mother took two packets of tea," he said later to his father. "Where should I write it down?"

The old man did not answer, but stood thinking, moving his eyebrows, and then went upstairs to his wife.

"Varvarushka, dearest," he said tenderly, "if you ever need anything from the shop, take it. You're welcome to take it, don't think twice."

And the next day the deaf son, running across the yard, called out to her:

"Mother, if you need anything—take it!"

In her giving of alms there was something new, something cheerful and light, as with the icon lamps and red flowers. When, on the eve of a fast or a major feast that lasted three days, they sold rotten corned beef to the peasants, which gave off such a strong stench that it was hard to stand near the barrel, and took scythes, hats, and their wives' shawls as pledges from drunken men, when factory workers stupefied by bad vodka lay about in the mud, and sin, condensing, seemed to hang like murk in the air, then it came as something of a relief to think that there, in the house, was a quiet, neat woman who had nothing to do with corned beef or vodka; in those oppressive, murky days her alms worked like a safety valve on an engine.

The days were busy in Tsybukin's house. The sun was not up yet, and Aksinya was already snorting as she washed in the front hall, the samovar was boiling in the kitchen and humming, boding something ill. Old Grigory Petrovich, dressed in a long black frock coat and cotton trousers, with tall, shiny boots, so clean and small, walked through the rooms, tapping his heels like the dear father-in-law in the famous song. The shop was opened. When day came, a light droshky was drawn up to the porch and the old man dashingly climbed into it, pulling his big visored cap down to his ears, and nobody looking at him would have said he was fifty-six years old. His wife and daughter-in-law would see him off, and at that time, when he was wearing a fine, clean frock coat and the droshky was harnessed to a huge black stallion worth three hundred roubles, the old man did not like to have peasants approach him with their petitions and complaints; he hated the peasants and scorned them, and if he saw some peasant waiting at the gate, he would shout wrathfully:

"No standing there! Move on!"

Or, if it was a beggar, he would shout:

"God will provide!"

He would drive off on business; his wife, in a dark dress with a black apron, would tidy the rooms or help in the kitchen. Aksinya tended the shop, and from the yard came the clink of bottles and money, Aksinya's laughter and shouting, or the angry voices of customers she had offended; at the same time it could be noted that the secret sale of vodka was already going on in the shop. The deaf man also sat in the shop, or else walked around outside, hatless, his hands in his pockets, gazing distractedly now at the cottages, now up at the sky. Six times a day they had tea in the house; four times they sat down to eat. In the evenings they counted the receipts and wrote them down, then slept soundly.

In Ukleyevo, all three cotton mills were connected by telephone with the quarters of the owners, the Khrymin Seniors, the Khrymin Juniors, and Kostiukov. A telephone was also installed in the local administrative office, but there it soon stopped working, because it got infested with bedbugs and cockroaches. The local headman was barely literate and began every word in official documents with a capital letter, but when the telephone broke down, he said:

"Yes, it'll be hard for us now without a telephone."

The Khrymin Seniors were constantly taking the Khrymin

Juniors to court, the Juniors also sometimes quarreled with each other and went to court, and then their factory would stop working for a month or two, until they made peace, and this entertained the populace of Ukleyevo, because there would be much talk and gossip on the occasion of each quarrel. On holidays Kostiukov and the Khrymin Juniors organized drives and raced around Ukleyevo, running down calves. Aksinya, her starched skirts rustling, all dressed up, would stroll outside near her shop; the Juniors would pick her up and drive away with her as if by force. Then old Tsybukin would also drive out, to show off his new horse, and take Varvara with him.

In the evening, after the drives, when everyone was in bed, an expensive accordion would begin to play in the Juniors' yard, and if the moon was out, these sounds would disturb and delight the heart, and Ukleyevo would no longer seem like a hole.

II

The elder son Anisim came home very rarely, only on major feasts, but to make up for it he often sent presents home with his fellow villagers and letters written in someone else's hand, a very beautiful one, each time on a sheet of writing paper, with the look of a petition. The letters were full of expressions such as Anisim never used in conversation: "My gentle mama and papa, I am sending you a pound of chamomile tea for the satisfaction of your physical needs."

At the bottom of each page "Anisim Tsybukin" was scrawled, as if with a broken pen, and below it, in the same beautiful hand: "Agent."

The letters would be read aloud several times, and the old man, moved, flushed with excitement, would say:

"See, he didn't want to live at home, he got into the learned line. So, let him! Each to his own place."

Once just before Lent there was a heavy rain with hail; the old man and Varvara went to the window to look, and—lo and behold, Anisim was driving up in a sledge from the station. They were not expecting him at all. He came in uneasy and alarmed at something; and so he remained all the while afterwards; and his behavior was somehow casual. He was in no hurry to leave, and it looked as if he had been dismissed from his job. Varvara was glad he had come; she kept glancing at him somehow slyly, sighing and shaking her head.

"How can it be, dear hearts?" she said. "Why, the lad's nearly twenty-eight and he's still going around a bachelor—oh, tush, tush . . ."

From the other room all that could be heard of her soft, even speech was: "Oh, tush, tush." She began to whisper with the old man and Aksinya, and their faces, too, acquired a sly and mysterious expression, as with conspirators.

They decided to get Anisim married.

"Oh, tush, tush! . . . The younger brother's been married a long time," said Varvara, "and you go on without a mate, like a cock at the market. What sort of thing is that? You'll get married, God willing, then go to work if you like, and the wife can stay home and help us. There's no order in your life, lad, and I can see you've forgotten all order. Oh, tush, tush, there's nothing but sin with you townsfolk."

When the Tsybukins married, the most beautiful brides were chosen for them, since they were rich. For Anisim, too, a beautiful girl was found. He himself was of uninteresting, unremarkable appearance; along with his weak, sickly build and small stature, he had full, plump cheeks, as if he puffed them out; his eyes never blinked, and their gaze was sharp; he had a sparse red beard, and when he pondered, he kept putting it in his mouth and chewing it; besides, he drank often, and it showed in his face and gait. But when he was told that they had a very beautiful bride for him, he said:

"Well, and I'm not so lopsided myself. All of us Tsybukins are handsome, I must say."

Just below the town was the village of Torguyevo. Half of it had recently been incorporated into the town, the other half remained a village. In the first half, in her own little house, lived a certain widow; she had a sister, completely poor, who did day labor, and this sister had a daughter, Lipa, a young girl who also did day labor. Lipa's beauty was already being talked about in Torguyevo, only everybody was disheartened by her terrible poverty; they reasoned that some older man or widower would marry her, overlooking her poverty, or would take her for himself "just so," and her mother would be fed along with her. Varvara found out about Lipa from the matchmakers and paid a visit to Torguyevo.

Then a showing was arranged in the aunt's house, quite properly, with food and wine, and Lipa wore a new pink dress specially made for the occasion, and a crimson ribbon shone like a flame in her hair. She was thin, frail, wan, with fine, tender features, darkened from working in the open air; a sad, timid smile never left her face, and her gaze was childlike—trusting and full of curiosity.

She was young, still a girl, with barely noticeable breasts, but she could already marry, since she was of age. She was indeed beautiful, and the only thing that could be found displeasing in her was her big, mannish hands, which now hung down idly like two big claws.

"There's no dowry, but we don't mind," the old man said to the aunt, "we also took one from a poor family for our son Stepan, and now we can't praise her enough. Around the house, or at work—a golden touch."

Lipa stood by the door and it was as if she wanted to say: "Do what you like with me, I trust you," but her mother Praskovya, the day laborer, hid in the kitchen, dying from timidity. Once, when she was still young, a merchant whose floors she used to scrub stamped his feet at her in anger, and she was so badly frightened, so mortified, that the fear remained in her soul for the rest of her life. And from fear her hands and feet always trembled, her cheeks trembled. Sitting in the kitchen, she tried to overhear what the guests were talking about and kept crossing herself, pressing her fingers to her forehead and glancing at the icon. Anisim, slightly drunk, opened the kitchen door and said casually:

"What are you sitting in here for, precious mother? We miss you."

And Praskovya, turning shy, pressing her hands to her skinny, emaciated breast, answered:

"Ah, mercy, sir . . . We're much pleased with you, sir."

After the showing, the day of the wedding was set. Then, at home, Anisim kept pacing the rooms, whistling, or, suddenly remembering something, would lapse into thought and stare at the floor, fixedly, piercingly, as if he wanted to penetrate deep into the ground with his gaze. He expressed neither pleasure at getting married, married soon, on Krasnaya Gorka,[1] nor any desire to see his fiancée, but simply whistled. And it was obvious that he was getting married only because his father and stepmother wanted it and because it was a village custom: a son should marry so that there would be a helper in the house. Going away, he was in no hurry and generally behaved differently than on his previous visits—was somehow especially casual and said things that were out of place.

III

In the village of Shikalovo lived two dressmakers, sisters, who belonged to the Flagellants.[2] They were hired to make new dresses for the wedding, and they often came for fittings and lingered a long time over tea. Varvara had a brown dress made, with black lace and bugles, and Aksinya a light green dress with a yellow front and train. When the dressmakers were done, Tsybukin paid them not in cash but in goods from his shop, and they went away from him sadly, carrying bundles of stearine candles and sardines, which they did not need at all, and when they got out of the village into the fields, they sat down on a knoll and began to cry.

Anisim came three days before the wedding in all new clothes. He wore shiny rubber galoshes and a red string tipped with beads instead of a tie, and over his shoulders hung a coat, also new, his arms not in the sleeves.

After gravely saying a prayer, he greeted his father and gave him ten silver roubles and ten half roubles; he gave the same amount to Varvara, and to Aksinya twenty quarter roubles. The main charm of this present was precisely that all the coins, as if specially chosen, were new and glittered in the sun. Trying to look grave and serious, Anisim strained his face and puffed his cheeks, and he gave off a smell of drink—he had probably rushed out to the buffet at every station. And again there was some sort of casualness, something superfluous in the man. Later Anisim and the old man had tea and a bite to eat, while Varvara fingered the new roubles and asked about local people who were living in town.

"It's all right, thank God, they have a good life," said Anisim. "Only Ivan Yegorov had something happen in his family: his old woman, Sofya Nikiforovna, died. Of consumption. They ordered a memorial dinner for the repose of her soul at a confectioner's, two roubles fifty a person. And there was grape wine. Peasants came—our locals—it was two-fifty for them, too. They didn't eat anything. What does a peasant know about sauce!"

"Two-fifty!" said the old man and shook his head.

"And so what? It's not a village. You stop at a restaurant to have a bite to eat, you order this and that, a company gathers, you have a drink—lo and behold, it's daybreak and three or four roubles each, if you please. And when it's with Samorodov, he likes to top it all off with coffee and cognac, and cognac's sixty kopecks a glass, sir."

"And it's all a pack of lies," the old man said admiringly. "A pack of lies!"

"I'm always with Samorodov now. It's that same Samorodov who writes my letters. He writes magnificently. And if I was to tell you, mother," Anisim went on merrily, addressing Varvara, "what sort of man that same Samorodov is, you wouldn't believe it. We all call him Mukhtar,³ because he's got the looks of an Armenian—all dark. I can see through him, I know all his dealings like the palm of my hand, mother, and he feels it and keeps following me, never leaves me, and now we're inseparable. He seems a little scared, but he can't live without me. Wherever I go, he goes. I've got a true and trusty eye, mother. I see a peasant selling a shirt at the flea market. 'Stop! That's a stolen shirt!' And it turns out to be so: the shirt's stolen."

"But how do you know?" asked Varvara.

"No idea, I've got that sort of eye. I don't know anything about this shirt, only for some reason I'm just drawn to it: it's stolen and that's that. They say in the department: 'Well, Anisim's gone hunting woodcock!' That means looking for stolen goods. Yes . . . Anybody can steal, but how to hold on to it! It's a big world, but there's nowhere to hide stolen goods."

"And in our village the Guntorevs had a ram and two ewes stolen last week," Varvara said and sighed. "And there's nobody to go looking for them . . . Oh, tush, tush . . ."

"So what? It could be done. Nothing to it."

The day of the wedding came. It was a cool but bright and cheerful April day. From early morning troikas and pairs, bells jingling, drove around Ukleyevo, their manes and yokes decorated with multicolored ribbons. The rooks, disturbed by this driving, squawked in the pussywillows, and the starlings sang incessantly, straining their voices, as if rejoicing that there was a wedding at the Tsybukins'.

In the house the tables were already laid with long fish, hams, and stuffed fowl, tins of sprats, various salted and pickled things, and numerous bottles of vodka and wine, and there was a smell of smoked sausage and spoiled lobster. And around the table, tapping his heels and sharpening one knife against another, walked the old

man. Someone was calling Varvara all the time, asking for something, and she, with a lost look, breathing hard, kept running to
the kitchen, where a chef sent by Kostiukov and a kitchen maid
from the Khrymin Juniors had been working since dawn. Aksinya,
her hair curled, with no dress on, in a corset and creaking new
boots, rushed about the yard like a whirlwind, and only her bare
knees and breast kept flashing. It was noisy, oaths and curses were
heard; passersby stopped at the flung-open gates, and it all felt as if
something extraordinary was being prepared.

"They've gone for the bride!"

Harness bells rang out and faded away far beyond the village . . .
Between two and three o'clock people came running: again the
bells were heard, they were bringing the bride! The church was
packed, the big chandelier was lit, the choir, at old Tsybukin's wish,
sang from books. The shining lights and bright dresses dazzled
Lipa, it seemed to her that the loud voices of the choir were beating
on her head with hammers; her corset, which she was wearing for
the first time in her life, and her high shoes squeezed her, and she
looked as if she had just come out of a swoon—her eyes wide and
uncomprehending. Anisim, in a black frock coat, with a red string
instead of a tie, stared pensively at one spot, and each time the
choir gave a loud cry, he quickly crossed himself. He was moved in
his heart, he felt like weeping. This church had been familiar to
him from childhood; his late mother had brought him there for
communion; he had sung in the choir with the other boys; for him
every little corner, every icon had its memories. Now he was getting
married, he had to have a wife for propriety's sake, but he no longer
thought about that, he somehow did not remember, he completely
forgot the wedding. Tears prevented him from seeing the icons,
something pressed on his heart; he prayed and asked God that the
inevitable misfortunes which were ready to break over him any day
might somehow pass him by, as storm clouds in a time of drought
pass by a village without giving a drop of rain. And so many sins
had already been heaped up in the past, so many sins, and everything was so inextricable, irreparable, that it somehow even made
no sense to ask forgiveness. Yet he did ask forgiveness, and even
sobbed loudly, but nobody paid attention to it, thinking he was
drunk.

An anxious child's crying was heard:

"Mummy dear, take me home!"

"Quiet there," shouted the priest.

As they returned from church, people ran after them; by the shop, by the gates, and under the windows in the yard there was also a crowd. Peasant women came to chant praises. The young couple had barely crossed the threshold when the choir, already standing in the front hall with their books, struck up loudly, with all their might; musicians, specially invited from town, began to play. Sparkling Don wine was brought in tall glasses, and the carpenter-contractor Yelizarov, a tall, lean old man with such thick eyebrows that his eyes were barely visible, said, addressing the young couple:

"Anisim, and you, little girl, love each other, lead a godly life, my little ones, and the Queen of Heaven will not abandon you." He fell on the old man's shoulder and sobbed. "Grigory Petrovich, let us weep, let us weep for joy!" he said in a high little voice and straightaway suddenly guffawed and went on loudly, in a bass voice: "Ho, ho, ho! And this daughter-in-law of yours is a fine one, too! She's got everything in the right place, I'd say, all smooth, no rattling, the whole mechanism's in order, plenty of screws."

He was a native of the Yegoriev district, but from an early age he had been working in Ukleyevo at the factories and around the district and was at home there. He had long been known as the same tall and lean old man he was now, and had long been called Crutch. For over forty years he had done nothing but repair work at the factories, and that was perhaps the reason why he judged every person or object from the point of view of sturdiness alone: by whether or not it needed repair. And before sitting down at the table he tried several chairs to see if they were sturdy, and also poked the whitefish.

After the sparkling wine they all began to sit down at the table. The guests talked, moved chairs. The choir sang in the front hall, the music played, and at the same time the peasant women were singing in the courtyard, all as one voice—and the result was some terrible, wild mixture of sounds, which made one's head spin.

Crutch fidgeted in his chair and nudged his neighbors with his elbows, preventing them from talking, and now wept, now laughed.

"Little ones, little ones, little ones . . ." he muttered quickly. "Aksinyushka dear, Varvarushka, let's all live in peace and harmony, my gentle little hatchets . . ."

He drank rarely, and now became drunk from one glass of English bitters. This disgusting bitters, made of God knows what, stupefied everyone who drank it, as if it hit them on the head. Tongues became confused.

The clergy were there, the factory managers and their wives, merchants and tavernkeepers from other villages. The local headman and the local clerk, who had been serving together for fourteen years and in all that time had never signed a single paper nor allowed a single person to leave their office without having cheated and insulted him, were now sitting side by side, both fat, well fed, and it seemed they were so saturated with falsehood that even the skin of their faces was of some special fraudulent sort. The clerk's wife, an emaciated, cross-eyed woman, had brought all her children with her, and, like a bird of prey, cast sidelong glances at the plates, snatched everything she could lay her hands on, and hid it in her own and her children's pockets.

Lipa sat petrified, with the same look that she had in church. Since making her acquaintance, Anisim had not said a single word to her, so that he did not know to that day what her voice was like; and now, sitting beside her, he still kept silent and drank English bitters, but when he got drunk he began to speak, addressing her aunt, who was sitting opposite him:

"I have a friend whose last name is Samorodov. He's a special man. A personally honorable citizen and a capable speaker. But I can see through him, auntie, and he feels it. Allow me, auntie, to drink with you to Samorodov's health!"

Varvara, tired and confused, walked around the table offering things to the guests, and was clearly pleased that there was so much food and all of it so high-class—now no one could find fault with them. The sun set and the dinner went on; they no longer knew what they were eating, what they were drinking, it was impossible to hear anything that was said, and only from time to time, when the music died down, could some peasant woman in the yard be heard shouting:

"You've sucked enough of our blood, you Herods, a plague upon you!"

In the evening there was dancing to the music. The Khrymin Juniors came with their wine, and one of them, during the quadrille, held a bottle in each hand and a glass in his mouth, and that made everyone laugh. In the middle of the quadrille, someone would start a squatting dance; the green Aksinya only flitted about, and a breeze blew from her train. Someone stepped on her flounce, and Crutch shouted:

"Hey, the plinth got torn off below! Little ones!"

Aksinya had gray, naïve eyes that seldom blinked, and a naïve smile constantly played over her face. And there was something snakelike in those unblinking eyes, and in that small head on its long neck, and in her shapely build; green with a yellow front, smiling, she gazed the way a viper in springtime, stretched out and head up, gazes from the young rye at someone going past. The Khrymins behaved freely with her, and it was quite obvious that she had a long-standing intimacy with the older one. And her deaf husband, who understood nothing, did not look at her; he sat with his legs crossed eating nuts, and cracked them so loudly that it was as if he were firing a pistol.

But now old man Tsybukin himself stepped out to the middle and waved his handkerchief, giving a sign that he, too, wanted to dance a Russian dance, and a hum of approval ran through the whole house and the crowd in the courtyard:

"*Himself* stepped out! *Himself*!"

Varvara danced, while the old man just waved the handkerchief and shifted from one heel to the other, but those who were hanging over each other there in the yard, peeking through the windows, were delighted and for a moment forgave him everything—his wealth and his offenses.

"Good boy, Grigory Petrovich!" came from the crowd. "Keep it up! So you can still go to it! Ha, ha!"

It all ended late, past one o'clock in the morning. Anisim went around unsteadily to all the singers and musicians and gave each of them a new half rouble. And the old man, not swaying but somehow favoring one foot, saw the guests off and told each of them:

"The wedding cost two thousand."

As people were leaving, somebody exchanged the Shikalovo tavernkeeper's good vest for an old one, and Anisim suddenly flared up and started shouting:

"Stop! I'll find him at once! I know who stole it! Stop!"

He ran outside, chasing after someone; they caught him, took him under the arms, brought him home, shoved him, drunk, flushed with anger, wet, into the room where the aunt was already undressing Lipa, and locked the door.

IV

Five days passed. Anisim got ready to leave and went upstairs to say good-bye to Varvara. She had all the icon lamps burning, there was a smell of incense, and she herself was sitting by the window knitting a red woolen stocking.

"You didn't spend long with us," she said. "Boring, was it? Oh, tush, tush . . . We have a good life, there's plenty of everything, and your wedding was celebrated properly, the right way. The old man says two thousand went into it. In short, we live like merchants, only it's boring here. We do people much wrong. My heart aches, my friend—oh, God, how we wrong them! We trade a horse, or buy something, or hire a workman—there's cheating in all of it. Cheating and cheating. The vegetable oil in the shop is bitter, rancid, the people's tar is better. Tell me, for pity's sake, isn't it impossible to sell good oil?"

"Each to his own place, mother."

"But don't we all have to die? Ah, no, really, you should talk with your father! . . ."

"Why don't you talk with him yourself."

"Well, well! I tell him what I think, and he says the same as you, word for word: each to his own place. In the other world they're not going to sort out who had which place. God's judgment is righteous."

"Of course, nobody's going to sort it out," Anisim said and sighed. "And anyhow God doesn't exist, mother. What's there to sort out!"

Varvara looked at him with astonishment and laughed and clasped her hands. Because she was so sincerely astonished at his words and looked at him as if he were a freak, he became embarrassed.

"Or maybe God does exist, only there's no faith," he said. "As I was being married, I felt out of sorts. Like when you take an egg from under a hen and there's a chick peeping in it, so my conscience suddenly peeped in me, and all the while I was being married, I kept thinking: God exists! But as soon as I stepped out of the church—there was nothing. And how should I know if God exists or not? We weren't taught that when we were little, but here's a baby still at his mother's breast, and he's taught just one thing: each to his own place. Papa doesn't believe in God either. You told me that time that the Guntorevs had their sheep stolen . . . I found out: it was a Shikalovo peasant who stole them; he stole them, but papa got the skins . . . There's faith for you!"

Anisim winked an eye and shook his head.

"And the headman doesn't believe in God either," he went on, "neither does the clerk or the beadle. If they go to church and keep the fasts, it's so that people won't speak ill of them, and in case there may really be a Judgment Day. Now they say the end of the world has come, because people have grown weak, don't honor their parents, and so on. That's nonsense. My understanding, mother, is that all troubles come from people having too little conscience. I can see through things, mother, and I understand. If a man's wearing a stolen shirt, I see it. A man's sitting in a tavern, and it looks to you like he's having tea and nothing else, but, tea or no tea, I can also see that he's got no conscience. You walk around the whole day, and there's not a single person with any conscience. And the whole reason is that they don't know whether God exists or not . . . Well, good-bye, mother. Keep alive and well, and think no evil of me."

Anisim bowed to the ground in front of Varvara.

"I thank you for everything, mother," he said. "You've been a great benefit to our family. You're a very decent woman, and I'm much pleased with you."

Feeling moved, Anisim went out, but came back again and said:

"Samorodov got me involved in a certain business: I'll be rich or I'll perish. If anything happens, mother, you must comfort my father."

"Well, now! Oh, tush, tush . . . God is merciful. And you, Anisim, you should be more tender with your wife—the two of you just look at each other and pout. You could at least smile, really."

"Yes, she's sort of a strange . . ." Anisim said and sighed. "She doesn't understand anything, keeps silent. She's too young, let her grow up."

At the porch a tall, sleek white stallion already stood hitched to a charabanc.

Old Tsybukin made a run, leaped up dashingly on the box, and took the reins. Anisim kissed Varvara, Aksinya, and his brother. Lipa also stood on the porch, stood motionless and looked aside, as though she had not come out to say good-bye but just so, for no reason. Anisim went up to her and brushed her cheek with his lips, barely, lightly.

"Good-bye," he said.

And she smiled somehow strangely, without looking at him; her face quivered, and for some reason everyone felt sorry for her. Anisim also hopped up and sat arms akimbo, because he considered himself a handsome man.

As they drove up out of the ravine, Anisim kept looking back at the village. It was a warm, clear day. The cattle were being taken out to pasture for the first time, and girls and women walked beside the herd in their Sunday dresses. A brown bull bellowed, rejoicing in his freedom, and dug his front hooves into the earth. Larks were singing all around, above and below. Anisim looked back at the church, shapely, white—it had recently been whitewashed—and remembered praying in it five days ago; he turned to look at the school with its green roof, at the river, where he once used to swim and fish, and joy leaped in his breast, and he wished that a wall might suddenly grow up from the ground and keep him from going further, so that he could remain only with his past.

At the station they went to the buffet and drank a glass of sherry each. The old man went to his pocket for his purse, in order to pay.

"It's on me!" said Anisim.

The old man went soft, slapped him on the shoulder, and winked at the bartender: See what a son I've got.

"Why don't you stay home, Anisim," the old man said, "you'd be priceless in the business! I'd shower you with gold, sonny."

"I just can't, papa."

The sherry was sourish and smelled of sealing wax, but they drank another glass each.

When the old man came back from the station, for the first moment he did not recognize his younger daughter-in-law. As soon as her husband drove out of the yard, Lipa was transformed and suddenly became cheerful. Barefoot, in an old, tattered skirt, her sleeves rolled up to the shoulders, she was washing the stairs in the front hall and singing in a high, silvery little voice, and when she carried the big tub of dirty water outside and looked up at the sun with her childlike smile, it seemed that she, too, was a lark.

An old workman who was passing by the porch shook his head and grunted:

"Yes, Grigory Petrovich, what daughters-in-law God sent you!" he said. "Not women, but pure treasures!"

V

On July 8, a Friday, Yelizarov, nicknamed Crutch, and Lipa were coming back from the village of Kazanskoe, where they had gone on a pilgrimage, the occasion being the feast of the church there—the Kazan Mother of God.[4] Far behind them walked Lipa's mother Praskovya, who could never keep up, because she was ill and short of breath. It was getting towards evening.

"A-a-ah! . . ." Crutch was surprised as he listened to Lipa. "A-ah! . . . We-e-ll?"

"I'm a great lover of preserves, Ilya Makarych," said Lipa. "I sit myself down in a little corner and drink tea with preserves. Or I drink together with Varvara Nikolaevna, and she tells me some touching story. They've got lots of preserves—four jars. 'Eat, Lipa,' they say, 'don't have any second thoughts.' "

"A-a-ah! . . . Four jars!"

"It's a rich man's life. Tea with white bread, and as much beef as you like. A rich man's life, only it's scary there, Ilya Makarych. It's so scary!"

"What are you scared of, little one?" asked Crutch, and he turned around to see how far Praskovya was lagging behind.

"First, right after the wedding, I was afraid of Anisim Grigoryich. He was all right, he never hurt me, only as soon as he comes near me I get chills all over, in every little bone. I didn't sleep a single night, I kept shivering and praying to God. And now I'm afraid of Aksinya, Ilya Makarych. She's all right, she just smiles, only sometimes she looks out the window, and her eyes are so angry and they burn green, like with a sheep in the barn. The Khrymin Juniors keep egging her on: 'Your old man has a lot in Butyokino,' they say, 'about a hundred acres, and there's sand and water there,' they say, 'so you build yourself a brickworks, Aksiusha, and we'll go shares with you.' Bricks now cost twenty roubles a thousand. It's a going trade. So yesterday at dinner Aksinya says to the old man, 'I want to build a brickworks in Butyokino, to be a merchant in my own right.' She says it and smiles. But Grigory Petrovich goes dark in the face; obviously he doesn't like it. 'As long as I'm alive,' he says, 'we can't do things separately, it must be all together.' And she flashed her eyes at him, ground her teeth . . . They served pancakes—she didn't eat!"

"A-a-ah! . . ." Crutch was astonished. "She didn't eat!"

"And tell me, please, when does she sleep?" Lipa went on. "She sleeps a wee half hour, then pops up, walks around, walks around all the time, checking whether the peasants are setting fire to something or stealing . . . It's scary with her, Ilya Makarych! And the Khrymin Juniors didn't even go to bed after the wedding, they went to court in town, and people say it's all because of Aksinya. Two of the brothers promised to build her the brickworks, but the third took it wrong, and the factory has stood still for a month, and my uncle Prokhor is out of work and goes from door to door begging for a crust. 'Uncle,' I say to him, 'don't shame yourself, go and do plowing meanwhile, or cut lumber!' 'I've lost the feel for peasant work, Lipynka,' he says, 'I can't do anything . . . '"

They stopped near a grove of young aspens to rest and wait for Praskovya. Yelizarov had been a contractor for a long time, yet he did not keep a horse, but went about the whole district on foot, with nothing but a little sack in which he kept bread and onion, and he took long strides, swinging his arms. It was hard to keep up with him.

At the entrance to the grove stood a boundary post. Yelizarov touched it to see if it was sturdy. Praskovya came up, out of breath. Her wrinkled, perpetually frightened face was radiant with happiness: she had been in church today, like other people, then had gone to the fair, and there she had drunk pear kvass! That rarely happened to her, and it even seemed to her now that she had lived for her own pleasure for the first time in her life. After resting, all three went on together. The sun was setting, and its rays penetrated the grove, shone on the tree trunks. Loud voices rang out ahead. The Ukleyevo girls had gone ahead long ago, but had tarried there in the grove, probably picking mushrooms.

"Hey, gi-i-irls!" shouted Yelizarov. "Hey, you beauties!"

He was answered with laughter.

"Crutch is coming! Crutch! The old coot!"

And the echo laughed, too. Now the grove was behind them. They could already see the tops of the factory smokestacks; the cross on the belfry flashed: this was the village, "the one where the verger ate all the caviar at the funeral." They were almost home; they only had to go down into the big ravine. Lipa and Praskovya, who went barefoot, sat down on the grass to put their shoes on; the contractor sat down with them. Looked at from above, Ukleyevo, with its pussywillows, white church, and river, seemed beautiful, peaceful, an impression only spoiled by the factory roofs, painted a gloomy, savage color for the sake of economy. On the opposite slope one could see rye—stacked up, or in sheaves here and there, as if scattered by a storm, or in just-cut rows; the oats, too, were ripe and gleamed in the sun now, like mother-of-pearl. It was harvest time. Today was a feast day, tomorrow, a Saturday, they had to gather the rye and get the hay in, then Sunday was a feast day again; every day distant thunder rumbled; the weather was sultry, it felt like rain, and, looking at the fields now, each one hoped that God would grant them to finish the harvest in time, and was merry, and joyful, and uneasy at heart.

"Mowers cost a lot these days," said Praskovya. "A rouble forty a day!"

And people kept on coming from the fair in Kazanskoe; peasant women, factory workers in new visored caps, beggars, children . . . A cart drove past, raising dust, with an unsold horse running behind it, looking as if it were glad it had not been sold; then a resisting cow was led past by the horns, then came another cart carrying drunken peasants, their legs dangling down. An old woman led a boy in a big hat and big boots; the boy was exhausted from the heat and the heavy boots, which did not let him bend his knees, but even so he kept blowing with all his might on a toy trumpet; they had already gone down and turned off on a side street, and the trumpet could still be heard.

"And our factory-owners are a bit out of sorts . . ." said Yelizarov. "It's bad! Kostiukov got angry with me. He said, 'Too much lumber went into the cornices.' Too much? 'As much as was needed, Vassily Danilych,' I say, 'that's how much went into them. I don't eat it with my kasha, your lumber.' 'How can you speak to me like that?' he says. 'A blockhead, that's what you are! Don't forget yourself! It was I,' he shouts, 'who made you a contractor!' 'Some feat,' I say. 'Before I was a contractor,' I say, 'I still drank tea every day.' 'You're all crooks,' he says . . . I kept quiet. We're crooks in this world, I thought, and you'll be crooks in the next. Ho, ho, ho! The next day he softened. 'Don't be angry with me for my words, Makarych,' he said. 'If I said something unnecessary, still there's the fact that I'm a merchant of the first guild, superior to you—you ought to keep quiet.' 'You're a merchant of the first guild,' I say, 'and I'm a carpenter, that's correct. And Saint Joseph,' I say, 'was also a carpenter. Our business is righteous, pleasing to God, and if,' I say, 'you want to be superior, go ahead, Vassily Danilych.' And later—that is, after the conversation—I thought: but who's the superior one? A merchant of the first guild or a carpenter? Turns out it's the carpenter, little ones!"

Crutch thought briefly and added:

"So it is, little ones. He who labors, he who endures, is the superior one."

The sun had set, and a thick mist, white as milk, was rising above the river, in the churchyard and the clearings around the mills. Now, when darkness was falling quickly and lights flashed below, and when it seemed that the mist concealed a bottomless abyss beneath it, Lipa and her mother, who were born destitute and were prepared to live out their days that way, giving everything to others except their meek, frightened souls, might have imagined for a moment that in this vast, mysterious world, among an endless number of lives, they, too, were a force and were superior to someone else; it felt good to sit up there, they smiled happily and forgot that they had to go back down all the same.

Finally they returned home. Mowers were sitting on the ground by the gates and near the shop. Ordinarily the local Ukleyevo people did not work for Tsybukin, and he had to hire outsiders, and now in the darkness it looked as if people with long black beards were sitting there. The shop was open, and through the doorway the deaf man could be seen playing checkers with a boy. The mowers sang softly, in barely audible voices, or loudly demanded to be paid for the past day's work, but they were not paid, so that they would not leave before the next day. Old Tsybukin, without a frock coat, in just his waistcoat, sat with Aksinya under a birch tree by the porch and drank tea; and a lamp burned on the table.

"Grandpa-a-a!" a mower repeated outside the gates, as if teasing him. "Pay us at least half! Grandpa-a-a!"

And at once laughter was heard, and then barely audible singing . . . Crutch also sat down to have tea.

"So we were at the fair," he began telling them. "We had a good time, little ones, a very good time, thank the Lord. And this thing

happened, not very nice: the blacksmith Sashka bought some tobacco and so he gave the shopkeeper a half rouble. And the half
rouble was false," Crutch went on and glanced around; he meant to
speak in a whisper, but instead spoke in a hoarse, muffled voice,
and everybody could hear him. "And it turned out the half rouble
was false. They ask him: 'Where'd you get it?' And he says, 'Anisim
Tsybukin gave it to me. When I was making merry at his wedding,'
he says . . . They called a policeman and took him away . . . Watch
out, Petrovich, or something may come of it, some talk . . ."

"Grandpa-a-a!" the same teasing voice came from outside the
gate. "Grandpa-a-a!"

Silence ensued.

"Ah, little ones, little ones, little ones . . ." Crutch muttered
rapidly and got up; drowsiness was coming over him. "Well, thanks
for the tea and the sugar, little ones. It's time for bed. I've gone
crumbly, the beams are all rotten in me. Ho, ho, ho!"

And, walking off, he said:

"Must be time I died!"

And he sobbed. Old Tsybukin did not finish his tea, but went on
sitting, thinking; he looked as if he were listening to Crutch's footsteps far down the street.

"Sashka the blacksmith lied, I expect," said Aksinya, guessing his
thoughts.

He went into the house and came back a little later with a package; he unwrapped it—roubles gleamed, perfectly new. He took
one, tried it with his teeth, dropped it on the tray; tried another,
dropped it . . .

"It's a fact, the roubles are false . . ." he said, looking at Aksinya
as if in perplexity. "They're the ones . . . Anisim brought that time,
they're his present. You take them, daughter," he whispered and
shoved the package into her hands, "take them, throw them down
the well . . . Away with them! And watch yourself, don't go talking
about it. Or something may happen . . . Take the samovar away,
put out the lamp . . ."

Lipa and Praskovya, sitting in the shed, saw the lights go out one
after another; only Varvara's blue and red icon lamps shone upstairs,
and from there came a breath of peace, contentment, and unaware-
ness. Praskovya could not get used to the fact that her daughter had
married a rich man, and when she came, she huddled timidly in the
front hall, smiled entreatingly, and had tea and sugar sent out to

her. Lipa could not get used to it either, and after her husband left, she slept not in her own bed but wherever she happened to be—in the kitchen or the shed—and every day she washed the floors or did the laundry, and it seemed to her that she was doing day labor. And now, on returning from the pilgrimage, they had tea in the kitchen with the cook, then went to the shed and lay down on the floor between the sledges and the wall. It was dark there and smelled of horse collars. The lights went out around the house, then the deaf man was heard locking up the shop and the mowers settling down to sleep in the yard. In the distance, at the Khrymin Juniors, someone was playing the expensive accordion . . . Praskovya and Lipa began to doze off.

And when someone's footsteps awakened them, it was bright with moonlight; at the entrance of the shed stood Aksinya, holding her bedding in her arms.

"Maybe it's cooler here . . ." she said, then came in and lay down almost on the threshold itself, and the moon cast its light all over her.

She did not sleep and sighed heavily, tossing about from the heat and throwing almost everything off—and in the magic light of the moon, what a beautiful, what a proud animal she was! A short time passed and again footsteps were heard: the old man appeared in the doorway, all white.

"Aksinya!" he called. "Are you here or what?"

"Well?" she replied angrily.

"I told you earlier to throw the money down the well. Did you do it?"

"What an idea, throwing goods into the water! I gave it to the mowers . . ."

"Oh, my God!" said the old man in amazement and fright. "Mischievous woman . . . Oh, my God!"

He clasped his hands and left, muttering something as he went. A little later Aksinya sat up, sighed heavily and vexedly, then got up and, collecting her bedding, went out.

"Why did you give me to them, mama?" said Lipa.

"You had to be married, daughter. It's not we who set it up that way."

And a feeling of inconsolable grief was about to come over them. But it seemed to them that someone was looking down from the heights of the sky, from the blue, from where the stars are, saw everything that went on in Ukleyevo, and was watching over them. And, however great the evil, the night was still peaceful and beautiful, and there still was and would be righteousness in God's world, just as peaceful and beautiful, and everything on earth was only waiting to merge with righteousness, as moonlight merges with the night.

And the two women, comforted, pressed close to each other and fell asleep.

VI

The news had come long ago that Anisim had been put in prison for making and passing counterfeit money. Months went by, more than half a year went by, the long winter was over, spring came, and at home and in the village they got used to the fact that Anisim was in prison. And when anyone passed the house or the shop at night, they remembered that Anisim was in prison; and when the cemetery bell tolled, they also remembered for some reason that he was in prison and awaiting trial.

It was as if a shadow had been cast over the yard. The house became darker, the roof rusted, the ironclad door of the shop, heavy, painted green, became discolored, or, as the deaf man said, "got gristled"; and it was as if old man Tsybukin himself grew darker. He had long ceased cutting his hair and beard, was all overgrown, no longer leaped as he got into the tarantass, nor shouted "God will provide!" to the beggars. His strength was waning, and that was noticeable in everything. People were less afraid of him now, and the local policeman drew up a report on the shop, though he still collected what was owed him; and three times he was summoned to court in town for secret trading in vodka, but the hearing kept being postponed owing to the non-appearance of the witnesses, and this wore the old man out.

He visited his son frequently, hired someone, petitioned someone, donated somewhere for a church banner. He offered the warden of the prison in which Anisim was kept the gift of a silver tea-glass holder with "The soul knows moderation" inscribed on the enamel and with a long teaspoon.

"There's nobody, nobody to intervene properly for us," said Varvara. "Oh, tush, tush . . . You should ask someone of the gentry to write to the head officials . . . At least they'd release him till the trial! Why torment the lad?"

She, too, was upset, but she grew plumper, whiter, lit the icon lamps in her room as before, and saw to it that the house was clean, and treated guests to preserves and apple comfit. The deaf son and Aksinya tended the shop. They started a new business—a brickworks in Butyokino—and Aksinya went there almost every day in the tarantass; she drove herself and on meeting acquaintances stretched her neck like a snake from the young rye and smiled naïvely and mysteriously. And Lipa played all the time with her baby, who was born to her just before Lent. He was a small baby, skinny and pitiful, and it was strange that he cried, looked about, and that he was considered a person and was even named Nikifor. He would lie in his cradle, Lipa would go to the door and say, bowing:

"How do you do, Nikifor Anisimych!"

And she would rush headlong to him and kiss him. Then she would go to the door, bow, and say again:

"How do you do, Nikifor Anisimych!"

And he would stick up his little red legs, and his crying was mixed with laughter, as with the carpenter Yelizarov.

At last the day of the trial was set. The old man left five days ahead of time. Then it was heard that peasants called as witnesses had been sent from the village; the old hired workman also received a summons, and he left.

The trial was on a Thursday. But Sunday had already passed, and the old man had still not come back, and there was no news. On Tuesday, before evening, Varvara sat by the open window listening for the old man coming. In the next room Lipa was playing with her baby. She tossed him in her arms and said in admiration:

"You'll grow so-o-o big, so-o-o-big! You'll be a man, we'll do day labor together! Day labor together!"

"We-e-ell!" Varvara became offended. "What kind of day labor have you thought up, silly girl? He'll be a merchant for us! . . ."

Lipa started to sing softly, but a little later forgot herself and began again:

"You'll grow so-o-o big, so-o-o big, you'll be a man, we'll go to day labor together!"

"We-e-ell! You're at it again!"

Lipa stood in the doorway with Nikifor in her arms and asked:

"Mama, why do I love him so? Why do I pity him so?" she went on in a quavering voice, and her eyes glistened with tears. "Who is he? How is he? Light as a feather, a crumb, and I love him, I love him like a real person. He can't do anything, can't speak, but I understand everything he wishes with his dear eyes."

Varvara listened: there was the sound of the evening train coming into the station. Was the old man on it? She no longer heard or understood what Lipa was saying, did not notice the time going by, but only trembled all over, and that not with fear but with intense curiosity. She saw a cart filled with peasants drive past quickly, with a rumble. It was the returning witnesses coming from the station. As the cart drove past the shop, the old workman jumped off and came into the yard. One could hear him being greeted in the yard, being questioned about something . . .

"Loss of rights and all property," he said loudly, "and six years' hard labor in Siberia."

Aksinya could be seen coming out the back door of the shop; she had just been selling kerosene and was holding a bottle in one hand and a funnel in the other, and there were silver coins in her mouth.

"And where's papa?" she asked, lisping.

"At the station," the workman replied. " 'When it gets darker,' he says, 'then I'll come.' "

And when it became known in the yard that Anisim had been sentenced to hard labor, the cook in the kitchen began to wail as over a dead man, thinking that propriety demanded it:

"Why have you abandoned us, Anisim Grigoryich, our bright falcon . . ."

The dogs barked in alarm. Varvara ran to the window and in a flurry of anguish began shouting to the cook, straining her voice as much as she could:

"Eno-o-ough, Stepanida, eno-o-ough! Don't torment us, for Christ's sake!"

They forgot to prepare the samovar, they were no longer thinking well. Only Lipa could not understand what was the matter and went on fussing over her baby.

When the old man came home from the station, they did not ask him about anything. He greeted everyone, then walked silently through all the rooms; he ate no supper.

"There's nobody to intercede . . ." Varvara began, when they were left alone. "I said to ask the gentry—you didn't listen then . . . A petition might . . ."

"I interceded myself!" said the old man, waving his hand. "When they sentenced Anisim, I went to the gentleman who defended him. 'Impossible to do anything now, it's too late.' And Anisim says so himself: it's too late. But all the same, as I was leaving the court, I made an arrangement with a lawyer, gave him an advance . . . I'll wait a week and then go back. It's as God wills."

The old man walked silently through all the rooms again, and when he came back to Varvara, he said:

"I must be sick. Something in my head . . . A fog. My thoughts are clouded."

He shut the door so that Lipa would not hear and went on softly:

"I don't feel right about money. Remember, Anisim brought me new roubles and half roubles before the wedding, on St. Thomas's Sunday?[5] I stashed one package away then, and the rest I mixed in with my own . . . When my uncle Dmitri Filatych, God rest his soul, was still alive, he used to go for goods all the time, now to Moscow, now to the Crimea. He had a wife, and that same wife, while he went for goods, as I said, used to play around with other men. There were six children. So my uncle would have a drink and start laughing: 'I just can't sort out which are mine and which aren't.' An easygoing character, that is. And so now I can't figure out which coins are real and which are false. And it seems like they're all false."

"Ah, no, God help you!"

"I'm buying a ticket at the station, I hand over three roubles, and I think to myself, maybe they're false. And it scares me. I must be sick."

"What can I say, we all walk before God . . . Oh, tush, tush . . ." said Varvara, and she shook her head. "You ought to give it some thought, Petrovich . . . What if something bad happens? You're not a young man. You'll die, and for all I know they may wrong our grandson. Aie, they'll do Nikifor wrong, I'm afraid they will! His father can be counted as not there, his mother's young, foolish . . . You ought at least to leave that land to him, to the boy, that Butyokino, Petrovich, really! Just think!" Varvara went on persuading him. "A nice little boy, it's a pity! Go tomorrow and draw up the paper. Why wait?"

"And here I was forgetting about my grandson . . ." said

Tsybukin. "I must go and say hello. So you say he's a nice boy? Well, let him grow up. God grant it!"

He opened the door and beckoned to Lipa with a bent finger. She came up to him with the baby in her arms.

"If you need anything, Lipynka, just ask," he said. "And eat whatever you like, we won't begrudge it, as long as you're healthy . . ." He made a cross over the baby. "And take care of my grandson. The son's gone, at least the grandson is left."

Tears ran down his cheeks; he sobbed and turned away. A little later he went to bed and fell fast asleep, after seven sleepless nights.

VII

The old man made a short trip to town. Somebody told Aksinya that he had gone to the notary to write a will, and that he was leaving Butyokino, the same place where she baked bricks, to his grandson Nikifor. She was told of it in the morning, when the old man and Varvara were sitting under the birch tree by the porch drinking tea. She locked up the shop front and back, collected all the keys she had, and flung them down at the old man's feet.

"I won't work for you anymore!" she cried loudly, and suddenly began to sob. "It turns out I'm not your daughter-in-law, but a hired worker! Everybody laughs: 'Look,' they say, 'what a worker the Tsybukins found for themselves!' I'm not your charwoman! I'm not a beggar, not some kind of slut, I've got a father and mother."

Without wiping her tears, she turned her eyes, tear-flooded, spiteful, crossed with anger, on the old man; her face and neck were red and strained, because she was shouting with all her might.

"I don't want to serve you anymore!" she went on. "I'm worn out! When it's work, when it's sitting in the shop day after day, and sneaking out at night to get vodka—then it's me, but when it's giving away land—then it's the convict's wife with her little devil! She's the mistress, she's the lady here, and I'm her servant! Give her everything, the jailbird's wife, let her choke on it, I'm going home! Find yourselves another fool, you cursed Herods!"

Never in his life had the old man scolded or punished his children, and he could not admit even the thought that anyone in the family could say rude words to him or behave disrespectfully; and now he got very frightened, ran into the house, and hid behind a wardrobe. And Varvara was so taken aback that she could not get up from her place, but only waved both arms as if warding off a bee.

"Ah, saints alive, what is this?" she murmured in horror. "Why is she shouting? Oh, tush, tush . . . People will hear! Not so loud . . . Ah, not so loud!"

"You gave Butyokino to the jailbird's wife," Aksinya went on shouting, "so give her everything now—I don't need anything from you! Perish the lot of you! You're all one gang here! I've had enough of looking at you! You've robbed everybody walking or riding by, you've robbed them old and young! Who sold vodka without a license? And the false money? You've stuffed your coffers with false money—now you don't need me anymore!"

A crowd had already gathered by the open gates and was looking into the yard.

"Let people stare!" Aksinya shouted. "I'll disgrace you! You'll burn with shame! You'll grovel at my feet! Hey, Stepan!" she called the deaf man. "Let's go home this very minute! Let's go to my father and mother, I don't want to live with criminals! Get ready!"

Laundry was hanging on lines stretched across the yard; she tore down her still-wet skirts and blouses and flung them into the deaf man's arms. Then she rushed furiously about the yard, tearing down all the laundry, hers or not hers, flinging it to the ground and trampling on it.

"Ah, saints alive, calm her down!" Varvara groaned. "What's the matter with her? Give her Butyokino, give it to her for the sake of Christ in Heaven!"

"Well, some wo-o-oman!" people were saying by the gate. "There's a wo-o-oman for you! Got herself going—something awful!"

Aksinya ran to the kitchen where the laundry was being done just then. Lipa was doing it alone, while the cook went to the river to do the rinsing. Steam rose from the tub and the cauldron by the stove, and the kitchen was stuffy and dim with mist. There was still a pile of unwashed laundry on the floor, and on the bench beside it, his red legs sticking up, lay Nikifor, so that if he fell, he would not be hurt. Just as Aksinya came in, Lipa took a shift of hers from the pile, put it into the tub, and reached for the big dipper of boiling water that stood on the table . . .

"Give it here!" said Aksinya, looking at her with hatred and snatching the shift from the tub. "You've got no business touching my underwear! You're a convict's wife, and you should know your place and what you are!"

Lipa stared at her, bewildered, and did not understand, but suddenly she caught the glance that the woman shot at the baby, and suddenly she understood and went dead all over . . .

"You took my land, so there's for you!"

As she said it, Aksinya seized the dipper of boiling water and dashed it over Nikifor.

After that a cry was heard such as had never yet been heard in Ukleyevo, and it was hard to believe that such a small, weak being as Lipa could scream like that. And it suddenly became hushed in the yard. Aksinya went into the house silently, with her former naïve smile . . . The deaf man kept walking about the yard with the laundry in his arms, then began to hang it up again, silently, unhurriedly. And until the cook came back from the river, nobody dared go into the kitchen and see what had happened there.

VIII

Nikifor was taken to the regional hospital, and towards evening he died there. Lipa did not wait till they came for her, but wrapped the dead boy in a blanket and carried him home.

The hospital, new, built recently, with big windows, stood high on a hill; it was all lit up by the setting sun and looked as if it were burning inside. At the bottom was a village. Lipa descended by the road and, before reaching the village, sat down near a small pond. Some woman brought a horse to water, but the horse would not drink.

"What else do you want?" the woman said softly, in perplexity. "What do you want?"

A boy in a red shirt, sitting right by the water, was washing his father's boots. And there was not another soul to be seen either in the village or on the hill.

"He won't drink . . ." said Lipa, looking at the horse.

But the woman and the boy with the boots left, and now there was no one to be seen. The sun went to sleep, covering itself with purple and gold brocade, and long clouds, crimson and lilac, watched over its rest, stretching across the sky. Somewhere far away, God knows where, a bittern gave a mournful, muted cry, like a cow locked in a barn. The cry of this mysterious bird was heard every spring, but no one knew what it looked like or where it lived. Up by the hospital, in the bushes just by the pond, beyond the village, and in the surrounding fields, nightingales were pouring out their song. The cuckoo was counting out someone's years and kept losing count and starting over again. In the pond angry, straining frogs called to each other, and one could even make out the words: "You're such a one! You're such a one!" How noisy it was! It seemed that all these creatures were calling and singing on purpose so that no one would sleep on that spring evening, so that all, even the angry frogs, might value and enjoy every minute: for life is given only once!

A silver crescent moon shone in the sky, there were many stars. Lipa could not remember how long she had been sitting by the pond, but when she got up and left, everybody in the village was asleep, and there was not a single light. Home was probably some eight miles away, but she did not have strength enough, she could not figure out how to go; the moon shone now ahead, now to the right, and the same cuckoo kept calling, its voice grown hoarse, laughing, as if mocking her: oh-oh, watch out, you'll lose your way! Lipa walked quickly, lost the kerchief from her head . . . She gazed at the sky and thought about where the soul of her boy was then: was it following her, or flitting about up there near the stars and no longer thinking of its mother! Oh, how lonely it is in the fields at night, amidst this singing, when you yourself cannot sing, amidst the ceaseless cries of joy, when you yourself cannot be joyful, when the moon looks down from the sky, also lonely, careless whether it is spring now or winter, whether people live or die . . . When your soul grieves, it is hard to be without people. If only her mother Praskovya was with her, or Crutch, or the cook, or some peasant!

"Boo-o-o!" cried the bittern. "Boo-o-o!"

And suddenly she clearly heard human speech:

"Harness up, Vavila!"

Ahead, just by the road, a campfire was burning; there were no longer any flames, just red embers glowing. She could hear horses munching. Two carts stood out against the darkness—one with a barrel, the other, slightly lower, with sacks—and two men: one was leading a horse in order to harness up, the other stood motionless by the fire, his hands behind his back. A dog growled near the cart. The man leading the horse stopped and said:

"Seems like somebody's coming down the road."

"Quiet, Sharik!" the other shouted at the dog.

And from his voice it was clear this other was an old man. Lipa stopped and said:

"God be with you!"

The old man approached her and replied after a moment:

"Good evening!"

"Your dog won't bite, grandpa?"

"Never mind, come on. He won't touch you."

"I was at the hospital," said Lipa, after a pause. "My little son died there. I'm taking him home."

It must have been unpleasant for the old man to hear that, because he stepped away and said hastily:

"Never mind, dear. It's God's will. You're taking too long, lad!" he said, turning to his companion. "Get a move on!"

"Your yoke's gone," said the lad. "I don't see it."

"You're unyoked yourself, Vavila!"

The old man picked up an ember, blew it to flame—lighting up only his eyes and nose—then, when the yoke was found, went over to Lipa with the light and looked at her; his eyes expressed compassion and tenderness.

"You're a mother," he said. "Every mother feels sorry for her wee one."

And with that he sighed and shook his head. Vavila threw something on the fire, trampled on it—and all at once it became very dark; everything vanished, and as before there were only the fields, the sky with its stars, and the birds making noise, keeping each other from sleeping. And a corncrake called, seemingly from the very place where the campfire had been.

But a minute passed, and again the carts, and the old man, and the lanky Vavila could be seen. The carts creaked as they drove out onto the road.

"Are you holy people?" Lipa asked the old man.

"No. We're from Firsanovo."

"You looked at me just now and my heart softened. And the lad's quiet. So I thought: they must be holy people."

"Are you going far?"

"To Ukleyevo."

"Get in, we'll give you a ride to Kuzmenki. From there you go straight and we go left."

Vavila sat on the cart with the barrel, the old man and Lipa on the other. They went at a walk, Vavila in the lead.

"My little son suffered the whole day," said Lipa. "He looked with his little eyes and said nothing, he wanted to speak but he couldn't. Lord God, Queen of Heaven! I just kept falling on the floor from grief. I'd stand up and fall down beside the bed. And tell me, grandpa, why should a little one suffer before death? When a grown man or woman suffers, their sins are forgiven, but why a little one who has no sins? Why?"

"Who knows!" said the old man.

They rode for half an hour in silence.

"You can't know the why and how of everything," said the old man. "A bird's given two wings, not four, because it can fly with two; so a man's not given to know everything, but only a half or a quarter. As much as he needs to know in order to live, so much he knows."

"It would be easier for me to walk, grandpa. Now my heart's all shaky."

"Never mind. Just sit."

The old man yawned and made a cross over his mouth.

"Never mind . . ." he repeated. "Your grief is half a grief. Life is long, there'll be more of good and bad, there'll be everything. Mother Russia is vast!" he said, and he looked to both sides. "I've been all over Russia and seen all there is in her, and believe what I say, my dear. There will be good and there will be bad. I went on foot to Siberia, I went to the Amur and to the Altai, and I moved to live in Siberia, worked the land there, then I began to miss Mother Russia and came back to my native village. We came back to Russia on foot; and I remember us going on a ferry, and I was skinny as could be, all tattered, barefoot, chilled, sucking on a crust, and some gentleman traveler was there on the ferry—if he's dead, God rest his soul—he looked at me pitifully, the tears pouring down. 'Ah,' he says, 'black is your bread, black are your days . . .' And when I got home I had neither stick nor stone, as they say; there was a wife, but she stayed in Siberia, buried. So I just live as a hired hand. And so what? I'll tell you: since then there's been bad and there's been good. But I'm not up to dying, my dear, I wouldn't mind living another twenty years—which means there's been more good. And Mother Russia is vast!" he said and again looked to both sides and behind him.

"Grandpa," asked Lipa, "when a man dies, how many days after does his soul wander the earth?"

"Who knows! Let's ask Vavila, he went to school. They teach everything now. Vavila!" the old man called.

"Eh!"

"Vavila, after a man dies, how many days does his soul wander the earth?"

Vavila stopped the horse and only then replied:

"Nine days. My uncle Kyrill died, and his soul lived in our cottage thirteen days after."

"How do you know?"

"There was a knocking in the stove for thirteen days."

"Well, all right. Drive on," said the old man, and it was clear that he did not believe any of it.

Near Kuzmenki the carts turned onto the high road, and Lipa kept on straight. Day was breaking. As she went down into the ravine, the cottages and church of Ukleyevo were hidden in mist. It was cold, and it seemed to her that the same cuckoo was calling.

When Lipa came home, the cattle had not gone to pasture yet: everyone was asleep. She sat on the porch and waited. The old man was the first to come out; he understood at once, from the first glance, what had happened, and for a long time could not say a word, but only smacked his lips.

"Eh, Lipa," he said, "you didn't take care of my grandson . . ."

Varvara was awakened. She clasped her hands and burst into sobs, and they immediately began laying the child out.

"And he was such a pretty little boy . . ." she kept saying. "Oh, tush, tush . . . One little boy you had, and you didn't take care of him, foolish girl . . ."

They served a panikhida in the morning and in the evening. The next day was the funeral, and after the funeral the guests and clergy ate a great deal and with such greed as if they had not eaten for a long time. Lipa served at the table, and the priest, raising a fork with a pickled mushroom on it, said to her:

"Don't grieve over the baby. Of such is the Kingdom of Heaven."

And only after everyone left did Lipa realize properly that there was no more Nikifor and never would be, realize it and begin to weep. And she did not know which room to go to in order to weep, because she felt that, after the boy's death, there was no place for her in this house, that she had no part in it and was superfluous; and the others felt it, too.

"Well, what are you howling here for?" Aksinya suddenly shouted, appearing in the doorway; for the occasion of the funeral she had put on all new clothes and powdered her face. "Shut up!"

Lipa wanted to stop but could not, and wept still louder.

"Do you hear?" Aksinya shouted and stamped her foot in great wrath. I'm speaking to you! Get out and don't ever set foot here, you convict's wife! Out!"

"Well, well, well! . . ." the old man started fussing. "Aksiuta, calm down, dear . . . She's crying, it's an understandable thing . . . her wee one's dead . . ."

"An understandable thing . . ." Aksinya mocked him. "Let her stay the night, but tomorrow there better not be a breath of her left here! An understandable thing! . . ." she mocked once more and, laughing, headed for the shop.

The next day, early in the morning, Lipa went to her mother in Torguyevo.

IX

At the present time the roof and door of the shop have been painted and are shining like new; cheerful geraniums are blooming in the windows as before, and what took place three years ago in the house and yard of the Tsybukins is almost forgotten.

Old Grigory Petrovich is considered the proprietor, as before, but in fact everything has passed into Aksinya's hands; she sells and buys, and nothing can be done without her consent. The brickworks is going well; owing to the demand for bricks for the railway, the price has gone up to twenty-four roubles a thousand; women and girls cart bricks to the station and load them on the cars, and get twenty-five kopecks a day for it.

Aksinya has gone shares with the Khrymins, and their factory is now called "Khrymin Junior and Co." They've opened a tavern by the station, and now play the expensive accordion not at the factory but in this tavern, and the place is frequented by the postmaster, who has also started some sort of business, and by the stationmaster. The Khrymin Juniors have presented deaf Stepan with a gold watch, and he is forever taking it out of his pocket and holding it to his ear.

In the village they say of Aksinya that she has acquired great power; and it is true that when she goes to her brickworks in the morning, with her naïve smile, beautiful, happy, and then when she gives orders at the brickworks, great power is felt in her. Everyone fears her at home, and in the village, and in the brickworks. When she comes to the post office, the postmaster jumps to his feet and says to her:

"I humbly beg you to be seated, Xenia Abramovna."

A certain landowner, a fop in a fine flannel jacket and high patent-leather boots, an elderly man, was once selling her a horse, and got so carried away by his conversation with her that he let the horse go for what she offered. He held her hand for a long time and, looking into her merry, sly, naïve eyes, said:

"For a woman like you, Xenia Abramovna, I'm ready to do any pleasure. Only tell me when we can see each other, so that no one will bother us?"

"Why, whenever you like!"

And since then the elderly fop comes to the shop almost every day to drink beer. The beer is terribly bitter, like wormwood. The landowner wags his head but drinks.

Old Tsybukin no longer mixes in the business. He carries no money on him, because he cannot distinguish real money from false, but he keeps mum and tells no one about this weakness of his. He has become somehow forgetful, and if he is not given anything to eat, he will not ask himself; they are already used to eating without him, and Varvara often says:

"Our man went to bed again last night without eating."

And she says it indifferently, because she is used to it. For some reason, summer and winter alike, he goes about in a fur coat and only on very hot days does not go out but sits at home. Ordinarily, he puts his coat on and turns up the collar, wraps himself up, and strolls around the village, along the road to the station, or else sits from morning till evening on a bench by the church gate. He sits and does not stir. Passersby bow to him, but he does not respond, because he dislikes peasants as much as ever. When someone asks him something, he replies quite reasonably and politely, but briefly.

The talk going round the village is that his daughter-in-law has driven him out of his own house and gives him nothing to eat, and that he supposedly lives by begging: some are glad, others are sorry.

Varvara has grown still more plump and white and does good deeds as before, and Aksinya does not interfere with her. There is now such a quantity of preserves that there is no time to eat it before the new berries come; it crystallizes, and Varvara all but weeps, not knowing what to do with it.

They have begun to forget about Anisim. A letter came from him once, written in verse, on a big sheet of paper with the look of a petition, in the same magnificent hand. Evidently his friend Samorodov was serving his term together with him. Below the verses, in a poor, barely legible hand, a single line was written: "I'm sick all the time here, it's hard for me, help me, for Christ's sake."

Once—this was on a clear autumn day, before evening—old man Tsybukin was sitting by the church gates, the collar of his coat turned up, so that only his nose and the visor of his cap could be seen. At the other end of the long bench sat the contractor Yelizarov and beside him the school watchman, Yakov, a toothless old man of about seventy. Crutch and the watchman were talking.

"Children must give their old parents food and drink . . . honor thy father and mother," Yakov was saying with vexation, "but she, this daughter-in-law, has driven her father-in-law out of his ownest house. The old man's got nothing to eat, nothing to drink—where's he to go? It's the third day he hasn't eaten."

"The third day!" Crutch said in surprise.

"He just sits like that, saying nothing. He's grown weak. And why say nothing? If he goes to court, the court's not going to praise her for it."

"What's the court going to praise?" asked Crutch, who had not heard well.

"Eh?"

"She's an all-right woman, works hard. In that business you can't get by without it . . . sin, I mean . . ."

"From his ownest house," Yakov went on in vexation. "Earn yourself a house, then drive people out. Eh, she's a fine one, she is! A pla-a-ague!"

Tsybukin listened without stirring.

"Your own house or somebody else's, it makes no difference, so long as it's warm and the women don't yell at you . . ." said Crutch, and he laughed. "When I was still a young man, I pitied my Nastasya very much. She was a quiet little woman. She used to say: 'Buy a house, Makarych! Buy a house, Makarych! And buy a horse, Makarych!' She was dying, and she kept saying: 'Buy yourself a droshky, Makarych, so as not to go on foot.' But I only ever bought her gingerbread."

"Her husband's deaf and stupid," Yakov went on, not listening to Crutch, "a fool of fools, the same as a goose. Does he understand anything? Hit a goose on the head with a stick—it still won't understand."

Crutch got up to go home to the factory. Yakov also got up, and the two went off together, still talking. When they were fifty paces away, old Tsybukin also got up and trudged after them, stepping uncertainly, as if on slippery ice.

The village was already sunk in evening twilight, and the sun shone only up above, on the road that ran snakelike down the slope. The old women were coming back from the forest, and the children with them; they were carrying baskets of mushrooms. Women and girls were coming in a crowd from the station, where they had been loading bricks on the cars, and their noses and cheeks under their eyes were covered with red brick dust. They were singing. Ahead of them all went Lipa, and she sang in a high voice, pouring out her song as she looked up at the sky, as if celebrating and rejoicing that the day, thank God, was over and they could rest. Her mother was in the crowd, the day laborer Praskovya, walking with a bundle in her arms and breathing heavily as always.

"Good evening, Makarych!" said Lipa, seeing Crutch. "Good evening, dear heart!"

"Good evening, Lipynka!" said Crutch, delighted. "Dear women, dear girls, love the rich carpenter! Ho, ho! Little ones, my little ones," Crutch sobbed. "My gentle little hatchets."

Crutch and Yakov walked on, and could still be heard talking. After them the crowd met with old Tsybukin, and it suddenly became very quiet. Lipa and Praskovya had dropped behind a little, and when the old man came abreast of them, Lipa bowed low and said:

"Good evening, Grigory Petrovich!"

And her mother also bowed. The old man stopped and looked at the two women without saying anything; his lips trembled and his eyes were filled with tears. Lipa took a piece of kasha pie from her mother's bundle and gave it to him. He took it and began to eat.

The sun had set completely; its glow had gone out even on the road above. It was growing dark and cool. Lipa and Praskovya walked on and kept crossing themselves for a long time.

JANUARY 1900

The Bishop

I

On the eve of Palm Sunday the vigil was going on in the Old Petrovsky Convent. It was almost ten o'clock when they began to hand out the pussywillows,[1] the lights were dim, the wicks were sooty, everything was as if in a mist. In the twilight of the church, the crowd heaved like the sea, and to Bishop Pyotr, who had been unwell for three days, it seemed that all the faces—old and young, men's and women's—were alike, that everyone who came up to get a branch had the same expression in their eyes. The doors could not be seen in the mist, the crowd kept moving, and it looked as if there was and would be no end to it. A women's choir was singing, a nun was reading the canon.

How hot it was, how stifling! How long the vigil was! Bishop Pyotr was tired. His breathing was labored, short, dry, his shoulders ached with fatigue, his legs trembled. And it was unpleasantly disturbing that some holy fool cried out now and then from the gallery. Besides, the bishop suddenly imagined, as if in sleep or delirium, that his own mother, Marya Timofeevna, whom he had not seen for nine years, or else an old woman resembling his mother, came up to him in the crowd, and, receiving a branch from him, stepped away, all the while gazing happily at him, with a kind, joyful smile, until she mingled with the crowd again. And for some reason tears poured down his face. His soul was at peace, all was well, yet he gazed fixedly at the choir on the left, where they were reading, where not a single person could be made out in the evening darkness—and wept. Tears glistened on his face, his beard. Then someone else began to weep near him, then someone else further away, then another and another, and the church was gradually filled with quiet weeping. But in a short while, some five minutes, the convent choir began to sing, there was no more weeping, everything was as before.

The service was soon over. As the bishop was getting into his carriage to go home, the whole moonlit garden was filled with the merry, beautiful ringing of the expensive, heavy bells. The white walls, the white crosses on the graves, the white birches and black shadows, and the distant moon in the sky, which stood directly over the convent, now seemed to live their own special life, incomprehensible, yet close to mankind. April was just beginning, and after the warm spring day it turned cooler, slightly frosty, and a breath of spring could be felt in the soft, cold air. The road from the convent to town was sandy, they had to go at a walking pace; and on both sides of the carriage, in the bright, still moonlight, pilgrims trudged over the sand. And everyone was silent, deep in thought, everything around was welcoming, young, so near—the trees, the sky, even the moon—and one wanted to think it would always be so.

At last the carriage drove into town and rolled down the main street. The shops were closed, except that of the merchant Yerakin, the millionaire, where they were trying out electric lighting, which was flickering badly, and people crowded around. Then came wide, dark streets, one after another, deserted, then the high road outside town, the fields, the smell of pines. And suddenly there rose up before his eyes a white, crenellated wall, and behind it a tall bell tower, all flooded with light, and beside it five big, shining, golden domes—this was St. Pankraty's Monastery, where Bishop Pyotr lived. And here, too, high above the monastery hung the quiet, pensive moon. The carriage drove through the gate, creaking over the sand, here and there the black figures of monks flashed in the moonlight, footsteps were heard on the flagstones . . .

"Your mother came while you were away, Your Grace," the cell attendant reported, when the bishop came to his quarters.

"Mama? When did she come?"

"Before the vigil. She first asked where you were, and then went to the convent."

"That means it was her I saw in church! Oh, Lord!"

And the bishop laughed with joy.

"She asked me to tell Your Grace," the attendant went on, "that she will come tomorrow. There's a girl with her, probably a grand-daughter. They're staying at Ovsyannikov's inn."

"What time is it now?"

"Just after eleven."

"Ah, how vexing!"

The bishop sat for a while in the drawing room, pondering and as if not believing it was so late. His arms and legs ached, there was a pain in the back of his head. He felt hot and uncomfortable. Having rested, he went to his bedroom and there, too, sat for a while, still thinking about his mother. He heard the attendant leave and Father Sisoy, a hieromonk, cough on the other side of the wall. The monastery clock struck the quarter hour.

The bishop changed his clothes and began to read the prayers before going to sleep. He read these old, long-familiar prayers at-tentively, and at the same time thought about his mother. She had nine children and around forty grandchildren. Once she had lived with her husband, a deacon, in a poor village, lived there for a long time, from the age of seventeen to the age of sixty. The bishop re-membered her from early childhood, almost from when he was three—and how he loved her! Sweet, dear, unforgettable childhood! Why does this forever gone, irretrievable time, why does it seem brighter, more festive and rich, than it was in reality? When he had been sick as a child or a youth, how tender and sensitive his mother had been! And now his prayers were mixed with memories that burned ever brighter, like flames, and the prayers did not interfere with his thoughts of his mother.

When he finished praying, he undressed and lay down, and at once, as soon as it was dark around him, he pictured his late father, his mother, his native village Lesopolye . . . Wheels creaking, sheep bleating, church bells ringing on bright summer mornings, gypsies under the windows—oh, how sweet to think of it! He remembered the priest of Lesopolye, Father Simeon, meek, placid, good-natured; he was skinny and short himself, but his son, a seminarian, was of enormous height and spoke in a furious bass; once he got angry with the cook and yelled at her: "Ah, you Iehudiel's ass!" and Father Simeon, who heard it, did not say a word and was only ashamed because he could not remember where in holy scripture there was mention of such an ass.[2] After him the priest in Lesopolye was Father Demyan, who was a heavy drinker and was sometimes drunk to the point of seeing a green serpent, and he was even nicknamed "Demyan the Serpent-seer." The schoolmaster in Lesopolye was Matvei Nikolaich, a former seminarian, a kind man, not stupid, but also a drunkard; he never beat his students, but for some reason always had a bundle of birch switches hanging on the wall with a perfectly meaningless Latin inscription under it—*Betula kinderbalsamica secuta*.[3] He had a shaggy black dog that he called Syntax.

And the bishop laughed. Five miles from Lesopolye was the village of Obnino, with its wonder-working icon. In summer the icon was carried in procession to all the neighboring villages, and bells rang the whole day, now in one village, now in another, and to the bishop it had seemed then that the air was vibrant with joy, and he (he was then called Pavlusha) had followed after the icon, hatless, barefoot, with naïve faith, with a naïve smile, infinitely happy. In Obnino, he now recalled, there were always many people, and the priest there, Father Alexei, in order to manage the proskomedia, made his deaf nephew Ilarion read the lists "for the living" and "for the dead" sent in with the prosphoras;[4] Ilarion read them, getting five or ten kopecks every once in a while for a liturgy, and only when he was gray and bald, when life had passed, did he suddenly notice written on one slip: "What a fool you are, Ilarion!" At least till the age of fifteen, Pavlusha remained undeveloped and a poor student, so that they even wanted to take him from theological school and send him to work in a shop; once, when he went to the Obnino post office for letters, he looked at the clerks for a long time and then said: "Allow me to ask, how do you receive your salary—monthly or daily?"

The bishop crossed himself and turned over on the other side, in order to sleep and not think anymore.

"My mother has come . . ." he remembered and laughed.

The moon looked in the window, the floor was lit up, and shadows lay on it. A cricket called. In the next room, on the other side of the wall, Father Sisoy snored, and something lonely, orphaned, even vagrant could be heard in his old man's snoring. Sisoy had once been the steward of the diocesan bishop, and now he was called "the former father steward"; he was seventy years old, lived in the monastery ten miles from town, also lived in town, or wherever he happened to be. Three days ago he had come to St. Pankraty's Monastery, and the bishop had let him stay with him, in order to talk with him somehow in leisure moments about various things, local ways . . .

At half past one the bell rang for matins. He heard Father Sisoy cough, grumble something in a displeased voice, then get up and walk barefoot through the rooms.

"Father Sisoy!" the bishop called.

Sisoy went to his room and shortly afterwards appeared, wearing boots now and holding a candle; over his underclothes he had a cassock, on his head an old, faded skullcap.

"I can't sleep," said the bishop, sitting up. "I must be unwell. And what it is, I don't know. A fever!"

"You must've caught cold, Your Grace. You should be rubbed with tallow."

Sisoy stood for a while and yawned: "O Lord, forgive me, a sinner."

"At Yerakin's today they burned electricity," he said. "I doan like it!"

Father Sisoy was old, lean, bent, always displeased with something, and his eyes were angry, protruding, like a crayfish's.

"Doan like it!" he said, going out. "Doan like it, God help 'em all!"

II

The next day, Palm Sunday, the bishop served the liturgy in the town cathedral, then visited the diocesan bishop, visited a certain very sick old general's widow, and finally went home. Between one and two o'clock he had dinner with two dear guests: his old mother and his niece Katya, a girl of about eight. All through dinner the spring sun looked through the window from outside, shining merrily on the white tablecloth and in Katya's red hair. Through the double windows one could hear the noise of rooks in the garden and the singing of starlings.

"It's nine years since we saw each other," the old woman said, "but yesterday in the convent, when I looked at you—Lord! You haven't changed a bit, only you've lost weight, and your beard has grown longer. Ah, Queen of Heaven, Holy Mother! And yesterday during the vigil, nobody could help themselves, everybody wept. Looking at you, I suddenly wept, too—though why, I don't know. It's God's holy will!"

And, in spite of the tenderness with which she said it, she was clearly embarrassed, as if she did not know whether to address him formally or informally, to laugh or not, and seemed to feel more like a deacon's widow than his mother. But Katya gazed without blinking at her uncle, the bishop, as if trying to figure out what sort of man he was. Her hair rose from under the comb and velvet ribbon and stood out like a halo, her nose was turned up, her eyes were sly. Before sitting down to dinner she had broken a tea glass, and now her grandmother, as she talked, kept moving glasses and cups away from her. The bishop listened to his mother and remembered how, many years ago, she used to take him and his brothers and sisters to visit relatives whom she considered wealthy; she was solicitous for her children then, and for her grandchildren now, and so she had brought Katya . . .

"Your sister Varenka has four children," she told him. "Katya here is the oldest, and, God knows what was the cause of it, but my son-in-law, Father Ivan, took sick and died three days before the Dormition.⁵ And my Varenka is now fit to go begging through the world."

"And how is Nikanor?" the bishop asked about his oldest brother.

"All right, thank God. He's all right, and able to get by, Lord be blessed. Only there's one thing: his son Nikolasha, my grandson, didn't want to follow the clerical line, but went to the university to become a doctor. He thinks it's better, but who knows! It's God's holy will."

"Nikolasha cuts up dead people," said Katya, and she spilled water in her lap.

"Sit still, child," the grandmother remarked calmly and took the glass from her. "Pray when you eat."

"We haven't seen each other for so long!" the bishop said and tenderly stroked his mother's shoulder and arm. "I missed you when I was abroad, mama, I missed you terribly."

"I thank you."

"I used to sit by the open window in the evening, alone as could be, they'd start playing music, and homesickness would suddenly come over me, and I thought I'd give anything to go home, to see you . . ."

His mother smiled, brightened up, but at once made a serious face and said:

"I thank you."

His mood changed somehow suddenly. He looked at his mother and could not understand where she got that timid, deferential expression in her face and voice, or why it was there, and he did not recognize her. He felt sad, vexed. Besides, his head ached just as yesterday, he had bad pain in his legs, the fish seemed insipid, tasteless, and he was thirsty all the time . . .

After dinner two rich ladies, landowners, came and spent an hour and a half sitting silently with long faces; the archimandrite,[6] taciturn and slightly deaf, came on business. Then the bells rang for vespers, the sun set behind the woods, and the day was gone. Returning from church, the bishop hastily said his prayers, went to bed, and covered himself warmly.

The memory of the fish he had eaten at dinner was unpleasant. The moonlight disturbed him, and then he heard talking. In a neighboring room, probably the drawing room, Father Sisoy was discussing politics:

"The Japanese are at war now. They're fighting. The Japanese, my dear, are the same as the Montenegrins, the same tribe. They were both under the Turkish yoke."

And then came the voice of Marya Timofeevna:

"So we said our prayers and had tea, and so then we went to see Father Yegor in Novokhatnoe, which is . . ."

And it was "we had tea" or "we drank a glass" time and again, as if all she ever did in her life was drink tea. The bishop slowly, listlessly remembered the seminary, the theological academy. For three years he had taught Greek at the seminary, by which time he could no longer read without glasses; then he was tonsured a monk and was made a school inspector. Then he defended his thesis. When he was thirty-two, they made him rector of the seminary, he was consecrated archimandrite, and life then was so easy, pleasant, it seemed so very long that he could see no end to it. Then he fell ill, lost weight, nearly went blind, and on his doctors' advice had to abandon everything and go abroad.

"And what then?" Sisoy asked in the neighboring room.

"And then we had tea . . ." answered Marya Timofeevna.

"Father, your beard is green!" Katya suddenly said in surprise and laughed.

The bishop recalled that the gray-haired Father Sisoy's beard did indeed have a green tinge, and he laughed.

"Lord God, what a punishment the girl is!" Sisoy said loudly, getting angry. "Spoiled as they come! Sit still!"

The bishop remembered the white church, perfectly new, in which he served when he lived abroad, remembered the sound of the warm sea. His apartment consisted of five rooms, high-ceilinged and bright, there was a new desk in the study, a library. He read a lot, wrote often. And he remembered how homesick he was, how a blind beggar woman sang of love and played the guitar outside his window every day, and each time he listened to her, for some reason he thought of the past. Eight years passed and he was recalled to Russia, and now he was installed as an auxiliary bishop, and the past had all withdrawn somewhere into the distance, the mist, as if it had been a dream . . .

Father Sisoy came into his bedroom with a candle.

"Well," he was surprised, "you're already asleep, Your Grace?"

"Why not?"

"But it's early, ten o'clock, or not even that. I bought a candle to-day, I wanted to rub you with tallow."

"I have a fever . . ." said the bishop, and he sat up. "In fact, I do need something. My head doesn't feel right . . ."

Sisoy removed his shirt and began to rub his chest and back with candle tallow.

"There . . . there . . ." he said. "Lord Jesus Christ . . . There. Today I went to town, visited—what's his name?—the archpriest Sidonsky . . . Had tea with him . . . I doan like him! Lord Jesus Christ . . . There . . . Doan like him at all!"

III

The diocesan bishop, old, very fat, was suffering from rheumatism or gout and had not left his bed for a month. Bishop Pyotr went to see him almost every day and received petitioners in his stead. And now, when he was unwell, he was struck by the emptiness, the pettiness of all that people asked about and wept about; he was angered by their backwardness, their timidity; and the mass of all these petty and unnecessary things oppressed him, and it seemed to him that he now understood the diocesan bishop, who once, when he was young, had written *Lessons on Freedom of Will,* but now seemed totally immersed in trifles, had forgotten everything, and did not think of God. The bishop must have grown unaccustomed to Russian life while abroad, and it was not easy for him; he found the people coarse, the women petitioners boring and stupid, the seminarians and their teachers uncultivated, sometimes savage. And the papers, incoming and outgoing, numbering in the tens of thousands, and what papers! Rural deans throughout the diocese gave the priests, young and old, and even their wives and children, marks for behavior, A's and B's, and sometimes also C's, and it was necessary to talk, read, and write serious papers about all that. And he decidedly did not have a single free moment, his soul trembled all day, and Bishop Pyotr found peace only when he was in church.

He also could not get used to the fear which, without wishing it, he aroused in people, despite his quiet, modest nature. All the people of the province, when he looked at them, seemed to him small, frightened, guilty. In his presence they all grew timid, even old archpriests, they all "plopped down" at his feet, and recently a woman petitioner, the elderly wife of a village priest, had been unable to utter a single word from fear, and so had gone away with nothing. And he, who in his sermons never dared to speak badly of people, never reproached them, because he felt pity for them, lost his temper with petitioners, became angry, flung their petitions to the floor. In all the time he had been there, not a single person had spoken to him sincerely, simply, humanly; even his old mother seemed not the same, not the same at all! And why, one asked, did she talk incessantly and laugh so much with Sisoy, while with him, her son, she was serious, usually silent, bashful, which did not become her at all? The only person who behaved freely in his presence and said whatever he liked was old Sisoy, who had been around bishops all his life and had outlived eleven of them. And that was why he felt at ease with him, though he was unquestionably a difficult, fussy man.

On Tuesday after the liturgy the bishop was at the diocesan bishop's house and received petitioners there, became upset, angry, then went home. He was still unwell and felt like going to bed; but he had no sooner come home than he was informed that Yerakin, a young merchant, a donor, had come on very important business. He had to be received. Yerakin stayed for about an hour, talked very loudly, almost shouted, and it was difficult to understand what he said.

"God grant that!" he said, going out. "Most unfailingly! Depending on the circumstances, Your Episcopal Grace! I wish that!"

After him came an abbess from a distant convent. And when she left, the bells rang for vespers, and he had to go to church.

In the evening the monks sang harmoniously, inspiredly, the office was celebrated by a young hieromonk with a black beard; and the bishop, listening to the verses about the Bridegroom who cometh at midnight and about the chamber that is adorned,[7] felt, not repentance for his sins, not sorrow, but inner peace, silence, and was carried in his thoughts into the distant past, into his childhood and youth, when they had also sung about the Bridegroom and the chamber, and now that past appeared alive, beautiful, joyful, as it probably never had been. And perhaps in the other world, in the other life, we shall remember the distant past, our life here, with the same feeling. Who knows! The bishop sat in the sanctuary, it was dark there. Tears flowed down his face. He was thinking that here he had achieved everything possible for a man in his position, he had faith, and yet not everything was clear, something was still lacking, he did not want to die; and it still seemed that there was some most important thing which he did not have, of which he had once vaguely dreamed, and in the present he was stirred by the same hope for the future that he had had in childhood, and in the academy, and abroad.

"They're singing so well today!" he thought, listening to the choir. "So well!"

IV

On Thursday he served the liturgy in the cathedral, and there was the washing of feet.[8] When the church service ended and people were going home, it was sunny, warm, cheerful, the water ran noisily in the ditches, and from the fields outside town came the ceaseless singing of larks, tender, calling all to peace. The trees were awake and smiled amiably, and over them, God knows how far, went the fathomless, boundless blue sky.

On coming home, Bishop Pyotr had tea, then changed his clothes, went to bed, and told his cell attendant to close the window blinds. The bedroom became dark. What weariness, though, what pain in his legs and back, a heavy, cold pain, and what a ringing in his ears! He lay without sleeping for a long time, as it now seemed to him, for a very long time, and it was some trifle that kept him from sleeping, that flickered in his brain as soon as his eyes closed. As on the previous day, voices, the clink of glasses and teaspoons came through the wall from neighboring rooms . . . Marya Timofeevna, merry and bantering, was telling Father Sisoy something, and he responded sullenly, in a displeased voice: "Oh, them! Hah! What else!" And again the bishop felt vexed and then hurt that the old woman behaved in an ordinary and simple way with strangers, but with him, her son, was timid, spoke rarely, and did not say what she wanted to say, and even, as it had seemed to him all those days, kept looking for an excuse to stand up, because she was embarrassed to sit in his presence. And his father? If he were alive, he would probably be unable to utter a single word before him . . .

Something fell on the floor in the next room and smashed; it must have been Katya dropping a cup or a saucer, because Father Sisoy suddenly spat and said angrily:

"The girl's a sheer punishment, Lord, forgive me, a sinner! There's never enough with her!"

Then it became quiet, only sounds from outside reached him. And when the bishop opened his eyes, he saw Katya in his room, standing motionless and looking at him. Her red hair, as usual, rose from behind her comb like a halo.

"It's you, Katya?" he asked. "Who keeps opening and closing the door downstairs?"

"I don't hear it," Katya said and listened.

"There, somebody just passed by."

"It's in your stomach, uncle!"

He laughed and patted her head.

"So you say cousin Nikolasha cuts up dead people?" he asked after a pause.

"Yes. He's studying."

"Is he kind?"

"Kind enough. Only he drinks a lot of vodka."

"And what illness did your father die of?"

"Papa was weak and very, very thin, and suddenly—in his throat. I got sick then and so did my brother Fedya, all in the throat. Papa died, and we got well."

Her chin trembled and tears welled up in her eyes and rolled slowly down her cheeks.

"Your Grace," she said in a high little voice, now crying bitterly, "mama and all of us were left in such misery . . . Give us a little money . . . Be so kind . . . dear uncle! . . ."

He, too, became tearful and for a long time was too upset to utter a word, then he patted her head, touched her shoulder, and said:

"Very well, very well, child. The bright resurrection of Christ will come, and then we'll talk . . . I'll help you . . . I will . . ."

Quietly, timidly, his mother came in and crossed herself before the icons. Noticing that he was not asleep, she asked:

"Would you like some soup?"

"No, thank you . . ." he replied. "I don't want any."

"You don't look well . . . seems to me. But then how could you not get sick! On your feet the whole day, the whole day—my God, it's painful even to look at you. Well, Easter's not far off, God grant you'll be able to rest, then we can talk, and I won't bother you with my talk now. Let's go, Katechka, let His Grace sleep."

And he remembered how, a long, long time ago, when he was still a boy, she had spoken with a rural dean in just the same jokingly deferential tone . . . Only by her extraordinarily kind eyes and the timid, worried glance she cast at him as she left the room, could one see that she was his mother. He closed his eyes and it seemed he slept, but twice he heard the clock strike and Father Sisoy cough on the other side of the wall. His mother came in once more and gazed at him timidly for a moment. Someone drove up to the porch in a coach or a carriage, judging by the sound. Suddenly there came a knock, the bang of a door: the attendant came into his bedroom.

"Your Grace!" he called.

"What?"

"The horses are ready, it's time to go to the Lord's Passion."[9]

"What time is it?"

"A quarter past seven."

He dressed and drove to the cathedral. He had to stand motionless in the middle of the church through all twelve Gospel readings, and the first Gospel, the longest, the most beautiful, he read himself. A vigorous, healthy mood came over him. The first Gospel—

"Now is the Son of Man glorified"[10]—he knew by heart; and as he read, he raised his eyes from time to time and saw on both sides a whole sea of lights, heard the sizzle of candles, but, as in previous years, he was unable to see the people, and it seemed to him that they were the same people as in his childhood and youth, that they would be the same every year, but for how long—God only knew.

His father had been a deacon, his grandfather a priest, his great-grandfather a deacon, and all his ancestry, perhaps since the time when Russia embraced Christianity,[11] had belonged to the clergy, and the love for church services, the clergy, the ringing of bells, was innate in him, deep, ineradicable; in church, especially when he celebrated the office himself, he felt active, vigorous, happy. And so he did now. Only when the eighth Gospel had been read, he felt that his voice had weakened, even his coughing had become inaudible, his head ached badly, and he was troubled by a fear that he was about to fall down. And indeed his legs had gone quite numb, so that he gradually ceased to feel them, and it was incomprehensible to him how and on what he was standing, and why he did not fall down . . .

When the service ended, it was a quarter to twelve. Returning home, the bishop undressed at once and lay down, without even saying his prayers. He was unable to speak, and it seemed to him that he would now be unable to stand. As he pulled the blanket over him, he suddenly had a longing to be abroad, an unbearable longing! He thought he would give his life only not to see those pathetic, cheap blinds, the low ceilings, not to breathe that oppressive monastery smell. If there had been just one person to whom he could talk, unburden his soul!

For a long time he heard someone's footsteps in the next room and could not remember who it was. At last the door opened and Sisoy came in, holding a candle and a teacup.

"In bed already, Your Grace?" he asked. "And I've come because I want to rub you with vodka and vinegar. If you rub it in well, it can be of great benefit. Lord Jesus Christ . . . There . . . There . . . And I've just been to our monastery . . . I doan like it! I'll leave here tomorrow, Your Grace, I want no more of it. Lord Jesus Christ . . . There . . ."

Sisoy was unable to stay long in one place, and it seemed to him that he had been living in St. Pankraty's Monastery for a whole year by then. And, above all, listening to him, it was hard to understand where his home was, whether he loved anyone or anything, whether he believed in God . . . He did not understand himself why he was a monk, and he did not think about it, and the time of his tonsuring had long been erased from his memory; it looked as if he had simply been born a monk.

"I'll leave tomorrow. God bless the lot of them!"

"I'd like to talk with you . . . I never can get around to it," the bishop said softly, forcing himself. "I don't know anyone or anything here."

"So be it, if you like I'll stay till Sunday, but no longer. I want none of it! Pah!"

"What sort of bishop am I?" the bishop went on softly. "I should be a village priest, a deacon . . . or a simple monk . . . All this oppresses me, oppresses me . . ."

"What? Lord Jesus Christ . . . There . . . Well, go to sleep, Your Grace! . . . No point! Forget it! Good night!"

The bishop did not sleep all night. And in the morning, around eight o'clock, he began to have intestinal bleeding. The cell attendant became frightened and ran first to the archimandrite, then for the monastery doctor, Ivan Andreich, who lived in town. The doctor, a stout old man with a long gray beard, examined the bishop for a long time, and kept shaking his head and scowling, then said:

"You know, Your Grace, you've got typhoid fever."

Within an hour the bishop became very thin from the bleeding, pale, pinched, his face shrank, his eyes were now big, he looked older, smaller, and it seemed to him that he was thinner, weaker, more insignificant than anyone, that all that had once been had gone somewhere very far away and would no longer repeat itself, would not be continued.

"How good!" he thought. "How good!"

His old mother came. Seeing his shrunken face and big eyes, she became frightened, fell on her knees by his bed, and started kissing his face, shoulders, hands. And to her, too, it seemed that he was thinner, weaker, and more insignificant than anyone, and she no longer remembered that he was a bishop, and she kissed him like a child very near and dear to her.

"Pavlusha, my darling," she said, "my dear one! . . . My little son! . . . What makes you like this? Pavlusha, answer me!"

Katya, pale, stern, stood nearby and did not understand what was the matter with her uncle, why there was such suffering on her grandmother's face, why she was saying such touching, sad words. And he could no longer say a word, he understood nothing, and imagined that he was now a simple, ordinary man, walking briskly, merrily across the fields, tapping his stick, and over him was the broad sky, flooded with sunlight, and he was free as a bird and could go wherever he liked!

"My little son, Pavlusha, answer me!" said the old woman. "What's the matter with you? My dear one!"

"Don't trouble His Grace," Sisoy said crossly, passing through the room. "Let him sleep . . . there's no point . . . forget it! . . ."

Three doctors came, held a consultation, then left. The day was long, unbelievably long, then night came and lasted a very, very long time, and towards morning on Saturday the cell attendant went up to the old woman, who was lying on a sofa in the drawing room, and asked her to go to the bedroom: the bishop had bid the world farewell.

The next day was Easter. There were forty-two churches and six monasteries in the town; a resounding, joyful ringing of bells hung over the town from morning till evening, never silent, stirring up the spring air; the birds sang, the sun shone brightly. It was noisy on the big market square, swings were swinging, barrel organs playing, accordions shrieked, drunken voices shouted. In the afternoon people went driving about the main streets—in short, all was cheerful, all was well, just as it had been the year before, and as it would also be, in all probability, the year after.

A month later a new auxiliary bishop was appointed, and no one thought of Bishop Pyotr anymore. Soon he was completely forgotten. And only the old woman, the mother of the deceased, who now lives with her deacon son-in-law in a forsaken little provincial town, when she went out before evening to meet her cow, and got together by the pasture with other women, would begin telling them about her children and grandchildren, and how she once had a son who was a bishop, and she said it timidly, afraid they would not believe her . . .

And indeed not everyone believed her.

APRIL 1902

The Fiancée

I

It was ten o'clock in the evening, and a full moon was shining over the garden. In the Shumins' house the vigil ordered by the grandmother, Marfa Mikhailovna, had just ended, and now Nadya—she had gone out to the garden for a moment—could see the table being set for a light meal in the reception room, and her grandmother bustling about in her magnificent silk dress; Father Andrei, the archpriest of the cathedral, was talking about something with Nadya's mother, Nina Ivanovna, and now, through the window in the evening light, her mother for some reason looked very young; next to her stood Father Andrei's son, Andrei Andreich, listening attentively.

The garden was quiet, cool, and shadows lay dark and peaceful on the ground. From somewhere far away, very far, probably outside town, came the calling of frogs. May, sweet May, was in the air! She breathed deeply and wanted to think that, not here, but somewhere under the sky, above the trees, far outside town, in the fields and woods, spring's own life was now unfolding, mysterious, beautiful, rich, and holy, inaccessible to the understanding of weak, sinful human beings. And for some reason she wanted to cry.

She, Nadya, was already twenty-three years old; since the age of sixteen she had been dreaming passionately of marriage, and now at last she was the fiancée of Andrei Andreich, the same one who was standing behind the window; she liked him, the wedding was already set for the seventh of July, and yet there was no joy, she slept badly at night, her gaiety had vanished . . . From the open window to the basement, where the kitchen was, came the sounds of people hurrying about, of knives chopping, of the door slamming shut on its pulley; there was a smell of roast turkey and pickled cherries. And for some reason it seemed that it would be like this all her life, without change, without end!

Now someone came out of the house and stood on the porch; it was Alexander Timofeich, or simply Sasha, a guest, come from Moscow ten days before. Long ago a distant relative, Marya Petrovna, an impoverished widow, a small, thin, ailing gentlewoman, used to come to the grandmother for charity. She had a son Sasha. For some reason he was said to be a wonderful artist, and when his mother died, the grandmother, for the salvation of her soul, sent him to Komissarov's school in Moscow; two years later he transferred to a school of fine arts, stayed there for nearly fifteen years, and finished up none too brilliantly in architecture, but he did not go into architecture anyway, but worked in one of the Moscow printing houses. He came to the grandmother's almost every summer, usually very sick, to rest and recuperate.

He was now wearing a buttoned-up frock coat and shabby duck trousers frayed at the bottoms. His shirt was unironed, and his entire look was somehow unfresh. Very thin, with large eyes and long, slender fingers, bearded, dark, but, for all that, handsome. He was accustomed to the Shumins, as to his own family, and felt at home with them. And the room he lived in there had long been known as Sasha's room.

Standing on the porch, he saw Nadya and went over to her.

"It's nice here," he said.

"Of course it's nice. You ought to stay till autumn."

"Yes, that's probably so. Perhaps I'll stay with you till September."

He laughed for no reason and sat down beside her.

"And I'm sitting here and looking at mama," said Nadya. "She looks so young from here! My mama has her weaknesses, of course," she added after a pause, "but still she's an extraordinary woman."

"Yes, she's nice . . ." Sasha agreed. "Your mama is, of course, a very kind and dear woman in her own way, but . . . how shall I put it? Early this morning I went to your kitchen, and there were four servants sleeping right on the floor, no beds, rags instead of sheets, stench, bedbugs, cockroaches . . . The same as it was twenty years ago, no change at all. Well, your grandmother, God be with her, that's how grandmothers are; but your mama speaks French, takes part in theatricals. It seems she might understand."

When Sasha spoke, he held up two long, skinny fingers in front of his listener.

"I find everything here somehow wild, because I'm unused to it," he went on. "Devil knows, nobody's doing anything. Your mother spends the whole day strolling about like some sort of duchess, your grandmother also doesn't do anything, and neither do you. And your fiancé, Andrei Andreich, doesn't do anything either."

Nadya had heard it all last year and, it seemed, the year before last, and she knew that Sasha could not think differently, and it used to make her laugh, but now for some reason she felt annoyed.

"That's all the same old, boring stuff," she said and got up. "Try to invent something newer."

He laughed and also got up, and they both went towards the house. Tall, beautiful, trim, she now looked very healthy and well-dressed beside him; she sensed it and felt sorry for him and, for some reason, slightly awkward.

"And you say a lot that's unnecessary," she said. "You just talked about my Andrei, but you don't know him."

"My Andrei . . . God be with your Andrei! It's your youth I feel sorry for."

When they went into the reception room, everyone was just sitting down to supper. The grandmother, or granny, as she was known at home, very stout, homely, with thick eyebrows and a little mustache, spoke loudly, and from her voice and manner of speaking it was clear that she was the head of the household. She owned the shopping stalls in the market and the old house with columns and a garden, but every morning she prayed that God would save her from ruin, and with tears at that. Her daughter-in-law, Nadya's mother, Nina Ivanovna, blond, tightly corseted, in a pince-nez, and with diamonds on every finger; and Father Andrei, an old man, lean, toothless, and with a look as if he were about to say something very funny; and his son, Andrei Andreich, Nadya's fiancé, stout and handsome, with wavy hair, resembling an actor or an artist—all three were talking about hypnotism.

"You'll recover after a week with me," said granny, addressing

Sasha, "only you must eat more. Just look at you!" she said. "It's frightful! A real prodigal son, if I ever saw one!"

"I have scattered the riches which thou gavest me," Father Andrei said slowly, with laughing eyes. "Accursed, I have fed with senseless swine . . ."[1]

"I love my papa," said Andrei Andreich, touching his father's shoulder. "A nice old man. A kind old man."

They all fell silent. Sasha suddenly burst out laughing and put his napkin to his mouth.

"So you believe in hypnotism?" Father Andrei asked Nina Ivanovna.

"I cannot, of course, maintain that I believe in it," Nina Ivanovna replied, giving her face a serious, even stern, expression, "but I must admit that there is much in nature that is mysterious and incomprehensible."

"I fully agree with you, though I must add for my own part that faith considerably diminishes the sphere of the mysterious for us."

A big, very fat turkey was served. Father Andrei and Nina Ivanovna continued their conversation. The diamonds glittered on Nina Ivanovna's fingers, then tears began to glitter in her eyes, she became upset.

"Though I dare not argue with you," she said, "you must agree that there are a great many insoluble riddles in life."

"Not a single one, I dare assure you."

After supper Andrei Andreich played the violin and Nina Ivanovna accompanied him on the piano. Ten years ago he had graduated from the university with a degree in philology, but he did not work anywhere, had no definite occupation, and only participated occasionally in concerts of a charitable nature; and in town he was called an artiste.

Andrei Andreich played; everyone listened silently. The samovar boiled quietly on the table, and only Sasha drank tea. Then, as it struck twelve, a string suddenly broke on the violin; everyone laughed and began bustling about and saying good-bye.

After seeing her fiancé off, Nadya went to her room upstairs, where she lived with her mother (the grandmother occupied the lower floor). Below, in the reception room, the lights were being put out, but Sasha still sat and drank tea. He always drank tea for a long time, Moscow-style, up to seven glasses at a time. Long after she had undressed and gone to bed, Nadya could hear the servants tidying up downstairs, and her grandmother being angry. At last everything quieted down, and all that could be heard was Sasha coughing occasionally in a bass voice downstairs in his room.

II

When Nadya woke up, it must have been about two o'clock. Dawn was breaking. Somewhere far away a night watchman was rapping. She did not want to sleep, her bed was very soft, uncomfortable. Nadya, as on all previous nights that May, sat up in bed and began to think. Her thoughts were the same as last night, monotonous, superfluous, importunate—thoughts of how Andrei Andreich had begun courting her and proposed to her, how she had accepted and had then gradually come to appreciate this kind, intelligent man. But now, for some reason, with less than a month to go till the wedding, she had begun to experience fear, anxiety, as if something uncertain and oppressive awaited her.

"Tick-tock, tick-tock . . ." the watchman rapped lazily. "Tick-tock . . ."

Through the big old window she can see the garden, and further away the densely flowering lilac bushes, sleepy and languid from the cold; and dense white mist is slowly drifting towards the lilacs, wanting to cover them. Drowsy rooks are cawing in the distant trees.

"My God, what makes it so oppressive for me?"

Perhaps every fiancée feels the same way before her wedding. Who knows! Or is it Sasha's influence? But Sasha has been saying the same thing for several years on end, as if by rote, and when he says it, it seems naïve and strange. But, anyway, why can she not get Sasha out of her head? Why?

The watchman had stopped rapping long ago. Under the window and in the garden birds began making noise, the mist left the garden, everything around brightened up with the light of spring, as with a smile. Soon the whole garden revived, warmed and caressed by the sun, and dewdrops sparkled like diamonds on the leaves; and that morning the old, long-neglected garden seemed so young, so festive.

Granny was already awake. Sasha coughed in a rough bass. There was the sound of the samovar being prepared downstairs, of chairs being moved around.

The hours passed slowly. Nadya had long been up and strolling in the garden, but the morning still dragged on.

Then Nina Ivanovna came, teary-eyed, with a glass of mineral water. She was taken up with spiritism, homeopathy, read a lot, liked to talk of the doubts to which she was susceptible, and all that, as it seemed to Nadya, contained a deep, mysterious meaning. Now Nadya kissed her mother and walked beside her.

"What were you crying about, mother?" she asked.

"Last night I began reading a story describing an old man and his daughter. The old man works in some office and, well, so his superior falls in love with his daughter. I didn't finish it, but there's a passage where I couldn't help crying," said Nina Ivanovna, and she sipped from the glass. "This morning I remembered it and cried a little more."

"And I've been feeling so cheerless all these days," said Nadya, after some silence. "Why can't I sleep nights?"

"I don't know, dear. When I can't sleep at night, I close my eyes very, very tight, like this, and picture Anna Karenina to myself, how she walks and speaks, or I picture something historical, from the ancient world . . ."

Nadya felt that her mother did not and could not understand her. She felt it for the first time in her life, and even became frightened, wanted to hide herself; and she went to her room.

At two o'clock they sat down to dinner. It was Wednesday, a fast day, and therefore the grandmother was served a meatless borscht and bream with kasha.

To tease the grandmother, Sasha ate both his own meat soup and the meatless borscht. He joked all the while they were eating, but his jokes came out clumsy, invariably calculated to moralize, and it came out as not funny at all when, before producing a witticism, he raised his very long, emaciated, dead-looking fingers, and the thought occurred to one that he was very ill and was perhaps not long for this world, and one pitied him to the point of tears.

After dinner the grandmother went to her room to rest. Nina Ivanovna played the piano for a little while and then she also left.

"Ah, dear Nadya," Sasha began his usual after-dinner conversation, "if only you would listen to me! If only you would!"

She was sitting deep in an old armchair, her eyes closed, while he quietly paced up and down the room.

"If you'd just go and study!" he said. "Only enlightened and holy people are interesting, only they are needed. The more such people there are, the sooner the Kingdom of God will come on earth. Of your town then there will gradually be no stone left upon stone—everything will turn upside down, everything will change as if by magic. And there will be huge, magnificent houses here, wonderful gardens, extraordinary fountains, remarkable people . . . But that's not the main thing. The main thing is that the crowd as we think of it, as it is now, this evil will not exist then, because every man will have faith, and every man will know what he lives for, and no one will seek support from the crowd. My dear, my darling, go! Show them all that this stagnant, gray, sinful life is sickening to you. Show it to yourself at least!"

"Impossible, Sasha. I'm getting married."

"Ah, enough! Who needs that?"

They went out to the garden and strolled a bit.

"And however it may be, my dear, you must perceive, you must understand, how impure, how immoral this idle life of yours is," Sasha went on. "You must understand, for instance, that if you, and your mother, and your dear granny do nothing, it means that someone else is working for you, that you are feeding on someone else's life, and is that pure, is it not dirty?"

Nadya wanted to say: "Yes, that's true," she wanted to say that she understood, but tears came to her eyes, she suddenly grew quiet, shrank into herself, and went to her room.

Towards evening Andrei Andreich came and, as usual, played his violin for a long time. Generally he was untalkative, and liked the violin, perhaps, because he could be silent while he played. After ten, going home, with his coat already on, he embraced Nadya and greedily began kissing her face, shoulders, hands.

"My dear, my sweet, my lovely! . . ." he murmured. "Oh, how happy I am! I'm mad with ecstasy!"

And it seemed to her that she had already heard it long ago, very long ago, or read it somewhere . . . in a novel, old, tattered, long since abandoned.

In the reception room Sasha sat at the table and drank tea, the saucer perched on his five long fingers; granny was playing patience, Nina Ivanovna was reading. The flame sputtered in the icon lamp, and everything seemed quiet and happy. Nadya said good night, went upstairs to her room, lay down, and fell asleep at once. But, as on the previous night, she awoke with the first light of dawn. She did not want to sleep, her soul was uneasy, heavy. She sat, her head resting on her knees, and thought about her fiancé, about the wedding . . . She remembered for some reason that her mother had not loved her deceased husband and now owned nothing and was totally dependent on her mother-in-law, granny. And, think as she might, Nadya could not figure out why up to now she had seen something special, extraordinary, in her mother, why she had failed to notice the simple, ordinary, unhappy woman.

And Sasha was not asleep downstairs—she could hear him coughing. He is a strange, naïve man, thought Nadya, and there is something absurd in his dreams, in all his wonderful gardens and extraordinary fountains. But for some reason there was so much that was beautiful in his naïveté, even in that absurdity, that the moment she merely thought whether she should go and study, her whole heart, her whole breast felt a cold shiver and was flooded with a feeling of joy, ecstasy.

"But better not think, better not think . . ." she whispered. "I mustn't think of it."

"Tick-tock . . ." the watchman rapped somewhere far away. "Tick-tock . . . tick-tock . . ."

III

In the middle of June Sasha suddenly became bored and began preparing to go to Moscow.

"I can't live in this town," he said glumly. "No running water, no drains! I feel queasy eating dinner—there's the most impossible filth in the kitchen . . ."

"Wait a bit, prodigal son!" the grandmother persuaded him, for some reason in a whisper. "The wedding's on the seventh!"

"I don't want to."

"You were going to stay with us till September."

"But now I don't want to. I must work!"

The summer had turned damp and cold, the trees were wet, everything in the garden looked dismal, uninviting, one did indeed feel like working. In the rooms downstairs and upstairs, unfamiliar women's voices were heard, the grandmother's sewing machine clattered: they were hurrying with the trousseau. Of fur coats alone Nadya was to come with six, and the cheapest of them, in the grandmother's words, cost three hundred roubles! The fuss annoyed Sasha; he sat in his room and felt angry; but they still persuaded him to stay, and he promised not to leave before the first of July.

The time passed quickly. On St. Peter's day,[2] after dinner, Andrei Andreich and Nadya went to Moscovskaya Street for one more look at the house that had been rented and long since prepared for the young couple. It was a two-story house, but so far only the upper story was furnished. In the reception room a shiny floor, painted to look like parquet, bentwood chairs, a grand piano, a music stand for the violin. It smelled of paint. On the wall hung a big oil painting in a gilt frame: a naked lady, and beside her a purple jug with the handle broken off.

"A wonderful painting," said Andrei Andreich, sighing with respect. "By the artist Shishmachevsky."

Further on was the drawing room, with a round table, a sofa, and armchairs upholstered in bright blue material. Over the sofa, a big photographic portrait of Father Andrei wearing a kamilavka[3] and medals. Then they went into the dining room with its cupboard, then into the bedroom; there in the half-darkness two beds stood next to each other, and it looked as if, when the bedroom was being decorated, it was with the idea that it should always be good there and could not be otherwise. Andrei Andreich led Nadya through the rooms, his arm all the while around her waist; and she felt herself weak, guilty, she hated all these rooms, beds, armchairs, was nauseated by the naked lady. It was clear to her now that she had stopped loving Andrei Andreich, or perhaps had never loved him; but how to say it, whom to say it to, and why, she did not and could not figure out, though she thought about it every day and every night . . . He held her by the waist, spoke so tenderly, so modestly, was so happy going around this apartment of his; while in all of it she saw only banality, stupid, naïve, unbearable banality, and his arm that encircled her waist seemed to her as hard and cold as an iron hoop. And she was ready to run away, to burst into tears, to throw herself out the window at any moment. Andrei Andreich brought her to the bathroom and touched the faucet built into the wall, and water suddenly flowed.

"How about that?" he said and laughed. "I ordered a hundred-bucket cistern installed in the attic, and now you and I will have water."

They strolled through the courtyard, then went out to the street and got into a cab. Dust flew up in thick clouds, and it looked as if it was about to rain.

"You're not cold?" asked Andrei Andreich, squinting from the dust.

She did not answer.

"Yesterday, you remember, Sasha reproached me for not doing anything," he said after a short pause. "Well, he's right! Infinitely right! I don't do anything and can't do anything. Why is that, my dear? Why am I repulsed even by the thought that one day I might stick a cockade to my forehead and go into government service?[4] Why am I so ill at ease when I see a lawyer or a Latin teacher, or a member of the town council? O Mother Russia! O Mother Russia, how many idle and useless people you still carry on your back! How many you have who are like me, O long-suffering one!"

And he generalized from the fact that he did nothing, and saw it as a sign of the times.

"When we're married," he went on, "we'll go to the country together, my dear, we'll work there! We'll buy a small piece of land with a garden, a river, we'll work, observe life . . . Oh, how good it will be!"

He took his hat off and his hair flew in the wind, and she listened to him, thinking: "God, I want to be home! God!" Almost in front of the house they overtook Father Andrei.

"There goes my father!" Andrei Andreich joyfully waved his hat. "I love my papa, I really do," he said as he paid the cabby. "A nice old man. A kind old man."

Nadya went into the house angry, unwell, thinking that there would be guests all night, that she would have to entertain them, smile, listen to the violin, listen to all sorts of nonsense, and talk only of the wedding. Her grandmother, imposing, magnificent in her silk dress, haughty, as she always seemed when there were guests, sat by the samovar. Father Andrei came in with his sly smile.

"I have the pleasure and blessed consolation of finding you in good health," he said to the grandmother, and it was hard to tell whether he was joking or serious.

IV

The wind rapped on the windows, on the roof; a whistling was heard, and the household goblin in the stove sang his little song, plaintively and gloomily. It was past midnight. Everyone in the house was already in bed, but no one slept, and Nadya kept having the feeling that someone was playing the violin downstairs. There was a sharp knock, probably a blind being torn off its hinge. A moment later Nina Ivanovna came in in just her nightgown, holding a candle.

"What was that knocking, Nadya?"

Her mother, her hair plaited in a single braid, smiling timidly, seemed older, smaller, plainer on this stormy night. Nadya recalled how still recently she had considered her mother an extraordinary woman and had proudly listened to the words she spoke; and now she could not recall those words; everything that came to her mind was so weak, so useless.

From the stove came the singing of several basses, and one could even hear: "O-o-oh, my Go-o-od!" Nadya sat up in bed and suddenly seized herself strongly by the hair and broke into sobs.

"Mama, mama," she said, "my dear mama, if only you knew what's happening to me! I beg you, I implore you, let me go away! I implore you!"

"Where?" asked Nina Ivanovna, not understanding, and she sat on the bed. "Go away where?"

Nadya wept for a long time and could not utter a word.

"Let me go away from this town!" she said at last. "There should not be and will not be any wedding, understand that! I don't love this man . . . I can't even speak of him."

"No, my dear, no," Nina Ivanovna began speaking quickly, terribly frightened. "Calm yourself—it's because you're in a bad mood. It will pass. It happens. You've probably had a falling out with Andrei, but lovers' trials end in smiles."

"Oh, leave me, mama, leave me!" Nadya sobbed.

"Yes," said Nina Ivanovna after a silence. "Not long ago you were a child, a little girl, and now you're already a fiancée. There's a constant turnover of matter in nature. And you won't notice how you yourself become a mother and an old woman and have a daughter as rebellious as mine is."

"My dear, kind one, you're intelligent, you're unhappy," said Nadya, "you're very unhappy—why do you talk in banalities? For God's sake, why?"

Nina Ivanovna wanted to say something but was unable to utter a word, sobbed, and went to her room. The basses droned in the stove again, and it suddenly became frightening. Nadya jumped out of bed and went quickly to her mother. Nina Ivanovna, her face tear-stained, lay in bed with a blue blanket over her, holding a book.

"Mama, listen to me!" said Nadya. "I implore you to perceive and understand! Simply understand how shallow and humiliating our life is. My eyes have been opened and I see it all now. And what is your Andrei Andreich? He's not intelligent, mama! Lord God! Understand, mama, he's stupid!"

Nina Ivanovna sat up abruptly.

"You and your grandmother torment me!" she said with a sob. "I want to live! To live!" she repeated and beat her breast twice with her little fist. "Give me freedom! I'm still young, I want to live, and you've made an old woman out of me! . . ."

She wept bitterly, lay down, and curled up under her blanket, and looked so small, pitiful, silly. Nadya went to her room, got dressed, and, sitting by the window, waited for morning. She sat all night thinking, and someone outside kept rapping on the blinds and whistling away.

In the morning the grandmother complained that during the night the wind had blown down all the apples in the orchard and broken an old plum tree. It was a gray, dull, joyless day, fit for lighting the lamps; everyone complained about the cold, and rain rapped on the windows. After tea Nadya went to Sasha's room and, without saying a word, knelt by the armchair in the corner and covered her face with her hands.

"What is it?" asked Sasha.

"I can't . . ." she said. "How could I have lived here before, I can't understand, I can't perceive! I despise my fiancé, I despise myself, I despise all this idle, meaningless life . . ."

"Well, well . . ." said Sasha, not yet understanding what was the matter. "It's nothing . . . It's all right."

"This life is hateful to me," Nadya went on, "I can't stand it here one more day. Tomorrow I'll go away. Take me with you, for God's sake!"

For a moment Sasha looked at her in amazement; finally he understood and was happy as a child. He waved his arms and began shuffling in his slippers, as if dancing for joy.

"Splendid!" he said, rubbing his hands. "God, how good!"

And she looked at him without blinking, with big, enamoured eyes, as if spellbound, expecting him to say something significant at once, something of boundless importance; he had not said anything yet, but it seemed to her that something vast and new was opening out before her, something she had not known before, and she now looked at him, filled with expectations, ready for anything, even death.

"I'm leaving tomorrow," he said, after some thought, "and you will come to the station to see me off . . . I'll bring your luggage in my trunk and buy you a ticket; at the third bell you'll get on the train, and—off we'll go. You'll keep me company as far as Moscow and then go on by yourself to Petersburg. You have a passport?"[5]

"Yes."

"I swear you won't regret it and won't repent of it," Sasha said with enthusiasm. "You'll go, you'll study, and then let your destiny carry you on. Once you've turned your life around, the rest will change. The main thing is to turn your life around, and the rest doesn't matter. So, then, tomorrow we go?"

"Oh, yes! For God's sake!"

It seemed to Nadya that she was very agitated, that her soul was heavy as never before, that now, right up to their departure, she would have to suffer and have tormenting thoughts; but as soon as she went to her room upstairs and lay down on the bed, she fell asleep and slept soundly, her face tear-stained and smiling, till evening.

V

They sent for a cab. Nadya, already in her hat and coat, went upstairs to look once more at her mother and at all that had been hers; she stood in her room by the still-warm bed, looked around, then went quietly to her mother. Nina Ivanovna was asleep, it was quiet in the room. Nadya kissed her mother and straightened her hair, stood there for a minute or two . . . Then she unhurriedly went downstairs.

Outside it was raining hard. A cab with its top up, all wet, was standing by the porch.

"There won't be room enough for you, Nadya," said the grandmother, as a servant began putting in the trunks. "Who wants to go and see him off in such weather! Stay home! Look how it's raining!"

Nadya wanted to say something and could not. Sasha helped her into the cab, and covered her legs with a plaid. Then he got in beside her.

"Have a good trip! God bless you!" the grandmother called from the porch. "And you, Sasha, write to us from Moscow!"

"All right. Good-bye, granny!"

"May the Queen of Heaven keep you!"

"Well, some weather!" said Sasha.

Only now did Nadya begin to cry. Now it was clear to her that she was bound to leave, something she had not yet believed when she was saying good-bye to her grandmother, when she was looking at her mother. Farewell, town! And suddenly she remembered everything: Andrei, and his father, and the new apartment, and the naked lady with the vase; and now it was all not frightening, not oppressive, but naïve, petty, and dropping further and further behind her. And when they got in the carriage and the train started, this whole past, so big and serious, shrank into a little lump, and a vast, expansive future, which until now had been so little noticeable, began to unfold. Rain rapped on the carriage windows, only green fields could be seen, telegraph poles with birds on the wires flashed by, and joy suddenly took her breath away: she remembered that she was on the way to freedom, on the way to study, and it was the same as what very long ago was called going to the Cossacks.[6] She laughed, and wept, and prayed.

"It's all ri-i-ight!" said Sasha, grinning. "It's all ri-i-ight!"

VI

Autumn passed, then winter passed. Nadya was already very homesick, and thought every day of her mother, her grandmother, thought of Sasha. The letters that came from home were quiet, kind, and everything seemed to have been forgiven and forgotten. In May after examinations she went home, healthy and cheerful, and stopped in Moscow on her way to see Sasha. He was the same as last summer: bearded, his hair disheveled, in the same frock coat and duck trousers, with the same large, beautiful eyes; but he looked unhealthy, worn out, had aged and lost weight, and kept coughing. And for some reason Nadya found him gray, provincial.

"My God, Nadya's come!" he said and laughed merrily. "My dearest, my darling!"

They sat for a while in the printing shop, where it was smoky and smelled strongly, suffocatingly, of India ink and paint; then they went to his room, where it was also smoky, messy; on the table, next to the cold samovar, was a cracked plate with a piece of dark paper, and on the table and the floor a multitude of dead flies.[7] And here everything showed that Sasha's personal life was slovenly, that he lived anyhow, with a total disdain of comfort, and if anyone had begun talking to him about his personal happiness, about his personal life, about anyone's love for him, he would have understood none of it and would only have laughed.

"It's all right, everything worked out very well," Nadya told him hurriedly. "Mama came to see me in Petersburg during the autumn and told me that my grandmother wasn't angry, but only kept going into my room and crossing the walls."

Sasha looked cheerful, but kept coughing and spoke in a cracked voice, and Nadya peered at him and could not understand whether he was indeed seriously ill or it only seemed so to her.

"Sasha, my dear," she said, "you're quite ill!"

"No, it's nothing. I'm sick, but not very . . ."

"Ah, my God!" Nadya said worriedly, "why don't you go to a doctor, why don't you look after your health? My dear, sweet Sasha," she said, and tears poured from her eyes, and for some reason Andrei Andreich appeared in her imagination, and the naked lady with the vase, and all her past life, which now seemed as distant as her childhood; and she wept because Sasha no longer seemed so new, intelligent, interesting to her as he had last year. "Dear Sasha, you're very, very ill. I don't know what I wouldn't do to keep you from being so pale and thin. I owe you so much! You can't even imagine how much you've done for me, my good Sasha! In fact, you're now the nearest and dearest person for me."

They sat and talked for a while; and now, after Nadya had spent a winter in Petersburg, there was in Sasha, in his words, in his smile, and in his whole figure, the air of something outlived, old-fashioned, long sung, and perhaps already gone to its grave.

"I'm leaving for the Volga the day after tomorrow," said Sasha, "and then for a kumys cure.[8] I want to drink kumys. A friend of mine and his wife are coming with me. His wife is an amazing woman; I keep whipping her up, convincing her to go and study. I want her to turn her life around."

Having talked, they went to the station. Sasha treated her to tea and apples; and when the train started and he smiled and waved his handkerchief, she could tell even from his legs that he was very ill and would hardly live long.

Nadya arrived in her town at noon. As she drove home from the station, the streets seemed very wide and the houses very small, flattened; there were no people, and she met only the German piano tuner in his faded brown coat. And all the houses seemed covered with dust. Her grandmother, quite old now, stout and homely as before, put her arms around Nadya, and wept for a long time, pressing her face to Nadya's shoulder, unable to tear herself away. Nina Ivanovna had also aged considerably and looked bad, somehow all pinched, but was still as tightly corseted as before, and the diamonds sparkled on her fingers.

"My dear!" she said, trembling all over. "My dear!"

Then they sat and wept silently. It was evident that both her grandmother and her mother felt that the past was lost forever and irretrievably: gone now was their position in society, gone their former honor, and their right to invite people; so it happens when, amidst a carefree, easy life, the police suddenly come at night, make a search, and it turns out that the master of the house is an embezzler, a counterfeiter—and then farewell forever to the carefree, easy life!

Nadya went upstairs and saw the same bed, the same windows with the naïve white curtains, and through the windows the same garden, flooded with light, cheerful, noisy. She touched her table, sat, thought a little. And she ate well, and drank tea with rich, delicious cream, but something was lacking now, there was a feeling of emptiness in the rooms, and the ceilings were low. In the evening she went to bed, covered herself up, and for some reason it was funny to be lying in that warm, very soft bed.

Nina Ivanovna came in for a moment and sat down, as guilty people do, timidly and furtively.

"Well, how is it, Nadya?" she asked, after some silence. "Are you content? Quite content?"

"I am, mama."

Nina Ivanovna stood up and made a cross over Nadya and over the windows.

"And I, as you see, have become religious," she said. "You know, I've taken up philosophy and keep thinking, thinking . . . And many things have become clear as day to me now. First of all, I think, the whole of life must pass as if through a prism."

"Tell me, mama, how is grandmother?"

"She seems all right. When you left then with Sasha, and the telegram came from you, your grandmother read it and collapsed; for three days she lay in bed without moving. Then she prayed to God and wept all the time. But now it's all right."

She got up and paced about the room.

"Tick-tock . . ." the watchman rapped. "Tick-tock, tick-tock . . ."

"First of all, the whole of life must pass as if through a prism," she said, "that is, in other words, life must be broken down into the simplest elements, as if into the seven primary colors, and each element must be studied separately."

What else Nina Ivanovna said, and when she left, Nadya did not hear, because she soon fell asleep.

May passed, June came. Nadya was accustomed to home now. Her grandmother fussed over the samovar and sighed deeply; Nina Ivanovna talked in the evenings about her philosophy; as before, she lived in the house as a hanger-on and had to turn to the grandmother for every penny. There were lots of flies in the house, and the ceilings of the rooms seemed to get lower and lower. Granny and Nina Ivanovna did not go out, for fear of meeting Father Andrei and Andrei Andreich. Nadya walked in the garden, in the street, looked at the houses, at the gray fences, and it seemed to her that everything in the town had long since grown old, outlived itself, and was only waiting for the end, or for the beginning of something young, fresh. Oh, if only this new, bright life would come sooner, when one could look one's fate directly and boldly in the eye, be conscious of one's rightness, be cheerful, free! And this life would come sooner or later! There would be a time when of grandmother's house, where everything was so arranged that four maids could not live otherwise than in a single basement room, in filth—there would be a time when no trace of this house would remain, it would be forgotten, no one would remember it. And

Nadya's only entertainment came from the boys in the neighboring yard; when she strolled in the garden, they rapped on the fence and teased her, laughing:

"The fiancée! The fiancée!"

A letter came from Sasha in Saratov. In his merry, dancing hand he wrote that the trip down the Volga had been quite successful, but that he had fallen slightly ill in Saratov, had lost his voice, and had been in the hospital for two weeks now. She realized what it meant, and a foreboding that amounted to certainty came over her. And she found it unpleasant that this foreboding and her thoughts of Sasha did not trouble her as before. She wanted passionately to live, wanted to be in Petersburg, and her acquaintance with Sasha now seemed to her something dear, but long, long past! She did not sleep all night and in the morning sat by the window, listening. And, indeed, voices could be heard downstairs; her grandmother was quickly, anxiously asking about something. Then someone began to weep . . . When Nadya came downstairs, her grandmother was standing in the corner and praying, and her face was wet with tears. On the table lay a telegram.

Nadya paced the room for a long time, listening to her grandmother's weeping, then picked up the telegram and read it. It said that on the previous morning, in Saratov, there died of consumption Alexander Timofeich, or simply Sasha.

The grandmother and Nina Ivanovna went to church to order a panikhida, but Nadya still paced the rooms for a long time, thinking. She realized clearly that her life had been turned around, as Sasha had wanted, that here she was lonely, alien, not needed, and that she needed nothing here, that all former things had been torn from her and had vanished, as if they had been burned and their ashes scattered on the wind. She went into Sasha's room and stood there for a while.

"Farewell, dear Sasha!" she thought, and pictured before her a new, expansive, spacious life, and that life, still unclear, full of mysteries, lured and beckoned to her.

She went to her room upstairs to pack, and the next morning said good-bye to her family and, alive, cheerful, left town—as she thought, forever.

DECEMBER 1903

NOTES

THE DEATH OF A CLERK

1. The name Cherviakov comes from the Russian word *cherviak* ("worm").
2. A popular operetta by French composer Robert Planquette (1843–1903).
3. The name Brizzhalov suggests a combination of *bryzgat'* ("to spray") and *briuzzhat'* ("to grumble").

SMALL FRY

1. The name Nevyrazimov comes from *nevyrazimy* ("inexpressible"), also used as a euphemism for men's long underwear (*nevyrazimye,* i.e., unmentionables).
2. In the Eastern Orthodox Church, Easter Sunday and the days of the week following Easter are called "bright" days.
3. In Russia windows are double-glazed and sealed for the winter, but one pane can be opened for ventilation.
4. Easter is preceded by the forty-day fast known as the Great Lent, which continues through Holy Week and ends with a feast on Easter Day.
5. A kulich is a dense, sweet yeast bread that is traditionally eaten at Easter; the loaves are brought to church to be blessed.
6. Titular councillor was ninth of the fourteen ranks of the Russian imperial civil service established by Peter the Great, immortalized by Nikolai Gogol in the figure of the poor clerk Akaky Akakievich, hero of "The Overcoat."
7. The Order of St. Stanislas, a Polish civil order founded in 1792, began to be awarded in Russia in 1831; its decoration was in the form of a star.

PANIKHIDA

1. The church is named for a famous iconographic type of the Mother of God which Byzantine tradition traces back to an image painted by Saint Luke. There is no agreement among scholars on the origin and meaning of the word "Hodigitria."

2. An iconostasis is an icon-bearing partition with three doors that spans the width of an Orthodox church, separating the body of the church from the sanctuary.

3. A prosphora is a small, round loaf of leavened bread used for communion in the Orthodox Church. Prosphoras are sent in to the sanctuary by each of the faithful with a list of names of people to be commemorated during the offering, and are sent out again for distribution at the end of the liturgy.

4. The proskomedia is the office of preparation of the bread and wine for the sacrament of communion.

5. The forgiving of the harlot is recounted in John 8:3–11. Mary of Egypt, a fifth-century saint greatly venerated in Orthodoxy, was a prostitute who converted to Christianity and spent forty-seven years in the desert in prayer and repentance.

6. A panikhida, which gives the story its title, is an Orthodox prayer service in commemoration of the dead.

7. Kolivo, also known as kutya, is a special dish made of grain (wheat or rice) mixed with nuts, raisins, and honey, served in the church on occasions of commemoration of the dead.

8. Esau's selling of his birthright "for a mess of pottage" is told in Genesis 27:1–46, the punishment of Sodom in Genesis 18:20–19:29, and the account of Joseph in Genesis 37.

EASTER NIGHT

1. The exclamation "Christ is risen!" is heard during the Orthodox Easter service, and is also used as a greeting among Orthodox Christians during the forty days between Easter and the Ascension.

2. The words are from the first hymn (troparion) of Canticle IX of the Easter matins (*Service Book of the Holy Orthodox-Catholic Apostolic Church,* trans. by Isabel F. Hapgood, fifth edition, Englewood, N.J., 1975, p. 232).

3. An akathist (from the Greek "standing up") is a special canticle sung in honor of Christ, the Mother of God, or one of the saints.

4. An archimandrite is the Orthodox equivalent of an abbot, the superior of a monastery or superintendent of several monasteries.

5. Saint Nicholas, fourth-century bishop of Myra in Lycia (Asia Minor), is one of the most highly venerated saints in all Christendom.

6. The church is emptied and the people and clergy process around it with candles before going back in to begin the Easter service.

7. See note 5 to "Small Fry."

8. The royal doors are the central doors in the iconostasis (see note 2 to "Panikhida"); a large church would have several side chapels with their own iconostasis and royal doors; they are all left open throughout the Easter service, signifying that the Kingdom of Heaven is now open to all.

9. From the first hymn of Canticle VIII of the Easter matins (Hapgood, p. 231).

10. See note 4 to "Small Fry."

Vanka

1. Watchmen patrolled their territory at night rapping out the hours on an iron or wooden bar.

2. A village Christmas custom, commemorating the wise men's journey to Bethlehem (Matthew 2:1–12).

3. In a village church anyone who wanted to could sing in the choir; the choirs in large city churches could be more selective.

A Boring Story

1. See note 2 to "Panikhida." The iconostasis of a large church may be hung with a great many icons, large and small, often in gold or silver casings.

2. N. I. Pirogov (1810–81) was a great Russian surgeon and anatomist, active in questions of popular education. K. D. Kavelin (1818–85) was a liberal journalist and social activist. N. A. Nekrasov (1821–78) was a poet and liberal social critic, editor of the influential journal *The Contemporary*.

3. The reference is to the eminent Russian writer Ivan Turgenev (1818–83); we are unable to identify the heroine Nikolai Stepanovich has in mind.

4. A novel by the German writer Friedrich Spielhagen (1829–1911).

5. "History of the illness" (Latin), the heading on the blank page to be filled in by the doctor.

6. V. L. Gruber (1814–85) was a Russian anatomist. A. I. Babukhin (1835–91) was a histologist and physiologist.

7. M. D. Skobelev (1843–82) was a Russian general prominent at the time of the Russo-Turkish war of 1877–78.

8. Professor V. G. Perov (1833–82), Russian artist, was head of the Russian Academy of Art in Petersburg.

9. Adelina Patti (1843–1919), Italian opera singer, was one of the great sopranos of her time, known especially for her performances of Mozart, Rossini, and Verdi.

10. Cf. *Hamlet,* II, 2, 562: "What's Hecuba to him or he to Hecuba . . . ?"

11. The phrase, become proverbial, is from Part I, chapter 8 of *Dead Souls,* by Nikolai Gogol (1809–52).

12. Chatsky is the hero of the comedy in verse *Woe from Wit* (1822–23), the first real masterpiece of the Russian theater, by Alexander S. Griboedov (1795–1829).

13. Having the civil service rank of privy councillor, third of the fourteen degrees established by Peter the Great and equivalent to the military rank of general, Nikolai Stepanovich is also entitled to be addressed as "Your Excellency."

14. Nikolai Stepanovich lists some of the homeliest and most comforting staples of Russian peasant cooking, including kasha, most often made from buckwheat.

15. Seminary education was open to poorer people who could not afford private tutors or expensive schools, and did not necessarily mean that the student was preparing for a church career.

16. The first line of the poem "Reflection," by Mikhail Lermontov (1814–41).

17. N. A. Dobrolyubov (1836–61) was a radical literary critic of the earnest materialist sort, with a prominent forehead and tubercular pallor.

18. A. A. Arakcheev (1769–1834), all-powerful minister under emperors Paul I and Alexander I, was an extreme reactionary and strict disciplinarian.

19. "Final argument" (Latin). The full phrase, *ultima ratio regum* ("the final argument of kings"), was the motto Louis XIV had engraved on his cannons.

20. 2 Kings 2:23.

21. There are several important Orthodox feast days during the summer months: the feast of Sts. Peter and Paul on June 29, the feast of the Transfiguration on August 6, and of the Dormition of the Mother of God (Assumption) on August 15. However, Chekhov also commonly refers to ordinary Sundays as feast days.

22. A distortion of the opening line of the old Latin students' song *Gaudeamus igitur, juvenes dum sumus* ("Let us make merry while we are young").

23. N. I. Krylov (1807–79) was a famous Russian jurist. Revel is the old name of Tallinn, capital of Estonia.

24. A quotation from the fable "The Eagle and the Hens," by the Russian poet and fabulist I. A. Krylov (1768–1844).

25. Berdichev, a town in the Ukraine, is synonymous with deep provinciality.

26. Actual illustrated magazines of the time.

27. A reference to the Russian law requiring the use of internal passports for citizens traveling within the country. At the time, Russia was the only European country to have such a system.

28. These words (*Gnôthi seauton* in Greek) were inscribed on the pediment of the oracular temple of Apollo at Delphi; Socrates adopted them as his personal motto.

Gusev

1. Captain Kopeikin is the hero of an inset story in Gogol's *Dead Souls*. Midshipman Dyrka (his name means "hole") is referred to in Gogol's play *The Marriage*.

2. A Turco-Tartar people who settled on the Black Sea in the ninth century A.D. They were exterminated by the Byzantine emperor John II Comnenus in 1123. For Pavel Ivanych the word simply means primitive, savage people.

3. The proper preparation for death for an Orthodox Christian. The sacrament of anointing with oil is in fact a sacrament of healing, but has come to be considered a part of the "last rites."

4. Germans, being Lutherans, were not thought of as Christians in the Russian popular mind.

5. The prayer "Memory Eternal" (*Vechnaya pamyat'*) is sung at the end of the Orthodox funeral service and the panikhida.

Peasant Women

1. The words "where there is no sickness or sighing" come from the panikhida, the Russian Orthodox memorial service.

2. Holy Week is the week preceding Easter, during which the events of Christ's Passion are remembered. Thursday is a day of particular holiness when the Last Supper is commemorated.

3. In Russia "Trinity" is another name for Pentecost, the feast that

falls on the fiftieth day after Easter and celebrates the descent of the Holy Spirit.

4. Churches and homes are traditionally decorated at Pentecost with green branches and flowers, symbolizing the life-giving action of the Holy Spirit.

5. He means "the fiery Gehenna," synonymous with Hell in Jewish and Christian tradition. The words are somewhat closer in Russian. The actual Gehenna is the Hinnom valley just outside the walls of Jerusalem, which in ancient times was a refuse dump where fires constantly smoldered.

THE FIDGET

1. See note 6 to "Small Fry."

2. A dacha is a summer residence for city dwellers—a cottage, part of a big house, or a whole house, depending on a person's means. "Going to dacha" also signifies the whole way of life in the summer.

3. A. Mazzini (1845–1926) was an Italian opera singer.

4. The words come from the poem "Reflections at the Front Entrance," by Nikolai Nekrasov (see note 2 to "A Boring Story"), which became very popular in its musical setting.

5. V. D. Polenov (1844–1927) was a Russian landscape and historical painter.

6. L. Barnay (1842–1924) was a German actor.

7. Osip is the servant of Khlestakov, impostor-hero of Gogol's comedy *Revizor* ("The Inspector General").

IN EXILE

1. See note 21 to "A Boring Story."

WARD NO. 6

1. These "calendars" included edifying little stories and helpful advice as well as the days of the year.

2. See note 7 to "Small Fry."

3. The Swedish Order of the Polar Star was also awarded in Russia.

4. The zemstvo was an elective provincial council with powers of local government; it came to be very important for reform-minded Russians in the latter nineteenth century.

5. See note 3 to "Easter Night."

6. The 1860s in Russia were a period when liberalism became radicalized and the material and practical were exalted above the ideal.

7. See note 2 to "A Boring Story."

8. "In the future" (Latin).

9. The French biochemist Louis Pasteur (1822–95) and the German doctor and microbiologist Robert Koch (1843–1910) were pioneers in the study of microbes and contagious diseases. Koch discovered the tuberculosis bacillus.

10. Mt. Elbrus in Georgia, at 18,481 feet, is the highest peak of the Caucasus and the highest mountain in Europe.

11. An old-fashioned method of treatment for various respiratory ailments, which consisted in applying a number of small heated glasses to the patient's back. The heat would cause suction and draw the blood to the surface.

12. In *The Brothers Karamazov* (Part I, Book 1, chapter 4) Fyodor Pavlovich Karamazov does indeed produce a variant of Voltaire's famous saying: *Si Dieu n'existait pas, il faudrait l'inventer* ("If God did not exist, he would have to be invented").

13. The Greek philosopher Diogenes the Cynic (412?–323 B.C.) came to Athens from his native Sinope as a penniless vagabond and was so scornful of wealth and social convention that he lived in a barrel.

14. Marcus Aurelius (121–180 A.D.), Roman emperor and Stoic philosopher, taught the wisdom of self-restraint and indifference to both pleasure and pain.

15. See Matthew 26:39 (also Mark 14:36 and Luke 22:42).

16. The itinerary includes some of the standard tourist sights in Moscow. The Iverskaya icon of the Mother of God was an ancient miracle-working icon which, in Chekhov's time, was kept in a specially built chapel between the arches of the Iversky Gate at the entrance to Red Square; it disappeared soon after the revolution. Zamoskvorechye is the part of Moscow across the river from the Kremlin. The Rumiantsev Museum was the first public museum in Russia, opened in the early nineteenth century in Pashkov House; it contained anthropological collections, books, manuscripts, antiquities, and paintings.

17. A reference to the phrase "and out of me burdock will grow," spoken by Bazarov in Turgenev's *Fathers and Sons* (1862), which became proverbial in Russia (see note 3 to "A Boring Story").

18. "Bad tone" (French), meaning socially unacceptable.

19. See Genesis 1:26: "Then God said, 'Let us make man in our image, after our likeness.' "

THE BLACK MONK

1. Lines from *Evgeny Onegin,* a novel in verse by Alexander Pushkin (1799–1837), used in the opera of the same name composed by P. I. Tchaikovsky (1840–93).

2. Gaetano Braga (1829–1907), Italian cellist and composer, was best known for his salon composition *La Serenata,* which was arranged for various instruments.

3. The words are a quotation from *Poltava,* a long poem by Pushkin. Kochubey, who appears in the poem, was a wealthy Ukrainian landowner.

4. "Let the other side be heard" and "sufficient for an intelligent man" (Latin).

5. See John 14:2.

6. "A sound mind in a sound body" (Latin), from the tenth *Satire* of the Roman poet Juvenal (c. 65–128 A.D.).

7. A two-week fast period preceding the feast of the Dormition on August 15.

8. Polycrates (d. 522 B.C.), tyrant of Samos, after enjoying forty years of happiness, became worried that his luck would not hold out. He thought he might bribe fate by throwing a precious ring into the sea, but it was found in the belly of a fish and brought back to him. Soon after that Samos was taken by the Persian general Orontes, and Polycrates was crucified.

9. See the first Epistle of Paul to the Thessalonians, 5:16.

10. July 20.

11. Kovrin confuses two stories here: Herod ordered the slaughter of all the male children under two years old in and around Bethlehem (Matthew 2:16–18); the Egyptian "first-born" were smitten by the Lord as a sign to Pharaoh that he should let Moses lead the people of Israel out of Egypt (Exodus 12:29–32).

ROTHSCHILD'S FIDDLE

1. See note 11 to "Ward No. 6."

2. The feast of St. John the Theologian, author of the fourth Gospel, is celebrated on May 8, and the feast of the relics of St. Nicholas (see note 5 to "Easter Night") on May 9, commemorating the "rescue" of the saint's relics a few days before the Turkish invasion of Myra in the eleventh century and their safe transfer to the Italian town of Bari, where they now lie.

THE STUDENT

1. Good Friday, commemorating the Passion of Christ, is a day of total fast.

2. Rurik (d. 879), a Viking chief, was invited by the people of Novgorod to become their prince, thus founding the first ruling dynasty of Russia; Ivan IV, the Terrible (Ioann is the Old Slavonic form of the name), born in 1530, ruled Russia from 1547 to 1584 and was the first to adopt the title of tsar; Peter I, the Great (1672–1725), the first to adopt the title of emperor, extended the power of Russia considerably and built the new capital of St. Petersburg.

3. According to an old Russian superstition, a person not immediately recognized by face or voice is destined to become rich.

4. A composite reading of twelve passages from the four Gospels describing the Crucifixion is part of the matins of Holy Friday, sometimes referred to simply as "the Twelve Gospels." The student gives his own summary of some of the readings in what follows.

ANNA ON THE NECK

1. Not a real pilgrimage, but a visit to a monastery, where hotel rooms could be had more cheaply than elsewhere.

2. The Order of St. Anna, named for the mother of the Virgin Mary, was founded in 1735 by Karl Friedrich, Duke of Schleswig-Holstein, in honor of his wife Anna Petrovna, daughter of the Russian emperor Peter the Great. It had four degrees, two civil and two military: the decoration for the first civil degree was worn on a ribbon around the neck, for the second, in the buttonhole.

3. Shchi (cabbage soup) and kasha (buckwheat gruel) were the most common Russian peasant dishes.

4. The Order of St. Vladimir, named for St. Vladimir, Prince of Kiev (956?–1015), who converted Russia to Christianity in 988 A.D., was founded by the empress Catherine the Great in 1782 and was generally awarded for long-term civil service.

THE HOUSE WITH THE MEZZANINE

1. N. A. Amosov (1787–1868) was an artillery officer and engineer. He invented a kind of stove that functioned pneumatically, which was introduced on the market in 1835. An Amosov heating system was installed in the imperial Winter Palace in Petersburg, bringing the inventor a reward of 5,400 acres of land.

2. See note 4 to "Ward No. 6."

3. A sign of protest; it was considered improper for a girl or woman to go out without covering her head.

4. Baikal is a sea-sized freshwater lake in Siberia famous for the depth and purity of its water; the Buryat are an Oriental nationality inhabiting the region around Baikal.

5. A folk motif: the hero cannot recover his lost beloved until he wears out a pair of iron shoes.

6. See note 19 to "Ward No. 6."

7. For Rurik see note 2 to "The Student." Petrushka, the peasant servant of Chichikov, hero of Gogol's *Dead Souls,* "liked not so much what he was reading about as the reading itself, or, better, the process of reading, the fact that letters are eternally forming some word, which sometimes even means the devil knows what" (Volume I, chapter 2).

8. A health spa in central France, known for its mineral waters.

9. A line from the fable "The Crow and the Fox," by I. A. Krylov (see note 24 to "A Boring Story"). The end of the fable is well known: the crow fails to hold on to the God-sent piece of cheese.

THE MAN IN A CASE

1. M. E. Saltykov-Shchedrin (1826–89) was a liberal journalist and satirist best known for his dark novel *The Golovlevs* and his satirical history of Russia, *The History of a Certain Town.*

2. Henry Thomas Buckle (1821–94) was a liberal historian, author of *The History of Civilization in England* (1857–61), in which he formulated the idea that the development of civilization leads to the cessation of war between nations. There was also a George Buckle (b. 1857), a biographer and editor of the English magazine *Life.*

3. Fish is "lenten" but butter is not—thus Belikov strikes a middle path. In addition to the four major fast periods during the year (the Advent fast before Christmas, the Great Lent before Easter, the Peter and Paul fast, and the Dormition fast), Wednesdays and Fridays are also fast days in the Orthodox Church.

GOOSEBERRIES

1. Cantonists were sons of career soldiers, who were assigned to the department of the army from birth and educated in special schools at state expense.

2. Bast is the pliant inner bark of the linden tree, which when

stripped from the outer bark was put to a variety of uses in Russia, as material for roofing, shoes, wagon covers, and so forth.

3. An altered quotation from the poem "The Hero," by Alexander Pushkin; it should read, "Dearer to me than a host of base truths is the illusion that exalts."

A Medical Case

1. The reader will realize from this and other stories in the collection that summer nights in northern Russia are extremely short and dawn may come as early as two o'clock in the morning.

2. See note 16 to "A Boring Story." Tamara is the heroine of the long poem *The Demon* (1839).

The Darling

1. *Faust Inside Out* may be the Russian title of *Le Petit Faust* ("The Little Faust"), an operetta by French composer Florimond Hervé (1825–92). *Orpheus in the Underworld* is an operetta by Jacques Offenbach (1819–80), French composer of German origin.

On Official Business

1. See note 4 to "Ward No. 6."

2. That is, the emancipation of the serfs in 1861.

3. A line from *Evgeny Onegin,* by Alexander Pushkin.

4. "A little glass of Cliquot" (French). Cliquot is one of the finest champagnes.

5. "The Queen of Spades," a short story by Pushkin, was made into an opera by Tchaikovsky.

The Lady with the Little Dog

1. See note 4 to "Gusev."

2. Selyanka is a casserole of cabbage and meat or fish, served in its own baking pan.

3. The Slavyansky Bazaar was a highly respectable hotel and restaurant in Moscow, frequented in Chekhov's time by artists, actors, and writers.

At Christmastime

1. Jean-Martin Charcot (1825–93), a French doctor known for his work on nervous ailments, invented a method of treatment by means of cold showers.

IN THE RAVINE

1. Krasnaya Gorka ("Pretty little hill") is the Tuesday of the second week after Easter, when the graves of dead relations are visited and decorated. It was usual to celebrate weddings after Easter, because they could not be celebrated in church during Lent.

2. The Flagellants were a sect in Russia (with its counterparts elsewhere) that believed in flagellation as a means of spiritual purification. They had their own prophets and scriptures, and were always rejected by the Orthodox Church.

3. A Persian term meaning "plenipotentiary," the title of the highest Persian ministers, but here used simply by association with things Middle Eastern.

4. The church is named after the icon of the Mother of God from the city of Kazan, a sixteenth-century wonder-working icon the type of which is one of the most widespread in Russia.

5. The first Sunday after Easter, commemorating the disciple who doubted Christ's resurrection.

THE BISHOP

1. In Russia on Palm Sunday, the feast celebrating Christ's entry into Jerusalem a week before the Crucifixion, pussywillows are handed out to the people in church, for lack of palms. The day is known as "Pussywillow Sunday."

2. Father Simeon is right: there is no mention of Iehudiel or his ass in the Bible.

3. A Latin-German macaronic phrase meaning "child-curing whipping birch."

4. See notes 3 and 4 to "Panikhida."

5. See note 21 to "A Boring Story."

6. See note 4 to "Easter Night."

7. The words come from hymns sung during the services known as "Bridegroom services" celebrated on the first three days of Holy Week: "Behold, the Bridegroom cometh at midnight, and blessed is the servant whom He shall find watching; and again, unworthy is the servant whom He shall find heedless . . ." and "Thy bridal chamber I see adorned, O my Savior, and I have no wedding garment that I may enter . . ."

8. The washing of feet is part of the liturgy of Holy Thursday when it is served by a bishop. It commemorates Christ's washing of his disciples' feet before the Last Supper (John 13:3–15).

9. See note 1 to "The Student."

10. John 13:31–18:1, the longest of the twelve Gospel readings.

11. See note 4 to "Anna on the Neck."

THE FIANCÉE

1. Quotations from the hymns of matins of the Sunday of the Prodigal Son, three weeks before the beginning of Lent (see Luke 15:11–32).

2. That is, June 29.

3. A straight-sided hat, usually made of velvet, awarded to Orthodox priests as a token of distinguished service. The Russian *kamilavka* is a distortion of the Greek *kalimavka* ("beautiful hat").

4. Russian civil servants wore uniforms similar to military uniforms, including hats with cockades.

5. See note 27 to "A Boring Story."

6. The Cossack territory in the southeastern Ukraine enjoyed some measure of freedom and autonomy before it was fully annexed by Catherine the Great in the late eighteenth century. "Going to the Cossacks" meant living a life free of restrictions and conventions.

7. As a means of killing flies, a piece of paper treated with poison would be left to soak in a dish of water. The flies would drink the water and die.

8. *Kumys* is the Tartar word for fermented mare's milk, which was believed to strengthen the lungs. Leo Tolstoy, among others, was an advocate of the "kumys cure," which he took several times while visiting his property in Samara province during the summer.

MODERN LIBRARY IS ONLINE AT
WWW.MODERNLIBRARY.COM

MODERN LIBRARY ONLINE IS YOUR GUIDE TO CLASSIC LITERATURE ON THE WEB

THE MODERN LIBRARY E-NEWSLETTER

Our free e-mail newsletter is sent to subscribers, and features sample chapters, interviews with and essays by our authors, upcoming books, special promotions, announcements, and news. To subscribe to the Modern Library e-newsletter, visit **www.modernlibrary.com**

THE MODERN LIBRARY WEBSITE

Check out the Modern Library website at
www.modernlibrary.com for:

- The Modern Library e-newsletter
- A list of our current and upcoming titles and series
- Reading Group Guides and exclusive author spotlights
- Special features with information on the classics and other paperback series
- Excerpts from new releases and other titles
- A list of our e-books and information on where to buy them
- The Modern Library Editorial Board's 100 Best Novels and 100 Best Nonfiction Books of the Twentieth Century written in the English language
- News and announcements

Questions? E-mail us at **modernlibrary@randomhouse.com**.
For questions about examination or desk copies, please visit
the Random House Academic Resources site at
www.randomhouse.com/academic.